CLIVE CUSSLER

TWO COMPLETE NOVELS

FLOOD TIDE & CYCLOPS

Wings Books®
New York

This 2001 edition is published by Wings Books®, an imprint of Random House Value Publishing, Inc., 280 Park Avenue, New York, NY 10017, by arrangement with Simon & Schuster Publishing, Inc.

Wings Books® and design are registered trademarks of Random House Value Publishing, Inc.

DIRK PITT® is a registered trademark of Clive Cussler

Illustrations for FLOOD TIDE by Beauchamp Group
Design for FLOOD TIDE by Deirdre C. Amthor

In CYCLOPS, the author is grateful for permission to reprint lines from the following songs: "Supercalifragilisticexpialidocious." Words and music by Richard M. Sherman and Robert B. Sherman. Copyright © 1963 Wonderland Music Company, Inc. "Yankee Doodle Boy" (George M. Cohan). Used by permission of George M. Cohan Music Publishing Company.

Random House
New York • Toronto • London • Sydney • Auckland
http://www.randomhouse.com/

Library of Congress Cataloging-in-Publication Data

Cussler, Clive.
    [Flood tide]
    Two complete novels / Clive Cussler.
       p. cm.
    Contents: Flood tide — Cyclops.
    ISBN 0-517-16277-6
    1. Pitt, Dirk (Fictitious character)—Fiction. 2. Adventure stories, American. I. Cussler, Clive. Cyclops. II. Title.

PS3553.U75 F58 2001
813'.54—dc21
                               00-065435

8 7 6 5 4 3 2

CONTENTS

FLOOD TIDE

ACKNOWLEDGMENTS

The author wishes to express his gratitude to the men and women of the Immigration and Naturalization Service for generously providing data and statistics on illegal immigration.

Thanks also to the Army Corps of Engineers for their help in describing the capricious natures of the Mississippi and Atchafalaya Rivers.

And to the dozens of people who kindly offered ideas and suggestions on obstacles for Dirk and Al to overcome.

REQUIEM
FOR
A PRINCESS

Princess Dou Wan

THE WAVES TURNED VICIOUS and worsened with every rush of wind. The calm weather of the morning transformed from Dr. Jekyll into a vehement Mr. Hyde by late evening. Whitecaps on the crests of towering waves were lashed into sheets of spray. The violent water and black clouds merged under the onslaught of a driving snowstorm. It was impossible to tell where water ended and sky began. As the passenger liner *Princess Dou Wan* fought through waves that rose like mountains before spilling over the ship, the men on board were unaware of the imminent disaster that was only minutes away.

The crazed waters were driven by northeast and northwest gales that simultaneously caused ferocious currents to smash against the ship from two sides. Winds soon reached a hundred miles an hour with waves that crested at thirty feet or more. Caught in the maelstrom, the *Princess Dou Wan* had no place to hide. Her bow pitched and drove under waves that swept over her open decks and flowed aft and then forward when her stern rose, throwing her wildly spinning propellers free of the water. Struck from all directions, she rolled thirty degrees, her starboard rail along the promenade deck disappearing in a torrent of water. Slowly, too slowly, she sluggishly righted herself and plunged on, steaming through the worst storm in recent history.

Freezing and unable to see through the blinding snowstorm, Second Mate Li Po, who stood watch, ducked back inside the wheelhouse and slammed the door. In all his days of sailing the China Sea, he had never seen swirling snow in the middle of a violent storm. Po did not think the gods were fair to hurl such devastating winds at the *Princess* after a voyage halfway around the world with less than two hundred miles to go before reaching port. In the past sixteen hours, she had only made forty miles.

Except for Captain Leigh Hunt and his chief engineer down below in the engine room, the entire crew were Nationalist Chinese. An old salt with twelve years in the Royal Navy and eighteen as an officer for three different shipping-company fleets, Hunt had served fifteen of those years as captain. As a boy he went fishing with his father out of Bridlington, a small city on the east coast of England, before shipping out as an ordinary seaman on a freighter to South Africa. A thin man with graying hair and sad, vacant eyes, he was deeply pessimistic about his ship's ability to weather the storm.

Two days earlier, one of the crewmen had called his attention to a crack in the starboard outer hull aft of the single smokestack. He would have given a month's pay to inspect the crack now that his ship was enduring incredible stress. He reluctantly brushed the thought aside. It would have been suicide to attempt an inspection under hundred-mile-an-hour winds and the raging water that spilled across the decks. He felt in his bones the *Princess* was in mortal danger, and accepted the fact that her fate was out of his hands.

Hunt stared into the blanket of snow that pelted the wheelhouse windows and spoke to his second mate without turning. "How bad is the ice, Mr. Po?"

"Building rapidly, Captain."

"Do you believe we're in danger of capsizing?"

Li Po shook his head slowly. "Not yet, sir, but by morning the load on the superstructure and decks could prove critical if we take on a heavy list."

Hunt thought for a moment, then spoke to the helmsman. "Stay on course, Mr. Tsung. Keep our bow into the wind and waves."

"Aye, sir," the Chinese helmsman replied, feet braced wide apart, hands tightly gripping the brass wheel.

Hunt's thoughts returned to the crack in the hull. He couldn't remember when the *Princess Dou Wan* had a proper marine inspection in dry dock. Strangely, the crew's uneasiness about leaks, badly rusted hull plates, and weakened and missing rivets was totally lacking. They appeared to ignore the corrosion and the constantly running bilge pumps that strained to carry off the heavy leakage during the voyage.

If the *Princess* had an Achilles' heel, it was her tired and worn hull. A ship that sails the oceans is considered old after twenty years. She had traveled hundreds of thousands of miles scathed by rough seas and typhoons during her thirty-five years since leaving the shipyards. It was little short of a miracle that she was still afloat.

Launched in 1913 as the *Lanai* by shipbuilders Harland and Wolff for Singapore Pacific Steamship Lines, her tonnage grossed out at 10,758. Her overall length was 497 feet from straight-up-and-down stem to champagne glass–shaped stern with a sixty-foot beam. Her triple-expansion steam engines put out five thousand horsepower and turned twin screws. In her prime she could cut the waves at a respectable seventeen knots. She went into service between Singapore and Honolulu until 1931, when she was sold to the Canton Lines and renamed *Princess Dou Wan*. After a refit, she was employed running passengers and cargo throughout Southeast Asian ports.

During World War II, she was taken over and fitted out by the Australian government as a troop transport. Heavily damaged after surviving attacks by Japanese aircraft during convoy duty, she was returned to the Canton Lines after the war and served briefly on short runs from Shanghai to Hong Kong, until the spring of 1948, when she was to be sold to the scrappers in Singapore.

Her accommodations were designed to carry fifty-five first-class passengers, eighty-five second-class, and 370 third-class. Normally she carried a crew of 190, but on what was to be her final voyage, she was manned by only thirty-eight.

Hunt thought of his ancient command as a tiny island on a turbulent sea engulfed in a drama without an audience. His attitude was fatalistic. He was ready for the beach and the *Princess* was ready for the scrap yard. Hunt felt compassion for his battle-scarred ship as she wrestled with the full brunt of the storm. She twisted and groaned when inundated by the titanic waves, but she always broke free and punched her bow into the next one. Hunt's only consolation was that her worn-out engines never missed a beat.

Down in the engine room the creaking and groaning of the hull were uncommonly clamorous. Rust danced and flaked off the bulkheads as water began to rise through the walkway gratings. Rivets holding the steel plates were sheering off. They popped out of the plates and shot through the air like missiles. Usually, the crew was apathetic. It was a common occurrence on ships built before the days of welding. But there was one man who was touched by the tentacles of fear.

Chief Engineer Ian "Hong Kong" Gallagher was an ox-shouldered, red-faced, hard-drinking, heavily mustached Irishman who knew a ship in the throes of breaking up when he saw and heard one. Yet fear was pushed from his mind as he calmly turned his thoughts to survival.

An orphan at the age of eleven, Ian Gallagher ran away from the slums of Belfast and went to sea as a cabin boy. Nurturing a natural talent for maintaining steam engines, he became a wiper and then a third assistant engineer. By the time he was twenty-seven, he had his papers as chief engineer and served on tramp freighters plying the waters between the islands of the South Pacific. The name Hong Kong was given to him after he fought an epic battle in one of the port city's saloons against eight Chinese dockworkers who tried to roll him. When he turned thirty, he signed on board the *Princess Dou Wan* in the summer of 1945.

Grim-faced, Gallagher turned to his second engineer, Chu Wen. "Get topside, put on a life vest and be ready to abandon ship when the captain gives the order."

The Chinese engineer pulled the stub of a cigar from his mouth and stared at Gallagher appraisingly. "You think we're going down?"

"I *know* we're going down," Gallagher replied firmly. "This old rust bucket won't last another hour."

"Did you tell the captain?"

"He'd have to be deaf, dumb and blind not to figure it out himself."

"You coming?" asked Chu Wen.

"I'll be right behind you," answered Gallagher.

Chu Wen wiped his oily hands on a rag, nodded at the chief engineer and made his way up a ladder to a hatch leading to the upper decks.

Gallagher took one final look at his beloved engines, certain they would soon be lying in the deep. He stiffened as an unusually loud screech echoed throughout the hull. The aged *Princess Dou Wan* was tormented by metal fatigue, a scourge suffered by aircraft as well as ships. Extremely difficult to distinguish in calm waters, it only becomes evident in a vessel pounded by vicious seas. Even when new, the *Princess* would have been hard-pressed to bear up under the onslaught of the waves that pounded her hull with a force of twenty thousand pounds per square inch.

Gallagher's heart froze when he saw a crack appear in a bulkhead

that spread downward and then sideways across the hull plates. Starting
on the port side, it widened as it progressed to starboard. He snatched
up the ship's phone and rang the bridge.

Li Po answered. "Bridge."

"Put the captain on!" Gallagher snapped.

A second's pause, and then, "This is the captain."

"Sir, we've got a hell of a crack in the engine room, and it's getting
worse by the minute."

Hunt was stunned. He had hoped against hope that they could make
port before the damage turned critical. "Are we taking on water?"

"The pumps are fighting a losing battle."

"Thank you, Mr. Gallagher. Can you keep the engines turning until
we reach land?"

"What time frame do you have in mind?"

"Another hour should put us in calmer waters."

"Doubtful," said Gallagher. "I give her ten minutes, no more."

"Thank you, Chief," Hunt said heavily. "You'd better leave the
engine room while you still can."

Hunt wearily replaced the receiver, turned and looked out the aft
wheelhouse windows. The ship had taken on a noticeable list and was
rolling heavily. Two of her boats had already been smashed and swept
overboard. Making for the nearest shore and running the ship safely
aground was now out of the question. To reach the smoother waters, he
would have to make a turn to starboard. The *Princess* would never
survive if she was caught broadside in the maddened waves. She could
easily be plunged into a trough without any hope of getting out. Whatever the circumstance, breaking up or the ice building on her superstructure and capsizing her, the ship was doomed.

His mind briefly traveled back sixty days in time and ten thousand
miles in distance to the dock on the Yangtze River at Shanghai, where
the furnishings from the *Princess Dou Wan*'s staterooms were being
stripped in preparation for her final voyage to the scrap yard in Singapore. The departure had been interrupted when General Kung Hui of
the Nationalist Chinese Army arrived on the dock in a Packard limousine and ordered Captain Hunt to converse with him inside the car.

"Please excuse my intrusion, Captain, but I am acting under the personal directive of Generalissimo Chiang Kai-shek." General Kung Hui,
skin and hands as smooth and white as a sheet of paper, sat fastidious

and immaculate in a tailored uniform that showed no sign of a crease. He took up the entire rear seat in the passengers' compartment as he spoke, while Captain Hunt was forced to sit uncomfortably twisted sideways on a jump seat. "You are hearby ordered to place your ship and crew in a state of readiness for a long voyage."

"I believe there has been a mistake," said Hunt. "The *Princess* is not in a state of readiness for an extended cruise. She is about to depart with barely enough men, fuel and supplies to make the scrap yard in Singapore."

"You can forget about Singapore," said Hui with an airy wave of one hand. "Ample fuel and food will be provided along with twenty men from our Nationalist Navy. Once your cargo is on board . . ." Hui paused to insert a cigarette in a long holder and light it. ". . . I should say in about ten days, you will be given your sailing orders."

"I must clear this with my company directors," argued Hunt.

"The directors of Canton Lines have been notified the *Princess Dou Wan* will be temporarily appropriated by the government."

"They agreed to it?"

Hui nodded. "Considering they were generously offered payment in gold by the generalissimo, they were most happy to cooperate."

"After we reach our, or should I say, your destination, what then?"

"Once the cargo is safely delivered ashore, you may continue on to Singapore."

"May I ask where we're bound for?"

"You may not."

"And the cargo?"

"Secrecy will dominate the entire mission. From this minute on, you and your crew will remain on board your ship. No one steps ashore. You will have no contact with friends or family. My men will guard the ship day and night to guarantee strict security."

"I see," said Hunt, but obviously he didn't. He could not recall seeing such shifty eyes.

"As we speak," Hui continued, "all your communications equipment is being either removed or destroyed."

Hunt was stunned. "Surely you can't expect me to attempt a voyage at sea without a radio. What if we encounter difficulties and have to send out a call for assistance?"

Hui idly held up his cigarette holder and studied it. "I foresee no difficulties."

"You are an optimist, General," said Hunt slowly. "The *Princess* is a tired ship far beyond her prime. She is ill-prepared to cope with heavy seas and violent storms."

"I cannot impress upon you the importance and great rewards if this mission is carried out successfully. Generalissimo Chiang Kai-shek will generously compensate you and your crew in gold after you success- fully reach port."

Hunt stared out the window of the limousine at the rusting hull of his ship. "A fortune in gold won't do me much good when I'm lying on the bottom of the sea."

"Then we will rest together for eternity." General Hui smiled with- out humor. "I will be coming along as your passenger."

Captain Hunt recalled the frantic activity that quickly erupted around the *Princess*. Fuel oil was pumped until the tanks were filled. The ship's cook was astounded by the quality and quantity of the food carried aboard and stored in the galley. A constant stream of trucks soon began arriving, stopping beneath the huge cranes on the dock. Their cargo of large wooden crates was then lifted onto the ship and stowed in the holds, which were soon filled to capacity.

The stream of trucks seemed unending. Crates small enough to be carried by one or two men were stowed in the empty passenger cabins, vacant passageways and every available compartment below decks. Every square foot of space was crammed to the overhead decks. The final six truckloads were lashed down on the promenade decks once strolled by the passengers. General Hui had been the last to board, along with a small cadre of heavily armed officers. His luggage consisted of ten steamer trunks and thirty cases of expensive wines and cognacs.

All for nothing, Hunt thought. Beaten in the homestretch by Mother Nature. The secrecy, the intricate deception, had been for nothing. From the time they left the Yangtze, the *Princess* sailed silent and alone. Without communications equipment, radio calls from other passing ships went unanswered.

The captain stared down at the recently installed radar, but its sweep showed no other ship within fifty miles of the *Princess*. Unable to send a distress signal, there could be no rescue. He looked up as General Hui stepped unsteadily into the wheelhouse, face deathly white, a soiled handkerchief held to his lips.

"Seasick, General?" said Hunt tauntingly.

"This damned storm," Hui murmured. "Will it never end?"

"We were prophetic, you and I."

"What are you talking about?"

"Resting together on the bottom for all eternity. It won't be long now."

Gallagher rushed topside and ran, clutching the handrail for support while sliding his hand along it down the passageway to his cabin. He was neither frantic nor confused but calm and composed. He knew exactly what he must do. He always kept the door locked because of what was inside, but did not waste time fumbling for the key. He kicked the door open, smashing it against the stop.

A woman with long blond hair, wearing a silk robe, lay stretched on the bed reading a magazine. She looked up startled from the sudden intrusion as a small dachshund jumped to its feet beside her and began barking. The woman's body was long and beautifully proportioned. Her complexion was smooth and flawless with high cheekbones, her eyes the vivid blue of a late-morning sky. If she stood, the top of her head would have come up to Gallagher's chin. She swung her legs to the deck gracefully and sat there on the edge of the bed.

"Come on, Katie." His hand on her wrist, he jerked her to her feet. "We've precious little time."

"Are we coming into port?" she asked in confusion.

"No, darlin'. The ship is about to sink."

Her hand flew to her mouth. "Oh God!" she gasped.

Gallagher was jerking open closet doors, tearing out drawers and throwing clothes at her over his shoulders. "Put on every piece of clothing you can get into, every pair of pants you've got and every pair of my socks you can slide over your feet. Dress in layers, thinner garb on the inside, heavier on the outside, and be quick about it. This old tub is heading for the bottom any minute."

The woman looked as if she was about to protest, then silently and quickly threw off the robe and began pulling on her underwear. She moved rapidly and purposely, wiggling first into her slacks and then Gallagher's pants. Five knit sweaters went on over three blouses. She felt fortunate indeed that she had packed a full suitcase for her rendezvous with her fiancé. When she could wear no more, Gallagher helped stuff her into one of his working jumpsuits. A pair of his boots went over her silk hose and several pairs of his socks.

The little dachshund darted between their legs, leaping up and down, ears flapping in excitement. He had been a gift from Gallagher along with an emerald engagement ring when he had proposed marriage. The dog wore a red leather collar with a gold dragon charm that swung wildly across his little chest.

"Fritz!" she scolded him. "Lie on the bed and be still."

Katrina Garin was a strong-minded woman who did not require detailed instructions. She was twelve years old when her British father, who was master of an interisland freighter, was lost at sea. Raised by her mother's White Russian family, she went to work at Canton Lines as a clerk and worked her way up to the director's executive secretary. The same age as Gallagher, she had met him at the steamship offices when he was called in to report on the conditions of the *Princess Dou Wan*'s engines, and she became attracted to him. Though she would have preferred a man with a touch of style and sophistication, his rough manners and jovial disposition reminded her of her father.

They met frequently in the following weeks and slept together, mostly in his cabin aboard ship. It was the added thrill of sneaking on board and making love under the noses of the captain and crew that she found especially exciting. Katie had been trapped on board when General Hui surrounded the ship and dock with a small army of security guards. Unable to go ashore despite pleas by Gallagher and an angry Captain Hunt when he was informed of her presence, General Hui insisted she remain on board for the duration of the voyage. Since leaving Shanghai, she had rarely stepped from the cabin; her only companion when Gallagher was on duty in the engine room was the little dog that she had taught tricks to pass the long hours at sea.

Gallagher hurriedly inserted their papers, passports and valuables in a waterproof oilcloth pouch. He threw on a heavy sailor's peacoat and looked at her through blue eyes clouded with concern. "You ready?"

She held up her arms and looked down at the bulky mass of clothing. "I'll never get a life jacket over all this," she said, a tremor in her voice. "Without one I'll sink like a stone in the water."

"Have you forgotten? General Hui gave orders that all life jackets be thrown overboard four weeks ago."

"We'll get away in the lifeboats then."

"The boats that haven't already been bashed to pieces can never be launched in these waters."

She looked at him steadily. "We're going to die, aren't we? If we don't drown, we'll freeze to death."

He pulled a stocking cap down over her blond hair and ears. "Warm

19

head makes for warm feet." Then he gently tilted her face upward between his massive hands and kissed her. "Darlin', didn't they ever tell you that Irishmen never drown?" Taking Katie by the hand, Gallagher dragged her roughly into the passageway and headed up a companionway to the deck above.

Forgotten in the bedlam, Fritz the dachshund stretched out obediently on the bed, believing his mistress would soon return, bewilderment in his brown eyes.

Those of the crew off duty who weren't sitting around playing dominoes or telling stories of other storms they survived were sleeping in their berths, oblivious to the ship about to break up around them. The cook and his galley help were cleaning up after dinner and serving coffee to those who lingered. Despite the battering from the storm, the crew was happy at the prospect of reaching port. Although their destination had been held from them, they knew their exact position within thirty miles.

There was no complacency in the wheelhouse. Hunt stared aft through the snow flurries, barely distinguishing the deck lights trailing toward the stern. In horrified fascination he watched as the stern appeared to rise on an angle downward amidships. Over the howl of the wind through the superstructure, he could hear the hull shrieking as it ground itself to pieces. He reached out and punched the emergency bell that rang the general alarm throughout the ship.

Hui knocked Hunt's hand away from the emergency bell button. "We cannot abandon ship." He spoke in a shocked whisper.

Hunt stared at him in disgust. "Die like a man, General."

"I must not be allowed to die. I vowed to see the cargo safely deposited in port."

"This ship is breaking in two," said Hunt. "Nothing can save you and your precious cargo."

"Then our position must be fixed so it can be salvaged."

"Fixed for whom? The lifeboats have been crushed and swept away. You demanded all life vests be cast overboard. You destroyed the ship's radio. We can't send out a Mayday call. You covered our tracks too well. We're not even supposed to be in these waters. Our location is unknown to the rest of the world. All Chiang Kai-shek will ever learn is that the *Princess Dou Wan* vanished with all hands six thousand miles south of here. You planned well, General, too well."

20

"No!" Hui gasped. "This cannot happen!"

Hunt actually found himself amused at the look of rage and help-lessness on the face of Hui. The shifty look in the dark eyes was gone.

The general could not bring himself to accept the inevitable. He tore open the door to the bridge wing and ran out into the storm gone berserk. He could see the ship twisting in its death throes. The stern was swinging on a pronounced angle to starboard now. Steam was erupting from the tear in the hull. He stood and watched in shock as the stern separated from the rest of the ship in a protest of the grinding and tearing sound of metal being ripped apart. Then all the lights aboard ship blinked out and he could see no more of the stern.

Crewmen burst from below onto decks covered in snow and ice. Frustrated by murderous waves that had smashed the lifeboats, they cursed the lack of life jackets. The end came so quickly, most all were caught unprepared. This time of year the frigid water was only thirty-four degrees, the air temperature only five degrees above zero. In panic they jumped over the side, seemingly unaware that the cold water would kill them in a matter of minutes, if not from hypothermia then from the stoppage of their hearts at the shock of having their bodies exposed to an instantaneous sixty degree drop in temperature.

The stern sank out of sight in less than four minutes. The hull amidships seemed to evaporate into nothingness, leaving a long gap between the sunken stern and the bow section forward of the smoke-stack. A small group of men struggled to lower the only partially damaged lifeboat, but a massive wave thundered over the forecastle and swept across the deck. Men and boat disappeared under the deluge, never to be seen again.

Holding Katie's hand in a death grip, Gallagher dragged her up a ladder and across the roof of the officers' cabins toward a life raft that was mounted aft of the wheelhouse. He was surprised to see that it was empty. Twice, they slipped on the ice coating the roof and fell. Spray flung by the gale stung their faces and blinded them. In the confusion none of the Chinese officers or crew had remembered the life raft atop the roof. Most all, including General Hui's soldiers, had headed for the remaining lifeboat or had thrown themselves into the deadly water.

"Fritz!" Katie cried in anguish. "We left Fritz in the cabin."

"No time to return," said Gallagher.

"We can't leave without him!"

He looked into her eyes solemnly. "You must forget Fritz. It's our lives or his."

Katie twisted away, but Gallagher held her tightly. "Climb in, darlin', and hold on tight." Then he pulled a knife from his boot and furiously slashed at the ropes securing the raft. Gallagher paused as he cut away the last rope and glanced through the windows of the wheelhouse. Dimly lit by the emergency lights, Captain Hunt stood calmly beside the helm, accepting his death without remorse.

Gallagher frantically waved at his captain through the windows, but Hunt did not turn. He merely shoved his hands inside the pockets of his coat and stared vacantly into the snow building around the windows.

Suddenly, a figure emerged from the bridge through the swirling blanket of white. He stumbled like a man chased by a banshee, thought Gallagher. The intruder bumped against the life raft, striking it above the knees, and tumbled inside. Only when he stared up, eyes fixed more in madness than in terror, did Gallagher recognize General Hui.

"Don't we have to cut the raft loose?" Hui shouted above the wind.

Gallagher shook his head. "I've done that chore."

"The suction from the sinking ship will drag us under."

"Not in this sea, General. We'll be swept clear in seconds. Now lie down on the bottom and get a good grip on the safety ropes."

Too numb with cold to reply, Hui did as he was instructed and took his place inside the raft.

A deep rumble swelled up from below as the cold water surged over the boilers, causing them to explode. The forward section of the ship shook and vibrated, then lurched downward amidships, sending the bow rising into the cold night. The cables supporting the tall, old-fashioned smokestack snapped under the strain, and it fell with a large splash. The water reached the level of the life raft, and its buoyancy lifted it from its mounts. The last Gallagher saw of Captain Hunt, water was surging through the doors of the wheelhouse and whirling around his legs. Determined to go down with his ship, he clutched the helm and stood as firm as if he had turned to granite.

It felt to Gallagher as if they were suspended in time. Waiting for the ship to drop from under them seemed an eternity. Yet it all happened in a few seconds. Then the raft was washed free and hurled into the chaotic waters.

Cries for help came in Mandarin and Cantonese dialects that were impossible to answer. Final pleas to friends slowly faded between the monster wave crests and their troughs and into the fury of the wind. There would be no rescue. No ships were close enough to notice them vanish from radar and no call for help went out. Gallagher and Katie watched with a feeling of horror as the bow rose higher and higher, as if clawing at the stormy sky. She hung suspended for nearly a minute, her ice-shrouded upper works giving her the look of an apparition. Then she gave up and slipped under the black waters. The *Princess Dou Wan* was no more.

"Gone," Hui muttered, his voice unheard above the storm. "All gone." He was staring with utter disbelief at where the ship had been.

"Huddle together for our combined body heat," ordered Gallagher. "If we can make it until morning, we stand a chance of being picked up."

Surrounded by the specter of death and a terrible sense of emptiness, the raft and its pitiful passengers were swallowed by the bitter-cold night and unrelenting fury of the storm.

By dawn the malignant waves were still pounding the small raft. The blackness of night had given way to a ghostly gray sky covered with dark clouds. The snow had turned to a chilling sleet. Mercifully, the wind had fallen to twenty miles an hour and the waves had dropped from thirty to ten feet. The raft was solid and sound but was an old model that lacked emergency equipment for survival. Its passengers were left with nothing but personal fortitude to keep up their spirits until rescue.

Bundled under the heavy layers of clothing, Gallagher and Katie had survived the night in fair shape. But General Hui, dressed only in his uniform and without a coat, was slowly, inexorably freezing to death. The wretched wind was cutting through his uniform like a thousand ice picks. His hair was coated with ice. Gallagher had taken off his heavy peacoat and given it to Hui, but it became obvious to Katie that the old war-horse was rapidly fading.

The raft was tossed over the crests and spun around by the brutal waves. It didn't seem possible that the frail craft could take the pounding. Yet it always recovered from the crush of the curling waves, righted herself, and steadied before facing the next onslaught. Never once did she cast her miserable passengers into the cold water.

Gallagher rose to his knees every hour and scanned the agitated waters from the top of the waves as the raft was thrown skyward before plummeting into the trough again. It was an exercise in futility. The waters were empty. During the awful night, they saw no sign of lights from another ship.

"There has to be a ship nearby," said Katie through chattering teeth.

Gallagher shook his head. "The water is as empty as a homeless waif's piggy bank." He didn't tell her that visibility was cut to less than fifty yards.

"I'll never forgive myself for abandoning Fritz," Katie whispered, the tears falling down her cheeks before turning to ice.

"My fault," Gallagher consoled her. "I should have grabbed him when we ran out of the cabin."

"Fritz?" queried Hui.

"My little dachshund," replied Katie.

"You lost a dog." Hui abruptly sat up. "You lost a dog?" he repeated. "I lost the heart and soul of my country—" He paused and went into a coughing spasm. Misery etched his face, despair clouded his eyes. He looked like a man whose life had lost all meaning. "I have failed in my duty. I must die."

"Don't be stupid, man," said Gallagher. "We'll come through. Just hang in a little longer."

Hui appeared not to hear him. He seemed to wither and give up. Katie was gazing into the general's eyes. It was as if a light behind them had suddenly switched off. They took on a glazed, unseeing look.

"I think he's dead," Katie murmured.

Gallagher checked to be sure. "Move over against his body and use it as a shield from the wind and spray. I'll lie on the other side of you."

It seemed ghoulish to her, but Katie found that she could hardly feel Hui's cadaver through the bulk of her clothing. The loss of her faithful little dog, the ship plunging under the black water, the insane wind and crazed waters all seemed unreal to her. She hoped that it was all a nightmare and soon she would wake up. She burrowed deeper between the two men, one alive, the other dead.

Through the rest of the day and following night the intensity of the storm had slowly abated, but they were still exposed to a murderous windchill factor. Katie could no longer feel her hands and feet. She began to slip in and out of consciousness. Fantasies ran through her mind. Oddly, she found it macabre that she might have eaten her last meal. She thought she saw a sandy beach beneath swaying palm trees. She imagined Fritz running across the sand, barking as he came toward her. She talked to Gallagher as though they were sitting at a table at a restaurant, ordering dinner. Her dead father appeared to her, dressed in his captain's uniform. He stood in the raft, looked down and smiled.

He told her she would live and not to worry. Land was only a short distance away. And then he was gone.

"What time is it?" she asked hoarsely.

"Sometime late in the afternoon, I should judge," answered Gallagher. "My watch stopped soon after we abandoned the *Princess.*"

"How long have we been adrift?"

"A rough guess would put it about thirty-eight hours since the *Princess* went down."

"We're near land," she muttered abruptly.

"What makes you say that, darlin'?"

"My father told me."

"He did, did he?" He smiled at her compassionately under a mustache and eyebrows caked white with ice. Icicles hanging from whatever hair was exposed, gave Gallagher the appearance of a monster risen from the depths of the South Pole in a science-fiction movie. Except for her lack of facial hair, Katie wondered if she looked the same.

"Can't you see it?"

Dreadfully stiff from the cold, Gallagher struggled to a sitting position and scanned the horizons of his restricted world. His view was blurred by the driving sleet, but he kept trying. Then he thought his eyes were deceiving him. He could just make out large boulders scattered along a shoreline. A short distance beyond, no more than fifty yards, snow blanketed trees swaying in the wind. He spotted what looked like the dark shape of a small cabin amid the trees.

His joints numb and unresponsive, Gallagher removed one boot and used it as a paddle. After a few minutes, the exertion seemed to warm his body and the effort became less arduous. "Take heart, darlin'. We'll be on dry land soon."

The current was working parallel to the shore, and Gallagher fought to break out of its clutches. He felt as if he was struggling against a stream filled with molasses. The gap narrowed with agonizing slowness. The trees seemed so close he could reach out and shake them, but they were still a good sixty yards away.

Just when Gallagher had reached the end of his endurance and was about to collapse from exhaustion, he could feel the raft bumping against underwater boulders. He looked down at Katie. She was shivering uncontrollably from the damp and chill. She could not last much longer.

He shoved his frozen foot back inside the boot. Then, sucking in his breath, he prayed that the water would not close over his head and jumped in. It was a hazard he had to risk. Thankfully, the soles of his boots struck hard rock before the water level reached his crotch.

"Katie!" he shouted in happy delirium. "We've made it. We're on land."

"That's nice," Katie murmured, too paralyzed and oblivious to care.

Gallagher dragged the raft onto a shore covered with wave-smoothed rocks and pebbles. The exhausting effort took the last of his strength, and he sagged like a lifeless rag doll and dropped onto the cold, wet rocks. He never knew how long he lay there, but when he finally recovered enough to crawl up to the life raft and peer over the side, he saw that Katie's skin was blue and mottled. Fearful, he reached in and pulled her toward him. He wasn't sure whether she was alive or dead. Then he noticed a wisp of vapor coming from her nose. He felt for a pulse in her neck. It was faint and slow; her strong heart was still pumping, but death was very close to her.

He looked up at the sky. It was no longer a thick quilt of dark gray. The clouds were forming into distinct shapes and turning white. The storm was passing, and already he could sense the gusting wind diminishing to a settled breeze. He had little time. If he did not find warmth quickly, he would lose her.

Taking a deep breath, Gallagher slid his arms under Katie's body and lifted her out of the raft. Out of hatred he kicked the raft with General Hui's frozen body away from the shoreline. He watched for a few moments as the current caught the raft and began carrying it back into deep water. Then, clutching her close to his chest, he began trudging toward the cabin in the trees. The frigid air seemed suddenly warmer, and he no longer felt stiff and tired.

Three days later, the cargo ship *Stephen Miller* reported sighting a body in a life raft, which was later recovered. The dead man was Chinese and looked as if he had been sculpted from ice. He was never identified. The life raft, a model not in use for nearly twenty years, was marked in Chinese. Later translation indicated it came from a ship called the *Princess Dou Wan*.

A search was launched; bits of floating debris were spotted but never retrieved for investigation. No oil slick was discovered. No ship had been reported missing. Nowhere, on ship or ashore, had any distress signal or cry of "Mayday" been picked up. All rescue stations monitoring the standard ship-distress frequency received nothing, hearing only static from the heavy snow.

The mystery deepened when it was learned that a ship named *Princess Dou Wan* had been reported sunk off the coast of Chile the month before. The body found in the life raft was buried, and the strange enigma was quickly forgotten.

PART I

THE KILLING WATER

Orion Lake

Golf Course

Qin Shang's Retreat

Guesthouses

Dock

Yacht

Orion Lake

Boathouse & Dock

Pitt's Cabin

Orion River

1

AS IF SHE WERE STRUGGLING out of a bottomless pit, consciousness slowly returned to Ling T'ai. Her whole upper body swam in pain.
She groaned through clenched teeth, wanting to scream out in agony.
She lifted a hand that was badly bruised and tenderly touched her
fingertips to her face. One coffee brown eye was swollen closed, the
other puffed but partially open. Her nose was broken, with blood still
trickling from the nostrils. Thankfully, she could feel her teeth still in
their gums, but her arms and shoulders were turning black-and-blue.
She could not begin to count the bruises.

Ling T'ai was not sure at first why she was singled out for interrogation. The explanation came later, just before she was brutally beaten.
There were others, to be sure, who were pulled from the mass of illegal
Chinese immigrants on board the ship, tormented and thrown into a
dark compartment in the cargo hold. Nothing was very clear to her,
everything seemed confused and obscure. She felt as if she was about
to lose her grip on consciousness and fall back into the pit.

The ship she had traveled on from the Chinese port of Qingdao
across the Pacific looked to all appearances like a typical cruise ship.
Named the *Indigo Star,* her hull was painted white from waterline to the
funnel. Comparable in size to most smaller cruise ships that carried between one hundred and one hundred fifty passengers in luxurious comfort, the *Indigo Star* crammed nearly twelve hundred illegal Chinese
immigrants into huge open bays within the hull and superstructure. She
was a facade, innocent on the outside, a human hellhole on the inside.

Ling T'ai could not have envisioned the insufferable conditions that she and over a thousand others had to endure. The food was minimal and hardly enough to exist on. Sanitary conditions were non-existent and toilet facilities deplorable. Some had died, mostly young children and the elderly, their bodies removed and never seen again. It seemed likely to Ling T'ai that they were simply thrown into the sea as if they were garbage.

The day before the *Indigo Star* was scheduled to reach the northeastern coast of the United States, a team of sadistic guards called enforcers, who maintained a climate of fear and intimidation on board the ship, had rounded up thirty or forty passengers and forced them to undergo an unexplained interrogation. When her turn finally came, she was ushered into a small, dark compartment and commanded to sit in a chair in front of four enforcers of the smuggling operation who were seated behind a table. Ling was then asked a series of questions.

"Your name!" demanded a thin man neatly attired in a gray pinstripe business suit. His smooth, brown face was intelligent but expressionless. The other three enforcers sat silently and glared malevolently. To the initiated, it was a classic act of interrogative coercion.

"My name is Ling T'ai."

"What province were you born?"

"Jiangsu."

"You lived there?" asked the thin man.

"Until I was twenty and finished my studies. Then I went to Canton, where I became a schoolteacher."

The questions came dispassionately and devoid of inflection. "Why do you want to go to the United States?"

"I knew the voyage would be extremely hazardous, but the promise of opportunity and a better life was too great," answered Ling T'ai. "I decided to leave my family and become an American."

"Where did you obtain the money for your passage?"

"I saved most of it from my teacher's pay over ten years. The rest I borrowed from my father."

"What is his occupation?"

"He is a professor of chemistry at the university in Beijing."

"Do you have friends or family in the United States?"

She shook her head. "I have no one."

The thin man looked at her in long, slow speculation, then pointed his finger at her. "You are a spy, sent to report on our smuggling operation."

32

The accusation came so abruptly, she sat frozen for a few moments before stammering. "I do not know what you mean. I am a schoolteacher. Why do you call me a spy?"

"You do not have the appearance of one born in China."

"Not true!"she cried in panic. "My mother and father are Chinese. So were my grandparents."

"Then explain why your height is as least four inches above average for a Chinese woman and your facial features have the faint touch of European ancestry."

"Who are you?" she demanded. "Why are you so cruel?"

"Not that it matters, my name is Ki Wong. I am the chief enforcer for the *Indigo Star.* Now please answer my last question."

Acting frightened, Ling explained that her great-grandfather had been a Dutch missionary who headed up a mission in the city of Longyan. He took a local peasant girl as a wife. "That is the only Western blood in me, I swear."

The inquisitors acted as if they did not credit her story. "You are lying."

"Please, you must believe me!"

"Do you speak English?"

"I know only a few words and phrases."

Then Wong got down to the real issue. "According to our records, you did not pay enough for your passage. You owe us another ten thousand dollars American."

Ling T'ai leaped to her feet and cried out. "But I have no more money!"

Wong shrugged indifferently. "Then you will have to be transported back to China."

"No, please, I can't go back, not now!" She wrung her hands until the knuckles went white.

The chief enforcer glanced smugly at the three other men, who sat like stone sculptures. Then his voice changed subtly. "There may be another way for you to enter the States."

"I will do anything," Ling T'ai pleaded.

"If we put you ashore, you will have to work off the rest of your passage fee. Since you can hardly speak English it will be impossible for you to find employment as a schoolteacher. Without friends or family you'll have no means of support. Therefore, we will take it upon ourselves to generously provide you with food, a place to live and an opportunity for work until such time as you can subsist on your own."

"What kind of work do you mean?" asked Ling T'ai hesitantly.

Wong paused, then grinned evilly. "You will engage in the art of satisfying men."

This then was what it was all about. Ling T'ai and most of the other smuggled aliens were never intended to be allowed to roam free in the United States. Once they landed on foreign soil, they were to become indentured slaves subject to torture and extortion.

"Prostitution?" Horrified, Ling T'ai shouted angrily, "I will never degrade myself!"

"A pity," said Wong impassively. "You are an attractive woman and could demand a good price."

He rose to his feet, stepped around the table and stood in front of her. The smirk on his face suddenly vanished and was replaced with a look of malice. Then he pulled what looked like a stiff rubber hose from his coat pocket and began lashing at her face and body. He stopped only when he began to break out in sweat, pausing to grip her chin with one hand, staring into her battered face. She moaned and pleaded with him to stop.

"Perhaps you've had a change of mind."

"Never," she muttered through a split and bleeding lip. "I will die first."

Then Wong's narrow lips curled into a cold smile. His arm was raised and then came down in a vicious swing as the hose caught her on the base of the skull. Ling T'ai was enveloped in blackness.

Her tormentor returned to the table and seated himself. He picked up a phone and spoke into the mouthpiece. "You may remove the woman and place her with those going to Orion Lake."

"You do not think she can be converted into a profitable piece of property?" said a heavy-bodied man at the end of the table.

Wong shook his head as he looked down on Ling T'ai, lying bleeding on the floor. "There is something about this woman I do not trust. It is best to play safe. None of us dare to incur the wrath of our esteemed superior by jeopardizing the enterprise. Ling T'ai will get her wish to die."

An elderly woman, who said she was a nurse, tenderly dabbed a wet cloth on Ling T'ai's face, cleaning away the caked blood and applying disinfectant from a small first-aid kit. After the old nurse finished tending the injuries, she moved off to console a young boy who was whimpering in his mother's arms. Ling T'ai half opened the eye that was only mildly swollen and fought off a sudden wave of nausea. Though suffering agonizing pain that erupted from every nerve ending, her mind was unmistakenly clear on every aspect of how she came to be in this predicament.

Her name was not Ling T'ai. The name on her American birth certificate read Julia Marie Lee, born in San Francisco, California. Her father had been an American financial analyst based in Hong Kong when he met and married the daughter of a wealthy Chinese banker. Except for dove-gray eyes under the brown contact lenses, she had favored her mother, who passed on beautiful blue-black hair and Asian facial features. Nor was she a schoolteacher from Jiangsu Province in China.

Julia Marie Lee was a special undercover agent for the International Affairs Investigations Division of the United States Immigration and Naturalization Service. By posing as Ling T'ai, she had paid a representative of an alien-smuggling syndicate in Beijing the equivalent of $30,000 in Chinese currency. Becoming part of the human cargo with its built-in misery, she compiled a wealth of information on the syndicate's activities and methods of operation.

Once she was smuggled on shore, her plan was to contact the field office of the assistant district director of investigations in Seattle, who was prepared and waiting for information to arrest the smugglers within territorial limits and break up the syndicate's pipeline into North America. Now her fate was uncertain, and she saw no avenue of escape.

Through some untapped reservoir of fortitude she did not know she possessed, Julia had somehow survived the torture. Months of hard training had never prepared her for a brutal beating. She cursed herself for choosing the wrong course. If she had meekly accepted her fate, her plan to escape would have most likely been achieved. But she thought that by playing the role of a frightened but proud Chinese woman she could have deceived the smugglers. As it turned out, it was a mistake. She realized now that any sign of resistance was shown no mercy. Many of the men and women, she began to see in the dim light, were also badly beaten.

The more Julia thought about her situation, the more she became certain she and everyone in the cargo hold around her were going to be murdered.

2

THE OWNER of the small general store at Orion Lake, ninety miles due west of Seattle, turned slightly and peered at the man who opened the door and stood momentarily on the threshold. Orion Lake was off the beaten track to most traffic, and Dick Colburn knew everyone in this rugged area of the Olympic Peninsula mountains. The stranger was either a tourist passing through or a fisherman from the city trying his luck with either the salmon or trout stocked in the nearby lake by the Forest Service. He wore a short leather jacket over an Irish knit sweater and corduroy pants. No hat covered a mass of wavy black hair that was streaked gray at the temples. Colburn watched as the stranger stared unblinkingly at the shelves and display cases before stepping inside.

Out of habit Colburn studied the man for a few moments. The stranger was tall; his head cleared the top of the door by less than three fingers. Not the face of an office worker, Colburn decided. The skin was too tan and craggy for a life spent indoors. The cheeks and chin were in need of a shave. The body seemed thin for the frame. There was the unmistakable look about him of a man who had seen too much, who had suffered hardship and grief. He appeared tired, not physically tired, but emotionally used up, someone who cared little about life anymore. It was almost as if he had been tapped on the shoulder by death but had somehow shrugged him off. Yet there was a quiet cheerfulness in the opaline-green eyes that broke through the haggard features, and an obscure sense of pride.

Colburn concealed his interest well and went about his business of stocking the shelves. "Can I help you with anything?" he asked over his shoulder.

"Just dropped by to pick up a few groceries," replied the stranger. Colburn's store was too small for shopping carts, so he picked up a basket, slinging the carrying handles over one arm.

"How's the fishing?"

"Haven't tried my luck yet."

"There's a good hole at the south end of the lake where they've been known to bite."

"I'll keep that in mind, thank you."

"Got you a fishing license yet?"

"No, but I'll bet you're authorized to sell me one."

"Resident or nonresident of the state of Washington?"

"Non."

The grocer pulled out a form from beneath the counter and handed the stranger a pen. "Just fill in the applicable blanks. I'll add the fee onto your groceries." To Colburn's practiced ear the accent was vaguely southwestern. "The eggs are fresh. Laid right here in town. There's a sale on cans of Shamus O'Malley's stew. And the smoked salmon and the elk steaks taste like they came from heaven."

For the first time a hint of a smile crossed the stranger's lips. "The elk steaks and the salmon sound good, but I think I'll pass on Mr. O'Malley's stew."

After nearly fifteen minutes the basket was full and set on the counter beside an antique brass cash register. Instead of the usual selection of canned goods picked by most fishermen, this basket was filled with mostly fruits and vegetables.

"You must be planning on staying awhile," said Colburn.

"An old family friend loaned me his cabin on the lake. You probably know him. His name is Sam Foley."

"I've known Sam for twenty years. His cabin is the only one that damned Chinaman hasn't bought up," Colburn grumbled. "Good thing too. If Sam sells out, there won't be an access for fishermen to launch their boats on the lake."

"I wondered why most of the cabins looked run-down and abandoned, all except that odd-looking building. The one on the north side of the lake opposite the mouth of that small river flowing west."

Colburn spoke as he rang up the groceries. "Used to be a fish cannery back in the forties until the company went broke. The Chinaman picked it up for a song and then remodeled it into a fancy mansion. Even built a nine-hole golf course. Then he began buying every piece of property that fronted on the lake. Your friend, Sam Foley, is the only holdout."

"It seems half the population of Washington and British Columbia is Chinese," commented the stranger.

"The Chinese have poured into the Pacific Northwest like a flood tide since the Communist government took over Hong Kong. They already own half of downtown Seattle and most of Vancouver. No telling what the population will look like in another fifty years." Colburn paused and punched the TOTAL lever on the cash register. "With the fishing permit, that'll be seventy-nine-thirty-five."

The stranger pulled his wallet from a hip pocket, handed Colburn a hundred-dollar bill and waited for the change. "The Chinaman you mentioned—what sort of business is he in?"

"All I heard is that he's a wealthy shipping tycoon from Hong Kong." Colburn began sacking the groceries while gossiping away. "Nobody has ever seen him. Never comes through town. Except for drivers of big delivery trucks, nobody goes in or out. Strange goings-on, if you ask most of the folks around here. He and his cronies don't fish in the daytime. You can only hear boat motors at night, and they don't run lights. Harry Daniels, who hunts and camps along the river, claims he's seen an odd-looking work boat traveling the lake after midnight, and never under a moon."

"Everybody loves a good mystery."

"If I can do anything for you while you're in the neighborhood, just ask. My name's Dick Colburn."

The stranger showed white, even teeth in a broad grin. "Dirk Pitt."

"You be from California, Mr. Pitt?"

"You'd do Professor Henry Higgins proud," said Pitt lightheartedly. "I was born and grew up in Southern California, but for the past fifteen years I've lived in Washington."

Colburn began to smell new ground. "You must work with the U.S. government."

"The National Underwater and Marine Agency. And before you misreckon, I came to Orion Lake strictly to relax and unwind. Nothing more."

"If you'll pardon me for saying so," said Colburn sympathetically, "you look like a man who could use some rest."

Pitt grinned. "What I really need is a good back rub."

"Cindy Elder. She tends bar over at the Sockeye Saloon and gives a great massage."

"I'll keep her in mind." Pitt took the grocery sacks in both arms and headed for the door. Just before stepping outside, he stopped and turned. "Out of curiosity, Mr. Colburn, what is the Chinaman's name?"

Colburn looked at Pitt, trying to read something in the eyes that wasn't there. "He calls himself Shang, Qin Shang."

"Did he ever say why he purchased the old canning factory?"

"Norman Selby, the real-estate agent who handled the transaction, said Shang wanted a secluded area on water to build a fancy retreat where he could entertain affluent clients." Colburn paused and looked positively belligerent. "You must have seen what he did to a perfectly good cannery. Only a matter of time before the State Historical Commission would have named it as a historic site. Shang turned it into a cross between a modern office building and a pagoda. An abortion, I say, a damned abortion."

"It does have a novel look about it," Pitt agreed. "No doubt Shang, as a neighborly gesture, invites the town citizens to parties and golf tournaments?"

"Are you kidding?" said Colburn, venting his anger. "Shang won't even allow the mayor and city council within a mile of his property. Would you believe he even erected a ten-foot chain-link fence with barbwire on the top around most of the lake?"

"Can he get away with that?"

"He can and did, by buying off politicians. He can't keep people off the lake. It belongs to the state. But he can make it hard for them to get on."

"Some people have a fetish for privacy," said Pitt.

"Shang's got more than a fetish. Security cameras and armed goons crawl through the woods all around the place. Hunters and fishermen who accidentally wander too close are hustled off the land and treated like common criminals."

"I must remember to stay on my side of the lake."

"Probably wouldn't be a bad idea."

"See you in a few days, Mr. Colburn."

"Come again, Mr. Pitt. Have a nice day."

Pitt looked up at the sky. Not much of the day was left. The late-afternoon sun was partially shaded by the tops of the fir trees rising behind Colburn's store. He set the grocery bags on the rear passenger seat of his rental car and climbed behind the wheel. He turned the ignition key, shifted into drive and pressed the accelerator. Five minutes later, he turned off the asphalt highway onto a dirt road leading to the

Foley cabin on Orion Lake. For two miles the road meandered through a forest of cedar, spruce and hemlock.

At the end of a quarter-mile straight, he came to a fork, each road skirting the shore of the lake in opposite directions until meeting up again on the far side, which happened to be Qin Shang's extravagant retreat. Pitt could not help but agree with the grocer's description. The former cannery had truly been transformed into an architectural miscarriage, totally inappropriate for a beautiful setting on an alpine lake. It was as though the builder had begun a modern structure of copper-tinted solar glass intermingled with exposed steel beams, then changed his mind and turned it over to a fifteenth-century Ming-dynasty contractor who topped the building with a golden tile roof straight off the majestic Hall of Supreme Harmony in the Forbidden City at Beijing.

After being told that the owner was cloistered by an elaborate security system, Pitt, while enjoying the solitude of the lake, now assumed his movements were being observed. He turned onto the road bearing left and continued for another half-mile before stopping beside a wooden stairway leading to a porch that ran around an attractive log cabin overlooking the lake. He remained sitting in the car for a minute, gazing at a pair of deer that were feeding in the woods.

The soreness had gone out of his injuries, and he could exercise movement almost as well as he could before the tragedy. The cuts and burns had for the most part healed. It was his mind and emotions that were taking longer.

He was ten pounds lighter and not making a concerted effort at putting the lost weight back on. He felt as if he had lost all sense of purpose. It was a case of actually feeling worse than he looked. But deep down there was a spark that was fanned by an inherent urge to peer into the unknown. The spark burst into flame soon after he carried the groceries inside the cabin and set them on the kitchen sink.

Something did not seem right. He couldn't put his finger on it, but it quietly gnawed at his mind, some unfathomable sixth sense that told him something was wrong. He stepped into the living room. Nothing out of the ordinary there. He cautiously entered the bedroom, glanced around, checked the closet and moved into the bathroom. And then he had it. The toiletry items from his shaving kit—razor, cologne, toothbrush, hairbrush—were always placed in neat order on the sink after he arrived at his destination. They were right where he had set them, all except the shaving kit itself. He distinctly recalled holding it by the outside strap and pushing it onto a shelf. Now the strap was facing the rear wall.

He went through the rooms now, carefully studying every loose object. Somebody, probably more than one person, had been over every inch of the cabin. They had to be professionals but became indifferent when they concluded that the resident was not a secret agent or a hired assassin but merely a guest of the cabin's owner enjoying a few peaceful days of relaxation. From the time Pitt left for town until he returned, they had a good forty-five minutes to do the job. At first the reason behind the search escaped Pitt, but then a light began to glow in the dim reaches of his brain.

There had to be something else. To an expert spy or gold-badge detective, the answer would be immediately transparent. But Pitt was neither. A former Air Force pilot and longtime special projects director for NUMA, his specialty was troubleshooting the agency's underwater projects, not undercover investigation. It took him a good sixty seconds to solve the dilemma.

He realized that the search was secondary. The real purpose was to install listening devices or miniature cameras. Someone doesn't trust me, Pitt thought. And that someone must be the chief of Qin Shang's security network.

Because listening bugs were no larger than pinheads they would be difficult to find without an electronic snooping device. But since Pitt had only himself to talk to, he decided to concentrate on the cameras. Assuming he was under surveillance and his every movement was being observed by someone sitting in front of a TV monitor on the other side of the lake, he sat down and pretended to read a newspaper while his mind churned. Let them see what they want in the living room and bedroom, he reasoned. The kitchen was another matter. That would be his war room.

He put down the paper and began putting away the groceries in the cupboards and refrigerator, using the activity as a distraction while his eyes darted into every nook and cranny. He found nothing conspicuous. Then he began casually glancing at the log walls of the cabin, peering into the cracks and chinking. He finally hit paydirt when he spotted a tiny lens pressed into a wormhole, burrowed when the log was the trunk of a growing tree. Playing the role of an actor in front of a camera, which indeed he was, Pitt swept the floor with a broom. When he was finished he turned the broom upside down and leaned the sweeper part against the wall directly in front of the camera.

41

As if given a shot to spur his adrenaline, he brushed off any feelings of fatigue and tension and stepped outside, walking thirty paces away from the cabin into the woods. He pulled a Motorola Iridium phone from the inside pocket of his jacket. After dialing a number, his signal was bounced over a network of sixty-six satellites around the world and down to the private line of the person he was calling at the NUMA headquarters in Washington, D.C.

After four rings, a voice with a slight New England twang answered. "This is Hiram Yaeger. Be brief, time is money."

"Your time isn't worth a dime stuck in gum on the bottom of a shoe."

"Am I the subject of mockery by NUMA's special projects director?"

"You are."

"What are you doing that's not worth repeating?" asked Yaeger facetiously. Yet his voice betrayed a trace of concern. He knew Pitt was still recovering from injuries suffered during a volcanic eruption on an island off Australia only the month before.

"I haven't time to leave you breathless with my daring adventures in the north woods. But I do need a favor."

"I'm drooling with anticipation."

"See what you can dig up on a Qin Shang."

"How's it spelled?"

"Probably like it sounds. If my limited knowledge of Chinese menus serves me correctly, the first name begins with a Q. Shang is a Chinese shipping magnate who operates out of Hong Kong. He also owns a private retreat on Orion Lake in Washington State."

"Is that where you're at?" asked Yaeger. "You never told anyone where you were going when you up and disappeared."

"I'd just as soon Admiral Sandecker was kept in the dark."

"He'll find out anyway. He always does. Just what is it that intrigues you about Shang?"

"You might say I'm irritated by nosy neighbors," replied Pitt.

"Why don't you go over and borrow a cup of sugar, have a few laughs and challenge him to a fast game of mah-jongg."

"According to the locals, no one can get within ten city blocks of his place. And at that, I doubt if he's at home. If Shang is like most wealthy celebrities, he has several different houses around the world."

"Why does this guy consume you with curiosity?"

"No upstanding citizen has a mania about security unless he has something to hide," said Pitt.

"Sounds to me like you're bored, lying around the primeval forest, watching moss grow on the rocks. You've missed one of life's pleasures if you haven't tried to outstare a moose for forty-five minutes."

"I've never been turned on by apathy."

"Any other requests while I'm in the mood?" asked Yaeger.

"Now that you mention it, I do have a wish list of Christmas goodies I'd like boxed and sent out tonight so I can have them no later than tomorrow afternoon."

"Fire away," said Yaeger. "I've turned on the recorder and will print them out when you're finished."

Pitt described the articles and equipment he required. When he finished, he added, "Throw in a Department of Natural Resources chart of Orion Lake showing bathymetric data and fish species, underwater wrecks and obstructions."

"The plot thickens. For a guy who was battered to a pulp and just released from a hospital, don't you think you're overdoing it?"

"Play along with me and I'll mail you five pounds of smoked salmon."

"I hate being a weenie," Yaeger sighed. "Okay, I'll take care of your toys before I make inquiries through proper and unproper channels on Qin Shang. With luck, I'll give you his blood type."

Pitt knew from experience that data buried and secreted in classified files was not immune to Yaeger's ferretlike talents. "Set those fat little fingers flying over your keyboard and call me at my Iridium number when you turn up something."

Yaeger hung up the phone, leaned back in his chair and stared thoughtfully at the ceiling for several moments. Yaeger looked more like a street-corner panhandler than he did a brilliant computer-systems analyst. He kept his graying hair in a ponytail and dressed like an aging hippie, which he was. Yaeger was head of NUMA's computer-data network, which contained a vast library on every book, article and thesis, whether scientific, historical fact or theory, ever recorded on the world's oceans.

Yaeger's computer domain took up the entire tenth floor of the NUMA building. It had taken years to put together the massive library. His boss had given him a free hand and unlimited funding for accumulating every recorded bit of knowledge on ocean science and technology so it could be available to ocean-science students, professional oceanographers, marine engineers and underwater archaeologists around the world. The job carried enormous responsibility, but it was a job Yaeger loved with a passion.

He turned his gaze on the expansive computer he had designed and built himself. "Fat fingers on a keyboard, hah!" There was no keyboard and no monitor. As with virtual reality, images were projected in three dimensions in front of the user. Instead of typing on keys, commands were spoken. A caricature of Yaeger, enhanced and fleshed out, stared back at him.

"Well, Max, you ready to go cruising?" Yaeger asked the image.

"I am prime," replied a disembodied voice.

"Acquire all available information on a Qin Shang, a Chinese shipping-company owner, whose main office is in Hong Kong."

"Data insufficient for a detailed report," said Max in a monotone.

"Not much to go on, I admit," said Yaeger, never quite getting the hang of talking to a nebulous image produced by a machine. "Do the best you can. Print out your findings when you've exhausted all the networks."

"I will get back to you shortly," droned Max.

Yaeger stared at the space vacated by his holographic likeness, his eyes narrow and questioning. Pitt had never asked him to research and build a file unless he had good reason. Something, Yaeger knew, was running around in his friend's head. Quandaries and enigmas followed Pitt around like puppy dogs. He was drawn to trouble like salmon to their spawning grounds. Yaeger hoped Pitt would reveal the mystery. He always did, he always had to when his projects went beyond the mere realm of casual interest.

"What in hell is the crazy bastard up to this time?" Yaeger muttered to his computer.

3

ORION LAKE was shaped like a slender teardrop whose lower end gently tapered into a small river. Not a large body of water but alluring and mystical, its shores were bordered by an ocean of dense green forests that sloped up the gray rock bluffs of the majestic, cloud-shrouded Olympic Mountains. Vividly colored spring wildflowers bloomed beneath the trees and in small meadows. Meltwater from high-country glaciers fed into the lake through several streams, carrying minerals that gave the water a crystal blue-green color. The cobalt sky above was garnished with fast-moving clouds, all reflecting off the water, which gave them a light turquoise tint.

The flow of water that drained from the lower tip of the teardrop was appropriately called the Orion River. Running peacefully through a canyon sliced between the mountains, the river traveled sixteen miles before emptying into the upper end of a fjordlike inlet called Grapevine Bay. Carved by an ancient glacier, Grapevine Bay opened into the Pacific Ocean. The river, once traveled by fishing boats that unloaded their catch at the old cannery, was now only used by pleasure boats and fishermen.

The next afternoon after his trip to town, Pitt stepped from the cabin onto the porch and inhaled. A light rain had come and passed, leaving the air like perfume to the lungs, pure and intoxicating. The sun had fallen behind the mountains, its final rays angling down through the ravines between the peaks. It was a timeless scene. Only the abandoned homes and cabins gave the lake a haunted look.

He stepped across a narrow wooden pier leading from the beach to a boathouse that floated on the water. He selected a key on a ring and sprung the heavy padlock sealing the weatherworn wooden door. The interior was dark. No bugs or cameras in here, he thought as he pushed the door wide open. Suspended over the water by cradles attached to an electric hoist, a little ten-foot sailboat and a twenty-one-foot 1933 Chris-Craft runabout with a double cockpit and a gleaming mahogany hull hung inside the boathouse. Two kayaks and a canoe sat in racks along both walls.

He walked over to an electric-circuit box and snapped on a single breaker. Then he took the control unit that was wired to the hoist and pushed a button. The hoist whirred as it moved over the sailboat. Pitt slid the hook that dangled from the hoist though a metal loop on the cradle and lowered it. For the first time in many months, the sailboat's fiberglass hull settled into the water.

Pitt removed the neatly folded sails from a locker and assembled the aluminum mast and added the rigging. Then he set the tiller in its spindles and inserted the centerboard. After nearly half an hour, the little boat was ready to fill her sails with wind. Only the mast had to be stepped, a small chore that could only take place after the hull was pushed from under the roof of the boathouse.

Satisfied everything was in order, Pitt casually walked back to the cabin and unpacked one of the two large cartons air-expressed by Yaeger. He sat down at the kitchen table and spread out the chart of Orion Lake he had requested. The depth soundings showed the lake bed sloping gently from the shore, then leveling off for a short distance at a depth of thirty feet before dropping off steeply in the middle of the lake to over four hundred feet. Far too deep for a diver without the proper equipment and a surface crew, Pitt figured. No man-made obstructions were marked. The only wreck shown was an old fishing boat that had sunk off the cannery. The lake's average water temperature was forty-one degrees Fahrenheit, far too cold for swimming but ideal for fishing and boating.

Pitt barbecued an elk steak for an early dinner, mixed a salad and ate at a table on the porch overlooking the lake. He leisurely sipped an Olympia beer before setting the bottle on the table and stepping into the kitchen, where he extended the tripod legs on a brass telescope. He set it in the middle of the kitchen away from the window to make it difficult for anyone from the outside to observe his activity in the shadows. He crouched over the eyepiece and focused on Qin Shang's retreat. The high-powered magnification made it possible for Pitt to observe two players on the golf course behind the house. Duffers, he deduced. They took four putts apiece to send their balls into the cup. His circular field of vision strayed to the guesthouses nestled under a grove of trees growing behind the main house. Except for a maid making the rounds, they looked unoccupied. There was no neatly manicured lawn in the open spaces. The grounds were left natural with meadow grass and wildflowers.

A huge porte cochere extended from the building over the driveway so VIP guests could get in and out of automobiles without getting wet in bad weather. The main entry was guarded by two great bronze reclining lions on each side of a stairway that led to rosewood doors standing the height of three men. He refocused the telescope and discerned the beautifully carved dragon motif on the panels. The expansive golden-tiled, pagoda-styled roof seemed utterly incongruous with the walls of copper-tinted solar glass that wrapped the entire lower structure. The three-story house itself was set in a spacious clearing a stone's throw from the shoreline.

He lowered the telescope a fraction and studied the dock that extended half the length of a football field into the waters of the lake. Two boats were tied alongside. Nothing fancy about the smaller one. The stubby twin catamaran hulls held a large, boxlike cabin with no portholes or windows. A wheelhouse was perched on the roof, and the entire vessel was painted as black as a hearse, not a color often seen on the upperworks of a boat. The second could have qualified as a ship. She was a looker, an elegant motor yacht with a skylounge on a hull over 120 feet in length, the kind that stopped people in their tracks. Pitt estimated her beam at nearly thirty feet. Designed for luxurious comfort, her classic lines enhanced her from a mere yacht to a floating masterwork. Probably built either in Singapore or Hong Kong, Pitt guessed. Even with a shallow draft, it would take a good pilot to navigate her through the river running from the lake to open water.

As he watched, diesel smoke trailed from the stack of the work boat. In a few moments its crew cast off the mooring lines, and it began moving across the lake toward the river outlet. A very strange craft, Pitt thought. It looked like a wooden shipping crate on two pontoons. He could not begin to imagine what its builder had in mind.

On land, except for the maid and two golfers, the premises looked deserted. There was no hint of security systems. He could find no visible sign of mounted video cameras, but he knew they had to be there. No guards patrolling the grounds either, unless they had learned the art of invisibility. The only objects that seemed out of place with the landscape were several windowless structures built out of logs. Similar to the hostel-type huts used by hunters and hikers, they were spaced at strategic locations around the lake. He counted three and guessed that more were hidden in the woods. The third one seemed curiously mislaid. It floated at the end of the dock and looked like a small boathouse. As with the strange black boat, there were no windows or doors. He gazed at it for nearly a full minute, trying to fathom its purpose and speculate on what was inside.

A slight shift in the telescope, and the focal point of his interest was rewarded. Only a small piece showed from behind a stand of spruce. Not much, but enough to lay to rest his curiosity about the security setup. The roof of a neatly hidden recreation vehicle revealed a small forest of antennae and reception dishes. In a short clearing beyond, what appeared to be a small aircraft hangar sat beside a narrow runway that was only fifty yards in length. Definitely not the sort of layout that would facilitate the use of a helicopter. Ultralight aircraft, perhaps? Pitt conjectured. Yes, that had to be the answer.

"A state-of-the-art setup," he muttered softly to himself.

And a state-of-the-art setup it was, too. He recognized the RV as a mobile command post of the type that presidential Secret Service agents often operated from when the President traveled away from Washington. Pitt began to understand the purpose of the log huts. The next step was to provoke a response.

It seemed silly to go to so much effort out of bored inquisitiveness. He had yet to receive Yaeger's report. For all he knew, Shang was a humanitarian, a philanthropist and a spiritual inspiration, someone Pitt could respect. Pitt wasn't an investigator, he was a marine engineer. Most of his work took place beneath the sea. Why he even bothered was a mystery. But a tiny flag went up in his mind. Shang's lifestyle didn't hold water. This wouldn't be the first time Pitt had meddled in something that didn't concern him. The most compelling reason to jump in was that Pitt's intuition was almost always right on the money.

As if on cue, the tone on his Iridium phone sounded. Only Hiram Yaeger knew his code. He stepped a safe distance outside the cabin before answering. "Hiram?"

"Your boy Shang is a real piece of work," Yaeger said without preamble.

"What have you got on him?" asked Pitt.

"This guy lives like a Roman emperor. Huge entourage. Palatial homes around the world, yachts, a bevy of gorgeous women, jet aircraft, an army of security people. If ever someone qualified for *Lifestyles of the Rich and Famous,* it's Shang."

"What did you learn about his operations?"

"Damned little. Every time Max—"

"Max?"

"Max is my buddy. He lives inside my computer."

"If you say so. Go on."

"Every time Max tried to get into a data file with Shang's name on it, computers from just about every intelligence agency in town blocked our inquiries and demanded to know our business. It seems you're not the only one interested in this guy."

"Sounds like we opened a can of worms," said Pitt. "Why would our own government throw a security lock around Shang?"

"My impression is our intelligence agencies are conducting a classified investigation and don't appreciate an outside probe slipping under their fence."

"The plot thickens. Shang can't be pure as the driven snow if he's under a secret government investigation."

"Either that or they're protecting him."

"Which is it?"

"Beats me," admitted Yaeger. "Until Max and I can carry out a heavy hacking project into the proper data sources, I'm in the dark as much as you are. All I can tell you is that he's not the second coming of the Messiah. Shang slithers around the world like an eel, making enormous profits from a myriad of what appear to be perfectly legal enterprises."

"Are you saying you have no evidence that he's involved with an organized-crime group?"

"Nothing shows on the surface," answered Yaeger. "Which doesn't mean he can't operate as an independent."

"Maybe he's Fu Manchu reincarnated," said Pitt lightly.

"Mind telling what you have against him?"

"His flunkies tossed my cabin. I'm not keen on strangers probing about my underwear."

"There is one thing you'd find interesting," said Yaeger.

"I'm listening."

"Not only do you and Shang have the same birthday, but you were born in the same year. Under his culture Shang was born in the year of the rat. In yours, under the sign of Cancer."

"That's the best the finest computer whiz in the business can come up with?" Pitt said dryly.

"I wish I had more to offer," Yaeger said regretfully. "I'll keep trying."

"I can ask no more."

"What do you plan to do now?"

"There isn't much I can do," said Pitt, "except go fishing."

He didn't fool Yaeger for an instant. "Watch your back," Yaeger said seriously, "or you may find yourself up that famous foul-smelling creek without means of propulsion."

"I'll be my old, usual cagey self."

He punched off the CALL button, reached up and set the Iridium phone in the fork of a tree. Not the greatest of hiding places, but better than allowing it to lie around the cabin in the event of another search while he was away.

Pitt hated brushing off Yaeger's loyal concern, but it was better the head computer guru at NUMA knew as little as possible. For what Pitt was about to do he could get arrested. And if he wasn't careful, the probability was even greater of getting shot. He only hoped to God there were no unforeseen consequences. He had a leaden feeling in the pit of his stomach that if he made a mistake, his body might never be found.

There were two hours of daylight left when Pitt walked the dock to the boathouse. In his arms he carried a jumbo-sized ice chest and a large mounted salmon that had hung over the cabin's fireplace mantel. Once inside he opened the ice chest and lifted out a small autonomous underwater vehicle built by Benthos Inc., an undersea systems technology designer. Inside a black housing no more than twenty-five inches in length by six inches wide, the AUV held a high-resolution color video camera. Its battery power supply could propel two counterrotating thrusters for slightly over two hours.

Pitt laid the compact little unit in the bottom of the sailboat along with a fishing rod and a tackle box. Next he opened the outer doors to the boathouse, climbed down and took his place at the tiller. Pushing off the dock with a boat hook until it was free of the boathouse, he stepped the mast, raised the sail and lowered the centerboard.

To an observing eye he looked like a garden-variety businessman on holiday leisurely sailing on the lake. The climate was pleasant but cool, and he was dressed warmly in a red wool lumberman's shirt and khaki pants. On his feet he wore sneakers and sweat socks. The only contrast with serious fishermen was that they would have used a powerboat or a rowboat with an outboard motor to go after salmon and trout, certainly not a sailboat. Pitt chose the slower of the two boats because the sail made a good shield from any video cameras at the resort.

He propelled the little craft further away from the boathouse by pushing the tiller back and forth until the afternoon breeze filled the sail, and he began gliding across the blue-green waters of Orion Lake. He tacked easily, skirting the deserted shoreline while keeping a respectful distance from the huge home at the lower end of the lake. In the deepest part of the lake less than a quarter mile from Shang's boat dock, Pitt came into the wind and dropped the sail, leaving just enough raised to flap in the breeze and hide his movements. The rope on the anchor was not nearly long enough to reach the bottom, but he lowered it as far as it could reach to act as a drag to keep the wind from pushing the sailboat too close to shore.

With the lowered sail facing one shore and his back to the opposite, he leaned over the side and peered into a bucket with a transparent bottom. The water was so crystal clear that Pitt could see a school of salmon swimming a good hundred and fifty feet below. Then he opened a fishing tackle box and removed a hook and lead sinkers. The only fish Pitt had caught in the past thirty years, he caught underwater with a spear gun. He hadn't held a rod and reel in his hands since he fished with his father, Senator George Pitt, off the coast of California when he was a young boy. Still, he managed to tie on lead sinkers, slip an unfortunate night crawler over a hook and cast it into the deep.

While under the pretense of fishing, he also uncoiled a reel of thin wire and placed a coffee cup–sized transponder that sent and received electronic signals over the side of the sailboat. He lowered it to a depth of twenty feet to assure that it was out of the acoustic shadow of the boat's hull. A similarly sized transponder was housed in the aft end of the AUV. These two units and the electronics inside the AUV casing formed the heart of the system by talking to each other acoustically, allowing underwater control and video signals to be received by a small recorder.

Next, he removed the AUV from the ice chest, carefully lowered it into the water and watched as it silently slipped beneath the surface, its black casing giving the appearance of some ugly creature from the abyss. Pitt had over two hundred hours operating tethered robotic underwater vehicles, but this was only the second time he had operated an autonomous system. His mouth felt slightly on the dry side as he watched the little vehicle that had cost NUMA two million dollars sink out of sight into the lake. The autonomous underwater system was a marvel of miniaturization and for the first time enabled NUMA scientists to send a robotic unit into areas that were previously impossible to reach.

He unfolded a laptop computer with an oversized, high-resolution, active-matrix display, and powered up the system. Satisfied a secure acoustic link was established, he scrolled through the control menus and selected a combination of "remote and live video." Under normal circumstances he would have preferred to concentrate on a live video display of the images recorded by the camera under the water, but this trip it was vital that he focus his attention on the events that he hoped to incite at the retreat. He intended only to view the progress of the AUV from time to time to keep it on course.

He moved the joystick on a small remote handbox. The vehicle immediately responded and went into a dive. The acoustic telemetry and control system performed flawlessly, and the vehicle shot forward at almost four knots. The counterrotating thrusters were balanced perfectly, preventing the vehicle from corkscrewing through the water.

"Every move a picture," Pitt said, staring in the direction of Shang's retreat as he stretched out on a pair of vinyl seat cushions that doubled as safety floats should the boat's occupants be thrown in the water. Then he propped his feet on a bench seat and nestled the remote-control box of the AUV between his legs. Using the levers and joystick on the remote he directed the vehicle's movements like a model submarine. He leveled it out at a depth of sixty feet and worked it slowly toward Shang's boat dock, sweeping it back and forth as though he were plowing a field.

To the uninformed it might have looked as if Pitt was playing with a toy, but the exercise was more than a game. He meant to test Shang's security systems. The first experiment was to detect any underwater sensors. After running several lines that gradually closed to within ten yards of the boat dock with no response, it seemed apparent Shang's security systems did not extend into the lake. They apparently failed to consider penetration from the water as a threat.

It's show time, Pitt thought silently. He pulled gently on the lever that sent the AUV rising to the surface. The little submersible broke water in plain sight a few yards to one side of the dock. He timed the response. Surprisingly, a full three minutes passed before the walls on the windowless huts swung up and guards with Steyr tactical machine pistols slung over their shoulders came charging out across the grounds on off-road motorcycles. They looked to Pitt like Chinese-made copies of the Japanese Suzuki RM 250cc supercross bike. They spread out in formation and took up positions along the sandy beach. Thirty seconds later, the wall on the hut at the end of the floating dock facing the lake also flew open as two guards riding Chinese-built personal watercraft, these designed along the lines of the Japanese Kawasaki Jet Ski, sprinted after the AUV.

Not what Pitt called a rapid deployment. He expected better from veteran security specialists. Even the ultralights remained hidden in their hangar. It seemed the incursion by the AUV did not warrant an all-out search effort.

Pitt immediately sent the submersible into a dive, and because it was visible in the clear water, he cut a steep turn that brought it under the yacht beside the dock. He needn't have worried about the guards on the watercraft sighting the little sub. They churned the surface of the water to such a froth by racing around in circles, it was impossible for them to see into the depths. Pitt observed that neither of the men on the watercraft wore any type of diving equipment, not even masks and snorkels, a solid indication they were not prepared to engage in under-water investigation. Professionals on land but amateurs in the water, Pitt mused.

Finding no hint of an intruder along the beach, the men guarding the grounds climbed off their dirt bikes and stood watching the antics of the water derby. Any attempt at piercing Shang's retreat by land could only be undertaken with any chance of success by a team from the Special Forces, who were experts in the art of stealth and camouflage. By water it was another story. A diver could easily swim under the dock and the yacht without fear of being discovered.

While he guided the AUV back to the sailboat, Pitt reeled in his fishing line until it was just under the surface. Then he sneaked the mounted salmon from the Foley cabin's fireplace into the water and ran the hook, still with the impaled night crawler, through the dried open mouth. Waving his arms conspicuously, he lifted the long-deceased salmon out of the water and held it in the air for all prying eyes to see. The two security guards on the watercraft circled him at less than fifty feet, rocking the sailboat in their wakes. Reasonably assured they would not attempt to seize him on state-government-owned water, he ignored them. Instead, Pitt faced the guards lining the shore and waved the fish back and forth like a signal flag. He watched as the guards, finding nothing suspicious they could put their teeth into, returned to the log security huts. Feeling there was no point in hanging around and greatly relieved the AUV hadn't been discovered by the guards, who seemed more interested in a fisherman than what was under the water, Pitt pulled up the anchor, raised the sail and, with the little robotic submersible following obediently behind and below the surface, headed back toward the Foleys' boathouse. After securing the sailboat and replacing the AUV in the ice chest, he removed an eight-millimeter videocassette from the camera and dropped it in his pocket.

After checking to see if the probing eye of the surveillance camera was still obstructed by the broom, he relaxed with a bottle of Martin Ray chardonnay. Pleased with himself but prudent and wary, Pitt laid his faithful, scratched and worn old Colt .45 automatic in his lap under a napkin. A gift from his father, the gun had saved his life on more than one occasion, and he never traveled without it. After he cleared up the kitchen and brewed a pot of coffee, he walked into the living room, inserted the cassette from the AUV's camera package in a special adapter and slipped it into the slot of a VCR mounted on top of the cabin's television set. Then he sat hunched directly in front of the screen so the images could not be exposed to any camera still undiscovered in the living room.

As he watched the underwater video recorded by the AUV, he hardly expected to see anything that did not belong on the lake's bottom. His primary interest was the area in and around the dock and the yacht moored beside it. He sat patiently as the submersible swept back and forth over the shallower slopes before passing over the deep hole in the middle of the lake during its roundabout voyage toward Shang's dock. The first few minutes revealed only an occasional fish that darted away from the mechanical intruder, weeds growing out of the silt, gnarled logs that had been washed down the feeding streams. He smiled to himself when he observed several children's toys and bicycles just off a beach, as well as a pre–World War II automobile in deeper water. Then, suddenly, odd patches of white appeared through the blue-green void.

Pitt stiffened and stared in horrified fascination as the patches of white materialized into human faces on heads attached to bodies heaped together or lying alone in the silt. The lake bed was littered with what must have been hundreds of them, some piled three and four deep, perhaps more, many more. They rested on the slope of the lake in forty feet of water and spread out of sight into the deepest part of the lake. To Pitt it was like staring from a stage at a vast audience through an opaque curtain. Those in the front seats were clear and distinct, but the mass of people seated further to the rear faded and were lost in the dark. He couldn't begin to estimate the numbers. The appalling thought that came to him was that the bodies scattered in the shallower waters were but a small portion of those that lay out of the AUV's camera range in the unseen deep of the lake.

The chilling fingers of revulsion touched the back of Pitt's neck as he saw a number of women and several children scattered among the sunken field of dead. Many of them were elderly. The icy, fresh water running down from the glaciers had maintained the bodies in a state of near-perfect preservation. They appeared to be lying peacefully, as if asleep, slightly indented in soft silt. On some the facial expressions were tranquil, on others the eyes bulged and mouths were thrust open in what was their final scream. They lay undisturbed, unaffected by the frigid water temperature and the daily sequences of light and dark. There was no sign of decay.

As the submersible passed directly within one meter of what looked like an entire family, he could see by the folds of the eyes and features of the faces that they were Oriental. He could also see that their hands were tied behind them, their mouths taped and their feet roped to iron weights.

They had died at the hands of mass murderers. There was no sign of gunshot or knife wounds. Despite the myth, death by drowning is not a pleasant way to die. Only fire can be more horrible. When sinking rapidly into the deep, the eardrums burst, water rushes into the nostrils, causing incredible sinus pain, and the lungs feel as if they are seared by hot coals. Nor was death swift. The terror as they were bound, transported to the middle of the lake in the dead of night and then thrown, he guessed, from under the center cabin of the mysterious twin-hulled black boat, their screams muffled by the black water. They were innocently trapped in some unknown conspiracy, and died terribly and in agony.

Orion Lake was more than a picture of idyllic, charming scenery, much more. It was a graveyard.

4

ALMOST THREE THOUSAND MILES to the east, a spring drizzle fell over the heart of the city as a black limousine rolled silently over the wet, empty streets. The darkened windows rolled up, its occupants unseen, the car seemed as if it was part of a nocturnal funeral procession carrying mourners to a cemetery.

The dominant capital in the world, Washington had a benign aura of antiquated grandeur. This was especially true late at night when the offices were dark, the phones stopped ringing, the copy machines went mute and the distortions and exaggerations stopped coursing through the halls of the bureaucracy. Its political transient residents had all gone home to sleep with visions of campaign fund-raisers dancing in their heads. But for the lights and minimal traffic, the city took on a look of an abandoned Babylon or Persepolis.

Neither of the two men in the passenger compartment spoke as the driver, seated at the wheel in front of the closed divider window, efficiently steered the limousine over the rain-slicked asphalt that mirrored the streetlights along the sidewalks. Admiral James Sandecker stared out the window, his eyes staying unfocused as the driver turned onto Pennsylvania Avenue. His mind was lost in thought. Dressed in expensive sport coat and slacks, he didn't look the least bit tired. When the call came from Morton Laird, the President's chief of staff, he was hosting a late-night supper for a group of visiting oceanographers from Japan in his office suite atop the NUMA building across the river in Arlington, Virginia.

Slight of build from jogging five miles a day and exercising in the NUMA employees' health center, Sandecker looked much younger than a man homing in on sixty-five years of age. The respected director of NUMA since its founding, he had built a federal bureau of ocean sciences that was the envy of every maritime nation in the world. Spirited and gutsy, he wasn't a man to take no for an answer. Thirty years in the Navy, highly decorated, he was picked by a former president to head up NUMA when there wasn't a dime in funding nor congressional approval. In fifteen years, Sandecker had stepped on many toes, made any number of enemies, but persevered until no member of Congress dared suggest he resign in favor of a political lackey. Egocentric yet simple, he vainly dyed the gray that was seeping into his flaming red hair and Vandyke beard.

The man beside him, Commander Rudi Gunn, wore a rumpled business suit. He hunched his shoulders and rubbed his hands briskly. The April nights in Washington could be far too chilly for comfort. A graduate of the Naval Academy, Gunn had served in submarines until he became the admiral's chief aide. When Sandecker resigned to form NUMA, Gunn had followed him and was appointed director in charge of operations. He looked across at Sandecker through horn-rimmed glasses, studied the luminescent dial of his watch and then broke the silence.

He spoke in a voice mixed with fatigue and irritation. "Do you have any idea, Admiral, why the President demanded to see us at one o'clock in the morning?"

Sandecker turned his gaze from the passing lights and shook his head. "I haven't a clue. Judging from Morton Laird's tone, it was an invitation we couldn't refuse."

"I'm not aware of any crisis going on," muttered Gunn wearily, "domestic or foreign, that calls for middle-of-the-night secrecy."

"Nor I."

"Does the man ever sleep?"

"Three hours between four and seven A.M., according to my sources inside the White House. Unlike the previous three presidents, who served in Congress and were good friends, this one, a two-term governor of Oklahoma, is almost a total stranger to me. In the short time he's been in office since the former chief executive had a debilitating stroke, this is the first chance we've had to talk."

Gunn glanced over in the darkness. "You never met Dean Cooper Wallace when he was vice president?"

Sandecker shook his head. "From what I'm told, he has no use for NUMA."

The limousine driver turned off Pennsylvania Avenue and circled into the barricaded drive to the White House, stopping at the northwest gate. "Here we are, Admiral," he announced as he came around and opened the rear door.

A uniformed member of the Secret Service checked Sandecker's and Gunn's IDs and crossed off their names on a visitors' list. Then they were escorted through the building's entrance and led to the West Wing reception room. The receptionist, an attractive lady in her late thirties with auburn hair tied in an old-fashioned bow, rose and smiled warmly. The sign on her desk read ROBIN CARR.

"Admiral Sandecker, Commander Gunn, a great pleasure to meet you."

"You work long hours," said Sandecker.

"Fortunately, my time clock ticks in unison with the President's."

"Any chance for a cup of coffee?" asked Gunn.

The smile faded. "I'm sorry, but I'm afraid there isn't time." She quickly sat down, picked up a phone and simply said, "The Admiral is here."

Within ten seconds, the new President's chief of staff, Morton Laird, who had replaced the hospitalized former president's right-hand man, Wilbur Hutton, appeared and shook hands. "Thank you for coming, gentlemen. The President will be pleased to see you."

Laird came from the old school. He was the only chief of staff in recent history who wore three-piece suits with vests that sported a large gold chain attached to a pocket watch. And unlike most of his predecessors, who came out of Ivy League schools, Laird was a former professor of communications from Stanford University. A tall, balding man with rimless spectacles, he peered through glistening fox-brown eyes beneath heavily thicketed eyebrows. He oozed charm and was one of the few men in the executive office whom everyone genuinely liked. He turned and motioned for Sandecker and Gunn to follow him into the Oval Office.

The famous room, whose walls had witnessed a thousand crises, the lonely burdens of power and agonized decisions that affected the lives of billions of people, was empty.

Before either Sandecker or Gunn could comment, Laird turned and said, "Gentlemen, what you will observe in the next twenty minutes is vital to our nation's security. You must swear never to breathe a word to anyone. Do I have your oath of honor?"

"I venture to say that in all my years of service to my government, I've learned and kept more secrets than you have, Mr. Laird," said Sandecker with total conviction. "I will vouch for Commander Gunn's integrity."

"Forgive me, Admiral," said Laird. "It comes with the territory." Laird walked over to one wall and tapped a concealed switch on the baseboard. A section of the wall slid aside, revealing the interior of an elevator. He bowed and extended his hand. "After you."

The elevator was small and could hold no more than four people. The walls were finished in a polished cedar. There were only two buttons on the control panel, one up, one down. Laird pressed DOWN. The false wall inside the Oval Office silently returned to its place as the elevator doors met and sealed. There was no sensation of speed, but Sandecker knew they were dropping at a rapid pace from the falling sensation in his stomach. In less than a minute the elevator slowed and came to a soft stop.

"We're not meeting the President in the situation room," said Sandecker, more as a statement than a question.

Laird looked at him questioningly. "You guessed?"

"No guess. I've been there on several occasions. The situation room sits much deeper than we've traveled."

"You're very astute, Admiral," replied Laird. "This elevator goes less than half the distance."

The doors smoothly parted, and Laird stepped out into a brightly lit, immaculately maintained tunnel. A Secret Service agent stood beside the open doors of a small, customized bus. The interior was fitted out like a small office, with plush leather chairs, a horseshoe-shaped desk, a well-stocked minibar and compact bathroom. Once everyone was comfortably seated, the Secret Service agent eased behind the wheel and spoke into a microphone with an earpiece placed on his head. "Swordfish is leaving the premises." Then he engaged the transmission, and the bus moved off soundlessly into a large tunnel.

"Swordfish is my code name with the Secret Service," Laird explained almost sheepishly.

"Electric motor," commented Sandecker on the silent running of the bus.

"More efficient than building a complicated ventilation system to draw off the exhaust fumes of gas engines," explained Laird.

Sandecker stared at the side entrances leading off from the main tunnel in which they were traveling. "There's more to underground Washington than most people imagine."

"The system of passages and thoroughfares beneath the city form an intricate maze well over a thousand miles in length. Not exactly public knowledge, of course, except for tunnels built for sewage, drainage, steam and electrical wiring, but there is an extensive network in daily use for vehicular transportation. It spreads from the White House to the Supreme Court, Capitol building, State Department, under the Potomac to the Pentagon, the Central Intelligence Agency headquarters in Langley, and about a dozen other strategic government buildings and military bases in and around the city."

"Something like the catacombs of Paris," said Gunn.

"The Paris catacombs pale in comparison to Washington's underground web," said Laird. "May I offer you gentlemen a drink?"

Sandecker shook his head. "I'll pass."

"Not for me, thank you," answered Gunn. He turned to the admiral. "Did you know about this, sir?"

"Mr. Laird forgets that I've been a Washington insider for many years. I've traveled a few of the tunnels from time to time. Because they run below the water tables, it takes a small army of maintenance people to fight the invading damp and slime to keep them dry. There are also the derelicts, drug dealers and criminals who use them for warehousing illegal goods, and the young people who get a high partying in dark and eerie chambers. And, of course, reckless daredevils driven by curiosity and a lack of claustrophobia who find sport in exploring the passageways. Many of them are experienced cavers who find unknown labyrinths a challenge."

. "With so many intruders wandering in and out, how can they be controlled?"

"The main arteries crucial for government operations are guarded by a special security force which monitors them by video and infrared sensors," Laird said by way of explanation. "Penetration into critical areas is next to impossible."

Gunn said slowly, "This is certainly news to me."

Sandecker smiled enigmatically. "The President's chief of staff neglected to mention the escape tubes."

Laird covered his surprise by pouring himself a small glass of vodka. "You're extraordinarily well informed, Admiral."

"Escape tubes?" Gunn asked mechanically.

"Shall I?" Sandecker asked almost apologetically.

Laird nodded and sighed. "It seems government secrets have a short life."

"A script straight out of science-fiction movies," Sandecker continued. "Until now, saving the President, his Cabinet and the military Chiefs of Staff during a nuclear strike by whisking them away by helicopter to an airfield or an underground operations center was a fallacy almost from the beginning. Submarine missiles fired from a few hundred miles out at sea during a surprise attack could rain down on the city in less than ten minutes. Not nearly enough time to carry out an emergency evacuation."

"There had to be another way," added Laird.

"And there is," Sandecker went on. "Underground tubes leading out of the city were constructed using electromagnetic technology that can hurl a convoy of canisters containing high-ranking people from the White House and classified material from the Pentagon to Andrews Air Force Base and into the basement of a hangar where an air-command-transport version of the B-2 bomber is prepared to take off within seconds of their arrival."

"I'm pleased to learn that I know something that you don't," Laird said cryptically.

"If I took a wrong turn, please set me straight."

"Andrews Air Force Base is too widely known for departure and arrival of aircraft carrying high-level personnel," said Laird. "You were quite correct about a facility for housing a B-2 modified as an airborne command post. But the plane is based underground at a secret site southeast of the city in Maryland."

"If you'll forgive me," said Gunn, "I don't doubt what you're saying, but it does have a ring of fantasy about it."

Laird cleared his throat and spoke directly to Gunn as if he was lecturing a schoolboy. "The American public would be knocked out of their socks if they had the slightest glimpse of the devious and circuitous maneuvers that take place around the nation's capital in the name of good government. I know I certainly was when I came here. I still am."

The bus slowed and came to a stop beside the entrance of a short passageway that led toward a steel door standing beneath two video cameras. The forbidding starkness was heightened by recessed fluorescent lighting that illuminated the narrow chamber with an intense brilliance. To Gunn it appeared as "the last mile" walked by condemned murderers on their way to the gas chamber. He remained in his chair, his eyes straying into the passageway when the driver came around and opened the side panel on the bus.

"Begging your pardon, sir, but one more question." Gunn shifted his gaze to Laird. "I'd be grateful to learn just where it is we're meeting with the President."

Laird looked speculatively at Gunn for a moment. Then at Sandecker. "How say you, Admiral?"

Sandecker shrugged. "In this circumstance I can only rely on speculation and rumor. I'm curious myself."

"Secrets are meant to be kept," said Laird seriously, "but since you've come this far and your history of honor in the service of your country goes unquestioned, I believe I can take it upon myself to induct you into what is a very exclusive fraternity." He paused and then continued tolerantly. "Our short journey has taken us to Fort McNair and directly beneath what was once the base hospital until it was abandoned after World War II."

"Why Fort McNair?" Gunn persisted. "It seems more convenient for the President to have met us at the White House."

"Unlike former chief executives, President Wallace almost never goes near the place at night." He said it as if it were a comment on the weather.

Gunn looked confused. "I don't understand."

"It's painfully simple, Commander. We live in a Machiavellian world. Leaders of unfriendly countries—enemies of the United States, if you will—armies of highly trained and skilled terrorists or just plain crazies, they all dream of destroying the White House and its live-in residents. Many have tried. We all remember the car that crashed through the gate, the lunatic who fired an automatic weapon through the fence on Pennsylvania Avenue, and the suicidal maniac who flew his plane onto the South Lawn. Any athlete with a good throwing arm could heave a rock from the street against the Oval Office windows. The sad fact is the White House is a tough target to miss—"

"That goes without saying," added Sandecker. "The number of attempts that were nipped in the bud by our intelligence services remains a deep secret."

"Admiral Sandecker is correct. The professionals who planned to assault the Executive Mansion were apprehended before their operation could get off the ground." Laird finished off his vodka and set the glass in a small sink before exiting the bus. "It is too dangerous for the First Family to eat and sleep in the White House. Except for public tours, occasional press conferences, social functions for visiting dignitaries and photo opportunities of the President meeting in the Rose Garden with the public, the First Family is seldom at home."

Gunn found it difficult to accept the revelation. "You're saying the executive branch of the government conducts business someplace other than the White House?"

"Ninety-five feet above us, to be precise."

"How long has this facade been going on?" asked Sandecker.

"Since the Clinton administration," answered Laird.

Gunn stared thoughtfully at the steel door. "When you consider the current situation at home and abroad, I guess now you see him, now you don't, does seem a practical solution."

"It seems a shame," said Sandecker solemnly, "to learn that what was once the revered home of our presidents has now been reduced to little more than a reception facility."

5

SANDECKER AND GUNN followed Laird out of the elevator across a circular reception room guarded by a Secret Service agent and into a library whose four walls were packed from floor to ceiling with over a thousand books. As the door was closed behind him, Sandecker saw the President standing in the center of the room, his eyes fixed on the admiral but showing no trace of recognition. There were three other men in the room. One Sandecker knew, the other two were unfamiliar. The President held a coffee cup in his left hand as Laird made the introductions.

"Mr. President, Admiral James Sandecker and Commander Rudi Gunn."

The President gave the impression of being older than he was. He looked sixty-five but was still in his late fifties. The premature gray hair, red veins streaming through his facial skin, the beady eyes that always seemed reddened, inspired political cartoonists often to caricature him as a wino, when in fact he rarely drank anything more than an occasional glass of beer. He was an intense man with a round face and low forehead and thin eyebrows. He was the consummate politician. Within days of replacing his ailing boss, no decision regarding his lifestyle or the state of the union was made without considering the potential for gathering votes for his run for office in the next election.

Dean Cooper Wallace would not become one of Sandecker's favorite presidents. It was no secret that Wallace detested Washington and re-fused to play the required social games. He and the Congress pulled in harness together like a lion and a bear, both wanting to eat the other. He was not an intellectual, but was adept at cutting deals and acting on intuition. Since replacing the man who had been duly elected, he had quickly surrounded himself with aides and advisers who shared his distrust of the entrenched bureaucracy and were always looking for innovative ways to circumvent tradition.

The President extended his free hand while still holding the coffee cup. "Admiral Sandecker, a pleasure to finally meet you."

Sandecker involuntarily blinked. The President's grip was anything but hardy, not what he expected from a politician who pressed flesh year in and year out. "Mr. President. I hope this will be only the first of many times we meet face-to-face."

"I expect so, since the prognosis for my predecessor is not good for a full recovery."

"I'm sorry to hear it. He is a good man."

Wallace did not reply. He merely nodded at Gunn, acknowledging his presence, as Laird continued playing host. The chief of staff took the admiral by the arm and led him over to the three men standing in front of a gas fire that burned in a stone fireplace.

"Duncan Monroe, commissioner of the Immigration and Naturalization Service, and his executive associate commissioner for field operations, Peter Harper." Monroe had a tough, no-nonsense look about him. Harper seemed as if he melted into the bookcase behind him. Laird turned to the third man. "Admiral Dale Ferguson, commandant of the Coast Guard."

"Dale and I are old friends," said Sandecker.

A large ruddy man with a ready smile, Ferguson gripped Sandecker by the shoulder. "Good to see you, Jim."

"How are Sally and the kids? I haven't seen them since we took that cruise together around Indonesia."

"Sally is still saving the forests, and the boys are wiping out my pension with their college expenses."

Impatient with the small talk, the President gathered them all around a conference table and kicked off the meeting. "I apologize for asking you to leave your beds on a rainy night, but Duncan has brought to my attention a crisis that is exploding on our doorstep that involves illegal immigration. I'm counting on you gentlemen to come up with a viable program to cut the flow of aliens, particularly the Chinese who are being smuggled across our shorelines in vast numbers."

Sandecker raised his eyebrows, puzzled. "I can certainly see, Mr.

President, where INS and the Coast Guard fit into the picture, but what does unlawful immigration have to do with the National Underwater and Marine Agency? Our work is based on underwater research. Chasing down Chinese smugglers is out of our territory."

"We're in dire need of any source that can help us," said Duncan Monroe. "With congressional budget cuts, INS is overstretched far beyond our capacity. Congress appropriated a sixty-percent increase in INS border-patrol agents, but provided no funds for expanding our investigations division. Our entire department has only eighteen hundred special agents to cover the entire United States and foreign investigations. The FBI has eleven hundred agents in New York City alone. Here in Washington twelve hundred Capitol police patrol an area that is measured in city blocks. Simply put, there are nowhere near enough INS criminal investigative assets to put a dent in the flow of illegal immigrants."

"Sounds like you're operating with an army of patrolmen on the beat but few detectives to back them up," said Sandecker.

"We fight a losing battle as it is with illegals pouring across our border with Mexico, many who come from as far away as Chile and Argentina," Monroe continued. "We might as well hold back ocean surf with kitchen sieves. People-smuggling has grown into a multibillion-dollar industry that rivals arms and drug smuggling. Moving human cargo in an underworld apathetic to borders and political ideologies, people-smuggling will be the major crime of the twenty-first century."

Harper inclined his head. "To make matters worse, large-scale alien smuggling from the People's Republic of China is reaching epidemic proportions. Smugglers, with the blessing and support of their government, who are looking to decrease their tremendous population any way they can, have launched a program to export tens of millions of their people to every corner of the globe, especially to Japan, the U.S. and Canada, Europe and South America. Strange as it sounds, they're even infiltrating the whole of Africa from Capetown to Algiers."

Harper continued for his boss. "The smuggling syndicates have organized a complex labyrinth of transportation routes. Air, sea, and land are all used to smuggle human cargo. Over forty advanced staging and dispersion areas have been set up throughout Eastern Europe, Central America and Africa."

"The Russians are especially hard hit," added Monroe. "They see massive, uncontrolled migration of Chinese nationals into Mongolia and Siberia as a threat to their security. The intelligence directorate of the Russian Defense Ministry has warned their leaders that Russia is on the verge of losing its Far Eastern territories because the flow of Chinese is already accounting for a greater part of the population in the region."

"Mongolia is already a lost cause," said the President. "Russia has allowed her power base to slip through her fingers. Siberia is next."

As if reading lines from a play, Harper chimed in again. "Before Russia forfeits her ports in the Pacific, with rich deposits of gold, oil and gas, all vital for her entry into the exploding Asia-Pacific economy, her president and his parliament may out of desperation declare war on China. That would make for an impossible situation for the United States to choose sides."

"There is also another cataclysm in the making," said the President. "The gradual takeover of eastern Russia is only the tip of the iceberg. The Chinese think in the long term. Besides the impoverished peasants being rounded up and loaded aboard ships, a great many migrants are by no means poor. Many have the financial means to buy property and launch businesses in whichever country they settle. Given enough time this can lead to enormous changes in political and economic influence, particularly if their culture and loyalty remain tied to the mother country."

"If the tide of Chinese migration goes unchecked," said Laird, "there is no predicting the enormous upheaval the world will experience in the next hundred years."

"It sounds to me like you're implying the People's Republic of China is engaged in a Machiavellian scheme to take over the world," said Sandecker.

Monroe nodded. "They're in it up to their necks. China's mass of humanity is growing by twenty-one million people a year. Their population of one-point-two billion represents twenty-two percent of the world's total people. Yet their land area is only seven percent. Starvation is a fact of life over there. Laws enacted to allow couples only one child to slow the birthrate are a drop in the bucket. Poverty breeds children despite threats of prison. China's leaders see illegal immigration as a simple and inexpensive solution to their population problem. By literally licensing criminal syndicates that specialize in smuggling, they capitalize on both ends of the spectrum. The profits can be nearly as high as trafficking in drugs, and they decrease the numbers of those who drain their economy."

Gunn looked across the table at the INS commissioners. "It was always my impression that organized-crime syndicates directed the smuggling operations."

Monroe nodded toward Harper. "I'll let Peter reply, since he is our expert on Asian organized crime and transnational criminal groups."

"There are two sides to the smuggling," explained Harper. "One *is* operated by an alliance of criminal groups that also deals in drugs, extortion, prostitution and international car theft. They account for nearly thirty percent of aliens smuggled into Europe and the Western Hemisphere. The second is legitimate business fronts that engage in the traffic from behind the cloak of respectability, licensed and supported by their governments. This part of the activity accounts for seventy percent of all aliens run across world borders.

"Although many illegal Chinese immigrants come in by air, the great mass cross into foreign countries by sea. Air requires passports and heavy bribery. The use of ships to smuggle aliens has become more widespread. The overhead costs are lower, many more bodies can be transported in one operation, the logistics are simpler and the profits are higher."

Admiral Ferguson cleared his throat and said, "When the flood was a trickle, old dilapidated and run-down tramp freighters were used to transport the immigrants before sending them ashore in leaky boats and rafts. Many were given life jackets and thrown over the side. Hundreds drowned before reaching the beach. Now, the smugglers have become far more sophisticated, secreting the immigrants in commercial shipping and, in an increasing number of cases, the smugglers sail brazenly into port before sneaking them past immigration agents."

"What happens after the immigrants safely arrive in the country?" asked Gunn.

"Local Asian crime gangs take over," Harper answered. "Those immigrants lucky enough to have money or relatives already living in the U.S. are released directly into their destination community. Most, however, cannot pay the fee for entry. Consequently, they are forced to remain concealed, generally in remote warehouses. Here, they're locked away for weeks or even months, and threatened by being told that if they try to escape they will be turned over to American law enforcement and imprisoned for half their lives merely because they are illegal entrants. The gangs frequently use torture, beatings and rape to frighten the captives into signing their lives away as indentured servants. Once the aliens cave in they are forced to work for the crime syndicates in drug dealing, prostitution, in illegal sweatshops and other gang-related activities. Those in good physical condition, usually the younger men, must sign a contract requiring them to repay their smuggling fee at high rates of interest. Then they are found jobs in laundries, restaurants or manufacturing working fourteen hours a day, seven days a week. It takes from six to eight years for the illegal immigrant to pay off his debt."

"After obtaining the necessary forged documents, many of them become bona fide American citizens," Monroe continued. "As long as the United States has a demand for cheap labor, efficient smuggling enterprises will exploit it with illegal immigration that is already increasing to epidemic proportions."

"There must be any number of ways to cut off the flow," Sandecker said, helping himself to a cup of coffee from a silver urn on a nearby cart.

"Short of throwing up an international blockade around the Chinese mainland, how can you stop them?" asked Gunn.

"The answer is simple," replied Laird. "We can't, certainly not under international law. Our hands are tied. All any nation can do, including the United States, is recognize the threat as a major international security concern and take whatever emergency measures that are required to protect its borders."

"Like calling out the Army and Marines to defend the beaches and repel invaders," suggested Sandecker wryly.

The President gave Sandecker a sharp look. "You seemed to have missed the point, Admiral. What we're facing is a peaceful invasion. I simply can't whistle up a curtain of missiles against unarmed men, women and children."

Sandecker pressed on. "Then what's stopping you, Mr. President, from directing a joint operation by the armed forces to effectively seal our borders? By doing so, you'd probably cut the flow of illegal drugs into the country as well."

The President shrugged. "The thought has crossed smarter minds than mine."

"Stopping illegals is not the mission of the Pentagon," said Laird firmly.

"Perhaps I've been misinformed. But I've always been under the impression that the mission of our armed forces was to protect and defend the security of the United States. Peaceful or not, I still read this as an invasion of our sovereign shores. I see no reason why Army infantry and Marine divisions can't help Mr. Monroe's understaffed border patrolmen, why the Navy can't back up Admiral Ferguson's overextended Coast Guard and why the Air Force can't fly aerial reconnaissance missions."

"There are political considerations beyond my control," the President said, a certain hardness creeping into his voice.

"Like not retaliating with tough trade sanctions on Chinese imports because they buy billions of dollars' worth of industrial and agricultural products from us every year?"

"While you're on that subject, Admiral," said Laird with emphasis, "you should be aware that the Chinese have replaced the Japanese as the biggest purchaser of U.S. Treasury bonds. It is not in our best interest to harass them."

Gunn could see the anger reddening his chief's face, while the President's was turning pale. He stepped into the debate quietly. "I'm sure Admiral Sandecker understands your difficulties, Mr. President, but I believe we're both in the dark as to how NUMA can help."

"I'll be happy to brief you on your involvement, Jim," said Ferguson to his old friend.

"Please do," Sandecker said testily.

"It's no secret the Coast Guard is stretched too thin. Over the past year we've seized thirty-two vessels and intercepted over four thousand illegal Chinese aliens off Hawaii and the East and West coasts. NUMA has a small fleet of research vessels—"

"Stop right there," interrupted Sandecker. "There is no way I will permit my ships and scientists to stop and board vessels suspected of carrying illegal immigrants."

"Not our intention to put weapons in the hands of marine biologists," Ferguson assured the admiral, his voice calm and unperturbed. "What we need from NUMA is information on possible alien landing sites, undersea conditions and geology along our coastlines, bays and inlets that the smugglers can take advantage of. Put your best people on it, Jim. Where would *they* offload their human cargo if *they* were the smugglers?"

"Also," added Monroe, "your people and vessels can act as intelligence gatherers. NUMA's turquoise-painted ships are known and respected throughout the world as ocean-science research vessels. Any one of them could sail within a hundred yards of a suspected ship filled with aliens without arousing the suspicions of the smugglers. They can report what they observe and continue on with their research."

"You must understand," said the President wearily to Sandecker, "I'm not asking you to drop your agency's priorities. But I am ordering you and NUMA to give whatever assistance possible to Mr. Monroe and Admiral Ferguson to reduce the flow of illegal aliens from China into the United States."

"There are two particular areas we'd like your people to investigate," said Harper.

"I'm listening," muttered Sandecker, beginning to show a faint trace of curiosity.

"Are you familiar with a man by the name of Qin Shang?" asked Harper.

"I am," answered Sandecker. "He owns a shipping empire called Qin Shang Maritime Limited out of Hong Kong that operates a fleet of over a hundred cargo ships, oil tankers and cruise ships. He once made a personal request through a Chinese historian to search our data files for a shipwreck he was interested in finding.

"If it floats, Shang probably owns it, including dockside facilities and warehouses in nearly every major port city in the world. He is as shrewd and canny as they come."

"Isn't Shang the Chinese mogul who built that huge port facility in Louisiana?" asked Gunn.

"One and the same," answered Ferguson. "On Atchafalaya Bay near Morgan City. Nothing but marshlands and bayous. According to every developer we questioned, there is absolutely no logic in pouring hundreds of millions of dollars into a shipping port eighty miles from the nearest major city and with no transportation network leading from it."

"Has it got a name?" inquired Gunn.

"The port is called Sungari."

"Shang must have a damned good reason for throwing big money into a swamp," said Sandecker.

"Whatever his logic, we've yet to learn what it is," Monroe admitted. "That's one of two areas where NUMA can help us."

"You'd like to use a NUMA research ship and its technology to nose around Shang's newly constructed shipping port," assumed Gunn.

Ferguson nodded. "You get the picture, Commander. There's more to Sungari than what meets the eye, and it's probably out of sight underwater."

The President stared pointedly at Sandecker with a faint smile. "No other government agency has the brains and technology of NUMA for underwater investigation."

Sandecker stared back. "You haven't made it clear what Shang has to do with alien smuggling."

"According to our intelligence sources, Shang is the mastermind responsible for fifty percent of the Chinese smuggled into the Western Hemisphere, and the number is growing rapidly."

"So if you stop Shang, you cut off the head of the snake."

The President nodded briefly. "That's pretty much our theory."

"You mentioned two areas for us to investigate," Sandecker probed.

Ferguson held up a hand to field the question. "The second is a ship. Another of Shang's projects we can't fathom was his purchase of the former transatlantic ocean liner, the S.S. *United States.*"

"The *United States* went out of service and was laid up at Norfolk, Virginia, for thirty years," said Gunn.

Monroe shook his head. "Ten years ago she was sold to a Turkish millionaire who advertised that he was going to refit and put her into service as a floating university."

"Not a practical scheme," Sandecker said bluntly. "No matter how she's refitted, by today's standards she's too large and too expensive to operate and maintain."

"A deception." For the first time Monroe grinned. "The rich Turk turned out to be our friend Qin Shang. The *United States* was towed from Norfolk across the sea into the Mediterranean, past Istanbul and into the Black Sea to Sevastopol. The Chinese do not have a dry dock that can take a ship that size. Shang hired the Russians to convert her into a modern cruise ship."

"It makes no sense. He'll lose his shirt, he must know that."

"It makes a lot of sense if Shang intends to use the *United States* as a cover to move illegal aliens," said Ferguson. "The CIA also thinks the People's Republic bankrolled Shang. The Chinese have a small navy. If they should ever get serious about invading Taiwan, they'll need troop transports. The *United States* could transport an entire division, including their heavy arms and equipment."

"I fully understand that sinister threats call for urgent measures." Sandecker paused and massaged his temples with his fingertips for a few moments. Then he announced, "The resources of NUMA are at your command. We'll give it our best effort."

The President nodded as though he had expected that. "Thank you, Admiral. I'm sure Mr. Monroe and Admiral Ferguson join me in expressing our gratitude."

Gunn's thoughts were already on the job ahead. "It would be most helpful," he said, his eyes on Monroe and Harper, "if you had agents on the inside of Shang's organization to feed us information."

Monroe made a helpless gesture with his hands. "Shang's security is incredibly tight. He's hired a top group of former Russian KGB agents to form an impenetrable ring that even the CIA has yet to infiltrate. They have a computerized personnel identification and investigation system that is second to none. There is no one within Shang's own management circles who is not under constant surveillance."

"To date," added Harper, "we've lost two special agents who attempted to penetrate Shang's organization. Except for one of our agents who posed as an immigrant and bought her passage on board one of Shang's smuggling ships, our undercover missions are in shambles. I hate to admit such failure, but those are the hard facts."

"Your agent is a woman?" asked Sandecker.

"Comes from a wealthy Chinese family. She's one of our best."

"Any idea where the smugglers will put your agent ashore?" asked Gunn.

Harper shook his head. "We're not in contact with her. They could drop her and the rest of the illegal immigrants anywhere between San Francisco and Anchorage."

"How do you know Shang's security people haven't already caught on to her as they did your other two agents?"

Harper's eyes remained fixed in space for a long time. Finally, he admitted solemnly, "We don't. All we can do is wait and hope until she makes contact with one of our West Coast district offices."

"And if you never hear from her?"

Harper gazed down at the polished surface of the table as if seeing the unthinkable. "Then I send a letter of condolence to her parents and assign someone else to follow in her footsteps."

The meeting finally concluded at four o'clock in the morning. Sandecker and Gunn were ushered from the President's secret quarters and returned through the tunnel to the White House. As they were driven to their respective homes in the limousine, each man was lost in gloomy thoughts. Finally Sandecker broke the somber mood.

"They must be desperate if they need NUMA to help bail them out."

"I'd probably call in the Marines, the New York Stock Exchange and the Boy Scouts too if I was in the President's shoes," said Gunn.

"A farce," snorted Sandecker. "My sources in the White House tell me the President has been in bed with Qin Shang since he was governor of Oklahoma."

Gunn looked at him. "But the President said—"

"I know what he said, but what he meant is a different thing. Naturally, he wants the flow of illegal immigrants stopped, but he won't order any measures that might upset Beijing. Qin Shang is President Wallace's chief campaign fund-raiser in Asia. Many millions of dollars from the Chinese government were funneled through Hong Kong and Qin Shang Maritime into Wallace's campaign fund. It's corrupt influence peddling of the highest order. That's why Wallace stops short of any head-to-head confrontation. His administration is riddled with people working on China's behalf. The man has sold his soul to the detriment of American citizens."

"Then what does he hope to gain if we nail Qin Shang's ass to the wall?"

"It won't happen," said Sandecker acidly. "Qin Shang will never be indicted nor convicted of criminal activities, certainly not in the United States."

"Then I gather it's your plan to push ahead in the investigation," said Gunn, "regardless of the consequences."

Sandecker nodded. "Do we have a research ship operating in the Gulf?"

"The *Marine Denizen*. Her scientific team is conducting a study on the diminishing coral reefs off Yucatán."

"She's served NUMA for a long time," Sandecker said, visualizing the ship.

"The oldest in our fleet," Gunn acknowledged. "This is her final voyage. After she returns to port in Norfolk, we're donating her to the Lampack University of Oceanography."

"The university will have to wait a while longer. An old marine-research ship with a crew of biologists should prove an ideal cover to investigate Shang's port facility."

"Who have you in mind to lead the investigation?"

Sandecker turned to Gunn. "Our special projects director, who do you think?"

Gunn hesitated. "Asking a bit much from Dirk, aren't we?"

"Can you think of a better man?"

"No, but he took quite a beating on the last project. When I saw him a few days ago, he looked like death warmed over. He needs more time to mend."

"Pitt is a fast healer," Sandecker said confidently. "A challenge is just what he needs to get back into the swim of things. Track him down and tell him it's essential he contact me immediately."

"I don't know where to reach him," Gunn said vaguely. "After you gave him a month's leave, he just took off without saying where he was going."

"He's in Washington State, up to his old tricks at a place called Orion Lake."

Gunn looked at the admiral suspiciously. "How do you know that?"

"Hiram Yaeger sent him a truckload of underwater gear," said Sandecker, his eyes glinting like a fox's. "Hiram thought he did it on the sly, but word has a funny way of filtering up to my office."

"Not much goes on around NUMA that you don't know about."

"The only mystery I haven't solved is how Al Giordino smokes my expensive Nicaraguan cigars when I never find any missing."

"Did it ever occur to you that you both might have the same source?"

"Impossible," snorted Sandecker. "My cigars are rolled by a family who are close friends of mine in Managua. Giordino couldn't possibly know them. And while we're on the subject, where is Giordino?"

"Lying on a beach in Hawaii," answered Gunn. "He decided it was as good a time as any to take a vacation until Dirk got back in the saddle again."

"Those two are usually as thick as thieves. It's a rare moment when they're not causing mischief together."

"You want me to brief Al on the situation and then send him out to Orion Lake to bring Dirk back to Washington?"

Sandecker nodded. "A good idea. Pitt will listen to Giordino. You go along as backup. Knowing Dirk, if I called and ordered him to report back to work, he'd hang up the phone."

"You're absolutely right, Admiral," Gunn said, smiling. "That's exactly what he would do."

6

JULIA LEE'S THOUGHTS, certain beliefs rather, centered around an overwhelming sense of defeat. Deep down, she knew she had botched her mission. She had made the wrong moves, said the wrong things. There was a feeling of emptiness, shrouded by despair in her mind. She had learned much about the smugglers' operation. There were ashes in her mouth as she realized that it was all for nothing. The vital information she had obtained might never be passed on to the Immigration and Naturalization Service so they could apprehend the smugglers.

She felt a sea of pain from her sadistically inflicted injuries, sick and empty and debased. She was also deathly tired and hungry. Her self-assurance had gotten the better of her. She failed by not acting meek and subjugated. By using the skills taught her during her training as a special INS agent and given enough time, she could have easily escaped her captors before being submitted to a life of rape. Now it was too late. Julia was too badly hurt to make an all-out physical effort. It was all she could do to stand upright without getting dizzy and losing her balance before falling to her knees.

Because of dedication to her work, Julia had few close friends. The men in her life had passed through as if they were part of a reception line, little more than acquaintances. Sadness settled over her at the thought of never seeing her mother and father again. Strangely, she was conscious of no fear or revulsion. Whatever was to happen to her in the next few hours, nothing could change it.

Through the steel deck she sensed the engines coming to a stop.

Without headway the ship began rolling in the swells. A minute later the anchor chain clattered through the hawsehole. The *Indigo Star* had anchored just outside the territorial limits of the United States to evade law enforcement action.

Julia's watch had been taken from her during the interrogation, and all she could be certain about the time was that it was sometime in the middle of the night. She looked around at the other forty or more pathetic individuals huddled in the cargo hold, thrown in there after the interrogations. They all began chattering excitedly, thinking they had at last reached America and were going ashore to begin a new life. Julia might have felt the same, but she knew better. The truth would strike savagely and with cold indifference. Any expectation of happiness was short-lived. They had all been deceived. These were the intelligent ones, those of wealth and substance. They had been defrauded and robbed by the smugglers, and yet they still had the look of hope about them.

Julia was certain their immediate future would be one of terror and extortion. She looked with great sadness at two families with young children and prayed they would live to escape the smugglers and the domination by the criminal cartels waiting on shore.

Two hours was all the time the crew of smugglers needed to transfer the illegal Chinese aliens onto trawlers belonging to a fishing fleet owned by Qin Shang Maritime. Manned by documented Chinese who had taken out their citizenship papers, the fleet carried out legitimate fishing operations when not transporting illegal immigrants from the mother ship to transit points in small harbors and coves along the Olympic Peninsula coast. There, buses and cargo trucks waited to carry them to destinations throughout the country.

Julia, the last one to be taken from the cargo hold, was led roughly by an enforcer to the outer deck. She could barely walk, and he half dragged her. Ki Wong was standing by the disembarkation ramp. He held up a hand and stopped the enforcer before he could escort her down the ramp to a strange-looking black boat, bobbing in the waves beside the ship.

"One final word, Ling T'ai," he said in a low, cold voice. "Now that you've had a chance to think over my offer, perhaps you've had a change of mind."

"If I agree to become your slave," she murmured through her swollen lips. "What then?"

He gave her his best jackal grin. "Why nothing. I don't expect you to become a slave. That opportunity has long since passed."

"Then what do you want from me?"

"Your cooperation. I'd like you to tell me who else was working with you on board the *Indigo Star.*"

"I don't know what you're talking about," she muttered contemptuously.

He stared at her and shrugged smugly. Then he reached in his coat pocket, drew out a piece of paper and pushed it at her. "Read this, and see that I was right about you."

"You read it," she said with her last shred of defiance.

He held the paper under a deck light and squinted his eyes. "'The fingerprint and description you sent via satellite were analyzed and identified. The woman Ling T'ai is an INS agent by the name of Julia Marie Lee. Suggest you deal with her in an expeditious manner.'"

If Julia had a tiny thread of hope, it was abruptly swept away. They must have taken her prints after she was battered unconscious. But how was it possible for a band of Chinese smugglers to make her ID within a few hours from any source but the FBI in Washington, D.C.? The organization had to be far more complex and sophisticated than she and the field investigators at the INS suspected. She was not about to give Wong the slightest degree of satisfaction.

"I am Ling T'ai. I have nothing more to say."

"Then neither do I." Wong made a gesture with his hand toward the waiting black boat. "Goodbye, Miss Lee."

As the enforcer took her by the arm and pulled her off the counterfeit cruise ship, Julia looked back up the ramp at Wong, who still stood on the cruise ship's deck. The bastard was sneering at her. She stared up at him with pure hatred in her eyes.

"You will die, Ki Wong," she said caustically. "You will die very soon."

He returned her stare more out of amusement than annoyance. "No, Miss Lee. It is you who will die soon."

STILL SICKENED by what the AUV had discovered, Pitt spent the final hour of daylight staring across the lake at Qin Shang's retreat through his telescope. The maid on her rounds at the guesthouses, the same two golfers knocking balls all over the landscape—they were the only people he ever observed. Most curious, he thought. No cars or delivery trucks entered or left the grounds, nor did the security guards ever reveal themselves again. Pitt could not believe they stayed shut up in the little windowless huts day and night without relief.

He called no one at NUMA to inform them of the grisly discovery, nor did he contact local law enforcement. He took it upon himself to attempt to uncover the mystery of how the bodies came to be carpeting the bottom of the lake. That Qin Shang was using the lake depths as a depository for his murder victims seemed obvious. But there was more to learn before he blew the whistle.

Satisfied there was nothing more to see, he set the telescope aside and carried the second big carton sent by Yaeger into the boathouse. It was so heavy and bulky he had to use a small hand truck to roll the carton and its contents across the dock. Cutting open the lid, he removed a compact portable electric compressor and plugged its cord into an overhead light socket. Then he connected the compressor to the dual-manifold air valve on twin eighty-cubic-foot diver's air cylinders. It popped away with less noise than the exhaust of an idling car engine.

He returned to the cabin and lazily watched the sun descend over the small range of mountains between Orion Lake and the sea. After darkness settled over the lake, Pitt ate a light dinner and then watched satellite television. At ten o'clock he made ready for bed and turned out the lights. Gambling the surveillance cameras in the cabin did not work on infrared, he stripped naked, crept outside, crawled into the water and, holding his breath, swam up inside the boathouse.

The water was frigid, but his mind was too occupied to notice. He toweled his body dry and pulled on a one-piece Shellpro nylon-and-polyester undergarment. The compressor had automatically shut off when the cylinders were topped off with the required air pressure. He attached a U.S. Divers Micra air regulator to the manifold valve and checked the straps to the backpack. Then he climbed into a custom-made, dark gray Viking vulcanized-rubber dry suit with attached hood, gloves and traction-soled boots. He preferred the dry suit over a wet suit for better thermal protection in cold water.

Next came a U.S. Divers military buoyancy compensator and a Sigma Systems console with depth gauge, air pressure gauge, compass and dive timer. For weights, he used an integrated system with part of the weight in the backpack and the balance on his weight belt. A dive knife was strapped to his calf and an underwater miner's-type light was slipped over his hood.

Finally, he slung a belt that looked like an old western bandit's bandolier over one shoulder. Its holster contained a compressed air gun that fired wicked-looking barbs on short shafts. Slots in the belt held twenty barbs.

He was in a hurry to be on his way. He had a long swim ahead of him and many things to do and see. He sat on the edge of the dock, pulled on his fins, twisted his body to prevent the air tanks on his back from snagging the boards and splashed into the water. Before diving, he vented the air out of the dry suit. He saw not the slightest reason in the world why he should physically extend himself and waste the precious air in his tanks, so he lifted a compact, battery-powered Sting-ray diver-propulsion vehicle from the dock, extended it out in front of him by the handgrips, pressed the FAST speed switch to its stop and was instantly propelled from under the floats of the boathouse.

Getting his bearings on a moonless night did not present a problem. His destination across the lake was bathed in as much light as a football stadium. The brilliance lit up the surrounding forest. Why such a dazzling display of illumination? Pitt wondered. It seemed too excessive for average security purposes. Only the dock appeared devoid of lighting, but it was hardly needed, considering the radiance from shore. Pitt pushed the face mask to the top of his head and tilted the lens of the dive light backward to prevent any alert guards from spotting a reflection.

If the surveillance cameras didn't pierce the dark with infrared, there would be a guard with night glasses pressed against his eyes, watching for night fishermen, hunters, lost Boy Scout masters or even Bigfoot. It was a sure bet he wasn't peering into the heavens at the rings of Saturn. Pitt was not overly concerned. He made too small a target to be spotted at this distance. A quarter of a mile nearer and it would be a different story.

One of the fallacies of sneaking around in the dead of night is that black makes for the perfect concealment. Supposedly a person wearing black blends into the shadows. To some degree, yes. But because no night is totally black—there is often light from the stars—the perfect shade for near invisibility is dark gray. A black object *can* be distinguished against a shadowed background on a dark night, whereas gray blends in.

Pitt knew his chances of being detected were remote indeed. Only the white of his wake, as he was pulled along at nearly three knots by the Stingray twin motors, broke the sheer blackness of the water. After less than five minutes, he reached the midway point. He adjusted his face mask, ducked his head under the water and began breathing through the snorkel. Another four minutes put him a hundred yards from the retreat's boat dock. The work boat was still gone, but the yacht still tugged at her mooring lines.

This was as far as he dared go on the surface. He spit out the snorkel and clamped his teeth on the mouthpiece to his breathing regulator. Accompanied by the hiss of his exhaust, he tilted the Stingray downward and dropped into the depths, leveling out about ten feet above the bottom, hovering motionless for a few moments while adding air to his dry suit to achieve neutral buoyancy, then snorting and clearing his ears from the increase of water pressure. The lights of the retreat cast a translucent glow beneath the water. Pitt felt as if the propulsion vehicle was pulling him through liquid glass coated in an eerie green. He averted his eyes from the graveyard below as visibility increased from practically nil to thirty feet the closer Pitt approached the dock. Fortunately, he could not be discerned from above because the reflection on the surface of the water caused a glare that prevented all but a very limited view of the depths.

He decreased the Stingray's speed and moved slowly under the keel of the yacht. The hull was clean and free of any marine growth. Finding nothing of interest except a school of small fish, Pitt cautiously approached the floating log hut from which the guards on their Chinese-built personal watercraft had burst the previous afternoon. His heartbeat increased as he measured his opportunities of escape if he was discovered. They flat didn't exist. A swimmer stood little chance of outrunning a pair of personal watercraft with a top speed of thirty miles per hour. Unless they were prepared to come after him underwater, all they had to do was outwait him until he exhausted his air supply.

He had to be very careful. There would be no light reflection on the surface inside the hut. To anyone sitting in a darkened room over calm water it would be like staring into the depths from a glass-bottomed boat. He yearned for a passing school of fish to hide among, but none appeared. This is madness, he thought. If he had an ounce of gray matter he'd make his getaway while he was yet unseen, swim back across the lake to the cabin and call the police. That's what any sane man would have done.

Pitt felt no fear but a degree of trepidation at not knowing whether he would find himself looking up into the muzzle of an automatic rifle. But he was determined to find out why all those people had died, and he had to find out now or there would never be another chance. He drew the air gun from its holster and held it vertically, barrel and barb pointing upward. Slowly, so no sudden movement would be noticed, he released the speed switch to the Stingray's twin motors and gently kicked his fins until he eased under the floats of the hut. He peered upward through the water inside the boathouse, holding his breath so that his air bubbles would not advertise his arrival. The view looking up from less than two feet underwater was similar to gazing through six inches of gossamer.

Except for the two watercraft, the interior appeared dark and empty. He reset the dive light on his head, surfaced and beamed it around the floating hut. The fiberglass hulls of the watercraft were set snugly between two docks that were open at the front. Once the door of the hut was thrown aside, their riders could speed directly onto the lake. He reached out, rapped the door with his fist and received a hollow sound. The logs were fake, painted on a thin sheet of plywood. With no small amount of effort, Pitt hoisted himself and his equipment onto one of the docks. He removed his air tanks, fins and weight belt. and parked them in a watercraft. The Stingray, because it was slightly buoyant, he allowed to drift beside the dock.

Gripping the air gun, he moved quietly toward a closed door at the rear of the hut. He lightly laid his fingers on the latch, slowly turned it and eased the door open half an inch, just enough to see that it opened onto a passageway that led down a long ramp. Pitt moved like a wraith —at least he wanted to move like a wraith. His every footstep in the rubber dive boots sounded to him like the beat of a bass drum, when actually they touched the concrete floor without so much as a whisper. The ramp dropped into a narrow concrete passageway barely wide enough for Pitt's shoulders. Lit by overhead recessed lights, it appeared to lead under the water toward the shoreline. It was a reasonable assumption that the passageway extended from the boathouse to a basement below the main building. That was why it took so long for the guards who rode the watercraft to respond after the AUV was sighted. Unable to ride even a bicycle through the narrow passageway, they had to sprint nearly two hundred yards.

A quick look to see if his movements were covered by surveillance cameras—he saw none—and Pitt cautiously began to advance along the tightly spaced walls, having to turn slightly sideways to pass through. He cursed the contractor who poured the concrete with the smaller Chinese physique in mind. The passage ended at another ramp that rose and widened through an archway. Beyond, a corridor stretched off into the distance with doors on either side.

He moved to the first door that was slightly ajar. A glance from a wary eye through the crack revealed a low bed occupied by a sleeping man wearing a skullcap. There was a closet with hanging clothes, a dresser with several small drawers, a nightstand and lamp. One rack on a wall held a variety of weapons: a sniper's rifle with a scope, two different automatic rifles and four automatic pistols of different calibers. Pitt quickly realized that he had walked into the lions' den. This was the living quarters for the security guards.

Voices came from another room farther down the corridor along with the pungent aroma of incense. He dropped prone and sneaked a peek across the threshold with half an eye and nose he hoped would not be as obvious low to the floor. Four Asians were seated around a table playing dominoes. Their conversation was unintelligible to Pitt. To his untrained ear the Mandarin dialect sounded like a fast pitch by a used-car dealer in a television commercial that was speeded up and played backward. Through the doors of other rooms he could hear the strange, twangy sounds that Orientals call music.

It seemed like a good idea to move out of the area quickly. There was no way of telling when one of the unsuspecting guards might happen to step into the corridor and demand to know why a Caucasian was slinking around outside his bedroom. Pitt moved on until he found an iron spiral staircase. Still no shouts of discovery, no gunshots, no sirens or alarm bells. He was more than happy to find that Shang's security people were less concerned about trespassers on the inside than on the outside.

The staircase rose past two levels that were empty, great open areas with no interior walls. They appeared to Pitt as if the contractor and his workers had walked off the job before it was completed. He finally reached the top landing and stopped at a massive steel door that looked like it came off a bank vault. There was no time or combination lock, only a thick horizontal handle. He stood there for a solid minute, listening intently but hearing nothing while pushing down on the handle with firm but gentle pressure. Sweat poured from his body beneath the dry suit. Swimming back to the cabin in the frigid water of the lake began to sound good to him. He decided that one quick look inside the main house and he was out of there.

The shafts slid smoothly and silently out of their slots. Pitt hesitated for several moments before he began, ever so delicately at first, to pull open the massive door. Soon he had to exert most of his strength until it cracked enough to see beyond. What he saw was another door, but this one had bars. No cat burglar could have been half as surprised to find the house he came to rob of precious jewels and valuables was a maximum-security prison.

This was no elegant estate built by a man with unusual taste in architecture. This had no correlation to an estate at all. The entire interior of Shang's huge house was a cell block straight out of Alcatraz. The revelation struck Pitt like a blow to the head by a meteor. The retreat built to entertain Shang's clients and business associates was a facade, he realized, a damned facade. The maid who played at making up rooms with no furniture, the two golfers who played for all eternity —they were all frosted figures on a cake. The security that was carried to extremes was designed to keep captives in rather than intruders out. It now became obvious that the copper-tinted solar glass panes were backed by reinforced concrete walls.

Three tiers of jail cells faced an open square with a cage mounted on columns in the center. Inside the cage, two guards in gray, unmarked uniforms monitored a bank of video screens. The upper walkways that passed by the cells were shielded from the open square by mesh screens. The cell doors were solid except for peepholes barely large enough to insert a small plate of food and a cup of water. The most hardened incarcerated criminal would have had a tough time figuring an escape route out of this place.

There was no way for Pitt to tell how many poor souls were locked behind the doors. Nor could he guess who they were or what offense they had committed against Shang. Recalling the AUV's video of the sickening spectacle on the lake bed, he began to grasp that instead of staring at a penal colony he was staring at one huge death row.

Pitt felt a cold chill, but sweat was trickling down his face in streams. He had overstayed his welcome. It was time to head home and blow the whistle. Very carefully, he pushed the steel door closed and locked it in place. Lucky, lucky, he thought. Only the inside door with the bars was wired to sound an alarm when opened without permission by the guards at the security monitors. He was on the fourth step going down when he heard footsteps coming up.

There were two of them, no doubt a change of a shift for the men monitoring the video surveillance around the outer grounds and inside the prison cells. Neither had call to be apprehensive or suspicious of intruders. They casually moved up the stairs chatting to each other, and due to the human habit of watching one's feet when climbing a staircase, neither looked up and spied Pitt. Their only weapons were automatic pistols firmly clipped in their holsters.

Pitt had to move fast if he wanted the advantage of surprise, and he used it to the hilt. Foolhardy or not, he rushed down the stairs and leaped, crashing into the lead guard before he literally knew what hit him and throwing him backward into his friend.

Accustomed to cowering and frightened captives, the two Chinese guards were petrified with shock at being attacked by a reckless crazy man in a rubber suit whose body was considerably larger than either of theirs. Both men, caught off balance, stumbled and fell backward, arms and legs flailing, locked together back to chest. Pitt piled on the man on the top and rode them down the steps to the second landing before they all crumpled against a railing. The bottom man struck his head on a step and was immediately knocked unconscious. His friend, less injured but stunned with surprise, snatched feverishly at his holstered automatic.

Pitt could have killed him, could have killed them both, by shooting a pair of barbs through their heads. But he settled for gripping the air gun by the barrel and clubbing the guard on the side of the head with the butt. He didn't doubt for an instant that if their positions were reversed, they'd have had no misgivings whatsoever about blowing his brains out.

He dragged them into the vacant second level and propped them against the far wall in the shadows. He tore off their uniforms and ripped them into strips. Then he bound their hands and legs, and gagged them. If, as he suspected, they were on their way to work, they'd be missed in less than five or ten minutes at the most. Once they were found knocked unconscious and bound with shreds of their uniforms, all hell would erupt when an intrusion was reported to Shang or his murder advisory board. Once they became aware their security had been penetrated by an unknown force, there was no second-guessing the consequences. He didn't want to think about what might happen to the unfortunates still locked in the cells if it was decided all evidence to whatever was going on had to be destroyed and all eyewitnesses killed. If the bodies on the bottom of the lake were any indication, whatever this bunch of slime lacked, it certainly wasn't a willingness to murder by the numbers.

Pitt crept back through the corridor of the guards' living quarters with the finesse of Don Juan flitting out of a lady's bedroom. The luck he had of not being seen going in carried with him going out. He reached the passageway to the boathouse and hurried through as best he could without scraping the shoulders of his dry suit to shreds. Not in the mood for an exciting pursuit by incensed Chinese with lethal weapons, he briefly considered working over the motors of the watercraft, but thought better of wasting the time. If they couldn't find the AUV in broad daylight, they would never find him thirty feet underwater in the dark.

After hurriedly putting on his dive gear, he dropped into the water, swam around the dock and retrieved the Stingray. Pitt hadn't traveled a hundred yards along the lake bed when he heard the throb of an engine exhaust and the beat of propellers from a boat coming out of the darkness in the distance. The sound carried through the water faster than the air, making it seem as if the boat was almost on top of him when in fact it was just coming off the river outlet onto the lake. Inclining the Stingray, he let its thrust pull him to the surface. He spotted the boat as it moved out of the shadows and became illuminated under the lights from shore. He identified the approaching vessel as the black catamaran he'd observed the day before.

He figured that unless one of the boat's crew ate a bushel of carrots every day and took large doses of vitamin A for acute night vision, their chances of picking out a nearly invisible head on dark waters were unlikely. Then suddenly, the boat's motor died to an idle and it drifted to a stop not fifty feet away.

Pitt should have ignored the boat and moved on. There was still plenty of juice left in the Stingray's batteries to take him back to the cabin. He should have moved on, having seen more than he was ever meant to see. Law-enforcement authorities had to be notified quickly before any further harm came to the unknown human beings imprisoned inside the retreat. He was cold and exhausted and looked forward to a shot of tequila and a chair in front of a warm fire. He should have listened to an inner voice telling him to get the hell away from Orion Lake while the getting was still good. His inner voice might as well have pleaded with his sinus passages for all the good it did.

Some unfathomable fascination attracted him to the eerie-looking catamaran. There was something sinister about its appearance in the night. No one walked the decks, no lights showed anywhere.

Downright diabolic, he thought. A strange, indescribable malignance seem to vent from its decks. Then it began to dawn on Pitt that this just might be the ferry that transported dead souls across the River Styx. He rolled beneath the surface and aimed the Stingray in a downward and then upward arc that would bring him beneath the twin hulls of the mysterious vessel.

8

THE FORTY-EIGHT MEN, women and children were crammed so tightly inside the square cabin of the black boat that there was no room for anyone to sit. They all stood pressed together, breathing the stale air. The night outside the cabin was cool, but inside the body heat made it hot and stifling. The only ventilation came from a small grate in the cabin roof. A few were already unconscious, having collapsed from the terror induced by claustrophobia, but their bodies were unable to fall. Instead their heads sagged and rolled with the rocking of the boat. Everyone was strangely silent. Perhaps defeated and powerless to dictate their fate, the prisoners lapsed into a strange lethargy like those sent by the Nazis to the concentration camps in World War II.

Julia stood listening to the sound of the waves lapping against the hull of the boat and the soft beat of the twin diesel engines, wondering where she was being taken. The water was smooth now. The swells of the ocean had been left behind twenty minutes ago. She assumed they were inside a quiet bay or traveling on a river. She knew with reasonable clarity that she was back somewhere in the United States. This was her home ground. She refused to let herself become pliant, and though she was still weak and dizzy, she was determined to fight her way out of this insane predicament and survive. Too much depended on her survival. By escaping and reporting the information she had gathered on the smuggling syndicate to her superiors at INS, she could stop the ghastly suffering and killing of thousands of illegal immigrants.

In the wheelhouse above the cabinlike prison, two of the smuggling crew's four enforcers began cutting rope into short lengths while the captain, who stood at the helm, threaded his way up the Orion River in the dark. The only light came from the stars, and his eyes never strayed from the radar screen. After another ten minutes, he alerted the others to the fact that they were passing from the river into the lake. Just as the black boat was about to come under the bright lights positioned at Qin Shang's retreat, the helmsman picked up the boat's phone and spoke a few words in Chinese. Almost before he set the phone back in its cradle, the lights inside the main building and those placed around the shore blinked out, throwing the entire lake into a cloak of blackness. Guided by a small red light on a buoy, the helmsman expertly slipped the catamaran around the broad transom of Shang's magnificent yacht and came alongside the pilings on the opposite side of the dock. Two enforcers jumped clear and slipped the mooring lines over their cleats as the helmsman set the twin diesel engines on idle.

For the next three or four minutes there was no sound outside the crowded cabin. A flurry of questions, a swarm of anxieties, framed themselves in the thoughts of Julia and the illegal immigrants. But they didn't know in what order to assess them, and the continuing nightmare of their voyage still overshadowed any attempt at clear thinking. And then the door was opened on the rear wall of the cabin. The fresh air that came from a breeze drifting down from the mountains seemed like a miracle. At first, all they could see outside was darkness; then an enforcer moved into the doorway.

"When you hear your name, step out onto the dock," he instructed them.

At first it was difficult for those in the middle or the back to squeeze through the overcrowded cabin, but as each body exited through the door those who remained gave a collective sigh of relief. Most of those who left the boat were poorer immigrants, the ones who could not pay the exorbitant fare to reach land, any land, so long as it didn't belong to the People's Republic of China. Unknowingly, they had signed away their souls to a life of servitude to the smugglers, who in turn sold them to criminal syndicates already established in the U.S.

Soon, only Julia, a mother and father weak from lack of food, along with their two small children, who looked like they might be suffering from rickets, and eight elderly men and women were left standing in the cabin. These were the castoffs, thought Julia, those who had been bled dry of their possessions, who had no more money to give and were too helpless and frail for any type of heavy work. These were the ones, including herself, who were not going ashore.

As if to confirm her worst fears, the door was slammed shut, the lines were cast off and the diesels were shifted into reverse, increasing their throb. It seemed as though the boat had only traveled a short distance when the engines slowed and idled again. The door was thrown open and four enforcers entered. Without a word they began binding everyone's hands and feet. Mouths were sealed with duct tape and heavy iron weights tied to their ankles. The mother and father made a feeble defense of their children but were easily subdued.

This was it then, death by drowning. Julia's whole mind, her every nerve became instantly concentrated on escaping. She sprinted toward the door, intent on reaching the outside deck and throwing herself into the water, making a swim for the nearest shore. The attempt was doomed before she hit the door. Debilitated from her beating the day before, she stumbled rather than ran, and was easily swept off her feet by one of the enforcers and knocked to the deck. She tried to fight them, pounding, scratching, biting as they bound her feet and ankles. Then the tape was adhered across her lips and the weight tied to her ankles.

She watched in icy horror as a hatch in the middle of the deck was lifted open and the first body dropped through into the water.

Pitt removed his thumb from the speed switch on the Stingray and hovered in the water ten feet below the center cabin of the catamaran. He had planned to surface between the two hulls and inspect the bottom of the boat when suddenly a light showed above him and a heavy splash broke the water followed in succession by several more.

What in God's name is happening? Pitt wondered as bodies came raining down around him. Though disbelieving at what he saw and shocked at the abhorrent sight, his reaction time was nothing short of incredible. In a series of lightning movements he released his grip on the Stingray, switched on the dive light and snatched his dive knife out of its sheath. In movements blurred in time, he began grabbing bodies, slicing the ropes binding the hands and ankles and slashing away the iron weights. Once the ropes were cut free, he pushed the body toward the surface and swam to the next one. He worked frantically, hoping against hope that none slipped past him into the black depths of the lake, never knowing at first whether the victims were already dead, but fighting to save them all regardless of his fears. Then he found they were alive when he gripped a young girl no more than ten, who stared back at him through terror-stricken eyes. She looked like she was Chinese. He prayed she could swim as he thrust her toward the night air.

At first, he kept slightly ahead of the flow of victims, but he soon struggled furiously to keep pace. Desperation was replaced with sheer anger as he saved a little boy no more than four years old. He mentally cursed the monsters who were capable of such inhumanity. Not taking any chances, he kicked his fins upward, quickly found the floating Stingray and placed the boy's arms around it. He switched off the dive light and took a quick glance at the boat to see if the crew had observed their victims popping to the surface. All on board appeared quiet. There was no hint of alarm. He dove under again, turning on the dive light. Its beam picked out what seemed to be the last body dumped from the boat. It was already falling past twenty feet when he caught up with it. This one was a young woman.

Before her turn came, Julia had breathed deeply in and out, hyper-ventilating her lungs, then holding her breath as the enforcers kicked her through the hatch into the water. She fought desperately to free herself from the ropes. Deeper and deeper she fell in the black void, furiously snorting through her nose to relieve the pressure building in the eustachian tubes of her ears. One minute, maybe two, and her oxygen would be gone and she'd die an agonizing death.

Suddenly, a pair of arms wrapped around her waist, and she could feel the iron weight dropping away from her feet. Then her hands came free and a hand snatched her arm in a grip and began towing her upward. As her head broke the surface she winced as the tape was ripped from her mouth. The first thing she saw was an apparition in a hood with a face mask and light protruding from its head.

"Can you understand me?" a voice asked in English.

"I can understand you," she gasped.

"Are you a good swimmer?"

She only nodded her reply.

"Good. Help save as many people as you can, try and gather them into a group. Tell them to follow my light. I'll lead you all into shallow water along the shore."

Pitt left her and swam off toward the boy clutching the Stingray in a death grip. He swung the boy behind him, clasping the small hands around his neck. Then he engaged the speed switch and searched for the little girl, finding her and circling his arm around her only seconds before she was about to slip out of sight.

On board the boat two of the enforcers climbed to the wheelhouse and stepped inside. "All are drowned," one said to the helmsman. "Our job is done."

The captain at the helm nodded and gently pushed the twin throttles forward. The propellers bit the water, and the black catamaran began to move back toward the dock. Before it had traveled a hundred feet, a call came over the boat's phone.

"Chu Deng?"

"This is Chu Deng," the captain responded.

"Lo Han, chief of compound security. Why are you ignoring your instructions?"

"I have followed the plan. All immigrants are disposed of. What is your problem?"

"You are showing a light."

Chu Deng stepped from the wheel and glanced over the boat. "You ate too much spicy Szechuan chicken for dinner, Lo Han. Your stomach is telling lies to your eyes. There are no lights showing on this boat."

"Then what am I seeing toward the eastern shoreline?"

As supervisor for transporting the illegal immigrants from the mother ships, Chu Deng was also responsible for the execution of those unfit for slave labor. He did not work under the chief of security for the imprisoned immigrants. Both merciless men, both on equal footing, neither got along with the other.

Lo Han was a big bull of a man built like a beer keg with a massive, square-jawed head and eyes that were always bloodshot. Deng considered him little better than an untrained dog. He turned and stared to the east. Only then did he spot a dim light low in the water. "I see it, about two hundred yards off the starboard beam. Must be a local fisherman," he said to Lo Han.

"Take no chances. You must investigate."

"I shall make a search."

"If you see anything suspicious," said Lo Han, "contact me immediately and I will switch the lights on again."

Chu Deng acknowledged and hung up the phone. Then he twisted the wheel, swinging the catamaran to starboard. As he set the twin bows on a course toward the dim light bobbing on the surface of the lake, he called to the pair of enforcers still below on the main deck. "Go forward and closely observe that light on the water dead ahead."

"What do you think it is?" asked a small man with expressionless eyes as he unslung his machine pistol.

Chu Deng shrugged. "Probably fishermen. It's not the first time we've seen them troll for salmon at night."

"And if they aren't fishermen?"

Chu Deng turned from the wheel and grinned with every tooth. "In that case, see that they join the others."

Pitt saw the boat coming toward the small group of people struggling through the water and was certain they'd been seen. He could hear voices on the bow, actually more of a platform extending across the forward section between the hulls, shouting in Chinese, no doubt telling their skipper there were people swimming in the lake. He didn't mentally have to do an equation to know they had been attracted by his dive light. He was guilty of being damned if it was on and damned if it was off. With no light the people he'd rescued from a watery death would have floundered off in all directions, become lost and eventually drowned.

Keeping the frightened boy on his shoulders, he stopped the Stingray and passed off the little girl to the young woman, who'd been helping an elderly man and woman paddle through the water. Now both his hands were free and he flicked off his dive light, twisted around to face the boat that was looming above him and blocking off the stars. He noted that it was passing less than three feet from him, and he could see two shadowy figures move down a ladder from the cabin to the bow platform deck. One of them leaned over, spotted Pitt in the water and gestured at him.

Before the other enforcer could fix Pitt in his flashlight's beam, a barb from Pitt's air gun hissed through the darkness and buried itself in the man's temple above the ear. Before his partner knew what happened, he fell dead with a barb protruding from his throat. There was no hesitation or grain of misgiving in Pitt's mind. These men had murdered countless innocent people. They did not deserve a warning or a chance to defend themselves. They deserved no more chance than those they killed.

Both had fallen silently backward, crumpled on the catamaran's forward deck. Pitt reloaded another barb and slowly swam on his back, waving his dive fins behind. The young boy buried his head in Pitt's shoulder and held on to his savior's neck with every ounce of strength in his little arms.

Pitt watched in amazement as the boat passed on, circled and continued on toward the dock as if nothing had occurred, seemingly unaware of the dead bodies on the forward deck. He barely discerned the shadow of a man at the helm through the wheelhouse windows. Strangely, the helmsman didn't act as if he knew his men were terminated. Pitt could only speculate that the helmsman's attention was focused elsewhere when he'd killed his partners in crime.

Pitt didn't have the slightest doubt that the boat would return, and return quickly once the two bodies were found. He had bought four, maybe five, minutes, certainly no more. He kept his eyes on the catamaran as its phantom outline glided away in the darkness. The craft was halfway back to the dock when her shape gradually began to alter, and he reckoned that she was turning broadside and circling back.

He thought it odd that no light blinked on and swept the lake. He thought it odd for all of about ten seconds, when the lights at the prison retreat burst on again and danced on the waves created by the wake of the catamaran.

Caught like floating decoy ducks in the water was as bad as it could get. Caught after reaching the shore but before finding cover was only slightly less bad. Then suddenly the Stingray pulled him into the shallows, and he found he could stand up in water to his lower hips. He waded ashore and set the boy on the lake's bank, which rose about eighteen inches out of the water. Then he returned for the others, towing them in until they could wade onto dry land. These people were either too old or too young and too played out to do more than crawl into the trees.

He motioned to the girl, who was rising out of the water a few feet away with the little girl on her shoulders and one arm around an old woman who looked near death. "Take the boy!" he snapped. "Hurry these people into the trees and make them lie down!"

"Where will you . . . you be?" she asked haltingly.

He shot another look at the boat. "Horatius at the bridge, Custer standing alone at Little Big Horn, that's me," Pitt said. Before Julia could reply, the stranger who had saved their lives had vanished back into the water.

Chu Deng was scared down to his boots. In the darkness he had failed to see the deaths of his enforcers. He had been concentrating on keeping the boat from running aground when they were murdered. After discovering the dead bodies, Chu Deng had panicked. There was no going to the dock and reporting two of his enforcers murdered by unknown assassins without his witnessing the act. His employer would never accept vague and inexplicable excuses. He would be punished for inefficient actions—he knew that with total certainty.

He had no choice but to confront his assailants. It never entered his mind that there was only one. He assumed it had to be a planned operation by professionals. He stationed his remaining two men—one aft on the stern deck between the hulls, the other on the forward deck. After requesting Lo Han to turn on the lights, he spotted several people stumbling out of the water onto the lake bank. Then to add disaster to catastrophe, he recognized them as the immigrants who were supposed to be drowned. He went rigid in astonishment. How could they have escaped? Impossible unless they had help. It had to be a special force of trained agents, he thought wildly.

Qin Shang would surely order him sent to the bottom of the lake if he didn't capture the escaped immigrants before they reached American authorities. In the light from across the lake, Chu Deng counted nearly a dozen men and women and two children staggering and crawling from the water's edge toward a forest of trees. Caught up in fear of a short future and without regard to the circumstances, Chu Deng turned the catamaran directly toward a low bank running along the shoreline.

"There they are!" he screamed wildly to the enforcer on the forward deck. "Shoot them, shoot them before they reach the trees!"

He stared mesmerized as his man on the forward platform of the catamaran raised his weapon and stood watching as if a film was running in slow motion when a dark form rose out of the water in front of the boat like some abominable creature out of a nightmare. The enforcer suddenly stiffened, dropping the machine pistol and clutching his shoulder. Seconds later an ugly barb suddenly protruded from the enforcer's left eye. Chu Deng froze in bewildered shock as his enforcer tumbled into the cold waters of the lake.

There are many advantages to a craft with catamaran twin hulls. Repelling boarders is not one of them. A boat with a single high bow is next to impossible to climb aboard, much less to find a means of hanging on to the hull. But the straight-across platform deck forward of the main cabin and wheelhouse sat only fourteen inches above the water, making it relatively simple for a person in the water to grab hold of the leading edge.

Propelled by the Stingray, Pitt burst free of the water just as the black boat was about to run him down. With timing based more on luck than expertise, he cast off the propulsion vehicle, threw up one arm and clamped it over the edge of the forward deck. The shock of the rapidly moving boat as it abruptly jerked his body through the water felt as if his arm was torn from its socket. Fortunately, it remained in place, and Pitt shot the man who was aiming a machine pistol at the people on shore before he could pull the trigger. In three seconds, Pitt had reloaded and fired a barb that punched upward through the man's eye, penetrating his brain.

The catamaran was now on a collision course with the shore, which was less than thirty feet away when Pitt slipped off the forward part of the boat and floated on his back. While the raised cabin advanced over him, he calmly reloaded the air gun. After the propellers thrashed by harmlessly on both sides, he twisted around and stroked powerfully in the wake of the boat. He swam only a short distance before the catamaran smashed into the lake bank, crunching the bows and coming to a stop as abruptly as if it had struck a steel wall. The engines raced for several seconds and then sputtered and died. The momentum and the impact had thrown the enforcer on the aft platform against the cabin with such extraordinary force that he broke his neck.

Unbuckling the straps to the backpack that held his air cylinders and dropping his weight belt, Pitt heaved himself up onto the aft platform. No figure showed inside the wheelhouse. He climbed the ladder and kicked in the door.

A man lay on the deck, his head and shoulders propped against the forward counter, hands clutching his chest. Broke his ribs from the impact, Pitt quickly suspected. Injured or not, the man was a killer. Pitt took no chances. Not with men like this. He raised his air gun in the same instant as Chu Deng thrust out a small, .32-caliber automatic pistol he'd been shielding with the hands across his chest. The deadly crack of the automatic overpowered the hiss of the barb from the air gun, both missiles passing in the same microsecond. The bullet plowed a small hole through the outer flesh of Pitt's hip at the same time the barb plunged into Chu Deng's forehead.

Pitt did not judge his wound as serious. There was minor bleeding and pain to be sure, but it did not slow his physical movements. He ran stiffly from the wheelhouse, down the ladder and jumped off the forward platform onto the shore. He found the frightened immigrants huddled behind a clump of bushes.

"Where is the lady who speaks English?" he asked between pants of breath.

"I'm here," answered Julia. She rose to her feet and approached until she stood in front of him, more imagined than seen.

"How many did I lose?" he asked, fearful of the answer.

"By rough count," she answered, "three are missing."

"Damn!" Pitt muttered in frustration. "I'd hoped I got them all."

"You did," said Julia. "They became lost on the way to shore."

"I'm sorry," Pitt said honestly.

"You needn't be. It was a miracle you saved any of us."

"Can they travel?"

"I believe so."

"Follow the shore to your left as you face the lake," he instructed her. "After about three hundred yards, you'll come to a cabin. Hide everyone in the woods outside but do not enter. I repeat, do not enter. I'll follow as soon as I can."

"Where will you be?" she asked.

"We're not dealing with people who like to be fooled. They'll wonder what happened to their boat and come scouring the lakefront within the next ten minutes. I'm going to create a little diversion. You might call it a little payback for the person responsible for your misery."

It was too dark for him to see the sudden look of caring in her face. "Please be careful, Mr. . . . ?"

"Pitt, my name is Dirk Pitt."

"I'm Julia Lee."

He started to say something, but broke off and hurried back to the catamaran, returning to the wheelhouse just as the phone buzzed. He groped for it in the dark, found and picked it up. Someone was conversing in Chinese on the other end. When the voice paused, Pitt muttered unintelligible vowels, clicked the receiver and laid the phone on the bridge counter. Using the dive light on his hood, he soon found the boat's ignition switches and throttles. He engaged the starters and worked the throttles back and forth until both engines coughed into life again.

The catamaran's bows were stuck fast in the mud of the bank. Pitt shifted to full throttle in reverse and spun the helm, swinging the boat's twin sterns back and forth in an effort to loosen the suction of the mud. One agonizing inch at a time, the black boat warped backwards until the suction relaxed its grip and the bows broke free. The boat surged into deeper water, where Pitt swung her around and then pushed the throttles forward, pointing the damaged bows toward the dock and Qin Shang's yacht, its elegant, seemingly deserted salons sparkling with light.

He jammed his dive knife between the spokes of the wheel, sticking the point into the wooden compass box beyond to hold the boat on course. Then he set the throttles on slow and exited the wheelhouse, scrambling down the ladder to the engine compartment in the starboard hull. There was no time to build a fancy incendiary bomb, so he spun off the big refueling cap to the fuel tank, found several oily rags used to clean the engine fittings and quickly knotted them together. Then he stuffed a length of rags inside the tank, soaked them with diesel fuel and trailed the rest onto the engine-compartment deck. Next, he arranged the rags into a small, circlelike dam and poured fuel inside it. Not overly pleased with his handiwork, but satisfied that under the circumstances it was the best he could do, Pitt returned to the wheelhouse and rummaged the storage cabinets until he found what he knew had to be there somewhere. Loading the emergency flare gun, he laid it on the counter beside the phone in front of the helm. Only then did he pull his knife from the wheel and grip the spokes.

The yacht and the dock were only two hundred yards distant now.

Water gushing through cracks in the bows, crushed from their collision with the lake bank, rapidly filled the forward section of the twin hulls, dragging them down. Pitt shoved the throttles against their stops. The propellers bit and churned the water to froth, their drive power raising the bows out of the water. Fifteen, eighteen, then twenty knots, the ungainly catamaran skipped over the water. The helm vibrated under Pitt's hands as the yacht loomed ever larger through the windshield. He cut a broad arc until the twin hulls were lined up square in the middle of the yacht's port beam.

When the distance closed to seventy, going on sixty, yards, Pitt dashed through the wheelhouse door, dropped to the aft-deck platform, aimed the flare gun down through the open hatch of the engine compartment at the fuel-soaked rags and pulled the trigger. Trusting his aim was accurate, he leaped into the water, striking it at twenty knots with such force that his buoyancy compensator was torn from his body.

Four seconds later, there was a splintering crash as the catamaran smashed through the hull of the yacht, followed by an explosion that filled the night sky with flame and flying debris. The black catamaran that had acted as an execution chamber disintegrated. All that remained of it was a flaming oil slick. Almost immediately, fire was shooting through every port and varnished door of the yacht. Pitt was stunned at how quickly she became a flaming torch. He backstroked around the yacht's stern toward the floating hut at the end of the dock, watching as the luxurious skylounge and dining salon collapsed into the fire. Slowly, very slowly, the yacht settled into the cold waters of the lake amid a huge cloud of hissing steam, until nothing remained of her except the upper half of a radar antenna.

The reaction time for the security guards, as Pitt had previously estimated, was slow. He had reached the floating hut before they came racing from the retreat on their dirt bikes toward the dock, which had also ignited and was now going up in flames. For the second time in an hour he surfaced inside the hut. Feet could be heard pounding through the passageway. He slammed the door, but finding no lock, wedged his trusty dive knife between the outer edge and the frame, effectively jamming it closed.

An old hand at riding watercraft, he jumped astride the nearest one and pressed the starter button. He squeezed the thumb throttle, and the motor immediately whirred into life. The thrusters dug in the water and threw the craft and Pitt forward. Together, they struck the flimsy door, shattering it into splinters before racing across the lake. Cold, wet, exhausted and bleeding from the bullet wound in his hip, Pitt felt like a man who had just won the lottery, the sweepstakes and broke the bank at Monte Carlo. But only for the time it took to reach the dock beside his cabin.

Then reality set in, and he knew the worst was yet to come.

9

LO HAN STARED DUMBSTRUCK at the monitors inside the mobile security vehicle revealing the black catamaran suddenly making a wide swing around the lake and homing in on the yacht, ramming the beautiful vessel square amidships. The resulting explosion rocked the security vehicle, temporarily knocking out the surveillance systems. Lo Han ran outside and down to the shoreline to witness the disaster firsthand.

There will be a heavy price to pay, he thought, staring at the yacht as it sank under the lake in a cloud of steam. Qin Shang was not a man who easily forgave. He would not be pleased when he learned that one of his four yachts had been destroyed. Already Lo Han was mentally creating ways to blame that stupid Chu Deng.

After he had demanded that Chu Deng investigate the mysterious light, there had been no coherent communication from the black boat and its crew of enforcers. He had to believe that they were drunk and had passed out in a stupor. What other explanation could there be? What reason for purposely committing suicide? The last thing to cross his mind was the specter of an outside source who was responsible for this disaster.

Two of his guards came running up to him. Lo Han recognized them as the men from his water patrol.

"Lo Han," one of the men panted, out of breath after running nearly four hundred yards out and back through the passageway to the floating log hut.

He stared at them angrily. "Wang Hui, Li San, why aren't you men on the water with your craft?"

"We couldn't reach them," explained Wang Hui. "The door was locked. Before we could force it open the hut was on fire, and we had to escape back into the tunnel or be burned alive."

"The door was locked!" Lo Han bellowed. "Impossible. I personally instructed that no lock be installed."

"I swear to you, Lo Han," said Li San, "the door was barred from the inside."

"Perhaps it became blocked from the explosion," offered Wang Hui.

"Nonsense—" Lo Han broke off as a voice came over his portable radio. "Yes, what is it?" he snapped.

The quiet, competent voice of his second in command, Kung Chong, came through the earpiece. "The two men who were late in relieving the cell-block security guards . . ."

"Yes, what about them?"

"They have been found bound and beaten on the vacant second level of the building."

"Bound and beaten," blurted Lo Han. "There is no mistake?"

"It looks like the work of a professional," stated Kung Chong flatly.

"Are you saying our security has been infiltrated?"

"It would seem so."

"Launch an immediate search of the grounds," demanded Lo Han.

"I have already given the order."

Lo Han slipped the radio into his pocket and gazed at the dock that was still blazing from end to end. There has to be a connection between the men who were assaulted in the prison building and the insane collision of the yacht by the catamaran, he thought. Still ignorant of Pitt's rescue of the doomed immigrants, Han could not bring himself to believe that American law-enforcement agents had sent an undercover team to destroy Qin Shang's operation. He eliminated that thought as unrealistic, considering the situation. That would make them responsible for the murders of Chu Deng and his crew of enforcers, an act not generally conceived by FBI or INS agents. No, if American investigators had the slightest clue of the covert activities taking place on Orion Lake, a tactical assault team would already be swarming over the grounds. It was painfully obvious to Lo Han that this was no professionally planned intrusion by an army of trained agents. It was an operation conducted by one, surely no more than two, men.

But whom were they working for? Who was paying them? Certainly not a competing smuggling operation or one of the established criminal syndicates. They wouldn't be so stupid as to start a territory fight, not while Qin Shang had the backing of the People's Republic of China.

Han's gaze traveled from the burning pier and the sunken ships to the cabin across the lake. He stood there transfixed and recalled the arrogant fisherman who flaunted his catch the day before. He may not be what he seemed. Probably no fisherman or a simple businessman on vacation, Lo Han deduced, and yet he did not act like an agent of the Immigration Service or the FBI. Whatever his motive, the fisherman was Lo Han's only suspect within a hundred miles.

Content that he had eliminated the worst-case scenario, Lo Han began to breathe a little easier. He took his radio and called a name. The voice of Kung Chong answered.

"Are there suspicious sightings of vehicles?" Lo Han asked.

"The roads and skies are empty," Kung Chong assured him.

"Any unusual activity across the lake?"

"Our cameras reveal some movement among the trees behind the cabin but no signs of the occupant inside."

"I want a raid on that cabin. I must know who we're dealing with."

"A raid will take time to organize," said Kung Chong.

"Buy time by sending in a man to sabotage his automobile so he can't escape."

"Should something go wrong, won't we be risking a confrontation with the local law authorities?"

"The last of my worries. If my instincts are correct, the man is dangerous and a threat to our employer who pays us and pays us well."

"Do you wish to terminate him?"

"I believe that to be the safest alternative," Lo Han said, nodding to himself. "Be warned. There must be no mistakes. It is not wise to incur the wrath of Qin Shang."

"Mr. Pitt?" Julia Lee's whisper was barely audible in the darkness.

"Yes." Pitt had parked the watercraft in a small inlet that opened onto the lake beside the cabin, approaching through the woods until he found Julia and her brood. He sat down heavily on a fallen tree and began pulling off his dry suit. "Is everyone all right?"

"They're alive," she answered in a soft voice with just a trace of huskiness. "But they're not all right. They're soaked to the skin and freezing. Everyone needs dry clothes and medical attention."

Pitt gently touched the bullet wound in his hip. "I'll second that."

"Why can't they go inside your cabin where they can be warm and find something to eat?"

He shook his head. "Not a good idea. I haven't been to town for almost two days and my cupboard is bare. Better we herd them into the boathouse. I'll bring them whatever food I have left and every blanket I can find."

"You're not making sense," she said flatly. "They'd be more comfortable in the cabin than some smelly old boathouse."

A stubborn woman, this one, Pitt thought, and self-sufficient too. "Did I forget to mention the surveillance cameras and listening bugs that grow like mushrooms in nearly every room? I think it best if your friends across the lake observe no one but me. If they suddenly see the ghosts of the people they believe they drowned watching television and drinking my tequila, they'll come charging in here with every gun blazing before our side's posse arrives. No sense in getting them all riled up before their time."

"They've been monitoring you from across the lake?" she asked, puzzled.

"Someone over there thinks I have beady eyes and can't be trusted."

She looked at his face, trying to distinguish his features, but saw no details in the dark. "Who are you, Mr. Pitt?"

"Me?" he said, pulling his feet out of the dry suit. "I'm just an ordinary guy who came to the lake to unwind and fish."

"You are far from ordinary," she said softly, turning and gazing at the dying flames and smoldering embers of the dock. "No ordinary man could have accomplished what you did tonight."

"And you, Ms. Lee? Why is a highly intelligent lady who speaks flawless English and associates with a bunch of illegal immigrants thrown into a lake with weights tied around her ankles?"

"You know they're illegals?"

"If they're not, they don't hide it very well."

She shrugged. "I guess it's useless to pretend I'm somebody I'm not. I can't flash my badge, but I'm a special undercover agent with the Immigration and Naturalization Service. And I would be most grateful if you could get me to a telephone."

"I've always been putty in the hands of women." He walked over to a tree, reached up under the branches and returned. He handed her his Iridium satellite phone. "Call your superiors and tell them what's going on here," he advised. "Tell them the building on the lake is a prison for illegal immigrants. For what purpose, I can't say. Tell them the lake bed is littered with hundreds, maybe thousands of dead bodies. Why, I can't say. Tell them the security is first-rate and the guards are heavily armed, and tell them to get here fast before the evidence is either shot, drowned or burned to death. Then tell them to call Admiral James Sandecker at the National Underwater and Marine Agency and say his special projects director wants to come home and to send a taxi.''

Julia looked at Pitt's face in the dim starlight, trying to read something, her eyes wide and questioning, her lips slowly forming the words. "You are an amazing man, Dirk Pitt. A director of NUMA. I'd have never guessed in a thousand years. Since when do they train marine scientists to be assassins and arsonists?''

"Since midnight," he said briefly as he turned and set off for the cabin. "And I'm not a scientist, I'm an engineer. Now make your call, and hurry. As sure as the sun sets in the west, we're going to have company very soon.''

Ten minutes later Pitt returned from the house loaded down with a small box of food and ten blankets. He had also hurriedly changed into more practical clothes. He failed to hear the silenced pair of bullets that smashed into the radiator of his rental car. He only caught the antifreeze flooding the ground under the front bumper when it reflected off the night-lights he'd left burning on the porch of the cabin.

"So much for driving out of here," he said quietly to Julia as she distributed what little food he had, and he passed out the blankets to the shivering Chinese.

"What do you mean?" she asked.

"Your friends just punctured my radiator. We wouldn't make the main highway before the engine heated up and the bearings froze.''

"I wish you'd stop calling them my friends," she said flippantly.

"Merely a form of speech.''

"I fail to see a problem. The lake will be crawling with INS and FBI agents in another hour.''

"Too late," said Pitt seriously. "Shang's men will be all over us long before they arrive. By disabling my car, they bought time to organize a raiding party. They're probably closing off the road and forming a net around the cabin while we stand here.''

"You can't expect these people to hike miles through the woods in the dark," said Julia firmly. "They can endure no more. There must be another way to get them to safety. You have to think of something.''

"Why does it always have to be me?''

"Because you're all we've got.''

Feminine logic, Pitt mused. How do they come by it? "Are you in the mood for romance?"

"Romance?" She was completely taken aback. "At a time like this? Are you crazy?"

"Not really," said Pitt casually. "But you must admit, it's a lovely night for a boat ride under the stars."

They came to kill Pitt shortly before dawn. They came quietly and deliberately, surrounding and approaching the cabin in a well-timed and organized operation. Kung Chong spoke softly into his portable radio, coordinating his men's movements. Kung Chong was an old hand at conducting raids on houses of dissidents when he was an agent with the People's Republic intelligence service. He did not like what he saw of the cabin from the woods. The outside floodlights were on around the porch, playing havoc with the raiders' night vision. The lights of every room were also turned on, and country-western music blasted from a radio.

His team of twenty men had converged on the cabin along the road and through the forest after his advance scout radioed that he had shot holes in the radiator of the occupant's car. Kung Chong was certain that all paths of escape were cut off and that no one had passed through his cordon. Whoever was living in the cabin had to be there. And yet Kung Chong sensed all was not going according to plan.

Throwing light around a darkened building usually indicated an ambush by people waiting to open fire inside. The brightly lit yard canceled the use of night glasses. But this situation was different. The illuminated interior rooms and the loud music puzzled Kung Chong. Total surprise seemed out of the question. Until his men could gain the relative safety of the cabin walls and break through the doors, they were sitting ducks to anyone with automatic weapons as they rushed across the yard. He moved from position to position around the cabin, peering through the windows with a pair of binoculars, observing a solitary man who sat at a table in the kitchen, the only room unrecorded by interior surveillance cameras. He wore a baseball cap and reading glasses and was bent over the table seemingly reading a book. A cabin ablaze with lights. The radio turned up at full volume. A man fully dressed and reading a book at five-thirty in the morning? Kung Chong sniffed the air and smelled a setup.

He sent for one of his men who carried a sniper rifle with a scope and a long suppressor on the muzzle. "You see the man sitting in the kitchen?" he asked quietly.

The sniper nodded silently.

"Shoot him."

Anything less than a hundred yards was child's play. A good shot with a handgun could have hit the target. The sniper ignored the scope and sighted in on the man seated at the table with the gun's iron sights. The shot sounded like the quick clap of hands followed by a tinkle of glass. Kung Chong peered through his binoculars. The bullet had made a small hole in the windowpane, but the figure remained upright at the table as if nothing had happened.

"You fool," he growled. "You failed to hit him."

The sniper shook his head. "At this distance it is impossible to miss."

"Shoot again."

The sniper shrugged, lined up the shot and pulled the trigger. The man at the table remained immobile. "Either the target is already dead or he is in a coma. I struck him above the bridge of the nose. See the hole for yourself."

Kung Chong focused his glasses on the face of the man in the kitchen. There *was* a neat round hole above the bridge of the nose above the reading glasses, and it wasn't bleeding.

"Curse that devil!" Kung Chong snarled. No stealth. No orders quietly issued over his radio. He shouted wildly across the clearing in front of the cabin, "Move in! Move in!"

Men dressed in black materialized from the shadows cast by the trees and ran across the yard, past the car and burst through the front door of the cabin. They spread through the rooms like a flood, weapons at the ready, poised to shoot at the first hint of resistance. Kung Chong was the fifth man into the living room. He rushed past his men and burst into the kitchen.

"What manner of devil is he?" Kung Chong muttered as he picked up the dummy sitting in the chair and threw it on the floor. The baseball hat fell away and the reading glasses shattered, revealing a crude face hurriedly molded out of wet newspaper and painted sloppily with vegetable dyes.

Kung Chong's second in command came up to him. "The cabin is empty. No sign of our quarry."

His lips pressed together in a thin line as he nodded, not surprised by the report. He touched the transmit button on his radio and spoke a name. Lo Han's voice responded immediately.

"Report."

"He has escaped," said Kung Chong simply.

There was a moment's pause, then Lo Han said irritably, "How is it possible he sidestepped your men?"

"No one larger than a rat could have slipped through the cordon. He cannot be far away."

"Most odd. Not in the cabin, not in the forest, where could he have gone?"

Kung Chong stared out the window at the boathouse that was being searched by his men. "The lake," he answered. "He can only be on the lake."

He skirted the dummy lying on the floor and ran out the back door across the porch and onto the dock. He shoved aside his men and stepped inside the boathouse. The sailboat was hanging in its cradle, the kayaks and canoe still in their wall racks. He stood numb, aware of the enormity of his blunder, the incredible ease with which he had been deceived. He should have known, at least guessed, how the man in the cabin had slipped through his fingers.

The old boat, the Chris-Craft runabout that Kung Chong had observed earlier after a personal search of the cabin and boathouse, was missing.

Nearly two miles away, it was a sight to stir the blood of those fortunate people who lived in the past. The beautifully designed mahogany hull, contoured in what old-timers called a tumble-home stern, curved gracefully from the transom forward to the engine compartment, which sat between the forward and aft cockpits. Weighted down with twelve adults and two children packed into its dual cockpits, the sixty-seven-year-old 125-horsepower Chrysler marine engine lifted the bow and thrust the boat over the water at nearly thirty miles an hour, casting twin sheets of water to the sides and leaving a rooster tail in her wake. Pitt sat behind the wheel of the Foleys' 1933 Chris-Craft runabout with the little Chinese boy on his lap as the boat planed over the waters of the Orion River toward Grapevine Bay.

After explaining his latest plot to Julia, Pitt had quickly put two of the elderly Chinese men to work siphoning gas out of the car's tank and transferring it into the tank of the runabout. Because the big Chrysler marine engine had not turned over for several months, Pitt also replaced the battery with the one from his car. With Julia Lee translating, he instructed the senior citizens to take the paddles from the kayaks and canoe, and demonstrated the proper method of propelling the runabout without undue splashing noises. Considering the fatigue of the elderly immigrants and drawback of working in the dark, the enterprise went surprisingly smoothly.

Suddenly Pitt turned and rushed out of the boathouse.

"Where are you going?" shouted Julia.

"I almost forgot my best pal," he yelled back, running across the dock to the cabin. He was back in two minutes with a small bundle under one arm wrapped in a towel.

"That's your best pal?" asked Julia.

"I never leave home without him," he said.

Without further explanation he began helping everyone in the boat. When the drawn and hollow-eyed immigrants were stuffed into the confined dual cockpits, Pitt opened the boathouse door and whispered the order for everyone to paddle. They had hardly traveled little more than a quarter of a mile, staying along the shoreline in the shadows, when the weary Chinese began giving up from the effects of exposure and exhaustion. Pitt continued stroking until the runabout was at last caught in the current of the river. Only then did he lay his paddle aside and catch his breath for a few moments. Luck was with them; they had yet to be discovered. He waited until they had drifted down the river out of earshot of the lake before he tried to start up the engine. He primed the twin carburetors Foley had installed to update the intake manifold. Then he made a wish on every star in sight and pushed the starter button on the dashboard.

The big, straight-eight Chrysler turned over slowly until the oil circulated, and then increased its revolutions. After grinding away for several seconds, Pitt disengaged the starter. As he primed the carburetors again he could have sworn that everyone in the boat was holding his breath. On the next attempt a pair of cylinders popped to life, then another pair until the engine was hitting on all eight. Pitt pushed the floor lever into forward and let the boat move only on the engine's idle speed. He steered with the little Chinese boy sitting in his lap. Still no shouts from the shore, no searchlight stabbing across the lake. He looked back at the cabin. He could see tiny figures appearing out of the forest and running into the lights he'd left on.

The first rays of the sun were spreading over the mountains to the east when Pitt turned to Julia, who was sitting beside him, her arms clasped around the young girl. He looked over at her, seeing her face in the light for the first time, shocked at the punishment inflicted on what must have been delicate features, and fully appreciating her courage and stamina in surviving her ordeal.

Cold anger suddenly overwhelmed him. "My God, those bastards really worked you over."

"I haven't looked in a mirror, but I suspect I won't be showing my face in public for a while," she said gamely.

"If your superiors at INS give out medals, you'd rate a chestfull."

"A certificate of merit in my file is the best I can hope for."

"Tell everybody to hold on tight," he advised her. "We're coming into rapids."

"After we reach the mouth of the river, what then?" she asked.

"According to my calculations, any place on a map called Grapevine Bay must have grapes and grapes mean vineyards and vineyards mean people. The more, the merrier. Shang's mad dogs wouldn't dare attack us with a hundred U.S. citizens looking on."

"I'd better call the INS field agents again and alert them to the fact that we've left the area and give them our destination."

"A good idea," said Pitt, pushing the throttle forward to its stop with one hand while handing her the phone with the other. "They can concentrate their forces on the retreat instead of worrying about us at the cabin."

"Did you hear from your NUMA people?" Julia shouted above the increased roar of the exhaust.

"They're supposed to meet and pick me up after we reach Grapevine Bay."

"Do they use little open aircraft painted yellow?"

He shook his head. "NUMA leases executive jets and helicopters with turquoise color schemes. Why do you ask?"

Julia tapped Pitt on the shoulder and pointed over the stern at a yellow ultralight that was chasing them down the river. "If they're not friends, they must be foes."

10

PITT TOOK A FAST LOOK over his shoulder at the aircraft rapidly closing over the wake of the Chris-Craft. He recognized it as an ultralight, a pusher-engined, high-winged monoplane with tricycle landing gear and tandem seats for two people. The pilot sat forward, out in the open, with his passenger behind and slightly elevated. The airframe consisted of aluminum tubing braced with thin cable. Propelled by a lightweight, reduction-drive, fifty-horsepower engine, it could move fast. Pitt guessed it was capable of 120 miles an hour.

The pilot was flying directly over the middle of the river no more than forty feet off the water. He was good, Pitt admitted. The air currents swirled through the narrow canyon in a series of strong wind gusts, but the pilot compensated and kept the ultralight on a straight and level course. He was coming after the runabout intentionally and purposefully, like someone who knew exactly what he was about to do. There was no hesitation and no uncertainty about who was going to end up the loser in the coming unequal contest. God knows Pitt had no doubts, not when he saw a man strapped in the seat behind the pilot holding a stubby machine pistol in his hands.

"Force everyone to get down as low as they can," Pitt ordered Julia.

She spoke in Chinese, passing on Pitt's command, but the runabout's passengers were already so overcrowded in the small cockpits they had no place to go. All they could do was settle as low as humanly possible in the leather seats and duck their heads.

"Oh, dear lord," gasped Julia. "There are two more of them about a mile behind the first."

"I wish you hadn't told me," said Pitt, hunched over the steering wheel, willing the runabout to go faster. "They're not about to let us escape and spread the gospel about their shady operation."

The lead ultralight roared so low over the speeding Chris-Craft, the draft from its propeller blades whirled a cloud of spray that dampened the occupants of the boat. Pitt expected to hear gunshots, see holes appear in the smoothly varnished mahogany, but the aircraft passed on without attacking. It pulled up sharply, its tricycle landing wheels missing the runabout's windshield by no more than five feet.

Kung Chong sat strapped into the rear seat of the ultralight bringing up the rear and gazed with smug satisfaction at the speeding runabout below. He spoke into the transmitter attached to his crash helmet. "We have the boat in sight," he reported.

"Have you commenced your attack?" asked Lo Han from the mobile security vehicle.

"Not yet. The lead plane reports our quarry is not alone."

"As we suspected, there were two of them."

"Not two," said Kung Chong. "More like ten or twelve. The boat appears crowded with old people and young children."

"The devil must have found a family camping along the river and forced them into the boat to act as hostages. Our adversary, it seems, will stop at nothing to preserve his life."

Kung Chong raised a pair of binoculars with one hand and peered at the passengers huddled in the dual cockpits. "I believe we have an unforeseen problem, Lo Han."

"We've had nothing but problems for the past twelve hours. What is it now?"

"I can't be certain, but it appears the occupants of the boat are immigrants."

"Impossible, the only aliens brought ashore are either confined, on their way inland or dead."

"I could be mistaken."

"Let's hope you are," said Lo Han. "Can you fly close enough to identify their nationality?" asked Lo Han.

"For what purpose? For me to eliminate the devil responsible for the destruction of Qin Shang's yacht and the infiltration into the alien holding cells, those who are with him must die too. What difference if they are Chinese or American?"

"You are right, Kung Chong," acknowledged Lo Han. "Do whatever you must to protect the enterprise."

"I shall give orders to launch the attack."

"Be certain there are no spectators in the vicinity."

"The river is clear of recreational craft, and the shorelines are empty of people."

"Very well, but keep a sharp eye. We cannot afford eyewitnesses."

"As you command," said Kung Chong. "But time is running out. If we do not destroy the boat and those in it within the next few minutes, all opportunity will be lost."

"Why didn't he fire?" asked Julia, squinting against the glare from the morning sun on the surface of the river.

"A hitch in their assassination plans. They thought I worked alone. He's reporting to his boss that I'm loaded to the gunwales with passengers."

"How far to Grapevine Bay?"

"A good twelve or thirteen miles."

"Can't we pull onto shore and take cover in the trees and rocks?"

"Not a practical idea," he said. "All they'd have to do is land in the nearest clearing and hunt us down. The river is our only chance, slim as it is. You and the others keep your heads down. Let them wonder where I picked up a load of passengers. If they're looking closely they'll spot the folds on your eyelids and realize you're not the descendants of European ancestry on a picnic."

The venerable Chris-Craft covered another two miles of river before the lead ultralight dipped low over the river and increased speed, its nose aimed menacingly at the runabout. "No more peaceful intentions," said Pitt calmly. "He means business this time. How good are you with a handgun?"

"My qualifying scores on the range are higher than most of the male agents I know," she said as matter-of-factly as if she was describing her latest hairdo.

He took the bundle from under his seat, unwrapped the towel and handed her his old automatic pistol. "Ever shoot a Colt forty-five?"

"No," she answered. "When required, most of us at INS pack a Beretta forty-caliber automatic."

"Here are two spare clips. Don't waste your shells firing at the engine or fuel tank. As a target, it's too small to hit on an aircraft passing overhead at more than fifty miles an hour. Aim for the pilot and the gunner. One good body shot and they'll either crash or head for home."

She took the .45, twisted around in the seat so she was facing backward, flipped off the safety and cocked the hammer. "He's almost on us," she warned Pitt.

"The pilot will roll and come over us slightly off to one side, giving his gunner a clear shot downward," Pitt said coolly. "The instant he lines us up in his sights, shout out which side he's passing, left or right, so I can zigzag under him."

Without questioning Pitt's instructions, Julia gripped the old Colt with both hands, raised the barrel and lined up the sights on the two men perched in front of the wings and engine as it soared down the river. Her face showed more concentration than fear as her finger tightened on the trigger.

"On your left!" she called out.

Pitt threw the runabout in a sharp turn to the left, staying with the ultralight. He heard the quiet staccato burp of an automatic weapon with a suppressor on its muzzle, mingled with the loud thunder of the old Colt, and saw bullets lace the water only three feet alongside the hull as he cut under the ultralight, using its underside to mask the runabout from the gunner's view.

As the ultralight shot ahead, Pitt saw no trace of injury to the pilot or copilot. They looked as if they were enjoying themselves. "You missed!" he snapped.

"I could have sworn I scored," she snapped back furiously.

"Ever hear of a deflection shot?" Pitt lectured her. "You've got to lead a moving target. Haven't you ever hunted ducks?"

"I could never bring myself to shoot a harmless bird," she said loftily as she expertly ejected an empty clip and pumped a full one inside the handgrip of the Colt.

Feminine logic again, thought Pitt. Can't shoot an animal or bird, but not hesitating to blow a man's head off. "If he comes at the same speed and altitude, aim a good ten feet ahead of the pilot."

The ultralight circled around for another attack while its sister craft hung back in the distance. The droning whir of the engine's exhaust echoed off the rock walls of the canyon. The pilot swooped low over the shoreline, the airflow churned out by the propeller blades whipping the tops of the trees along the banks. The serene and picturesque river and the slopes of the forested canyon seemed the wrong location for a life-and-death struggle. The clear green water flowed past banks that were lined with trees marching up the rocky sides of the mountains until they thinned and stopped at the timberline. The yellow aircraft stood out like a colored gemstone, a Mexican fire opal against a sapphire sky. All things considered, Pitt thought fleetingly, there are worse places to die.

The ultralight leveled out and came directly toward the Chris-Craft's bow on this run. Now Pitt had an open field of vision and could see the angle of the gunner's trajectory for himself. Unless the pilot is a certified cretin, Pitt thought, he won't fall for the same sidestep again. Pitt had to reach down in his bag of tricks for another dodge. Maintaining his course until the last possible second, he felt like a herring taunting a shark.

Julia leveled the Colt over the windshield. She almost looked comical, her head slightly tilted to one side as she aimed with the only eye that was partially open. The pilot of the ultralight was sideslipping up the river to give his gunner additional shooting time and a wider range of fire. He knew his stuff and wasn't about to be fooled twice. On this strafing run he hugged the riverbank, cutting off any attempt by Pitt to slip under the plane's narrow belly. The pilot was also playing a more cautious game. Some of Julia's bullets had struck the wing and made him realize his prey had a sting.

Pitt knew with sickening certainty that they were going to take hits. No tricky maneuvers, no fancy footwork, could save them this time around. Unless Julia scored big-time, they were all dead, literally. He watched the ultralight loom up through the windshield. It was like standing in the middle of a bridge over a thousand-foot ravine with an express train hurtling toward him.

And then there was the despairing thought that even if they were successful in downing the first ultralight, they weren't even halfway home. The second and third craft were lagging back, staying out of range and clear of stray bullets while awaiting their turn. Take one out of the game and two substitutes were suited up and ready for action. The moment of trepidation ended as bullets struck and gouged the water, the line of splashes moving inexorably toward the boat.

Pitt jerked the steering wheel, sending the runabout on a skidding turn to his right. The gunner compensated, but too late. Pitt swung the boat in a flat curve to the left, throwing off his aim. He feinted again, but the gunner merely swiveled his weapon and laid down an S pattern. Then, as if he had touched a switch, Julia began blasting away.

This was the moment. As bullets stitched a groove of holes across the lustrous mahogany bow of the Chris-Craft, Pitt took the gear lever in both hands and yanked it back while the boat was at full speed. There was a horrifying grinding noise as the gearbox howled in protest. The engine revolutions raced past the red line on the tachometer, and the boat came to an abrupt stop. Then it leaped backward in a tight arc. Several bullets shattered the windshield but miraculously missed hitting anyone. And then the hail of fire, like a passing rainstorm, moved behind the boat. Julia tracked her target and fired until the last shell flipped out of the firing chamber.

Pitt glanced back and saw a beautiful sight. The ultralight was out of control, the racing engine shrieking like a banshee as fragments of the propeller spiraled in the air, spraying in every direction. He could see the pilot fighting the controls in a futile gesture as the craft hung poised in the air as if tied to a string. Then the nose dipped, and it plunged lifeless into the middle of the river, making a crater in the water and causing a huge splash before bobbing back to the surface for a few moments and then sinking rapidly until it vanished.

"Nice shooting," Pitt complimented Julia. "Wyatt Earp would be proud of you."

"I was lucky," Julia said modestly, not about to admit that she had been aiming at the pilot.

"You put the fear of God in the pilot of the other two. They're not about to make the same mistakes as his buddy. They'll lay back out of range of your Colt, take their time and pepper away at us at a safer altitude."

"How much farther until we're out of the canyon?"

"Four, maybe five miles."

They exchanged looks, she seeing the fierce determination in his eyes, he seeing her head and shoulders sag from severe fatigue, mental and physical. It didn't take a physician to see Julia was half-dead from lack of sleep. She had run on sheer guts as far as she could go, and had come to the end of the road. She turned slightly and stared at the bullet holes that had splintered the bow of the Chris-Craft.

"We're not going to make it, are we?" she muttered the words dully.

"Hell yes, we're going to make it!" he answered as if he truly believed it. "I didn't interrupt my vacation and go to all the work of bringing you and these people this far to let it end now."

She gazed at his dark, craggy face for a long moment, then shook her head in defeat. "I can't get off a straight shot if the ultralights stay more than a hundred yards away, not at that distance against a moving target from a boat that's bounding all over the place."

"Do the best you can." Hardly brilliant words of encouragement, Pitt conceded, but his mind was on other matters as he swerved around a series of large boulders protruding from the river. "Another ten minutes and we'll be home free."

"What if they both come at the same time?"

"You can bet on it. Take your time and divide your fire, two shots at one then two shots at the other. Maintain a show of resistance, just enough to keep them from getting too cocky and coming in too close. The farther they stay away, the more difficult for the gunners to fire with any accuracy. I'll throw the boat all over the river to spoil their aim."

Pitt had read Kung Chong's mind correctly. The Chinaman ordered his pilots to attack from a higher altitude. "I have lost one aircraft and two good men," he dutifully reported to Lo Han.

"How?" asked Lo Han simply.

"By gunfire from the boat."

"Not inconceivable that professionals would carry automatic weapons."

"I am ashamed to say, Lo Han, the defensive fire comes from a woman with one automatic pistol."

"A woman!" Lo Han's voice came through Kung Chong's earpiece as angry as he ever heard it. "We have lost face, you and I. Conclude this unfortunate occasion and do it now."

"Yes, Lo Han. I will faithfully carry out your orders."

"I anxiously await your announcement of victory."

"Soon, very soon," Kung Chong said confidently. "Success or death. I promise you one or the other."

During the next three miles, the tactics worked. The two remaining ultralights pressed home their attack, weaving violently from side to side to escape the few pathetic shells sent in their direction, but making it next to impossible for the gunners to train their machine pistols. Two hundred yards away from the Chris-Craft they split apart and closed in on the runabout from two sides. It was a shrewd maneuver that enabled them to converge their fire.

Julia took her time and fired a round whenever she saw an opportunity for a remote hit while Pitt madly twisted the wheel and sent the speeding runabout zigzagging from one bank to the other in an effort to escape the sporadic spray of bullets that splattered the water around them. He stiffened when he heard the thud of strikes behind him as one burst of gunfire cut across the mahogany hatch over the engine compartment between the dual cockpits. But the big Chrysler marine engine's throaty roar never slackened. On instinct his eyes swept the instrument panel, and he noted ominously that the needle on the oil-pressure gauge was suddenly falling into the red zone.

Sam Foley will be madder than hell when he gets his boat back, Pitt thought.

Two miles to go. The stench of scorched oil began to waft from the engine compartment. The engine revolutions were slowly dropping off, and Pitt mentally pictured metal grinding against metal from lack of oil. It was only a matter of minutes before the bearings burned out and the engine froze. All the ultralight pilots have to do now, Pitt savvied, is circle over the boat and blast everyone to bloody bits. He pounded the steering wheel in maddened frustration as they came at him to-gether, wingtip to wingtip.

They came head-on with no deviation, and much lower this time, knowing time was running out, keenly aware that once the boat and its occupants broke into the open bay, there would be spectators to report the murders.

Then, magically, the pilot of the ultralight that rolled off to the left of the Chris-Craft suddenly slumped in his seat and his arms fell to his sides. One of Julia's bullets had taken the pilot in the chest and torn through his heart. The aircraft sheered off violently, its wingtip brushed the water and then it cartwheeled crazily across the wake of the boat before disappearing into the uncaring river.

There was no time to celebrate Julia's phenomenal shot. Their situation went from bad to worse as she fired her last shell. The pilot on the last ultralight, seeing the return fire slacken and finally die, and the Chris-Craft slow considerably with smoke beginning to curl from the engine compartment, threw caution to the winds and came at them no more than five feet above the water.

The Chris-Craft was limping along at less than ten miles an hour. The race for survival was almost over. Pitt looked up and saw the Chinese gunner in the inner ultralight. The eyes were covered by stylish sunglasses, and his lips stretched in a tight grin. He waved a salute and lifted his weapon, finger tightening on the trigger.

In a final act of defiance, Pitt shook his fist in the air and raised the third digit. Then he threw his body over Julia and the two children in what he knew was a futile effort to use his body as a shield. He tensed, waiting for the bullets to tear into his back.

11

THE OLD MAN with the scythe, to Pitt's great relief, either decided
he had urgent business at a catastrophe elsewhere, or Pitt wasn't worth
taking and threw him back. The bullets Pitt expected to feel plowing
through his flesh never came because they were never fired.

He firmly believed the last sound he was about to hear in this life
was the soft report of a suppressed machine pistol. Instead, the rapid
beat of rotor blades reverberated in the air, rotor blades whirling at top
speed, drowning out the exhaust and unpleasant noises from inside the
big Chrysler. With a thundering roar accompanied by a great gust of
wind that flattened every hair on every head, a huge shadow flashed
over the Chris-Craft. Before anyone comprehended what was happening, a big turquoise helicopter with the letters NUMA painted on its tail
boom, swept down the river straight at the yellow ultralight like an
avenging hawk swooping on a canary.

"Oh God no!" Julia moaned.

"Never fear!" Pitt shouted jubilantly. "This one's on our side."

He recognized the McDonnell Douglas Explorer, a fast, no–tail rotor
helicopter with twin engines and a top speed in excess of 170 miles an
hour, as a craft he'd often flown. The forward fuselage looked like those
on most rotorcraft, but the tail boom, with its dual vertical stabilizers,
extended to the rear like a thin corona cigar.

"Where did it come from?"

"My ride showed up early," Pitt said, swearing to put the pilot in his
will.

Every pair of eyes in the runabout and on the remaining ultralight were trained on the intruder as it charged through the air. Two figures could be seen through the transparent bow of the helicopter. The copilot was wearing a baseball cap turned backward and peered through horn-rim glasses. The pilot wore a reed hat like those woven on tropical beaches and a brightly flowered Hawaiian aloha shirt. A gargantuan cigar was clenched between his teeth.

Kung Chong was no longer grinning. His expression was one of abject shock and fear. It flashed through his mind that the new bully on the playground wasn't about to back off. He took stock and saw that the runabout, though barely making headway, would soon reach the mouth of the river leading into Grapevine Bay. From his height he could already see a small fleet of fishing boats heading out to sea around the final bend in the river. Houses on the outskirts of a town perched along the shoreline. People walked along the beaches. His chance for terminating the escaped immigrants and the devil responsible for the chaos at Orion Lake had evaporated. Kung Chong had no choice but to order his pilot to break off the attack. In an attempt to dodge its attacker, the ultralight pulled up sharply and curled a turn so tight its wing tipped on a vertical angle.

The pilot of the NUMA helicopter had been there before. He easily second-guessed his opponent. There was never a flicker of pity or indecision. The face was expressionless as he easily matched the ultralight's steep turn and closed the distance between them. Then came a crunching sound as the landing skids of the helicopter ripped through the ultralight's flimsy wing.

The men in the open seats froze as their craft twisted in maddened torment, seeking desperately, hopelessly to cling to the sky. Then the shredded wing folded in the middle, and the little craft dove and crashed into a shoreline filled with large rocks. There was no explosion, as only a small cloud of dust and debris sprayed the air. All that remained was a distorted mass of wreckage with two bodies fused amid the shattered struts and tubing.

The helicopter hovered over the crippled Chris-Craft as the pilot and the man sitting in the copilot's seat both leaned out the cockpit windows and waved.

Julia waved back and threw them kisses. "Whoever those wonderful men are, they saved our lives."

"Their names are Al Giordino and Rudi Gunn."

"Friends of yours?"

"For many, many years," Pitt said, beaming like a lighthouse.

The struggling old Chrysler marine engine almost carried them to the end of their harrowing voyage, but not quite. Its bearings and pistons finally froze from lack of oil, and it gave up the ghost only two hundred yards from the dock that extended from the main street of the seaside village of Grapevine. A young teenager with an outboard boat towed the battered Chris-Craft and its weary passengers to the dock, where two men and one woman waited. None of the tourists strolling the wooden pier nor any of the local residents fishing over the railings would have guessed by the casual clothing that the three people standing at the end of the dock were INS agents about to collect a group of illegal immigrants.

"Your people?" Pitt asked Julia.

She nodded. "I've never met him but I assume one of them is the district director of investigations."

Pitt held up the little boy, made a funny face and was rewarded with a smile and a laugh. "What will happen to these people now?"

"They're illegal aliens. Under the law they must be sent back to China."

He looked at her and scowled. "After what they've endured, it would be a crime to send them back."

"I agree," said Julia. "But my hands are tied. I can fill out the required paperwork and recommend they be allowed to stay. But their final disposition is beyond my control."

"Paperwork!" Pitt nearly spat the word. "You can do better than that. The minute they step foot in their homeland, Shang's people will have them killed, and you damned well know it. They wouldn't be alive if you hadn't shot down the ultralights. You know the rule, save someone's life and you're forever responsible for them. You can't wash your hands of them and not care about their fate."

"I do care," Julia said firmly. She looked at Pitt the way women usually look at men when they feel as if they're talking to the village idiot. "And I'm not about to wash my hands of them. And because it is entirely possible, as you suggest, that they might be murdered if they returned to the Chinese mainland, it goes without saying that they'll be given every opportunity to apply for political asylum. There are laws, Mr. Pitt, whether you or I like them or not. But they're for a purpose and must be followed. I promise you that if it is humanly possible for these people to become United States citizens, it shall be."

"I'll hold you to that promise," Pitt said quietly.

"Believe me," she said earnestly, "I'll do everything in my power to help them."

"Should you run into problems, please contact me through NUMA. I have a bit of political influence and might arrange for the Senate to back their cause."

She looked at him skeptically. "How could a marine engineer with NUMA possibly have political influence in the Senate?"

"Would it help if I told you my father is Senator George Pitt of California?"

"Yes," she murmured, properly awed. "I can see you might prove useful."

The boy in the outboard cast off the towline, and the Chris-Craft bumped against the dock pilings. The Chinese immigrants were all smiles. They were happy at not being shot at any longer, and elated to have at last reached safety in America. Any apprehension about their fate was set aside for the moment. Pitt passed up the little boy and girl to the waiting hands of the INS agents and then turned to help the mother and father step up to the dock.

A tall, jovial-looking man with twinkling eyes stepped up to Julia and put his arm around her. The look on his face was one of compassion at seeing the bruised and swollen face with blood caked around the split lips. "Ms. Lee, I'm George Simmons."

"Yes, the assistant district director. I spoke to you over the phone from the cabin."

"You don't know how happy we are to see you alive, how grateful for your information."

"Not as happy as I am," she said, wincing with pain as she tried to crack a smile.

"Jack Farrar, the district director, would have greeted you himself, but he's directing the cleanup operation on Orion Lake."

"It's started?"

"Our agents dropped onto the grounds by helicopter eight minutes ago."

"The prisoners inside the building?"

"All alive, but in need of medical care."

"The security guards?"

"Rounded up without a fight. At last report only their head man had yet to be apprehended. But he should be in custody shortly."

Julia turned to Pitt, who was helping the last of the elderly immigrants out of the runabout. "Mr. Simmons, may I introduce Mr. Dirk Pitt of NUMA, who made your raid possible."

Simmons stuck out his hand to Pitt. "Ms. Lee didn't have time to fill me in on the details, Mr. Pitt, but I gather that you pulled off a remarkable achievement."

"They call it being in the right place at the right time," said Pitt, gripping the INS agent's hand.

"Seems to me it was more like the right man being where it counts most," said Simmons. "If you don't mind, I'd like a report of your activities over the past two days."

Pitt nodded and then pointed at the Chinese who were being herded by the other INS agents to a waiting bus at the end of the dock. "These people have gone through the worst ordeal imaginable. I hope they'll be treated in a humane manner."

"I can safely say, Mr. Pitt, they will be given every consideration."

"Thank you, Mr. Simmons. I appreciate your concern."

Simmons nodded at Julia. "If you feel up to it, Ms. Lee, my boss would like your presence at the retreat to assist as a translator."

"I think I can stay awake a little longer," she said stoutly. She turned and looked up at Pitt, who stood beside her. "I guess this is good-bye."

He grinned. "I'm sorry I proved to be a lousy date."

She ignored the pain and smiled. "I can't say it was romantic, but it was exciting."

"I promise to show more savoir faire the next time."

"Are you going back to Washington?"

"I haven't received my marching orders yet," he replied, "but I suspect they came with my pals, Giordino and Gunn. And you? Where will the needs of the service send you?"

"My home office is in San Francisco. I assume that's where they'll want me."

He moved forward and took her in his arms, kissing her gently on the forehead. "Next time we meet," he said softly, tenderly touching his fingertips to her cut and swollen lips, "I'll kiss you full on the mouth."

"Are you a good kisser?"

"Girls come from miles around to kiss me."

"If there is a next time," she murmured softly, "I'll return the favor."

Then she was walking with Simmons to a waiting car. Pitt stood alone by the forlorn Chris-Craft and watched until the car rounded a streetcorner. He was standing there when Giordino and Gunn came bounding across the dock, shouting like madmen.

They had remained in the air until the runabout was safely tied to the

123

town dock. Seeing an INS helicopter sitting in a field about a mile north of town, Giordino would have none of it. He set the NUMA helicopter down in a parking lot less than a block from the dock, much to the annoyance of a deputy sheriff, who threatened him with arrest. Giordino pacified him by claiming they were scouting locations for a Hollywood production company and promised they would recommend Grapevine as the perfect backdrop for a new big-budget horror movie. Suitably charmed by NUMA's most renowned con artist, the deputy insisted on driving Giordino and Rudi Gunn to the dock.

Standing only five feet four inches but with shoulders nearly as wide as he was tall, Giordino lifted Pitt off his feet in a great bear hug. "What is it with you?" he said, elated to see Pitt alive. "Every time I let you out of my sight you get into trouble."

"Natural instinct, I guess," Pitt grunted while being crushed.

Gunn was more sedate. He simply put his hand on Pitt's shoulder. "Good to see you again, Dirk."

"I've missed you, Rudi," said Pitt, taking a deep breath after Giordino released him.

"Who were those guys in the ultralights?" asked Giordino.

"Smugglers of illegal aliens."

Giordino stared down at the bullet holes in the Chris-Craft. "You ruined a perfectly good boat."

Pitt also studied the shattered windshield, the splintered engine hatch, the holes stitched across the bow, the wisp of dark smoke rising from the engine compartment. "If you'd arrived two seconds later, Admiral Sandecker would be stuck with the chore of writing my eulogy."

"When we flew over Foley's cabin, the place was swarming with guys in black ninja suits. Naturally thinking the worst, I shoved the throttles to the board and we took off after you. After finding you being strafed by a bunch of shady characters flying ultralights, we just naturally crashed the party."

"And saved a dozen lives," Pitt added. "But where in hell did you come from? The last I heard you were in Hawaii and Rudi was in Washington."

"Lucky for you," said Gunn, "Admiral Sandecker was handed a priority project by the President. As much as he disliked cutting off your rest and recuperation, he ordered Giordino and me to meet in Seattle. We both arrived last night, then borrowed a helicopter at the NUMA marine-science center at Bremerton to come pick you up. After you called the admiral this morning and told him what you'd discovered and that you were making a run for it down the river, Al and I took off and dashed across the Olympic Peninsula in forty minutes flat."

"That Machiavellian old sea dog sent you thousands of miles just to put me back to work?" Pitt asked in mild amazement.

Gunn smiled. "He told me that he was reasonably certain that if he'd called himself, you'd have uttered unrepeatable words over the phone."

"That old man knows me pretty well," Pitt admitted.

"You've had a rough time," said Gunn sympathetically. "Perhaps I can talk him into letting you lay low for a few days longer."

"Not a bad idea," Giordino added candidly. "You look like the rat the cat dragged in."

"Some vacation," Pitt said finally. "I hope I never have another like it. I'd like to think of it as being over."

Gunn motioned toward the edge of the dock. "The helicopter isn't far. Think you can make it okay?"

"There are a few things I'd like to take care of before you rush me off," Pitt said, giving both men a cold eye. "First, I'd like to get Sam Foley's Chris-Craft to the nearest boat yard for repairs and an engine overhaul. Second, it might be nice if we found a doctor who wouldn't ask a lot of questions while he attends to a gunshot wound in my hip. And third, I'm starved. I'm not going anywhere until I've been fed breakfast."

"You're wounded?" both men said in unison.

"Hardly a life-threatening puncture, but I'm not keen to get gangrene."

The show of obstinacy was tremendously effective. Giordino nodded at Gunn. "You find Dirk a doctor, I'll take care of the boat. Then we'll check out the nearest restaurant. This looks like a good town for boiled crab."

"There is one more thing," said Pitt.

The two men stared at him expectantly.

"What's this urgent project I have to drop everything for?"

"It involves an underwater investigation of a strange shipping port near Morgan City, Louisiana," answered Gunn.

"What's so strange about a shipping port?"

"Its location in a swamp, for one thing. That, and the fact the developer is the head of a large-scale international alien-smuggling empire."

"Heaven help me," Pitt said piously, throwing up his hands. "Say it isn't true."

"You have a problem?" Giordino asked.

"I've been up to my ears in illegal immigrants for the past twelve hours—that's the problem."

"It's truly amazing how you can gather on-the-job experience with such ease."

Pitt fixed his friend with an icy stare. "I suppose our divine government thinks the port is being used to smuggle in aliens."

"The facility is far too elaborate for that alone," replied Gunn. "We've been given the job of discovering its true purpose."

"Who built and developed the port?"

"An outfit by the name of Qin Shang Maritime Limited out of Hong Kong."

Pitt didn't throw an apoplectic fit. He didn't even bat an eyelid. He *did* look, however, as if he'd been punched in the pit of his stomach. His face took on the expression of a man in a horror movie who just found out his wife ran away with the monster. His fingers bit deeply, painfully, into Gunn's arm. "You *did* say Qin Shang?"

"That's right," answered Gunn, wondering how he would explain the black-and-blue marks at his gym. "He directs an empire of malignant activities. Possibly the fourth-richest man in the world. You act as though you know him."

"We've never met, but I'm safe in saying he hates my guts."

"You're kidding," said Giordino.

Gunn looked puzzled. "Why would a man who has more money than a New York City bank hate an ordinary screwup like you?"

"Because," Pitt said with a fiendish grin, "I torched his yacht."

When Kung Chong failed to report the destruction of the runabout, and efforts to contact him were returned by silence, Lo Han knew his trusted assistant and the five men who flew with him were all dead. The realization was accompanied by the sickening certainty that the devil who caused so much grief had escaped.

He sat alone in the mobile security vehicle, trying to make some sense of the disaster. His black eyes had a vacant stare, his face was tight and cold. Kung Chong had reported seeing immigrants in the runabout. Their appearance seemed a mystery since all the prisoners were accounted for in their cells. Then a thought exploded in his mind. Chu Deng. That idiot on the catamaran must have somehow allowed the immigrants marked for execution to escape. There was no other conclusion. The man who was taking them to safety must have been in the pay of the American government.

Then, as if to ram home the revelation, his eyes traveled to the video monitors and observed two large helicopters landing beside the main building. In a synchronized assault armored cars broke through the barricade on the road leading to the main highway. Men poured from the aircraft and vehicles and rushed into the building. There was no pause, no demand for those inside to lay down their weapons and surrender peacefully.

The raiders burst inside the prison compound before Lo Han's guards knew what was happening. It was as if the INS agents knew the prisoners were to be killed in the event of a raid. It became obvious that they were well informed by someone who had made a reconnaissance of the retreat.

Quickly realizing that resistance against a large force of armed law-enforcement agents was hopeless, Lo Han's security force meekly submitted individually and in groups. Numb with defeat, Lo Han leaned back in his chair and entered a series of codes into his satellite communication system and waited for a reply from Hong Kong.

A voice answered in Chinese. "You have reached Lotus II."

"This is Bamboo VI," said Lo Han. "Operation Orion has been compromised."

"Say again."

"Operation Orion is in the process of being closed down by American agents."

"This is not welcome news," replied the voice on the other end.

"I regret we could not have remained in business until Operation Iberville was completed."

"Were the prisoners terminated so they could not talk?"

"No, the raid was conducted with astonishing speed."

"Our chairman will be most displeased to hear of your failure."

"I accept all blame for my mismanagement."

"Can you make good your escape?"

"No, it is too late," said Lo Han solemnly.

"You cannot be arrested, Bamboo VI. You know that. Nor your subordinates. There can be no trail for the Americans to follow."

"Those who were aware of our association are dead. My security guards are merely mercenaries who were hired to do a job, nothing more. They are ignorant of who paid them."

"Then you are the only link," said the voice without inflection.

"I have lost face and must pay the price."

"This, then, is our final communication."

"I have one final act to perform," Lo Han said quietly.

"Do not fail," the voice demanded coldly.

"Good-bye, Lotus II."

"Good-bye, Bamboo VI."

Lo Han watched the monitors as they revealed a group of men rushing toward the mobile security vehicle. They were attacking the locked door when he removed a small, nickel-plated revolver from the drawer of his desk. He placed the barrel inside his mouth pointing upward. His finger was tightening on the trigger when the first INS agent burst through the doorway. The blast stopped the agent dead in his tracks, his gun leveled, a look of surprise in his eyes as Lo Han jerked back in his chair, then fell forward, head and shoulders falling on the desk as the revolver dropped from his hand onto the floor.

PART II

THE LAST
OF THE
GREYHOUNDS

United States

12

April 20, 2000
Hong Kong, China

QIN SHANG DID NOT HAVE the appearance of a corrupt and depraved sociopath who had indiscriminately murdered untold thousands of innocent people. He did not have serpent's fangs, vertical slit eyes, nor a forked tongue that flicked in and out. There was no aura of evil about him. Sitting at a desk in his palatial four-level penthouse atop the fifty-story mirrored tower of Qin Shang Maritime Limited, he looked no different than any other Chinese businessman working in the financial hub of Hong Kong. Like most mass murderers throughout history, Qin Shang went unobtrusive and unnoticed whenever he strolled down the street.

Tall for most Asian men at five feet, eleven inches, he was heavy around the waist, weighing in at 210 pounds, not solid but what you might call chubby, the aftereffects of a taste and appetite for good Chinese cooking. The black hair was thick and cut short, with a part down the middle. The head and face were not round but narrow and almost feline, and matched the long and slender hands. The mouth, oddly and deceptively, seemed fixed in a permanent smile. Outwardly, Qin Shang seemed as threatening as a shoe salesman.

No one who met him could forget his eyes. They were the color of the purest green jade and revealed a black depth that belied a good-tempered man. They burned with a frightening degree of malevolence and were so penetrating that men who knew him swore he could look through your skull and read the latest stock market quotes. The inward man behind the eyes was a different story. Qin Shang was as sadistic and unscrupulous as a Serengeti hyena. He thrived on manipulation so long as it led to spiraling wealth and power. As an orphan begging on the streets of Kowloon across Victoria Harbor from the island of Hong Kong, he developed an uncanny talent for exploiting people for their money. By the age of ten, he had saved enough to buy a sampan and used it to ferry people and transport whatever cargo he could talk merchants into letting him carry.

In two years, he had a fleet of ten sampans. Before he was eighteen, he sold his thriving little fleet and bought an ancient intercoastal tramp steamer. This tired old rust bucket became the foundation for Qin Shang's shipping empire. The freight line flourished during the next decade because Qin Shang's competitors in the freight trade strangely fell by the wayside when many of their ships mysteriously disappeared at sea without a trace with all hands aboard. Finding their profit margins dropping into the red, the owners of the doomed ships always seemed to find a ready buyer for their remaining vessels and dwindling assets. Operating out of Japan, the company that did the buying was known as Yokohama Ship Sales & Scrap Corporation. In reality it was a front whose parental ties stretched across the China Sea to Qin Shang Maritime Limited.

In time, Qin Shang took a different course from his business peers in Hong Kong, who established alliances with European financial institutions and Western exporters and importers. In a shrewd move, he turned his focus on the People's Republic of China, creating friendships with high government officials in preparation for the day when they would take control of Hong Kong from the British. He conducted behind-the-scenes negotiations with Yin Tsang, chief director of the People's Republic's Ministry of Internal Affairs, an obscure department of the government that was involved with everything from foreign espionage of scientific technology to the international smuggling of immigrants to relieve the country's overcrowded population. In return for his services Qin Shang was allowed to register his ships in China without the usual exorbitant fees.

The partnership proved incredibly profitable to Qin Shang. The clandestine transportation and trade in undocumented aliens, in concert with the legitimate hauling of Chinese goods and oil exclusively by Qin Shang's freighters and tankers, brought hundreds of millions of dollars over several years into the company's many hidden bank accounts around the world.

Qin Shang soon amassed more money than he could spend in a

thousand lifetimes. Yet there was a fixed determination in his sinister brain to amass even more wealth, more power. Once he had built one of the largest cargo and passenger fleets in the world, the challenge was gone and the moral and legitimate end of the business began to bore him. But there was excitement in the covert side of his operation. The rush of adrenaline and the intoxication of taking risks excited him like a steep slope of moguls in front of an expert skier. Little did his fellow conspirators in the People's Republic know he was also smuggling drugs and guns along with the illegal immigrants. It was a very lucrative sideline, and he used the profits to develop his landmark port facility in Louisiana. Playing the ends against the middle gave him glorious hours of exhilaration.

Qin Shang was an egomaniac with a stratospheric level of insane optimism. He held the firm belief that his day of reckoning would never come. Even if it did, he was too rich, too omnipotent, to be broken. He already paid enormous bribes to high-level officials in half the governments of the world. In the United States alone, there were over one hundred people in every agency of the federal government on his payroll. As far as Qin Shang was concerned the future was wrapped in a nebulous fog that never fully materialized. But just for added insurance, he maintained a small army of bodyguards and professional assassins he'd pirated away from the most efficient intelligence agencies in Europe, Israel and America.

His receptionist's voice came over a small speaker on his desk. "You have a visitor arriving on your private elevator."

Qin Shang rose from behind his immense rosewood desk, raised on legs intricately carved in the shape of tigers, and walked across the cavernous room toward the elevator. The office looked like the vastly expanded interior of a captain's cabin in an old sailing ship. Heavy oak planking was laid for the floor. Thick oak beams supported a skylighted ceiling with teak paneling throughout. Large builder's models of Qin Shang Maritime ships sailed on plaster seas inside glass cases on one side of the room while on the opposite wall a collection of old diver's suits with their lead boots and brass helmets hung suspended by their air hoses, as if they still contained the bodies of their owners. Qin Shang stopped in front of the elevator as its doors opened and greeted his visitor, a short man with dense gray hair. His eyes bulged as they protruded from fleshy pouches. He smiled as he came forward and shook Qin Shang's outstretched hand.

"Qin Shang," he said with a taut little grin.

"Yin Tsang, always an honor to see you," Qin Shang said graciously. "I did not expect you until next Thursday."

"I hope you'll forgive this unpardonable interruption," said Yin Tsang, the minister of China's internal affairs, "but I wished to speak with you privately on a matter of some delicacy."

"I am always available anytime to you, old friend. Come and sit down. Would you like some tea?"

Yin Tsang nodded. "Your own special blend? I'd like nothing better."

Qin Shang called his private secretary and ordered the tea. "Now then, what is this delicate matter that brings you to Hong Kong a week ahead of your scheduled visit?"

"Disturbing news has reached Beijing concerning your operation at Orion Lake in the state of Washington."

Qin Shang shrugged carelessly. "Yes, an unfortunate incident beyond my control."

"My sources tell me the holding station for the immigrants was raided by the Immigration and Naturalization Service."

"It was," Qin Shang freely admitted. "My best men were killed and our security people were captured in a lightning raid that was totally unexpected."

Yin Tsang looked at him. "How could this happen? I can't believe you failed to prepare for such a possibility. Didn't your agents in Washington, D.C., alert you?"

Qin Shang shook his head. "I've since learned the raid did not originate in the INS national headquarters. It was a spur-of-the-moment operation conducted by the local district director, who took it upon himself to launch an assault on the holding station. I was given no warning by any of my agents within the American government."

"Your entire North American operation has been compromised. The Americans now have broken a link in the chain that will surely lead directly to you."

"Not to worry, Yin Tsang," Qin Shang said calmly. "American investigators have no evidence that directly ties me to illegal immigrant smuggling. They may have their pitiful and insignificant suspicions, but nothing else. My other staging sites along the American coastline are still in operation and can easily absorb all future shipments programmed for Orion Lake."

"President Lin Loyang and my fellow ministers will be happy to hear you have everything under your control," said Yin Tsang. "But I still have my reservations. Once the Americans scent a crack in your organization, they will hound you unrelentingly."

"You are afraid?"

"I am concerned. Too much is at stake to allow a man more interested in profit than the aims of our party to remain in control."

"What are you suggesting?"

Yin Tsang looked at Qin Shang steadily. "I shall recommend to President Lin Loyang that you resign from the smuggling operation and be replaced."

"And my contract to carry the bulk of national Chinese cargo and passengers?"

"Revoked."

The expected response of surprise and anger did not materialize. Nor was there the slightest sign of annoyance. Qin Shang merely shrugged impassively. "You think that I can be that easily replaced?"

"Someone with your special qualifications has already been selected."

"Anyone I know?"

"One of your competitors, Quan Ting, chairman of China & Pacific Lines, has agreed to fill your shoes."

"Quan Ting?" Qin Shang's eyebrow rose a millimeter. "His ships are little better than rusting barges."

"Soon he will be in a position to launch new ships." The words came with a veiled implication that Quan Ting would be financed by the Chinese government with Yin Tsang's blessing and endorsement.

"You insult my intelligence. You have used the Orion Lake mishap as an excuse to cancel my association with the People's Republic of China so you can go into partnership on the sly and rake in the profits yourself."

"You are no stranger to greed, Qin Shang. You would do the same in my shoes."

"And my new facility in Louisiana?" asked Qin Shang. "Am I to lose that too?"

"You will be compensated for your half of the investment, of course."

"Of course," Qin Shang repeated acidly, knowing full well he would never receive a cent. "Naturally, it will be given to my successor and you, his silent partner."

"That will be my counsel at the next party conference in Beijing."

"May I inquire as to whom else you've discussed my expulsion with?"

"Only Quan Ting," answered Yin Tsang. "I thought it best to keep the matter quiet until the proper time."

Qin Shang's private secretary stepped into the room and moved to the sitting area with the grace of a Balinese dancing girl, which is exactly what she was until Qin Shang hired and trained her. She was only one of several beautiful girls who served as Shang's aides. Women he trusted more than men. Unmarried, Shang kept nearly a dozen mistresses—three lived in his penthouse—but he followed a policy of never becoming intimate with the women close to his business dealings. He nodded his appreciation as his secretary set a tray with two cups and two teapots on the low table between the men.

"The green teapot is your special blend," she said softly to Qin Shang. "The blue teapot is jasmine."

"Jasmine!" Yin Tsang snorted. "How can you drink tea that tastes like women's perfume when your special blend is far superior?"

"Variety." Qin Shang smiled. As a show of courtesy he poured the tea. Relaxing in his chair while he cradled the steaming cup in his hands, he watched as Yin Tsang sipped until his tea was gone. Then Qin Shang politely poured him another cup.

"You realize, of course, that Quan Ting has no cruise ships available to carry passengers."

"They can either be purchased or leased from other cruise lines," said Yin Tsang offhandedly. "Let us face the light. You have made immense profits over the past few years. You are not about to go bankrupt. It will be a simple matter for you to diversify Qin Shang Maritime Limited into Western markets. You are a shrewd businessman, Qin Shang. You will survive without the People's Republic of China's benevolence."

"The flight of a hawk cannot be accomplished with the wings of a sparrow," said Qin Shang philosophically.

Yin Tsang set down his cup and rose to his feet. "I must leave you now. My plane is waiting to fly me back to Beijing."

"I understand," Qin Shang said dryly. "As minister of internal affairs, you are a busy man who must make many decisions."

Yin Tsang noted the contempt but said no more. His unpleasant duty performed, he gave a curt bow and entered the elevator. As soon as the doors closed, Qin Shang returned to his desk and spoke into the intercom. "Send me Pavel Gavrovich."

Five minutes later, a tall, medium-built man with Slavic facial features and thick black hair greased and combed back across his head with no part stepped from the elevator. He strode across the room and stopped in front of Qin Shang's desk.

Qin Shang looked up at his chief enforcer, once the finest and most ruthless undercover agent in all of Russia. A professional assassin with few equals in the martial arts, Pavel Gavrovich was offered an exorbitant salary to leave a high-level position in the Russian Defense Ministry to come to work for Qin Shang. Gavrovich had taken less than one minute to accept.

"A competitor of mine who owns an inferior shipping line is proving to be an irritant to me. His name is Quan Ting. Please arrange an accident for him."

Gavrovich nodded silently, turned on his heels and reentered the waiting elevator, never having spoken a word.

The following morning, as Qin Shang sat in the dining room of his penthouse suite alone and scanned several newspapers, foreign and domestic, he was pleased to discover a pair of articles in the Hong Kong *Journal.* The first read,

Quan Ting, chairman and managing director of the China & Pacific Shipping Line, and his wife were killed late last night when their limousine was struck broadside by a large truck transporting electrical cable as Mr. Quan and his wife were leaving the Mandarin Hotel after dinner with friends. Their chauffeur was also killed. The driver of the truck vanished from the scene of the accident and has yet to be found by police.

The second article in the newspaper read,

It was announced in Beijing today by the Chinese government that Yin Tsang had died. The untimely death of China's minister of internal affairs, who succumbed to a heart attack while on a flight to Beijing, was sudden and unexpected. Though he had no known history of heart problems, all efforts to revive him failed, and he was pronounced dead upon arrival at the Beijing Airport. Deputy Minister Lei Chau is expected to succeed Yin Tsang.

A great pity, Qin Shang thought wickedly. My special blend of tea must not have agreed with Yin Tsang's stomach. He made a mental note to tell his secretary to send his condolences to President Lin Loyang and set up a meeting with Lei Chau, who had been nurtured with the necessary bribes and was known to be not nearly as avaricious as his predecessor.

Putting aside the newspapers, Qin Shang took a final sip of his coffee. He drank tea in public, but in private he preferred Southern-style American coffee with chicory. A soft chime warned him that his private secretary was about to enter the dining room. She approached and set a leather-bound file on the table beside him.

"Here is the information you requested from your agent at the Federal Bureau of Investigation."

"Wait one moment will you, Su Zhong. I'd like your opinion on something."

Qin Shang opened the file and began studying the contents. He held up a photograph of a man standing beside an old classic car who stared back at the camera. The man was dressed casually in slacks and a golf shirt under a sport coat. A crooked, almost shy grin curled the lips on a face that was tanned and weathered. The eyes, laughter lines wrinkling from their edges, were locked on the camera lens and had a probing quality about them, almost as if they were measuring whoever peered at the photo. They were accented by dark, thick eyebrows. The photo was in black-and-white, so it was impossible to assess the exact color of the irises. Qin Shang wrongly guessed them as blue.

The black hair was dense and wavy and slightly unkempt. The shoulders were broad and tapered to a slim waist and narrow hips. The data in the file gave his body size as six feet, three inches, 185 pounds. The hands looked like the hands of a field worker, the palms large with small scars and calluses, and the fingers long. The eyes, it was stated, were green and not blue.

"You have an inner sense about men, Su Zhong. You can envision things others like me cannot see. Look at this picture. Look inside the man and tell me what you find."

Su Zhong swept her long black hair back from her face as she leaned over Qin Shang and gazed at the photograph. "He is handsome in a rugged sort of way. I sense a magnetism about him. He has the look of an adventurer whose love is exploring the unknown, especially what lies under the sea. No rings on his fingers suggests that he is unpretentious. Women are drawn to him. They do not consider him a threat. He enjoys their company. There is an aura of kindness and tenderness about him. A man you can trust. All indications of a good lover. He is sentimental about old objects and probably collects them. His life is dedicated to achievement. Little of what he has accomplished was for personal gain. He thrives on challenges. This is a man who does not like to fail but can accept failure if he has tried his best. There is also a cold hardness in the eyes. He also has the capacity to kill. To friends he is extremely loyal. To enemies, extremely dangerous. All in all, a most unusual man who should have lived in another time."

"What you're saying is that he is a throwback to the past."

Su Zhong nodded. "He would have been at home on the deck of a pirate ship, fighting in the crusades or driving a stagecoach through the deserts of the old American West."

"Thank you, my dear, for your extraordinary insight."

"My pleasure is to serve you." Su Zhong bowed her head and quietly left the room, closing the door behind her.

Qin Shang turned over the photograph and began reading the data in the file, noting with amusement that he and the subject were born on the same day in the same year. There, any similarity ended. The subject was the son of Senator George Pitt of California. His mother was the former Barbara Knight. He attended Newport Beach High School in California and then the Air Force Academy in Colorado. Academically, he was above average, finishing thirty-fifth in his class. Played on the football team and won several athletic trophies. After flight training, he achieved a distinguished military career during the closing days of the Vietnam War. Rose to the rank of major before transferring from the Air Force to the National Underwater and Marine Agency. Later promoted to lieutenant colonel.

A collector of old automobiles and aircraft, he kept them stored in an old hangar at the edge of Washington's National Airport. He lived in an apartment above the collection. His accomplishments at NUMA while serving as special projects director under his boss, Admiral James Sandecker, read like an adventure novel. From heading the project to raise the *Titanic* to discovering the long-lost artifacts from the Alexandria Library to stopping a red tide in the oceans that would have ultimately decimated life on earth, during the past fifteen years the subject was directly responsible for operations that either saved a great many lives or were of inestimable benefit to archaeology or the environment. The list of projects he directed to successful conclusions covered nearly twenty pages.

Qin Shang's agent had also included a list of men Pitt reportedly had killed. Qin Shang was stunned by several of the names. They consisted of men who were wealthy and powerful as well as common criminals and professional murderers. Su Zhong was correct in her evaluation. This man could be an extremely dangerous enemy.

After nearly an hour, Qin Shang laid aside the documents and picked up the photograph. He stared at the figure standing beside an old car intently, wondering what drove such a man. It became clearer with each passing minute that their paths would cross.

"So, Mr. Dirk Pitt, you are the man responsible for the disaster at Orion Lake," said Qin Shang, speaking to the photograph as though Pitt were standing in the room before him. "Your motive for destroying my immigrant staging area and yacht is as yet a mystery to me. But I have this to say to you: You have qualities that I respect, but you have come to the end of your career. The next addendum and final postscript to your file will be your obituary."

13

ORDERS CAME DOWN from Washington for Special Agent Julia Lee to be flown immediately from Seattle to San Francisco, where she was placed in a hospital for medical treatment and observation. The nurse assigned to her audibly gasped when she removed the hospital gown so the doctor could make his examination. There was hardly a square inch of Julia's body that wasn't black-and-blue or marked by reddish bruises. The expression in the nurse's eyes also made it evident that Julia's face was still grotesque from the swelling and discoloration, reinforcing Julia's determination not to look at herself in a mirror for at least a week.

"Did you know you had three cracked ribs?" asked the doctor, a jolly, rotund man with a bald head and closely cropped gray beard.

"I guessed from the stabbing pain every time I sat down and then stood after going to the bathroom," she said lightheartedly. "Will you have to put a cast around my chest?"

The doctor laughed. "Binding fractured ribs went out with leeches and bleeding. Now we just let them mend on their own. You'll suffer some discomfort when you make sudden movements for the next few weeks, but that will soon diminish."

"How about the rest of the damage? Is it reparable?"

"I've already set your nose back in place, medication will soon reduce the swelling and all signs of bruising should disappear fairly quickly. I predict that by this time next month you'll be voted queen of the prom."

"All women should have a doctor like you," Julia complimented him.

"Funny," he said, smiling, "my wife never says that." He squeezed her hand reassuringly. "If you're feeling up to it, you can go home the day after tomorrow. By the way, there's a couple of important characters from Washington on their way up from the reception desk to see you. They should be stepping off the elevator about now. In old movies visitors in a hospital are always told not to stay too long. But to my way of thinking, going back to work speeds the healing process. Just don't overdo it."

"I won't, and thank you for your courtesy."

"Not at all. I'll look in on you this evening."

"Shall I stay?" asked the nurse.

The doctor shook his head as two somber-looking men carrying briefcases entered the room. "Official government business. You'll want to talk with Ms. Lee in private. Right, gentlemen?"

"Quite right, doctor," said Julia's boss, Arthur Russell, director of the INS San Francisco district office. Russell was gray-haired, his body reasonably trim from daily workouts in a home exercise room. He smiled and looked at Julia through eyes warm with sympathy.

The other man, with thinning blond hair, his gray eyes peering through rimless spectacles, was a stranger to Julia. There was no hint of sympathy in his eyes. If anything, he looked as if he was about to sell her an insurance policy.

"Julia," said Russell, "I'd like to introduce Peter Harper. He flew in from Washington to debrief you."

"Yes, of course," said Julia, struggling to sit up in bed, wincing from the pain that shot through her chest. "You're the executive associate commissioner for field operations. I'm happy to meet you. Your reputation is a bit of a legend throughout the Service."

"I'm flattered." Harper shook Julia's outstretched hand and was surprised at the firmness of her grip. "You've had a tough time of it," he said. "Commissioner Monroe sends his congratulations and thanks, and wishes me to say that the Service is proud of your performance."

He makes it sound as if I was taking a curtain call after a play, Julia thought. "But for one man, I wouldn't be here to receive the compliment."

"Yes, we'll come to him later. Right now, I'd like a verbal accounting of your mission to infiltrate the smugglers' operation."

"We didn't mean to put you back in harness so soon," interrupted

Russell in a quiet voice. "A full written report of your activities can wait until you're up and about. But for now, we'd like you to tell us everything you've learned about the smugglers and their procedures."

"From the time I became Ling T'ai and paid the smugglers for passage in Beijing?" Julia asked.

"From the beginning," said Harper, taking a tape recorder from his briefcase and setting it on the bed. "Starting with your entry into China. We'd like to hear it all."

Julia looked at Harper as she began. "As Arthur can tell you, I traveled to Beijing, China, with a group of Canadian tourists. After we arrived in the city I deserted the group during a walking tour of the city. Being of Chinese descent and speaking the language, I had no problem with melting into the people crowding the streets. After changing into more suitable clothes, I began making discreet inquiries about emigrating to a foreign country. As it turned out the newspapers ran stories and advertisements promoting emigration outside China's borders. I answered an ad by an outfit calling themselves Jingzi International Passages. Their offices, coincidentally, were on the third floor of a modern building owned by Qin Shang Maritime Limited. The price to be smuggled into the United States was the equivalent of thirty thousand American dollars. When I attempted to haggle, I was told in no uncertain terms to pay up or leave. I paid."

Then Julia related the story of her terrible ordeal after boarding the outwardly luxurious cruise ship that became a hell ship. She told of the inhuman cruelty; the lack of food and sanitation facilities; the brutality of the enforcers; her interrogation and beating; the transfer of the able-bodied to boats that took them unknowingly to a life of slavery ashore while those of some wealth were diverted to the prison at Orion Lake and placed in cages until they could be squeezed for more money. The very young, the elderly and those who could not physically endure a life of servitude were quietly murdered by drowning in the lake.

She narrated in exacting detail the entire smuggling operation calmly and unemotionally, covering every foot of the mother ship and drawing illustrations of the smaller craft used to ferry the aliens into the U.S. Using her trained skills in identification, she described the facial features and approximate body measurements of every smuggler she came in contact with, supplying whatever names she was able to obtain.

She told how she, the elderly aliens and the family with two children were forced into the confining cabin of the black catamaran; how they were eventually bound and their feet tied with iron weights before

143

being dropped through an open hatch into the lake. She told how a man in diving gear had miraculously appeared and cut them all loose before they drowned. Then she described how he herded everyone to the temporary safety of the shore; how he comforted and fed them at his cabin and provided a means of escape minutes before the arrival of the smugglers' security force. She told how that enduring man of iron killed five of the enforcers who were set on murdering the escaped immigrants, how he took a bullet in the hip and acted as if it never happened. She gave an account of his blowing up the dock and yacht at the retreat, the harrowing battle down the river to Grapevine Bay, her shooting the two ultralights out of the sky, and the indomitable courage of the man at the wheel of the runabout who threw his body over the children when it was thought they were about to be blasted out of the water.

Julia told them everything she had witnessed since leaving China. But she couldn't explain how or why the man from NUMA came to be under the catamaran at the exact moment she and the others were dropped into the cold waters of the lake, nor could she explain why he made a reconnaissance of the prison building on his own initiative. She did not know his incentive. It was as though Pitt's involvement was a dream sequence. How else could she explain his presence and actions on Orion Lake? Finally, she ended her account by saying his name, her voice trailing off into silence.

"Dirk Pitt, the special projects director for NUMA?" Harper blurted.

Russell turned to Harper, who was staring at Julia in disbelief. "It's true. Pitt was the one who helped reveal the retreat as a prison and provided the people in our district office in Seattle with vital information to conduct the raid. Without his timely appearance and exceptional courage, Agent Lee would have died and the mass killing at Orion Lake would have gone on indefinitely. Thanks to him, the macabre operation was exposed, enabling our Seattle district office to shut it down."

Harper looked at Julia steadily. "A man materializes in the dead of night underwater who is not a trained undercover agent nor a member of the Special Forces but a marine engineer with the National Underwater and Marine Agency and singlehandedly kills the crew of a murder boat and destroys a yacht and an entire dock. Then he leads you through a gauntlet of smugglers who strafe a boatload of illegal immigrants from light aircraft while they're speeding down a river in a seventy-year-old boat. An incredible story, to say the least, Ms. Lee."

"And every word of it true," said Julia firmly.

"Commissioner Monroe and I met with Admiral Sandecker of NUMA only a few nights ago, asking for their help in combating Qin Shang's smuggling operation. It seems unimaginable that they could have acted so quickly."

"Although we never had time to compare notes, I'm certain Dirk acted on his own without orders from his superior."

By the time Harper and Russell had asked her a barrage of questions and changed the cassette in the recorder four times, Julia was fighting a losing battle with fatigue. She had journeyed far beyond the call of duty, and now all she wanted was sleep. After her face returned to an assemblage of normality, she hoped to see her family, but not before.

Almost in a trancelike state, she wondered how Dirk Pitt would have described the events had he been there. She smiled, knowing that he would have probably reacted by making a joke out of the whole exploit, making light of his actions and participation. How odd, she thought, that I can predict his reactions and thoughts when I knew him for less than a few hours.

"You've been through more than any of us had any right to expect," said Russell, seeing that Julia was having a hard time keeping her eyes open.

"You're a credit to the service," Harper said sincerely as he switched off the recorder. "A fine report. Because of you an important link in the smuggling of illegal immigrants is history."

"They'll just pop up somewhere else," said Julia, stifling a yawn.

Russell shrugged. "Too bad we don't have enough evidence to convict Qin Shang in an international court of law."

Julia suddenly became alert. "What are you saying? Not enough evidence? I have proof the phony cruise ship, filled with illegal aliens, was registered to Qin Shang Maritime Limited. That alone, plus the bodies lying in Orion Lake, should be enough to indict and convict Qin Shang."

Harper shook his head. "We checked. The ship was legally registered to an obscure shipping company in Korea. And though Shang's representatives handled all real-estate transactions, the Orion Lake property is in the name of a holding company in Vancouver, Canada, by the name of Nanchang Investments. Offshore corporations with one dummy corporation leading to another in different countries is quite common, and makes it tough to trace the thread to the mother company and its owner, directors and stockholders. As rotten as it sounds, no international court of law would convict Qin Shang."

Julia looked vacantly through the window of her room. Between two buildings she could just make out the gray, ominous buildings of Alcatraz, the famous and now abandoned prison. "Then everything," she said disgustedly, "the sacrifice of innocent people in the lake, my ordeal, Pitt's heroic efforts, the raid on the retreat—all for nothing. Qin Shang will laugh up his sleeve and go on operating as if it was all a minor inconvenience."

"On the contrary," Harper assured her. "Your information is invaluable. Nothing comes easy, and it will take time, but sooner or later we're going to put Qin Shang and his kind out of business."

"Peter is right," added Russell. "We've only won a minor skirmish in the war, but we've cut off an important tentacle of the octopus. We also have a new insight into China's smuggling-operations policy. Our jobs have become a bit easier now that we know which back alleys to investigate."

Harper gathered up his briefcase and headed for the door. "We'll be on our way and let you rest."

Russell patted her gently on the shoulder. "I wish I could send you on extended leave, courtesy of the INS, but headquarters wants you in Washington as soon as you're up and about."

"I'd like to ask a favor," said Julia, stopping both men at the door.

"Name it," said Russell.

"Except for a brief visit with my mother and father here in San Francisco, I would like to return to duty by the beginning of next week. I formally request that I remain on the investigation of Qin Shang."

Russell looked at Harper, who smiled. "That goes without saying," said Russell. "Why do you think they want you in Washington? Who in INS knows more about Shang's alien-smuggling operation than you?"

After they left, Julia made one last effort to fight off creeping drowsiness. She picked up the bedside phone, dialed an outside line and then the area code and number for long-distance information. Obtaining the number, she called the NUMA headquarters building in Washington and asked for Dirk Pitt.

She was put through to his secretary, who informed her that Pitt was out on vacation and had not returned to work yet. Julia hung up the phone and settled her head into the pillows. In some odd manner she felt transformed. Here I am acting like a brazen hustler, she thought, pursuing a man I hardly know. Why, she wondered, of all the men in all the world, why did someone like Dirk Pitt have to walk into my life?

14

PITT AND GIORDINO never made it back to Washington. When they returned the helicopter to the NUMA marine-science laboratory in Bremerton through a rainstorm, they found Admiral Sandecker waiting for them. Most men in Sandecker's position would have remained in a dry office, sitting comfortably on a couch drinking coffee, making others come to him. But he did not march to the same drummer as most. Sandecker stood outside in a misting rain, raising his arm to shield his face from the clouds of spray that swirled beneath the rotor blades of the aircraft. He remained standing until the blades spun to a stop before stepping toward the hatch. He waited patiently until Gunn swung it open and dropped to the ground, followed by Giordino.

"I expected you over an hour ago," grunted Sandecker.

"We weren't forewarned you'd be here, Admiral," said Gunn. "When last we spoke, you elected to remain in Washington."

"I changed my mind," Sandecker said gruffly. Not seeing anyone left in the cockpit, he looked at Giordino. "Didn't you bring Dirk with you?"

"He slept like a rock between Grapevine Bay and here," answered Giordino without his usual grin. "He's not in the best of shape. As if he wasn't already a classic case of battle fatigue when he arrived at Orion Lake, he had to go and get himself shot again."

"Shot?" Sandecker's face clouded. "Nobody told me he'd been shot. How bad is it?"

"Not serious. Luckily, the bullet just missed the pelvis, going in and coming out the upper side of his right buttock. A doctor in Grapevine examined and dressed the wound. He insisted that Dirk shouldn't be up and running around, but our friend laughed and demanded on finding a bar, claiming a couple shots of tequila would make him as good as new."

"Did two shots of tequila do it?" Sandecker asked cynically.

"More like four." Giordino turned as Pitt emerged from the helicopter. "See for yourself."

Sandecker looked up and found himself looking at a man dressed like a backwoods hiker, thin and played out, as if he'd been existing on little else but berries in a forest. His hair was tangled in every direction, face drawn and haggard but split by a smile as broad as a highway billboard with eyes clear and intense.

"By God, it's the admiral," Pitt boomed. "You're the last man I expected to see standing out in the rain."

Sandecker wanted to laugh, but he fixed a frown on his face and spoke as if angered. "I thought it might be nice to demonstrate my charitable disposition and save you a five-thousand-mile round trip."

"You don't want me back at my desk?"

"No. You and Al are leaving for Manila."

"Manila," said Pitt, puzzled. "That's in the Philippines."

"It hasn't been moved that I was aware of," Sandecker said.

"When?"

"Within the hour."

"Within the hour?" Pitt stared at him.

"I've booked you on a commercial flight across the Pacific. You and Al *will* be on it."

"What are we supposed to do once we get to Manila?"

"If you'll come in out of the rain before we drown, I'll tell you."

After Pitt was ordered to drink two cups of coffee, Sandecker gathered his finest team of ocean engineers in the privacy of an aquarium. Sitting among tanks filled with North Pacific sea life under study by NUMA marine biologists, the admiral briefed Pitt and Giordino on the meeting he and Gunn had with the President and officials of the Immigration and Naturalization Service.

"The man whose criminal operation you screwed up at Orion Lake directs a vast smuggling empire that traffics in illegal immigrants, transporting them into nearly every country of the world. He literally smuggles millions of Chinese into the Americas, Europe and South America. Under a shroud of secrecy, he is supported and often funded by the Chinese government. The more people he can remove from the over-populated country and place in positions of influence overseas, the better the potential to achieve international power bases working under directives from the mother country. It is a worldwide conspiracy with incredible consequences if Qin Shang continues unchecked.''

''The man is responsible for hundreds of dead bodies lying on the bottom of Orion Lake,'' said Pitt angrily. ''You're telling me he can't be charged with mass murder and hanged?''

''Charging him and convicting him are different sides of the street,'' answered Sandecker. ''Qin Shang has more corporate barriers around him than waves pounding a shore. I'm told by the commissioner of INS, Duncan Monroe, that Qin Shang is so far removed, politically and financially, there is no direct evidence linking him to the mass murders on Orion Lake.''

''The man seems impregnable,'' said Gunn.

Pitt said in a measured tone, ''No man is impregnable. We all have an Achilles' heel.''

''How do we nail the bastard?'' Giordino asked bluntly.

Sandecker answered partially by explaining the two objectives the President had ordered NUMA to investigate, the old ocean liner *United States* and Qin Shang's shipping port of Sungari in Louisiana. He concluded by saying, ''Rudi here will be in charge of a special team for an underwater probe of Sungari. Dirk and Al will examine the former ocean liner.''

''Where do we find the *United States?*'' asked Pitt.

''Until three days ago, she was at Sevastopol in the Black Sea undergoing a refit. But according to satellite surveillance photos, she's left dry dock and passed through the Dardanelles on her way to the Suez Canal.''

''That's covering a lot of territory for a fifty-year-old ship,'' said Giordino.

''Not unusual,'' said Pitt, staring at the ceiling as if retrieving something once cataloged in his mind. ''The *United States* could leave the best of them in her wake. She beat the *Queen Mary*'s best time across the Atlantic by an amazing ten hours. On her maiden voyage she set a speed record between New York and England, averaging thirty-five knots, that still stands.''

''She must have been fast,'' said Gunn admiringly. ''That works out to about forty-one miles an hour.''

Sandecker nodded. ''She's still faster than any commercial ship built before or since.''

"How did Qin Shang get his hands on her?" asked Pitt. "It was my understanding that the U.S. Maritime Administration would not sell her unless she remained under the American flag."

"Qin Shang easily got around that by purchasing the ship through an American company who in turn could then sell it to a buyer who represented a friendly nation. In this case a Turkish businessman. Too late, American authorities discovered that a Chinese national bought the ship, posing as the Turkish buyer."

"Why would Qin Shang want the *United States?*" Pitt asked, still in the dark.

"He's in league with the Chinese People's Liberation Army," replied Gunn. "The deal he struck with them gives him the right to operate the ship, possibly to smuggle illegal aliens under the guise of a cruise ship. The Chinese military, for their purposes, has the option of commandeering the ship and quickly converting it to a troop transport."

"You'd have thought our defense department would have seen the light and converted her years ago," said Giordino. "She could have moved an entire division of troops from the States to Saudi Arabia during the Gulf War in less than five days."

Sandecker stroked his beard in thought. "Airlifts are the thing to transport men these days. Ships are used primarily to haul in supplies and equipment. Any way you look at it, the former pride of the transatlantic greyhounds was way past her prime."

"So what's our job?" Pitt asked with diminishing forbearance. "If the President wants to prevent the *United States* from smuggling aliens into the country, why doesn't he order a nuclear submarine to quietly put a couple of Mark XII torpedoes into her side."

"And give the Chinese military a bona fide excuse to retaliate by blasting a cruise ship filled with American tourists out of the water?" Sandecker said sharply. "I don't think so. There are more practical and less hazardous ways of cutting Qin Shang off at the knees."

"Like what?" Giordino asked guardedly.

"Answers!" Sandecker snapped back. "There are perplexing questions that must be answered before the INS can take action."

"We're not undercover specialists," said Pitt, unmoved by it all. "What does he expect us to do? Pay our ticket, reserve a stateroom and then send questionnaires to the captain and crew?"

"I am aware that you find this uninspiring," said Sandecker, seeing that both Pitt and Giordino were regarding their mission with a marked lack of enthusiasm, "but I'm dead serious when I say that the information you're to obtain is vital to the future welfare of the country. Illegal immigration cannot continue in an uncontrolled flood. Sleaze like Qin Shang are conducting modern versions of the slave trade." Sandecker paused and gazed at Pitt. "From what I've been told, you saw an example of their inhumanity with your own eyes."

Pitt nodded almost imperceptibly. "Yes, I saw the horror."

"There must be something the government can do to rescue these people from bondage," said Gunn.

"You can't protect people who are illegally in your country if they've disappeared and gone underground after they were smuggled in," Sandecker replied.

"Can't a task force be formed to search them out, free them and release them into society?" Gunn persisted.

"The INS has sixteen hundred investigators in the fifty states, not counting those working in foreign countries, who made over three hundred thousand arrests of illegal aliens engaged in criminal activities. It would take twice that number of investigators just to stay even."

"How many illegals are coming into the Unites States each year?" asked Pitt.

"There is no way to achieve an accurate count," answered Sandecker. "Estimates run as high as two million aliens who poured in last year from China and Central America alone."

Pitt stared out the window at the calm waters of Puget Sound. The rain had passed, and the clouds were becoming scattered. A rainbow slowly formed over the docks. "Has anybody a clue to where it will all end?"

"With a heil of a lot of people," Sandecker said. "The last census put the U.S. population at roughly two hundred and fifty million. With the coming increase in births and immigration, legal and illegal, the population will soar to three hundred and sixty million by the year twenty fifty."

"Another hundred million in the next fifty years," said Giordino dolefully. "I hope I'm gone by then."

Gunn said thoughtfully, "Hard to imagine the changes in store for the country."

"Every great nation or civilization either fell by corruption from within or was altered forever by foreign migration," said Sandecker.

Giordino's face registered indifference. The future was of little concern to him. Unlike Pitt, who found pleasure in the past, Giordino lived only for the present. Gunn, contemplative as ever, stared down at the floor, trying to picture the problems a population increase of fifty percent would bring with it.

Pitt said dryly, "And so the President in his infinite wisdom expects us to plug the dike with our fingers."

"Just how are we supposed to conduct this crusade?" asked Giordino, carefully removing a huge cigar from a cedar wrapper and slowly, very slowly, rolling the end over the flame from a lighter.

Sandecker stared at the cigar, his face reddening as he recognized it as one from his private cache. "When you arrive in Manila at the international airport, you will be met by a man named John Smith—"

"That's original," Giordino muttered. "I've always wanted to meet the guy whose signature I see above mine on motel registers."

To a stranger sitting in on the discussion, it would seem none of the NUMA men had the slightest respect for one another, and that there was a cloud of animosity hanging over them. Nothing could be further from the truth. Pitt and Giordino had nothing but total and unabridged admiration for Sandecker. They were as close to him as to their own fathers. Without the slightest hesitation, they had on more than one occasion risked their own lives to save his. The give-and-take was a game they had played many times over the years. The apathy was a sham. Pitt and Giordino were too wildly independent to accept instructions without a display of rebellion. Nor were they known to jump up and salute before dashing out the door to do their duty with an overabundance of fervor. It was a scene of puppets pulling the strings of puppets with an underlying sense of humor.

"We land in Manila and wait for a John Smith to make himself known," said Pitt. "I hope there's more to the plan than that."

Sandecker went on. "Smith will escort you to the dock area, where you'll board a tired old intercoastal freighter. A singularly uncommon vessel, as you will discover. By the time you set foot on the deck, NUMA's *Sea Dog II* submersible will be secured aboard. Your job, when the opportunity arises, will be to inspect and photograph the hull of the *United States* below the waterline."

Pitt shook his head, his expression one of incredulity. "We cruise around, examining the bottom of a ship that's the length of three football fields. Shouldn't take more than forty-eight hours of downtime. Naturally, Qin Shang's security people wouldn't think of dropping sensors around the hull for just such an intrusion." He looked at Giordino. "How do you see it?"

"Like giving a nipple to a baby," Giordino said casually. "My only problem is, how does a submersible with a top speed of four knots keep up with a ship that cruises at thirty-five knots?"

Sandecker gave Giordino a long, sour look, then answered the question. "You conduct your underwater survey while the ship is docked in port. That goes without saying."

"What port have you got in mind?" asked Pitt.

"CIA informants in Sevastopol report that the ship's destination is Hong Kong, where the final interiors and furnishings will be fitted before she takes on passengers for voyages in and around port cities of the United States."

"The CIA is in on this?"

"Every investigative agency in the government is cooperating with INS until they can work together to bring the situation under control."

"The intercoastal freighter," said Pitt. "Who owns and operates it?"

"I know what you're thinking," Sandecker replied. "You can forget any connection with an intelligence agency. The vessel is privately owned. That's all I can tell you."

Giordino exhaled a large blue cloud of cigar smoke toward a tank full of fish. "There must be over a thousand miles of water between Manila and Hong Kong. Any old tramp steamer I've ever seen seldom made more than eight or nine knots. We're looking at a voyage of almost five days. Do we have the luxury of that much time?"

"You'll be docked in Hong Kong less than a quarter of a mile from the *United States* and staring up at her keel within forty-eight hours after leaving the Philippines," answered Sandecker.

"That," said Giordino, his eyebrows raised in skepticism, "should prove interesting."

15

IT WAS ELEVEN O'CLOCK in the evening, Philippines time, when
Pitt and Giordino stepped off a commercial flight from Seattle, passed
through customs and entered the main terminal lobby of the Ninoy
Aquino International Airport. Off to the side of a milling crowd they
found a man holding a crudely lettered cardboard sign. Placards in the
hands of greeters usually advertised the names of arriving passengers.
This one simply said SMITH.

He was a great slob of a man. He might have been an Olympic
weight lifter at one time, but his body had gone to seed and his stomach
had grown into an immense watermelon. It sagged and hung over a pair
of soiled pants and an overstressed leather belt three sizes too small.
The face appeared scarred from dozens of fights, and his great hooked
nose had been broken so often it veered to one side across the left
cheek. Stubble covered the lips and chin. It was difficult to tell whether
his eyes looked bloodshot from too much booze or too little sleep. The
black hair was plastered over his head like some kind of greasy skullcap, and the teeth were irregular and yellow. His biceps and forearms
seemed remarkably taut and muscled in comparison with the rest of
him, and were laden with tattoos. He wore a grimy yachtsman's cap
and dingy coveralls. "Shiver me timbers," muttered Giordino, "if it
isn't old Blackbeard hisself."

Pitt walked up to the mangy derelict and said, "Good of you to meet
us, Mr. Smith."

"Happy to have you aboard," Smith said with a cheerful smile. "The
captain's expecting you."

Carrying only a few articles of underwear, toiletries and work shirts and pants picked up at a surplus store on the way to the Seattle airport, and all stuffed in a pair of small carry-on tote bags, Pitt and Giordino had no reason to wait at the baggage carousel. They fell in behind Smith and walked out of the terminal into the airport parking lot. Smith stopped at a Toyota van that looked as if it spent its life in endurance runs around the Himalayan Mountains. Half the windows were broken out and taped closed with plywood boards. The body paint was faded to the primer, and the rocker panels were rusted away. Pitt observed the deeply treaded off-road tires and listened with interest to the throaty roar of a powerful engine as it immediately kicked to life when Smith pressed the starter.

The van moved off with Pitt and Giordino sitting on the torn and worn vinyl upholstery. Pitt lightly prodded his friend with his elbow to get his attention and spoke loud enough for the driver to hear. "Tell me, Mr. Giordino, is it true you're a very observant person?"

"That I am," Giordino came back, picking up Pitt's intent instantly. "Nothing escapes me. And let us not forget you, Mr. Pitt. Your powers of prognostication are also world-renowned. Would you like to demonstrate your talents?"

"I would indeed."

"Let me begin by asking, what do you make of this vehicle?"

"I have to say it looks like a prop out of a Hollywood movie that no self-respecting hippie would be caught dead in, and yet it sports expensive tires and an engine that puts out around four hundred horsepower. Most peculiar, wouldn't you say?"

"Very astute, Mr. Pitt. My vision exactly."

"And you, Mr. Giordino. What does your remarkable insight see in our bon vivant driver?"

"A man obsessed with chicanery, skulduggery and connivery; in short, a rip-off artist." Giordino was in his element and on the verge of getting carried away. "Have you noticed his bulging stomach?"

"A poorly positioned pillow?"

"Exactly," Giordino exclaimed as if it were a revelation. "Then there are the scars on the face and the flattened nose."

"Poorly applied makeup?" Pitt asked innocently.

"There's no fooling you, is there?" The driver's ugly face twisted in a scowl through the rearview mirror, but there was no stopping Giordino. "Of course you caught the hairpiece floating in pomade."

"I most certainly did."

"How do you read his tattoos?"

"Inscribed by pen and ink?" offered Pitt.

Giordino shook his head. "I'm disappointed in you, Mr. Pitt. Stencils. Any apprentice remote viewer would envision them being stenciled on the skin."

"I stand rebuked."

Unable to remain quiet, the driver snapped over his shoulder. "You two pretty boys think you're smart."

"We do what we can," said Pitt lightly.

Having done their dirty work and advertised the fact that they had not fallen off a pumpkin wagon, Pitt and Giordino remained silent as the van drove onto a pier of a shipping terminal. Smith dodged around huge overhead cranes and stacked freight, finally stopping opposite an opening in a railing along the pier's edge. Without a word of instruction, he stepped from the vehicle and walked toward a ramp leading to a launch that was tied to a small floating dock. The two NUMA men obediently followed and climbed into the launch. The sailor standing at the helm in the stern of the boat was a concert in black—black pants, black T-shirt and black stocking cap pulled down over the ears despite the tropical heat and humidity.

The launch eased away from the wooden pilings and turned her bow toward a ship that lay anchored about two-thirds of a mile from the terminal. Around her were the lights from other ships waiting for their turn to load or unload cargo under the great cranes. The atmosphere was as clear as cut glass, and far across Manila Bay the colored lights of fishing boats sparkled like gemstones against the black sky.

The shape of the ship began to rise in the night, and Pitt could see that she was not the typical tramp steamer that plowed the South Seas from island to island. He correctly identified her as a Pacific Coast lumber hauler with clean, unencumbered holds and no amidships superstructure. Her engine room was in the stern below the crew's quarters. A single stack rose just aft of the wheelhouse and behind it, a tall mast. A second, smaller mast rose from the forecastle on the bow. Pitt guessed her at somewhere between four and five thousand tons with a length of just under three hundred feet and a forty-five-foot beam. A vessel her size could have carried nearly three million board feet of lumber. Her time had long come and gone. Her sister ships, which had carried the product of saw mills, had settled into the silt of the boneyard almost fifty years earlier, having been replaced by more modern towboats and barges.

"What's her name?" Pitt asked Smith.

"The *Oregon*."

"I imagine she carried a goodly amount of lumber in her day."

Smith looked at Pitt across the launch, inspecting him closely. "How could a pretty boy like you know that?"

"When my father was a young man, he crewed on a lumber ship. He made ten runs between San Diego and Portland before finishing college. He has a picture of the ship on his office wall."

"The *Oregon* sailed from Vancouver to San Francisco for close to twenty-five years before she was retired."

"I wonder when she was built."

"Long before you or I were born," said Smith.

The helmsman swung the launch alongside the hull, once painted a dark orange but now discolored by rust, as revealed by the running lights on the masts and the glow from the starboard navigation light. There was no gangway, only a rope boarding ladder with wood rungs.

"After you, pretty boy," said Smith, gesturing topside.

Pitt went first, trailed by Giordino. On the way up, Pitt wiped his fingers across a large scale of rust. The patch felt smooth, and no smudge dirtied his fingertips. The hatches on the deck were closed and the cargo booms sloppily stowed. Several large wooden crates stacked on the deck looked like they had been secured by untrained chimpanzees. To all appearances the crew ran what was often called "a loose ship." None of them were seen, and the decks seemed deserted. The only indication of life was a radio playing a Strauss waltz. The music was inconsistent with the ship's overall appearance. Pitt thought an ode to a trash dump would have been more appropriate. He saw no sign of the *Sea Dog II.*

"Did our submersible arrive?" Pitt asked Smith.

"She's stowed in that large crate just behind the forecastle."

"Which way to the captain's cabin?"

The mangy escort lifted a plate in the deck that revealed a ladder leading into what seemed a cargo compartment. "You'll find him down there."

"Ship captains aren't generally quartered in concealed compartments." Pitt looked up at the superstructure on the stern. "On any ship I've known the captain's cabin is below the wheelhouse."

"Down there, pretty boy," Smith repeated.

"What in hell has Sandecker gotten us into," murmured Giordino suspiciously as he turned his back to Pitt's and instinctively went into a fighting crouch.

Calmly, as if it was the most natural thing in the world, Pitt laid his tote bag on the deck, unzipped a pocket and retrieved his old .45 Colt. Before Smith knew what was happening the muzzle was jammed under his chin. "Forgive me for not mentioning it, but I blew the head off the last jerk who called me pretty boy."

"Okay, pal," Smith said without a hint of fear. "I recognize a gun when I see one. Not one in mint condition, but obviously well used. Please point it somewhere else. You wouldn't want to get hurt now, would you?"

"I don't think it's me who's going to get hurt," Pitt said conversationally.

"You might be wise to look around you."

It was the oldest trick in the book, but Pitt had nothing to lose. He glanced around the deck as men stepped out of the shadows. Not two men, nor four, but six men every bit as disreputable as Smith, each holding automatic weapons pointed at Pitt and Giordino. Big, silent men dressed as mangily as Smith.

Pitt pulled back the hammer and pressed the Colt another quarter inch into the flesh under Smith's chin. "Would it matter if I said, if I go, you go with me?"

"And allow your friend to be killed too?" said Smith with an ungodly grin. "From what little I know about you, Pitt, you're not that dumb."

"Just what *do* you know about me?"

"Put the gun away, and we'll talk."

"I can hear you perfectly well from where I stand."

"Relax, boys," said Smith to his men. "We must show a little class and treat our guests with respect."

Incredibly, the crew of the *Oregon* lowered their guns and began laughing. "Serves you right, skipper," one of them said. "You said they were probably a couple nerds from NUMA who drank milk and ate broccoli."

Giordino smoothly joined the act. "You guys got any beer on this tub?"

"Ten different brands," said a crewman, slapping him on the back. "Glad to have passengers with a little guts on board."

Pitt lowered the gun and eased the hammer back in the safety position. "I get the feeling we've been had."

"Sorry to inconvenience you," said Smith heartily, "but we can't let our guard down for even a moment." He turned to his men and issued an order. "Weigh anchor, boys, and get under way for Hong Kong."

"Admiral Sandecker said this was a singularly uncommon ship," said Pitt, replacing the automatic in his tote bag. "But he didn't say anything about the crew."

"If we can dispense with the theatrics," said Smith, "I'll show you below." He dropped down the ladder through the narrow hatch and disappeared. Pitt and Giordino followed, finding themselves in a brightly lit, carpeted hallway whose walls were painted in pastel colors. Smith opened a smoothly varnished door and nodded inside. "You can share this cabin. Stow your gear, get comfortable, use the head and then I'll introduce you to the captain. You'll find his cabin behind the fourth door on the port side aft."

Pitt stepped inside and switched on the light. This was no Spartan cabin on a decrepit freighter. It was every bit as swank as any stateroom on a luxury cruise ship. Ornately decorated and elegantly furnished, all that was missing were sliding doors leading to a private veranda. The only suggestion of the outside world was a porthole painted black.

"What," exclaimed Giordino, "no bowl of fruit?"

Pitt stared around the cabin in fascination. "I wonder if we have to dress formal when we dine with the captain."

They heard the anchor chain rattle up out of the water and felt the engines begin to throb through the deck under their feet as the *Oregon* began beating her way across Manila Bay toward her destination in Hong Kong. A few minutes later they knocked on the door to the captain's cabin. A voice on the other side responded. "Please come in."

If their cabin resembled a deluxe stateroom, this one would have easily rated as the penthouse suite. It resembled a decorator showroom on Rodeo Drive in Beverly Hills. The furniture was expensive yet tasteful. The walls, or bulkheads in nautical terms, were either richly paneled or covered by curtains. The carpet was thick and plush. Two of the paneled walls were covered by original oil paintings. Pitt walked up to one and studied it. The painting inside an ornate frame was a seascape depicting a black man lying on the deck of a small, demasted sloop with a school of sharks swimming around its hull.

"Winslow Homer's *Gulf Stream*," said Pitt. "I thought it was hanging in a New York museum."

"The original is," said a man standing beside a large antique rolltop desk. "What you see are forgeries. In my line of business no insurance company would insure the real thing." A handsome man in his mid-forties with blue eyes and blond hair in a crewcut stepped forward and

159

stuck out a manicured hand. "Chairman Juan Rodriguez Cabrillo, at your service." He pronounced Cabrillo as *Ka-bree-yo*.

"Chairman, like in chairman of the board?"

"A departure from maritime tradition," Cabrillo explained. "This ship is run like a business, a corporation if you will. The personnel prefer to be assigned corporate titles."

"That's a twist," Giordino said equably. "Don't tell me, I'm keen to guess. Your first officer is president."

Cabrillo shook his head. "No, my chief engineer is president. My first officer is executive vice president."

Giordino lifted an eyebrow. "This is the first I've heard the Kingdom of Oz owns a ship."

"You'll get used to it," Cabrillo said tolerantly.

"If I recall my California history," said Pitt, "you discovered California in the early fifteen hundreds."

Cabrillo laughed. "My father always claimed Cabrillo the explorer as an ancestor, but I've had my doubts. My grandparents walked across the border at Nogales from Sonora, Mexico, in nineteen thirty-one and became American citizens five years later. In honor of my birth they insisted my mother and father name me after a famous historical figure in California."

"I believe we've met before," said Pitt.

"Like about twenty minutes ago," added Giordino.

"Your imitation of a waterfront derelict, Chairman Cabrillo, alias Mr. Smith, was very professional."

Cabrillo laughed merrily. "You gentlemen are the first to see through my disguise as a rum-soaked barnacle." Unlike his staged character, Cabrillo was well-built and slightly on the thin side. The hook nose was gone, along with the tattoos and the overstuffed belly.

"I must admit, you had me fooled until I saw the van."

"Yes, our shore transportation is not quite what it appears."

"This ship," said Pitt, "your playacting, the facade, what's it all about?"

Cabrillo gestured for them to sit in a leather sofa. He walked over to a teak bar. "A glass of wine?"

"Yes, thank you."

"I'd prefer a beer," said Giordino.

Cabrillo poured and held out a mug to Giordino. "A Philippine San Miguel." Then a wineglass to Pitt. "Wattle Creek chardonnay from Alexander Valley, California."

"You have excellent taste," Pitt complimented Cabrillo. "I have the feeling it extends to your kitchen."

Cabrillo smiled. "I pirated my chef from a very exclusive restaurant in Brussels, Belgium. I might also add that should you get heartburn or indigestion from overindulging, we have an excellent hospital staffed by a top surgeon who doubles as a dentist."

"I'm curious, Mr. Cabrillo, what sort of trade is the *Oregon* engaged in, and who exactly do you work for?"

"This ship is a state-of-the-art intelligence-gathering vessel," Cabrillo replied without hesitation. "We go where no U.S. Navy warship can go, enter ports closed to most commercial shipping and transport highly secret cargo without arousing suspicion. We work for any United States government agency that requires our unique array of services."

"Then you're not under the CIA."

Cabrillo shook his head. "Although we're staffed by a few ex-intelligence agents, the *Oregon* is operated by an elite crew of former naval men and naval officers, all of whom are retired."

"I couldn't tell in the dark. What flag do you fly?"

"Iran," replied Cabrillo with a faint smile. "The last country any port authority would identify with the United States."

"Am I correct in assuming," said Pitt, "you're all mercenaries?"

"I can honestly say we're in business to make a profit, yes. By performing a variety of clandestine services for our country, we are paid extremely well."

"Who owns the ship?" asked Giordino.

"Everyone on board is a stockholder in the corporation," answered Cabrillo. "Some of us own more stock than others, but there isn't a single crew member who hasn't at least five million dollars stashed away in foreign investments."

"Does the IRS know about you?"

"The government has a secret fund for operations like ours," Cabrillo explained. "We have an arrangement whereby they pay our fees through a network of banks in countries that do not open their records to IRS auditors."

Pitt took a sip of his wine. "A sweet setup."

"But one that isn't unknown to peril and occasional disaster. The *Oregon* is our third ship. The others were destroyed by unfriendly forces. I might add that over thirteen years we've been in operation, we've lost no fewer than twenty men."

"Foreign agents caught on to you?"

"No, we've yet to be unmasked. There were other circumstances." Whatever they were, Cabrillo didn't explain them.

"Who authorized this trip?" inquired Giordino.

"Between you and me and the nearest porthole, our sailing orders came from within the White House."

"That's about as high as you can go."

Pitt looked at the captain. "Do you think you can put us reasonably close to the *United States?* We have a couple of acres of hull to inspect, and our time underwater is limited due to the *Sea Dog II*'s battery power. If you have to moor the *Oregon* a mile or more away, just getting to the liner and back will cut our downtime considerably."

Cabrillo stared back at him confidently. "I'll put you near enough to fly a kite over her funnels." Then he poured himself another glass of the chardonnay and held it up. "To a very successful voyage."

16

PITT WENT OUT ON DECK and looked up at the mast light as it swayed back and forth across the Milky Way. He planted his arms on the railing and gazed across the water at the island of Corregidor as the *Oregon* sailed out of Manila Bay. The indefinable black mass rose from the night, guarding the entrance to the bay in tomblike silence. A few lights glimmered on the interior of the island along with red warning lights on a transmitter tower. It was difficult for Pitt to imagine the onslaught of death and destruction that inundated the rocky outcropping during the war years. The number of men who died there, Americans in 1942, Japanese in 1945, numbered in the thousands. A small village of huts sat near the decaying dock from which General Douglas MacArthur had boarded Commander Buckley's torpedo boat for the initial stage of his journey to Australia and later return.

Pitt smelled the pungent odor of cigar smoke and turned as a crewman moved beside him at the railing. Under the running lights, Pitt could see a man who was in his late fifties. He recognized Max Hanley, who had been introduced earlier, not as the chief engineer or first officer, but as the corporate vice president in charge of operational systems.

Once safely out to sea, Hanley, like the rest of the dedicated crew members, transformed himself into a different person by donning comfortably casual clothes better suited for a golf course. He wore sneakers and was dressed in white shorts and a maroon polo shirt. He held a cup of coffee in one hand. His skin was reddened with no trace of tan, the brown eyes alert, a bulbous nose and only a wisp of auburn hair splayed across his head.

"A lot of history on that old rock," said Hanley. "I always come topside when we slip past her."

"She's pretty quiet now," replied Pitt.

"My father died over there in 'forty-two when the big gun he was manning took a direct hit from a Japanese bomber."

"A lot of good men died with him."

"That they did." Hanley looked into Pitt's eyes. "I'll be directing the descent into the water and retrieval of your submersible. Anything me or my engineers can help you with in regard to your equipment and electronics, you just holler."

"There is something."

"Name it."

"Could your crew do a quick repaint of the *Sea Dog II?* The NUMA turquoise trademark color is highly visible in shallow water from the surface."

"What color would you like?" asked Hanley.

"A medium green," explained Pitt, "a shade that blends with the water in the harbor."

"I'll get my boys on it first thing." Hanley turned and leaned against the rail with his back, staring up at the wisp of smoke drifting from the ship's funnel. "Seems to me it might have been a whole lot simpler to use one of them underwater robotic vehicles."

"Or an autonomous underwater vehicle," said Pitt, smiling. "Neither would prove as efficient as a manned submersible for inspecting the bottom of a hull the size of the *United States.* The sub's manipulator arm may also prove useful. There are certain projects where human eyesight is advantageous over video cameras. This happens to be one of them."

Hanley read the dial of an old pocket watch whose chain was hooked to a belt loop. "Time to program the engine and navigation systems. Now that we've reached open water, the chairman will want to triple our speed."

"We must be doing close to nine or ten knots now," said Pitt, his curiosity piqued.

"Strictly a performance," Hanley said candidly. "Whenever the old *Oregon* is in sight of prying eyes around the harbor or other ships that pass at sea, we like to make her look as if her antique engines and screws are straining to make headway. Which is the way she should appear for an old tub. In truth, she's been modified with two screws turned by twin diesel turbine engines that can push her past forty knots."

"But with a full load of cargo, your hull is riding low in the water and causing a heavy drag."

Hanley tilted his head toward the cargo hatches and the wooden crates tied to the deck. "All empty. We ride low because we fill specially installed ballast tanks to give the appearance of a heavily laden ship. Once they're pumped out, she'll rise six feet and take off four times faster than when she was built."

"A fox in disguise."

"With the teeth to match. Ask Chairman Cabrillo to show you how we bite back if we're attacked."

"I'll do that."

"Good night, Mr. Pitt."

"Good night, Mr. Hanley."

Ten minutes later Pitt felt the ship come to life as the vibrations from the engines increased dramatically. The wake turned from a white spreading scar to a boiling cauldron. The stern sank by a good three feet, the bow raised in an equal proportion and creamed white. The water rushed along the hull as if swept away by a giant broom. The sea shimmered under an awning of stars that outlined a scattering of thunderclouds on the horizon. It was a postcard South China Sea evening with an orange-tinted sky to the west.

The *Oregon* approached the outer reaches of Hong Kong Harbor two days later, making landfall at sunset. She had made the crossing from Manila in remarkable time. Twice, upon meeting other freighters during daylight, Cabrillo gave the order for slow speed. Several of the crew always quickly dressed in their shabby coveralls, assembled on deck and peered across the gap between the passing ships, staring blankly at what Cabrillo called a show of dummies. In an unwritten tradition of the sea, the crews of overtaking or passing ships coming together at sea never showed any animation. Only their eyeballs moved and blinked. Passengers wave, but merchant seamen always act uneasy when looking at crewmen on another ship. Usually, they offer a stiff little wave from a hand draped over the rail before disappearing inside their ship. Once the strange vessel was a safe distance in the *Oregon*'s wake, Cabrillo ordered a return to fast cruising speed.

Pitt and Giordino were given a tour of the remarkable ship. The wheelhouse above the aft house or superstructure was kept in a grimy and dirty state to mislead visiting port officials and harbor pilots. The unused officer and crew quarters below the wheelhouse were also kept in a slovenly mess to avoid suspicion. There was, however, no way of masquerading the engine room to make it look like a scrap heap. Vice president Hanley wouldn't hear of it. If any customs or harbor inspector came on board and wanted to see his engines, Hanley fixed up a passageway with enough dirty oil and sludge covering the deck and bulkheads to discourage even the most zealous officials from wanting to enter. None ever realized that the hatch beyond the filthy passageway opened onto an engine room as immaculate as a hospital's operating room.

The actual officer and crew cabins were concealed under the cargo holds. For defense the *Oregon* fairly bristled with weaponry. Like the German raiders of both wars and the British Q-ships of World War I, whose sides dropped away to reveal six-inch guns and vicious torpedo tubes, the *Oregon*'s hull secreted an array of sea-to-sea and sea-to-air missile launchers. The ship was remarkably different from any whose decks Pitt had set foot on before. It was a masterwork of deception and fabrication. He suspected there was no other like it on the seas.

He ate an early dinner with Giordino before going to the wheelhouse for a conference with Cabrillo. He was introduced to the ship's chef, Marie du Gard, a lady from Belgium with credentials that would send any restaurant or hotel owner on his knees begging her to work as his *chef de cuisine*. She was on board the *Oregon* because Cabrillo made her an offer she couldn't refuse. Through wise investments of her considerable fee as the ship's chef, she planned on opening her own restaurant in midtown Manhattan after two more undercover operations.

The menu was extraordinary. Giordino's tastebuds were mundane, so he settled for the *boeuf à la mode,* braised beef covered with aspic and glazed vegetables. Pitt opted for *ris de veau ou cervelles au beurre noir,* sweetbreads in brown butter sauce served with baked mushroom caps stuffed with crab enhanced by a boiled artichoke with hollandaise sauce. He allowed the chef to select for him a fine 1992 Ferrari-Carano Siena from Sonoma County. Pitt could not boast of having eaten a more savory meal, and certainly not on board a ship such as the *Oregon*.

After an espresso, Pitt and Giordino took a companionway up to the wheelhouse. Here pipes and iron fittings were stained with rust. Paint was flaking from bulkheads and window frames. The deck was deeply marred and spotted with old cigarette burns. Very little equipment seemed up-to-date. Only the brass on the old-fashioned binnacle and telegraph gleamed under the antiquated light fixtures still containing sixty-watt bulbs.

Chairman Cabrillo was standing on a bridge wing, pipe firmly clamped between his teeth. The ship had entered the West Lamma Channel leading to Hong Kong Harbor. Traffic was heavy, and Cabrillo ordered slow speed in preparation of taking on the harbor pilot. Her ballast tanks refilled when twenty miles out, the *Oregon* looked like any one of a hundred old freighters fully laden with cargo entering the busy harbor. The ruby lights on the television and microwave antennas atop Mount Victoria blinked on and off as a warning to low-flying aircraft. The thousands of lights decorating the palatial Jumbo Floating Restaurant near Aberdeen on Hong Kong Island sprinkled the water like clouds of fireflies.

If there was any risk and danger attached to the planned covert activity, the men and officers congregated in the wheelhouse demonstrated an utter immunity to it. The chartroom and the deck around the helm had become a corporate boardroom. The merits of different Asian stocks and bonds were being weighed. They were savvy investors who followed the market with seemingly more interest than they showed for the coming spy job on the *United States.*

Cabrillo stepped in from the bridge wing, noticed Pitt and Giordino, and approached them. "My friends in Hong Kong have informed me that the *United States* is tied up at Qin Shang Maritime's terminal dock at Kwai Chung north of Kowloon. The proper harbor officials have been bribed, and we've been given a berth in the channel about five hundred yards from the liner."

"A thousand-yard round trip," said Pitt, mentally calculating the submersible's downtime.

"*Sea Dog II*'s batteries—how far can you stretch them?" asked Cabrillo.

"Fourteen hours if we treat them gently," replied Giordino.

"Can you be towed behind a launch while underwater and out of sight?"

Pitt nodded. "A tow to and from would give us an extra hour under the liner's hull. I must warn you, though, the submersible is no lightweight. Its underwater drag will make ponderous going for a small launch."

Cabrillo smiled evenly. "You don't know what type of engines power our shore launch and lifeboats."

"I'm not even going to ask," said Pitt. "But I'm guessing they could hold their own in a Gold Cup hydro race."

"We've given away enough of the *Oregon*'s technical secrets for you to write a book on her." Cabrillo turned and peered through the bridge window as the pilot boat came out from the harbor, made a 180-degree turn and came alongside. The ladder was dropped, and the pilot stepped from his boat and climbed to the deck while both vessels were still under way. He went directly to the bridge, greeted Cabrillo and took charge of the helm.

Pitt walked outside onto the bridge wing and viewed the incredible carnival of colored lights of Kowloon and Hong Kong as the ship slipped through the channel to her assigned anchorage northwest of the central harbor. Along the waterfront of Victoria Harbor, the skyscrapers were illuminated like a forest of giant Christmas trees. In appearance, the city had changed little after it was taken over in 1997 by the People's Republic of China. For most of the residents life went on as before. It was the wealthy, along with many of the giant corporations, who had moved, primarily to the West Coast of the United States.

He was joined by Giordino as the ship closed on Qin Shang's dock terminal. The transatlantic ocean liner that was once the pride of America's maritime fleet appeared and grew larger.

During the flight to Manila he and Giordino had studied a lengthy report on the *United States*. The brainchild of the famed ship designer William Francis Gibbs, she was built by the Newport News Ship Building & Dry Dock Company, who laid her keel in 1950. Gibbs, a genius and a genuine character, was to marine engineering and design what Frank Lloyd Wright was to dry-land architecture. His dream was to create the fastest and most beautiful passenger liner yet built. He achieved his dream, and his masterpiece became the pride and apex of America during the age of great liners. She was truly the ultimate in elegant refinement and speed.

Gibbs was fanatical about weight and fireproofing. He insisted on using aluminum whenever possible. From the 1.2 million rivets driven into her hull to the lifeboats and their oars, stateroom furnishings and bathroom fixtures, baby's high chairs, even coat hangers and picture frames, all had to be aluminum. The only wood on the entire ship was a fireproof Steinway piano and the chef's butcher block. In the end, Gibbs had reduced the weight of the superstructure by 2,500 tons. The result was a ship of remarkable stability.

Considered huge then and now with a gross tonnage of 53,329 and measuring 990 feet in length with a 101-foot beam, she was not the world's largest liner. At the time of her construction the *Queen Mary* outweighed her by over 30,000 tons and the *Queen Elizabeth* was forty-one feet longer. The Cunard Line Queens may have provided a more ornate and baroque atmosphere, but the American ship's lack of rich wood paneling and fancy decor in favor of tasteful restraint, and her speed and safety were the elements that set the *United States* apart from her contemporaries. Unlike foreign competing liners, the *Big U,* as her crew had affectionately called her, gave her passengers 694 unusually spacious staterooms and air conditioning. Nineteen elevators carried passengers between the decks. Besides the usual gift shops, they could enjoy three libraries and two cinemas and could worship in a chapel.

But her two greatest assets were a military secret at the time of her building and operation. Not until several years later did it become known that she could be converted into a military transport capable of carrying 14,000 troops within a few weeks. Powered by eight massive boilers creating superheated steam, her four Westinghouse-geared turbines could put out 240,000 horsepower, 60,000 for each of her four propeller shafts, and drive her through the water just under fifty miles an hour. She was one of the few liners that could slip through the Panama Canal, charge across the Pacific to Singapore and back to San Francisco without refueling. In 1952, the *United States* won the prestigious Blue Riband, awarded for the fastest speed across the Atlantic. No liner has won it since.

A decade after she left the shipyard, she had become an anachronism. Commercial airplanes were already becoming competition to the famed greyhounds of the sea. By 1969, rising operating costs and the public's desire to reach their destination in the shortest time possible by air, spelled the end for America's greatest ocean liner. She was retired and laid up for thirty years at Norfolk, Virginia, before eventually finding her way to China.

Borrowing a pair of binoculars, Pitt studied the huge ship from the bridge of the *Oregon.* Her hull was still painted black, her superstructure white, her two great, magnificent funnels red, white and blue. She looked as magnificent as the day she broke the transatlantic record.

He was puzzled to see her ablaze with light. The sounds of activity echoed across the water. It puzzled him that Qin Shang's shipyard crews were working on her around the clock without any attempt at secrecy. Then, curiously, all sounds and activity suddenly stopped.

The pilot nodded at Cabrillo, who rang the ancient telegraph to STOP ENGINES. Unknown to the pilot, the telegraph was nonfunctional and Cabrillo muttered orders through a hand-held radio. The vibration died, and the *Oregon* went as quiet as a tomb as she slowly moved forward under her own momentum. Then the command came for slow astern, followed shortly by all stop.

Cabrillo gave the order to let go the anchor. The chain rattled, and it fell with a splash into the water. Then he shook hands with the pilot after signing the usual affidavits and logging the mooring. He waited until the pilot was on board the pilot boat before motioning to Pitt and Giordino. "Come join me in the chartroom and we'll go over tomorrow's program."

"Why wait another twenty-four hours?" asked Giordino.

Cabrillo shook his head. "Tomorrow after dark is soon enough. We still have customs officials due aboard. No sense in alerting suspicions."

Pitt said, "I think we have a breakdown in communications."

Cabrillo looked at him. "You see a problem?"

"We have to go during daylight. We have no visibility at night."

"Can't you use underwater lights?"

"In black water any bright light stands out like a beacon. We'd be discovered ten seconds after we switched on our floods."

"We'll be inconspicous when we're under the keel," Giordino added. "It's when we're inspecting the hull on the sides below the waterline that we're vulnerable to detection from above."

"What about the darkness caused by the shadow of the hull?" asked Cabrillo. "What if underwater visibility is lousy? What then?"

"We'd have to rely on artificial lighting, but it would be imperceptible to anyone staring over the side of the dock with sun over their head."

Cabrillo nodded. "I understand your dilemma. Romantic adventure novels say it's darkest before dawn. We'll drop you and your submersible over the side and tow you within spitting distance of the *United States,* putting you on station before sunup."

"Sounds good to me," Pitt said gratefully.

"Can I ask you a question, Mr. Chairman?" inquired Giordino.

"Go right ahead."

"If you carry no cargo, how do you justify entering and exiting a port?"

Cabrillo gave Giordino a canny look. "The empty wooden crates you see on the deck and the ones in the cargo holds above our concealed cabins and galley are stage props. They will be off-loaded onto the dock, then consigned to an agent who works for me and transported to a warehouse. After a proper length of time, the crates are re-marked with different descriptions, returned to the dock and loaded back on board. As far as the Chinese are concerned, we dumped one cargo and took on another."

"Your operation never ceases to amaze," said Pitt.

"You were given a tour of our computer compartment in the bow of the ship," said Cabrillo. "So you know that ninety percent of the *Oregon*'s operation is under the command of computer-automated systems. We go manual when entering and departing a port."

Pitt handed the binoculars to Cabrillo. "You're an old pro at stealth and covert activities. Doesn't it strike you odd that Qin Shang is converting the *United States* into a first-class smugglers' transport right out in the open under the eyes of anyone looking on? Crewmen on cargo ships, passengers on ferries and tour boats?"

"It does seem peculiar," Cabrillo admitted. He lowered the glasses momentarily in thought, puffed on his pipe, and peered through the lenses again. "It's also peculiar that all work on the ship appears to have stopped. No sign of tight security either."

"Tell you anything?" asked Giordino.

"It either tells Qin Shang is uncommonly careless or our renowned intelligence agencies have been outsmarted by him," said Cabrillo quietly.

"We'll know better after we check out the ship's bottom," said Pitt. "If he intends to smuggle illegal aliens into foreign countries under the noses of their immigration officials, he'd have to have a technique for removing them off the ship undetected. That can only mean some kind of watertight passage beneath the waterline to shore or even possibly a submarine."

Cabrillo tapped his pipe on the rail, watching as the ashes spiraled down into the harbor. Then he looked thoughtfully across the water at the former pride of America's passenger fleet, her superstructure and two rakish funnels brilliantly lit like a movie set. When he spoke it was slowly and solemnly. "You fully realize, I assume, that if something should go wrong, a minor mishap, an overlooked detail, and you are caught in what is considered an act of espionage by the People's Republic of China, you will be treated accordingly."

"Like being tortured and shot," said Giordino.

Cabrillo nodded. "And without anyone in our government so much as lifting their little finger to stop the execution."

"Al and I are fully aware of the consequences," said Pitt. "But you're placed in the hazardous position of risking your entire crew and your ship. I wouldn't fault you for a second if you wanted to toss us in the bay and steam off into the sunset."

Cabrillo stared at him and smiled craftily. "Are you serious? Skip out on you? I'd never consider it. Certainly not for the enormous sum of money a certain secret government fund is paying me and the crew. As far as I'm concerned, this has far less risk than robbing a bank."

"In excess of seven figures?" Pitt asked.

"More like eight," replied Cabrillo, suggesting a fee of over ten million dollars.

Giordino looked over at Pitt sadly. "When I think of what our pitiful monthly stipend from NUMA adds up to, I can't help wondering where we went wrong."

17

UNDER THE COVER of predawn darkness, the submersible *Sea Dog II,* with Pitt and Giordino inside, was lifted from her crate by the loading crane, swung over the side of the ship and slowly lowered into the water. A crewman standing on top of the submersible unhooked the cable and was hauled back on board. Then the *Oregon's* shore launch pulled alongside and attached a towline. Giordino stood in the open hatch that was raised three feet above the water while Pitt continued ticking off the instrument and equipment checklist.

"Ready when you are," announced Max Hanley from the launch.

"We'll descend to ten feet," said Giordino. "When we reach that level you can get under way."

"Understood."

Giordino closed the hatch and stretched out beside Pitt in the submersible, which had the appearance of a fat Siamese cigar with stubby wings on each side that curved to vertical on the tips. The twenty-foot long, eight-foot wide, 3,200-pound vehicle may have looked ungainly on the surface, but underwater she dived and turned with the grace of a baby whale. She was propelled with three thrusters in the twin tail section that impelled water through the front intake and expelled it out the rear. With a light touch on the two handgrips, one controlling pitch and dive, the other banks and turns, along with the speed-control lever, the *Sea Dog II* could glide smoothly a few feet under the surface of the sea or dive to a depth of two thousand feet in a matter of minutes. The pilots, who lay prone with their heads and shoulders extending into a single transparent glass bow, had a much wider range of visibility than provided by most submersibles with only small viewing ports.

Visibility beneath the surface was nil. The water enclosed the sub like a thick quilt. Looking up and ahead, they could just barely make out the shadowy outline of the launch. Then came a deep rumble as Cabrillo increased the rpms of the powerful Rodeck 539-cubic-inch, 1,500-horsepower engine that drove the big double-ender launch. The propeller thrashed the water, the stern dug in and the launch strained before surging forward with the bulky submersible in tow. Like a diesel locomotive pulling a long train up a grade, the launch struggled to gain momentum, finally increasing its speed until it was dragging the deadweight below the water at a respectable eight knots. Unknown to Pitt and Giordino, Cabrillo had the throttle of the powerful engine set at only one-third power.

During the short journey from the *Oregon* to the *United States,* Pitt programmed the on-board computer analyzer that automatically set and monitored the oxygen level, electronics and the depth control systems. Giordino activated the manipulator arm by running it through a series of exercises.

"Is the communications antenna up?" Pitt asked him.

Lying next to him, Giordino nodded slightly. "I let out the cable to a maximum length of sixty feet as soon as we entered the water. She's dragging on the surface behind us."

"How did you disguise it?"

Giordino shrugged. "Another cunning ploy of the great Albert Giordino. I encased it in a hollowed-out cantaloupe."

"Stolen from the chef, no doubt."

Giordino gave Pitt a hurt look. "Waste not, want not. It was overripe and she was going to throw it in her garbage collector."

Pitt spoke into a tiny microphone. "Chairman Cabrillo, do you read me?"

"Like you were sitting next to me, Mr. Pitt," Cabrillo came back quickly. Like the other five men in the launch, he was dressed as a local fisherman.

"As soon as we reach our drop zone, I'll release the communications-relay antenna so we can remain in contact after you've returned to the *Oregon.* When I drop the antenna, its weighted line will settle into the silt and it will act as a buoy."

"What is your range?"

"Underwater, we can transmit and receive up to fifteen hundred yards."

"Understood," said Cabrillo. "Stand by, we're only a short distance away from the liner's stern. I won't be able to come in much closer than fifty yards."

"Any sign of a security force?"

"The whole ship and dock look as dead as a crypt in winter."

"Standing by."

Cabrillo was better than his word. He slowed the launch until it barely maintained headway and steered it almost directly under the stern of the *United States*. The sun was coming up as a diver slipped over the side and descended down the towline to the submersible. "Diver is down," Cabrillo announced.

"We see him," answered Pitt, looking up through the transparent nose. He watched as the diver released the connection mechanism mounted on top of the submersible between the twin tubes and gave the familiar "okay" sign with one hand before disappearing up the towline. "We are free."

"Make a turn forty degrees to your starboard," directed Cabrillo. "You are only eighty feet west of the stern."

Giordino gestured up through the murky depth at the immense shadow that gave the illusion it was passing over *them*. The seemingly unending shape was enhanced by the sunlight filtering between the dock and the gigantic hull. "We have her."

"You're on your own. Rendezvous will be at four-thirty. I'll have a diver waiting at your antenna mooring."

"Thank you, Juan," said Pitt, feeling free to use the chairman's first name. "We couldn't have done it without you and your exceptional crew."

"I wouldn't have it any other way," Cabrillo came back cheerfully.

Giordino gazed in awe at the monstrous rudder looming overhead and pressed the lever that dropped the antenna's anchor into the silt on the bottom. From their position the hull seemed to travel off into infinity. "She appears to be riding high. Do you recall her draft?"

"I'd have to make a wild guess," said Pitt. "Somewhere around forty feet, give or take?"

"Judging from the look of her, your guess is a good five feet on the low side."

Pitt made Cabrillo's course correction and dipped the *Sea Dog II*'s bows into deeper water. "I'd better be careful or we'll bump our heads."

Pitt and Giordino had worked as a team on countless dives into the abyss and operated a score of submersibles on various NUMA projects.

Without any discussion each man spontaneously assumed his well-practiced responsibilities. Pitt acted as pilot while Giordino kept an eye on the systems monitor, operated the video camera and worked the manipulator arm.

Pitt gently eased the throttle lever forward, directing the sub's movement by angling and tilting the three thrusters with the handgrip controls, dodging beneath the giant rudder and banking around the two starboard screws. Like some nocturnal flying machine, the submersible slipped around the three-bladed bronze propellers that spanned the watery gloom like great, beautifully curved fans. The *Sea Dog II* continued silently through the water, which became an eerie opaque green.

The bottom appeared as distant land through a fog. Assorted trash dumped off ships and the dock over the years lay partially embedded in the silt. They soared over a rusting deck grate that was home to a small school of squid that drifted in and out of the parallel rows of square openings. Pitt guessed that it had simply been dumped by dockyard workers sometime in the past. He stopped the thrusters and settled the craft into the soft bottom beneath the liner's stern. A small cloud of silt filtered up and outward like a brown vapor, momentarily obscuring any view through the forward canopy.

Overhead, the hull of the *United States* stretched above them into the dusky water like a dark, ominous shroud. There was a sense of loneliness on the desolate bottom. The real world above did not exist.

"I think it best if we took a few minutes and thought this thing out," said Pitt.

"Don't ask me why," said Giordino, "but a dumb joke from my childhood suddenly popped into my head."

"What joke is that?"

"The goldfish that blushed when it saw the *Queen Mary*'s bottom."

Pitt made a sour face. "The simple things that come from simple minds. You should rot in purgatory for resurrecting that old turkey."

Giordino acted as if he didn't hear. "Not to change the titillating subject, but I wonder if these clowns thought of using eavesdropping sensors around the hull."

"Unless we bump into one dangling from the dock, we have no way of telling."

"Still pretty dark to make out any detail."

"I'm thinking we can set our light beams on the low end and begin inspecting the keel. Our chances of being spotted that deep beneath the hull are unlikely."

"Then as the sun rises higher in the sky, we can work out and up toward the waterline."

Pitt nodded. "Hardly a brilliant plan, but it's the best I can come up with under the circumstances."

"Then we'd better get a move on," said Giordino, "if we don't want to suck our oxygen dry."

Pitt engaged the thrusters, and the submersible slowly rose from the silt until it was only four feet below the keel. He concentrated on keeping the *Sea Dog II* on an even plane, glancing every few seconds at his positioning monitor to guide him on a straight track while Giordino peered upward, his eyes searching for any irregularity that indicated an exit or entry hatch that had been riveted in the bottom of the hull, taping any suspicious piece or workmanship with the video camera. After a few minutes, Pitt found it more expedient to ignore the monitor and simply follow the horizontal seams between the hull plates through the transparent canopy.

On the surface, the sun's rays pierced the depths, increasing visibility. Pitt switched off the exterior lights. The steel plates, black in the earlier darkness, now became a dull red as the antifouling paint became more evident. There was a slight current caused by the outgoing tide, but Pitt held the submersible steady as the inspection continued. For the next two hours they glided back and forth as if mowing a lawn, each man strangely silent, intent on his job.

Suddenly, Cabrillo's voice broke the silence. "Care to make a progress report, gentlemen?"

"No progress to report," Pitt answered. "One more sweep and we'll have finished the bottom of the hull. Then it's up the sides toward the waterline."

"Let's hope your new paint job makes it tough to spot you from the surface."

"Max Hanley and his crew laid on a darker green tint than I'd planned," said Pitt. "But if nobody stares down in the water, we should be okay."

"The ship still looks deserted."

"I'm glad to hear it."

"See you in two hours and eighteen minutes," said Cabrillo jovially. "Try not to be late."

"We'll be there," Pitt promised. "Al and I don't want to hang around down here any longer than we have to."

"Standing by and out."

Pitt leaned his head toward Giordino without looking at him. "How's our oxygen supply?" he asked.

"Tolerable," Giordino replied briefly. "Battery power still reads steady, but it's creeping slowly toward the red line."

They finished the final run working out from the keel. Pitt guided the little craft along the section of the hull that curved upward toward the waterline. The next hour passed with agonizing slowness, and nothing out of the ordinary was revealed. The tide turned and began flowing in from the sea, bringing cleaner water and increasing visibility to nearly thirty feet. Swinging around the bow they began working the starboard side, which was moored next to the dock, not rising to within ten feet of the surface.

"Time remaining?" Pitt asked tersely without lifting a hand to glance at his Doxa dive watch.

"Fifty-seven minutes to rendezvous with the *Oregon*'s launch," replied Giordino.

"This trip definitely wasn't worth the effort. If Qin Shang is sneaking aliens on and off the *United States,* it isn't by means of an underwater passage or submarine-type vessel."

"Doesn't figure he'd do it topside in the open," said Giordino. "Not in enough numbers to make it pay. Immigration agents would tag the operation ten minutes after the boat hit port."

"Nothing more we can do here. Let's wrap up and head home."

"That may present a problem."

Pitt glanced sideways at Giordino. "How so?"

Giordino nodded through the canopy. "We have visitors."

Ahead of the submersible, three divers materialized out of the green void, swimming toward them like evil demons in their black wet suits.

"What do you think the fine is for trespassing in these parts?"

"I don't know, but I'll bet it's more than a slap on the wrist."

Giordino studied the divers who were approaching, one in the center, the other two circling from the flank. "Most odd they didn't spot us earlier, long before we made our last run just under the waterline."

"Somebody must have looked over the side and reported a funny green monster," Pitt said facetiously.

"I'm serious. It's almost as if they sat back observing us until the last minute."

"Do they look mad?"

"They ain't bringing flowers and candy."

"Weapons?"

"Looks like Mosby underwater rifles."

The Mosby was a nasty weapon that fired a missile with a small explosive head through water. Though devastating against human body tissue, Pitt didn't believe it could cause serious damage to a submersible able to withstand the pressures of the deep. "The worst we can expect is scratched paint and a few dents."

"Don't get cocky just yet," said Giordino, staring at the approaching divers as a doctor might study an X ray. "These guys are making a coordinated assault. Their helmets must contain miniature radios. Our pressure hull may take a few good knocks, but one lucky shot into the impellers of our thrusters and we'll end up desecrated."

"We can outrun them," said Pitt confidently. He banked the *Sea Dog II* in a tight turn, set the thrusters on HIGH, and steered for the stern of the liner. "This boat can travel a good six knots faster than any diver encumbered with air tanks."

"Life isn't fair," Giordino muttered, more annoyed than fearful as they unexpectedly found themselves confronting another seven divers hovering in a semicircle beneath the ship's mammoth propellers, blocking off their avenue of escape. "It seems the goddess of serendipity has turned her back on us."

Pitt switched on his microphone and hailed Cabrillo over the radio. "This is *Sea Dog II*. We have a total of ten villains in hot pursuit."

"I read you, *Sea Dog,* and will take appropriate steps. No need to contact me further, out."

"Not good," said Pitt grimly. "We might dodge past two or three but the rest can get close enough to do us real damage." Then a notion struck him. "Unless . . ."

"Unless what?"

Pitt didn't answer. Orchestrating the handgrip controls, he threw the *Sea Dog II* into a dive, then leveling out less than a foot off the bottom and began a search pattern. Within ten short seconds, he found what he was looking for. The deck grate he'd seen earlier loomed up out of the silt.

"Can you lift that thing out of the muck with the manipulator arm?" he asked Giordino.

"The arm can handle the weight, but the suction is an unknown. It depends on how deep the grate is buried."

"Try."

Giordino nodded silently and quickly slipped his hands over the ball-shaped controls to the mechanical arm and tightened his fingers.

179

Exercising a delicate touch, he rotated the balls in a manner similar to moving the mouse on a computer. He extended the arm, which was articulated at the elbow and wrist like human joints. Next, he placed the mechanical handgrip over the top of the grate and tightened the three hinged fingers.

"One grate in hand," he announced. "Give me all the vertical thrust in the cupboard."

Pitt tilted the thrusters upward and poured on every ounce of their remaining battery power as the divers from Qin Shang's security force closed to within twenty feet. For a tormenting few seconds nothing happened. Then the grate slowly began to slip from the silt, stirring up a great cloud of silt as the sub pulled it free.

"Twist the arm until the grate is in a horizontal position," ordered Pitt. "Then hold it over the front of the thruster intakes."

"They can still shoot an explosive up our tail."

"Only if they carry muck-penetrating radar," said Pitt, reversing the thrusters and tilting them down so their exhaust blasted into the bottom, raising great billows of swirling silt. "Now you see us, now you don't."

Giordino grinned approvingly. "An armored shield, a self-induced smoke screen—what more could we ask? Now let's get the hell out of here."

Pitt needed no coaching. He sent the submersible careening across the bottom, stirring up silt as he went. Traveling every bit as visually blind as the divers through the agitated sediment but not nearly as confused, he had the advantage of an acoustics system that homed him in on the antenna buoy. He had traveled only a short distance when the submersible experienced a hard thump.

"They hit us?" Pitt asked.

Giordino shook his head. "No, I think you can scratch one of our attackers off as a road kill. You almost tore his head off with the starboard wing."

"He won't be the only casualty if they blindly miss and shoot each other—"

Pitt was cut off as an explosive thud rocked the *Sea Dog II.* Two more followed in quick succession. The submersible's speed fell off by a third.

"There's that lucky shot I was talking about," said Giordino matter-of-factly. "They must have slipped one under the grate."

Pitt glanced at his instruments. "They caught the port thruster."

Giordino placed a hand on the transparent nose, which had a series of tiny cracks and stars on its outer surface. "They pitted the hell out of the windshield too."

"Where did the third missile strike?"

"Impossible to see through this stuff, but I suspect the vertical stabilizer on the starboard wing is gone."

"I figured as much," said Pitt. "She's pulling to the port."

Unknown to them, the team of ten divers was down to six. Besides the one Pitt crashed into, the others, shooting indiscriminately through the brownout, had struck and killed three of their own number. Firing and reloading their Mosby underwater rifles as fast as they could insert a new explosive charge, the divers overlooked the danger to themselves. One was brushed by the submersible as it surged past and he fired point-blank.

"Another hit," reported Giordino. He twisted his body in the confined space and gazed back along the submersible's starboard hull. "This time they caught the battery case."

"Those Mosby explosive heads must be more powerful than I was led to believe."

Giordino jerked his eyes back and to the side as another explosion burst on the frame between the starboard hull and the nose-viewing shield. Water began to spurt in where metal met glass. "Those things do more than scratch paint and make dents," said Giordino. "I can vouch for it."

"We're losing power to the thrusters," came Pitt's voice in a precision display of unruffled coolness. "That last strike must have caused a short in the system. Dump the grate. It's causing too much drag."

Giordino complied, working the manipulator controls and releasing the grate. Through the silt cloud he could see several places in the grate where the rusting iron had been gouged away by the explosive charges. He watched it fall out of sight back into the sediment on the bottom. "So long, old pal, you served your purpose."

Pitt stared briefly at a small navigation monitor. "Two hundred feet to the antenna. I make us about to pass under the liner's screws."

"No hits in the last minute," said Giordino. "We must have left our angry friends behind in the fog. I suggest you cut back on your throttles and conserve whatever battery power is left."

"Nothing left to conserve," replied Pitt, pointing to the instrument dial indicating battery power. "We're down to one knot and the needle is in the red."

Giordino smiled tightly. "It would make my day if Shang's divers got lost and gave up the chase."

"We'll know soon," said Pitt. "I'm going to angle up and out of the cloud. The instant we break into clear water, look astern and tell me what you see."

"If they're still hanging around," said Giordino, "and they spot us limping along at half a knot, they'll be all over us like maddened wasps."

Pitt said nothing as the *Sea Dog II* emerged from the swirling mud storm. He squinted his eyes, trying to pierce the velvet-green water, searching for the antenna line and Cabrillo's diver. A vague silhouette wavering seventy to eighty feet ahead and slightly to port slowly evolved into the bottom of the launch rocking in the waves rolling across the harbor.

"We're almost home!" Pitt exclaimed, his spirits lifted.

"Stubborn little devils," said Giordino morosely. "Five of them are swimming like sharks up our tail."

"Smart fellas to catch on so quick. They must have kept one man in the clear as a lookout. Soon as he caught us rising out of the gunk, he alerted his pals by radio."

An explosive charge smashed against one of the *Sea Dog II*'s tail stabilizers and blew it away. A second charge narrowly missed the hemispherical nose section. Pitt fought for control, urging, willing the submersible on a straight course toward the launch. The instant he saw one of Shang's divers out of the corner of his eyes, overtaking and coming in from the flank of the sub, he knew it was all but over. Without battery power and help from Cabrillo, there was no escape.

"So near, yet so far," Giordino mumbled, staring upward at the keel of the launch as he waited helpless but unperturbed for the inevitable final assault.

Then suddenly a series of concussions swamped and reverberated all around the submersible. Pitt and Giordino were thrown about the interior like rats inside a rolling pipe. The water around them erupted in a mass of froth and bubbles that raged crazily in all directions before heading for the surface. The divers, who were about to close in on the *Sea Dog II*, died instantly, their bodies crushed to gelatin by the sledgehammer blows. The men inside the sub were both stunned and deafened by underwater detonations. They were saved from serious injury by the pressure hull.

It took several moments for Pitt to realize that Cabrillo, forewarned of the chase in progress, waited until the submersible and its attackers were close enough to the *Oregon*'s launch to throw concussion grenades into the water. Through the ringing in his ears, Pitt heard someone calling over the radio.

"You guys all right down there?" came Cabrillo's welcome voice.

"My kidneys will never be the same," Pitt answered back, "but we're behaving ourselves."

"How about the vigilantes?"

"They look like they came out of a Jell-o mold," replied Giordino.

"If we were attacked underwater," Pitt warned Cabrillo, "it stands to reason they'll come after you on the surface."

"Funny you should mention that," said Cabrillo airily. "There just happens to be a small cruiser coming this way as we speak. Nothing we can't handle, of course. Sit tight. I'll have my diver hook you up to the towline after we greet our callers."

"Sit tight," Giordino repeated acidly. "We have no power. We're dead in the water. He must think we're in an underwater amusement park."

"He means well," Pitt sighed as the tension inside the sub eased. He lay there idly, his hands loosely holding the handgrips of his now nonfunctioning controls, staring through the transparent canopy at the bottom of the launch, wondering what cards Cabrillo was about to deal.

"They mean business," Cabrillo said to Eddie Seng, the *Oregon*'s former CIA agent who was their man in Beijing for nearly twenty years before he was forced to make a sudden departure back to the States and retirement. Cabrillo peered through a small, single-lens telescope at the rapidly approaching cabin cruiser. Its configuration reminded him of a U.S. Coast Guard rescue boat, except that this one was not in the business of saving lives. "They figured the game when they detected the submersible, but they can't be sure we're tied in until they board and investigate."

"How many do you make out?" asked Seng.

"About five, all carrying arms except the helmsman."

"Any good-sized weapons mounted on the boat?" asked Seng.

"None that I can make out. They're on a fishing expedition and not looking for trouble. They'll leave two men behind to cover us, while the other three come on board." Cabrillo turned to Seng. "Tell Pete James and Bob Meadows to slip over the unobserved side of the launch.

They're both strong swimmers. When the boat comes alongside, tell them to swim under our craft and hang in the water between the hulls. If my plan works, the two guards remaining behind on their boat will instinctively react to an unexpected situation. We've got to take all five without guns. Nothing that makes noise. There'll be enough prying eyes on the dock and ship as it is. We'll just have to tough it out the best we can without drums and bugles."

James and Meadows slipped over the side under a tarpaulin and waited in the water for the signal to swim under the launch. The rest of Cabrillo's men lounged around the decks as if dozing. One or two acted as if they were fishing off the stern.

Now Cabrillo could plainly see that Qin Shang Maritime's security men were wearing showy, dark maroon uniforms that were better suited for a Gilbert and Sullivan operetta. Four of them clutched what looked to Cabrillo like the latest-model machine pistols manufactured by the Chinese. The boat's captain wore the indecipherable, hard expression of a Chinese in authority.

"Remain where you are!" he shouted in Mandarin. "We are coming aboard!"

"What do you want?" Seng yelled back.

"Dockyard Security. We want to inspect your boat."

"You're not the Harbor Patrol," said Seng indignantly. "You have no authority over us."

"You have thirty seconds to comply or we shoot," the captain said with icy persistence.

"You'd shoot poor fishermen?" Seng said bitterly. "You're mad." He turned to the others and shrugged. "We'd better do as they say. They're just crazy enough to do what they threaten."

"All right," he said to the Qin Shang Maritime security captain, "come aboard. But don't think I'm not going to report you to the People's Republic harbor authorities."

Cabrillo leaned over the helm, shielding his face with a straw hat so the security guards couldn't see his Western eyes. He casually flipped a few coins over the side as the signal for James and Meadows to swim under the launch. Slowly, one of his hands snaked onto the throttle lever. Then, just as the captain of the security boat and his men were in the midst of leaping across the narrow gap separating the two craft, Cabrillo cracked the throttle open and just as quickly pulled it back, abruptly widening the gap between the two boats.

As if the action was a rehearsed comedy routine, the security cruiser captain and his two men fell into the water between the two boats. Acting on impulse, as Cabrillo predicted, the two men still on the security boat dropped their weapons and fell to their knees, reaching out to their superior in an attempt to haul him out of the water. Their rescue attempt failed as two pairs of arms reached up out of the water, grabbed them each by the throat and pulled them overboard with a wild splash. Then, taking one man at a time by the feet, James and Meadows hauled them under the launch to the opposite side, where they were rendered unconscious by a none too gentle rap on the back of the head before being pushed aboard and roughly dumped in a small cargo hold.

Cabrillo scanned the stern of the *United States* and the end of the dock for witnesses. He counted no more than three or four shipyard workers who had paused to watch the activity on the two boats. None appeared unduly concerned. The cabin on the security cruiser had blocked off most of the view the workers had from the dock and the liner. As far as they could see, it looked like a normal investigation by the security force. All they could see was Cabrillo's crew still dozing and fishing off the stern of the launch. The shipyard workers soon returned to their jobs, showing no signs of alarm.

James and Meadows climbed back on board and, along with Eddie Seng, quickly stripped the security commander and two of his men of their clothes. A few minutes later all three reappeared on deck wearing the security guards' uniforms.

"Not a bad fit," said Eddie, modeling his damp attire for Cabrillo, "considering that the suit is soaking wet. "

"Mine is about four sizes too small," grumbled Meadows, who was a big man.

"Join the club," said James, holding out an arm and demonstrating a sleeve that barely passed the elbow.

"You don't have to walk down the runway at a fashion show," said Cabrillo while jockeying the launch next to the security boat. "Jump over and take the helm. As soon as we've got the submersible under tow, follow along in our wake as though you were escorting us to the Hong Kong Harbor Patrol dock. Once we're out of sight of Qin Shang's shipyard, we'll cruise around until dark. Then we'll head back to the *Oregon* and scuttle the security boat."

"What about the five drenched rats in the hold?" asked Seng.

Cabrillo turned from the helm and leered. "We'll enjoy seeing the expressions on their faces when they wake up and find they've been abandoned on an island off the Philippines."

Not having enough oxygen supply to remain underwater, the *Sea Dog II* was towed on the surface with the upper hatch partially open. Pitt and Giordino remained inside while the security boat cruised alongside and screened any view of it from passing ships and shore. Thirty minutes later the *Sea Dog II* was quickly lifted back onto the deck of the *Oregon.* Cabrillo was there to help Pitt and Giordino out of the submersible. With muscles stiff and numb from the many hours of tight confinement, they were grateful for his help.

"I apologize for leaving you cooped up like that, but as you know, we ran into a little difficulty."

"And you handled it very well," Pitt complimented him.

"You boys did a pretty fair job of fighting off the bad guys yourselves."

"We'd still be sitting on the bottom if you hadn't lobbed those grenades."

"What did you find?" asked Cabrillo.

Pitt shook his head wearily. "Nothing, absolutely nothing. The hull below the waterline is clean, no modifications, no concealed hatches or pressurized doors. The bottom has been scraped and recoated with antifouling paint and looks as unaltered as the day she was launched. If Qin Shang has a shifty method of slipping illegal aliens ashore in a foreign port, it's not from below the waterline."

"So where does that leave us?"

Pitt gave Cabrillo a steady look. "We've got to get inside the ship. Can you manage it?"

"As the resident whiz, yes, I believe I can arrange a guided tour of the ship's interior. But consider this. One, maybe two hours from now is all we have before the security guards we kidnapped are discovered as missing. The chief of Qin Shang's shipyard security will put two and two together and figure the intruders came from the *Oregon.* No doubt he's already wondering how and why ten of his divers went missing. Once he alerts the Chinese Navy they'll come after us as sure as women bear babies. With a head start the *Oregon* can outdistance most any ship in the Chinese fleet. If they send planes after us before we can get out of their territorial waters, we're dead."

"You're well armed," said Giordino.

Cabrillo tightened his lips. "But not immune to warships with heavy guns and aircraft with missiles. The sooner we get the hell out of Hong Kong and onto the high seas, the safer we'll be."

"Then you're pulling up anchor and skipping town," said Pitt.

"I didn't say that." Cabrillo looked over at Seng, who had thankfully changed into dry clothes. "What say you, Eddie? Do you want to put the uniform of a Qin Shang security chief back on and parade around the shipyard like a big man on campus?"

Seng grinned. "I've always wanted to tour the inside of a big cruise ship without paying for a ticket."

"Then it's settled," said Cabrillo directly to Pitt. "Go now. See what you have to see and get back here fast, or we'll all regret not knowing our grandchildren."

18

"DON'T YOU THINK we're overdoing it a bit?" said Pitt less than an hour later.

Seng shrugged behind the wheel on the right-hand side of the driver's seat. "Who would suspect spies arriving at a security gate in a Rolls-Royce?" he asked innocently.

"Anyone who does doesn't suffer from glaucoma or cataracts," Giordino said wearily.

A collector of old classic cars, Pitt appreciated the fine workmanship of the Rolls. "Chairman of the Board Cabrillo is an amazing man."

"The best scrounger in the business," said Seng as he braked to a stop beside the main guard gate in front of the Qin Shang Maritime Limited shipyard. "He made a deal with the concierge of Hong Kong's finest five star hotel. They use the limo to pick up and deliver celebrity guests to the airport."

The late-afternoon sun was still perched above the horizon when two guards came out of the security shack to stare at the 1955 Rolls-Royce Silver Dawn with Hooper coachwork. The elegant body lines exemplified the classic "razor edge" saloon style that was popular with British coach-built cars in the 1950s. The front fenders gracefully swooped downward across the four doors to the skirted fenders at the rear, matching the sloping rear roof and trunk known as the "French curve" that was copied by Cadillac in the early eighties.

Seng flashed the identification he'd taken from the captain of the security boat. Though the two men could have passed for cousins, he did not allow the guards to study the photo on the ID card too closely. "Han Wan-Tzu, captain of the dockside security," he announced in Chinese.

One of the guards leaned in the rear window and peered at the two passengers in the rear seat who were wearing conservative blue pin-stripe business suits. His eyes slightly narrowed. "Who is with you?"

"Their names are Karl Mahler and Erich Grosse. They are respected marine engineers with the German shipbuilding firm of Voss and Heibert, here to inspect and consult on the turbine engines of the great ocean liner."

"I don't see them on the security list," said the guard, checking names on a clipboard.

"These gentlemen are here at the personal request of Qin Shang. If you have a problem with that, you can call him. Would you like his direct and personal number?"

"No, no," the guard stammered. "Since you accompany them, their entry must have been cleared."

"Contact no one," Seng ordered. "The services of these men are required immediately and their presence here is a closely guarded secret. Do you understand?"

The guard nodded fervently, backed away from the car, lifted the barrier and waved them through onto a road leading to the dock area. Seng steered the luxurious old car past several warehouses and parts depots and under tall gantries arched over the skeletons of ships under construction. He had little problem finding the *United States.* Her funnels towered over nearby terminal buildings. The Rolls came to a silent halt at one of the many gangways that led up and into the hull of the ship. The ship appeared strangely lifeless. There were no crewmen, shipyard workers or security guards anywhere to be seen. The gangways were deserted and unguarded.

"Odd," muttered Pitt. "All her lifeboats have been removed."

Giordino looked up at the wisps of light smoke trailing from the funnels. "If I didn't know better, I'd say she's getting ready to sail."

"She can't take passengers without carrying boats."

"The plot thickens," said Giordino, looking up at the silent ship.

Pitt nodded in agreement. "Nothing is what we were led to expect."

Seng came around and opened the rear door. "This is as far as I go. You guys are on your own. Good luck. I'll come back in thirty minutes."

"Thirty minutes," Giordino complained. "You've got to be kidding."

"A half an hour is not nearly enough time to inspect the interior of an ocean liner the size of a small city," protested Pitt.

"The best I can do. Chairman Cabrillo's orders. The sooner we abscond, the less chance we all have of being discovered as fakes. Besides, it'll be dark soon."

Pitt and Giordino stepped from the car and walked up a gangway leading through a pair of open doors and inside the ship. They entered what was once the purser's reception area. It seemed curiously bare of all furnishings and signs of life.

"Did I forget to mention," said Giordino, "that I can't speak with a German accent?"

Pitt looked at him. "You're Italian, aren't you?"

"My grandparents were, but what has that got to do with anything?"

"If you're confronted, talk with your hands. Nobody will know the difference."

"And you? How do you intend to pass as a kraut?"

Pitt shrugged. "I'll just say 'Ja' to anything I'm asked."

"We don't have much time. More territory can be covered if we split up."

"Agreed. I'll make a sweep of the cabin decks, you scan the engine room. While you're at it, look in the galley."

Giordino looked puzzled. "Galley?"

Pitt smiled down at the shorter Giordino. "You can always tell a home by its kitchen." Then he was walking swiftly up a circular staircase to the upper deck, which had accommodated the first-class dining room, cocktail lounges, gift shops and movie theater.

The etched-glass doors that opened to the first-class dining room had been removed. The walls, with their Spartan fifties decor and high-arched ceiling, stood guard over an empty room. It was the same everywhere he walked, his footsteps echoing on the salon deck, which had been stripped of its carpeting. The 352 seats of the theater had been torn out. The gift shops were bare of display shelving and cases. Each of the two cocktail lounges was little more than a hollow compartment. The ballroom, where the wealthy celebrities of their time danced their way across the Atlantic, was stripped down to the bare walls.

He hurried up a companionway to the crew's quarters and the wheelhouse. The bareness was repeated. The crew's cabins were devoid of any sign of furnishings or human presence. "An empty shell," Pitt muttered under his breath. "The entire ship is one big empty shell."

The wheelhouse was a different story. It was crammed from deck to ceiling with a maze of computerized electronic equipment whose multitude of colored lights and switches were mostly positioned in the ON mode. Pitt paused briefly to study the sophisticated ship's automated control system. He found it odd that the brass-spoked helm was the only piece of original equipment.

He checked his watch. Ten minutes was all he had left. Incredibly, he had seen no workers, no crewmen. It was as if the ship had become a graveyard. He dropped down the stairs to the first-class cabin deck and ran down the hallways separating the staterooms. It was the same as the salon deck. Where the passengers once slept in luxury from New York to Southampton and back, there was a ghostly emptiness. Even the doors had been taken from their hinges. What struck Pitt was the lack of trash or debris. The gutted interior appeared surprisingly immaculate, as if the entire interior had been sucked clean by a giant vacuum.

When he reached the entry door in the purser's reception area, Giordino was already waiting. "What did you find?" Pitt asked him.

"Damn little," Giordino came back. "The cabin class decks and cargo holds are barren voids. The engine room looks like the day the ship left on her maiden voyage. Beautifully maintained with steam up and ready to sail. Every other compartment was stripped clean."

"Did you get into the baggage and the forward cargo holds that were used to transport the passengers' cars?"

Giordino gave a negative shake of his head. "The cargo doors were welded shut. Same with entrances and exits to the crew's quarters on the lower deck. They must have been cleaned out as well."

"I got the same picture," said Pitt. "Did you run into any trouble?"

"That's the weird part. I didn't see a soul. If anyone was working in the engine room, they're either mute or invisible. You meet up with anyone?"

"Never encountered a body."

Suddenly the deck began to tremble beneath their feet. The ships big engines had come to life. Pitt and Giordino quickly headed down the gangway to the waiting Rolls-Royce. Eddie Seng stood beside an open door to the passengers' seat. "Enjoy your tour?" he greeted them.

"You don't know what you missed," said Giordino. "The food, the floor show, the girls."

Pitt motioned toward the dockworkers who were casting off the huge hawsers from the iron bollards on the dock. The big rail cranes lifted the gangways and laid them on the dock.

"Our timing was right on the money. She's pushing off."

"How is it possible," Giordino muttered, "with no one on board?"

"We'd better go too while the going is good," said Seng, herding them inside the car and closing the door. He hurried around the Rolls-Royce's flying-lady ornament on the radiator shell and leaped behind the wheel. This time they were passed through the security gate with the mere nod of the head. Two miles from the shipyard, his eyes darting in the rearview mirror to see if they were being followed, Seng pulled onto a dirt road and drove to an open field behind a school that was empty of children. A purple-and-silver unmarked helicopter was sitting in the middle of a playground, its rotor blades slowly turning.

"We're not returning to the *Oregon* by boat?" inquired Pitt.

"Too late," replied Seng. "Chairman Cabrillo thought it wiser to raise the anchor and put as much water as possible between the ship and Hong Kong before the fireworks start. The *Oregon* should be passing out of the West Lamma Channel into the China Sea about now. Thus, the helicopter."

"Did Cabrillo work a deal on the helicopter too?" said Giordino.

"A friend of a friend runs a charter service."

"He must not believe in advertising," observed Pitt, looking vainly for a name on the side of the tail boom.

Seng's mouth stretched in a broad smile. "His clientele prefers to travel in obscurity."

"If we're any example of his clientele, I'm not at all surprised."

A young man in a chauffeur's uniform stepped up to the Rolls and opened the door. Seng thanked him and slipped an envelope into his pocket. Then he motioned Pitt and Giordino to follow him into the aircraft. They were in the act of tightening their seat belts when the pilot lifted off the playground and leveled off at only twenty feet before ducking under a network of electrical power lines as if it was an everyday affair. He then set a course to the south and flew out across the waters of the harbor, passing over an oil tanker no more than a hundred feet above its funnel.

Pitt gazed with longing at the former crown colony in the distance. He would have given a month's pay to walk the winding streets and visit the multitude of small shops selling everything from tea to intricately carved furniture, dine on exotic Chinese cuisine in a suite at the Peninsula Hotel overlooking the lights of the harbor with an elegant and beautiful woman and a bottle of Veuve Clicquot-Ponsardin brut champagne . . .

His reverie was shattered into a kaleidoscope of pieces when Giordino suddenly exclaimed, "God, what I wouldn't give for a taco and a beer."

The sun was down and the western sky was a bluish gray when the helicopter caught up to the *Oregon* and landed on one of her cargo-hatch covers. Cabrillo was waiting for them in the galley with a glass of wine for Pitt and a bottle of beer for Giordino. "You two must have had a hard day," he said. "So our chef is fixing up something special."

Pitt removed the borrowed coat and loosened the tie. "A hard day and an extremely unproductive one."

"Discover anything of interest on board the *United States?*" asked Cabrillo.

"What we found was a ship that has been gutted from stem to stern," answered Pitt. "The entire interior is nothing but a vacuum with an operational engine room and a wheelhouse filled with automated navigation and control systems."

"The ship has already left her dock. She must be operating with a skeleton crew."

Pitt shook his head. "There is no crew. If, as you say, she's sailing out of the harbor, she's sailing without benefit of human hands. The entire ship is operated by computer and remote command."

"I can vouch for the fact there isn't a scrap of food in the galley," added Giordino. "Nor stove nor refrigerator nor even a knife and fork. Anybody taking a long voyage on that ship will surely starve."

"No ship can sail across the sea without an engine-room crew and seamen to monitor the navigation systems," Cabrillo protested.

"I've heard tell the U.S. Navy is experimenting with crewless ships," said Giordino.

"A ship void of a crew might cross the Pacific Ocean, but would she still require a captain on board to take on a pilot and handle payment with Panamanian officials for the passage through the Canal into the Caribbean."

"They could put on a temporary crew and captain before the ship reached Panama—" Pitt suddenly paused and stared at Cabrillo. "How do you know the *United States* is heading for the Panama Canal?"

"That's the latest word from my local source."

"Nice to know you have a man inside Qin Shang's organization who keeps us up-to-date on current events," said Giordino caustically. "A pity he didn't bother to tell us the ship was converted into a remote operated toy. He might have saved us a boatload of trouble."

"I have no man on the inside," explained Cabrillo. "I wish I had. The information was obtained from the Hong Kong agent for Qin Shang Maritime Limited. Commercial ship arrivals and departures are not classified secrets."

"What is the *United States*'s final destination?" asked Pitt.

"Qin Shang's port at Sungari."

Pitt stared at the wine in his glass in long silence, then said slowly, "For what purpose? Why would Qin Shang send a fully robotic ocean liner with its guts removed across an ocean to a miscarriage of a shipping port in Louisiana? What can be rolling around in his mind?"

Giordino finished off his beer and dug a tortilla chip into a bowl of salsa. "He could just as well divert the ship somewhere else."

"Possibly. But she can't hide. Not a ship her size. She'll be tracked by reconnaissance satellites."

"Do you suppose he intends to fill it with explosives and blow up something," offered Cabrillo, "like maybe the Panama Canal."

"Certainly not the Panama Canal or any other shipping facility," said Pitt. "He'd be cutting his own throat. His ships need access to ports on both oceans as much as any other shipping company. No, Qin Shang must have something else in mind, another motive, one just as menacing and just as deadly."

19

THE SHIP PLOWED easily through the swells in a slow rocking motion under a sky so brightly lit by a full moon that one could read a newspaper under its beam. The scene was deceptively peaceful. Cabrillo had not called for the ship's full cruising speed, so she loafed along at eight knots until they were far beyond the Chinese mainland. The whisper of the bows cutting the water and the aroma of fresh baked bread wafting up from the galley might have lulled the crew of any other cargo ship on the China Sea, but not the highly trained men on the *Oregon*.

Pitt and Giordino stood in the surveillance and countermeasures control room in the raised forecastle of the ship, acting strictly as observers while Cabrillo and his team of technicians focused their eyes and minds on the radar detection and identification systems.

"She's taking her sweet time," said the surveillance analyst, a woman by the name of Linda Ross who was seated in front of a computer monitor that showed the three-dimensional display of a warship. Ross was another prize from Cabrillo's headhunting expeditions for superior personnel. She had been chief fire-control officer on board a U.S. Navy Aegis guided-missile cruiser when she fell under Cabrillo's spell and an offer of incredible compensation that went far beyond any money she could make in the Navy. "With a maximum speed of thirty-four knots, she'll overhaul us within a half an hour."

"How do you read her?" asked Cabrillo.

"Configuration indicates that she's one of the Luhu Type 052 Class of big destroyers launched in the late nineties. Displaces forty-two hundred tons. Two gas turbine engines rated at fifty-five thousand horsepower. She carries two Harbine helicopters on her stern. Her complement consists of two hundred and thirty men, forty of them officers."

"Missiles?"

"Eight sea-skimming surface-to-surface missiles and a surface-to-air octuble launcher."

"If I was her captain I wouldn't be concerned with preparing a missile strike against a helpless-looking old scow like the *Oregon*. Guns?"

"Twin one-hundred-millimeter guns in a turret aft of the bow," said the analyst. "Eight thirty-seven millimeters mounted in pairs. She also carries six torpedoes in two triple tubes and twelve antisubmarine mortar launchers."

Cabrillo wiped his brow with a handkerchief. "By Chinese standards, this is an impressive warship."

"Where did she come from?" asked Pitt.

"Bad luck on our part," said Cabrillo. "She just happened to be cruising across our path when the alarm went out and harbor officials notified their navy. I timed our departure so that we sailed in the wake of an Australian freighter and a Bolivian ore carrier to confuse Chinese radar. The other two were probably stopped and searched by fast attack patrol craft before being allowed to continue to their destinations. We had the misfortune to draw a heavy destroyer."

"Qin Shang has a long arm to get that kind of cooperation from his government."

"I wish I had his influence with our Congress."

"Isn't it against international law for a nation's military to stop and search foreign ships outside their territorial waters?"

"Not since nineteen ninety-six. That was when Beijing implemented a U.N. Law of the Sea Treaty, expanding China's territorial waters from a twelve mile limit to two hundred miles."

"Which puts us well within their waters."

"About a hundred and forty miles inside," said Cabrillo.

"If you have missiles," said Pitt, "why not blast the destroyer before we come in range of its guns?"

"Although we carry a small, older version of the Harpoon surface-to-surface missile with more than enough explosive power to blast a light attack craft or a patrol boat out of the water, we'd have to get incredibly lucky with our first launch to take out a forty-two-hundred-ton destroyer bristling with enough weaponry to sink a fleet. Disadvantage belongs to us. Our first missiles might take her launchers out of action. And we can slam two Mark 46 torpedoes into her hull. But that still leaves her with enough thirty-seven and hundred-millimeter guns to blast us into the nearest scrap yard."

Pitt looked at Cabrillo steadily. "A lot of men are going to die in the next hour. Is there no way to avert the slaughter?"

"We can't fool a naval boarding party," said Cabrillo solemnly. "They'll see through our disguise two minutes after setting foot on deck. You seem to forget, as far as the Chinese are concerned, Mr. Pitt, you and I and everyone on board this ship are spies. And as such, we can all be executed in the blink of an eye. Also, once they get their hands on the *Oregon* and her technology and realize her potential, they won't hesitate to use her for intelligence operations against other nations. Once the first Chinese marine sets foot on our deck, the die is cast. We fight or die."

"Then our only option is surprise."

"The key is that we won't constitute a threat in the eyes of the captain of that Chinese destroyer," Cabrillo explained gruffly. "If you were him, standing on your bridge looking at us through night glasses, would you be trembling in your boots at what you saw? I doubt it. He might train the hundred millimeters on our bridge or one of the thirty-seven-millimeter twins at any crewman showing on deck. But once he sees his marines come on board and begin seizing the ship, he'll relax and call off the ship's alert, provided he even bothered to order one."

"You make it sound as cut and dried as a snowball fight," ventured Giordino.

Cabrillo gave Giordino a patiently worn look. "A what fight?"

"You'll have to excuse Al's regressive display of humor," said Pitt. "He gets mentally unstable when things don't go his way."

"You're just as weird," Cabrillo growled at Pitt. "Doesn't anything ever faze you two?"

"Think of it as a response to a nasty situation," Pitt said in mild protest. "You and your crew are trained and prepared for a fight. We're merely helpless bystanders."

"We'll require the services of every man and woman on board before this night is over."

Pitt studied the image on the monitor over Linda Ross's shoulder.

"If you don't mind me asking, just how do you intend to trash a heavy destroyer?"

"My plan, elementary as it is, is for the *Oregon* to come to a stop when ordered. Then comes a demand to board and inspect us. Once we sucker him into standing off within spitting distance, we act like innocent, ill-tempered seamen while they observe us at close range. Once the Chinese boarding party climbs on deck, we'll lull the captain even deeper into a state of inertia by lowering our Iranian ensign and raising the People's Republic of China flag."

"You have a Chinese flag?" asked Giordino.

"We carry flags and ensigns of every maritime country in the world," answered Cabrillo.

"After your show of surrender?" said Pitt. "Then what?"

"We hit him with everything we've got and pray that when we're through he has nothing left to throw back at us."

"It beats a long-range duel with missiles we couldn't win," said Max Hanley, who was sitting in a chair beside an electronics specialist manning a tactical data unit.

Like a football coach in the lockers before the kickoff, Cabrillo went over his game plan carefully with his players. No contingency was left undevised or unpolished, no detail overlooked, nothing left to chance. Tension was nonexistent. The men and women on board the *Oregon* prepared to go about their jobs as if it was a typical Monday morning in the big city. Their eyes were clear and fixed, they did not have the frightened look of the hunted.

When Cabrillo finished, he asked, "Any questions?" His voice was deep and low, with the tiniest trace of a Spanish accent, and although he was far too experienced and perceptive not to accept fear, no hint showed in his face and manner. Hearing no inquiries from his crew, he nodded. "Okay, that's it then. Good luck to you all. And when this little scrape is over, we'll throw the biggest party the *Oregon* has ever known."

Pitt raised a hand. "You said you needed every man. How can Al and I help?"

Cabrillo nodded. "You two gave evidence the other night that you're not afraid of a fight. Go to the ship's armory and pick up a pair of automatic weapons. You'll need more firepower than that forty-five-caliber popgun of yours. Also check out a couple of sets of body armor. After that check with the costume department for some grungy old clothes. Then join the deck crew. Your talents will come in handy in stopping the Chinese marines once they come on board. I can only spare a few men from more important duties, so you'll be slightly outnumbered. There probably won't be more than ten of them, not enough to matter since you'll have the element of surprise. If you're successful, and I'm counting on it, you can lend a hand at damage control. And you can bet there will be plenty of damage to go around."

"Will it be absolutely necessary to shoot down the boarding party without warning?" asked Linda Ross.

"Keep in mind," Cabrillo said to her bluntly, "these people do not intend to allow anybody on board this ship to reach port. Because they are no doubt aware of our involvement with the underwater search of the *United States,* there is not the slightest doubt they mean for all of us to sleep with fishes before morning."

Pitt's eyes raked Cabrillos, searching for a tinge of regret, a sign that he thought that what they were about to do was a colossal mistake, but there was none of it. "Does it bother you that we might be mistaken about their intentions and commit an act of war?"

Cabrillo pulled his pipe out of a breast pocket and scraped the bowl. Then he said, "I don't mind admitting that I'm a bit worried on that score, but we can't run from their air force, so we have no option but to bluff our way out, and if that fails, we must fight."

Like a gray ghost gliding over a black sea streaked by the full moon, the big Chinese destroyer overhauled the slow-moving *Oregon* with the malevolence of an Orca killer whale stalking a friendly manatee. But for its ungainly array of navigation, surface- and air-search detection and countermeasure systems that were perched above ugly towers, the ship might have had a sleek appearance. As it was, it looked like it was glued together by a small child who wasn't sure where all the pieces went.

Hali Kasim, the *Oregon*'s vice president in charge of communications, called through the speakerphone on the bridge wing to Cabrillo, who now stood observing the destroyer through night glasses.

"Mr. Cabrillo, they've ordered us to heave to."

"In what language?"

"English," answered Kasim.

"An amateurish attempt to get us to tip our hand. Answer them in Arabic."

There was a short pause. "They called our bluff, sir. They have someone on board who can speak Arabic."

"String them along for a little while. We don't want to appear too anxious to appease. Ask why we should obey their orders in international waters."

Cabrillo lit his pipe and waited. He looked down on the deck where Pitt, Giordino and three of his crew had assembled, all armed for a knock-down, drag-out fight.

"They're not buying it," came Hali Kasim's voice again. "They say if we don't stop immediately, they will blow us out of the water."

"Are they jamming in anticipation of us sending out a distress signal?"

"You can make book on it. Any message we transmit outside the immediate area will be received garbled."

"What are the chances of a friendly warship cruising in the neighborhood, like a nuclear submarine?"

"None," came the voice of Linda Ross in the countermeasures and surveillance room. "The only vessel within a hundred miles is a Japanese auto transporter."

"All right," Cabrillo sighed. "Signal them that we will comply and heave to. But inform them that we will protest this outrage to the World Board of Trade and International Maritime Council."

Cabrillo could then do nothing but wait and watch the Chinese destroyer emerge from the gloom. Besides his pair of unblinking eyes, the big warship was covered by the two concealed Harpoon missiles mounted in the center of the *Oregon*'s hull, the two Mark 46 torpedoes in their underwater tubes and the muzzles of twin Oerlikon thirty-millimeter guns that could spit seven hundred rounds per minute out of each barrel.

All that could be done in preparation had been done. Cabrillo was proud of his corporate team. If there was unease, none of them showed it. What was visible was a determination, a grim satisfaction, that they were going to tackle an opponent twice their size and ten times as powerful and see it through to the end. There would be no turning of the cheek after a slap. The point of no return had been passed, and it was they who were going to slap first.

The destroyer came to a stop and drifted no more than two hundred yards away from the *Oregon*. Through his night glasses, Cabrillo could read the big white numbers painted near the bow. He called down to Ross, "Can you give me an ID on Chinese destroyer number one hundred sixteen? I repeat, one sixteen."

He waited for a reply as he watched a boat being lowered from the destroyer's midships and clearing her davits. The boarding operation went smoothly, and the boat pushed off from the destroyer and headed across the gap between the two ships, coming alongside the hull of the simple-looking old freighter within twelve minutes. He noted with no little satisfaction that the turreted twin one-hundred-millimeter guns on the bow were the only weapons trained on the *Oregon*. The missile launchers appeared deserted and secured. The thirty-seven millimeter gun mounts had their barrels trained fore and aft.

"I have your ID," came back Ross. "Number one sixteen is called the *Chengdo*. She's the biggest and the best the Chinese Navy has to offer. She is captained by Commander Yu Tien. With enough time I could get you his bio."

"Thank you, Ross, don't bother. It's always nice to know the name of your enemy. Please stand by to fire all weapons."

"All weapons ready to fire when you are, Mr. Chairman," Ross answered, cool and unruffled.

The boarding ladder was thrown over the side, and the Chinese marines, led by a naval lieutenant and a captain of the marine contingent, quickly scrambled from their boat onto the deck. There was an almost festive air about the boarders, a complacency bordering more on a Boy Scout camping trip than an operation conducted by tough fighting men.

"Damn!" Cabrillo cursed. There were more than twice as many of them as he figured, and all armed to the teeth. He agonized over not being able to spare any more men for the approaching fight on the main deck. He looked down at Pete James and Bob Meadows, the ship's divers and former Navy SEALs, and at Eddie Seng, all three of them standing at the railing, their machine pistols held under their coats. Then he spotted Pitt and Giordino standing squarely in front of the Chinese officers, their hands held high in the air.

Cabrillo's immediate reaction was one of infuriation. With Pitt and Giordino surrendering without a fight, the other three crewman wouldn't stand a prayer against over twenty combat-trained marines. The Chinese would brush them aside and be all over the ship in a matter of minutes. "You yellow-bellied wimps!" he exploded, shaking his fist at Pitt and Giordino. "You dirty traitors."

"What's your count?" Pitt asked Giordino as the last of the Chinese marines came over the railing.

"Twenty-one," Giordino answered complacently. "Four to one against us. Not exactly what I'd call 'slightly outnumbered.' "

"I make the same odds."

They stood awkwardly, wearing long winter coats, their hands raised over their heads in apparent surrender. Eddie Seng, James and Meadows stared at the boarding Chinese sullenly, like crewmen irritated by any interruption of their normal shipboard routine. The effect had the results Pitt counted on. The Chinese marines, seeing the feeble reception, relaxed and held their weapons loosely, not expecting any resistance from a disreputable crew on a shabby ship.

The naval officer, arrogant and staring as if in disgust at the motley crew that greeted him, strutted up to Pitt and demanded to know in English where he could find the ship's captain.

Without the slightest indication of malice as he looked from the naval lieutenant to the marine captain, Pitt purred politely, "Which of you is Beavis and which is Butt-head?"

"What was that you said?" demanded the lieutenant. "If you don't want to get shot, lead me to your captain."

Pitt's expression took on a mask of pure fright. "Heh? You want captain? You should say so." He turned slightly and made a production of tilting his head toward Cabrillo on the bridge wing, who was cursing a blue streak in anger.

In a moment of sheer reflex, all heads and every eye followed Pitt's gesture toward the shouting man.

Then from the bridge, with sudden, startling clarity, Cabrillo understood what the two NUMA men were up to and gazed hypnotized at the bloody fight that erupted before his eyes. He watched in dazed astonishment as Pitt and Giordino suddenly sprouted another pair of hands from under their coats, each hand gripping a machine pistol, fingers locked on the triggers. They cut a deadly swath through the Chinese marines, who were caught totally off balance. The two officers were the first to fall, followed by the next six men behind them. They could never, never have been prepared for such a vicious onslaught, certainly not from men who appeared frightened and cowering. In a fraction of a minute the unexpected assault had cut the odds from four to a little more than two to one. An arrogant confrontation quickly turned into a gory rampage of chaos.

Aware in advance of the phony-arms deception, Seng, James and Meadows instantly leveled their weapons and opened fire less than a second after Pitt and Giordino. It was bedlam. Men falling, scattering, frantically trying to cut each other down. The Chinese marines were professional fighting men and a brave lot. They recovered quickly and stood their ground on the deck, now heaped with their fallen comrades, and fired back. In a lightning stroke of time every clip in every gun had gone empty in almost the same instant. Seng was hit and down on one knee. Meadows had taken a bullet in one shoulder but was swinging his gun like a club. With no time to reload, Pitt and Giordino threw their weapons at the eight Chinese marines still fighting and waded in slugging. Yet even during that raging flash when the two forces fell on each other in a cursing, punching horde of twisting bodies, Pitt was aware of Cabrillo's cry from the bridge.

"Fire, for God's sake, fire!"

A section of the *Oregon*'s hull snapped open in the blink of an eye and the two Harpoon missiles burst from their launchers in almost the same instant as the Mark 46 torpedoes shot from their tubes. A second later the twin Oerlikons opened up, aimed and fired by command from the combat control center, spitting a hail of shells against the *Chengdo*'s missile launchers, that knocked their systems out of action before they could be activated and launched against the unarmored freighter. Time froze to a stop as the *Oregon*'s first missile tore into the big destroyer's hull below the large single funnel and burst into the engine room. The second Harpoon struck the tower mounting the *Chengdo*'s communications systems, effectively silencing any transmission to her fleet command.

The slower torpedoes came next, exploding as one no more than thirty feet apart, throwing up a tremendous pair of geysers beside the *Chengdo*, rocking it nearly over on its beam ends. It settled back on an even keel for a moment, and then began to list to starboard as the water rushed in through two holes as large as barn doors.

Captain Yu Tien of the *Chengdo*, normally a cautious man, fell for the sleight of hand as he peered through binoculars at the seemingly innocent old ship, observing his marines board without the slightest show of resistance. He watched as the green, white and red Iranian national flag was lowered and replaced with the red ensign of the People's Republic of China, with its five gold stars. Then suddenly Captain Yu Tien was paralyzed in disbelieving shock. One minute his seemingly invincible ship was calmly overhauling what appeared to be a rusty old tramp steamer, the next the helpless tramp had inflicted a horrifying amount of damage to his vessel with sophisticated precision. Struck by missiles, torpedoes and a hail of small-weapons fire almost simultaneously, his ship was instantaneously mortally wounded. He thought it outrageous that such an innocent commercial vessel could possess so much firepower.

Yu Tien stiffened as he saw death and dishonor creeping out of the ventilators, hatches and companionways leading down to the bowels of his ship. What began as white puffs and orange flickers quickly became a torrent of red fire and black smoke from the shambles that had been an engine room but had now become a crematory of helpless men.

"Fire!" he cried out. "Destroy those deceiving dogs!"

"Reload!" Cabrillo yelled through the communications system. "Hurry and reload—"

His orders were interrupted by a tremendous roar followed by concussions reverberating all around him. The big guns on the destroyer's undamaged forward turret belched a torrent of fire as it sent its shells screaming toward the *Oregon.*

The first shrieked between the loading cranes and burst against the base of the aft mast, sheering it clean and sending it crashing over the cargo deck while hurling a fiery core of white-hot fragments and debris in every direction, causing several small fires but little serious damage. With a convulsive explosion, the second shell slammed into the fantail on the *Oregon*'s stern and tore it away, leaving a gaping hole above the rudderpost. The destruction was severe but not catastrophic.

Cabrillo involuntarily ducked as a storm of thirty-seven-millimeter shells from the *Chengdo*'s lighter gun mounts began raking the *Oregon* from forecastle to shattered stern. Almost immediately he was hailed by Ross, who was also manning the ship's fire-control systems.

"Sir, the Chinese light guns have knocked out the missile launcher's firing mechanisms. I hate to be the bearer of sad tidings, but our one-two punch is history."

"What about the torpedoes?"

"Three more minutes before they're ready for firing."

"Tell the men loading the tubes to do it in one!"

"Hanley!" Cabrillo shouted through the speakerphone to the engine room.

"I'm here, Juan," Hanley answered with quiet calmness.

"Any damage to your engines?"

"A few pipes have sprung leaks. Nothing we can't handle."

"Give me full speed, every knot you can coax out of your engines. We've got to get the hell out of here before the destroyer rips us apart."

"You got it."

It was then Cabrillo realized his Oerlikons had gone silent. He stood still and stared at the twin guns sitting dead in the center of a large wooden shipping crate with its four walls peeled out. The barrels pointed impotently at the destroyer as if neglected, their automated electronic controls severed by thirty-seven-millimeter shells. He knew with sick certainty that without its covering fire, their chances for survival were rapidly going down the drain. Too late did he feel the *Oregon*'s stern dip and her bow raise as Hanley's big engines kicked the ship forward. For the first time he felt fear and hopelessness as he stared down the twin throats of the destroyer's one-hundred-millimeter guns, waiting for them to destroy his dedicated crew and ship.

Having momentarily forgotten the fight raging on the deck in the midst of the destruction, he blinked and glanced downward. Bloodied bodies were heaped and scattered like a truckload of human refuse dumped in the street. He stared with bile welling up in his throat. The appalling carnage had taken less than two minutes, a gory rampage that had left no man still alive uninjured. Or so he thought.

Then, like the flicker of a camera shutter, he saw a figure sway to his feet and begin staggering drunkenly across the deck toward the Oerlikons.

Although protected by the body armor around their torsos, James and Meadows were both down with wounds in the legs. Seng had taken two bullets through his right arm. Sitting with his back against the railing, he tore off a shirtsleeve, wadded it up and calmly pressed it against his wounds to stem the flow of blood. Giordino lay beside him, barely conscious. One of the Chinese marines had clubbed him on the top of his head with the butt of an automatic rifle in almost the same instant as Giordino had savagely sunk his fist into his opponent's stomach nearly to the vertebra. Both men had toppled to the deck together, the marine withering in pain and gasping for air, Giordino knocked nearly senseless.

Pitt, seeing that his friend was not seriously wounded, threw off the coat with the mannequin arms and struggled painfully toward the silent Oerlikons, muttering to himself. "Twice. Would you believe it. Twice in the same place." He held one hand over the entry wound only an inch above the still-bandaged hole in his hip where he'd taken a bullet at Orion Lake. The other hand gripped a Chinese machine pistol he'd snatched off a dead marine.

From his vantage point on the bridge wing, Cabrillo stood rooted in awe of the unbelievable sight of Pitt contemptuously brushing aside the air filled with the maddening clatter of the *Chengdo*'s storm of thirty-seven-millimeter shells that scythed across the *Oregon*'s cargo deck. The fire splattered all around him like rain, chewing up the wooden crates stacked on the deck. He heard them shriek past his head and felt their demented breeze as they passed within inches of his face and neck. Miraculously, none struck him during his harrowing journey to the Oerlikons.

Pitt's face was not pleasant to see. To Cabrillo it seemed like a mask of unholy rage, the vivid green eyes burning with furious determination. It was a face Cabrillo would never forget. He had never seen a man with such a sardonic contempt for death.

At last, after achieving what seemed the impossible, Pitt lifted the machine pistol and shot away the shredded remnants of the cable leading to the fire-control room, giving the twin barrels freedom of movement. Then he moved behind the twin guns and took manual control, his right hand clutching the trigger grip, which had been installed but never operated. It was as if the old *Oregon* had come to life again, like a badly battered fighter who rose from the canvas at the count of nine and began punching. His aim was not what Cabrillo expected. Instead of spraying the *Chengdo*'s bridge and thirty-seven-millimeter-gun mounts, Pitt unleashed the Oerlikons' combined 1,400-round-per-minute firepower against the turret, whose hundred-millimeter guns were aimed at and about to devastate the freighter.

Though it seemed like a useless, defiant gesture—the hurricane of small shells merely splattered and ricocheted off the heavily armored turret—Cabrillo realized what Pitt was attempting to do. Stark madness, he thought, sheer, unfettered madness to attempt the impossible. Even with a solid support to rest the barrel of his rifle, only a superb marksman could have put a bullet down the barrel of any one of the turret's gun muzzles from a ship rising and falling on the ocean swells. But Cabrillo overlooked the awesome firepower of the Oerlikons at Pitt's command, not realizing the law of averages was on his side. Three shells, one directly behind the other, entered the muzzle of the center gun and swept down its barrel, impacting with the shell that had been freshly loaded in the breech and detonating its warhead at almost the same instant it was fired.

In a moment stolen from hell, the big one-hundred-millimeter shell burst, causing a sympathetic explosion inside that peeled the turret open like a tin can covering a Fourth of July cherry bomb, instantly turning it into a shambles of jagged steel. Then, as if on cue, the *Oregon*'s last two torpedoes smashed into the *Chengdo*'s hull, one of them miraculously entering through a previous hole made by one of its predecessors. The destroyer shuddered as a great thunderous roar exploded in her bowels, lifting her hull nearly clear of the water. A blossoming ball of fire bloomed around her, and then, like a great, mortally wounded animal, she shuddered and died. Three minutes later she was gone amid a great hissing sound and column of black smoke that spiraled upward and merged with the night sky, hiding the stars.

The shock wave swept against the *Oregon,* and the following tidal surge from the sinking destroyer rocked her as if she was landlocked in an earthquake. On the bridge, Cabrillo had not seen the final death throes of the *Chengdo*. Only seconds before Pitt's shrewdly directed fire turned her into a smoldering wreck, the destroyer's light guns had converged their fire on the bridge, pounding it into a shower of debris and shattered glass, as if struck by a thousand sledgehammers. Cabrillo felt the air tear apart around him in a concert of explosions. His arms flailed at the air as he was struck and hurled backward from the bridge into the wheelhouse. He fell to the deck, closed his eyes tightly and wrapped his arms around the brass binnacle and held on. A shell had smashed through his right leg below the knee, but Cabrillo experienced no pain. And then he heard a tremendous eruption and felt a rush of air, followed by an almost eerie silence.

On the deck below, Pitt released the trigger grip and retraced his steps through the wreckage littering the cargo deck. He reached Giordino and helped him upright. Giordino put his arm around Pitt's waist to steady himself, and then withdrew it, staring at a hand stained with red. "It appears to me that you've developed a leak."

Pitt gave him a tight grin. "I must remember to stick my finger in it."

Assured Pitt's wound was not serious, Giordino gestured at Seng and the others and said, "These guys are seriously injured. We must help them."

"Do what you can to make them comfortable until the ship's surgeon can tend to them," Pitt said as he looked up at the ruins of what had been the bridge, now a tangled mass of debris. "If Cabrillo is still alive I should try to help him."

The ladder to the bridge wing from the cargo deck was a tangled piece of scrap, and Pitt had to scale the shell-riddled, twisted mass of steel that had been the aft superstructure to reach the wheelhouse. The

shattered interior was deadly quiet. The only sounds came from
the racing beat of the engines and the rush of water along the hull as
the badly punished ship raced from the scene of the battle, strangely
enhancing the eerie silence. Pitt slowly entered Satan's scrap heap,
stepping over the rubble.

There were no bodies of a helmsman or first officer in the wheelhouse—all fire-combat systems had been operated from the control
center under the forecastle. Cabrillo had observed and directed the
battle alone on the seldom-used bridge. Through the edge of unconsciousness he saw a vague figure approach and push aside the splintered
remains of the door. Awkwardly, he struggled to sit up. One leg responded but the other proved powerless. His thoughts seemed lost in a
fog. He was only dimly aware of someone kneeling beside him.

"Your leg took a nasty hit," said Pitt as he tore off his shirt and
tightened it above the wound to stop the bleeding. "How's the rest of
you?"

Cabrillo held up the remains of a shattered pipe. "The bastards
ruined my best briar."

"You're lucky it wasn't your skull."

Reaching up, Cabrillo grasped Pitt's arm. "You made it through. I
thought you bought a tombstone for sure."

"Didn't someone tell you," he said, smiling, "I'm indestructible,
thanks in large part to the body armor you suggested I check out."

"The *Chengdo?*"

"Settling in the mud on the bottom of the China Sea about now."

"Survivors from the destroyer?"

"Hanley has his engines wound as tight as they'll go. I don't think
he has any inclination to slow down, turn around, go back and see."

"How badly were we mauled?" Cabrillo asked as his eyes began to
focus again.

"Other than looking like she was trampled by Godzilla, there isn't
any damage a few weeks in a shipyard won't cure."

"Casualties?"

"About five, maybe six wounded, including yourself," answered
Pitt. "No dead or injured below decks that I'm aware of."

"I want to thank you," said Cabrillo. He could feel himself getting
faint from loss of blood, and he wanted to get it in. "You fooled both
me and the Chinese boarding party with your fake-hands-in-the-air
routine. If you hadn't taken them out, the outcome might have been
different."

"I had help from four good men," Pitt said as he knotted the tourniquet on Cabrillo's leg.

"It took a ton of guts to run across that shell-swept deck to man the Oerlikons."

Having done all he could until Cabrillo could be carried to the ship's hospital, Pitt sat back and stared at the chairman of the board. "I believe they call it temporary insanity."

"Still," Cabrillo said in a weak voice, "you saved the ship and everyone on it."

Pitt looked at him tiredly and smiled. "Will the corporation vote me a bonus at the next board-of-directors meeting?"

Cabrillo started to say something, but he passed out just as Giordino, followed by two men and a woman, entered the ravaged wheelhouse. "How bad is he?" asked Giordino.

"His lower leg is hanging by a thread," said Pitt. "If the ship's surgeon is as skilled and professional as everyone else on this ship, I'm betting he can reattach it."

Giordino looked down on the blood seeping through Pitt's pants at the hip. "Did you ever consider painting a bull's-eye on your ass?"

"Why bother?" Pitt retorted with a twinkle in his eyes. "They'd never miss it anyway."

20

UNKNOWN TO MOST VISITORS of Hong Kong are the outlying islands, 235 of them. Considered the other face of the bustling business district across from Kowloon, the old fishing villages and peaceful open countryside are embellished by picturesque farms and ancient temples. Most of the islands are less accessible than Cheung Chau, Lamma and Lantau, whose populations run from 8,000 to 25,000, and many are still uninhabited.

Four miles southwest of the town of Aberdeen on Repulse Bay, Tia Nan Island rises from the waters of the East Lamma Channel across a narrow channel from the Stanley Peninsula. It is small, no more than a mile in diameter. At its peak, jutting from a promontory two hundred feet above the sea, stands a monument to wealth and power, a manifestation of supreme ego.

Originally a Taoist monastery built in 1789 and dedicated to Ho Hsie Ku, one of the immortals of Taoism, the main temple and its surrounding three smaller temples were abandoned in 1949. In 1990 it was purchased by Qin Shang, who became obsessed with creating a palatial estate that would become the envy of every affluent businessman and politician in southeast China.

Protected by a high wall and well-guarded gates, the enclosed gardens were artistically designed and planted with the world's rarest trees and flowers. Master craftsmen replicated ancient design motifs. Artisans from all over China were brought in to remodel the monastery into a glorious showplace of Chinese culture. The harmonious architecture was retained and enhanced to display Qin Shang's immense collection of art treasures. His thirty-year hunt netted art objects from China's prehistory to the end of the Ming dynasty in 1644. He pleaded, cajoled and bribed People's Republic bureaucrats into selling him priceless antiques and artwork, any cultural treasure he could get his hands on.

His agents combed the great auction houses of Europe and America, and scoured every private collection on every continent for exquisite Chinese objects. Qin Shang bought and bought with a fanaticism that stunned his few friends and business associates. After an appropriate time span, what could not be purchased was stolen and smuggled to his estate. What he couldn't display because of lack of space, or was documented as stolen, he stored in warehouses in Singapore and not Hong Kong because he didn't trust bureaucrats of the People's Republic government not to decide someday to confiscate his treasures for themselves.

Unlike so many of his superrich contemporaries, Qin Shang never settled into a "lifestyle of the rich and famous." From the time he hustled his first coin until he made his third billion, he never stopped working at extending his thriving shipping operations, nor did he cease his maniacal, unending drive to collect the cultural riches of China.

When he bought the monastery, Qin Shang's first project was to enlarge and pave the winding foot trail leading up to the temples from a small harbor so that construction materials and later his artwork and furnishings could be carried up the steep hill by vehicles. He wanted more than to rebuild and remodel the temples, much more; he wanted to create a stunning effect never achieved in a private residence or any other edifice so dedicated to the accumulation of cultural art by an individual, except perhaps the Hearst Castle at San Simeon, California.

It took five years from start to finish before the grounds inside the walls were lushly landscaped and the decor inside the temples was completed. Another six months passed before the art and furnishings were set in place. The main temple became Qin Shang's residence and entertainment complex, which included a lavishly decorated billiard room and a vast heated indoor/outdoor swimming pool that meandered in a circle for over a hundred yards. The complex also sported two tennis courts and a short nine-hole golf course. The other three smaller temples were turned into ornate guesthouses. In the end, Qin Shang called it the House of Tin Hau, the patroness and goddess of seafarers.

Qin Shang was an extremist when it came to perfection. He never ceased fine-tuning his beloved temples. The complex seemed in a constant state of activity as he redesigned and added costly details that enriched his creation. The expense was enormous, but he had more than enough money to indulge his passion. His fourteen thousand art objects were the envy of museums around the world. He was constantly besieged with offers by galleries and other collectors, but Qin Shang only bought. He never sold.

When completed, the House of Tin Hau was grand and magnificent, looming over the sea like a specter guarding Shang's secrets.

An invitation to visit the House of Tin Hau was always accepted with great pleasure among Asian and European royalty, world leaders, society people, financial tycoons and movie stars. Guests, who generally arrived at Hong Kong's international airport, were immediately flown by a huge executive helicopter to a landing pad just outside the temple complex. High state officials or those of a special elite status were carried by water on Qin Shang's incredible two-hundred-foot floating mansion, actually the size of a small cruise ship, which he designed and built in his own shipyard. Upon arrival the guests were met by a staff of servants who would direct them to luxurious vans for the short drive to their sleeping quarters, where they were assigned their own private maids and valets during their stay. They were also informed about dinner schedules and asked if they preferred any special dishes or particular wine.

Properly awed by the scope and splendor of the rebuilt temples, the guests relaxed in the gardens, lounged around the swimming pools or worked in the library, which was staffed with highly professional secretaries and specially equipped with the latest publications, computers and communications systems for businessmen and government officials so they could remain in convenient contact with their various offices.

Dinners were always formal. Guests gathered in an immense antechamber that was a lush tropical garden with waterfalls, reflection ponds filled with vividly colored carp and a light perfumed mist that filtered from jets in the ceiling. Women, to protect their hairstyles, sat under artistically dyed silk umbrellas. After cocktails, they gathered in the great hall of the temple that served as a dining room and sat in massive chairs exotically carved with dragon legs and armrests. Flatware was optional—chopsticks for Oriental guests, gold-plated utensils for those used to Western tastes. Instead of the traditional long rectangular table with the host seated at its head, Qin Shang preferred a huge circular table with the guests comfortably spaced around the outer circumference. A narrow aisle was cut in one section of the table so gorgeous, svelte Chinese women in beautiful, form-fitting silk dresses with thigh-high slits in the skirts could serve a multitude of national dishes conveniently from the inside. To Qin Shang's creative mind, this was far more practical than the time-honored method of serving over a guest's shoulder.

After everyone was seated, Qin Shang made his appearance in an elevator that came up through the floor. He usually wore the expensive silk robes of a mandarin lord and sat on an ancient throne elevated two inches above the chairs of his guests. Irrespective of status or nationality, Qin Shang acted as if every meal was a ceremonial occasion and he was the emperor.

Not surprisingly, ranking guests loved every minute of a stylishly staged dinner that was actually more of a feast. After dinner, Qin Shang led them to a lavish theater where they were shown the latest feature films flown in from around the world. They sat in soft, velvet chairs and wore earphones that translated the dialogue into their native language. By the end of the program it was close to midnight. A light buffet was laid out, and the guests mingled among themselves while Qin Shang would disappear into a private sitting room with a selected guest or two to discuss world markets or negotiate business deals.

This evening Qin Shang requested the presence of Zhu Kwan, the seventy-year-old scholar who was China's most respected historian. Kwan was a little man with a smiling face and small, heavily lidded brown eyes. He was invited to sit in a thickly cushioned wooden chair carved with lions and offered a small Ming-dynasty china cup of peach brandy.

Qin Shang smiled. "I wish to thank you for coming, Zhu Kwan."

"I am grateful for your invitation," Zhu Kwan replied graciously. "It is a great honor to be a guest in your magnificent home."

"You are our country's greatest authority on ancient Chinese history and culture. I requested your presence because I wanted to meet you and discuss a possible venture between us."

"I must assume you want me to do research."

Qin Shang nodded. "I do."

"How can I be of service?"

"Have you taken a close look at some of my treasures?"

"Yes indeed," answered Zhu Kwan. "It is a rare treat for a historian to study our country's greatest artworks firsthand. I had no idea so many pieces of our past still existed. It is thought many of them were lost. The magnificent bronze incense burners inlaid with gold and gemstones from the Chou dynasty, the bronze chariot with life-size driver and four horses from the Han dynasty—"

"Fakes, replicas!" Qin Shang snapped in a sudden display of torment. "What you consider masterworks of our ancestors were recreated from photographs of the originals."

Zhu Kwan was astonished and disillusioned at the same time. "They look so perfect, I was completely fooled."

"Not if you had time to study them under laboratory conditions."

"Your artisans are extraordinary. As skilled as those a thousand years ago. On today's market your commissioned works must be worth a fortune."

Qin Shang sat heavily in a chair opposite Zhu Kwan. "True, but reproductions are not priceless like the genuine objects. That is why I'm delighted you accepted my invitation. What I'd like you to do is compile an inventory of the art treasures that were known to exist prior to nineteen forty-eight, but have since disappeared."

Zhu Kwan eyed him steadily. "Are you prepared to pay a great sum of money for such a list?"

"I am."

"Then you shall have a complete inventory itemizing every known art treasure that has been missing in the last fifty to sixty years by the end of the week. You wish it delivered here or at your office in Hong Kong?"

Qin Shang looked at him quizzically. "That is quite an exceptional commitment. Are you sure you can fulfill my request in so short a time?"

"I have already accumulated a detailed description of the treasures over a period of thirty years," explained Zhu Kwan. "It was a labor of love for my own personal satisfaction. I only require a few days to put it in readable order. Then you may have it free of charge."

"That is most gracious of you, but I am not a man who asks for favors without compensation."

"I will accept no money, but there is one provision."

"You have but to name it."

"I humbly ask that you use your enormous resources in an attempt to locate the lost treasures so they can be returned to the people of China."

Qin Shang nodded solemnly. "I promise to use every source at my command. Though I have only spent fifteen years to your thirty on the search, I regret to say I have made little progress. The mystery is as deep as the disappearance of the bones of the Peking man."

"You have found no leads either?" inquired Zhu Kwan.

"The only key to a possible solution my own agents have turned up is a ship called the *Princess Dou Wan.*"

"I remember her well. I sailed on her with my mother and father to Singapore when I was a young boy. She was a fine ship. As I recall, she was owned by Canton Lines. I searched for clues to her disappearance myself some years ago. What is her connection with the lost art treasures?"

"Shortly after Chiang Kai-shek looted the national museums and plundered the private collections of our ancestors' art treasures, the *Princess Dou Wan* sailed for an unknown destination. She never reached it. My agents have failed to trace any eyewitnesses. It seems many of them also disappeared under mysterious circumstances. No doubt lying in unmarked graves, courtesy of Chiang Kai-shek, who wanted no secrets about the ship to leak to the Communists."

"You think Chiang Kai-shek tried to smuggle the treasures away on the *Princess Dou Wan?*"

"The coincidence and odd events lead me to believe so."

"That would answer many questions. The only records I could find on the *Princess Dou Wan* suggested that she was lost on the way to the scrappers at Singapore."

"Actually, her trail ends somewhere in the sea west of Chile, where a distress signal was reported received from a ship calling herself the *Princess Dou Wan* before she sank with all hands in a violent storm."

"You have done well, Qin Shang," said Zhu Kwan. "Perhaps now you can solve the puzzle?"

Qin Shang shook his head dejectedly. "Easier said than done. She could have gone down anywhere within a four-hundred-square-mile area. An American would compare it to looking for a needle in a field of haystacks."

"This is not a quest to cast aside as too difficult. A search must be conducted. Our most priceless national treasures must be recovered."

"I agree. That's why I built a search-and-survey ship precisely for that purpose. My salvage crew has been crisscrossing the site for six months and has seen no indication of a hulk on the seabed matching the size and description of the *Princess Dou Wan.*"

"I pray you do not give up," Zhu Kwan said solemnly. "To discover and return the artifacts for display in the People's museums and galleries would make you immortal."

"The reason I've asked you here tonight. I wish for you to put forth your greatest effort in finding a clue to the ship's final whereabouts. I will pay you well for any new information you discover."

"You are a great patriot, Qin Shang."

But any expectation Zhu Kwan had that Qin Shang was on a noble quest for the people of China was quickly dashed. Qin Shang looked at him and smiled. "I have achieved great wealth and power in my lifetime. I do not search for immortality. I do it because I cannot die unfulfilled. I shall never rest until the treasures are found and retrieved."

The veil shrouding Qin Shang's evil intentions was ripped away. The billionaire was no moralist. If he was fortunate enough to find the *Princess* and her priceless cargo, he had every intention of keeping it for himself. Every piece, no matter how large or small, would become part of a hidden collection that only Qin Shang would enjoy.

Qin Shang was lying in bed studying financial reports on his far-flung business empire when the phone beside his bed chimed softly. Unlike most unmarried men in his position, he usually slept alone. He admired women and summoned one when he occasionally felt desire, but business and finance were his passion. He thought smoking and drinking wasted time, as did seduction. He was too disciplined for a common affair. He felt only disgust for men of power and wealth who wasted themselves with dissipation and debauchery.

He picked up the phone. "Yes?"

"You asked me to call you regardless of time of night," came the voice of his secretary, Su Zhong.

"Yes, yes," he said impatiently, his train of thought interrupted. "What is the latest report on the *United States?*"

"She left her dock at seven o'clock this evening. All automated systems are functioning normally. Unless she encounters heavy storms at sea, she should make Panama in record time."

"Is a crew standing by to board and to take her through the canal?"

"Preparations have been made," answered Su Zhong. "Once the ship enters the Caribbean, the crew will reengage the automated systems for her journey to Sungari and disembark."

"Any word on the intruders at the shipyard?"

"Only that it was a very professional operation using a highly sophisticated submersible."

"And my underwater security team?"

"Their bodies have been recovered. None survived. Most appear to have died from concussion. The patrol boat was found at the Harbor Authority dock, but the crew has vanished."

"The Iranian-registered freighter that was moored nearby the shipyard—has she been boarded and investigated?"

"Her name is the *Oregon*. She departed slightly ahead of the *United States*. According to our sources at Naval Command, it was overtaken at your request by Captain Yu Tien of the cruiser *Chengdo*. His last message said that the freighter had heaved to and he was sending a boarding party of marines to inspect her."

"Nothing from Captain Yu Tien since then?" asked Qin Shang.

"Only silence."

"Perhaps his boarding party found incriminating evidence and he has seized the ship and disposed of the crew under strict secrecy."

"No doubt that is the situation," agreed Su Zhong.

"What else do you have for me?"

"Your agents are also questioning the guard at the main gate who claimed that three men, one of them wearing the uniform of a security officer, presented stolen credentials and entered the shipyard in a Rolls-Royce. It was thought they drove directly to the *United States,* but this cannot be verified since all guards were ordered off the dock just prior to her sailing."

"I want answers," Qin Shang said angrily. "I want to know what organization is responsible for spying on my operations. I want to know who is behind the intrusion and the deaths of our security people."

"Do you wish Pavel Gavrovich to head up the investigation?" asked Su Zhong.

Qin Shang thought a moment. "No, I want him to concentrate on eliminating Dirk Pitt."

"At last report, Pitt was in Manila."

"The Philippines?" Qin Shang said, his composure slipping away. "Pitt was in the Philippines, just two hours away from Hong Kong by air? Why wasn't I told of this?"

"Word only came in from Gavrovich an hour ago. He trailed Pitt to a dockyard in Manila, where he and his partner, Albert Giordino, were observed being taken aboard an Iranian cargo ship."

Qin Shang's voice became quiet and vicious. "The same Iranian freighter that stood off the *United States?*"

"A positive match has not yet been confirmed," said Su Zhong. "But every indication suggests that they are one and the same."

"Somehow, Pitt is mixed up in this affair. As the National Underwater and Marine Agency's special projects director, it stands to reason he can operate and pilot a submersible. But what possible interest can NUMA have in my operations?"

"His involvement at Orion Lake appears to be accidental," said Su Zhong. "But perhaps he is now working with another United States investigative agency such as the INS or CIA?"

"Very possible," said Qin Shang, the latent hostility reflected in his voice. "The devil has proven far more destructive than I ever conceived." A few seconds passed in silence. Then he said, "Inform Gavrovich that he is to be given full authority and an unlimited budget to uncover and stop any covert operation against Qin Shang Maritime."

"And Dirk Pitt?"

"Tell Gavrovich to postpone killing Pitt until he returns."

"To Manila?"

Qin Shang was breathing quickly, his mouth a thin white line. "No, when he returns to Washington."

"How can you be sure he'll go straight to the American capital?"

"Unlike you, Su Zhong, who can read people from photographs, I've studied the man's history from the time he was born until he devastated my operation at Orion Lake. Trust me when I say he will return to his home at the first opportunity."

Su Zhong shuddered slightly, knowing what was about to come. "Are you speaking of the aircraft hangar where he lives with his old car collection?"

"Exactly," Qin Shang hissed like a serpent. "Pitt will watch in horror as his precious automobiles go up in flames. I may even take the time and watch him burn with them."

"Your calendar does not put you in Washington next week. You're scheduled for meetings with your company directors in Hong Kong and government officials in Beijing."

"Cancel them," Shang said with an indifferent wave of one hand. "Set up meetings with my friends in Congress. Also arrange a meeting with the President. It's time I soothed any misgivings they might have about Sungari." He paused, and his lips tightened in a sinister smile. "Besides, I think it appropriate that I be on hand when Sungari becomes the premier shipping port in North America."

21

As THE SUN ROSE the *Oregon* bounded across a calm sea under clear skies at a speed of thirty knots. With her ballast tanks pumped dry to raise her hull out of the water to reduce drag, she made a strange sight with her stern dug deep in water thrashed white by wildly turning screws, her bows lifted nearly free of the troughs before bursting aside the crest of the next rolling swell. During the night the cargo deck had been cleared of debris while the ship's surgeon worked nonstop to bind wounds and operate on those who were seriously injured. The *Oregon* lost only one man, who had the misfortune of being struck in the head by fragments from the hundred-millimeter shell when it smashed into the upper section of the stern. None of the wounded were critical. The surgeon also managed to save all but six of the Chinese marines. Both officers had died and were dropped over the side with their men who had not survived.

The women who served aboard the *Oregon* quickly turned into angels of mercy, assisting the surgeon and tending to the wounded. Pitt's unlucky curse held tight. Instead of an attractive nurse to bandage his hip wound, his luck of the draw was the ship's quartermaster or mistress (her actual title in Cabrillo's corporate structure was supply and logistics coordinator), who stood six feet and weighed two hundred pounds if she weighed an ounce. Her name was Monica Crabtree, and she was as bright and resourceful as they came.

After she finished, she gave Pitt a slap on his exposed tail. "All finished. And may I say that you've got a nice set of buns."

"Why is it," Pitt said, pulling up his boxer briefs, "women always take advantage of me?"

"Because we're smart enough to see through that steely exterior and know that inside beats the heart of a sentimental slob."

Pitt looked at her. "Do you read palms, or more correctly, buns?"

"No, but I'm a whiz with tarot cards." Crabtree paused and gave him a come-hither smile. "Come over to my quarters sometime and I'll give you a reading."

Pitt would have rather rushed off for a root canal. "Sorry, knowing the future might upset my stomach."

Pitt limped through the open doorway to the chairman's cabin. No bunk for the chairman of the board. Cabrillo was lying in a king-size bed with a Balinese carved headboard on top of clean green sheets. Bottles on a stand containing clear fluids flowed into him through tubes. Considering his ordeal, he looked reasonably healthy as he sat propped up by pillows reading damage reports while smoking a pipe. Pitt was saddened to see that his leg had been amputated below the knee. The stump was elevated on a pillow, a red stain having spread through the bandage.

"Sorry about your leg," said Pitt. "I had hoped the surgeon might have somehow reattached it."

"Wishful thinking," said Cabrillo with extraordinary grit. "The bone was too shattered for the doc to glue it back on."

"I guess there is no sense in asking how you feel. Your constitution seems to be firing on all cylinders."

Cabrillo nodded at his missing limb. "Not so bad. At least it's below the knee. How do you think I'd look with a peg leg?"

Pitt looked down and shrugged. "Somehow I can't picture the chairman of the board stomping about the deck like some lecherous buccaneer."

"Why not? That's what I am."

"It's obvious," Pitt said, smiling, "that you don't need any sympathy."

"What I need is a good bottle of Beaujolais to replace my blood loss."

Pitt eased into a chair beside the bed. "I hear you've given orders to bypass the Philippines."

Cabrillo nodded. "You heard correct. All hell must have broken loose when the Chinese learned we sank one of their cruisers along with its crew. They'll use every arm-twisting scheme in the diplomatic book to have us arrested and the ship impounded the minute we sail into Manila."

"What then is our destination?"

"Guam," answered Cabrillo. "We'll be safe in American territory."

"I'm deeply sorry about the death and injuries to your crew and damage to your ship," said Pitt sincerely. "The blame belongs on my shoulders. If I hadn't insisted you delay your departure from Hong Kong to search inside the liner, the *Oregon* might have gotten clear."

"Blame?" Cabrillo said sharply. "You think you're the cause of all that's happened? Don't flatter yourself. I wasn't ordered by Dirk Pitt to covertly search the *United States*. I made a contract with the U.S. government to fulfill a mission. All decisions relating to the search were mine and mine alone."

"You and your crew paid a high price."

"Maybe so, but the corporation was damn well rewarded for it. In fact, we're already guaranteed a fat bonus."

"Still—"

"Still, hell. The mission would have been a bust if you and Giordino hadn't learned what you did. To someone, somewhere in the hallowed halls of our intelligence agencies the information will be considered vital to the nation's interest."

"All we really learned," said Pitt, "is that a former ocean liner, gutted of every nonessential piece of equipment and owned by a master criminal, is sailing without a crew to a port in the United States owned by the same master criminal."

"I'd say that's quite a store of information."

"What good is it if we've yet to fathom the motivation?"

"I have confidence you'll divine the answer when you get back to the States."

"We probably won't learn anything solid until Qin Shang tips his hand."

"The Ancient Mariner and the Flying Dutchman had ghostly crews."

"Yes, but they were works of classic fiction."

Cabrillo set his pipe in an ashtray; he was beginning to look tired. "My theory about the *United States* blowing up the Panama Canal might have held water if you'd found her bowels filled with high explosives."

"Like the old lend-lease destroyer during a commando raid at Saint-Nazaire, France, in World War II," said Pitt.

221

"The *Campbeltown*. I remember. The British packed her with several tons of explosives and rammed her into the big dry dock at the Saint-Nazaire shipyard so the Nazis couldn't use it to refit the *Tirpitz*. With the help of a timing device, she blew to pieces several hours later, destroying the dry dock and killing over a hundred Nazis who came to stare at her."

"You'd need several trainloads of explosives to blow a ship the size of the *United States* out of existence and everything within a mile around her."

"Qin Shang is capable of most anything. Could it be he got his hands on a nuclear bomb?"

"Suppose he did?" suggested Pitt. "What's his upside? Who'd waste a good nuclear bomb unless you've got a target of conspicuous magnitude? What could he gain by leveling San Francisco, New York or Boston? Why spend millions reconverting a nine-hundred-and-ninety-foot ocean liner into a bomb carrier when he could have used any one of a thousand old obsolete ships? No, Qin Shang is not a fanatical terrorist with a cause. His religion is domination and greed. Whatever his grand design, it has to be devious and brilliant, one that you and I wouldn't have thought of in a million years."

"You're right," Cabrillo sighed. "Devastating a city and killing thousands of people is a no-win situation for a man of wealth. Especially when you consider that the bomb carrier could be traced back directly to Qin Shang Maritime."

"Unless," Pitt added.

"Unless?"

Pitt gave Cabrillo a distant look. "Unless the scheme called for a minimal amount of explosives."

"For what purpose?"

"To blow the bottom out of the *United States* and scuttle her."

"Now there's a possibility." Cabrillo's eyelids were beginning to droop. "I do believe you may be onto something."

"That could explain why Al found all the doors to the crew's quarters and lower cargo holds welded shut."

"Now all you need is a crystal ball to predict where Qin Shang intends to sink her . . ." Cabrillo murmured softly. His voice trailed off as he drifted off to sleep.

Pitt started to say something, but saw that he would only be talking to himself. He quietly stepped from Cabrillo's cabin and softly closed the door.

Three days later the *Oregon* picked up the harbor pilot, passed through the shipping channel and slipped alongside the dock at Guam's commercial terminal. Except for the stump where her aft mast once stood and her pulverized stern, the ship looked little the worse for wear.

A string of ambulances was waiting on the dock to receive the wounded and transport them to the hospital at the island's naval station. The Chinese marines were the first to be taken away, followed by the ship's crew. Cabrillo was the last of the injured to leave the ship. After saying their goodbyes to the crew, Pitt and Giordino muscled aside the stretcher bearers and carried him down the gangway themselves.

"I feel like the sultan of Baghdad," said Cabrillo.

"You'll get our bill in the mail," Giordino told him.

They reached the ambulance and gently set the stretcher on the dock before loading it onto a gurney. Pitt knelt down and stared into Cabrillo's eyes. "It was an honor knowing you, Mr. Chairman."

"And a privilege to work with you, Mr. Special Projects Director. If you ever decide to leave NUMA and want a job sailing the seven seas to exotic ports, send me your résumé."

"I don't mean to criticize, but I didn't exactly find the cruise aboard your ship a benefit to my health." Pitt paused and looked up at the rusty sides of the *Oregon*. "Sounds strange to say so, but I'm going to miss the old boat."

"Likewise," Cabrillo agreed.

Pitt looked at him questioningly. "You'll mend and be back on board in no time."

Cabrillo shook his head. "Not after this trip. The *Oregon*'s next voyage is to the scrap yard."

"Why?" asked Giordino. "Are the ashtrays full?"

"She's outlived her usefulness."

"I don't understand," said Pitt. "She looks perfectly sound."

"She's been what is called in the spy trade 'compromised,'" explained Cabrillo. "The Chinese are wise to her facade. Within days every intelligence service around the world will be on the lookout for her. No, I'm afraid her days as disguised gatherer of classified information are over."

"Does that mean you're going to dissolve the corporation?"

Cabrillo sat up, his eyes gleaming. "Not in your life. Our grateful government has already offered to refit a new ship with state-of-the-art-technology, bigger, more powerful engines and a heavier weapons system. It may take a few operations to pay off the mortgage, but the stockholders and I are not about to close down operations."

Pitt shook the chairman's hand. "I wish you the best of luck. Perhaps we can do it again sometime."

Cabrillo rolled his eyes. "Oh God, I hope not."

Giordino took one of his magnificent cigars and slipped it into Cabrillo's shirt pocket. "A little something in case you tire of your smelly old pipe."

They waited as the attendants transferred Cabrillo to the gurney and lifted him inside the ambulance. Then the door was closed and the vehicle moved across the dock. They were standing there watching for a moment until it disappeared onto a street lined with palm trees when a man came up behind them.

"Mr. Pitt and Mr. Giordino?"

Pitt turned. "That's us."

A man in his middle sixties, with gray hair and beard, held up a leather-encased badge and identification. He was wearing white shorts, a flowered silk shirt and sandals. "I've been sent by my superiors to take you to the airport. An aircraft is waiting to fly you to Washington."

"Aren't you a little old to play secret agent?" said Giordino, studying the stranger's identification.

"We oldies but goodies can often pass unnoticed where you younger guys can't."

"Which way to your car?" asked Pitt conversationally.

The senior citizen pointed to a small Toyota van painted in the wild colors of a local taxi. "Your carriage awaits."

"I had no idea the CIA cut your budget so drastically," Giordino said sarcastically.

"We make do with what we've got."

They piled into the van, and twenty minutes later they were seated in a military cargo jet. As the plane rolled down the runway of Guam's Air Force base, Pitt looked out the window and saw the senior intelligence agent leaning against his van as if confirming that Pitt and Giordino had departed the island. In another minute they were flying above the often overlooked island paradise of the Pacific with its volcanic mountains, lush jungle waterfalls and miles of white-sand beaches graced with swaying coco palms. The Japanese swarmed into the hotels and onto the beaches of Guam, but not many Americans. He continued staring down as the plane passed over the turquoise waters inside the reef surrounding the island and headed out to sea.

As Giordino dozed off, Pitt turned his thoughts to the *United States,* sailing somewhere on the ocean below him. Something terrible was in the works, a terrible threat that only one man on earth could prevent. But Pitt knew with crystallized certainty that nothing, except perhaps an untimely death, would deflect Qin Shang from his purpose.

The world may be a place that is scarce of honest politicians, white buffalo, unpolluted rivers, saints and miracles, but there is no shortage of depraved villains. Some, like serial killers, may slay twenty or a hundred innocent victims. But given financial resources they might kill many more. Those like Qin Shang who possessed enormous affluence could hold themselves above the law and hire homicidal cretins to do their dirty work for them. The evil billionaire was not a general who felt remorse over losing a thousand men in battle to achieve an objective. Qin Shang was a cold-blooded sociopathic murderer who could drink a glass of champagne and eat a hearty dinner after condemning hundreds of illegal immigrants, many of them women and children, to a horrible death in the frigid waters of Orion Lake.

Pitt was committed to stopping Qin Shang whatever the consequences, whatever the cost, even killing him if the occasion presented itself. He was drawn in too deeply to struggle back over the edge. He fantasized what it would be like if they ever met. What would the circumstances be? What would he say to a mass slaughterer?

For a long time, Pitt sat there staring up at the cabin ceiling of the aircraft. There was no sense in anything. Whatever Qin Shang's plan had to be, if nothing else it was mad. And now Pitt's own mind was running amok. There is nothing to do, he thought finally, but to sleep it off and hope to see things with a sane eye when we reach Washington.

PART III

CANAL TO NOWHERE

22

April 23, 2000
Atchafalaya River, Louisiana

OF THE MAJOR RIVERS of the world, the Nile casts a romantic spell
from an ancient past, the Amazon conjures up images of adventure and
danger, while the Yangtze entwines the soul with the mysteries of the
Orient. Images of pharaohs lounging on royal barges rowed by a hundred men past the pyramids come to mind . . . the Spanish conquista-
dors struggling and dying in a green hell . . . Chinese junks and
sampans crowding water turned yellow-brown with flowing silt. But it
is the Mississippi that truly captures the imagination.

Thanks to the stories of Mark Twain of big side-paddle riverboats
coming around the bend with whistles blowing as they passed Huck
Finn and Tom Sawyer on a raft, and of battles up and down the river
by Union and Confederate ironclads during the Civil War, the Mississippi's past seems so near that one has but to pierce a thin veil to
experience it.

"The Father of Rivers," as the Indians called it, the Mississippi is
the only river in North America that ranks in the top ten of the world.
Third in length, third in drainage, fifth in volume, it stretches from the
headwaters in Montana of its longest tributary, the Missouri, 3,484
miles south to the Gulf of Mexico.

Almost as fluid as mercury, always searching for the path of least
resistance, the Mississippi has changed course many times throughout
the last five thousand years, especially after the seas finally reached
their present levels at the end of the last ice age. Between 1900 B.C. and
700 B.C. it flowed almost forty miles west of its present course. Rest-

lessly, the river shifted back and forth across the state of Louisiana, carving a channel before migrating and carving another. Almost half of Louisiana was formed by the Mississippi depositing tremendous amounts of silt and clay carried from as far north as Minnesota and Montana.

"The water looks quiet today," said a man in an elevated seat who gazed from the pilothouse of the *George B. Larson,* an Army Corps of Engineers survey boat.

Standing at the control console, the boat's captain, Lucas Giraud, merely nodded as he piloted the craft past the cattle grazing on the levees of the Mississippi River in southern Louisiana.

This was Cajun country, the last outpost of French Acadian culture. Pickup trucks parked under spreading trees next to tar-papered cabins raised on pylons. Nearby, small Baptist churches rose from the damp countryside, their paint-peeled wooden sides overlooking cemeteries with weathered tombs rising above the ground. Soybeans and corn rose from the rich soil between man-made ponds for the farming of catfish. Little hardware and feed stores stood across narrow roads from auto garages surrounded by rusting wrecked cars half-buried in green under-brush that sprouted through their broken windows.

Major General Frank Montaigne studied the passing scene as the big survey boat cruised down the river that was textured by a light morning mist. He was late fiftyish and wore a light gray suit and a striped blue shirt with a burgundy bow tie. A vest, embellished with a large gold watch chain spanning the pockets, was displayed through the open coat. An expensive Panama hat was perched at a jaunty angle over steel-gray hair that flowed back from the temples. The eyebrows had managed to remain black and arched over limpid eyes that were gray-blue. There was a polished look about him, burnished with a hardness that you knew was there but couldn't see. His trademark, a cane carved from a willow tree with a leaping frog for its handle, lay across his lap.

Montaigne was no stranger to the capricious nature of the Mississippi River. To him it was a monster that was condemned to move through a narrow passage for eternity. Mostly it slept, but occasionally it went into a rampage, overflowing its banks and causing disastrous floods. It was the job of General Montaigne and of the Army Corps of Engineers, which he represented, to control the monster and protect the millions of people who lived along its banks and levees.

As president of the Mississippi River Commission, Montaigne was required to inspect the flood-control projects once a year on an Army

Corps towboat that was fitted out almost as ostentatiously as a cruise ship. On those trips he was accompanied by a bevy of high-ranking officers of the Army as well as his civilian staff. Stopping at the many towns and ports along the river, he held conferences with the residents to hear their input and complaints about how the river was affecting their lives.

Montaigne disliked wining and dining local officials while surrounded by the pomp of his office. He much preferred unannounced inspection tours conducted from a workaday survey boat with no one but himself, Captain Giraud and his crew on board. Without distraction, he could study firsthand the workings of the revetments laid along the levees to reduce erosion, the condition of the levees themselves, the rock jetties and navigation locks leading to and from the river.

Why is the Army Corps of Engineers in command of the never-ending war against flooding? They launched their attack to tame the Mississippi River in the early eighteen hundreds. After building fortifications during the War of 1812 along the river to keep out British forces, it seemed expedient for them to turn their experience to civil works, and the Military Academy at West Point had the only school of engineering in the country. Today the organization almost seems like an anachronism when one considers that civilians who work for the Corps outnumber Army officers by a hundred and forty to one.

Frank (his birth certificate read François) Montaigne was born a Cajun in Plaquemines Parish below New Orleans and spent his boyhood in the French Acadian world of southern Louisiana. His father was a fisherman, or to be more exact a crawfisherman, who built a floating house in the swamp with his own hands, and made a great sum of money over the years, hauling his catch and selling directly to the restaurants of New Orleans. And, like most Cajuns, he never spent his profits and died a rich man.

Montaigne spoke French before he learned English, and his classmates at the academy called him Potpourri because he often mixed the two languages together when speaking. After a distinguished career as a combat engineer in Vietnam and the Gulf War, Montaigne was rapidly promoted after receiving several academic degrees in his spare time, including a Ph.D. in hydrology. At the age of fifty-five he was appointed commander of the entire Mississippi Valley from the Gulf up to the Missouri River where it joins the Mississippi near St. Louis. It was a job he was born for. Montaigne loved the river almost as much as he loved his wife, who was also a Cajun, the sister of his best boyhood friend, and his three daughters. But mixed with his love for the flowing waters was a fear that someday Mother Nature would turn violent and wipe out his efforts, sending the Mississippi raging over the levees and flooding millions of acres while cutting a new channel to the Gulf.

Earlier in the morning just before dawn, the *Larson,* named after an Army Corps engineer long deceased, had eased into the navigation locks that were constructed by the Army Corps for flood control and to stop the Atchafalaya from capturing the Mississippi. Giant control structures that are basically dams with spillways were built fifty miles above Baton Rouge at an old bend in the river where a hundred and seventy years before the Red River once entered into the Mississippi and the Atchafalaya flowed out. Then in 1831 a steamboat entrepreneur, Captain Henry Shreve, dug a channel across the neck of the bend. Now the Red River bypassed the Mississippi and flowed through remains of the bend that became known as the Old River. Almost as if it was a siren enticing an unwary sailor, the Atchafalaya, with only 142 miles to the Gulf versus the Mississippi's 315, beckons the main river into its waiting arms.

Montaigne had stepped out on deck as the gates swung and closed off the water of the Mississippi and watched as the walls of the lock seemed to rise toward the sky while the survey boat descended to the Atchafalaya. He waved to the lockmaster, who waved back. The waters of the Atchafalaya run fifteen feet lower than the Mississippi's, but it only took ten minutes before the west gates opened and the *Larson* moved out into the channel that led south to Morgan City and the Gulf beyond.

"What time do you estimate our rendezvous with the NUMA research ship below Sungari?" he asked the *Larson*'s captain.

"Around three o'clock, give or take," answered Giraud without indecision.

Montaigne nodded at a big towboat pushing a string of barges downriver. "Looks like a cargo of lumber," he said to Giraud.

"Must be heading for that new industrial development near Melville." Giraud looked like one of the Three Musketeers with his hawklike French features and flowing black mustache waxed and twisted at the ends. Like Montaigne, Giraud had grown up in the Cajun land, only he had never left it. A big man with a belly seldom empty of Dixie beer, he possessed a sardonic humor that was known up and down the river.

Montaigne watched as a small speedboat filled with four teenagers darted recklessly around the survey boat and cut in front of the barges, followed by four of their friends astride a pair of watercraft.

"Stupid kids," muttered Giraud. "If any of them lost their engines in front of the barges, there is no way the towboat could stop the momentum before running them over."

"I used to do the same thing with my father's eighteen foot aluminum fishing skiff with a little twenty-five horsepower outboard motor, and I'm still alive."

"Forgive me for saying so, General, but you were even dumber than them."

Montaigne knew that Giraud meant no disrespect. He was well aware the pilot had witnessed his share of accidents during the long years he'd piloted ships and towboats up and down the Mississippi river system. Ships running aground, oil spills, collisions, fires, he'd seen them all, and as with most old river pilots, he was a cautious man. No one was more aware that the Mississippi was an unforgiving river.

"Tell me, Lucas," said Montaigne, "do you think the Mississippi will flow into the Atchafalaya one day?"

"One great flood is all it will take for the river to tear away the levees and sweep into the Atchafalaya," replied Giraud stoically. "One year, ten years, maybe twenty, but sooner or later the river will run no more past New Orleans. It's only a matter of time."

"The Army Corps has fought a good battle to keep it in control."

"Man can't tell nature what to do for very long. I only hope I'm around to see it."

"The sight won't be pretty," said Montaigne. "The effects of the disaster will be appalling. Death, major flooding, mass destruction. Why would you want to be a witness to such devastation?"

Giraud turned from the wheel and stared at the general, a dreamlike look in his eyes. "The channel already carries the flow of the Red and Atchafalaya rivers. Just think what a mighty river will flow through southern Louisiana when the entire Mississippi breaks loose and adds its discharge to the other two. It will be a sight to behold."

"Yes," said Montaigne slowly, "a sight to behold, but one I hope I never live to see."

23

AT FIVE MINUTES before three o'clock in the afternoon, Lucas Giraud slipped the throttles to the big Caterpillar diesels to quarter speed as the *Larson* cruised past Morgan City at the lower end of the Atchafalaya River. After crossing the Intracoastal Waterway and dropping below Qin Shang Maritime's port of Sungari, the *Larson* entered the glassy-smooth waters of Sweet Bay Lake six miles from the Gulf of Mexico. He swung the boat toward a turquoise-colored research ship with NUMA painted in large block letters on the hull amidships. She has a no-nonsense, businesslike air about her, Giraud noted. As the *Larson* drew closer he could read the name on the bow, *Marine Denizen*. She looked like a ship that had seen her share of service. He judged her age at twenty-five years or more, old for a working ship.

The wind blew out of the southeast at fifteen miles an hour and the water had a light chop. Giraud ordered a crewman to drop the fenders over the side. He then eased the *Larson* against the *Marine Denizen* with a gentle bump, and held the survey boat against the research vessel just long enough for his passenger to step across a ramp that had been extended for his arrival.

On board the *Denizen*, Rudi Gunn raised his eyeglasses to the light streaming in through a porthole of the NUMA marine-survey ship, squinted his eyes and checked for smudges on the lenses. Seeing none, he replaced the rims and adjusted the earpieces. Then he looked down and studied the three-dimensional diorama of the Sungari shipping port that was beamed down on a horizontal surface by an overhead holographic projector. The image was processed from forty or more aerial photographs taken at low altitudes by a NUMA helicopter.

Constructed on newly made land in a swampland along both banks of the Atchafalaya River before it emptied into the Gulf of Mexico, the port was hailed as the most modern and efficient shipping terminus in the world. Covering two thousand acres and stretching over a mile on both sides of the Atchafalaya River, it was dredged to a navigational depth of thirty-two feet. The Port of Sungari consisted of over one million square feet of warehouse space, two grain elevators with loading slips, a six-hundred-thousand-barrel-capacity liquid bulk terminal and three general-cargo handling terminals that could load and unload twenty container ships at one time. The steel-faced docks on opposite sides of the river channel backed by landfill provided twelve thousand feet of deep-water berthage for all ships except heavily laden supertankers.

What made Sungari different from most port facilities was its architecture. No gray concrete buildings shaped in austere rectangles. The warehouses and office structures were constructed in the shape of pyramids, all covered with a gold galvanized material that blazed like fire when struck by the sun. The effect was electrifying, especially to planes flying overhead, and its glow could be seen from ships forty miles out in the Gulf.

A light rap came on the door behind Gunn. He stepped across the ship's conference room, used for meetings between the ship's scientists and technicians, and opened the door. General Frank Montaigne stood in the passageway outside, looking dapper in a gray suit with vest and leaning on his cane.

"Thank you for coming, General. I'm Rudi Gunn."

"Commander Gunn," said General Montaigne affably, "I've looked forward to meeting you. After my briefing by officials from the White House and INS, I'm delighted to find that I'm not the only one who believes Qin Shang to be a deviously clever menace."

"We seem to be members of a growing club."

Gunn showed the general to a chair beside the three-dimensional image of Sungari. Montaigne leaned toward the projected diorama, his hand and chin resting on the leaping frog atop his cane. "I see NUMA also uses holographic imagery to demonstrate their marine projects."

"I've heard the Army Corp of Engineers takes advantage of the same technology."

"It comes in handy to convince Congress to increase our funding.

The only difference is, our unit is designed to show fluid motion. When we brief the various committees in Washington, we like to impress them with a demonstration on the horrors of a disastrous flood."

"What's your opinion of Sungari?" asked Gunn.

Montaigne seemed lost in the image. "It's as if an alien culture came down from space and built a city in the middle of the Gobi Desert. It's all so pointless and unnecessary. I'm reminded of the old saying, All dressed up and no place to go."

"You're not impressed with it."

"As a shipping terminus, I find it about as useful as a second belly button on my forehead."

"Hard to believe Qin Shang got the necessary approval and permits for such a vast project with no profitable future," said Gunn.

"He submitted a comprehensive development plan that was approved by the Louisiana state legislature. Naturally, politicians will jump on any industrial development they think will increase employment and revenue that won't tap the taxpayers' pockets. With no obvious downside, who can blame them? The Army Corps also approved their permits for dredging because we saw no interruption in the natural flow of the Atchafalaya River. The environmentalists raised hell, of course, because of the virtual destruction of a vast area of wetlands. But all their objections and those of my own engineers concerning the future alteration of the Atchafalaya Delta were quickly brushed aside when Qin Shang's lobbyists sweet-talked Congress into fully authorizing the project. I've yet to meet a financial analyst or port-district commissioner who did not think Sungari was a failure before its plans came out of the computers."

"And yet, all permits were approved," said Gunn.

"Blessings were given by high officials in Washington, including President Wallace, who greased the path," conceded Montaigne. "Much of the acceptance was based around the new trade deals with China. Congress didn't want to upset the apple cart when Chinese trade reps threw Sungari into their proposals. And to be sure, there must have been heavy payoffs under the table by Qin Shang Maritime up and down the line."

Gunn moved around the three-dimensional projection and stared through a porthole at the actual complex two miles upriver from the *Marine Denizen*. The golden buildings were turning orange with the setting sun. But for two ships, the long docks were empty. "We're not dealing with a man who bets on a horse with long odds. There has to be a method to the madness for Shang to spend over a billion dollars to develop a terminus for overseas trade in such an impractical location."

"I wish someone would enlighten me as to what it is," Montaigne said cynically, "because I haven't a clue."

"And yet, Sungari does have access to State Highway 90 and the Southern Pacific rail line," Gunn pointed out.

"Wrong," snorted Montaigne. "Presently, there is no access. Qin Shang has refused to build a link to the main rail line and a paved thoroughfare to the highway. He says he's done enough. He insists that it is up to the state and federal governments to build access to his transportation network. But because of voter unrest and new budget restrictions, state bureaucrats are balking."

Gunn turned and looked at Montaigne, puzzled. "No means of ground transportation in and out of Sungari? That's insane."

Montaigne nodded at the holographic image. "Take a good look at your fancy display. Do you see an arterial roadway traveling north to Highway 90 or rail spurs connecting with the Southern Pacific tracks? The Intracoastal Waterway runs past a few miles north, but it's used mostly by pleasure craft and limited barge traffic."

Gunn studied the image closely and saw that the only access for freight up the Atchafalaya River to the north was by barge traffic. The entire port was surrounded by marshland. "This is crazy. How did he build and develop such a vast complex without construction materials trucked or shipped in by rail?"

"No materials came out of the United States. Virtually everything you see was shipped in from overseas on Qin Shang Maritime ships. The building materials, the construction equipment, all came from China, as did the engineers, supervisors and workmen. No American, Japanese or European had a hand in Sungari's development. The only material that didn't arrive from China was the landfill that came from an excavation sixty miles up the Atchafalaya."

"Couldn't he find landfill closer to the development?" asked Gunn.

"A mystery," replied Montaigne. "Qin Shang's builders barged millions of cubic yards of fill downriver by excavating a canal through the marshlands that goes nowhere."

Gunn sighed in exasperation. "How in the world does he expect to ever show a profit?"

"Until now, the cargoes of the few Chinese merchant ships that dock at Sungari have been carried inland by barge and towboat," explained Montaigne. "Even if he gave in and built a transportation system in and out of his dream port, who but the Chinese would come? Terminal facilities on the Mississippi have far superior access to major highways, rail links and an international airport. No shipping-company CEO with half a brain would divert vessels of his merchant fleet from New Orleans to Sungari."

"Could he barge cargo up and down the Atchafalaya and Red rivers to a transportation center farther north?"

"A losing proposition," Montaigne replied. "The Atchafalaya may be an inland navigable waterway, but it doesn't contain half the flow of the Mississippi. It's considered a shallow-draft artery and barge traffic is limited, unlike the Mississippi, which can accommodate great towboats with ten thousand horsepower pushing as many as fifty barges tied together in rows like a marching column stretching nearly a third of a mile. The Atchafalaya is a treacherous river. It may look calm and peaceful, but that is a mask that hides its true, ugly face. It waits like a gator with only its eyes and nostrils showing, ready to strike the unwary river pilot or pleasure-boat operator out for a weekend cruise. If Qin Shang thought he could build a commercial waterborne empire to support freight traffic up and down the Atchafalaya or across the Intracoastal Waterway, he was sadly mistaken. Neither channel has been improved to handle heavy barge traffic."

"The White House and Immigration Service suspect the chief purpose behind the building of Sungari is for a dispersal point for smuggling illegal immigrants, drugs and illegal weapons."

Montaigne shrugged. "So I was told. But why sink tons of money into a facility capable of handling millions of tons of ship cargoes and then use it only to smuggle illicit contraband? I fail to see the logic."

"There is big money in alien smuggling alone," said Gunn. "One thousand illegals brought in on one boat and ferried across the country at thirty thousand dollars a head, and you're talking real money."

"All right, if Sungari *is* a front for immigrant smuggling," said Montaigne, "I'd be interested in knowing how Qin Shang is going to get the immigrants and goods from point A to point B without some sort of underground transportation system. U.S. Customs and Immigration comb every ship docking at Sungari. All barge traffic inland is carefully monitored. It would be impossible for undocumented aliens to slip through their fingers."

"The reason NUMA is here." Gunn picked up a metal pointer and tapped the point inside the image of the Atchafalaya River that divided Sungari East from Sungari West. "Because there is no way for him to send human and drug cargo over land and water, he must be shipping them under the surface."

Montaigne sat erect and stared at Gunn through skeptical eyes. "By submarine?"

"Submarines capable of carrying large numbers of passengers and cargo are a possibility we can't ignore."

"Forgive me for saying so, but there is no way in hell you can get a submarine up the Atchafalaya River. The shoals and bends are a nightmare for experienced river pilots. Navigating below the surface upriver against the current is unthinkable."

"Then perhaps Shang's engineers have carved out hidden underwater-passage systems that we're not aware of."

Montaigne gave a negative shake of his head. "No way they could have excavated a tunnel network without discovery. Government building experts scrutinized every square inch of the site during construction to make sure the approved plans were followed to the letter. Qin Shang's contractors were incredibly cooperative and either complied with our criticisms or took as gospel any and all suggested changes without argument. In the end it was almost as if we had all been in on the design stage. If Qin Shang dug a tunnel under the noses of men and women whom I consider the best engineering and structural inspectors in the South, he could get himself elected Pope."

Gunn held up a pitcher and a glass. "Can I interest you in a glass of iced tea?"

"You wouldn't happen to have a bottle of bourbon lying about?"

Gunn smiled. "Admiral Sandecker follows Navy tradition and has a rule against alcohol on board NUMA research vessels. However, in honor of your presence, I do believe a bottle of Jack Daniels' Black Label whiskey somehow slipped on board."

"You, sir, are a saint," said Montaigne, his eyes gleaming in anticipation.

Gunn poured a glass. "Ice?"

"Never!" Montaigne held up the glass and studied the amber contents, then sniffed the aroma as if pondering a fine wine before sipping it. "Because nothing suspicious was observed above ground, I was told at my briefing that you're going to try your luck with an underwater search."

Gunn nodded. "I'm sending in an autonomous underwater vehicle for an exploratory search first thing in the morning. If anything questionable is recorded by its cameras, divers will investigate."

"The water is murky and running with silt, so I doubt if you'll see much."

"With high resolution and digital enhancement, our cameras can distinguish objects in murky water up to twenty feet. My only concern is Qin Shang's underwater security."

Montaigne laughed. "If it's anything like the security around the port," Montaigne said with a chuckle, "you can forget it. A ten-foot-high fence runs around the perimeter, but there is only one gate that leads to nowhere in the swamp with no guard. Any passing vessel, especially fishing boats out of Morgan City, are welcome to tie up at a dock. And there is an excellent helicopter landing pad with a small terminal building on the north end. I never heard of Shang's security turning away anybody who dropped in for a guided tour. They go out of their way to make the place accessible."

"Definitely not your ordinary Qin Shang operation."

"So I've been told."

"As a port," Gunn continued, "Sungari must have offices for customs and immigration agents?"

Montaigne laughed. "Like the Maytag man, they're the loneliest men in town."

"Dammit!" Gunn abruptly burst. "This has to be a gigantic scam. Qin Shang built Sungari to conduct criminal activities. I'd stake my government pension on it."

"If it was me, and my aim was to conduct an illegal operation, I'd have never designed the port to stand out like a Las Vegas casino."

"Nor I," Gunn conceded.

"There was, come to think of it," Montaigne said thoughtfully, "an odd bit of construction that puzzled inspecting engineers."

"What was that?"

"Shang's contractor built the upper level of their docks a good thirty feet higher than necessary from the water's surface. Instead of walking down a gangway to the dock from the deck of a ship, you actually have to negotiate a slight incline."

"Could it be insurance against hurricane tides or a hundred-year flood down the river?"

"Yes, but they magnified the threat," explained Montaigne. "Oh sure, there have been flood stages on the Mississippi that have reached huge heights, but not on the Atchafalaya. Ground level at Sungari was raised to a level far beyond anything that nature could throw at it."

"Qin Shang wouldn't be where he is by gambling with the elements."

"I suppose you're right." Montaigne finished off the Jack Daniels. He waved a hand at the image of Sungari. "So there it sits, a grand edifice to one man's ego. Look across the water. Two ships in a port built to take a hundred. Is that any way to run a profitable business?"

"No way that I'm aware of," said Gunn.

The general rose to his feet. "I should be on my way. It'll be dark soon. I think I'll instruct my pilot to go upriver to Morgan City and tie up there for the night before heading back to New Orleans."

"Thank you, General," Gunn said sincerely. "I appreciate you taking the time to see me. Please don't be a stranger."

"Not at all," Montaigne replied jovially. "Now that I know where to go for a free shot of good whiskey, rest assured, you'll see me again. And good luck on your investigation. Anytime you require the services of the Corps, you have but to call me."

"Thank you, I will."

Long after General Montaigne returned to his survey boat, Gunn sat staring at the holographic image of Sungari, his mind seeking answers that never revealed themselves.

"If you're worried about their security hassling us," said Frank Stewart, captain of the *Marine Denizen*, "we can conduct our survey from the middle of the river. They may own the buildings and land on both sides of the Atchafalaya, but free passage between the Gulf and Morgan City is guaranteed under maritime law."

Stewart, with brown hair cut short and slickly combed with a precision part on the right side, was a mariner from the old school. He still shot the sun with his sextant and figured latitude and longitude the old-fashioned way when a quick scan of his geophysical positioning system could tell him within a yard of where he was standing. Slim and tall with deep-set blue eyes, he was a man without a wife whose mistress was the sea.

Gunn stood beside the helm, staring through the wheelhouse windows at the deserted port. "We'd look as obvious as a wart on a movie star's nose if we anchored in the river between their docks and warehouses. General Montaigne said that security around Sungari was no heavier than any other port facility on the East and West coasts. If he's right, I see no reason to play cagey. Let's simply call the port master and request dock space to make repairs, and work in their backyard."

Stewart nodded and hailed the port master over a satellite phone, which had all but replaced ship-to-shore radio. "This is NUMA research ship *Marine Denizen*. We request dock space to make repairs to our rudder."

The port master was most congenial. He gave his name as Henry Pang and readily gave permission. "Sure, maintain your position and I'll send a boat to lead you to dock seventeen, where you can tie up. If there's one thing we've got, it's vacant moorings."

"Thank you, Mr. Pang," acknowledged Stewart.

"You guys looking for weird fish?" asked Pang.

"No, we're studying Gulf currents. We bumped over an unmarked shoal off the coast and damaged our rudder. It responds but not to its full arc."

"Enjoy your stay," said Pang politely. "If you need a marine mechanic or parts, please let me know."

"Thank you," said Stewart. "Standing by for your guide boat."

"General Montaigne was right," said Gunn. "So much for tight security."

A rainsquall rolled in and out during the night, leaving the decks of the *Marine Denizen* gleaming under the rising sun. Stewart had two of his crew lowered on a small platform over the rudder to act as though they were making repairs. The performance hardly seemed necessary. The docks and cranes were as dead as a football stadium in the middle of the week. Both of the Chinese cargo ships Gunn had observed the evening before had slipped out during the night. The *Marine Denizen* had the entire port to herself.

Inside the center section of the *Denizen*'s hull was a cavernous compartment called the moon pool. Two sliding divisions parted like horizontal elevator doors, allowing water to flow inside the moon pool until it leveled out after rising six feet. This was the heart of the research vessel, where divers could freely enter the water without being knocked about by waves, where submersibles could be lowered to explore the depths, and where scientific equipment that monitored and captured sea life could be raised for study in the ship's labs.

Lulled by the cemetery-like atmosphere of Sungari, the crew and scientists ate a leisurely breakfast before gathering around the work platforms in the moon pool. A Benthos autonomous underwater vehicle hung in a cradle over the water. This vehicle was three times the size of the compact AUV that Pitt used at Orion Lake. A rugged, streamlined unit with two horizontal thrusters, it could move at speeds up to five knots. The imagery equipment consisted of a Benthos video camera with low-light sensitivity and high resolution. The AUV also featured a digital still camera and a ground-penetrating radar unit that could detect a void through the steel casings, indicating a passage. A diver, wearing a wet suit purely as protection against jellyfish, lazily floated on his back while he waited for the AUV to be lowered.

Stewart looked through a doorway at Gunn, who was sitting in front of a computer monitor that was mounted beneath a large video screen. "Ready when you are, Rudi."

"Drop her in," said Gunn with the wave of a hand.

The winch attached to the cradle hummed and the AUV slowly settled into the perpetual gloom of the river. The diver uncoupled the cradle, swam to a ladder and climbed onto the work platform.

Stewart entered the small compartment that was filled from deck to roof with electronic equipment. He sat down next to Gunn, who was operating the AUV from a computer console while staring into the video monitor. All that was revealed was a long gray wall of steel casing that trailed off into the gloom. "Frankly, this seems like much ado about nothing."

"You'll get no argument from me," said Gunn. "The order to investigate Sungari from under the surface came direct from the White House."

"Do they really think Qin Shang would conduct his smuggling operations through underwater passageways that connect to the hulls of his ships?"

"Some hotshot in Washington must think so. That's why we're here."

"Like me to send for some coffee from the galley?" asked Stewart.

"I could use a cup," said Gunn without turning from the monitor.

The cook's galley assistant soon brought a tray of cups along with a filled coffeepot. Three hours later the cups and pot were as empty as the inspection project. Nothing showed on the monitor except a seemingly unending wall of steel casings that were driven deep into the silt to act as a barrier for the landfill that in turn acted as a foundation for the dock and terminal buildings. Finally, just before noon, Gunn turned to Stewart.

"So much for the west side of the port," Gunn said wearily. He rubbed his eyes to relieve the strain. "It gets awfully tedious staring at gray, shapeless casing for hours on end."

"See any hint of a door leading to a passage?"

"No so much as a crack or hinge."

"We can move the AUV across the river channel and, with luck, finish up the east side before dark," said Stewart.

"The sooner we wrap this up, the better." Gunn typed a command on the keyboard that sent the AUV on a course toward the opposite side of the port. Then he leaned back and relaxed in his chair.

"Sure you don't want to knock off for a sandwich?" asked Stewart.

Gunn shook his head. "I'll see it through and fill my empty stomach at dinner."

It took only ten minutes for the AUV to cross under the river to the east side of the port. Gunn then programmed the AUV's controls to start the run at the end of the casing wall, working north to south. The AUV had only covered two hundred yards when the phone beside him buzzed. "Can you take that?" he asked Stewart.

The *Marine Denizen*'s skipper picked up the receiver and then handed it to Gunn. "It's Dirk Pitt."

"Pitt." Gunn turned from the monitor, his eyebrows raised in surprise. He took the phone and spoke into the mouthpiece. "Dirk?"

"Hello, Rudi," came Pitt's familiar voice. "I'm calling from an airplane somewhere over the Nevada desert."

"How did your underwater search of the *United States* go?"

"Got a little hairy there for a while, but all Al and I found was a smooth hull and keel with no openings."

"If we don't find anything on this end in the next few hours, we'll join you."

"Are you using a submersible?" asked Pitt.

"Not necessary," replied Gunn. "An AUV is doing the job just fine."

"Keep a tight leash on it, or Qin Shang's underwater security people will steal it before your eyes. They're sneaky devils."

Gunn hesitated before he replied, wondering what Pitt meant. He was about to ask when Stewart came back. "They're serving lunch, Rudi. I'll talk to you after we reach Washington. Good luck, and give my best to Frank Stewart." Then the connection went dead.

"How is Dirk?" inquired Stewart. "I haven't seen him since we worked together on the *Lady Flamborough* cruise-ship search down off Tierra del Fuego a few years ago."

"Testy as ever. He gave me a strange warning."

"Warning?"

"He said Qin Shang's underwater security people might steal the AUV," Gunn answered, obviously confused.

"What underwater security?" said Stewart sarcastically.

Gunn didn't reply. His eyes suddenly widened and he pointed at the video monitor. "My God, look!"

Stewart's eyes followed Gunn's outstretched finger and stiffened.

A face wearing a diver mask filled the screen of the monitor. They stared in amazement as the diver pulled off the mask and revealed very Chinese-featured eyes, nose and mouth. Then he flashed a wide grin and waved as a child waves bye-bye.

Then the image went dark and was replaced with jagged gray and white streaks. Gunn frantically commanded the AUV to return to the *Marine Denizen,* but there was no response. The AUV had disappeared as if it had never been launched.

24

PITT KNEW SOMETHING was wrong the instant the NUMA driver stopped the car. A tiny indescribable alarm tingled inside his brain and traveled to the nape of his neck. Something was not as it should have been.

A life-threatening situation was the last thing on his mind on the ride from Andrews Air Force Base, where the NUMA jet had landed, to his home on a far corner of Washington's National Airport. Darkness had closed over the city, but he ignored the ocean of lights illuminating the buildings. He tried to relax and let his mind drift, but it kept returning to Orion Lake. He thought it odd that the story had not broken in the news media.

From the outside, the former aircraft-maintenance hangar that was built in 1937, the year Amelia Earhart disappeared, appeared forlorn and deserted. Weeds grew right up to its rusting, corrugated-metal walls, whose paint had long since vanished after decades of onslaught by the extremes of Washington's weather patterns. Though it had been condemned as an eyesore and scheduled to be demolished, Pitt had visualized the hangar's potential. Stepping in at the last minute, he thwarted FAA bureaucrats by winning a battle to have it placed on the national register of historic landmarks. Preventing its destruction, he purchased the building and surrounding acre of property and went to work on the interior, remodeling it into a combination living quarters and storage facility for his collection of classic automobiles and aircraft.

Pitt's grandfather had acquired a small fortune in developing Southern California real estate. On his death, he left his grandson a considerable inheritance. After paying the estate taxes, Pitt had chosen to invest in classic cars and aircraft rather than stocks and bonds. In twenty years, he had built up a collection that was highly unique.

Rather than bathe the hangar in a battery of floodlights, Pitt preferred that it appear desolate and empty. One small light atop an electrical pole that gave off a dim yellow glow was all that illuminated the unpaved road that ended at the hangar. He turned and stared through the car's window and studied the top of the pole. A red light that should have beamed from a concealed security camera was dark.

It was an indication as conspicuous to him as a blinking stop sign that something was drastically wrong.

Pitt's security system was designed and installed by a friend with an intelligence agency who was at the top of his trade. No one but a skilled professional could have come within a country mile of breaking the code and compromising it. He gazed around the barren landscape and detected the shadow of a van faintly visible fifty yards away under the reflected light from the city across the Potomac. Pitt didn't require the services of a psychic to know that someone or some group had gained entry into the hangar and was waiting to throw a welcome inside.

"What's your name?" Pitt asked the driver.

"Sam Greenberg."

"Sam, do you carry a satellite phone?"

"Yes, sir, I do," Greenberg replied.

"Contact Admiral Sandecker and tell him I have uninvited visitors and to please send a security force as quickly as possible."

Greenberg was young, no more than twenty, a student studying oceanography at a local university while earning extra money under a marine educational program with NUMA created by Admiral Sandecker. "Shouldn't I call the police?"

The kid is sharp, Pitt thought; he'd quickly grasped the situation. "Not a matter for local law enforcement. Please make the call as soon as you're away from the hangar. The admiral will know the drill."

"Are you going in alone?" the student asked as Pitt exited the car and retrieved his well-traveled duffel bag from the trunk.

Pitt looked at the young man and smiled. "A good host always entertains his guests." He stood and waited until the NUMA car's taillights faded into the dust cloud trailing the rear bumper. He paused to unzip his duffel bag to retrieve his old Colt .45 before remembering

247

that he'd failed to obtain any cartridges after Julia Lee had emptied the gun at the ultralight aircraft on the Orion River.

"Empty!" he said through his teeth. As he stood alone in the night he began to wonder if he had a permanently dislocated brain. There was nothing left but to act dumb and enter the hangar as if he suspected nothing, then attempt to reach one of his collector cars where he kept a shotgun secreted inside a walnut cabinet originally crafted to contain an umbrella.

He pulled a small remote transmitter from his pocket and whistled the first few bars of "Yankee Doodle." The sound-recognition signal electronically shut down the security systems and unlocked a shabby side door that looked as if it was last open in 1945. A green light on the remote flashed three times in series. It should have flashed four, he observed. Someone who was very clever at neutralizing security systems had broken his code. He closed his eyes, paused for a few moments and took a deep breath. As the door cracked open, he dropped to the ground on his hands and knees and reached around the frame and flicked on the interior lights.

The inside walls, floor and curved roof were painted a glossy white that accented a spectrum of vivid colors gleaming off the thirty beautifully painted cars spaced throughout the hangar. The visual effect was dazzling, which was what Pitt counted on to blind whoever was waiting in the blackened interior to ambush him. He reminded himself that the orange-bodied and brown-fendered 1929 Duesenberg convertible sedan containing the shotgun was the third car from the door.

The intruders were not on a social visit. His suspicions were abruptly confirmed when he heard what sounded like a series of muted pops and sensed rather than felt a torrent of bullets spraying the doorway. The suppressors on the killers' guns changed the character of the gunfire in such a way that it was not identifiable as gunshots. They were using silencers even though there wasn't another soul within a mile. His arm whipped around the door again, and he flicked the lights. Then he slithered like a snake under the hail of fire around the doorway and then crept beneath the first two collector cars, a 1932 Stutz and a 1931 L-29 Cord, blessing the old vehicles for sitting high off the ground. Reaching the Duesenberg unscathed, he leaped over the side door onto the floor of the rear seat. In almost the same motion he turned the knob on the door of the cabinet behind the front seat and pulled it open. Then he removed an Aserma 12-gauge Bulldog self-ejecting shotgun that held eleven rounds. The deadly, compact firearm lacked a buttstock but was mounted with a flash hider/muzzle brake. It was one of four guns Pitt secreted throughout the hangar for just such an occasion.

The interior of the hangar was as dark as the deepest reaches of a cave. If these guys are pros, Pitt considered, and there was almost no uncertainty about their being highly trained, they'll be using night-vision scopes and infrared laser sights. Assessing the trajectory of the bullets as they whistled through the doorway, Pitt guessed that there were two assassins probably armed with fully automatic machine pistols. One was somewhere on the ground floor, the other on the balcony to his living quarters thirty feet above one corner of the hangar. Whoever wanted him dead made certain there was a backup in case one assassin failed.

There was no attempt to rush the door. The killers knew that Pitt had entered and was somewhere on the floor of the hangar. Realizing their intended quarry had knowingly entered the trap would make them apprehensive and wary.

With no place to go, Pitt quietly cracked both rear doors on the Duesenberg, peered into the darkness and waited for his assailants to make the next move.

He tried to slow his breathing to hear any sounds of stealth, but all his ears could detect was the beat of his own heart. There was no overpowering sense of fright, no feeling of hopelessness, only a slight mist of fear to be sure. He wouldn't be human if he didn't experience a degree of dread at being a target for two professional killers. But he was on home ground, while the assassins were in a strange environment. If they were to fulfill their mission and kill him, they had to find their target in the dark amid thirty antique automobiles and airplanes. Whatever advantage they had before Pitt walked in the hangar was lost. And what they didn't know was that he was armed and deadly. All Pitt had to do was sit it out in the back of the Duesenberg and wait for them to make a mistake.

He began to wonder who they were and who sent them. The only enemy that came to mind whom he had antagonized in the past few weeks, and who was still among the living, had to be Qin Shang. He could think of no one else who wanted him dead. It was evident to him the Chinese billionaire nurtured a vindictive streak.

He laid the shotgun across his chest, cupped his ears and listened. The hangar was as quiet as a crypt at midnight in the middle of a churchyard. These guys were good. There was no soft patter of stockinged or bare feet, but then stockinged or bare feet did not make noise on concrete if stepped on carefully. They were probably biding their time, also listening. He decided against the old movie trick of throwing something against a wall to draw their fire. Master assassins were too savvy to give their position away with random gunfire.

One minute dragged by, two, then three—it seemed far longer than that. Time seemed to flow like a stream of molasses. He looked up and saw the beam of a red laser sweep across the windshield of the Duesenberg and move on. He was betting his assailants were beginning to wonder if he might have slipped out of the hangar and escaped the trap. There was no way of knowing when Admiral Sandecker, backed by a team of federal marshals, would arrive on the scene. But Pitt was prepared to wait all night if need be while he laid there waiting for a sound or shadow that betrayed movement.

A plan began to form in his mind. He normally made a habit of removing the batteries from all his collector cars because of the danger of creating a fire from an electrical short. But since he planned on driving the Duesenberg when he returned from Orion Lake, Pitt had arranged for the chief mechanic of NUMA's fleet of vehicles, who was entrusted to enter the hangar, to charge a battery and install it in the car. It now struck him that if the opportunity presented itself, he could use the headlights of the Duesenberg to illuminate the floor of the warehouse.

Prudently keeping his eyes locked on the laser beams that swept around the hangar like tiny guard-tower lights from an old prison movie, he silently rolled over the backrest and slipped into a horizontal position on the front seat. Taking a calculated gamble, he aimed the spotlight on the outer cowling beside the steering wheel upward until the lens faced in the general direction of the balcony on the outside of his apartment. Then he raised the shotgun over the upper frame of the windshield and switched on the light.

The bright beam shot aloft and pinpointed a figure in a black ninja suit with a hood covering the head and face crouched at the balcony railing and clutching a tactical machine pistol. The assassin's hand instinctively flew up to shield his eyes from the unexpected blinding glare. Pitt barely had time to adjust his aim before firing off two shots and blinking out the light, throwing the hangar into darkness again. The twin blast from the shotgun sounded like the firing of a cannon inside the metal-walled hangar. A surge of satisfaction swept through him as he heard the thud of a body against the concrete floor. Reckoning the

250

second assassin would be expecting him to hide by throwing himself under the car, he stretched out horizontal on the wide running board and waited for a hail of gunfire.

It never came.

The second killer failed to react because he was searching for Pitt inside an antique Pullman coach parked at one side of the hangar on a pair of rails. The car had once been part of the crack express train called the *Manhattan Limited* that ran between New York and Quebec, Canada, between 1912 and 1914. Pitt had acquired the old coach after finding it in a cave. The killer barely perceived the brief flash of light through a glass window of the Pullman before hearing the explosive roar of the shotgun. By the time he rushed to the rear platform, the hangar had been plunged back into blackness. He was too late to hear the impact on the floor of his accomplice's body or know what target to fire at. He crouched behind a massive Daimler convertible and panned his night-vision goggles around and beneath the maze of parked cars. As he peered through the binocular eyepiece connected to a single objective lens that was attached to his head with straps, giving him the look of a robotic Cyclops, the pitch-black interior of the hangar appeared bathed in a green light that distinguished surrounding objects. Twenty feet ahead of him he spotted the body of his accomplice crumpled on the cold, hard floor, a pool of blood spreading around the head. Any confusion as to why their prey had willingly and knowingly walked into the trap evaporated. He now realized Pitt had somehow armed himself with a weapon. They were warned that their target was a dangerous man, and yet they had still badly underestimated him.

It was essential for Pitt to make a move while he had an advantage, and move as quickly as possible before the remaining killer pinpointed his location. Pitt made no attempt at stealth. Speed was what counted. He scrambled around the front end of the cars toward the entrance door, keeping low and using the wheels and tires to shield his movement from the view of a night scope probing the floor beneath. He reached the door, threw it open and fell back behind a car as bullets sped through the opening into the night outside. Then Pitt crawled along the wall of the hangar until he could huddle against the wheel of a 1939 540-K Mercedes-Benz sedan.

The move was foolhardy and reckless, but he only paid a small price. Pitt could feel blood streaming from his left forearm where the flesh had been nicked by a bullet. Had the remaining assassin been given five long seconds to divine Pitt's intention, he would have never rushed headlong toward the door in the certain belief that his quarry had tried to escape from the hangar.

Pitt heard the soft drumming of supple rubber soles against concrete. Then a figure dressed from the top of the head to his feet in black became outlined in the doorway by the dim light outside on the electrical pole. All's fair in love and war, Pitt thought, as he pulled the trigger and cut down the killer with a shotgun blast through the back below the right shoulder.

The arms flew upward and outward, his tactical machine pistol clattering to the walkway in front of the hangar. The killer stood there a moment, tore off his night-vision goggles and slowly turned. He stared disbelievingly into Pitt's face as the hunted approached the hunter and saw the muzzle of vicious-looking shotgun aimed at his chest. The shocked realization of his deadly blunder, the awareness that his death was only seconds away, seemed more to anger than frighten him. The bitter, stunned expression in his now visible eyes gave Pitt a chill. It was not the look of a man afraid to die, it was the desperate look of a man who had failed his mission. He staggered toward Pitt in a hopeless gesture of tenacity, the lips that were faintly visible through the open slit in his black hood hideous in a blood-flecked snarl.

Pitt did not send another burst from the shotgun into the assassin's body. Nor did he use his gun as a club. He stepped forward and lashed out with one foot, kicking the man's legs out from under him and sending him crashing heavily to the ground.

Picking up the killer's weapon, Pitt did not immediately recognize it as Chinese-manufactured, but he was impressed with its advanced innovations: a plastic frame with integral electro-optics, a fifty-round magazine in line with the bore, and cased, telescoped cartridges with the ballistics of a rifle shell. It was a handgun for the twenty-first century.

He stepped back inside the hangar and switched on the lights again. Despite the harrowing ordeal, Pitt felt strangely unaffected. He walked the aisle separating the cars until he stood below the balcony of his apartment. Then he stared down at the second killer's body. The partner of the man he dropped in the doorway was as dead as a rat in a sprung trap. One of Pitt's shots had missed, but the other had taken off the top of the killer's head. Not a sight to remember at the dinner table.

Wearily, Pitt climbed a circular metal staircase and entered his apartment. There was no sense in calling 911. He expected federal marshals to come bounding up the road any minute. Methodically, he rinsed a glass with water, shook it partially dry and inverted it in a bowl of salt. Then he added crushed ice, a sliced lime, and two shots from a bottle of Don Julio silver tequila. Relaxing in a leather sofa, he savored the drink like a thirst-stricken bedouin who staggered onto an oasis.

Five minutes and a second tequila later, Admiral Sandecker arrived with a team of marshals. Pitt came down to the hangar floor and met them, drink in hand. "Good evening, Admiral, always good to see you."

Sandecker grunted something appropriate and then nodded at the body beneath the apartment. "You really must learn to pick up after yourself." The voice was caustic, but there was no mistaking the concern in his eyes.

Pitt smiled and shrugged. "The world needs murderers like it needs cancer."

Sandecker noticed the streak of blood on Pitt's arm. "You took a hit."

"Nothing a Band-Aid won't fix."

"Let's have the story," demanded Sandecker, all preliminaries over. "Where did they come from?"

"I haven't a clue. They were waiting for me."

"A miracle they didn't kill you."

"They didn't plan on me coming to the party prepared after I saw that my security system had been tampered with."

Sandecker looked at Pitt cautiously. "You might have waited until I arrived with the marshals."

Pitt motioned through the door toward the road and barren land outside the hangar. "If I made a run for it, they'd have cut me down before I got fifty yards. Better to go on the offensive. I felt my only chance was to do something quickly and catch them off balance."

Sandecker stared at Pitt shrewdly. He knew his special projects director would never attempt anything without a solid reason. His eyes took in the bullet-riddled doorway. "I hope you know a good handyman."

At that moment a man wearing casual clothes and a windbreaker over a ballistic armor vest with a Smith & Wesson model 442 .38 revolver in a shoulder holster approached. In one hand he held a hooded mask worn by the killer whom Pitt had dropped in the doorway. "Won't be easy to ID them. They were probably imported for the hit."

Sandecker made the introduction. "Dirk, this is Mr. Peter Harper, executive associate commissioner of field operations for the Immigration and Naturalization Service."

Harper shook Pitt's hand. "A pleasure to meet you, Mr. Pitt. It seems you had an unexpected homecoming."

"A dubious surprise I wasn't counting on." Pitt was not at all sure he could warm to Harper. The associate commissioner of the INS struck him as a man who spent his spare time working algebra problems. Despite the fact he carried a weapon, Harper looked benign and scholastic. "There is a van parked a short distance from the hangar."

"We already checked it out," said Harper. "It belongs to a rental-car agency. The name on the agreement is fictitious."

"Who do you suspect was behind this?" Sandecker asked.

"The name Qin Shang comes to mind," said Pitt. "I'm told he has a retaliatory nature."

"The obvious choice," Sandecker agreed.

"He won't be happy when he finds out his assassins failed," added Harper.

Sandecker's expression turned foxlike. "I think it only appropriate that Dirk tell him in person."

Pitt shook his head. "I hardly think that's a sensible idea. I'm persona non grata in Hong Kong."

Sandecker and Harper exchanged glances. Then Sandecker said, "Qin Shang saved you the trip. He recently arrived in Washington to grease his way out of any connection with Orion Lake. As a matter of fact, he's throwing a party at his residence in Chevy Chase to stroke congressmen and their staffers. If you hurry and dress, you can just make it."

Pitt looked as if he'd been sandbagged. "I hope you're joking."

"I was never more serious."

"I believe the admiral makes a good case," said Harper. "You and Qin Shang should meet face-to-face."

"Why? So he can provide a first-hand description of me to the next team he sends out to put me in a cemetery?"

"No," said Harper seriously. "To let Qin Shang know that despite his wealth and power he can't outclass the United States government. The man is not infallible. If your appearance can shake him up, he probably won't get the word you're alive until you walk in on him. The shock just might make him mad enough to make a mistake in the future. And that's when we step in."

"In essence you want me to create a chink in his armor."

Harper nodded. "Exactly."

"You realize, of course," said Pitt, "that what you're proposing will compromise my further involvement in investigating his illegal activities."

"Think of yourself as a distraction," said Sandecker. "The more Qin Shang concentrates on you as a threat to his operations, the easier it will be for the INS and the other intelligence services to nail him to the cross."

"Distraction hell. You want a decoy."

Harper shrugged. "A rose by any other name."

Pitt made as if to appear uneasy with the idea despite the fact it intrigued him. He thought of the bodies strewn on the bottom of Orion Lake, and the anger rose inside him like an uncontrollable flood. "Whatever it takes to hang the murdering scum."

Harper sighed in relief, but Sandecker never doubted for an instant that Pitt would acquiesce. The admiral had never known Pitt to turn down a challenge, no matter how impossible. Some men were indifferent, impassive. It was difficult to tell what they were thinking. Not Pitt. Sandecker understood him like no other man except Al Giordino. To women he was a mystery, a man they could reach out and touch but never restrain. He knew there were two Dirk Pitts, one that could be tender, considerate and humorous, the other cold and ruthless as a winter storm. Unvaryingly competent to the point of brilliance, his perception of events and people was uncanny. Pitt never made a conscious error. He had a knack for doing the right thing during incredibly difficult circumstances that was almost inhuman.

Harper was unable to read Pitt. All he saw was a marine engineer who had unbelievably killed two professional assassins who had come to murder him. "So you'll do it."

"I'll meet Qin Shang, but I wish someone would tell me how I'm going to crash his party without an invitation."

"It's all been arranged," explained Harper. "A good agent always has connections with the company that prints invitations."

"You were pretty sure of yourself."

"I admit I wasn't, but the admiral here assured me that you never turned down free drinks and food."

Pitt threw Sandecker a peevish look. "The admiral has made victimization an art form."

"I've even taken the liberty of arranging an escort for you," Harper continued. "A most attractive lady who will back you up in case of trouble."

"A baby-sitter," Pitt muttered, rolling his eyes upward. "As a matter of pure optimism I have to ask if she's seen combat."

"I'm told she shot down two aircraft and saved your ass on the Orion River."

"Julia Lee."

"The same."

Pitt's lips stretched into a wide grin. "It looks as if the evening won't turn out to be a bust after all."

25

PITT KNOCKED on the door of the address given him by Peter Harper. After a short wait, it was opened by Julia Lee. She stood radiant in a white silk cashmere dress that came slightly below the knees with open shoulders and back to the curve above her hips and was held up by a thin strap around the neck. Her black hair was swept back in a wrapped ponytail high on the head with spiky ends. Her only jewelry was a thin gold chain around her waist and a gold cuff necklace. Her legs were nude, her feet showing in open gold shoes.

Her eyes widened and she murmured, "Dirk, Dirk Pitt!"

"Oh, I hope so," he replied with a devilish grin.

After her initial shock at seeing Pitt standing there resplendent in a tuxedo with vest and gold watch chain, she recovered and threw herself against him, her arms encircling his neck. He was so surprised he barely caught himself from tumbling over backward down the steps. Impetuously, she kissed him hard on the mouth. Now it was Pitt's turn for his eyes to widen. He had never expected such a spontaneous reception.

"I thought I was the one who said I'd kiss you full on the mouth when next we meet." Reluctantly, he gripped Julia by the upper arms and gently eased her away. "Do you greet all your blind dates in that manner?"

Suddenly, she cast her dove-gray eyes to the ground shyly. "I don't know what came over me. Seeing you came as a shock. I wasn't told who was escorting me to Qin Shang's party. Peter Harper only said he arranged for a tall, dark, handsome man to act as my backup."

"The dirty sneak led me to believe that *you* were *my* backup. He should have been a theatrical producer. I'll bet he's drooling in anticipation of Qin Shang's reaction when the two people who queered his operation at Orion Lake walk in uninvited to his party."

"I hope you're not disappointed at having to escort me. Under all this makeup, I still look pretty awful."

He gently lifted her chin until he could look down into her misty eyes. He might have said something witty and clever, but it wasn't the moment. "About as disappointed as a man who has discovered a diamond mine."

"I didn't know you could say nice things to a girl."

"You wouldn't believe the hordes of women my silver tongue has seduced."

"Liar," she said softly as her lips broke into a smile.

"Enough of this endearing talk," he said, releasing her. "We'd better get a move on before the food runs out."

After Julia briefly returned inside the house to find her purse and coat, Pitt led her to the stately and majestic machine parked at the curb in front of the townhouse where she was staying with an old sorority sister from college. She stared in open astonishment at the mammoth car with its big chrome wire wheels and wide whitewall tires.

"Good Lord!" she exclaimed. "What kind of a car are we going in?"

"A nineteen-twenty-nine Duesenberg," answered Pitt. "Since we've been ordered to crash a party thrown by one of the world's richest men, I thought it only fitting and proper that we arrive in style."

"I've never ridden in a car this grand," said Julia admiringly as she slid onto the soft tan leather seat. She marveled at the hood that seemed to stretch halfway down the block as Pitt closed the door and came around behind the big steering wheel. "I've never heard of a Duesenberg."

"The Model J Duesenbergs were the finest examples of American automaking," Pitt explained. "Manufactured from nineteen-twenty-eight until nineteen-thirty-six, they were considered by many automobile connoisseurs as the handsomest cars ever built. Only about four hundred eighty chassis and engines came out of the factory and were sent to the most esteemed coachmakers in the country who produced magnificent designs. This car was custom-bodied by the Walter M. Murphy Company in Pasadena, California, and styled as a convertible sedan. Not cheap, they sold as high as twenty thousand dollars when the Ford Model A sold for around four hundred. They were owned by the wealthy celebrities of their day, particularly the Hollywood crowd, who bought Duesenbergs as a show of pride and prestige. If you drove a Duesy, you had made it big-time."

"She's beautiful," said Julia, admiring the artistically flowing lines. "She must be fast."

"The engine was an outgrowth of the Duesenberg racing engines. A straight eight-cylinder engine displacing four hundred twenty cubic inches, it produced two hundred sixty-five horsepower when most engines at the time put out less than seventy. Although this engine doesn't have the supercharger that was installed on later models, I made a few modifications when I restored the car. Under the right conditions she could touch one hundred forty miles an hour."

"I'll take your word for it without a demonstration."

"A pity we can't drive with the top down, but it's a cool night and I put it up to protect milady's hair."

"A woman loves a considerate man."

"I always aim to please."

She looked at the flat windshield and noticed a small hole in one corner of the glass with tiny cracks spreading from it. "Is that a bullet hole?"

"A souvenir from a couple of Qin Shang's flunkies."

"He sent men to kill you?" asked Julia, staring in fascination at the hole. "Where did this take place?"

"They dropped by the aircraft hangar where I live earlier in the evening," Pitt answered impassively.

"What happened?"

"They weren't the least bit sociable, so I sent them on their way."

Pitt hit the starter and the big engine turned over with a soft purr before the eight cylinders fired and broadcast a mellow roar through the big exhaust pipe. The low gears gave out a muted whir as Pitt shifted through the sequence from first to third. The great luxury car that has never been surpassed rolled through the streets of Washington, regal and majestic.

Julia decided it was hopeless to pry any more information out of Pitt. She relaxed in the wide leather seat and enjoyed the ride and the stares of other drivers and the people walking on the sidewalks.

Shortly after traveling up Wisconsin Avenue out of the District of Columbia, Pitt turned onto a meandering residential street canopied by huge trees sprouting new spring leaves until he reached the gate of the drive leading to Qin Shang's Chevy Chase mansion. The iron gates were a monstrosity of Chinese dragons entwined around the bars. Two Chinese guards dressed in elaborate uniforms stared strangely at the huge car for several moments before stepping forward and asking to see invitations. Pitt passed them through the open window and waited while the guards checked his and Julia's names against those on a guest list. Satisfied that Pitt and Julia were indeed invited, they bowed and pressed the code on a remote transmitter that opened the gates. Pitt threw them a brief wave and tooled the Duesenberg up the long driveway and stopped under the portico at the entrance to the house, whose exterior was lit up like a football stadium.

"I must remember to compliment Harper," said Pitt. "He not only provided us with invitations, but he somehow managed to sneak our names onto the guest list."

Julia's expression was that of a young girl approaching the Taj Mahal. "I've never attended a major-league Washington party before. I hope I won't embarrass you."

"You won't," Pitt assured her. "Just tell yourself that it's strictly a social theater. The powerful Washington elite throw posh functions because they have something to sell. It all comes down to people milling around, swilling booze, looking influential and exchanging gossip mixed with explicit information. Mostly, the city's society chronicles the foolish events from their petty little political worlds."

"You act as if you've been to them before."

"As I told you on the dock at Grapevine Bay, my father is a senator. In my bon vivant younger days I used to tag along and attempt to pick up congressional mistresses."

"Were you successful?"

"Almost never."

A stretch limo was disgorging several of Qin Shang's guests, who turned and gazed in frank admiration at the Duesenberg. Valet parking attendants appeared as if summoned. The valets were immune to limousines and expensive cars, most of them foreign, but this one staggered their minds. Almost reverently, they opened the doors.

Pitt eyed a man standing off to the side who took a particular interest in the newcomers and their means of transportation. Then he turned and hurried inside. No doubt, Pitt thought, to alert his boss to the arrival of guests who didn't fit the normal pattern.

As they swept arm in arm through the elegant colonnade entrance, Julia whispered to Pitt, "I hope I don't lose it when I meet that murdering bastard and spit in his face."

"Just tell him how much you enjoyed the cruise on his ship, and how you're looking forward to the next one."

The gray eyes flashed with fire. "Like hell I will."

"Now don't forget," said Pitt, "as an agent in good standing with the INS, you're here on assignment."

"And you?"

Pitt laughed. "I'm just along for the ride."

"How can you be so lackadaisical?" she snapped. "We may be lucky to get out of here with our heads."

"We'll be all right so long as we're in a crowd. Our problems come after we leave."

"Not to worry," she assured him. "Peter has arranged for a team of security people to stand by outside the house in case of trouble."

"Should Qin Shang get nasty, do we send up flares?"

"We'll be in constant communication. I have a radio in my purse."

Pitt stared at the tiny purse skeptically. "And a gun too?"

She shook her head. "No gun." Then she smiled slyly. "You forget, I've seen you in action. I'm counting on *you* to protect me."

"Dearheart, you're in big trouble."

They passed through the foyer into a vast hallway filled with Chinese art objects. The centerpiece was a seven-foot-tall bronze incense burner inlaid with gold. The upper section depicted flames leaping toward the sky interspersed with women, their arms and hands uplifted with offerings. Aromatic incense wreathed the flames in billowy clouds that scented the entire house. Pitt stepped up to the bronze masterwork and studied it closely, examining the inlaid gold that decorated the base.

"Beautiful, isn't it?" said Julia.

"Yes," Pitt said quietly. "The craftsmanship is quite unique."

"My father has a much smaller version that isn't nearly so ancient."

"The smell is a bit overwhelming."

"Not to me. I grew up surrounded by Chinese culture."

Pitt took Julia by the arm and led her into an immense room filled with Washington's rich and mighty. The scene reminded him of a Roman banquet out of a Cecil B. DeMille movie: slim women in designer dresses, congressmen, senators and the aristocracy of the city's attorneys, lobbyists and power brokers, all trying to look sophisticated and distinguished in their formal evening wear. There was such an ocean of fabrics between the guests and the furniture that the room was unnaturally silent despite a hundred voices talking at once.

If the furnishings had cost less than twenty million dollars, then Qin Shang had bought them at a discount house in New Jersey. The walls and ceiling were intricately carved and paneled in redwood, as was most of the furniture. The carpet alone must have taken twenty young girls half their adolescent lives to weave. It flowed in blue and gold like an ocean at sunset, and the depth of its pile made it seem as if one had to wade through it. The curtains alone would have put those in Buckingham Palace to shame. Julia had never seen so much silk in one space. The opulent upholstered chairs and settees looked like they might have been more at home in a museum.

No less than twenty stewards stood behind a buffet line whose mountains of lobster, crab and other seafood must have cleaned out the entire catch of a fishing fleet. Only the finest French champagne was served alongside vintage wines, none of which had labels from later than 1950. In one corner of the ornate room a string orchestra played themes from motion pictures. Though Julia had come from a wealthy family in San Francisco, she had seen nothing to compare with this affair. She stood in solemn awe as her eyes scanned the room. Finally, she recovered enough to say, "I can see what Peter meant when he said Qin Shang's invitation was the most desired in Washington aside from the White House."

"Frankly, I prefer the ambiance at the French-embassy parties. More elegant, more refined."

"I feel so . . . so plain among all these beautifully dressed women."

Pitt gave Julia an adoring look and squeezed her around the waist. "Stop belittling yourself. You're a class act. You'd have to be blind not to notice that every man in the room is devouring you."

Julia blushed at the flattery. It embarrassed her to see that he was right. The men were staring at her openly, as were many of the women. She also observed a dozen exquisite Chinese women dressed in silk sheath dresses mingling with the male guests. "It seems I'm not the only woman with Chinese ancestry."

Pitt made a passing, offhand glance at the women Julia referred to. "Daughters of joy."

"I beg your pardon."

"Hookers."

"What are you suggesting?"

"Qin Shang hires them to work the men who came along without their wives. You might call it a subtle form of political patronage. What influence he can't buy, he slips through the back door with sexual favors."

Julia looked bewildered. "I have a lot to learn about government lobbying."

"They are exotic, aren't they? A good thing I'm with someone who puts them to shame or they might prove a temptation I couldn't resist."

"You've got nothing Qin Shang wants," Julia said testily. "Perhaps we should find him and make our presence known."

Pitt gazed at her as if shocked. "What, and miss out on all the free food and drink? Not on your life. First things first. Let's head to the bar for champagne, and then indulge ourselves at the buffet. Later, we'll enjoy a cognac before making ourselves known to the arch-villain of the Orient."

Julia said to him, "I think you're the craziest, most complex and reckless man I've ever met."

"You left out charming and cuddly."

"I can't imagine any woman putting up with you for more than twenty-four hours."

"To know me is to love me." The mirth lines around his eyes crinkled, and he gave a tilt of his head toward the bar. "All this talk makes me thirsty."

They strolled across the crowded floor to the bar and casually sipped the offered champagne. Then they wandered to the buffet table and filled their plates. Pitt was profoundly surprised to find a large platter of fried abalone, a shellfish that was on the verge of extinction. He spotted an empty table by the fireplace and commandeered it. Julia could not keep her eyes from exploring the throng in the immense room. "I see several Chinese men, but I can't tell which one is Qin Shang. Peter failed to give me a description of him."

"For an investigative agent," said Pitt between bites of lobster, "your powers of observation are sadly lacking."

"You know his appearance."

"Never laid eyes on him. But if you look through the doorway on the west wall, guarded by a giant dressed in a dynastic costume, you'll find Qin Shang's private audience room. My guess is he sits in there and holds court."

Julia began to rise to her feet. "Let's get this over with."

Pitt held out a hand and restrained her. "Not so fast. I haven't had my after-dinner cognac yet."

"You're impossible."

"Women are always telling me that." A steward took their plates, and Pitt left Julia momentarily for the bar, returning in a few minutes with two crystal snifters containing a fifty-year-old cognac. Slowly, very slowly, as if he hadn't a care in the world, he savored the smooth flavor. As he held the snifter to his lips, he saw a man, reflected in the crystal, approach their table.

"Good evening," he said in a soft voice. "I hope you're enjoying yourselves. I am your host."

Julia froze as she looked up into the smiling face of Qin Shang. He looked nothing like what she imagined. She did not envision him as tall and stout. The face was not that of a cruel, cold-blooded murderer with vast power. There was no hint of authority behind the friendly tone, and yet she could sense an underlying coldness. He stood immaculate in a beautifully cut tuxedo embroidered with golden tigers.

"Yes, thank you," said Julia, barely able to remain polite. "It truly is a magnificent affair."

Pitt rose to his feet slowly in a conscious effort not to appear patronizing. "May I present Ms. Julia Lee."

"And you, sir?" asked Qin Shang."

"My name is Dirk Pitt."

There it was. No skyrockets, no drumroll. The guy has style, Pitt had to give him that. The smile remained fixed. If there was surprise at finding Pitt alive and breathing, Qin Shang didn't show it. The only detectable response was a slight shift of the eyes. For long moments jade-green eyes locked with opaline-green, neither man willing to break off. Pitt knew damned well it was stupid and saw no purpose in the staredown other than egotistical satisfaction by the winner. Gradually, his gaze lifted to Qin Shang's eyebrows, then forehead, lingered and moved to the hair. Then Pitt's eyes widened a fraction as if he found something, and his lips broke into a slight grin.

The ruse worked. Qin Shang's concentration was broken. He involuntarily raised his eyeballs to look upward. "May I ask what you find so amusing, Mr. Pitt?"

"I was just wondering who your hairstylist was," Pitt answered innocently.

"She is a Chinese lady who attends me once a day. I'd give you her name, but she is in my private employ."

"I envy you. My barber is a mad Hungarian with palsy."

There came a brief icy stare. "The photo of you in your dossier does not do you justice."

"I applaud a man who docs his homework."

"May I have a word with you in private, Mr. Pitt?"

Pitt nodded toward Julia. "Only if Ms. Lee is present."

"I'm afraid our conversation may not be of interest to the lovely lady."

Pitt realized that Qin Shang did not know Julia's credentials. "On the contrary. Rude of me not to mention that Ms. Lee is an agent with the Immigration and Naturalization Service. She was also a passenger on one of your cattle boats and had the misfortune of enjoying your hospitality at Orion Lake. You are familiar, I trust, with Orion Lake. It's in the state of Washington."

For an instant there was a red glare in the jade eyes, and then it was just as quickly extinguished. Qin Shang remained as impenetrable as marble. His voice came even and calm. "If you both will please follow me." He turned and strode away, knowing unquestionably Pitt and Julia would trail in his wake.

"I think the time has come," said Pitt as he helped Julia from her chair.

"You crafty dog," she murmured. "You knew all along he would seek us out."

"Shang didn't get where he's at without a healthy dose of curiosity."

Obediently, they followed Qin Shang through the milling congregation until he came to the costumed giant who opened the door for him. They entered a room unlike the heavily furnished and decorated one they just left. This room was modest and austere. The walls were merely painted in a soft blue. The only furnishings were a settee, two chairs and a desk whose surface was barren except for a telephone. He motioned for them to sit on the settee as he took his place behind the desk. Pitt was amused to see that the desk and chair were slightly elevated so that Qin Shang looked down at his visitors.

"Forgive me for mentioning it," Pitt said offhandedly, "but the bronze incense burner in the main entry. From the Liao dynasty, I believe."

"Why yes, you are quite correct."

"I assume you know that it's a fake."

"You are most observant, Mr. Pitt," said Qin Shang without taking offense. "The piece is not fake, but a well-executed replica. The original was lost in nineteen forty-eight during the war when the People's Army of Mao Tse-tung crushed the forces of Chiang Kai-shek."

"The burner is still in China?"

"No, it was on a ship with many other ancient treasures stolen from my country by Chiang that were lost at sea."

"The ship's final resting place is a mystery?"

"A mystery I have worked many years to solve. To find the ship and its cargo is my life's most passionate desire."

"It's been my experience that shipwrecks are never found until they want to be found."

"Very poetic," Qin Shang said, pausing to glance at his watch. "I must return and tend to my guests so I'll be brief before I have my security people escort you to the door. Please tell me the purpose behind your uninvited presence."

"I thought the purpose was transparent," Pitt replied conversationally. "Ms. Lee and I wanted to meet the man we're going to hang."

"You're very succinct, Mr. Pitt. I appreciate that in an adversary. But it is you who will be a casualty in the war."

"What war is that?"

"The economic war between the People's Republic of China and the United States. A war for extraordinary power and wealth for the winner."

"I have no ambitions on that score."

"Ah, but I do. That's the difference between us and between our countrymen. Like most of the rabble in America, you lack determination and zeal."

Pitt shrugged his shoulders. "If greed is your god, then you possess very little of true value."

"You think of me as a greedmonger?" Qin Shang asked pleasantly.

"I've seen little of your lifestyle that persuades me otherwise."

"All the great men of history were driven by ambition. It goes hand in hand with power. Contrary to public opinion, the world is not divided by good and evil, but between those who do and those who do not, the visionaries and the blind, the realists and the romanticists. The world does not turn on good deeds and sentiment, Mr. Pitt, but on achievement."

"What do you ultimately hope to gain in the end besides a pretentious edifice over your coffin?"

"You misunderstand me. My goal is to help China become the greatest nation the world has ever known."

"While you become even more filthy-rich than you already are. Where does it end, Mr. Shang?"

"There is no end, Mr. Pitt."

"You'll have a tough fight on your hands if you think China can surpass the United States."

"Ah, but the deed is done," Qin Shang said matter-of-factly. "You country has died a slow death as a world power while my country is in its ascendancy. Already we have passed the United States to become the largest economy in history. Already we have passed your trade deficit with Japan. Your government is impotent despite its nuclear arsenal. Soon it will be unthinkable for your leaders to intervene when we assume control of Taiwan and the rest of the Asian nations."

"So what does it really matter?" asked Pitt. "You'll still be playing catch-up to our standard of living for the next hundred years."

"Time is on our side. Not only will we erode America from the outside, but with the help of your own countrymen we will eventually cause it to crumble from within. If nothing else, future division and internal race wars will seal your fate as a great nation."

Pitt began to see Qin Shang's direction. "Aided and abetted by your doctrine of illegal immigration, is that it?"

Qin Shang looked at Julia. "Your Immigration and Naturalization Service estimates that nearly a million Chinese enter America and Canada legally and illegally each year. Actually, the figure is closer to two million. While you concentrated on keeping out your neighbors to the south, we have been flooding masses of my countrymen across the sea and across your shoreline. One day, sooner than you think, your coastal states and the Canadian provinces will be an extension of China."

To Pitt the concept was inconceivable. "I'll grade you with an A for wishful thinking and an F for practicality."

"Not as ridiculous as you may think," Qin Shang said patiently. "Consider how the boundaries of Europe have changed in the past hundred years. Migration through the centuries has shattered old empires and built new, only to have them fall again from new waves of migrants."

"An interesting theory," said Pitt. "But a theory nonetheless. The only way for your scenario to become reality is for the American people to lie down and play dead."

"Your countrymen have slept through the nineteen nineties," Qin Shang replied, a visceral, even menacing quality in his voice. "When they finally wake up, it will be a decade too late."

"You paint a grim picture for humanity," said Julia, visibly shaken.

Pitt went silent. He did not have the answer nor was he Nostradamus. His brain told him that Qin Shang's prophecy might indeed come to pass. But his heart refused to reject hope. He came to his feet and nodded at Julia. "I think we've heard enough of Mr. Shang's meaningless drivel. It's plain to see that he's a man who loves to hear himself talk. Let's clear out of this architectural monstrosity and its phony decor and breathe fresh air again."

Qin Shang leaped to his feet. "You dare mock me," he snarled.

Pitt moved to the desk and leaned across the surface until his face was bare inches away from Qin Shang's. "Mock you, Mr. Shang? That's putting it mildly. I'd rather have my Christmas stocking filled with cow dung than listen to your retarded philosophy on future affairs." Then he took Julia's hand. "Come on, we're out of here."

Julia made no effort to move; she appeared dazed. Pitt had to pull her along behind him. At the doorway he paused and looked back.

"Thank you, Mr. Shang, for a most provocative evening. I enjoyed your excellent champagne and seafood, especially the abalone."

The Chinese's face was tight and cold, twisted in a mask of malevolence. "No man speaks to Qin Shang in this manner."

"I'm sorry for you, Shang. On the surface you are fabulously rich and almighty, but underneath you're only a self-made man who worships his inventor."

Qin Shang fought to regain control of his emotions. When he spoke, his voice came as though out of an arctic mist. "You have made a fatal error, Mr. Pitt."

Pitt smiled thinly. "I was about to say the same about the two cretins you sent to kill me earlier this evening."

"Another time, another place, you may not be so fortunate."

Pitt said coldly, "Just so we keep a level playing field, please be advised that I have hired a team of professional assassins to terminate you, Mr. Shang. With luck, we'll never meet again."

Before Qin Shang could respond, Pitt and Julia were walking through the mass of guests toward the front entrance. Julia discreetly opened her purse, held it close to her face as though searching for cosmetics and spoke into the tiny radio.

"This is Dragon Lady. We're coming out."

"Dragon Lady," said Pitt. "Is that the best you could dream up for a code name?"

The dove-gray eyes gazed at him as if he was thick between the ears. "It fits," she said simply.

If Qin Shang's paid killers had any plans of following the Duesenberg and blasting its occupants at the first stoplight, they were quickly laid to rest as two unmarked vans fell into a convoy behind the big car.

"I hope they're on our side," said Pitt.

"Peter Harper is very thorough. The INS protects its own with specialists outside the service. The people in the vans are from a little-known security force that supplies teams of bodyguards on request from different branches of government."

"A great pity."

She looked at him quizzically. "Why do you say that?"

"With all these armed chaperons watching our every move, I can't very well take you to my place for a nightcap."

"Are you sure a nightcap is all you had in mind?" Julia replied in a sultry voice.

Pitt took one hand off the wheel and patted her bare knee. "Women have always been an enigma to me. I had hoped you might forget you were an agent of the government and throw caution to the winds."

She moved across the leather bench seat until her body was pressed against his and slid her hands around his arm. She found the muffled roar of the engine and the smell of the leather sensual. "I went off duty the minute we walked out of that scumbag's house," she said lovingly. "My time is your time."

"How do we get rid of your friends?"

"We don't. They're with us for the duration."

"In that case, do you think they'd mind if I took a detour?"

"Probably," she said, smiling. "But I'm sure you'll do it anyway."

Pitt went silent as he shifted gears and drove the Duesenberg effortlessly through traffic, watching in the rearview mirror with a touch of pride at seeing the vans struggle to keep pace. "I hope they don't shoot out my tires. They don't come cheap for a car like this."

"Did you mean what you said when you told Qin Shang you'd hired a team of hit men to kill him?"

Pitt grinned wolfishly. "A big, fat bluff, but he doesn't know that. I take great satisfaction in tormenting men like Qin Shang who are too used to having people jump at their beck and call. Do him good to stare at the ceiling nights and wonder if someone is lurking outside waiting to put a bullet in him."

"So what's with the detour?"

"I think I found the chink in Qin Shang's armor, his Achilles' heel if you'll pardon the cliché. Despite the seemingly impenetrable wall he's formed around his personal life, he has a vulnerable crack that can be pried open a mile wide."

Julia pulled her coat tightly around her bare legs to ward off the late-evening chill. "You must have divined something from what he said that escaped me."

"As I recall, his words were, 'My life's most passionate desire.' "

She looked curiously into his eyes, which never left the road. "He was talking about a vast cargo of Chinese art treasures that vanished on a ship."

"The same."

"He possesses more wealth and Chinese antiques than anyone else in the world. Why should a ship with a few historical objects be of serious interest to him?"

"Not a mere interest, gorgeous creature. Qin Shang is obsessed like all men down through the centuries who have searched for lost treasure. He won't die a happy man no matter how much wealth and power he's accumulated until he can replace every one of his art replicas with the genuine pieces. To own something no other man or woman on earth can own is the ultimate fulfillment to Qin Shang. I've known men like him. He'd trade thirty years of his life to find the shipwreck and its treasures."

"But how does one go about searching for a ship that vanished fifty years ago?" Julia asked. "Where do you begin to look?"

"You start," Pitt said casually, "by knocking on a door about six blocks up the street."

26

PITT STEERED the big Duesenberg over a narrow driveway between two homes with brick walls entirely blanketed with climbing ivy. He stopped the car in front of a spacious carriage house that fronted an expansive courtyard that was now roofed over.

"Who lives here?" asked Julia.

"A very interesting character," Pitt replied. He motioned toward a large bronze knocker on the door cast in the shape of a sailing ship. "Give it a rap, if you can."

"If you can?" Her hand reached for the knocker hesitantly. "Is there a trick to it?"

"Not what you're thinking. Go ahead, try to lift it."

But before Julia could touch the knocker, the door was swept open, revealing a huge, roly-poly man dressed in burgundy paisley silk pajamas under a matching robe. Julia gasped and took a step backward, bumping into Pitt who was laughing.

"He never fails."

"Fails to do what?" demanded the fat man.

"Open the door before a visitor knocks."

"Oh, that." The big man waved airily. "A chime sounds whenever someone comes up the drive."

"St. Julien," said Pitt. "Forgive the late visit."

"Nonsense!" boomed the man, who weighed four hundred pounds if he weighed an ounce. "You're welcome any hour of the day or night. Who's the lovely little lady?"

"Julia Lee, may I present St. Julien Perlmutter, gourmet, collector of fine wines and possessor of the world's largest library on shipwrecks."

Perlmutter bowed as far as his bulk allowed and kissed Julia's hand. "Always a pleasure to meet a friend of Dirk's." He stood back and swept out an arm, the silk sleeve flapping like a flag in a stiff breeze. "Don't stand out there in the night. Come in, come in. I was just about to open a bottle of forty-year-old Barros port. Please share it with me."

Julia stepped from the enclosed courtyard that once served to harness teams of horses to fancy carriages and gazed enraptured at the thousands of books that were massed over every square inch of open space inside the carriage house. Many were neatly spaced on endless shelves. Others were piled along walls, up stairs and on balconies. In bedrooms, bathrooms, closets, they were even clustered in the kitchen and dining room. There was barely enough room for a person to walk through a hallway, they were so thickly stacked.

Over fifty years, St. Julien Perlmutter had accumulated the finest and most extensive collection of historical ship literature ever assembled in one place. His library was the envy of every maritime archive in the world and second to none. What books and ship records he could not possess, he painstakingly copied. Fearful of fire or destruction, his fellow researchers pleaded with him to put his immense archive on-line, but he preferred to leave his collection in bound paper.

He generously shared it all without cost to anyone who came to his front door seeking information on a particular shipwreck. As long as Pitt had known him, Perlmutter had never turned down anyone who sought his extensive knowledge.

If the staggering hoard of books wasn't a colossal sight, Perlmutter was. Julia gazed openly at him. His face, turned crimson from a lifetime of excessive good food and drink, barely showed under a curly mass of gray hair and a thick, heavy beard. His nose under the sky-blue eyes was a little red knob. His lips were lost under a mustache twisted at the ends. He was obese but not sloppy-fat. No flab hung. He was solid as a massive wood sculpture. Most people who first met him thought he was probably much younger than he looked. But St. Julien Perlmutter was a year past seventy and as hearty as they came.

A close friend of Pitt's father, Senator George Pitt, Perlmutter had known Dirk almost from the time he was born. Over the years they had formed a close bond to the point where Perlmutter was like a favorite uncle. He sat Pitt and Julia down around a huge latticed hatch cover, reconstructed and lacquered to as high a sheen as a dining table's. He offered them crystal glasses that had once graced the first-class dining room of the former Italian luxury liner the *Andrea Doria.*

Julia studied the etched image of the ship on her glass as Perlmutter poured the aged port. "I thought the *Andrea Doria* rested on the bottom of the sea."

"She still does," said Perlmutter, twisting one end of the gray hair flowing from his lips. "Dirk here brought up a rack of wineglasses during a dive he made on the wreck five years ago and graciously gave them to me. Please tell what you think of the port."

Julia was flattered that such a gourmet would want her opinion. She sipped the ruby contents of the glass and made an expression of delight. "It tastes wonderful."

"Good, good." He gave Pitt a look reserved for a derelict on a park bench. "You I won't ask, since your taste runs to the mundane."

Pitt acted as if he was insulted. "You wouldn't know good port if you drowned in it. While I, on the other hand, was weaned on it."

"I hate myself for ever letting you through the front door," Perlmutter moaned.

Julia saw through the charade. "Do you two always go on like this?"

"Only when we meet," Pitt said, laughing.

"What brings you here this time of night?" asked Perlmutter, winking at Julia. "It couldn't have been my witty conversation."

"No," Pitt agreed, "it was to see if you ever heard of a ship that left China sometime around nineteen forty-eight with a cargo of historical Chinese art and then vanished."

Perlmutter held the port in front of his eyes and swirled it around in his glass. His eyes took on a reflective expression as his encyclopedic mind delved into his brain cells. "I seem to recall that the name of the ship was the *Princess Dou Wan.* She went missing with all hands somewhere off Central America. No trace of ship or crew was ever found."

"Was there a record of her cargo?"

Perlmutter shook his head. "The word that she was carrying a rich cargo of antiquities came from unsubstantiated reports only. Vague rumors actually. No evidence ever came to light to suggest it was true."

"How do you call it?" asked Pitt.

"Another mystery of the sea. There is very little I can tell you except the *Princess Dou Wan* was a passenger ship that had seen her day and was scheduled for the scrap yard. A pretty ship, in her prime she was known as the queen of the China Sea."

"Then how did she end up lost off Central America?"

Perlmutter shrugged. "As I said, another mystery of the sea."

Pitt shook his head vigorously. "I disagree. If there is an enigma, it is man-made. A ship simply doesn't vanish five thousand miles from where she is supposed to be."

"Let me dig out the record on the *Princess*. I believe it's in a book stacked under the piano." He lifted his bulk off a thankful chair and ambled out of the dining room. In less than two minutes, Pitt and Julia heard his voice roar out through the hall from another room. "Ah, here it is!"

"With all these books, he knows exactly where to find the one he's looking for?" she asked in amazement.

"He can tell you the title of every book in the house," said Pitt with certainty, "its exact location and what number it lies from the top of its stack or from the right side of its shelf."

Pitt had no sooner finished speaking than Perlmutter came into the room, his elbows brushing both frames of the doorway simultaneously. He held up a thick, leather-bound book. The title, lettered in gold, read, *History of the Orient Shipping Lines*. "This is the only official record I've ever come across on the *Princess Dou Wan* that gives details of her years afloat." Perlmutter sat down at the table, opened the book and began reading aloud.

"She was laid down and launched in the same year, nineteen thirteen, by Harland and Wolff shipbuilders of Belfast for the Singapore Pacific Steamship Lines. Her original name was *Lanai*. Gross tonnage of just under eleven thousand tons, overall length of four hundred and ninety-seven feet and a sixty-foot beam, she was rather a good-looking ship for her day." He paused and held up the book to show a photograph of the ship sailing over a flat sea with a trailing wisp of smoke from her single smokestack. The photo was tinted and revealed the traditional black hull with white superstructure topped by a tall green funnel. "She could carry five hundred and ten passengers, fifty-five of them first class," Perlmutter continued. "She was originally coal-fired but converted to oil-firing in nineteen twenty. Top speed of seventeen knots. Her maiden voyage took place in December of nineteen thirteen when she left Southhampton for Singapore. Until nineteen thirty-one, most of her voyages were between Singapore and Honolulu."

"It must have been a comfortable and relaxing experience sailing across the South Seas in those early days," said Julia.

"Passengers were not nearly so harried and occupied eighty years ago," Pitt agreed. He looked at Perlmutter. "When did the *Lanai* become the *Princess Dou Wan?*"

"She was sold to the Canton Lines out of Shanghai in nineteen thirty-one," Perlmutter answered. "From then until the war, she carried passengers and cargo to ports around the South China Sea. During the war, she served as an Australian troop transport. In nineteen forty-two, while unloading troops and their equipment off New Guinea, she was attacked by Japanese aircraft and severely damaged, but she returned to Sidney under her own power for repair and a refit. Her war record is quite impressive. From nineteen forty to nineteen forty-five, she transported over eighty thousand men in and out of the war zone, dodging enemy aircraft, submarines and warships and suffering extensive damage inflicted during seven different attacks."

"Five years of sailing through Japanese-infested waters," said Pitt. "It's a wonder she wasn't sunk."

"When the war ended, the *Princess Dou Wan* was returned to the Canton Lines and refitted as a passenger ship again. She then went into service between Hong Kong and Shanghai. Then in the late fall of nineteen forty-eight she was taken out of service and sent to the scrappers in Singapore for breaking up."

"Breaking up," Pitt echoed. "You said she sank off Central America."

"Her fate gets vague," said Perlmutter, pulling several loose sheets of paper from the book. "I accumulated what information I could find and condensed it into a brief report. All that's known for certain is that she didn't make it to the scrappers. The final account came from a naval station radio operator at Valparaiso, Chile. According to the radio operator's records, a ship calling herself the *Princess Dou Wan* sent out a series of distress signals, saying she was taking on water and badly listing under a violent storm two hundred miles west. Repeated inquiries brought no answers. Then her radio went dead and she was never heard from again. A search turned up no sign of her."

"Could there have been another *Princess Dou Wan?*" asked Julia.

Perlmutter shook his head negatively. "The *International Ships Registry* only lists one *Princess Dou Wan* between eighteen fifty and the present. The signal must have been sent as a red herring from another Chinese vessel."

"Where did the rumor originate that Chinese antiquities were on board?" asked Pitt.

Perlmutter held out his hands, palms upward in a sign of unknowing. "A myth, a legend, the sea is full of them. The only sources I'm aware of were unreliable dockworkers and Nationalist Chinese soldiers who were in charge of loading the ship. They were later captured and interrogated by the Communists. One claimed a crate broke open while it was being lifted aboard, revealing a life-size bronze prancing horse."

"How on earth did you find all this information?" said Julia, overwhelmed with Perlmutter's knowledge of maritime disasters.

He smiled. "From a fellow researcher in China. I have sources around the world that I rely on to send me books and information related to shipwrecks whenever they find it. They know that I pay top dollar for reports that contain new and uncovered ground. The story of the *Princess Dou Wan* came from an old friend who is China's top historian and researcher by the name of Zhu Kwan. We've corresponded and exchanged maritime information for many years. It was he who mentioned a legend surrounding the alleged treasure ship."

"Was Zhu Kwan able to give you a manifest of the treasure?" Pitt inquired.

"No, he claimed only that his research led him to believe that before Mao's troops marched into Shanghai, Chiang Kai-shek cleaned out the museums, galleries and private collections of Chinese antiquities. Records of art and artifacts before World War II in China are sketchy to say the least. It is pretty well known that after the Communists took over, there were few antiquities to be found. All that you see in China today were discovered and excavated since nineteen forty-eight."

"Not one of the lost treasures was ever found?"

"Not to my knowledge," Perlmutter admitted. "Nor has Zhu Kwan told me any different."

Pitt took the last swallow from his glass of the forty-year-old port. "So a vast part of China's heritage may lie on the bottom of the sea."

Julia's expression altered to curiosity. "This is all most interesting, but I fail to see what good any of this has to do with Qin Shang's illegal immigrant-smuggling operations."

Pitt took her hand and held it tightly. "Your Immigration and Naturalization Service, the Central Intelligence Agency and the Federal Bureau of Investigation can strike Qin Shang and his rotten empire from the front and sides. But his obsession with the lost antiquities of China opens the door for the National Underwater and Marine Agency to strike him from the rear, where he least expects it. St. Julien and I will have to play catch-up. But we're very good at what we do. Together, we make a better search team than any Qin Shang can put together." Pitt paused, and his expression lightened. "Now the only trick we have to perform is to find the *Princess Dou Wan* before Qin Shang."

27

THE NIGHT WAS STILL YOUNG when Pitt and Julia left St. Julien Perlmutter's carriage house. Pitt turned the Duesenberg around and drove out the driveway toward the street. He stopped before entering the traffic. The two Ford vans driven by the special bodyguards from the security company hired by Peter Harper were not parked and patiently waiting at the curb. They were nowhere in sight.

"It seems we've been abandoned," said Pitt, his foot firmly on the brake pedal of the Duesenberg.

Julia looked puzzled. "I don't understand. I can think of no reason why they would desert us."

"Maybe they decided we were boring, and they drove to a sports bar to watch basketball."

"Not funny," Julia said grimly.

"Then it's déjà vu all over again," Pitt noted with deceptive calm. He leaned across Julia, reached into a side pocket on the door, pulled out the old .45 Colt that he had reloaded, and handed it to her. "I hope you haven't lost your touch since our escapade on the Orion River."

She shook her head vigorously. "You're exaggerating the danger."

"No, I'm not," he argued. "Something is seriously wrong. Take the gun, and if you have to, use it."

"There must be a simple explanation for the vans' departure."

"One more prognostication of Pitt's precognition. The pockets of the Immigration and Naturalization Service are not as deep as the pockets of Qin Shang Maritime Limited. I suspect Harper's private security guards were paid double to pack up and go home."

Julia snatched the radio transmitter from her purse. "This is Dragon Lady. Come in, Shadow, and give me your position." She patiently waited for a response, but her only reply was static. She repeated the message four times but received no answer. "This is inexcusable!" Julia snapped.

"Can you raise anyone else with your call box?" Pitt asked cynically.

"No, it's only good for about two miles."

"Then it's time to—" Pitt stopped in midsentence as the two vans suddenly turned the corner of the block and pulled up at the curb, one on each side of the Duesenberg, which was still sitting in the driveway. They left barely enough room for the Duesenberg's wide, flowing fenders to pass into the street between them. They showed no headlights, only parking lights. The figures inside looked vague and shadowy through the darkened, solar-coated windows.

"I knew nothing was wrong," said Julia, squinting at Pitt with a know-it-all look. She spoke into her radio transmitter again. "Shadow, this is Dragon Lady, why did you leave your positions around the carriage house?"

This time a voice answered almost immediately. "Sorry Dragon Lady, we thought it best to circle the block and look for any suspicious vehicles. If you are ready to leave, please give us your destination."

"I don't buy it," Pitt said, eyeing the distance between the two parked vans while gauging the passing traffic on the street. "One van should have remained in position while the other circled the block. You're an agent. Why am I telling you?"

"Peter would not have hired irresponsible people," Julia said firmly. "He doesn't work that way."

"Don't answer just yet!" said Pitt harshly. Danger, like a red warning sign, began to flash in Pitt's brain. "We've been sold out. A dime will get you a dollar those are not the same men Harper hired."

For the first time Julia's eyes reflected a growing apprehension. "If you're right, what do I tell them?"

If Pitt thought their lives were in deadly peril, he didn't show it. His face was cool, his mind focused. "Say we're going to my place at the Washington National Airport."

"You live in an airport?" Julia asked, baffled.

"For almost twenty years. Actually, I live on the perimeter."

Julia shrugged in bewilderment and gave the instructions to the men in the vans as Pitt reached under the seat and produced a cellular phone. "Now get a hold of Harper. Explain the situation and say we're on our way toward the Lincoln Memorial. Tell him I'll try to stall off our arrival until he can arrange an intercept."

Julia dialed a number and waited for the party on the other end to answer. After giving her identification, she was put through to Peter Harper, who was at home relaxing with his family. After she gave him Pitt's message, she sat and listened in silence before punching off the phone. She looked at Pitt expressionless. "Help is on the way. Peter also said to tell you that considering what happened at your hangar earlier this evening, he regrets not being more alert to possible problems."

"Is he sending law-enforcement teams to the Memorial for the intercept?"

"He's contacting them now."

"You never told me what happened at your hangar."

"Not now."

Julia began to say something, thought better of it and said simply, "Shouldn't we have waited right here for help?"

Pitt studied the vans parked quietly and ominously at the curb. "I can't sit here any longer looking like I'm waiting for the traffic to ease or our friends will begin to think we're onto them. Once we reach Massachusetts Avenue and merge into the main stream of traffic, we'll be reasonably safe. They won't risk exposure by attacking us in front of a hundred witnesses."

"You could call nine-one-one on your cell phone and ask them to respond with a patrol car cruising the area."

"If you were a dispatcher, would you buy some bizarre story and take responsibility for ordering a fleet of patrol cars to charge to the Lincoln Memorial and look for an orange and brown nineteen-twenty-nine Duesenberg that is being pursued by killers?"

"I suppose not," Julia admitted.

"Better we left it to Harper to call out the posse."

He slipped the big stick shift on the floor into first gear and accelerated out into the street, turning to the left so the vans would lose time swinging a U-turn to follow him. He gained almost a hundred yards before he caught the lights of the lead van coming up on his rear bumper. Two blocks later he whipped the heavy Duesenberg onto Massachusetts Avenue and began snaking in and out of the nighttime traffic.

Julia tensed as she looked through the steering wheel and saw the needle creep up and waver at seventy miles an hour. "This car doesn't have seat belts."

"They didn't believe in them in nineteen twenty-nine."

"You're going awfully fast."

"I can't think of a better way to attract attention than by exceeding the speed limit in a seventy-year-old car that weighs almost four tons."

"I hope she has good brakes." Julia resigned herself to the chase, uncertainty still in her mind.

"They're not as sensitive as modern power brakes, but if I stomp on them they do the job just fine."

Julia gripped the Colt automatic but made no effort to remove the safety or aim it. She balked at accepting Pitt's assertion that their lives were in jeopardy. That their bodyguards had turned on them seemed too incredible to believe.

"Why me?" Pitt moaned as he careened the monster around Mount Vernon Square, the big tires howling in protest, heads turning on the sidewalks, people staring incredulously. "Would you believe this is the second time in a year a pretty girl and I had to escape sharks who chased us over the streets of Washington?"

She stared at him. "This happened to you before?"

"On that occasion I was driving a sports car and had a much easier time of it."

Pitt aimed the polished hood ornament on the radiator cap down New Jersey Avenue before hammering a right turn onto First Street and accelerated toward the nation's Capitol and its Mall. Cars that got in his way, he frightened aside with warning blasts from the big twin horns mounted beneath the massive headlights. He spun the thick rim of the steering wheel violently as they raced between the traffic on the crowded street.

The vans were still on his tail. Because of their faster acceleration, they had closed until their reflections loomed in the rearview mirror atop the center of the windshield. Although the Duesenberg could out-pull them if given a long enough straight stretch, it was not a car that would set records at a drag strip. Pitt had yet to shift from second to third, and the gears wailed like a banshee.

The giant engine with its twin overhead cams turned effortlessly at high rpms. The traffic on the street ahead thinned, and Pitt was able to push the Duesenberg as hard as she could go. He slewed the car into the circle around the Peace Monument behind the Capitol building.

Then another quick twist of the steering wheel and the Duesy drifted on all four wheels around the Garfield Monument, skirted the Reflecting Pool and shot down Maryland Avenue toward the Air & Space Museum.

From behind them, over the exhaust roar of the Duesenberg, they heard a brief staccato of gunfire. The mirror attached to the top of the spare-tire cover mounted in the left front fender abruptly disintegrated. The shooter quickly adjusted and a stream of bullets shredded the top frame of the windshield, shattering the glass, which showered across the hood of the car. Pitt slipped down low behind the wheel, his right hand grabbing Julia by the hair and yanking her horizontal on the leather seat.

"That concludes the entertainment part of the program," muttered Pitt. "No more chicken-hearted maneuvers."

"Oh, God, you were right!" Julia shouted in his ear. "They *are* out to kill us."

"I'm going to make a straight run so you can return their fire."

"Not in traffic, not on these streets," she retorted. "I couldn't live with myself if I hit an innocent child."

Her reply was a frenzied sideways motion as the car rocketed across Third Street. Instead of turning with the traffic, Pitt cut across the pavement and sent the Duesenberg leaping over the curb onto the grass of the Capitol Mall. The big 750-by-17-inch tires took the raised concrete as casually as a minor speed bump. Sod was ripped out of the ground by the spinning rear wheels and sprayed out and under the rear fenders like shrapnel.

Julia did what any sane woman would do under the same circumstances. She screamed and then cried out, "You can't drive down the middle of the Mall!"

"I damned well can and will so long as we live to tell about it!" Pitt shot back.

His seemingly crazy and totally unexpected maneuver had the desired results. The driver of the lead van tenaciously chased the Duesenberg over the curb onto the grassy Mall, and blew all four tires in the attempt. They struck the concrete barrier with such force that they exploded in a rapid series of loud pops. The much smaller, more modern tires on the vans could not jump over the curb with the ease of the Duesenberg's big doughnuts.

The second van's driver elected for discretion, checked his speed in time, braked and slowly drove over the curb without damaging his tires.

The men in the first van—there were two—frantically abandoned their vehicle and flung themselves through the open side door of the second one. Then they all stubbornly took up the chase again, pursuing the Duesenberg across the middle of the Mall to the astonishment of hundreds of onlookers who were heading for home after an open-air Marine Corps band concert at the Navy Memorial. The shocked expression on their faces ranged from frozen incomprehension to stunned astonishment at seeing the huge car with the artistically flowing lines tearing across the Mall between the National Air & Space Museum and the National Gallery of Art. Groups of people strolling or jogging along the Mall's paths were suddenly galvanized into chasing the speeding vehicles on foot, certain they were about to witness an accident.

The Duesenberg was still accelerating with Pitt's foot flat on the gas pedal. The long car flared as it tore across Seventh Street, skidding around passing cars, Pitt fighting the wheel with grim tenacity. The mammoth car was incredibly responsive. The faster the speed, the more solid the feeling of stability. All he had to do was point the car where he wanted to go, and she went. He breathed a brief sigh of relief at seeing no cross-traffic on Fourteenth Street, the next thoroughfare across the Mall. The sidemount mirror and the rearview mirror on the windshield had both been blown to pieces by the earlier burst of gunfire, and he could not spare a brief glance to see if the pursuing van was closing within accurate firing range again.

"Take a peek over the seat and see how close they are," he yelled to Julia.

She had thumbed off the side safety on the Colt and had it aimed over the backrest of the seat. "They slowed when bouncing over the curbs on the last two cross streets," she answered, "but they're gaining. I can almost see the whites of the driver's eyes."

"Then you can begin shooting back."

"This isn't the wilderness around Orion River. There are pedestrians all over the Mall. I can't risk striking anyone with a stray shot."

"Then wait until you can't miss."

The men firing out the sides of the van were not as considerate. They unleashed another burst at the Duesenberg, drilling the big trunk mounted on the rear of the body, the thuds of the bullets mingling with the pulsing bursts erupting from the guns' muzzles. Pitt wrenched desperately on the wheel, dodging the fusillade that whistled past the right side of the car.

"Those guys don't have your sensitivity toward others," he said, thankful that he had managed to swerve around any car that crossed his path without accident.

Wishing he had a magic wand to stop the traffic, he hurtled across Fifteenth Street, narrowly missing a newspaper truck and throwing the Duesenberg into a four-wheel slide to avoid a black Ford Crown Victoria sedan, which had replaced most of the government limousines. Fleetingly, he wondered what government VIP was riding inside. He felt a small surge of comfort at knowing the van had to drop back to negotiate the curbs.

The towering Washington Monument rose in front of the car's path. Pitt guided the car around the floodlit obelisk and sped down the slight slope on the opposite side. Julia was still unable to get a clear shot as Pitt concentrated on getting the Duesenberg past the Monument without losing control on the slippery grass. And then they were heading toward the Lincoln Memorial at the end of the Mall.

Seconds later he came to Seventeenth Street. Thankfully, there was a slot in the middle of the traffic and he shot toward the other side without endangering passing cars. Despite the violent chase through the avenues of Washington and across the Mall, he saw no flashing red lights nor heard sirens from pursuing police cars. If he had attempted the mad ride across the Mall on any other occasion, he'd have been stopped and arrested for reckless driving within the first hundred yards.

Pitt had a short breathing spell as they roared between the Reflecting Pool and Constitution Gardens. Almost directly ahead loomed the brilliantly illuminated Lincoln Memorial and the Potomac River beyond. He turned and looked over his shoulder at the van, which was coming up fast on the Duesenberg again. The van's twin headlights were so close he could have read a newspaper under them. The contest was too uneven. Despite the Duesenberg being a magnificent automobile by which all others were measured, it was a case of a big-game hunter in a bush vehicle chasing an elephant. He knew that they knew he was running out of space. If he cut and swung right toward Constitution Avenue, they could easily cut him off. To his left the long Reflecting Pool stretched almost to the great white marble Memorial. The water barrier looked impassable. Or was it?

He roughly pushed Julia off the seat onto the floor. "Keep down and hold on tight!"

"What are you going to do?"

"We're going boating."

"You're not only deranged, you've gone berserk."

"A rare combination," Pitt said calmly. His features were fixed in concentration, his eyes glistening like those of a hawk circling over a hare. There was a look of unfathomable detachment about him. To Julia, who stared up from her position on the floorboards under the dashboard, he looked as relentlessly determined as a comber surging toward a beach. Then she saw him snap the wheel to the left, sending the Duesenberg sliding sideways in the grass at nearly seventy miles an hour, the big rear wheels spinning crazily, ripping up the turf like giant meat grinders and just missing the large trees spaced twenty-two feet apart along the pool.

After what seemed like ages, the tires dug in and gripped the soft ground, sending the car beyond the point of no return, her immense bulk lunging forward into the Reflecting Pool.

The heavy steel chassis and aluminum body, driven by the full force of the powerful engine, smacked into the water with an enormous white explosion that leaped from her front and sides like Niagara Falls turned upside down. The sickening thump jarred the Duesenberg from bumper to bumper as her great weight sank, pushing her balloon tires onto the concrete bottom where their rubber treads bit and hurled the car forward like a bull whale charging through the sea after a female in heat.

The water gushed over the hood and flooded through the shattered windshield into the front compartment, drenching Pitt and nearly inundating Julia. Unaware exactly of Pitt's intentions, she was petrified at finding herself suddenly submerged under a deluge. To Pitt, taking the full brunt of the torrent, it seemed as if he was driving into raging breakers only a surfer could love.

There was no growth on the bottom of the Reflecting Pool. It was drained and cleaned by the Park Service on a regular basis. The distance between the surface of the water and the top of the edge along the sides measured only eight inches. The bottom of the pool was not flat but sloped from a depth of one foot around the walls to a maximum depth of two and a half feet in the middle. The distance from the pool floor to the top edge of the wall measured twenty inches.

Pitt prayed the engine wouldn't flood and die. The distributor, he knew, was a good four feet from the ground. No problem there. Nor with the carburetors, as they sat well over three feet high. But his main concern was the spark plugs. They rested between the twin overhead cam shafts at three feet on the nose.

The Reflecting Pool was exactly 160 feet in width. It seemed impossible for the Duesenberg to navigate such an obstacle. But she bulldozed a gaping valley through the water, her engine gamely producing torque to the rear wheels and not drowning out. She had pushed her way to within ten yards of the opposite edge of the pool when the water around her suddenly erupted in a cloud of small geysers.

"Obstinate bastards!" Pitt muttered to himself. He gripped the big steering wheel so hard his knuckles bleached white.

The chase van had stopped at the edge of the Reflecting Pool, her occupants tumbling out and firing wildly at the big car crashing through the water. Their shock and disbelief had cost them nearly a full minute, giving Pitt time almost to reach the other side. Realizing this was their final chance, they pumped shot after shot at the floundering Duesenberg seemingly deaf and dumb to the sirens and flashing lights that were converging on them from Twenty-Third Street and Constitution Avenue. Too late did they finally sense their predicament. Unless they followed Pitt across the Reflecting Pool, an act about as conceivable as producing wings and flying to the moon because of their modern, smaller wheels and tires, they were left with no alternative but to try to evade the rapidly approaching police patrol cars. Without the luxury of a conference, they leaped back in the van and spun a 180-degree turn before tearing back across the Mall toward the Washington Monument.

The Duesenberg was coming up the slope of the pool toward the edge now. Pitt slowed the car, carefully judging the height of the wall in relation to the size of the front tires. He backshifted the transmission into first, actually crammed it into gear. The gears inside the three-speed nonsynchromesh crash box shrieked in protest before they finally meshed in place. Then, ten feet before meeting the wall, Pitt stamped the gas pedal into the floorboard as hard as he could, taking advantage of the upward slope of the pool to lift the front end of the car. "Do it!" he implored the Duesenberg. "Go over the wall!"

As though she had a mechanical brain and heart, the old Duesenberg responded with a burst of acceleration that lifted the front end, barely clearing the bumper over the edge of the pool, the tires rolling up the wall until they shot over the edge onto flat ground.

The Duesenberg's ground clearance was almost a foot, but not high enough for the bottom of her chassis to run clear. She canted steeply, followed by a rendering crash. Then an ungodly scraping, tearing sound ripped the air. For a moment she seemed to hang, then her momentum propelled her forward and she leaped ahead, as if grinding her guts out over the concrete wall until all four wheels were on the grass of the Mall again.

Only at that instant did the engine begin to miss. Almost like a golden retriever exiting a river with a bird in its mouth, the Duesenberg shuddered, shook herself free of the water that filled her body, and limped ahead. After only a hundred yards the fan behind the radiator and the heat from the engine worked in unison to blow-dry the water that had splashed and shorted four of her spark plugs. Soon, she began hitting on all eight cylinders again.

Julia came up off the floor sputtering and peered over the back of the car at the van speeding away under pursuit by four police cars. She wrung the water from the hem of her dress and ran her fingers through her hair in a vain attempt to look presentable. "I'm a mess. My dress and coat are ruined." She looked at Pitt with a look of pure anger. Then her expression softened. "If you hadn't saved my life for the second time in as many weeks, I'd make you buy me a new outfit."

He turned to her and smiled as he set the Duesenberg on a course down Independence Avenue and across the Memorial Bridge toward the Washington National Airport and his hangar. "Tell you what. If you're a good girl, I'll take you to my place, dry your clothes and warm you up with a cup of coffee."

Her gray eyes were soft and unblinking. She laid a hand on his arm and murmured. "And if I'm a naughty girl?"

Pitt laughed, partly from the relief of escaping another death trap, partly from seeing Julia's bedraggled appearance and partly because she was trying without success to cover the parts of her body that were revealed through the wet dress. "Keep talking like that and I'll skip the coffee."

28

SUNLIGHT WAS SLIDING over the sills of the skylights when Julia slowly pushed aside the mist of sleep. She felt as if she was floating, her body totally weightless. It was a pleasurable sensation left over from the ardor of the night. She opened her eyes, shifted her mind into gear and began studying her surroundings. She found herself lying alone. The bed was king-size and sat in the middle of a room that looked like the captain's cabin from an old sailing ship, complete with mahogany-paneled walls and a small fireplace. The furnishings, including the dressers and cabinets, were nautical antiques.

Like most women, Julia was curious and intrigued about male bachelor apartments. She felt that the opposite gender could be read by their surroundings. Some men, ladies observed, lived like pack rats and never cleaned up after themselves, creating and preserving strange alien life-forms in their bathrooms and inside their refrigerators. Making beds was as foreign as processing goat cheese. Their laundry was piled beside and over washers and dryers that still had the instruction booklets attached to the knobs.

And then there were the neatness freaks who lived in an environment only a decontamination scientist could love. Dust, food scraps and toothpaste droppings were all furiously attacked and energetically eliminated. Every piece of furniture, every object of decor, was positioned with precision, never to migrate. The kitchen would have passed a white-glove inspection by the most diligent of sanitation inspectors.

Pitt's apartment was somewhere in between. Tidy and uncluttered, it had a masculine casualness about it that appealed to the women who visited occasionally rather than frequently. Julia could see that Pitt was a man who preferred to live in the past. There was nothing modern in the entire apartment. Even the brass plumbing fixtures in the bathroom and kitchen seemed to have come out of some old passenger liner that once traveled the seas.

She rolled over on her side and stared through the doorway into the living room, where shelves on two walls were filled with delicately built ship models of wrecks that Pitt and his NUMA crew had discovered and surveyed. The remaining walls held dockyard builders' half models and four seascape paintings by Richard DeRosset, a contemporary American artist, of nineteenth-century steamships. There was a feeling of comfort about the apartment, not the formal and grandiose atmosphere produced by an interior decorator.

Julia soon came to realize that Pitt's home made no allowances for a woman's touch. It was the sanctuary of an intensely private man who adored and admired women but who could never be fully controlled by them. He was the kind of man women were drawn to, had wild adventures and amorous affairs with, but never married.

She smelled coffee coming from the kitchen but saw no sign of Pitt. She sat up and set her bare feet on a wood-plank floor. Her dress and underwear were neatly hung in an open closet, dried and pressed. She padded across the plank floor into the bathroom and smiled at herself in the mirror when she found a tray with an unopened new toothbrush, women's moisturizers, bath gels, body oils, makeup accessories and an assortment of feminine hairbrushes. Julia could not help but wonder how many women had stood and looked into the same mirror before her. She showered inside of what looked like an upended copper tank, toweled and dried her hair with a blow-dryer. After she dressed, Julia stepped into the empty kitchen, helped herself to a cup of coffee and moved out onto the balcony.

Pitt was down on the main floor in coveralls replacing the shattered windshield on the Duesenberg. Before she greeted him, Julia's gaze swept over the immaculate machinery on the spacious floor below.

She did not recognize the makes of the classic cars parked in even rows, nor did she recognize the Ford Trimotor aircraft and the Messerschmitt 262 jet plane sitting side by side at one end of the hangar. There was a large, old-fashioned Pullman car sitting on a short section of track, while behind it a small bathtub with an outboard motor stood perched on a small platform beside a strange-looking craft that resembled the upper half of a sailboat that had been tied to the buoyancy tubes of a rubber boat. A mast rose from the middle with what seemed like palm fronds woven into a sail.

"Good morning," she called down.

He looked up and gave her a killer smile. "Nice to see you, lazybones."

"I could have stayed in bed all day."

"No chance of that," he said. "Admiral Sandecker called while you were in dreamland. He and your boss want our bodies at a conference in one hour."

"Your place or mine?" Julia asked in a humorous tone.

"Yours, the INS headquarters office."

"How did you ever clean and press my silk dress?"

"I soaked it in cold water after you fell asleep last night and hung it to dry. This morning I lightly ironed it through a cotton towel. As far as I can tell, it looks good as new."

"You're quite a guy, Dirk Pitt," she said. "I've never known a man so thoughtful, or innovative. Do you perform the same services for all the girls who sleep over?"

"Only exotic ladies of Chinese descent," he answered.

"May I fix breakfast?"

"Sounds good. You'll find whatever you need in the fridge and on the upper cupboards to your right. I already made coffee."

She hesitated as Pitt began removing the fragmented mirror on the side-mounted spare tire. "I'm sorry about your car," she said sincerely.

Pitt merely shrugged. "The damage is nothing I can't fix."

"Truly, she's a lovely car."

"Fortunately, the bullets failed to strike any vital parts."

"Speaking of Qin Shang's thugs . . ."

"Not to worry. There are enough hired guards patrolling outside to stage a coup on a third-world country."

"I'm embarrassed."

Pitt looked up at Julia leaning on the balcony railing and saw that her face was genuinely red with chagrin. "Why?"

"My superiors at INS and fellow agents must know I spent the night and are probably making snide remarks behind my back."

Pitt looked up at Julia on the balcony and grinned. "I'll tell anybody who asks that while you slept, I spent the night working on a rear end."

"That's not funny," she said reprovingly.

"Sorry, I meant to say differential."

"That's better," Julia said, turning flippantly with a toss of her ebony hair and strutting into the kitchen, having enjoyed Pitt's teasing of her.

Accompanied by two bodyguards in an armored sedan, Pitt and Julia were driven to her sorority sister's apartment so she could change into attire more fitting for a government agent. Then they were taken to the stark-looking Chester Arthur Building on Northwest I Street, which housed the headquarters of the Immigration and Naturalization Service. They entered the beige seven-story stone structure with its blackened windows from the underground parking area and were escorted up an elevator to the Investigations Division where they were met by Peter Harper's secretary, who showed them into a conference room.

Six men were already present in the room: Admiral Sandecker; Chief Commissioner Duncan Monroe and Peter Harper of the INS; Wilbur Hill, a director with the Central Intelligence Agency; Charles Davis, special assistant to the director of the Federal Bureau of Investigation; and Al Giordino. They all rose to their feet as Pitt and Julia entered the room. All, that is, except Giordino, who simply nodded silently and gave Julia an infectious smile. Introductions were quickly made before everyone settled in chairs around a long oak table.

"Well," said Monroe to Pitt, "I understand you and Ms. Lee had an interesting evening." The tone of his voice strongly suggested a double meaning.

"Harrowing would be closer to the truth," Julia answered quickly, prim and proper in a white blouse and blue business suit with the skirt cut just above her shapely knees.

Pitt stared evenly at Harper. "Things might have gone smoother if our hired bodyguards hadn't tried to send us to the morgue."

"I deeply regret the incident," said Harper seriously. "But circumstances went beyond our control."

Pitt noticed that Harper looked far from sheepish. "I'd be interested in knowing the circumstances," he came back coldly.

"The four men Peter hired to protect you and Ms. Lee were murdered," revealed Davis of the FBI. A tall man who sat half a head above the other men around the table, he had the eyes of a Saint Bernard that had just come across a garbage can behind a barbecue-steak restaurant.

"Oh God," murmured Julia. "All four?"

"Because their concentration was focused on observing Mr. Perlmutter's residence they left themselves vulnerable for an assault."

"I regret their deaths," said Pitt. "But it doesn't sound like they operated as true professionals."

Monroe cleared his throat. "A full investigation is under way, of course. Initial analysis suggests that they were approached and murdered by Qin Shang's men, who posed as city police officers checking on reports of suspicious behavior in the neighborhood."

"You have witnesses?"

Davis nodded. "A neighbor across the street from Mr. Perlmutter reported seeing a patrol car and four uniformed officers entering the vans and driving them away."

"After shooting the bodyguards with silenced weapons," Harper added.

Pitt looked at Harper. "Can you identify the men who attacked me at the hangar?"

Harper glanced at Davis, who turned up his palms in a dismayed gesture. "It seems their bodies disappeared on the way to the morgue."

"How is that possible?" demanded Sandecker explosively.

"Don't tell me," Giordino said sarcastically, "an investigation is under way."

"That goes without saying," replied Davis. "All we know is that they went missing after being unloaded from the ambulances at the morgue. We were lucky, however, in obtaining a make on one of your assassins when a paramedic pulled off a glove so he could try for a pulse. The corpse's hand lay flat on your polished hangar floor and left a set of three fingerprints. The Russians identified the killer for us as a Pavel Gavrovich, a former high-level Defense Ministry agent and assassin. For a marine engineer with NUMA to take out a professional hit man, Mr. Pitt, a man who had killed at least twenty-two people that we know of, is a polished achievement."

"Professional or not," said Pitt quietly, "Gavrovich made the mistake of underestimating his prey."

"I find it incredible that Qin Shang can make fools of the entire United States government with such ease," said Sandecker acidly.

Pitt sat back and stared down as if seeing something beneath the surface of the conference table. "He couldn't. Not unless he had inside help from the Justice Department and other agencies of the federal government."

Wilbur Hill of the CIA spoke for the first time. He was a blond man with a mustache, the pale blue eyes set widely apart, as if he could observe movements off to his sides. "I'll likely get into trouble for saying this, but we have strong suspicions that Qin Shang's influence reaches into the White House."

"As we speak," said Davis, "a congressional committee and Justice Department prosecutors are looking into tens of millions of dollars in fraudulent contributions by the People's Republic of China that were funneled into the President's future election campaign through Qin Shang."

"When we met with the President," said Sandecker, "he spoke as if the Chinese were the greatest scourge on the country since the Civil War. Now you tell me his fingers are in Qin Shang's wallet."

"There is simply no underestimating the morals of a politician," Giordino said with a sardonic twist of his lips.

"Be that as it may," Monroe said gravely, "political ethics are not the job of INS. Our primary concern at the moment is with the huge numbers of illegal Chinese aliens that are being smuggled into the country by Qin Shang Maritime Limited before being killed or enslaved by criminal syndicates."

"Commissioner Monroe is quite correct," said Harper. "The duty of INS is to plug the flow, not prosecute murders."

"I can't speak for Mr. Hill and the CIA," said Davis, "but the Bureau has been heavily involved with investigating Qin Shang's domestic crimes against the American people for three years."

"Our inquiries, on the other hand, are focused more on his overseas operations," offered CIA's Hill.

"An uphill battle on any front," said Pitt thoughtfully. "If Shang has forces within our own government working against your efforts, it will make all your jobs that much tougher."

"Nobody here thinks it will be a piece of cake," said Monroe formally.

Julia jumped in. "Aren't we overlooking the fact that besides being an international body smuggler, Qin Shang is a mass murderer. I experienced his ruthlessness firsthand. There is no counting the untold numbers of innocent people and children who lie dead because of his greed. The atrocities his henchmen have committed under his direction are hideous and monstrous. He deals in crimes against humanity. We must put an end to the slaughter, and quickly."

For a long moment no one said a word. Every man at the table knew of the horrors Julia had witnessed and suffered. Finally, Monroe broke the silence.

"We all understand your feelings, Ms. Lee, but all of us are working under laws and regulations that must be followed. I promise you that every possible effort is being made to stop Qin Shang. As long as I am at the helm of the INS, we won't rest until his operation is destroyed and he is arrested and convicted."

"I can safely say that goes for Mr. Hill and myself as well," added Davis.

"Not good enough," said Pitt quietly, turning every head.

"You doubt our resolve?" asked Monroe indignantly.

"No, but I totally disagree with your methods."

"Government policy dictates our actions," Davis said. "All of us must work under guidelines set by the American justice system."

Pitt's face went dark as a midnight sky. "I saw for myself a sea of dead on the bottom of Orion Lake. I saw the poor wretched souls locked up in cells. Four men died protecting Julia and me—"

"I know what you're driving at, Mr. Pitt," said Davis. "But we have no evidence directly linking Qin Shang to those crimes. Certainly not enough to call for an indictment."

"The man is shrewd," said Harper. "He's shielded himself from direct involvement. Without solid proof that he is in some way responsible, we can't nail him."

"If he's laughed in your face every step of the way," said Pitt, "what makes you think he's going to suddenly play dumb and fall into your waiting arms?"

"No man can defy the far-reaching investigative powers of our government indefinitely," said Hill earnestly. "I promise you that he will be tried, convicted and sentenced quite soon."

"The man is a foreign national," said Sandecker. "You arrest him anywhere in the United States and the Chinese government will raise every kind of hell with the White House and State Department. Boycotts, sanctions on trade goods, you name it. No way are they going to let you take their fair-haired boy out of circulation."

"The way I see it, Mr. Hill," said Giordino, "you whistle up one of your CIA hit squads and eliminate Shang neatly and cleanly. Problem solved."

"Despite what many think, the CIA does not do assassinations," said Hill testily.

"Madness," muttered Pitt. "Suppose Shang's hit men were successful last night and killed Julia and me. You'd still be sitting here claiming you didn't have enough cold evidence to indict the man who ordered our murders."

"Unfortunately, that's the way it is," said Monroe.

"Qin Shang isn't about to stop there," Julia said in frustration. "He fully intends to kill Dirk. He said as much at his party last night."

"And I informed him that it's only fair that we play by the same rules," said Pitt. "He now thinks I've hired a team of assassins to take him out too."

"You threatened Qin Shang to his face?" Harper asked incredulously. "How could you dare?"

"It was easy," Pitt answered casually. "Despite his wealth and power, he still puts his pants on one leg at a time the same as me. I thought it might be nice if he looks over his shoulder like the rest of his intended victims."

"You're joking, of course," said Monroe, scorn in his tone. "You don't really conspire to murder Shang."

Pitt answered in a smooth voice. "Oh, but I do. As they say in the old western movies, it's either him or me, and next time I intend to shoot first."

Monroe looked worried. He looked across the table at Hill and Davis. Then he focused on Sandecker. "Admiral, I called this meeting in the hope of enlisting Mr. Pitt in cooperating with our operation. But it seems he has become a loose cannon. Since he is under your authority, I strongly suggest you give him a leave of absence. Peter here will arrange for his protection in a safe house on the coast of Maine."

"What about Julia?" demanded Pitt. "How do you intend to keep her safe from further harm?"

"Ms. Lee is an agent with INS," said Harper in an official tone. "She will continue to work the case. A team of our agents will stand guard over her movements. I guarantee that she will be safe."

Pitt stared across the table at Sandecker. "How do you call it, Admiral?"

Sandecker pulled his red Vandyke to a point. Only Pitt and Giordino recognized the wolfish glint in his eyes. "It would appear we have little choice in the matter. A safe house might be the best place for you to lay low until Qin Shang and his criminal activities are terminated."

Pitt said soberly, "Well, I guess I have little say in the matter. A safe house it is."

Sandecker wasn't fooled for an instant by Pitt's easy acceptance. He knew his special projects director did not have the slightest intention of leaving the room like a lamb. "Then it's settled." Suddenly he laughed sharply.

"May I ask what you find so funny, Admiral?" asked Monroe irritably.

"Sorry, Mr. Monroe. But I'm relieved to assume that the INS, the FBI and CIA have no further use for NUMA."

"That is correct. After your people bungled their underwater investigations of Qin Shang Maritime's facilities in Hong Kong and Sungari, I see it as a wasted effort to involve your agency any further."

Monroe's cutting words produced no fury, no outrage, nor did they incite wrath. Pitt and Giordino sat there and took it in stride, expressing no emotions. Sandecker barely managed to reply to the commissioner's insulting remarks. He settled for clenching his fists out of sight under the table.

Pitt rose to his feet, followed by Giordino. "I know when I'm not wanted." He grinned at Sandecker. "I'll wait in the car." He paused to grasp lightly one of Julia's hands, raise it to his lips and kiss it. "Have you ever lain on the beach at Mazatlán and watched the sunset over the Sea of Cortez?" he whispered in her ear.

She looked self-consciously up and down at the faces around the table, her face reddening. "I've never even been to Mexico."

"You will," he promised, "you will." Then he released her hand and leisurely strolled from the conference room, trailed by Giordino and Sandecker.

Unlike most directors of U.S. governmental agencies, who demanded to be carried around Washington by limousine, Admiral Sandecker preferred to drive himself. After leaving the INS headquarters building, he steered the turquoise Jeep, which was one of the NUMA fleet of transportation vehicles, along the east side of the Potomac River on the Maryland shore. After dropping several miles below the city, he turned off the road and stopped the Jeep in a parking lot next to a small boat dock. Locking the car, Sandecker led the way across the floating wooden dock to a sixty-year-old double-ender whaleboat that had once served as Admiral Bull Halsey's shore boat during the war in the Pacific. After finding it in shabby condition, he had lovingly restored it to its original state. While he turned the handle that kicked the four-cylinder Buda diesel engine to life, Pitt and Giordino cast off the mooring lines. Then they climbed aboard as the little boat chugged out into the river.

"I thought we'd hold a little private talk before we returned to the

NUMA building," Sandecker said above the exhaust as he held the long tiller in the stern under one arm. "As ridiculous as it sounds, I'm leery of conversing in my own office."

"It does tend to make one gun-shy, knowing Qin Shang can and has bought off half the city," said Pitt.

"The guy has more tentacles than ten squids joined together at birth," added Giordino.

"Unlike the Russians, who paid paltry sums for secret information during the cold war," said Sandecker, "Qin Shang thinks nothing of paying out millions of dollars to buy people and information."

"Backed by the Chinese government," said Pitt, "his cash reserves are bottomless."

Giordino sat on a bench seat facing Sandecker. "What magic have you conjured up, Admiral?"

"Magic?"

"I've been around you too long to know you're not the kind to sit back and take contempt and ridicule. Something is cooking in your Machiavellian mind."

Pitt grinned. "I suspect the admiral and I are running on the same wavelength. We're not about to let NUMA be shut out of hanging Qin Shang from the nearest tree."

Sandecker's lips curled in a taut smile as he swung the boat in a wide arc to avoid a sailboat that was tacking upriver. "I hate it when I'm second-guessed by the hired help."

"Sungari?" asked Pitt.

Sandecker nodded. "I've kept Rudi Gunn and the *Marine Denizen* on station a few miles below Qin Shang Maritime's port facility in the Atchafalaya River. I'd like you two rogues to fly down and join him. Then wait for the *United States* to show up."

"Where is she now?" asked Giordino.

"The last report put her two hundred miles off the coast of Costa Rica."

"That should put her at the dock at Sungari in three days," remarked Pitt.

"You were right about a crew coming on board to take her through the Panama Canal."

"Did they remain on board?"

Sandecker shook his head. "After transit through the Canal, they disembarked. The *United States* is continuing toward Louisiana under remote control."

"A 'robo ship,' " Giordino muttered thoughtfully. "Hard to believe a ship the size of the *United States* is cruising the seas with no one on board."

"The Navy has been developing the 'robo ship' concept for ten years," explained Sandecker. "Ship designers and engineers have already built an arsenal ship that is basically a floating missile pad able to launch as many as five hundred missiles by remote control from another ship, an aircraft or a facility thousands of miles away, a radical departure from present aircraft carriers that require a five-thousand-man crew. It's the newest concept from the Navy since the nuclear ballistic missile submarine. Totally contained warships and bomber aircraft are not far behind."

"Whatever Qin Shang has in mind for the *United States*," said Giordino, "it's not as a missile platform. Dirk and I searched it from engine room to wheelhouse. There are no missile launchers."

"I read your report," said Sandecker. "You also found no indication that it would be used to smuggle illegal immigrants."

"That's true," acknowledged Pitt. "When Shang's operations are examined at first glance they appear to be conceived by a genius with a flair for sorcery, but tear away the veneer and you find a logical exercise. He has a valid function for the ship, you can bet on it."

Sandecker pulled the throttle lever another notch and increased the speed of the whaleboat. "So we're no closer to a solution than we were two weeks ago."

"Except for my personal theory that Shang intends to scuttle her," said Pitt.

Sandecker looked dubious. "Why scuttle a perfectly good ocean liner after he spent millions refitting her?"

"I don't have an answer," Pitt admitted.

"That's what I want you to find out. Take care of your immediate affairs and sign out a NUMA jet to fly yourselves to Morgan City. I'll call Rudi and tell him you're coming."

"Now that we're working without an endorsement from the INS and other investigative agencies, how far can we go with this thing?" Pitt asked.

"Do whatever it takes without getting yourselves killed," responded Sandecker firmly. "I'll be responsible and answer for your actions once Monroe and Harper get wise that we haven't stumbled off into the fog and gone home like good little boys."

Pitt studied Sandecker. "Why are you doing this, Admiral? Why are you jeopardizing your job as head of NUMA to stop Qin Shang?"

The admiral stared back at Pitt astutely. "You and Al were going to go behind my back and keep dogging Qin Shang anyway. Am I right?"

Giordino shrugged. "Yes, I guess you are."

"The instant Dirk played the cowardly lion and timidly submitted to Monroe's demand that you go to a safe house, I knew damned well you were going to jump ship. I'm only bowing to the inevitable."

Pitt had long ago become a shrewd judge of Sandecker's character. "Not you, Admiral. You never bow to anything or anybody."

The fire in Sandecker's eyes blazed for a moment, then smoldered. "If you must know, those spooks around the table pissed me off so bad that I'm counting on both of you and Rudi Gunn and every resource at NUMA to take out Qin Shang before they do."

"We're up against some pretty heavy competition," said Pitt.

"Maybe," said Sandecker, his eyes becoming urgent, commanding. "But Qin Shang Maritime operates on water, and that's where we have the advantage."

After the meeting broke up, Harper escorted Julia to his office and closed the door. When she was seated he came around and sat down behind his desk. "Julia, I have a tough assignment for you. Strictly on a volunteer basis. I'm not sure you're quite up to it just yet."

Julia's interest was piqued. "It won't hurt to give me a rundown."

Harper handed her a file folder. She opened it and examined a photograph of a woman her own age who was facing the camera with a blank expression on her face. Except for a scar on her chin, she and Julia could have passed for sisters. "Her name is Lin Wan Chu. She grew up on a farm in Jiangsu Province and ran away when her father wanted her to marry a man old enough to be her grandfather. After finding work in the kitchen of a restaurant in the port Qingdao, she eventually became a chef. Two years ago she signed on as a cook with Qin Shang Maritime and has since crewed on a container ship called the *Sung Lien Star.*"

Julia turned to a dossier on the woman and noted that it came from the CIA. She began reading as Harper sat back silently until she finished. "There is a definite resemblance," said Julia. "We're the same height and weight. I'm only four months older than Lin Wan Chu." She kept the file open in her lap and stared across the desk at Harper. "You want me to take her place? Is that the assignment?"

He nodded. "It is."

"My ID was made on the *Indigo Star.* Thanks to a double agent on Qin Shang's payroll, his security people have a file on me a mile long."

"The FBI thinks they have a prime suspect and are maintaining surveillance on him."

"I don't see how I could take Lin Wan Chu's identity and not be caught," Julia said solemnly. "Especially during a long voyage."

"You only have to be Lin Wan Chu for four, maybe five, hours at the most. Just enough time to slip into the ship's routine and hopefully discover how Qin Shang is smuggling his illegal cargo of immigrants onto land."

"You know for a fact the *Sung Lien Star* has aliens hidden on board?"

"A CIA undercover agent in Qingdao reported that he observed over a hundred men, women and children with luggage being unloaded from buses in the dead of night who were herded into a warehouse on the dock beside the ship. Two hours later, the *Sung Lien Star* sailed. At daylight, the agent found the warehouse empty. A hundred-some-odd people had mysteriously disappeared."

"And he thinks they were smuggled on board the ship?"

"The *Star* is a large container ship with the capacity to hide a hundred warm bodies, and its destination is the port of Sungari in Louisiana. There seems little doubt that she's another one of Qin Shang's illegal-immigrant smuggling vessels."

"They make me this time," said Julia seriously, "and I'll be shark bait in less time than it takes to tell about it."

"The risk is not as high as you think," Harper assured her. "You won't be working alone like you did on the *Indigo Star*. You'll carry a concealed radio and be monitored every minute. Backup will be no less than a mile away."

When it came to daring the unknown, Julia was as fearless as any man, more so than most. Her adrenaline was already rising at the thought of walking a tightrope.

"There is one problem," she said quietly.

"What is that?"

A little grimace twisted the shapely red mouth. "My mother and father taught me gourmet cooking. I've never prepared basic slop in quantity before."

29

THE MORNING WAS BRIGHT with a high clear sky flecked by small cloud puffs scattered about like popcorn spilled on a blue carpet as Pitt leveled out the little Skyfox flying boat and flew over the terminal buildings and docks of Sungari. He circled and made several passes, skimming less than a hundred feet above the tops of the big cranes that were lifting wooden cargo crates from the holds of the only freighter moored along an otherwise deserted dock. The merchant ship was sandwiched between the dock and a barge with a towboat.

"Must be a slow business day," observed Giordino from the copilot's seat.

"One ship offloading cargo at a port facility built to handle an entire fleet," said Pitt.

"Qin Shang Maritime Limited's profit-and-loss ledger must be awash in red ink."

"What do you make of the barge?" asked Pitt.

"Looks like trash day. The crew appears to be throwing plastic sacks over the side into the barge."

"See any signs of security?"

"The place sits in the middle of a swamp," said Giordino staring down into the surrounding marshlands. "The only duty for security guards would be to shoo off itinerant alligators, which I hear are hunted around these parts."

"A big business," Pitt said. "Their skins are used for shoes, boots and purses. Hopefully, laws will be passed to restrict the alligator killing long before they become an endangered species."

"That tugboat and garbage barge are beginning to pull away from the hull of the freighter. Make a swing over them when they get into open water."

"Not tugboat, you mean towboat."

"A misnomer. Why call them towboats when they push instead of pull barges through inland waterways?"

"A collection of connecting barges is called a tow, hence, towboat."

"They should be called pushboats," Giordino grumbled.

"I'll take your suggestion up at the next river pilot's annual high-water ball. Maybe they'll give you a free pass on a ferryboat."

"I already get one of those every time I buy ten gallons of gas."

"Coming around." Pitt tilted the control column slightly, banking the Lockheed Skyfox two-seater jet aircraft and leveling out for a few hundred yards before flying over the five-story-high towboat with its square bow burrowed against the stern of a single barge. A man stepped from the towboat's wheelhouse and furiously motioned the aircraft away. As the Skyfox skimmed over the towboat, Giordino caught a quick glimpse of a dirty, unfriendly look on a face that harbored suspicions.

"The captain acts paranoid about prying eyes."

"Maybe we should drop him a note asking directions to Ireland," Pitt said facetiously as he banked the Skyfox for another pass. Formerly a military jet trainer, the aircraft was purchased by NUMA and modified for water landings with a waterproof hull and retractable floats. With twin jet engines mounted on the fuselage behind the wings and cockpit, the Skyfox was often used by NUMA personnel when one of their larger executive jets was not required, and because it could land and take off from water, it was especially useful for offshore transportation.

This time Pitt came in no more than thirty feet over the towboat's funnel and electronic gear, which sprouted from the roof of the wheel-house. As they flashed past the boat and over the barge, Giordino spotted a pair of men throwing themselves prone amid the trash bags in an effort to make themselves indiscernible.

"I've got two men carrying automatic rifles who made a bad job of trying to look invisible," Giordino announced as calmly as if he was calling guests to dinner. "Methinks there is skulduggery afoot."

"We've seen all we're going to see," said Pitt. "Time to meet up with Rudi and the *Marine Denizen*." He made a sweeping turn and set the Skyfox on a course down the Atchafalaya River toward Sweet Bay

Lake. The research ship soon came into view, and he lowered the flaps and dropped the floats in preparation for landing. He flared the aircraft, allowing it gently to kiss the calm water and throw up a light sheet of spray from the floats. Then Pitt taxied alongside the research ship and killed the engines.

Giordino raised the canopy and waved up to Rudi Gunn and Captain Frank Stewart, who were standing at the railing. Stewart turned and shouted an order. The boom from the ship's crane swung around until it was hovering over the Skyfox. The cable was lowered and Giordino attached the hook and lines to the lifting rings on the top of the aircraft's wings and fuselage before catching guy ropes from the crew. A signal was given and the crane's engine shifted into gear and hoisted up the Skyfox. Water fell in cascades from the hull and floats as the Coast Guard crew manning the guy ropes pulled the aircraft into the proper attitude. Once clearance was achieved, the crane swung the aircraft over the side and lowered it onto a landing pad on the stern deck next to the ship's helicopter. Pitt and Giordino climbed from the cockpit and shook hands with Gunn and Stewart.

"We watched through binoculars," said Stewart. "If you had circled Sungari any lower you could have rented a headset and cassette and taken a self-guided tour of the place."

"See anything interesting from the air?" asked Gunn.

"Odd that you should mention that," said Giordino. "I do believe we just might have viewed something we weren't supposed to."

"Then you've seen more than we have," muttered Stewart.

Pitt gazed at a pelican that folded its wings and dove cleanly into the water, emerging with a small fish in its scooplike beak. "The admiral told us that you failed to find any openings in the landfill casings under the docks before their security snatched your AUV."

"Not so much as a crack," admitted Gunn. "If Qin Shang is planning on smuggling illegal aliens through Sungari, it isn't from a ship through underground tunnels to the warehouse terminals."

"You warned us they could be cagey," said Stewart. "And, we found out the hard way. Now NUMA is out an expensive piece of equipment and we don't dare ask for it back."

Gunn said bleakly, "We've accomplished nothing. All we've done for the last forty-eight hours is stare at empty docks and vacant buildings."

Pitt placed a hand on Gunn's shoulder. "Cheer up, Rudi. While we stand here feeling sorry for ourselves for acting deaf, dumb and blind, a boatload of illegal immigrants from China was offloaded at Sungari and are now on their way inland to a staging center."

Gunn stared into Pitt's eyes, startled, and saw them twinkle. "So tell us what you saw."

"The towboat and barges that left Sungari a short time ago," replied Pitt. "Al observed a couple of men on board the barges who were carrying weapons. When we passed over them they tried to hide."

"Nothing shady about a towboat crew carrying arms," said Stewart. "It's a fairly common practice if they're transporting valuable cargo."

"Valuable?" Pitt said, laughing. "The cargo was trash and garbage thrown off the ship that had accumulated after a long voyage across the sea. Armed men weren't on the barge to protect trash, they were there to keep their human cargo from escaping."

"How could you know that?" asked Gunn.

"A process of elimination." Pitt began to feel good. He was on a roll. "At the present time, the only way in and out of Sungari is by ocean ships and riverboats. The ships smuggle in the immigrants, but there is no way to secretly transport them to a staging area for dispersion around the country. And you've proven they're not herded from the ships through hidden passages under the docks and warehouses. So they must be carried inland by barges."

"Not possible," stated Stewart flat out. "Customs and immigration agents come on board the minute the ship docks and search it from bow to stern. All cargo must be offloaded and stored in the warehouses for inspection. Every bag of trash is examined. So how do Qin Shang's people deceive the inspectors?"

"I believe the illegal immigrants are secretly housed in an underwater craft beneath the hull of the merchant ship that transported them from China. After the ship comes into port, the submerged craft is somehow transferred under the barge tied alongside to receive the trash and garbage. While this is going on, the customs and immigration agents do their job but find no evidence of illegal immigrants. Then, moving to a landfill up the Atchafalaya River to dispose of the trash, they make a stop at some out-of-the-way place to disembark the aliens."

Gunn looked like a blind man whose sight had suddenly been restored by a faith healer in a revivalist tent. "You figured that out by simply flying over a garbage barge?"

"A theory at best," Pitt said modestly.

"But a theory that can easily be verified," pointed out Stewart.

"Then we're wasting time talking," said Gunn excitedly. "We put a launch over the side and follow the towboat. You and Al can keep an eye on them from the air."

"Worst thing we could do," cut in Giordino. "We've already put them on guard by buzzing the barge. The towboat captain will know if he's being tailed. I vote we lay low temporarily and play inconspicuous."

"Al's right," said Pitt. "The smugglers are not dumb. They have calculated every option. Their uncanny intelligence sources in Washington may have already given the Sungari security force photographs of everyone on board the *Marine Denizen*. It's best we take our time and keep any scouting expedition as discreet as possible."

"Shouldn't we at least notify the INS?" inquired Steward seriously.

Pitt shook his head. "Not until we can show them hard evidence."

"There's another problem," Giordino added. "Dirk and I are prohibited from working your side of the street."

Gunn grinned perceptively. "Admiral Sandecker told me. You're AWOL from a government safe house in Maine."

"They've probably got an all-points bulletin out on me for fleeing across state lines," Giordino said, laughing.

"So what do we do to keep busy?" asked Stewart. "And for how long?"

"Keep the *Marine Denizen* anchored right where she is for now," Pitt ordered. "After Qin Shang's security people stole your AUV, any cover you had as an innocent NUMA research project was blown. Maintain observation of Sungari as close as you can anchor."

"If they're onto us, wouldn't it be better to move the ship further downriver toward the Gulf?"

Pitt gave a negative shake of his head. "I don't think so. Stay in close. I'm betting they're overconfident and think their smuggling tactics and strategy are undetectable and foolproof. Qin Shang believes he is untouchable. Let him go right on thinking Chinese are artful and crafty devils while Americans all attend village-idiot school. Meanwhile, Al and I mount a little clandestine operation of our own upriver and pinpoint the staging center. Immigration agents will want to know where the smuggled aliens are unloaded and held before boarding buses or trucks for circulation around the country." Pitt paused. "Any questions, any comments?"

"If you've pegged Qin Shang's modus operandi," Stewart said happily, "we're halfway home."

"Sounds like a good plan to me," said Gunn. "How should we proceed?"

"Subterfuge will be the order of the day," explained Pitt. "Al and I will move into Morgan City, merge in with the locals and charter a fishing boat. Then head up the Atchafalaya and search out the staging center."

"You'll probably need a guide," Stewart suggested. "There are a thousand inlets, sloughs and bayous between here and the canal locks above Baton Rouge. Not being familiar with the river could cost you much time and wasted effort."

"Good thinking," agreed Giordino. "I do not wish to go off and perish in a quagmire and become a mystery like Amelia Earhart."

"Little danger of that," Stewart said, smiling.

"Detailed topographical maps should be the only guide we'll need." Pitt nodded at the *Marine Denizen*'s captain. "We'll keep you apprised of location and any progress over my satellite phone. You alert us to the next departure of the barge and towboat from the next ship to hit port."

"Won't hurt for you to pass on the information regarding the *United States* too," added Giordino. "I'd like to be around when she docks at Sungari."

Gunn and Stewart exchanged confused looks. "The *United States* isn't bound for Sungari," said Gunn.

Pitt's green eyes narrowed and his shoulders stiffened slightly. "I've heard nothing from Admiral Sandecker. Where did you get that bit of information?"

"The local newspaper," answered Stewart. "We send a launch up to Morgan City once a day for any needed supplies. Whoever volunteers for the trip always brings back a newspaper. The story has been big news around Louisiana."

"What story?" Pitt demanded.

"You haven't been told?" asked Gunn.

"Haven't been told what?"

"The *United States,*" Gunn muttered quietly. "She's heading up the Mississippi to New Orleans, where she's going to be remodeled into a hotel and gambling casino."

Both Pitt and Giordino looked as if they had been told their life's savings had vanished. Giordino twisted his mouth in a wry grimace. "It seems, old buddy, that we have been led down the garden path."

"That we have." When Pitt spoke again his voice carried a windchill factor of minus twenty, and he smiled a grim smile that seemed to portend something. "But then, things aren't always what they seem."

30

LATER THE SAME AFTERNOON, the Coast Guard cutter *Weehawken* moved easily over the low, breeze-ruffled waves and slowed as the order came down from the wheelhouse to the engine room to reduce speed. Captain Duane Lewis peered through his binoculars at the big container ship that was approaching from the south less than a nautical mile away. His expression was calm and relaxed, his cap tilted slightly back over a thicket of sandy hair. He lowered the glasses, revealing deep-set ivory brown eyes. He turned and smiled thinly at the woman standing beside him on the bridge wing who was dressed in the uniform of the United States Coast Guard.

"There's your ship," he said in a bass voice, "sailing as smugly as a wolf in sheep's clothing. She looks innocent enough."

Julia Lee gazed over the railing at the *Sung Lien Star.* "A deception. God only knows the human suffering that's being endured hidden within her hull."

She wore no makeup, and a fake scar ran across her chin. Her beautiful long black hair had been cropped short and styled like a man's, and was covered by a ship's baseball cap. In the beginning, she had second thoughts about clandestinely switching roles with Lin Wan Chu, but her burning hatred of Qin Shang, along with an unyielding confidence that she could succeed, made her more determined than ever to make the attempt. She felt a surge of optimism at knowing that she was not alone in this mission.

Lewis turned and aimed the binoculars toward the flat green shoreline and the mouth of the lower Atchafalaya River only three miles away. Except for a few shrimp boats, the water was empty. He gestured at a young officer standing at his side. "Lieutenant Stowe, signal her to come to a stop and stand by for a boarding inspection."

"Aye, sir," acknowledged Stowe as he stepped into the radio room. Tanned, blond and tall, Jefferson Stowe had the boyish good looks of a tennis instructor.

The *Weehawken* heeled slightly in response to her rudder as the helmsman brought the cutter around on a parallel course with the container ship that was flying the flag of the People's Republic of China. The decks were piled high with containers, and yet she rode strangely high in the water, Lewis observed. "Did they reply?" he asked loud enough to be heard across the wheelhouse.

"They answered in Chinese," Stowe called from the radio room.

"Shall I translate?" offered Julia.

"It's a dodge," Lewis said with a grin. "Half the foreign ships we stop have a habit of acting dumb. Most of their officers speak better English than we do."

Lewis waited patiently as the seventy-six-millimeter Mark 75 remote-controlled, rapid-firing gun on the bow turned and ominously aimed its muzzle at the container ship. "Please inform the captain, *in English,* to stop engines or I will fire into his bridge."

Stowe returned to the bridge wing with a smile stretched across his lips. "The captain answered in English," he said. "He reports he is stopping."

As if to underscore the compliance, the foam that spilled from around the bows fell away as the big container ship slowly drifted to a stop. Lewis looked at Julia with care written in his eyes. "Ready, Ms. Lee?"

She nodded. "Ready as I'll ever be."

"You've checked your radio." It was a statement rather than a question.

Julia glanced down at where the miniature radio was taped inside the cleavage of her breasts under her bra. "Working perfectly." Without being obvious, she pressed her legs together, feeling the little .25-caliber automatic that was strapped to the inside of her right thigh. A short Smith & Wesson First Response knife, whose blade could spring open in an eye blink and was strong enough to rip through sheet metal, was taped to her biceps under the sleeve of her uniform.

"Keep your transmitter on so we can monitor your every word," said Lewis. "The *Weehawken* will remain within range of your radio until the *Sung Lien Star* docks at Sungari and you signal that you are ready to be picked up. Hopefully the substitution will go as planned, but should you encounter a problem after you take the cook's identity, call out and we'll come running. I'll also have our helicopter and crew in the air ready to drop on board."

"I appreciate your concern, Captain." Julia paused, turned slightly and motioned to a burly man with a walrus mustache whose deep-set gray eyes peered from under the brim of a baseball cap. "Chief Cochran has been a dream to work with during our rehearsals for the switch."

"Chief Mickey Cochran has been called many names," said Lewis, laughing, "but never a dream."

"I'm sorry for putting everyone to so much trouble," Julia said softly.

"All on board the *Weehawken* feel responsible for your safety. Admiral Ferguson gave me strict orders to protect you regardless of the consequences. I don't envy you your job, Ms. Lee. But I promise we will do everything in our power to keep you out of harm's way."

She looked away, her face very controlled despite the tears forming in her eyes. "Thank you," she said simply. "Thank them all for me."

As Stowe gave the order to swing out the cutter's launch, Captain Lewis looked down at Julia and said, "It's time." Then he firmly shook her hand. "God bless, and best of luck."

Captain Li Hung-chang of the *Sung Lien Star* was not unduly annoyed at being stopped by the American Coast Guard and boarded. He had expected it long before now. He had been warned by Qin Shang Maritime directors that the United States's immigration agents were stepping up their efforts to halt the rise in illegal-alien smuggling. He felt impervious to any threat. The most diligent inspection would never discover the second hull attached beneath the bilges and keel of his ship that housed three hundred immigrants. Despite the cramped and insufferable conditions, he had not lost one. Hung-chang was assured that a generous Qin Shang would reward him with a fat bonus after his return to China, as in the past. This was his sixth voyage combining the legal transportation of cargo with smuggling, and already his compensation had built a fine house for his family in the upper-class section of Beijing.

He watched the bow wave fall off the Coast Guard cutter, his expression calm and outwardly relaxed. Hung-chang was still in his late forties, yet his hair was a gleaming salt-and-pepper under the sun, though his narrow mustache was still black. He stared through kindly-grandfather, dark-amber eyes, his lips tight with silence as the two ships drifted closer. Then a boat was lowered and began to motor toward the *Sung Lien Star.* He nodded to his first officer.

"Go to the boarding ladder and greet our guests. About ten by the look of it. Give them your fullest cooperation and allow them free access throughout the ship."

Then, as calm and relaxed as if he was sitting in the garden of his home, Captain Li Hung-chang ordered a cup of tea from the galley and watched the *Weehawken*'s boarding party climb onto the deck of his ship and begin their inspection.

Lieutenant Stowe paid his respects to Captain Hung-chang on the bridge and requested to see the ship's papers and manifest. The crew from the Coast Guard cutter began to split up, four searching the ship's compartments, three examining the cargo containers, and another three who headed for the crew's quarters. The Chinese acted indifferently to the intrusion and paid little attention to the three coast guardsmen who seemed more interested in the ship's mess, particularly the galley, instead of their individual cabins.

Only two of the *Sung Lien Star*'s crew were present in the mess room. Both were dressed in the white uniform and hats of galley workers. They sat around a table, one reading a Chinese newspaper while the other spooned a bowl of soup. Neither protested when Chief Cochran, using sign language, asked them to step into the passageway while a search of the dining area was conducted.

Disguised as one of the Coast Guard boarding crew, Julia walked directly into the galley, where she found Lin Wan Chu dressed in white shirt and pants leaning over a stove, a long wooden spoon in one hand, stirring a large copper vat of boiling shrimp. Under her captain's orders to cooperate with the Coast Guard inspectors, she looked up from the steam rising from the vat and flashed a toothy, friendly smile. She went on working unconcerned as Julia walked behind her, eyes routinely darting into pantries and storerooms.

Lin Wan Chu did not sense the needle of the syringe enter the flesh of her back. After a few seconds her eyes took on a puzzled look as the steam over the vat suddenly seemed to thicken into a dense cloud. Then a solid blackness swept over her. Much later, when she awoke on board

310

the *Weehawken,* her first thought was whether she had overboiled the shrimp.

In less than a minute and a half, and thanks to the results of well-practiced exercise, Julia was dressed in the cook's white kitchen clothes while Lin Wan Chu lay on the deck in the uniform of the U.S. Coast Guard. Another thirty seconds passed as Julia cut short the cook's hair before pulling a baseball cap with the Coast Guard insignia and the word *Weehawken* down over Lin Wan Chu's head. "Take her away," Julia said to Cochran, who was patiently guarding the doorway to the passage outside.

Cochran and the other member of his boarding party quickly picked up the Chinese cook, one on each side, and hung her arms over their shoulders so her head would sag on her chest and make identification difficult. The baseball cap was pulled down over her face before he gave Julia a final nod and said softly, so only she could hear, "I wish you a great performance." Then they half-dragged, half-carried, Lin Wan Chu back to the boarding launch.

Julia picked up the wooden spoon and continued stirring the boiling shrimp as if she'd been at it all afternoon.

"One of your men seems to have injured himself," said Captain Hung-chang at seeing the boarding party lower a limp body into the launch.

"The fool didn't watch where he was going and cracked his head on an overhead pipe," Stowe explained. "Probably has a concussion."

"Have you found anything interesting aboard my ship?" asked Hung-chang.

"No sir, your ship is clean."

"Always happy to oblige the American authorities," said Hung-chang condescendingly.

"Your destination is Sungari?"

"According to my sailing orders and the documents provided by Qin Shang Maritime."

"You may get under way as soon as we're clear," said Stowe, giving the Chinese captain a courtesy salute. "I regret that we had to detain you."

Twenty minutes after the Coast Guard launch had pulled away, the pilot boat arrived from Morgan City and swung alongside the *Sung Lien Star.* The pilot climbed aboard and made his way up to the bridge. Soon the container ship was moving through the deep-water channel of the lower Atchafalaya River and across Sweet Bay Lake toward the docks of Sungari.

Captain Hung-chang stood on the bridge wing beside the Cajun pilot as he took the automated helm and expertly guided the ship through the marshlands. Out of curiosity Hung-chang peered through a pair of binoculars at the turquoise ship anchored just out of the channel. Bold letters across the hull designated the vessel as a research ship belonging to the National Underwater and Marine Agency. Hung-chang had often seen them on scientific marine expeditions during his voyages around the world. He idly wondered what manner of experiments they were conducting here on the Atchafalaya River below Sungari.

As he panned the glasses along the deck of the research ship, he suddenly stopped and found himself peering at a tall man with thick, curly black hair who was staring back through his own binoculars. What struck Li Hung-chang odd was that the crewman on the research vessel wasn't focused on the container ship itself.

He seemed to be studying the wake directly behind the stern.

31

JULIA HAD TO STRUGGLE to decipher Lin Wan Chu's menus and recipes. Although Han Chinese is the most widely spoken language in the world, there are several different dialects reflected by regional differences. Julia's mother taught her to read, write and speak Mandarin, the most important of these, when she was a young girl. She had learned the most widespread of the three Mandarin variants, known as the Peking dialect. Because Lin Wan Chu had grown up in Jiangsu Province, she wrote and spoke another variant of Mandarin, the Nanking dialect. Fortunately, there were enough similarities for Julia to fake it and get by. As she worked over the stove she kept her head down and face away from anyone nearby.

Her two helpers, an assistant cook and a dishwasher/galley cleanup man, showed no sign of suspicion. They went about their business, speaking only when it concerned the evening meal, offering no small talk or gossip from the crew. Julia thought she caught the baker studying her with a peculiar look on his face, but when she ordered him to quit staring and get back to deep-frying wontons, he laughed, made a ribald remark and went back to work.

The stoves and the boiling pots and woks that were vigorously stirred soon turned the galley into a steam bath. Julia could not remember when she had sweat rivers. She drank glass after glass of water to maintain her bodily liquids. She gave a little prayer of thanks at watching the assistant cook take the initiative and prepare the watercress soup and the shredded chicken with bean sprouts. Julia gave a worthy performance of making the roast pork and noodles and the shrimp fried rice.

Captain Hung-chang wandered into the galley briefly for a quick snack of sesame-seed puffs after the *Sung Lien Star* was safely moored to the dock at Sungari. Then he returned to the bridge to receive the American customs and immigration officials. He looked Julia square in the face, but his eyes betrayed no sign other than simple recognition of who he thought was Lin Wan Chu.

Julia joined the rest of the crew as they lined up and produced their passports to the immigration official who came on board. Ordinarily, the captain would present the documents so the crew could go about their duties, but the INS was particularly strict with vessels entering the port owned by Qin Shang Maritime. The official examined Lin Wan Chu's passport, which Julia had uncovered in the cook's cabin, without looking up at her. All neat and very professional, she thought. By looking her in the face, the official might have made an expression of recognition no matter how inconsequential.

Once the crew cleared immigration, they came down for their evening meal. The galley was located between the officer's wardroom and the crew's mess. As chief cook, Julia served the ship's officers while her assistants ladled out food to the crew. She was anxious to roam about the ship, but until the crew was fed she had to play out her role to avoid suspicion.

Julia remained quiet throughout the meal, scurrying about the galley, occasionally flashing a smile at a crewman as they complimented her on the food and asked for seconds. She did not merely act like Lin Wan Chu; to everyone on board she *was* Lin Wan Chu. There was no scrutiny, no incredulity. No one took notice of the negligible differences in mannerisms, appearance or speech. To them, she was the same cook who prepared their meals on board the *Sung Lien Star* since the night they cast off in Qingdao.

Item by item, she went over her mission in her mind. So far things had gone smoothly, but there was a major hang-up. If three hundred illegal immigrants were on board the ship, how were they being fed? Certainly not out of her galley. According to Lin Wan Chu's menu and recipe entries, she only prepared food for thirty crewmen. It didn't make sense for there to be another shipboard galley to feed passengers. She checked out the storage compartment and lockers, finding the correct amount of food supplies to feed the *Sung Lien Star*'s crew for the voyage from China to Sungari. She began to wonder if Peter Harper's

CIA source in Qingdao had been mistaken and somehow gotten the name of the ship confused with another.

Calmly, she sat in Lin Wan Chu's little office and acted as if she was working on the menu for the following day. Out of the corner of one eye she watched as her assistant put away the leftover food in the locker and the cleanup man wiped off the tables before attacking the dirty dishes, pots and pans.

Casually, she left the office and walked through the officer's ward-room and into the passageway, pleased that the two galley men took no notice of her leaving. She climbed a companionway and stepped out onto the deck below the wheelhouse and bridge wings. Already the big cranes on the dock were swinging into position to unload the containers stacked on the cargo decks.

She looked over the side and watched as a towboat pushed a barge alongside the hull of the ship. The crew looked to be Chinese. Two of them began throwing plastic bags bloated with trash through a cargo hatch into the barge. The procedure was conducted under the scrutiny of a drug-enforcement agent who probed and examined each sack before it was dropped overboard.

The entire dockyard scene appeared completely innocent of any illegitimate activity. Julia could see nothing that raised questions. The ship had been searched by the Coast Guard, customs and immigration officials for illegal aliens and drugs, and nothing illicit had been found. The containers were filled with manufactured trade goods, including clothing, rubber and plastic shoes, children's toys and games, radios and television sets, all produced by cheap Red Chinese labor to the detriment of thousands of American workers who had lost their jobs.

She returned to the galley and filled a bucket with the sesame-seed puffs (scallions and sesame seeds in a dough wrapper) that she knew were a favorite of Captain Hung-chang. Then she began moving through the bowels of the ship, checking out the compartments below the waterline. Most of the crew were working above, unloading the ship's cargo containers. The few who remained below appeared pleased when she wandered past and offered them a snack from her bucket. She skirted the engine room, reasonably assured no immigrants were hidden there. No chief engineer worth his salt would have permitted passengers near his precious engines.

The only sickening moment of panic occurred when she became lost in the long compartment that held the ship's fuel tanks. She was startled by a crewman who came up behind her and demanded to know what she was doing there. Julia smiled, offered him her sesame-seed puffs and told him that it was the captain's birthday and he wanted everyone to celebrate. The ordinary seaman, having no reason to suspect the ship's cook, gratefully accepted a handful of puffs and smiled happily.

After a fruitless search looking into any compartment of the *Sung Lien Star* capable of holding and feeding scores of passengers and finding nothing suspicious, she made her way back to the open starboard deck. Standing at the railing as if she was idly wishing she could go ashore, and making certain no one was within earshot, she inserted a small receiver in her ear and began talking into the transmitter between her breasts.

"I regret saying this, but the ship appears clean. I searched every deck and found no indication of illegal immigrants."

Captain Lewis on board the *Weehawken* replied without hesitation. "Are you secure?"

"Yes, I was accepted without reservation."

"Do you wish to disembark?"

"Not yet. I'd like to hang around a bit longer."

"Please keep me advised," said Lewis, "and be careful."

Lewis's parting words came muffled, as the air trembled suddenly with a thumping sound followed by the exhaust roar of the *Weehawken*'s helicopter sweeping over the dock. Julia suppressed an urge to wave. She remained leisurely hunched over the railing, gazing at the aircraft with detached curiosity. She felt a wave of pleasure just knowing that she was watched over by a pair of U.S. coast guardsmen who were acting as her angels.

She was relieved that her job was done and angered that she had failed to discover any criminal activity. From the looks of it, Qin Shang had outsmarted everyone once again. If her mind ran in a practical vein, she could call Lewis to come get her or simply jump ship into the arms of the nearest immigration agent. But she could not bring herself to quit by default. There had to be an answer, and Julia was determined to find it.

She moved around the stern to the lower portside deck until she could look directly down into the barge that was now half filled with plastic trash bags. She stood at the railing for a long minute, studying the barge and the towboat as its captain engaged the powerful engines to pull away from the *Sung Lien Star*. The wash from the twin propellers began beating the calm brownish water into foam.

Julia was seized with frustration. There was no crowd of immigrants huddled in sordid conditions on board the *Sung Lien Star*. Of that she was positive. Nor did she truly doubt the CIA agent's veracity who reported from Qingdao. Qin Shang was a shrewd customer. He must have devised a method that had fooled the best government investigators in the business.

There were no hard and fast answers. If there was a solution, perhaps it was connected with the towboat and barge pulling away from the ship. She was left with no other options. Failure was staring her in the face again. She felt overwhelmed by a sense of inadequacy and self-anger. She knew then, beyond all doubt, that she had to act.

One swift glance told her that the cargo door had been closed and there were no crewmen to be seen working the side of the ship's hull that faced the water opposite the dock. The captain of the towboat was standing at the helm while one crewman acted as lookout on the bridge wing and another stood forward on the bow of the barge, their eyes focused on the waters ahead. None were looking aft.

As the towboat passed her position she looked down on its stern deck. There was a long length of rope coiled aft of the funnel. She estimated the drop at ten feet, and climbed over the railing. There was no time to call Lewis and explain her action. Any hesitation was brushed aside, for Julia was a woman of quick decision. She took a deep breath and leaped.

Julia's dive into the barge was observed, not by any of the *Sung Lien Star*'s crew, but by Pitt on board the *Marine Denizen,* which was anchored at the entrance to the port. For the past hour he had sat in the captain's chair on the bridge wing, tolerant of the sun and occasional passing rain shower, and scrutinized the activity swirling around the container ship through a pair of powerful binoculars. He was especially intrigued by the barge and towboat alongside. He watched intently as the trash accumulated on the long voyage from China was tied neatly in bags and dropped from a hatch in the ship's hull to the barge below. When the last trash bag was tossed overboard and the hatch closed, Pitt was about to turn his attention to the containers being hoisted onto the dock by the cranes when, unpredictably, he saw a figure climb the railing along the deck above and drop onto the roof of the towboat. "What the hell!" he burst.

Rudi Gunn, who was standing near Pitt, stiffened. "See something interesting?"

"Somebody just took a dive off the ship onto the towboat."

"Probably a crewman jumping ship."

"It looked like the ship's cook," Pitt said, keeping the glasses fixed on the boat.

"I hope he didn't injure himself," said Gunn.

"I think a coil of rope broke his fall. He appears to be uninjured."

"Have you discovered anything that still makes you think there is a some sort of submerged craft that can be moved from beneath the ship and under the barge?"

"Nothing that would hold up in court," Pitt admitted. Then the opaline-green eyes became intense and a faint glint radiated from them. "But all that could change in the next forty-eight hours."

32

THE *MARINE DENIZEN*'S little jet boat sped across the Intracoastal Waterway and then slowed as it cruised past the Morgan City waterfront. The town was protected from a flooding river by a concrete levee eight feet high and a giant seawall that rose twenty feet and faced the Gulf. Two highway bridges and a railway bridge span the Atchafalaya River in Morgan City, the white headlights and red taillights of the traffic moving like beads slipped through a woman's fingers. The lights of the buildings played across the water, wavering in the wash from passing boats. With a population of 15,000, Morgan City was the largest community in St. Mary Parish (Louisiana's civil divisions are called parishes instead of counties, as with most states). The city faced west overlooking a wide stretch of the Atchafalaya River called Berwick Bay. To the south ran Bayou Boeuf, which circled the town like a vast moat and ran into Lake Palourde.

Morgan City is the only town on the banks of the Atchafalaya and sits low, making it susceptible to floods and extreme high tides, especially during hurricanes, but the residents never bother to look southward toward the Gulf for menacing black clouds. California has its earthquakes, Kansas has it tornadoes and Montana has its blizzards, "so why should we worry" is the prevailing sentiment.

The community is a bit more urbane than most other towns and small cities throughout the Louisiana bayou country. It functions as a seaport, catering to fishermen, oil companies and boat builders, and yet it has the flavor of a river town much like those along the Missouri and Ohio rivers, with the majority of the buildings facing water.

A procession of fishing boats passed. The sharp-prowed boats, with high freeboards and the cabins mounted well forward, masts and net booms aft on the stern, were heading into deep water in the Gulf. The boats that stayed in shallower water had flat bottoms for less draft, lower freeboards, rounded bows with the masts forward and little cabins at the stern. Both types trawled for shrimp. Oyster luggers were another breed. Since they mostly worked the inland waters they had no masts. One chugged by the NUMA jet boat, its decks barely above the surface and heaped with a small mountain of unshucked oyster shells piled six to seven feet high.

"Where do you want to be dropped off?" asked Gunn, who sat behind the wheel of the propless runabout.

"The nearest waterfront saloon would be a good place to meet the river men," said Pitt.

Giordino pointed toward a rambling block of wooden structures stretching along a dock. A neon sign over one building read, CHARLIE'S FISH DOCK, SEAFOOD AND BOOZE. "Looks like our kind of place."

"The packing house next door must be where fishermen bring their catch," Pitt observed. "As good a spot as any to ask about unusual goings-on upriver."

Gunn slowed the runabout and steered her between a small fleet of trawlers before coming to a stop at the bottom of a wooden ladder. "Good luck," he said, smiling, as Pitt and Giordino began climbing onto the dock. "Don't forget to write."

"We'll stay in touch," Pitt assured him.

Gunn waved, pushed away from the dock and turned the little jet boat back downriver toward the *Marine Denizen*.

The dock reeked of fish, the authentic aroma made even more pungent by the nighttime humidity. Giordino nodded at a hill of shucked oyster shells that rose almost to the roof of the waterfront bar and café. "A Dixie beer and a dozen succulent Gulf oysters would suit me just fine about now," he said in happy anticipation.

"I'll bet their gumbo is world-class too."

Walking through the doors of Charlie's Fish Dock saloon was like walking back in time. The ancient air-conditioning had long ago lost the war against human sweat and tobacco smoke. The wooden floor was worn smooth from the tread of fisherman boots and was scarred by hundreds of cigarette burns. The tables that had been cut and varnished from the hatch covers of old boats showed their share of cigarette burns, too. The tired captain's chairs looked patched and glued after years of bar fights. Covering the walls were rusty metal signs advertising everything from Aunt Bea's Ginger Ale to Old South Whiskey to Goober's Bait Shack. All had been liberally peppered with bullet holes at one time or another. There were none of the modern promotional beer signs that proliferated in most watering holes around the country. The shelves behind the bar, which held nearly a hundred different brands of liquor, some distilled locally, looked like they had been haphazardly nailed to the wall during the Civil War. The bar came from the deck of a long-abandoned fishing boat and could have used a good caulking job.

The clientele was a mixed bag of fishermen, local boatyard and construction workers, and oilmen who worked the offshore rigs. They were a rugged lot. This was the land of the Cajuns, and several conversed in French. Two big dogs snoozed peacefully under an empty table. At least thirty men filled the bar with no women to be seen, not even a barmaid. All drinks were served by the bartender. No glasses came with the beer. You either got a bottle or a can. Only the liquor rated a cracked and chipped glass. A waiter who looked as if he wrestled on Thursday nights at the local arena served the food.

"What do you think?" Pitt asked Giordino.

"Now I know where old cockroaches go to die."

"Just remember to smile and say 'sir' to any of these hulks who ask you the time."

"This would be the last place I'd start a fight," Giordino agreed.

"Good thing we're not dressed like tourists off a cruise ship," said Pitt, reexamining the soiled and patched work clothes the crew of the *Marine Denizen* had scrounged together for them. "Though I doubt it makes any difference. They know we don't belong by the clean smell."

"I knew it was a mistake to bathe last month," Giordino said wryly.

Pitt bowed and gestured toward an empty table. "Shall we dine?"

"Yes, lets," Giordino countered with a bow as he pulled back a chair and sat down.

After twenty minutes with no service, Giordino yawned and said, "It would appear our waiter has refined the professional technique of pretending not to notice our table."

"He must have heard you," Pitt said, grinning. "Here he comes."

The waiter, dressed only in cutoff jeans and wearing a T-shirt with a longhorn steer skiing down a hill of brown that said, IF GOD MEANT TEXANS TO SKI, HE'D HAVE MADE COWSHIT WHITE.

"Can I get you something from the kitchen?" he asked in a surprisingly high-pitched voice.

"How about a dozen oysters and a Dixie beer?" said Giordino.

"You got it," answered the waiter. "And you?"

"A bowl of your famous gumbo."

The waiter grunted. "I didn't know it was famous, but it *is* good-tastin'. Whatta you want to drink?"

"Got tequila behind the bar?"

"Sure, we get a lot of Central American fishermen in here."

"Tequila on the rocks with a lime."

The waiter turned and began walking toward the kitchen, but not before he looked at them and said, "I'll be back."

"I hope he doesn't think he's Arnold Schwarzenegger and drives a car through the wall," Giordino muttered.

"Relax," said Pitt. "Enjoy the local color, the ambience, the smoke-filled environment."

"I might as well take advantage of the stale atmosphere and add to it," said Giordino, lighting up one of his exotic cigars.

Pitt surveyed the room, searching for an appropriate character to probe for information. He eliminated a group of oil riggers gathered round one end of the bar and who were playing pool. The dockyard workers were a good possibility, but they did not look like they took kindly to strangers. He began focusing on the fishermen. A number of them were sitting at community tables pulled together and playing poker. An older man, in what Pitt guessed was his mid-sixties, straddled a chair nearby but did not join in. He played the role of a loner, but there was a humorous and friendly gleam in his blue-green eyes. His hair was gray and matched a mustache that fell and met a beard around the chin. He watched the others as they tossed their money on the poker table as though he was a psychologist studying behavioral patterns of laboratory mice.

The waiter brought the drinks, no tray, a glass in one hand and a bottle in the other. Pitt looked up and asked, "What brand of tequila did the bartender have?"

"I think it's called Pancho Villa."

"If I know my tequilas, Pancho Villa comes in a plastic bottle."

The waiter twisted his lips as if trying to dredge up a vision seen many years previously. Then his face lit up. "Yeah, you're right. It does come in a plastic bottle. Great medicine for what ails you."

"Nothing ails me at the moment," said Pitt.

Giordino came as close to a smirk as he could get. "How much residue lies on the bottom of the bottle, and how much does it cost?"

"I bought a bottle in the Sonoran Desert during the Inca Gold project for a dollar sixty-seven," said Pitt.

"Is it safe to drink?"

Pitt held his glass up to the light before taking a healthy swallow. Then he jokingly crossed his eyes and said, "Any port in a storm."

The waiter returned from the kitchen with Giordino's oysters along with Pitt's gumbo. They decided on a main course of jambalaya and catfish. The Gulf oysters were so large that Giordino had to cut them apart as he would a steak. Pitt's bowl of gumbo would have satisfied a hungry lion. After stuffing their stomachs with a heaping platter of jambalaya, then ordering another Dixie beer and Pancho Villa tequila, they sat at the table and loosened their belts.

All during dinner, Pitt had rarely taken his eyes off the old man observing the poker players. "Who's the old fellow over there straddling the chair?" he asked the waiter. "I know him but can't place where we met."

The waiter swiveled his eyes around the bar, stopping them on the old man. "Oh, him. He owns a fleet of fishing boats. Mostly trawls for crab and shrimp. Owns a big catfish farm, too. Wouldn't know it to look at him, but he's a wealthy man."

"Do you know if he charters boats?"

"Dunno. You'll have to ask him."

Pitt looked at Giordino. "Why don't you work the bar and see if you can learn where Qin Shang Maritime's towboats dump their trash?"

"And you?"

"I'll ask about the dredging operations upriver."

Giordino nodded silently and rose from the table. Soon he was laughing amid several fishermen, regaling them with inflated stories of his fishing days off California. Pitt moved over to the old fisherman and stood beside him.

"Excuse me, sir, but I wonder if I might have a word with you."

The gray-bearded man's blue-green eyes slowly examined Pitt from his belt buckle to his black curly hair. Then he nodded slowly, rose from his chair and motioned Pitt to a booth in one corner of the bar. After he settled in and ordered another beer, the fisherman said, "What can I do for you Mr. . . . ."

"Pitt."

"Mr. Pitt. You're not from around the bayou country."

"No, I'm with the National Underwater and Marine Agency out of Washington."

"You doing marine research?"

"Not this trip," said Pitt. "My colleagues and I are cooperating with the Immigration Service in trying to stop the illegal smuggling of aliens."

The old man pulled a cigar stub from the pocket of an old windbreaker and lit it. "How can I help?"

"I would like to charter a boat to investigate an excavation upriver—"

"The canal dug by Qin Shang Maritime for landfill at Sungari?" the fisherman interrupted knowledgeably.

"The same."

"Not much to see," said the fisherman. "Except a big ditch where the Mystic Bayou used to be. Folks call it the Mystic Canal now."

"I can't believe it took that much fill to build the port," said Pitt.

"What muck dredged from the canal that wasn't used for landfill was barged out to sea and dumped out in the Gulf," answered the fisherman.

"Is there a nearby community?" asked Pitt.

"Used to be a town called Calzas that sat at the end of the bayou a short ways off the Mississippi River. But it's gone."

"Calzas no longer exists?" asked Pitt.

"The Chinese spread the word that they was doing the townspeople a service by providing them with boating access to the Atchafalaya. The truth is, they bought out the landowners. Paid them three times what the property was worth. What's left standing is a ghost town. The rest was bulldozed into the marsh."

Pitt was confused. "Then what was the purpose of excavating a dead-end canal when they could have just as easily dug fill anywhere in the Atchafalaya Valley?"

"Everybody up and down the river is curious about that, too," said the fisherman. "The problem is that friends of mine who have fished that bayou for thirty years are no longer welcome. The Chinese have run a chain across their new canal and no longer give access to fishermen. Nor hunters either."

"Do they use the canal for barge traffic?"

The fisherman shook his head. "If you're thinking they smuggle illegal aliens up the canal, you can forget it. The only towboats and barges that come upriver out of Sungari turn northwest up Bayou Teche and stop at a landing beside an old abandoned sugar mill about ten miles from Morgan City. Qin Shang Maritime bought it when they was building Sungari. A rail yard that used to run alongside the mill was restored by the Chinese."

"Where does it connect?"

"To the main Southern Pacific line."

The muddy waters were beginning to clear. Pitt didn't say anything for several moments as he sat there, staring off into space. The wake he had observed behind the *Sung Lien Star* showed an unusual, yet defined roll beneath the churned surface that was not normal for the basic hull design of a cargo ship. It seemed to him the hull either displaced more water than was consistent with the ship's design, or carried a second, outer hull. In his mind he began to visualize a separate vessel, perhaps a submarine, attached to the keel of the container ship. Finally he asked, "Is there a name for the landing?"

"Used to be called Bartholomeaux after the man who built the mill back in nineteen-oh-nine."

"In order to get close enough to check out Bartholomeaux without raising suspicion, I'll need to charter some type of fishing boat."

The old fisherman stared across the table at Pitt and then he gave a little shrug and smiled. "I can do better than that. What you fellows need is a shantyboat."

"A shantyboat?"

"Some call them campboats. People use them to wander up and down the waterways, mooring in the bayous beside towns or farms before moving on again. Often they're left moored in the same location and used as vacation cabins. Not many people live full-time on them anymore."

"A shantyboat must be like a houseboat," said Pitt.

"Except a houseboat doesn't usually travel about under its own power," said the gray-bearded fisherman. "But I have a boat that's livable and has a good engine tucked away inside the hull. It's yours if you think it's suitable. And since you intend to use it for the good of the country, you can have it at no charge. Just so long as you bring it back as good as you found it."

"I think the man has made us an offer we can't refuse," said Giordino, who had wandered over from the bar and was eavesdropping on the conversation.

"Thank you," Pitt said sincerely. "We accept."

"You'll find the shantyboat about a mile up the Atchafalaya tied at a dock on the left bank called Wheeler's Landing. Nearby is a small boatyard and a grocery store run by an old friend and neighbor, Doug Wheeler. You can buy your provisions from him. I'll see that the fuel tank is filled. If anybody questions you, just say you're friends of the Bayou Kid. That's what some people call me around here. Except for my old fishing pal, Tom Straight, the bartender. He still calls me by my given name."

"Is the engine powerful enough to move it upriver against the current?" asked Pitt naively.

"I think you'll find she can do the job."

Pitt and Giordino were elated and grateful for the old fisherman's significant cooperation. "We'll bring your shantyboat back in the condition we found it," Pitt promised.

Giordino reached across the table and shook the old man's hand. When he spoke it was with uncharacteristic humility. "I don't think you'll ever know how many people will benefit from your kindness."

The fisherman stroked his beard and waved an airy hand. "Glad to be of help. I wish you fellas luck. The illegal business of smuggling, especially that of human beings, is a rotten way to make money."

He watched thoughtfully as Pitt and Giordino left Charlie's Fish Dock and stepped into the night outside. He sat and finished his beer. It had been a long day, and he was tired.

"Did you learn anything at the bar?" Pitt asked Giordino as they walked from the dock down an alley to a busy street.

"The rivermen aren't real friendly toward Qin Shang Maritime," answered Giordino. "The Chinese refuse to use local labor or boat companies. All towboat and barge traffic out of Sungari is conducted by Chinese boats and crews who live at the port and never come into Morgan City. There is an undercurrent of anger that just might erupt into a small-scale war if Qin Shang doesn't begin showing more respect to St. Mary Parish residents."

"I doubt if Shang ever cultivated an affinity for dealing with peasants," commented Pitt drolly.

"What's the plan?"

"First we find a local bed and breakfast. Then, soon as the sun comes up, we'll board the shantyboat, travel upriver and canvass the canal to nowhere."

"And Bartholomeaux?" Giordino persisted. "Aren't you curious to see if that's where the barge dumps human cargo?"

"Curious, yes. Desperate, no. We're not working under a deadline. We can size up Bartholomeaux after we check the canal."

"If you want to conduct an underwater search," said Giordino, "we'll need diving equipment."

"Soon as we're settled in, I'll call Rudi and have him ferry our gear to wherever we're staying."

"And Bartholomeaux?" Giordino continued. "Should we prove the old sugar mill is a staging and distribution depot for smuggled aliens, then what?"

"We'll turn the chore of conducting a raid over to INS agents, but only after we give Admiral Sandecker the satisfaction of informing Peter Harper that NUMA has uncovered another one of Qin Shang's illicit operations without his help."

"I believe that is what you call poetic justice."

Pitt grinned at his friend. "Now comes the hard part."

"Hard part?"

"We have to find a taxi."

As they stood on the curb Giordino turned and looked back over his shoulder at the bar and grill. "Did that old fisherman look familiar to you?"

"Now that you mention it, there was something about him that struck a chord."

"We never did get his name."

"Next time we see him," said Pitt, "we'll have to ask if we've ever met."

Back in Charlie's Fish Dock restaurant and bar, the old fisherman glanced up at the bar as the bartender yelled across the room at him.

"Hey, Cussler. You want another beer?"

"Why not?" The old man nodded. "One more brew before I hit the road won't hurt."

33

"OUR HOME AWAY FROM HOME," said Giordino at his first look of the shantyboat he and Pitt were borrowing from the old fisherman. "Hardly bigger than a North Dakota outhouse."

"Not fancy but functional," Pitt said as he paid the taxi driver and studied the ancient boat that was moored at the end of a rickety, sagging dock that extended from the riverbank on waterlogged pilings. Inside the dock, several small aluminum fishing boats bobbed in the green water, their outboard motors showing rust and grease from long, hard use.

"Talk about roughing it," Giordino groaned as he unloaded their underwater equipment from the trunk of the taxi. "No central heating or air-conditioning. I'll bet this tub doesn't have running water or electricity to operate lights and a television."

"You don't need running water," said Pitt. "You can bathe in the river."

"What about a toilet?"

Pitt smiled. "Use your imagination."

Giordino pointed to a small reception dish on the roof. "Radar," he muttered incredulously, "It has radar."

The shantyboat's hull was broad and flat with easy rakes, much like that of a small barge. The black paint was heavily scarred from a hundred sideswipes against dock pilings and other boats, but the bottom that could be seen below the waterline appeared scraped clean of marine growth. A square box with windows and doors, which was the house, rose about seven feet, its weathered blue walls nearly flush with the sides of the hull. A small, roofed-over veranda sporting lawn chairs stretched across the bow. Above, centered on the house roof, as if it was an afterthought, sat a low, raised bridgelike structure that acted as a skylight and a small pilothouse. On the roof lay a short skiff with paddles lashed upside down. The black chimney pipe from a wood-burning potbellied stove stuck up from the aft end of the house.

Giordino shook his head sadly. "I've slept on bus benches that had more class than this. Kick me the next time I complain about my motel room."

"Oh, ye of little faith, stop griping. Keep telling yourself that it didn't cost us anything."

"I've got to admit that it has character."

Pitt aimed the chronically complaining Giordino toward the shantyboat. "Go load up the equipment and check out the engine. I'll go over to the store and buy some groceries."

"I can't wait to see our motive power," Giordino groused. "Ten to one it doubles as an eggbeater."

Pitt walked a boardwalk through a boatyard leading down the bank into the river. A worker was giving a wooden fishing boat set inside a cradle on rails a new coat of antifouling paint on the keel and hull. Next door, Pitt came to a wooden structure under a sign that proclaimed WHEELER'S LANDING. A long porch ran around the building, which was raised off the ground by rows of short pilings. The walls were painted a bright green with yellow shutters framing the windows. Inside, Pitt found it incredible that so much merchandise could be crammed in so small a space. Boating parts took up one end of the store, fishing and hunting supplies the other. The center was devoted to groceries. A compact refrigerator stocked with five times as much beer as soft drinks and dairy products stood against one wall.

Pitt picked up a hand basket and made out very well, selecting enough foodstuffs to feed him and Giordino three or four days, and, as with most men, he probably bought more than they could eat, especially specialty items and condiments. Setting the overloaded basket on the counter by the cash register, he introduced himself to the portly owner of the store who was busily stocking canned goods.

"Mr. Wheeler. My name is Dirk Pitt. My friend and I have charted the Bayou Kid's shantyboat."

Wheeler brushed his thick mustache with the light touch of a finger and stuck out his hand. "Been expectin' you. The Kid said you'd be by this mornin'. She's all ready to go. Fuel tank filled, battery charged and topped off with oil."

"Thank you for your trouble. We should be back in a few days."

"I hear y'all is goin' up to the canal them Chinks built."

Pitt nodded. "Word travels."

"Y'all got charts of the river?" asked Wheeler.

"I was hoping you might supply them."

Wheeler turned and checked the labels taped on a slotted cabinet hanging on the wall containing rolled nautical charts of the local waterways and topographical maps of the surrounding marshlands. He pulled out several and spread them on the counter. "Here's a chart showing depths of the river and a few topo maps of the Atchafalaya Valley. One of them shows the area around the canal."

"You're a great help, Mr. Wheeler," said Pitt sincerely. "Thank you."

"I guess y'all know the Chinks won't let you on the canal. They've got it chained off."

"Is there another way in?" asked Pitt.

"Sure, at least two of them." Wheeler took a pencil and began marking the maps. "You can take either Hooker's or Mortimer's bayous. Both run parallel to the canal and empty into it about eight miles from the Atchafalaya. Y'all'll find Hooker's to be the easiest to navigate the shantyboat."

"Does Qin Shang Maritime own the property around Hooker's Bayou, too?"

Wheeler shook his head. "Their borders only run a hundred yards on either side of the canal."

"What happens if you cross the barrier?"

"Local fishermen and hunters sneak in sometimes. More often than not, they're caught and thrown out by an armed boatload of automatic rifle–totin' Chinks who patrol the canal."

"Then security is tight," said Pitt.

"Not so much at night. Y'all could probably get in, see what y'all want to see, since we're havin' a quarter moon for the next two nights before it wanes, and get out before they know y'all been there."

"Has anyone reported seeing anything strange in and around the canal?"

"Nothin' worth writin' home about. Nobody can figure why the fuss to keep people out of a ditch through a swamp."

"Any barge or boat traffic in and out?"

Wheeler shook his head. "None. The chain barrier is fixed in place and can't be opened unless ya blast it with TNT."

"Does the canal have a name?"

"Use to be known as Mystic Bayou," Wheeler said wistfully. "And a pretty bayou it was, too, before it was dug all to hell. Lots of deer, ducks and alligator to hunt. Catfish, bream and bass to fish. Mystic Bayou was a sportsman's paradise. Now it's all gone, and what's left is off limits."

"Hopefully my friend and I will have some answers in the next forty-eight hours," said Pitt as he loaded the groceries in an empty cardboard box offered by Wheeler.

The boat-landing owner penciled several numbers on the corner of a map. "Y'all get into trouble, call my cell-phone number. Y'all hear? I'll see that you get help real quick."

Pitt was touched by the amiable and intelligent people in southern Louisiana who had offered their advice and assistance. They were contacts to be treasured. He thanked Wheeler and carried the groceries down the dock to the shantyboat. As he stepped on board the veranda, Giordino stood in the doorway shaking his head in wonderment.

"You're not going to believe what you see in here," he said.

"It's worse than you thought?"

"Not at all. The interior is clean and Spartan. It's the engine and our passenger that boggle the mind."

"What passenger?"

Giordino handed Pitt a note he'd found pinned to the door. It read,

Mr. Pitt and Mr. Giordino. I thought that since you wanted to look like locals on a fishing trip, you should have a companion. So I loaned you Romberg to embellish your image as rivermen. He'll eat any kind of fish you throw at him.

Luck,
The Bayou Kid

"Who's Romberg?" asked Pitt.

Giordino stepped out of the doorway and without comment pointed inside at a bloodhound lying on his back with his paws in the air, big floppy ears splayed to the sides, his tongue half hanging out.

"Is he dead?"

"He might as well be, for all the enthusiasm he's shown at my

331

presence," said Giordino. "He hasn't twitched or blinked an eye since I came on board."

"What is so unusual about the engine?"

"You've got to see this." Giordino led the way through the one room that composed the living room, bedroom, and kitchen of the shantyboat to a trapdoor in the floor. He lifted the cover and pointed below into the compact engine room in the hull. "A Ford 427-cubic-inch V-8 with dual quad carburetors. An oldie but goodie. It's got to have at least four hundred horsepower."

"Probably closer to four hundred twenty-five," said Pitt, admiring the powerful engine that appeared in immaculate condition. "How the old man must have laughed after I asked him if the engine could move the boat against the river current."

"As big as this floating shack is," said Giordino, "I'd guess we could make close to twenty-five miles an hour if we had to."

"Keep it slow and easy. We don't want to look like we're in a hurry."

"How far is the canal?"

"I haven't measured the distance, but it looks to be close to sixty miles."

"We'll want to get there sometime before sunset," said Giordino, mentally calculating a leisurely cruising speed.

"I'll cast off. You take the helm and head her into the channel while I store the groceries."

Giordino needed no coaxing. He couldn't wait to start the big 427 Ford and feel its torque. He hit the starter and it rumbled into life with a mean and nasty growl. He let it idle for a few moments, savoring the sound. It did not turn over smoothly, but loped. It was too good to believe, Giordino thought to himself. The engine was not stock. It was modified and tuned for racing. "My God," he murmured to himself, "It's far more powerful than we thought."

Knowing without a shade of doubt Giordino would soon get carried away and push the engine throttle to its stop, Pitt secured the groceries so they wouldn't end up on the deck. Then he stepped over the sleeping Romberg, went out onto the forward veranda and relaxed in a lawn chair, but not before bracing his feet against the bulwark and wrapping his arm around the railing.

Giordino waited until the Atchafalaya River was clear and there were no boats in sight. He laid out the nautical chart of the river provided by Doug Wheeler and studied the river depths ahead. Then, true to form, he increased the speed of the old shantyboat until the flat nose bow was a good foot above the water and the stern was burrowed, cutting a wide groove across the surface. To see such an ungainly craft barreling upriver at better than thirty-five miles an hour was an extraordinary and incongruous sight. On the forward veranda, the wind resistance and the raised angle of the bow pressed Pitt back against the wall of the house with such force he felt constrained and barely able to move.

Finally, after about two miles of spreading a three-foot-high wash behind the shantyboat that swept into the marshlands and splayed the unbroken green mat of water hyacinth that spread from the river channel, Giordino observed two small fishing boats approaching on their way to Morgan City. He eased back the throttle and brought the shantyboat to a crawl. The water hyacinth is a pretty plant but is a disaster to inland waterways, growing at a prolific rate and choking off streams and bayous. They are kept afloat by their stems full of air bladders. The hyacinth sprouts beautiful lavender-pink flowers, but unlike most other flowering plants, it smells like a fertilizer factory when pulled from the water.

Feeling as if he had survived a roller-coaster ride, Pitt returned inside, retrieved the topographical map and began studying the twists and turns in the river as well as familiarizing himself with the network of swampy bayous and lakes between Wheeler's Landing and the canal dug by Qin Shang Maritime. He traced and compared the landmarks and river bends with those on the map. It was refreshing to sit comfortably in the shade of the veranda overhang and experience the pleasant sensation of traveling smoothly over timeless waters that only a boat can provide. Riverbank vegetation varied from mile to mile. Thick forests with willows, cottonwoods and cypresses interspersed with berry bushes, and wild grapevines slowly gave way to a moist, primeval swamp, a prairie of soaring reeds swaying under a light breeze that swept off to the horizon. A lone cypress rose majestically out of the grass like a frigate on the sea. He saw herons walking on their long, sticklike legs along the fringe of water, their necks bent into an S shape as they pecked for food in the mud.

To a hunter kayaking or paddling a canoe through the swamps of southern Louisiana, the trick was to find a firm piece of ground on which to pitch a tent for the night. Duckweed and hyacinth floated on much of the open water. Forests grew from the brackish muck, not dry land. It was hard for Pitt to imagine that all the water he could see came from as far away as Ontario and Manitoba, North Dakota and Minnesota, and every state below. Only behind the safety of thousands of miles of levee systems did people cultivate farms and build cities and towns. It was a landscape unlike any he'd ever seen.

The day was pleasantly cool, with just enough breeze to make small waves across the surface of the water. The hours rolled by as if time was as limitless as space. As idyllic as the lazy cruise up the river seemed, they were on serious business that could easily be the cause of their deaths. There could be no mistakes, no errors in planning their reconnaissance of the mysterious canal.

A few minutes after noon, Pitt took a salami sandwich and a bottle of beer up to Giordino in the little wheelhouse on the roof. Pitt offered to take the helm, but Giordino wouldn't hear of it. He was having too much fun, so Pitt returned to his chair on the veranda.

Although time seemed to have no meaning, Pitt's hours were neither idle nor aimless. He spent the time laying out their diving equipment. He unpacked and adjusted the controls on the little AUV he had used at Orion Lake. Lastly, he removed the night-vision goggles from their case and laid them on the cushions of an old, worn sofa.

Shortly after five o'clock in the afternoon, Pitt stepped inside the house and stood at the base of the ladder leading up to the pilothouse on the roof. "One half mile before we reach the mouth of the canal," he alerted Giordino. "Move on past another half mile to the next bayou. Then swing a turn to starboard."

"What's it called?" asked Giordino.

"Hooker's Bayou, but don't bother looking for a sign at the intersection. Take it for about six miles to where the map shows an abandoned dock by a capped oil well. We'll tie up there and have dinner while we wait for darkness."

Giordino eased the shantyboat around a long string of barges pushed downriver by a large towboat. The captain of the towboat gave a blast from his air horn as they passed, no doubt thinking the owner was on board the shantyboat. Pitt had returned to his chair on the bow and waved. Using a pair of binoculars, he scrutinized the canal as they crossed its mouth. It was carved in a perfectly straight course nearly a quarter of a mile wide that seemed to roll like a green carpet over the horizon. A rusty chain stretched across the mouth and was attached to concrete pilings. Large, billboard-sized signs were raised with red letters against a background of white that said, NO TRESPASSING. ANYONE CAUGHT ON QIN SHANG MARITIME PROPERTY WILL BE PROSECUTED.

Small wonder the local residents hate Qin Shang, thought Pitt. He seriously doubted that the local sheriff would go out of his way to arrest friends and neighbors for hunting or fishing on foreign-owned property.

Forty minutes later, Giordino eased back on the throttle and swung the bulky shantyboat from the narrow channel of Hooker's Bayou and crept to a halt toward the remains of a concrete pier, nudging the flat, raked bow onto a low bank. Stenciled lettering on the concrete pilings read, CHEROKEE OIL COMPANY, BATON ROUGE, LOUISIANA. The boat had no anchor, so they took up long poles that were tied to the catwalks for the purpose and rammed them into the mud. Then they tied the mooring lines from the boat to the poles. Lastly, a gangplank was run out onto firm ground.

"I have a contact on radar moving across the marsh from the southeast," Giordino calmly reported.

"They're coming from the direction of the Mystic Canal."

"They're coming fast," Giordino said in a deliberate tone.

"Shang's security didn't waste any time tagging us." Pitt went inside and returned with a large square net with vertical supports he'd found on the aft veranda. "Drag Romberg out here and get yourself a bottle of beer."

Giordino looked at the net. "You think you're going to catch crab for dinner?"

"No," Pitt answered, catching a glint from the setting sun on a shiny object far away in the ocean of grass. "The trick is to look like I know what I'm doing."

"A helicopter," Giordino said in a deliberate tone, "or an ultralight like Washington."

"Too low, more likely a hovercraft."

"Are we on Qin Shang's real estate?"

"According to the map, we're a good three hundred yards off their property line. They must be paying a social call to check us out."

"What's the scenario?" asked Giordino.

"I'll play a crab fisherman, you act like a redneck swilling beer and Romberg can play Romberg."

"Not easy for an Italian to pretend he's French Cajun."

"Chew on some okra."

The dog cooperated when dragged out onto the veranda, not out of obedience, but out of necessity. He walked slowly across the gangplank and did his duty. The hound has an iron bladder, Giordino thought, to have lasted this long. Then Romberg abruptly became alert, barked at a rabbit that darted through the grass and chased after him. "No Academy

Award nomination for you, Romberg!" Giordino yelled at the dog as it took off onto a path leading along the bank. Then he flopped in a lawn chair, removed his sneakers and socks and propped his bare feet up on a railing, a bottle of Dixie beer clutched in one hand.

Onstage for the opening act, Pitt with his old .45 Colt stashed in a bucket at his feet and covered by a rag, Giordino with the Aserma 12-gauge shotgun from Pitt's hangar resting beneath the pad on his lawn chair, they watched the black dot that was the hovercraft grow in size as it flew over the marshlands, swirling and flattening a swath through the reeds. It was an amphibious craft that could make the transition from water to land. Propelled by twin aircraft engines with propellers at the stern, the hovercraft was supported by a cushion of air contained within a heavy rubber structure and produced by a smaller engine attached to a horizontal fan. Control was accomplished with a set of rudders much like those used on aircraft. Pitt and Giordino watched as it moved effortlessly and rapidly over the marshlands and mud flats.

"She's fast," commented Pitt. "Capable of fifty miles an hour. About twenty feet long with a small cabin. By the look of her, she can carry six people."

"And none of them are smiling," muttered Giordino as the hovercraft approached the shantyboat and slowed. At that moment, Romberg came bounding from the swamp grass, barking up a storm.

"Good old Romberg," said Pitt. "Right on cue."

The hovercraft came to a stop ten feet away, its skirted hull resting in the bayou. The engines died away to a dull murmur. The five men on board all wore side arms but carried no rifles. They were wearing the same Qin Shang security uniforms Pitt had seen at Orion Lake. Every eye had the unmistakable slant of an Asian. They weren't smiling; their sunburned faces looked dead serious. This was clearly an attempt at intimidation.

"What are you doing here?" asked a hard-faced individual in fluent English. He wore the insignia on his shoulders and hat of someone in command, and he looked like a man who would enjoy sticking pins in living insects, a man who would welcome the opportunity to shoot another human being. He eyed Romberg with a gleam in his eye.

"We're havin' fun," Pitt said casually. "What's y'alls problem?"

"This is private property," the hovercraft's commander said coldly. "You cannot moor here."

"Ah happen to know for a fact that the land around Hooker's Bayou belongs to the Cherokee Oil Company." Pitt actually wasn't certain who owned the property, but he assumed it had to be Cherokee Oil.

The commander turned to his men and they jabbered among themselves in Chinese. Then the commander stepped to the side of the hovercraft and announced, "We are coming aboard."

Pitt tensed and readied himself to snatch up the old Colt. Then he realized the demand to come aboard was a deception. But Giordino didn't fall for it. "The hell y'all are," said Giordino, threateningly. "Y'all got no authority. Now get your ass out of here before we call the sheriff."

The commander looked at the weathered shantyboat and the faded and shabby clothing worn by Pitt and Giordino. "You have a radio or a cellular phone on that boat?"

"A flare gun," Giordino answered, scratching an imaginary itch between the toes of one foot. "We shoot flares and the law comes a-runnin'."

The hovercraft's commander's eyes narrowed. "I do not find that believable."

"Exhibiting a pompous attitude toward intellectual impeccability will get you nowhere," Pitt suddenly said smartly.

The commander tensed. "What was that?" he demanded. "What did you say?"

"Ah said, leave us alone," Pitt drawled. "We ain't hurtin' nothin'."

Another conference between the commander and his men. Then he pointed a finger at Pitt. "I warn you. Do not enter Qin Shang Maritime property."

"Who'd want to?" Giordino said nastily. "Y'all's company ruined the swamp, killed the fish and drove off the wildlife with your dredging. No reason to go in there anyways."

The commander arrogantly turned his back and dismissed them as the first drops of a rainsquall began to splatter on the roof of the shantyboat. He gave the still barking Romberg a withering stare and said something to his crew. The engines accelerated and the hovercraft began moving off in the direction of the canal. A moment later they disappeared from view as the rain poured down in blinding torrents.

Giordino sat enjoying the rain splashing on his bare feet as they dangled over the railing. He cringed as Romberg shook his wet fur, sending a barrage of water flying in every direction. "A glittering performance except for your attempt at a drawing-room put-down."

Pitt laughed. "A bit of keen and boisterous freewheeling humor never fails to get a rise."

"You might have given us away."

"I *wanted* them to record our arrogance. Did you catch the video camera on top of the cabin? At this moment, our pictures are being sent by satellite to Shang's security headquarters in Hong Kong for identification. A pity we can't be there to see Shang's face when he's informed that we're poking around another one of his sensitive projects."

"Then our friends will be back."

"You can bet the farm on it."

"Romberg will protect us," Giordino said jokingly.

Pitt looked around for the dog and found him curled up inside the shantyboat, having quickly returned to his catatonic state. *"That* I seriously doubt."

34

AFTER THE RAINSQUALL PASSED and before the last rays of the sun vanished beyond the marshlands in the west, Pitt and Giordino moved the shantyboat into a narrow tributary of Hooker's Bayou and moored it beneath a huge cottonwood tree to cloak it from the hovercraft's radar. Then they camouflaged the boat with reeds and dead branches from the cottonwood. Romberg only came alive when Pitt fed him a bowl filled with catfish. Giordino offered him some hamburger, but Romberg wouldn't touch it, happily licking his chops and drooling from his flews while consuming the fish.

After closing the shutters and hanging blankets over the windows and doors to black out interior light, Pitt spread the topo map on the dining table and traced out a plan of action. "If Shang's security force runs true to form, they'll have a command post somewhere along the banks of the canal, probably in the center so they can cover both ends quickly against trespassing locals."

"A canal by any other name is a canal," said Giordino. "What exactly are we looking for?"

Pitt shrugged. "Your guess is as good as mine."

"Bodies like you found in Orion Lake?"

"God, I hope not," Pitt said soberly. "But if Qin Shang is smuggling illegals through Sungari, you can bet he's got a killing ground somewhere in the area. Dead bodies are easy to hide in the marshlands. But according to Doug Wheeler, boat traffic from the river into the canal is nonexistent."

"Qin Shang didn't excavate an eighteen-mile trench as an exercise in futility."

"Not him," Pitt said acridly. "The catch is that two miles of excavation could have easily supplied all the fill he required to build Sungari. And the question is, why dig another sixteen miles?"

"Where do we begin?" asked Giordino.

"We'll take the skiff because it's less likely to be detected by their security systems. After loading the equipment, we paddle up Hooker's Bayou until it empties into the canal. Then continue east to Calzas. After we see whatever there is of interest, we work back toward the Atchafalaya and around to the shantyboat."

"They must have detection systems to spot trespassers."

"I'm counting on them using the same limited technology they had at Orion Lake. If they have laser detectors, the beams must be set to sweep above the marsh grass. Hunters with swamp vehicles or fishermen standing in their boat to throw a net can be distinguished from five miles away. By keeping low in the skiff and skirting the banks, we can stay below any sweeping beam."

Giordino listened to Pitt's plan of action and remained silent for a few moments after he finished. He sat with his Etruscan features twisted in a scowling expression, looking like a mask from a voodoo ceremony. Then he slowly moved his head from side to side, visualizing long, aching hours of paddling the skiff.

"Well," he said finally, "Mrs. Giordino's boy is going to have a pair of sore arms before this night is over."

Doug Wheeler's forecast of a waning quarter moon was correct. Leaving a sated and dormant Romberg to guard the shantyboat, they pushed off and began paddling up the bayou, easily finding their way along the twists and turns by the lunar light. A narrow boat with graceful lines, the skiff moved smoothly with little exertion on their part. Whenever a cloud passed over the slim crescent of the moon, Pitt relied on the night-vision goggles to guide their course as the bayou narrowed to little more than five feet in width.

The marshlands came alive at night. The squadrons of mosquitoes winged into the night air, searching for juicy targets. But Pitt and Giordino, shielded by their wet suits and an ample layer of bug repellent on their faces, necks and hands, ignored them. The frogs croaked in a chorus of thousands, rising in a crescendo, then breaking off suddenly into total silence before beginning again. It seemed as if their night song was orchestrated and led by an unseen maestro. The marsh grass became decorated with millions of lightning bugs, blinking their lights on and off like falling sparkles from dying fireworks. An hour and a half later, Pitt and Giordino paddled out of Hooker's Bayou into the canal.

The security force command post was lit up like a football stadium. Floodlights spaced around two acres of dry land illuminated an old plantation house sheltered by live oak trees on a weed-infested lawn that rolled down a slight incline to the bank of the canal. Three stories high with siding that was warped and barely hanging on to support beams by rusty nails, the structure looked similar in architecture to the house in the movie *Psycho,* but not in nearly as good a condition. Several of the shutters hung off kilter on rusting hinges, and the attic windows were broken. Wooden pillars stood in rigid formation across a sagging front porch, their cornices supporting a long, sloping roof.

The smell of Chinese cooking permeated the air. Men in uniform could be seen through the uncurtained windows moving around inside. Chinese music, a scourge to the ears of Westerners, and sung by a female who screeched as if she was giving birth, grated over the marsh-lands. The living room of the old manor was cluttered with a maze of communication and security-detection antennas. Like Orion Lake, there were no guards patrolling the command-center grounds. They had no fear of attack and placed their faith in the electronic systems. The hovercraft was tied to a little dock that floated on empty oil drums. No one was on board.

"Head toward the opposite bank and paddle very slowly," Pitt whispered. "Keep movement to a minimum."

Giordino nodded silently and dipped his paddle carefully into the water, stroking as if in slow motion. Like wraiths gliding through the night, they passed through the shadows of the canal bank, past the command post and up the canal for a hundred yards before Pitt called for a brief rest stop. Stealth was not an option but rather a necessity, since they had not packed their weapons in the overloaded skiff to save weight and space.

"From what I've experienced of their security," said Pitt, "this setup is more slipshod than Orion Lake. The detection network is in place, but they don't seem conscientious about monitoring it."

"They caught on to us damned quick this afternoon," Giordino reminded him.

"No trick to spot a ten-foot-high houseboat on a flat field of grass from five miles. If this was Orion Lake, they would have been observing our every movement five seconds after we stepped into the skiff. Yet here, we move right under their noses as if it was a piece of cake."

"It's beginning to look a lot like Christmas," Giordino observed. "No presents under the tree that contain deep dark secrets. But you've got to like them for giving us free passage."

"Let's move on," said Pitt. "Nothing promising here. We've got a lot of territory to cover. The security force may be lax at night, but they'd have to be blind not to discover us if we don't reach the shantyboat before the sun comes up."

With growing confidence, they cast off any thoughts of caution and began stroking vigorously up the canal. The moon's dim glow fell over the bayou and cast its reflection on the water like a road narrowing to a pinpoint as it traveled over the horizon. The end of the canal seemed impossibly remote, as unattainable as a mirage in the desert. Giordino worked his paddle, easily, powerfully, each stroke moving the skiff four feet to Pitt's three. The night air was balmy but damp. Beneath the wet suits they sweated like lobsters in a pot, but they dared not remove them. Their light skin, although tanned, was revealed under the dying moon like faces in a black velvet painting. Ahead, they could see clouds outlined and glowing from an unseen light source. The headlights from cars and trucks could also be seen, sweeping back and forth on a distant highway.

Buildings from the deserted ghost town of Calzas loomed up on both banks, the canal having split the community in two. The houses huddled eerily in ragged clusters on a large section of land that rose above the marshlands. It was a place haunted by former residents who could no longer return. The town's old hotel stood silent and gaunt across from a gas station whose pumps still stood on islands outside the office and mechanic's bays. A church rose forlorn and empty beside a cemetery, the tombs raised above the round, little shrines weathered and bleached white. The abandoned town was soon left in the wake of the skiff.

At long last they finally ran out of canal. All excavation ended at an embankment leading up to a major highway. At the base of the highway embankment, rising out of the water in the canal, they found a concrete structure that looked like the entrance to a huge underground bunker. It was sealed tight by a massive steel door that was welded closed.

"What do you suppose they keep in there?" queried Giordino.

"Nothing they need to get at fast," Pitt replied, studying the door through the night-vision goggles. "It would take an hour or more just to torch it open." He also spied an electrical conduit that ran from the door and vanished into the muck of the canal. He removed the goggles from his head and gestured toward the shore. "Come on, let's beach the skiff and climb to the highway."

Giordino looked upward speculatively and nodded. They paddled to the bank and pulled the skiff ashore. The embankment was not steep but more of a long, sloping grade. They reached the top and climbed over a traffic guardrail and were almost blown back down the slope by a giant truck and trailer that thundered past. Embellished by the crescent moon, the countryside was bathed in a panoramic sea of lights.

The view was not quite what they expected. The headlights from the traffic, strung out along the highway like fluorescent beads on a snake, twisted around a wide expanse of water. As they stood there, a huge towboat the size of a condominium building moved past, shoving twenty barges that stretched nearly a quarter of a mile. Above and below a large city on the opposite shore, they could see the brilliantly lit white tanks of oil refineries and petrochemical plants.

"Well," said Giordino without any particular expression in his voice, "is now a good time for a chorus of 'Old Man River'?"

"The Mississippi," Pitt muttered. "That's Baton Rouge to the north across the river. The end of the line. Why dig a canal to this particular spot?"

"Who knows what weird machinations lurk in the mind of Qin Shang?" Giordino said philosophically. "Maybe he has plans to access the highway."

"What for? There's no turnoff. The road shoulder is barely wide enough to hold one car. There has to be another reason." Pitt sat on the guardrail and gazed thoughtfully at the river. Then he said slowly, "The highway runs straight as an arrow along here."

Giordino looked at Pitt, his eyebrows raised. "What's so novel about a linear road?"

"Was it a coincidence or a well-conceived plan to end the canal at the exact point where the river curls westward and nearly touches the highway?"

"What difference does it make? Shang's engineers could have ended the canal anywhere."

"A big difference, as I'm beginning to see it, a very big difference indeed."

Giordino's mind was not running on the same channel as Pitt's. Giordino checked the dial on his dive watch under the lights of an approaching car. "If we want to finish the job while it's still dark, I suggest we row our boat gently down the stream, and be quick about it."

They still had the entire eighteen miles of the canal to search using the autonomous underwater vehicle. After dropping back down the slope to the skiff, they removed the AUV from its case and slipped it over the side of the skiff and watched it slip out of sight beneath the dark surface. Then, while Giordino paddled, Pitt worked the remote control, engaging the AUV's motors, switching on its lights and leveling it off five feet from the bottom mud of the canal. Because of the high algae content of the brackish water, which limited visibility to no more than six feet, there was the danger of the AUV striking a submerged object before he could divert it.

Giordino paddled with long even strokes that never slowed as the precious hours passed, making it easy for Pitt to pace the AUV's progress with that of the skiff. Only when they reached the outer fringe of light around the old plantation headquarters of Qin Shang's security force did they move furtively along the opposite bank at a snail's speed.

This time of night most of the security force should have been sleeping, but the plantation house had suddenly come alive with activity as guards began rushing across the lawn to the little dock where the hovercraft was moored. Pitt and Giordino pressed into the shadows and watched as the hovercraft was loaded with automatic weapons. Two men lifted a long, heavy, tubelike object into the boat.

"They're going for bear," said Giordino softly. "Unless I'm mistaken that's a rocket launcher."

"You're not mistaken," Pitt murmured. "I do believe Shang's chief of security in Hong Kong has identified us and sent word that we're evildoers out to spy on another one of his nasty ventures."

"The shantyboat. It's evident they plan to blow it and anyone in it to smithereens."

"Not polite of us to allow them to destroy the Bayou Kid's property. And then we've got Romberg to consider. The Society for the Prevention of Cruelty to Animals would put us on their blacklist for life if we let poor old Romberg go to dog heaven in a blaze of rocket fire."

"Two unarmed bon vivants against a horde of barbarians armed to the teeth," muttered Giordino. "Not very healthy odds, wouldn't you say?"

Pitt slipped a dive mask over his head and picked up an air tank. "I've got to get across the canal before they cast off. You take the skiff and wait for me a hundred yards beyond the plantation."

"Let me guess. You're going to take your little dive knife and slash the hell out of the hovercraft's inflatable skirt."

Pitt grinned. "If it leaks, it won't lift."

"What about the AUV?"

"Keep it submerged. It might be worth seeing what kind of trash they throw in the canal in front of their quarters."

In ten seconds Pitt was gone. He eased into the water without making a sound or a splash, while at the same time strapping on the air tank and its backpack. He had already kicked twenty feet from the boat before he inserted the regulator in his mouth and began breathing underwater. After leveling out, he quickly got his bearings and swam across the canal toward the lights flickering on the water in front of the plantation. The mud on the bottom below looked dark and forbidding, and the water itself was tepid as a bathtub's. Pitt swam aggressively, his arms out in front forming a V to reduce water resistance, kicking his feet and fins as hard and fast as his leg muscles would allow.

A good diver can sense the water as an animal senses a change in weather or the presence of a predator. The brackish water of the canal had a warm and friendly feel to it, nothing like the sinister and malignant force he experienced in the deep cold of Orion Lake. His only fear now was that one of the security guards might glance out into the canal and see his air bubbles, a possibility he didn't think likely because they were wrapped up in preparing to attack the shantyboat and had no time to stare at the water surface above Pitt for even half a second.

The light became brighter underwater as he neared the source. Soon the shadow of the hovercraft loomed ahead. He was certain it was loaded and the crew was aboard to launch the search and attack. Only the lack of sound told him the engines had yet to start. He swam harder, determined to stop the hovercraft before it hurtled from the dock.

From his vantage point across the canal, Giordino began to have grave doubts that Pitt would reach the hovercraft in time. He cursed himself for not working harder on the return trip so they might have arrived earlier. But then, how could he have known the guards were preparing to assault the shantyboat before daylight? He kept in the shadows and paddled the skiff slowly, so no sudden movement would be caught by the men on the other side of the canal. "Do it!" he muttered under his breath as if Pitt was in earshot. "Do it!"

Pitt felt a growing numbness from overexertion in his arms and legs, his lungs gasping from fatigue. He gathered his waning strength for a final surge, a last effort before his exhausted body refused his demands. He couldn't believe he was killing himself to save a dog that he swore was bitten by a tsetse fly when a pup and suffered from chronic sleeping sickness.

Abruptly, the light from above faded and he swam into a dark hole. His head broke the surface just inside the flexible sleeve, called a skirt, that contains the cushion of air and suspends the hovercraft. He floated for several moments, his chest heaving, his arms too numb to move, while he regained his strength and studied the interior of the skirt. Of the three types fitted to hovercraft, this one was called a bag skirt, consisting of a rubber tube that encircled the hull and when inflated served to contain the air cushion while providing lift. He also recognized that this hovercraft used an aluminum propeller as a lift fan to inflate the bag tube and feed air into the cushion.

As Pitt reached down to pull his dive knife out of its sheath strapped to his leg to begin slicing holes in the rubberized fabric, his moment of victory was snatched away by the sound of the starter motors as they began to turn over the engines. Then the propeller's blades started to spin, their speed increasing with every revolution. The skirt began to flare, and the water inside was whipped into a maelstrom. Too late to slash the rubber cushion and prevent the craft from moving.

Out of irreversible despair, he unsnapped the buckle to his air tank's backpack, spit out the breathing regulator and pulled the tank up and over his head. Then, in one movement, he thrust it upward into the spinning lift propeller and ducked under the skirt as it was starting to inflate. The propeller blades struck the tank and shattered. It was an act born of desperation. Pitt knew he had gambled recklessly and pushed his luck too far.

The disintegration of the propeller as its blades struck a solid, ungiving object was followed by a hurricane of metal shards that ripped through the walls of the rubber skirt like shrapnel from a bomb. Then came a second, more massive explosion as the tank's walls were penetrated and it burst from the sudden release of eighty cubic feet of air pressurized at three thousand pounds. Not content to be left out, the fuel tanks added to the cataclysm by erupting in a blazing conflagration that sent a firestorm into the air and fiery particles of the hovercraft flying onto the roof of the plantation house and quickly setting the wooden structure ablaze.

Giordino was stunned in horror as he watched the hovercraft lift out of the water and then violently shred itself into a thousand flaming fragments. Bodies spun through the air like drunken circus acrobats and splashed into the water with the inert stiffness of mannequins dropped from a helicopter. The windows of the plantation house were blown into jagged shards. The explosion rumbled over the surface of the canal and struck Giordino's exposed face like a punch thrown by the gloved fist of a boxer. A waterspout of fiery fuel enveloped the hovercraft, and when it fell away and the spray had scattered into the night, the burning remains of the craft were sinking into the waters of the canal amid a great hiss of steam and dark smoke that swirled and quickly became lost in the black sky.

In growing fear, Giordino frantically paddled the skiff toward the shattered wreckage. Reaching the outer perimeter of the burning debris, he strapped on his air tank and rolled into the canal. Lit by a field of flames on the surface, the water beneath took on a look of eerie candescence, ghostly and threatening. In a strange kind of restrained frenzy, he searched through the mangled remains of the hovercraft, tearing aside the shreds of the skirt and probing underneath. He was still dazed with shock as he desperately tried to find the body of his friend. He groped about the shambles created by Pitt, and his hands touched what remained of a man, stripped of his clothing, a sliced and gutted thing with no legs. One black eye, wide open and unseeing, was all he required to know it wasn't Pitt.

He fought off a sickening fear that it seemed impossible anyone could have survived that holocaust. He searched unavailingly, hopelessly, for some sight of a living body. God, where is he? Giordino cried in his mind. He began to feel beyond weary in his bones and was almost ready to give up in despair when something reached out of the darkness of the muck below him and grabbed his ankle. Giordino experienced an icy chill of panic that gave way to disbelief when he felt the hard grip of a living human. He spun around and saw a face leering at him, green eyes squinting to see through the liquid gloom, blood flowing from the nose and dissolving in the water.

As if risen from the dead, Pitt's lips tightened in a crooked little grin. His wet suit was in tatters and the dive mask had been torn from his head, but he was alive. He pointed up, released his hold on Giordino's ankle and kicked toward the surface a short five feet away. They broke the surface at the same time, Giordino grasping Pitt around the shoulders in a great bear hug.

"Damn you!" Giordino shouted. "You're alive."

"Damn me if I'm not," Pitt came back, laughing.

"How in God's name did you do it?"

"Dumb luck. After I heaved my air tank into the hovercraft's lift propeller and dove under the skirt, a stupid move by the way, I got no farther than eight feet when the tank exploded. The explosion blew outward and the resulting blast from the fuel tanks burst upward. I was unscathed until the concussion tore into me. I was blown into the muddy bottom, which cushioned my impact. It was a miracle my eardrums didn't burst. My ears are still ringing. I ache in places I didn't know existed. Every square inch of my body must be black-and-blue. Things went vague and woolly. I was knocked silly for a few moments but quickly recovered when I sucked on my regulator mouthpiece and found only my tongue along with a gush of swamp water. Gagging and retching, I made for the surface and floated around while pulling my mind and body together until I saw your air bubbles trail by."

"I thought for sure you bought the farm this time," said Giordino.

"Me too," Pitt agreed. He gingerly fingered his nose and a split lip. "Something struck my face when I was mashed into the canal bed—" He broke off and made a grimace. "Broken, my nose is broken. First time ever."

Giordino nodded his head at the devastation, the plantation house that had become a blazing inferno. "Did you ever determine which side of the family passed on your uncanny knack for causing destruction?"

"No pyromaniac ancestors that I know of."

Three security guards were still alive, one crawling away from the house, smoke curling from smoldering holes in the back of his uniform, the second lying dazed on the edge of the bank, weaving back and forth, his hands cupped to ears whose eardrums had burst. Four bodies floated in the flame-lit waters. The rest of the security force had disappeared. The third living guard stood in shock, staring dumbly at the shattered wreckage of the hovercraft with blood from a gash across one cheek flowing down his neck and dyeing his shirt crimson.

Pitt swam to the bank, came to his feet and walked ashore. The guard stared wide-eyed at the black-suited apparition from the canal as if he was an alien creature from the swamp. He convulsively reached for the gun in his side holster, but it had been torn away by the explosions. He turned and tried to run, staggered a few steps and fell. The apparition, with blood streaming from his nose, stared down.

"You speak English, my friend?"

"Yes," the guard nodded, replying in a voice hoarse with shock. "I learned American vocabulary."

"Good. You tell your boss, Qin Shang, that Dirk Pitt wants to know if he still stoops over and picks up bananas. You got that?"

The guard stumbled several times, repeating the sentence, but with Pitt's coaching he finally got it right. "Dirk Pitt wants to know if the esteemed Qin Shang still stoops over and picks up bananas."

"Nice going," Pitt said jovially. "You move to the head of the class."

Then Pitt casually strolled back to the canal and waded out to Giordino, who was waiting in the skiff.

35

JULIA WAS THANKFUL when darkness arrived. Moving through the shadows along the outside deck of the towboat toward the bow, she slipped over the side onto the barge and hid amid the black plastic bags of trash. She was not happy about the faint light thrown by a waning moon, but it enabled her to keep track of crew movements on board the towboat and to observe the countryside for geographical references as to location. She also followed the direction of her progress by glancing up every few minutes at Polaris, the North Star.

Unlike the featureless landscape of the central Atchafalaya Valley, the grassy banks of Bayou Teche supported a thick canopy of live oak trees, interspersed with stately cypresses and lithe willows. But like the edge of a checkerboard, the tree belt opened up every mile to reveal lights of farmhouses and dim, moonlit fields of newly planted crops. Behind fenced pastures, Julia could make out the shapes of cattle grazing. She recognized the sound of a meadowlark and fleetingly wished that she had a family and a home. She knew the day was not far off when her superiors at INS would curtail her hazardous attempts to stop Chinese immigrant-smuggling operations and put her behind a desk.

The towboat and barge passed what seemed a picturesque fishing town that Julia would later learn was Patterson. Docks lined the waterfront with fishing trawlers taking up almost every slip. She made a mental note of how the town was laid out along the bayou as it receded in the distance. The towboat captain blew his air horn as a drawbridge drew into sight. The bridge tender dutifully tooted his horn in reply and raised the span to allow passage.

A few miles above Patterson the towboat slackened its speed and began easing toward the west bank. Peering over the side of the barge, Julia could see a large, warehouselike brick structure with several outer buildings that were spaced around a long dock. A high chain-link fence with barbwire strung along the top encircled the compound. A few scattered floodlights with dim and dusty bulbs in their sockets ineffectually illuminated the open area between the dock and warehouse. The only sign of life Julia could see was a guard who exited a little shack and stood at a closed gate on the end of the dock. She noted that he was wearing the common uniform sold by private security services. Through a window of the shack, she could see the reflected images of a television screen.

Her heart gave a leap when she spied a pair of railroad tracks that ran down a concrete culvert under the big warehouse. She believed with growing certainty that this was the main staging center from where the illegals were transported to their predetermined destinations. Once there, they were either enslaved or released into heavily populated metropolitan cities.

She burrowed under the trash bags as the Chinese crew came aboard the barge and tied it to the dock. When the barge was secure, they leaped back on board the towboat. There was no word spoken between the captain, crew and the guard behind the gate. The captain gave a brief blast on his air horn to signal his intentions to a small shrimp boat about to pass by. The towboat slowly reversed away from the barge, swinging its stern wide until a 180-degree turn was completed and the flat-nosed bow was pointing down the bayou. Then the captain engaged FORWARD, increased speed and set the towboat on a course back toward Sungari.

The next twenty minutes were spent in a strange silence that began to frighten Julia. Not from personal fear of her safety, but a dread that perhaps she had made a mistake. The guard had long since returned to his shack and his television. The barge full of trash lay moored to the dock, dismissed and neglected.

Julia had contacted Captain Lewis aboard the *Weehawken* soon after her leap onto the towboat and informed him of her reckless enterprise. Lewis was not a happy camper when he realized that the woman whose safety was in his hands had taken a terrible risk. Professional that he was, he brushed aside his frustration and ordered a launch full of armed men under Lieutenant Stowe to follow the towboat and barge as a backup to the helicopter. His only order to Stowe was to keep a respectful distance behind the towboat and not arouse suspicion. Julia could hear the whine of the helicopter's engines and see its navigation lights in the night sky.

She well knew the fate that awaited her if Qin Shang's smuggling enforcers apprehended her, and it gave her a warm feeling to know she was being watched over by men who were willing to lay their lives on the line to save her if worst came to worst.

She had long before removed Lin Wan Chu's cook clothes and crammed them into a plastic trash bag, not so much because they were now incongruous but because the white cloth would have made her visible to anyone on the towboat when she stood up to stare over the side of the barge during the journey from Sungari. Underneath, she wore simple shorts and a blouse.

For the first time in nearly an hour, she spoke into her miniature radio and hailed Lieutenant Stowe. "The towboat has dropped off the barge and moored it alongside a dock near what looks like a large warehouse."

Lieutenant Jefferson Stowe, in command of the launch, answered quickly over the transmitter and receiver set around his head. "We confirm. The towboat is about to pass us going in the opposite direction. What is your situation?"

"About as exciting as watching a tree become petrified. Except for a security guard on the other side of a tall fence, who's busy watching a TV program in his shack, there isn't another soul in sight."

"Are you saying your objective is a washout?" asked Stowe.

"I need more time for an investigation," answered Julia.

"Not too long, I hope. Captain Lewis is hardly a patient man, and the helicopter only has another hour of fuel left. And that's only the half of it."

"What's the other half?"

"Your decision to jump on the towboat came so fast none of my crew or I got dinner."

"You're joking."

"Not about growing coast guardsmen missing a meal," Stowe said humorously.

"You *will* stand by, and not desert me."

"Of course," replied Stowe, the humor in his voice quickly fading. "I only hope the towboat didn't simply park the barge overnight in expectation of moving it to a trash fill in the morning."

"I don't think that's the case," said Julia. "One of the buildings has a railroad siding leading in and out of it. This place would make an ideal layout to transport smuggled immigrants to destinations around the country."

"I'll request Captain Lewis to check the railroad company for freight-train schedules that call for stops at the mill," Stowe offered reasonably. "Meanwhile, I'll run the launch into a small inlet across the bayou about a hundred yards south of you. We'll stand by here until I hear otherwise." There was a slight pause. "Ms. Lee."

"Yes."

"Don't get your hopes up," said Stowe evenly. "I've just spotted a shabby, run-down sign that's sitting at a crazy angle on the bank of the bayou. Would you like to know what it says?"

"Yes, do tell me," Julia answered, deliberately robbing her words of irritation.

"Felix Bartholomeaux Sugar Processing Plant Number One. Established 1883. You're apparently moored at a long-abandoned sugar mill. From my vantage point, the complex looks deader than a fossilized dinosaur egg."

"Then why would it be protected by a security guard?"

"I don't know," Stowe replied honestly.

"Hold on!" Julia snapped unexpectedly. "I heard something."

She went quietly, listening, and Stowe cooperated by asking no questions. As if far away, she heard the muted clank of metal against metal. At first, she thought it came from somewhere within the deserted sugar mill, but then she realized the sound was muffled by the water beneath the barge. Furiously, she threw the plastic trash bags aside until she could squirm a passage down to the bottom of the barge's hull. Then she pressed her ear against the damp, rusting metal of the bilge keel.

This time she heard muffled voices whose vibrations telegraphed through the steel. She could not distinguish words, but what she heard came through as men shouting harshly. Julia fought her way back to the top of the trash-bag pile, checked to see the guard was still occupied and then leaned over the side of the barge, peering down into the water. There were no telltale lights in the depths, and it was too dark to see more than a few inches past the surface.

"Lieutenant Stowe," she said softly.

"I'm here."

"Can you see anything in the water between the dock and the barge?"

"Not from here. But I have you in view."

Julia instinctively turned and stared across the bayou, but all she saw was darkness. "You can follow my actions?"

"Through a night-vision scope. I didn't want anybody sneaking up on you without you knowing about it."

Good old faithful Lieutenant Stowe. Another time, another place, she might have felt a growing affection for him. But any thought of love, no matter how fleeting, created an image of Dirk Pitt in her mind. For the first time in her life she was infatuated with a man, and her independent spirit was not sure how to accept the situation. Almost reluctantly, she refocused her concentration on discovering the covert methods of Qin Shang's smuggling operation.

"I believe there must be another vessel or compartment connected to the bottom of the barge," she reported.

"What are the indications?" asked Stowe.

"I heard voices through the keel. That would explain how the Chinese were able to smuggle the illegal immigrants through Sungari and past immigration, customs and the Coast Guard."

"I'd like to buy your theory, Ms. Lee, but an underwater compartment that is carried across two oceans from China and then shifted under a barge for a voyage up a Louisiana bayou to a railroad terminal in an abandoned sugar mill may get you an award for literary fiction, but it won't score you any points with pragmatic minds."

"I'll stake my career on it," Julia said positively.

"May I ask your intent?" Stowe's tone went from friendly to official.

"I intend to gain entry into the mill and make a search."

"Not a smart move. Better to wait until morning."

"That may be too late. The immigrants could be herded into freight cars and transported away by then."

"Ms. Lee," said Stowe coldly. "I strongly urge you to think this thing out and back off. I'll swing the launch across the bayou and pick you up off the barge."

Julia did not feel that she had come this far suddenly to walk away. "No thank you, Lieutenant Stowe. I'm going in. If I find what I hope to find, you and your men can come running."

"Ms. Lee, I must remind you that although you're under the protection of the Coast Guard, we are not a Justice Department SWAT team. My advice, if you wish to take it, is to wait until daylight, obtain a search warrant from a parish judge and then send in the local sheriff to investigate. You'll score more points with your superiors that way."

It was as though Julia had not heard Stowe. "Please ask Captain

Lewis to notify Peter Harper in Washington and alert the INS office in New Orleans. Good night, Lieutenant Stowe. Let's do lunch tomorrow."

Stowe tried several times to raise Julia, but she had turned off her little radio. He looked across the bayou through his night-vision scope and saw her jump from the barge and run the length of the dock, disappearing around a moss-covered oak tree outside the chain-link fence.

Julia stopped when she reached the oak and hid for a few minutes under the moss that hung from the branches above. Her eyes slowly panned around the seemingly deserted buildings of the sugar mill. No lights inside the doors and windows leaked through the weathered cracks. She listened but only heard the rhythmic whine and rasp of cicadas, an indication that summer was just around the corner. The balmy air lay heavy and damp with no breeze to cool skin moist with sweat.

The main building in the complex, solid and substantial, stood three stories tall. The founder must have been influenced by medieval architecture. Ramparts traveled around the roof with four turrets that once held the company's offices. The walls showed only enough windows to provide daylight for the interior, but to the men and women who had once labored there, the lack of ventilation must have caused incredibly oppressive working conditions. The red-clay bricks looked as if they had long defied the mugginess, but green moss and climbing vines were slowly invading their mortared seams, loosening their grip. Already, a large number of them had fallen to the damp earth below. To Julia the unearthly scene of a once-thriving business humming with activity, crowded with people but now abandoned, wore the expectant air of a place long overdue for the wrecker's ball.

She worked her way through the shadows of the vegetation growing along the fence until she came to the railroad tracks leading through a heavily padlocked gate, down the culvert and ending at a massive wooden door opening into the basement of the main warehouse. She bent down and studied the rails under a light on a nearby pole. The steel was shiny and free of rust. Her cocksure conviction was now becoming more firmly established.

She continued her reconnaissance, flitting silently with the grace of a cat through the underbrush until she came to a small drainage pipe two feet in diameter that ran under the fence before emptying in a ditch parallel to the old mill. She made a quick survey of the immediate area to check that she was still unobserved and began crawling into the pipe, pushing herself feet first so she could scramble forward if it proved to be a dead end.

Julia was by no means lulled into a false sense of security. It puzzled her that only one guard appeared to be working for a security service other than Qin Shang Maritime. The lack of extra guards and brighter floodlighting suggested that this was a facility holding little of value— perhaps the very image that was meant to be projected. She was too much the professional not to consider the likely possibility that her movements were recorded by concealed infrared video cameras from the time she jumped from the barge until now. But she had come too far to quit. If this *was* a staging area for illegal immigrants, then Qin Shang wasn't operating under his usual formula of fanatical secrecy and tight security.

A broad-shouldered man might never have squirmed through the drainage pipe, but Julia had inches to spare. At first, all she saw when she looked between her feet was blackness. But after negotiating a slight bend in the pipe, she saw a circle of moonlight playing in a reflection of water. At last she emerged into a concrete ditch filled with several inches of muck that ran around the main warehouse building to catch the rainwater that dropped from drain spouts on the roof.

She went immobile as she gazed to her left and right. No sirens, no mad attack dogs, no searchlights greeted her entry into the sugar-mill compound. Content that her presence wasn't detected, she stealthily moved along the building, searching for a way to enter. She pressed her back against the moss-covered brick walls, deciding on which direction to take around the sugar mill. The side where the railroad tracks sloped off into a basement was open and washed from the light on the pole, so she chose the opposite course, which offered dark shadows from a grove of cypress trees. She stepped as noiselessly as possible, careful not to fall over any old rubbish that lay scattered about the ground.

A small thicket of brush blocked her way, and Julia crawled under it. Her outstretched, probing fingers touched a stone step, and then a second one leading downward. Squinting her eyes, she peered into the shadows and discovered a stairway dropping to the basement of the mill. The steps were covered with debris, and she carefully had to step around and over it. The door at the bottom of the stairs had seen better days. Stout and made of oak, at one time it could have stopped a battering ram. But a century of damp climate had rusted out the hinges, and Julia found that all she had to do was give it a hearty kick for the door to creak open just far enough to allow her to squeeze past.

Julia hesitated only long enough to see that she was in a concrete-walled passage. There was a faint glow of light at the other end a good fifty feet away, she guessed. The dank smell from the long-unused passage lay heavy. The floor was dripping-damp and puddled in places where rainwater had seeped in from the outer door. Debris and old furniture cast into the passageway when the sugar mill closed down made it difficult to pass through without undue sounds. She became extra cautious when she reached the dim light that shone through the dirty glass window of a heavy oak door blocking the way. She carefully turned a rusting door handle. Unexpectedly, the bolt slid whisper-silent from its slot. Then she painstakingly eased the door open a crack. It swung on its hinges as smoothly as if it had been oiled only the day before.

She softly stepped inside with the expectation of a woman anticipating trouble. She found herself inside an office furnished in the heavy oak furniture so popular in the early part of the twentieth century. Julia froze. The room was immaculately clean. There wasn't a speck of dust or a cobweb to be seen. It was like entering a time capsule. She had also stepped into a trap.

She felt as if she had been punched in the stomach when the oak door clunked shut behind her and three men stepped from behind a screen that shielded a sitting room at the other end of the office. All of the men were dressed in business suits, two carrying briefcases as though they had just come from a board-of-directors meeting.

Before she could transmit over her hidden radio, her arms were pinned and her mouth taped shut.

"You are a most obstinate young lady, Ling T'ai, or should I call you Julia Lee?" said Ki Wong, Qin Shang's chief enforcer, as he gave a curt bow and grinned satanically. "You don't know how happy I am to meet you again."

Stowe stared across the bayou as he pressed the receiver against his ear with one hand and held the microphone of the transmitter until it nearly touched his lips. "Ms. Lee. If you read me, please answer."

He heard what seemed to be stifled voices for a moment before all communications with Julia went dead. His first instinct was to rush across the bayou and charge the gate on the wharf. But he could not be certain Julia had encountered a life-threatening situation. Surely not certain enough to risk the lives of his men in a combat engagement. Another factor that preyed on his mind was the possibility of ambush on territory that was unknown. Stowe took the route used by astute officers since the first military force was formed: He laid the responsibility on his superior officer.

"Weehawken, this is Lieutenant Stowe."

"We read you," came the voice of Captain Lewis.

"Sir, I believe we have a situation."

"Please explain."

"Contact has been lost with Ms. Lee."

There was a few moments' pause. Then Lewis replied slowly. "Remain in your position and keep the sugar mill under surveillance. Report any new information. I'll get back to you."

Stowe stood in the launch and gazed across the bayou at the silent and dark buildings. "God help you if you've run into trouble," Stowe muttered softly, "because I can't."

36

THERE WAS NO FEVERISH HURRY after Pitt and Giordino left the burning hovercraft and command post. It seemed reasonable to assume that all communications between the security force and Qin Shang's headquarters were cut off when the plantation burned to the ground. They continued their project of photographing the bed of the canal with the AUV as if no interruption ever occurred. Neither man was of a mind to do a rushed, botched job.

They reached the Atchafalaya River and returned up Hooker's Bayou to the shantyboat just as the eastern sky was beginning to lighten from black to blue-gray. Romberg greeted their arrival by opening his eyes only long enough to recognize them before instantly dropping off into dog dreamland again.

Without delay, they unloaded the dive equipment and the AUV. Once the skiff was stowed on the roof, Giordino started the big Ford 427 engine as Pitt pulled the mooring stakes from the mud under the boat. The sun had still to put in an appearance when the shantyboat swung onto the Atchafalaya and headed downriver.

"Where to?" Giordino shouted down into the main cabin from the pilothouse.

"Bartholomeaux," Pitt yelled back over the roar of the engine.

Giordino said no more. Boat traffic was not as light as he expected this early in the morning. The oyster and crawfish boats were already on the river heading toward their favored fishing grounds. Towboats with their trains of barges came south after passing through the Old

River Canal Lock from the Mississippi into the Atchafalaya north of Baton Rouge. He skirted the other vessels respectfully, but once past he took the big 427 up to half throttle, sending it barreling down the river at twenty-five miles an hour.

Inside the little house, Pitt sat on a small sofa and played the videotape shot by the cameras of the AUV of the canal bed beginning at the highway bordering the Mississippi and ending at the entrance to the Atchafalaya. From start to finish the totally dull and boring show ran nearly six hours. Except for a few fish, a passing turtle and a runty baby gator no more than a foot in length, the bottom of the canal was nothing but barren muck. Pitt was relieved to find no bodies, nor was he surprised. Qin Shang's incredibly complicated plan had a small crack in it. The canal was the key, and Pitt was onto its purpose now. But he still found himself on the short side of tangibility. He had no proof. Only a vague theory that even he found almost impossible to accept.

He turned off the TV monitor and sat back in the sofa. He didn't dare close his eyes. He could have easily slipped off to sleep, but it wouldn't be fair to Giordino. There was still much to do. He fixed breakfast and called Giordino down to a table laid with a plate of scrambled eggs and ham. He'd brewed coffee in an old-fashioned pot and set out a carton of orange juice. To save time, he spelled Giordino at the helm while his friend ate.

He turned the shantyboat into Berwick Bay several miles above Morgan City and traveled south through the Wax Lake Canal, entering Bayou Teche just above Patterson, only two miles from the old sugar mill at Bartholomeaux. He gave the wheel back to Giordino and sat in his lawn chair on the veranda with Romberg curled up beside him.

They had made good time, and it was still shy of twelve noon when Giordino slowed the shantyboat as the abandoned sugar mill came into view around a bend just under a mile ahead. Pitt stared through a pair of binoculars, scanning the buildings and the long wharf that trailed along a stone breakwater. A tight smile curled his lips at seeing the barge still loaded with trash. He stood, leaned over the veranda railing, called up to Giordino and pointed down the bayou. "That must be the place. The barge moored to the wharf looks like the same one we saw at Sungari."

Giordino picked up a brass telescope he'd found in a drawer next to the helm. His right eye squinted through the lenses, scanning the wharf and buildings. "The barge is still full. Looks like they haven't gotten around to dumping the trash."

"Unlike the ramshackle condition of the buildings, the wharf looks no more than a year or two old. Can you make out anyone inside the guard shack by the gate?"

Giordino swung the telescope and refocused. "I have a single security guard sitting on his ass inside, watching a TV set."

"Any sign we might be sailing into an ambush?"

"I've seen cemeteries with more life than this place," Giordino said mildly. "Word must not have come down about our party on the canal."

"I'm going over the side and check out the bottom of the barge," said Pitt. "I lost my dive gear at the plantation so I'll borrow yours. Take it slow, as if you're having engine problems. As soon as I'm in the water, tie up to the wharf and give the guard another of your sterling performances."

"After mastering the manipulation of unsympathetic audiences," Giordino pontificated, "Romberg and I may form an act and go to Hollywood."

"Don't get your hopes up," Pitt replied sourly.

Giordino pulled back the throttle two notches above the idle position and flicked the ignition key on and off to simulate misfiring cylinders within the engine. As soon as he saw Pitt in his wet suit stepping over the catwalk on the side of the shantyboat out of sight of the guard, he turned the wheel toward the wharf. A few seconds later, when he glanced downward, Pitt was gone.

He watched Pitt's bubbles approach the barge, and then steadily scatter as he passed under its bottom edge. It looked to Giordino as if Pitt was working deeper and deeper. Then the bubbles rising beside the barge disappeared altogether.

Giordino slowly raised a hand to shield the sun from his eyes and expertly steered the shantyboat around the barge and along the pilings without scratching the paint on the hull. Then he dropped down a ladder to the catwalk, jumped onto the wharf and began looping mooring lines around a pair of rusty bollards.

The guard came out of his shack, unlocked the gate and rushed up to the shantyboat. He cautiously eyed Romberg, who acted happy to see him. The guard looked Asian but he spoke with a West Coast accent. He was a good four inches taller than Giordino but much thinner. He wore a baseball cap and World War II pilot's sunglasses.

"You must leave. This is a private dock. The owners do not allow boats to moor here."

"Ah cain't help it," Giordino moaned. "Mah engine died on me. Just give me twenty minutes, and Ah'll have it fixed."

The guard was not to be refused. He began untying the lines. "You must leave."

Giordino walked over and grasped the guard's wrist in an iron grip. "Qin Shang will not be happy when I report your offensive behavior to one of his inspectors."

The guard looked at Giordino queerly. "Qin Shang? Who the hell is Qin Shang? I was hired by the Butterfield Freight Corporation."

Now it was Giordino's turn to make a queer expression. He unconsciously glanced over the side into the water where he'd last seen Pitt's air bubbles and wondered if they'd made a big mistake. "You were hired to do what? Keep crows off the corn?"

"No," said the guard defensively, unable to shake Giordino's grip and contemplating whether he was dealing with a madman and should draw his holstered revolver. "Butterfield uses the old buildings to store furniture and equipment from their offices around the country. My job, and the guards who work the other shifts, is to keep vandals off the property."

Giordino released the guard's arm. He was far too wise and cynical to fall for the lie. He was almost thrown off the track in the first moments of the conversation. But now he knew with solid conviction there was more to the abandoned sugar mill at Bartholomeaux than met the eye.

"Tell me, friend. Would it be worth a bottle of Black Label Jack Daniel's whiskey to let me stay here just long enough to fix my engine?"

"I don't think so," the guard said testily as he rubbed his wrist.

Giordino fell back into his back country accent. "Look, Ah'm in a bind. If Ah just drift out in the river while workin' down on the engine, Ah could be busted in two by a towboat."

"That's not my problem."

"Two bottles of Black Label Jack Daniel's whiskey?"

A sly look gleamed in the guard's eyes. "Four bottles."

Giordino stuck out his hand. "Done." Then he motioned through the door leading inside the shantyboat from the veranda. Come on board and Ah'll put 'em in a sack for ya."

The guard looked apprehensively at Romberg. "Does he bite?"

"Only if ya put your hand in his mouth and step on his jaws."

Unwittingly drawn into the web, the guard stepped around Romberg and entered the shantyboat's main cabin. It was the last thing he remembered until he woke up four hours later. Giordino hit him on the nape of the neck. Not a judo chop, but a huge fist swung like a club that sent the guard crashing heavily to the deck, out for the long count.

Ten minutes later, Giordino, wearing the guard's uniform, pants and sleeves too long by inches but the shirt straining at its buttons as his chest and shoulders stretched the seams, stepped out on the shantyboat's veranda. With the guard's baseball cap pulled down over the old, wide-style sunglasses, Giordino leisurely walked to the gate, closed it behind him and pretended to lock it. Then he went inside the guard shack and sat in front of the television set while his eyes roamed the grounds of the sugar mill, picking out the security cameras placed about the property.

Pitt sank to the bottom before swimming up and under the flat bottom of the barge. He was surprised to encounter the bed of the bayou at thirty feet beside the wharf—far deeper than was necessary for barge traffic. The depth must have been dredged to accept a deep-hulled ship.

It was as if a cloud had passed over the sun. The shadow of the barge cut off nearly fifty percent of the light from the surface. The water was an opaque green and filled with plant particles. He swam fast and had hardly passed under the barge when a vague shape appeared in the gloom and stopped his progress.

Hanging from the keel of the barge was an immense cylindrical tube with tapered ends. Pitt instantly recognized what it was, and his heart began to pump faster with excitement. The size and regular shape was similar to the hull of an early submarine. He swam along the hull slightly above it. There were no visible ports, and he could see that it was attached to the barge by a system of rails. These, Pitt immediately determined, were used to move the submerged container from the seagoing ship to the barge and back again.

He estimated the size of the underwater container at ninety feet in length by nearly fifteen feet in diameter by ten feet high. Without being able to peer inside, Pitt quickly realized that it was capable of housing anywhere from two hundred to four hundred people, depending on how tightly they were packed inside.

Quickly, he swam around the vessel to the other side, looking for a hatch connecting with an underwater passage from the vessel to inside the breakwater that anchored the wharf. He found it thirty feet aft of the bow, a small watertight tunnel just large enough for two people to pass through at the same time.

Pitt could find no way to enter, certainly not from the water. He was about to give up and swim back to the shantyboat when he spotted a small round portal embedded in the stone breakwater. The portal was above the surface of the water but just below the planking on the wharf. It was covered by an iron door that was secured by three dog levers. Its purpose eluded him. A sewer outlet? A drainage pipe? A maintenance tunnel? A closer inspection of the lettering stamped by the manufacturer on the iron door cleared up the mystery.

MANUFACTURED BY THE ACADIA CHUTE COMPANY
NEW ORLEANS, LOUISIANA

It was a chute that was used when the mill was in operation to load the raw sugar onto barges. The old wharf had been demolished and a new one constructed that was five feet higher to accommodate the passage of illegal immigrants under the water without being visible on the surface. The newer, raised wharf now sat a good foot over the early loading chute.

The dog levers were badly rusted and probably hadn't been opened in eighty years. But the bayou water did not have the salt content of the sea. The corrosion was not deep. Pitt gripped a dog lever with both hands, positioned his feet against the upper planks of the wharf and pulled downward.

To his delight, the lever gave and moved an inch on the first try. The next heave took it three inches; then it turned more easily. Finally, he twisted it out against its stop. The second dog lever came slightly easier, but the third fought him every inch of the way. Gasping and panting, Pitt rested for a minute before pulling the door open. It fought too. He had to put both feet against the breakwater and pull with every ounce of strength he had left.

At last the iron door grudgingly squeaked open on its rusting hinges. Pitt peered inside, but all he could see was darkness. He turned and swam under the wharf, stopping just before he reached the shantyboat's hull. He called up softly. "Al, are you there?"

His only response came from Romberg. Curious, the hound strolled onto the wharf and sniffed through the cracks in the planking just above Pitt's head. "Not you. I want Giordino."

Romberg began wagging his tail. He stretched out his front paws, and lay down on the wharf and playfully tried to dig through the wooden planking.

Inside the guard shack, Giordino turned every minute or two and stared at the shantyboat for an indication of Pitt's return. Seeing Romberg pawing and scratching on the wharf for something underneath made him curious. He slowly walked through the gate and stopped by the dog. "What are you sniffing at?" he asked.

"Me!" Pitt whispered through the planking.

"Jeez!" muttered Giordino. "For a second I thought Romberg could talk."

Pitt stared up between the cracks in the planks. "Where did you get the uniform?"

"The guard decided to take a nap, and charitable, benevolent fellow that I am, I offered to stand his watch."

"Even with my limited view I can tell it's a lousy fit."

"You might be interested to learn," said Giordino, facing away from the sugar mill and rubbing a two-day-whiskered chin to cover his lip movements, "this place is owned by the Butterfield Freight Corporation, not Qin Shang Maritime. Also, the guard may have Asian ancestry, but I figure he went to school in either L.A. or San Francisco."

"Butterfield has to be a corporate front used by Shang to move people in and out of here. There's a submerged vehicle connected to the bottom of the barge that has the capacity to transport close to four hundred bodies."

"Then we've found the mother lode."

"We'll know shortly, just as soon as I get inside."

"How?" asked Giordino simply.

"I found a chute that was used to load sugar onto barges. It appears to lead toward the main building."

"Watch your step and make it fast. I don't know how much longer I can fool whoever is monitoring me."

"They have a camera on you?" asked Pitt.

"I've counted three and suspect there may be a few more around the perimeter I haven't spotted yet," Giordino answered.

"Can you drop my forty-five over the side? I don't want to go in naked."

"I'll lower it over the side."

"You're okay, Al. I don't care what they say about you," said Pitt.

"If I hear a gunshot," said Giordino as he walked toward the shantyboat, "Romberg and I will come running."

"That should be a sight to behold."

Giordino entered the shantyboat, took Pitt's Colt automatic and shift-

365

ily lowered it on a string through a window until it hung just above the water surface opposite the wharf. He felt a sharp tug on the line and the gun was gone. Then he slowly made his way back to the guard shack, where he unholstered the impressive Wesson Firearms .357 Magnum revolver that he'd taken off the unconscious guard, and waited for something to happen.

Pitt dropped his air tank, weight belt and the rest of the dive gear below the shantyboat. Clad only in his wet suit and carrying the Colt above his head to keep it dry, he stroked under the wharf to the chute portal and climbed inside. It was a tight squeeze, and he had to pull his body along a few inches at a time. The Colt he slipped under the collar of his wet suit against his upper chest, making it easy merely to bend his arm and retrieve it should an unpleasant occasion arise. The light decreased the farther he penetrated the chute, his body blocking off a fair share of it. But he could still see well enough to pick out any obstacles that lay ahead. He fervently hoped he wouldn't run up against a poisonous snake. With almost no room to maneuver, he would either have to club it to death with the old Colt or shoot it. One event risked a bite from fangs, the other detection by security guards.

Then a belated fear flooded his mind. What if the other end was blocked by another iron door that could only be opened from the opposite side? There was no denying the possibility. But the gamble was worth the effort, he rationalized. Nothing ventured and all that. He forged on until the chute began to slope upward. The going became more difficult as gravity began to work against him.

Fingertips scraped raw from clawing the corroded lining of the chute, Pitt continued forward. A vivid imagination could have easily conjured up visions of nightmare monsters from an alien world lurking in the darkness ahead, but reality revealed an empty, hollow chute, nothing more. Slowly, almost imperceptibly, the chute began to widen, as if blossoming into the upper half of a giant funnel. Then suddenly and completely unanticipatedly, he found himself crawling into a large bin that flared upward and out to the sides. The upper lip was only four feet away. He struggled upward, gaining a grip and pulling himself higher, then climbing toward the upper rim of the chute.

Automatic grasped in one hand and only dimly aware of the curious prickling sensation moving up the nape of his neck, he heard voices drifting into the chute, voices that were not speaking English. He also became strongly aware of the heavy, sickening odor of human bodies packed too long in a stifling atmosphere. Pitt raised his head until his eyes could see over the edge of the chute. He found himself gazing down from a height of twelve feet into a large chamber scarcely lit by a small dirty skylight in the ceiling. The walls of the chamber were dingy brick, the floor concrete.

Standing, lying or crouched in the stale atmosphere of the chamber, packed together shoulder to shoulder with little or no room to move about, were over three hundred men, women and children in varying states of sickness, malnutrition and fatigue. All appeared to be Chinese. Pitt scanned the chamber but saw no guards. The mass of humanity below was sealed in what was once the sugar-processing room; the only entrance was barred by a thick wooden door.

As he watched, the door abruptly swung open, and an Asian wearing the same uniform Giordino had taken off the guard at the dock roughly pushed a man into the crowded chamber. A woman, who Pitt assumed was the man's wife, had her arms tightly pinned by another guard in a passage outside. The door slammed shut with an echoing thud, and the man, in a highly emotional state, pounded on it and cried out in Chinese, clearly begging the guards not to take the woman away.

Without misgivings or thoughts of personal risk, Pitt dropped out of the chute opening onto the floor below, landing on his feet between two women, knocking both into people packed around them, creating a ripple in the mass. The women stared at him in startled curiosity but said nothing. No one else gave indication of his sudden appearance.

Pitt didn't bother to beg their pardon. He moved quickly through the huddled crowd of bodies toward the door. Reaching it, he gently pushed the sobbing man aside and then rapped on the door with the butt of his Colt. It was a familiar knock, one long, four short, two long, often given by someone friendly with the occupants on the other side. After the second try, Pitt's brazenness was rewarded. As he'd hoped, the guard's curiosity was aroused by the incomprehensible rap instead of the crazed pounding from a distraught husband.

The lock clacked and the door was thrown open again, only this time with Pitt standing behind it. A guard burst back into the chamber, grabbing the husband by the collar and shaking him like a fruit tree. The other guard still stood in the passage, pinning the woman's arms cruelly behind her back. He spoke angrily in perfect English.

"Tell that dumb bastard for the last time, he isn't getting his wife back until he forks over another ten thousand U.S. dollars."

367

Pitt's arm whirled in a blurred arc downward, the butt of the Colt in his hand connecting solidly on the side of the first guard's head, sending him unconscious to the concrete floor. Then Pitt stepped into the open doorway, gun pointed steadily at the head of the man with the young woman.

"I don't mean to intrude, but I believe you have something that belongs to someone else."

The guard's jaw, already open at seeing his colleague crumpled in a heap, dead to the world, began working furiously as he stared pop-eyed at the apparition in the black wet suit. "Who the hell are you?"

"I was hired by your captives to act as their agent," Pitt said, smiling. "Now let the girl go."

The guard had guts, Pitt had to admit that. One arm moved up and encircled the young woman's neck. "Drop the gun or by God I'll snap her neck."

Pitt stepped forward and raised the Colt until the muzzle was only a few inches from the guard's left eye. "I'll blow your eyes out if you do. Is that what you want, to spend the rest of your days as a blind man?"

The guard was smart enough to know he was in a no-win situation. He looked up and down the passageway in hope of finding help. But he was alone. Slowly, he acted as if his hold was loosening around the woman's neck while his other hand inched toward a gun in a holster at his hip.

Pitt caught the movement and rammed the muzzle of the Colt into the guard's eye. "Not a wise gamble, my friend." He smiled pleasantly, his teeth gleaming in the pale light.

The guard gasped in pain, dropped his hold on the woman and clutched both hands to his eye. "Oh God, you blinded me!"

"No such luck," Pitt said briefly as he yanked the guard into the chamber by the collar. He didn't have to order the woman; she had already rushed by him and thrown herself into her husband's arms. "The worst you can expect is a bloodshot eyeball for a few days."

Pitt kicked the big door closed, crouched down and hurriedly removed the guards' revolvers from their holsters. Then he searched them for concealed weapons. The guard he'd knocked unconscious carried a small .32-caliber automatic strapped to his pants belt behind his back; the other had a bowie knife stuffed in one boot. Then he checked them for size to see which one came closest in height and weight. They were both considerably shorter, but one nearly matched his chest and waist measurements.

As he began to switch clothes, Pitt spoke to the hushed horde who stared back at him as if he was some kind of deity. "Do any of you speak English?"

Two people made their way toward him. One was an elderly man with a long white beard, the other an attractive woman in her mid-thirties. "My father and I can speak English," she said. "We both taught languages at Chungking University."

Pitt swept his hand around the chamber. "Please tell them to bind and gag these men and hide their bodies as far away from the door as possible, where they can't be easily found."

The father and daughter nodded. "We understand," he replied. "We will also caution them to remain quiet."

"Thank you," said Pitt, as he stripped off his wet suit. "Am I correct in saying that you have all been treated badly by the smugglers who are extorting you for more money?"

"Yes," answered the woman, "all you say is true. We were subjected to unspeakable conditions during the voyage from China. After we arrived in the United States, we were brought here by the enforcers from Qin Shang Maritime, where we were turned over to an American-Chinese crime syndicate. It is they who are extorting us for more money by threatening to either kill or force us into indentured slavery if we do not pay."

"Tell them all to take heart," said Pitt solemnly. "Help is on the way."

He finished dressing, grinning when he noticed that a good three inches of socks showed between the guard's shoes—two sizes too small—and the bottom cuffs of the trousers. While the guards were dragged to the other end of the chamber and bound, Pitt slipped one revolver and the Colt automatic inside his pants and buttoned the shirt over them. Next he adjusted the holster containing the second guard's revolver at his side. Then, with a quick look of encouragement to the poor wretched immigrants, he stepped into the passage, quietly closed the door and locked it.

Twenty feet to the left of the door the passage ended in a tangled mass of old rusty machinery that filled it from floor to ceiling. Pitt went right and came to a stairway ascending to a corridor that opened onto a series of rooms with huge copper pots that had corroded over the decades until the once-bright metal had changed to a patinated green.

Pitt entered one of what had been the sugar cane cooking rooms and peered through a long row of dusty windows. Below him was a vast storage and shipping terminal. A pair of railroad tracks ran between two loading docks before stopping at a concrete barrier. Broad doors on one end of the floor were spread open to accommodate three freight cars that were being backed down a slope by a diesel-electric locomotive painted in the blue and orange colors of the Louisiana & Southern Railroad.

Next to the building near the railroad tracks, Pitt could see a parked pair of white stretch limousines, their drivers talking together while watching with interest as the train rolled past.

It became startlingly clear to Pitt that the immigrants he'd just left were about to be loaded on the freight cars. Accompanied by a growing knot in his stomach, he also observed that the loading docks were manned by nearly a dozen guards. After seeing all there was to see, he sat down below the window, back to the wall, and considered the situation.

Stopping the smugglers from boarding the immigrants onto the train looked grim. Stalling them was a tactic that lay open, but what good would delaying the inevitable do? He might take out four or five of the guards before they recovered from surprise and blasted him, but where were the percentages in that? There was almost no hope of terminating the departure, but there was a slim chance of bringing it to a standstill, at least for the next few hours.

Pitt removed his small arsenal and studied the two .357 magnum revolvers, the bowie knife and his steadfast old Colt. The six-shot revolvers gave him twelve rounds. Many years ago he had redesigned the grip on the Colt to hold a twelve-shot magazine. The revolvers were loaded with hollow-point cartridges, excellent for stopping power and producing extreme tissue damage in man and animal, but not efficient for what Pitt had in mind. His .45 packed Winchester 185-grain Silvertips, which were not as brutal on flesh but had better penetration. He had twenty-four chances to stop the train's departure. Only one lucky shot would do it. The problem was that although he had more than enough killing power, he was woefully short in the metal-piercing department. His intent was to strike a vital part of the diesel engines and electric generators, shutting down all power to the drive wheels.

Pitt sighed, rose to his knees, took the revolvers in both hands and commenced firing, aiming at the louvered sides of the locomotive.

37

JULIA HAD NO IDEA of how long she had been unconscious. The last thing she remembered was the soft face of a woman, a very beautiful woman, dressed in a red Oriental–silk sheath dress slit up the sides, tearing Julia's blouse from her shoulders. As the haze lifted she became aware of a fiery, burning sensation that coursed through her body. She also discovered that her hands and feet were in manacles with chains running around her waist and snaking through the bars of a gate, brutally pulling her arms out of their sockets, leaving her toes barely touching the floor. The chains were worked tight and looped over the door, making it impossible for her to move even fractionally.

Only the cool, damp air that touched and tingled her bare skin gave her relief from the searing fire flowing in her veins. She slowly came to realize that her clothes were gone and she was dressed in little else but her bra and panties.

The woman, who looked Eurasian, stared at Julia from a nearby chair. She sat with her legs curled under her and smiled a catlike smile that sent a shiver running through Julia. Her hair was shiny black and fell in a long cascade down her back. Her shoulders were broad, her breasts nicely rounded, her slim waist neatly merging with trim hips. She wore makeup with skill and her nails were incredibly long. But it was her eyes that drew Julia's interest. The scientific term was heterochromia. One of her eyes was nearly black while the other was a light gray. The effect was hypnotic.

"Well?" she said sociably. "Welcome back to reality."

"Who *are* you?"

"My name is May Ching. I serve the Dragon Triad."

"Not Qin Shang?"

"No."

"Not very sporting of you to drug me," Julia whispered angrily, fighting off the internal torment raging inside her body.

"I suspect you did no less to Lin Wan Chu, the cook on board the *Sung Lien Star,*" said May Ching. "Where is she, by the way?"

"She's being treated better than I am."

May Ching casually lit a cigarette and blew the smoke toward Julia. "We had quite a chat, you and I."

"I was interrogated?" Julia exclaimed. "I don't remember."

"You wouldn't. The very latest in truth serums. Not only does it reverse the mind to a child of five, but it makes the body feel as if your blood turned into molten lava. Between the madness and the agony, no man or woman, regardless of how strong-willed, can refuse honest answers to intimate questions. By the way, just so you won't feel unduly embarrassed, it was I who undressed and searched you. Clever hiding places for your little automatic and knife. Most men wouldn't have thought to look between your legs and inside your biceps. Being a woman, however, your radio was exactly where I thought it would be."

"You're not Chinese."

"Only on my mother's side," answered May Ching. "My father was British."

At that moment Ki Wong entered the room with another man whose facial features were also Eurasian. They both stood in front of Julia, staring at her lewdly. Wong's sallow skin stretched tautly and contrasted with his companion's suntanned face and neck. As he stared at her, he seemed to revel in a perverse satisfaction.

"Excellently done," he informed May Ching. "You obtained an incredible supply of information that will be most useful. Discovering that Miss Lee is working in cooperation with the Coast Guard, who has our facility under surveillance from across the bayou, has given us the necessary time to remove all immigrants and any evidence of their presence before local authorities and immigration agents can marshal their forces to conduct a raid."

"Fifteen more minutes and all they'll find are abandoned ruins," said the other man. His eyes were black and vapid, like those of a raccoon. A scavenger's eyes, bright without warmth. His hair was long, black and tied in a ponytail that came halfway down his back. His face portrayed someone who lived high, a party animal, a Las Vegas gambler, a womanizer. The skin was taut from more than one face-lift. Nothing done by a surgeon hid the fact that he would never see fifty again. He was dressed fashionably for a Hollywood lifestyle.

He stepped over to Julia, reached out, took a handful of hair and cruelly pulled her head back until she was staring up at the ceiling. "My name is Jack Loo," he said icily. "You belong to me."

"I belong to no one," Julia gasped through lips taut from the sudden pain.

"Not so," said Wong. "Qin Shang's orders were to kill you on sight. But Mr. Loo made an offer I cannot refuse. For a tidy sum, I sold you to him."

"You sick beast," Julia flashed at him, fear beginning to spread in her eyes.

"Do not entirely blame me," Wong said as if wounded. "Your future is now in the hands of the Dragon Triad, Qin Shang Maritime's partners in crime, you might say. We export and the Dragon Triad imports. We smuggle and sell; they buy, be it drugs, aliens or weapons. In return, Mr. Loo, who is their chief executive officer, and his partners provide Qin Shang with stolen luxury automobiles, yachts, consumer goods, high technology, and counterfeit currency, credit cards and government documents for shipment to China."

"A most profitable arrangement for both sides," said Loo, twisting Julia's hair viciously until she screamed. Then he slapped her hard across the buttocks and began removing the chains. "You and I are going for a nice, long ride in my limo. By the time we reach New Orleans, we'll be on very close terms."

"You will pay," Julia murmured as she was released from the door, her wrists and ankles free of the manacles. Unable to stand, she sagged into Loo's arms. "I am an agent of the United States government. Kill me and they'll never rest until you're brought to justice."

Wong laughed off her threat. "You have no one but yourself to blame for your plight. Qin Shang sent a force of no less than twenty men to track you and Mr. Pitt down for the purpose of killing you both. They lost your trail and certainly never expected you to walk through our front door."

"I was stupid."

Wong shrugged in agreement. "Granted, impulsive behavior is not what makes a good government agent—" Wong was suddenly interrupted by the sound of gunfire from somewhere within the building. He stared at Loo, who removed a portable phone from a pocket of his expensive sport coat and spoke into the receiver.

"Where is the gunfire coming from?" demanded Loo. "Are we being raided?"

"No, Mr. Loo," his chief of security answered from the monitoring-systems room. "There is no raid. All grounds and wharf are clear. The gunfire is coming from a room above the train-loading dock. We do not yet know who is behind the attack nor his purpose."

"Are there casualties?"

"No," answered the security chief. "Whoever is shooting is not aiming at our guards."

"Keep me informed!" Loo snapped. He nodded at Wong. "It is time to go." He had barely spoken the words when the shooting stopped. "What has happened?" he inquired, snatching up the radio again.

The security chief's voice came back. "We must have hit him. I am sending a team upstairs to examine the body."

"I wonder who it can be," Wong muttered thoughtfully.

"We'll know shortly," Loo muttered. He threw Julia over his shoulder as lightly as if she was a large pillow. He shook hands with Wong. "Good doing business with you, Mr. Wong. I suggest you find a new staging depot. This one is no longer safe."

Wong smiled without the slightest expression of agitation. "Three days from now Qin Shang Maritime's new operation will be firmly established and the Americans will have bigger problems on their minds."

With Wong in the lead, they left the office together and hurried down a circular staircase that opened onto a wide corridor leading past empty storage and equipment rooms last used when the sugar mill was in operation. They were halfway down the corridor when Loo's beeper went off on his radio. "Yes, what is it?" he said irritably.

"Our security agents stationed throughout St. Mary Parish report a small fleet of Coast Guard boats entering Bayou Teche, and a pair of helicopters with government markings just now passing over Morgan City, headed in this direction."

"How long before they arrive?" asked Loo.

"The helicopters," said his security chief, "fifteen, maybe eighteen minutes. Add half an hour for the boats."

"All right, close down all systems and follow the plan for evacuation and dispersal of all personnel."

"Shutting down now."

"We should be in our limos and on the road in less than three minutes," said Loo, shifting Julia to his other shoulder.

"More than enough time to put a safe distance between us and the mill," Wong acknowledged.

When they reached a doorway leading to stairs that dropped to the basement shipping terminal, they heard the shouting of voices but no sounds from the locomotive. Then the voices died and it became clear that something was very, very wrong. They burst through a doorway onto a landing high above the loading dock. Wong, ahead of the rest, stopped and froze in shock.

The freight cars had been loaded with the immigrants and their doors shut and locked. But the engine sat idle, with blue smoke curling up through bullet holes on the panels covering the diesel engines and electric generating compartment. The engineers stood looking at the damage, their expressions reflecting helplessness and bafflement. The security guards who worked for the Triad had already climbed into a truck that quickly drove off toward the main highway the instant it was loaded.

Suddenly Loo realized why the unknown assailant did not shoot at the guards. Fear and confusion swept over him as he understood that the train was not going anywhere. Three hundred immigrants and a cargo of illegal goods worth nearly thirty million dollars was going to be captured and confiscated by United States government agents. He turned to Wong. "I'm sorry, my friend, but because the transfer of goods was not able to take place, I must hold Qin Shang responsible."

"What are you saying?" demanded Wong.

"Simple," explained Loo. "I'm saying the Dragon Triad is not paying for this shipment."

"Qin Shang Maritime delivered as agreed," Wong said thickly. If Loo and the Dragon Triad reneged on their deal with his boss, Wong knew that he would be held responsible. Failure of this magnitude meant death when one was in the employ of Qin Shang. "The goods and property were turned over and placed in your hands. You *will* be held accountable."

"Without us, Qin Shang cannot do business in the United States," Loo said smugly. "The way I see it, he is powerless to do anything but accept the loss."

"He is far more powerful than you think," said Wong. "You are making a grave mistake."

"You tell Qin Shang that Jack Loo is not afraid of him. Valuable friends are not to be cast off like old clothes. He is too wise not to accept a minor defeat that he can recoup in a week."

Wong gazed ferretlike at Loo. "Then our little deal is off concerning Miss Lee. She reverts back to me."

Loo considered that for a moment, then he laughed. "Didn't you say Qin Shang wants her dead?"

"Yes, that is true," Wong said, nodding.

Loo lifted Julia above his head with both hands. "The drop from here onto the steel rails of the track bed is thirty feet. Suppose I fulfill Qin Shang's wish to kill Miss Lee and make reparation for our financial differences."

Wong glanced down at the steel rails lying directly below and between the rear of the last freight car and the concrete stop barrier. "Yes, you make an excellent point. I think Qin Shang might be appeased for his loss. But please make it now. We can no longer afford to waste time. We must leave quickly."

Loo extended his arms and tensed. Julia screamed. Wong and May Ching were waiting in sadistic anticipation. None of them noticed a tall, curly-haired man in an ill-fitting security uniform who had stepped silently down the stairs behind them. "Forgive me for interrupting," said Pitt, jamming the muzzle of his Colt against the base of Loo's skull, "but if anyone so much as scratches their nose, I'll blow their gray matter into the next parish."

They all turned instinctively toward the strange voice, each forming different expressions on their faces at his abrupt appearance. Loo's tan features went pallid, his eyes blank with incredulity. May Ching's features went taut with dread. Wong looked downright curious.

"Who are you?" Wong asked.

Pitt ignored him. When he spoke, it was to Loo. "Put the lady down gently." To emphasize his demand, Pitt jammed the .45 solidly into the flesh of Loo's neck below the skull.

"Don't shoot, please don't shoot," pleaded Loo as he slowly lowered Julia to her feet, his beady eyes glazed with fear.

Julia crumpled to her knees. It was then that Pitt saw the terrible bruises on Julia's wrists and ankles. Without a second's hesitation, he clubbed Loo on the temple with the barrel of the Colt, watching with grim satisfaction as the Triad director dropped and rolled down the stairs.

Unable to believe the voice was really his, Julia looked up and saw the opaline-green eyes and the crooked grin. "Dirk!" she muttered dazedly as she reached up and gently touched the bandage on his broken nose. "Oh God, oh God, you're here. How, how in the world . . . ?"

Pitt wanted desperately to lift her up and hold her in his arms, but he didn't dare take his eyes off of Wong. He read the expression and knew Qin Shang's enforcer was coiled to strike like a snake. With foresight, he also predicted May Ching had nothing to lose now that her boss was a broken body at the foot of the stairs. She stared at him with a look of cold hatred no woman had ever speared him with before. Pitt kept his eyes on her and the gun trained on Wong's forehead. "I just happened to be passing by and thought I'd drop in and say hello."

"Your name is Dirk?" Wong said tightly. "Am I to presume you are Dirk Pitt?"

"I certainly hope so. And you?"

"Ki Wong, and the lady is May Ching. What do you intend to do with us?"

"Ki Wong," said Pitt thoughtfully. "Where have I heard that name before?"

Julia was astute. Without jeopardizing Pitt's vigilance, she circled her arms around his waist from the back so as not to restrict his movements. "He's Qin Shang's chief enforcer," said Julia, slowly struggling to her feet. "He interrogates the immigrants and decides who lives and dies. He was the one who tortured me on board the *Indigo Star.*"

"You're not a very nice man, are you?" said Pitt conversationally. "I've seen your handiwork."

Without warning a guard appeared from nowhere. Too late, Pitt caught the unexpected presence from May Ching's eyes as they flashed from hatred to triumph at seeing the uniformed guard. Desperately he whirled around to face his attacker as Wong threw himself at Pitt. May Ching screamed.

"Kill him! Kill him!"

"I always respect a lady's wishes," said the intruder without emotion. The .357 magnum revolver in his hand spat fire, the deafening blast reverberating around the landing as if it came from a cannon. Wong's eyes burst from their sockets as the bullet's impact struck him square, just above the bridge of the nose. He reeled backward, arms outstretched, and careened over the railing, his already dead body crashing onto the rails far below.

Giordino regarded his handiwork modestly. "I hope I did the right thing."

"And high time too," said Pitt, hoping his heart would start pumping again.

"Damn you!" shrieked May Ching, leaping at Pitt, her fingers with their long nails curled to gouge out his eyes.

She only took one step before Julia's fist rammed into May Ching's mouth, splitting the lips and sending a spurt of blood down the front of the red silk dress. "You bitch!" said Julia fiercely. "That's for drugging me." Another convulsive movement, and Julia's next blow took May Ching in the stomach, sending the lady from the Dragon Triad to her knees, gasping for breath. "And that's for leaving me half naked in front of men."

"Remind me never to make you mad," Pitt said with a grin.

She massaged her fist and stared up at him, her face sad and strained. "If only we could have caught them in the act of transporting illegal immigrants. God only know how many lives we could have saved. Now it's too late."

Pitt hugged her tenderly, favoring her cracked ribs. "Didn't you know?"

"Know?" she said, puzzled. "Know what?"

He motioned toward the train below. "There are over three hundred of them locked into freight cars down there."

Caught off balance, she stiffened as if Pitt had struck her. She stared uncomprehending at the train. "They were here and I never saw them."

"How did you get to the sugar mill?" he asked her.

"I sneaked on board the trash barge as it left the *Sung Lien Star.*"

"Then you rode on top of them from Sungari. They came across the sea from China in a submerged container that was moved by an underwater rail system from under the *Sung Lien Star* to the barge that brought them here."

Her voice suddenly became hard. "We've got to free them before the train leaves."

"Not to worry," said Pitt with a canny smile. "Even Mussolini couldn't make that train run on time."

They were unlocking the freight cars and helping the illegal immigrants onto the loading docks when the Immigration and Naturalization Service agents and coast guardsmen arrived and took over.

38

PRESIDENT DEAN COOPER WALLACE came from behind his desk as Qin Shang stepped into the oval office of the White House. He put out a hand and said, "My dear Qin Shang, how good to see you."

Qin Shang pressed the President's hand in both of his. "It's so kind of you to see me in light of your busy schedule."

"Nonsense, I'm deeply in your debt."

"Will you be needing me?" asked Morton Laird, who had escorted Qin Shang from the reception room.

"Please stay, Morton," said the President. "I'd like you to be present."

The President showed Qin Shang to a pair of sofas that faced across a coffee table, and they sat down. "I wish you to convey my deep appreciation to Premier Wu Kwong for his generous contribution to my presidential campaign. And please tell him he has my promise of close cooperation between our two governments."

"Premier Kwong will be happy to hear it," said Qin Shang affably.

"What can I do for you, Qin Shang?" asked the President, setting the discussion in a firm direction.

"As you know, certain members of Congress have been calling my country a slave state and condemning what they call human-rights abuses. They are currently proposing a bill to reject our most-favored-nation status. Premier Wu Kwong fears they may muster enough votes to push through the bill's passage."

"Rest assured," the President said, smiling, "I fully intend to veto any bill Congress passes that jeopardizes trade between our two countries. I've also gone on record as stating that mutual trade benefits are the best opportunity to eliminate the human-rights questions."

"Do I have your word on that, Mr. President?" asked Qin Shang, his aggressiveness pulling a negative expression from Chief of Staff Laird.

"You can tell Premier Wu Kwong that he has my personal assurance."

Laird marveled at the conciliatory atmosphere in the room between the shipping tycoon and the President when the air should have crackled with antagonism.

"The other matter of concern is the harassment by your Coast Guard and immigration agents of my ships. Search boardings have become more numerous and extensive in the past months, and shipping-schedule delays have proved very costly."

"I understand your concern, Qin Shang," said Wallace flatly. "At last count by the INS there were six million people living illegally in the United States. A good percentage of them, so the Immigration and Naturalization Service claims, were smuggled into the country in your ships, and the fiasco at Orion Lake was not an easy event to conceal. By rights I should have you arrested as you stand in my office and indicted for mass murder."

There was no display of indignation from Qin Shang. He stared at the most powerful man in the world without blinking. "Yes, under your laws you have every right to do so. But then you run the risk of much delicate information being leaked to the American public about your secret dealings with Qin Shang Maritime and the People's Republic of China."

"Are you threatening blackmail against the President of the United States?" Wallace demanded, suddenly disturbed.

"Please forgive me," Qin Shang acquiesced quickly. "I merely wished to remind the President of possible contingencies."

"I will not condone mass murder."

"An unfortunate event caused by criminal syndicates in your own country," Qin Shang countered.

"*Not* in the report I read."

"You have my solemn oath there will be no repetition of Orion Lake."

"In return, you want your ships left alone. Is that it?"

Qin Shang nodded. "I would be most grateful."

Wallace looked at Laird. "Inform Admiral Ferguson and Duncan

Monroe that I wish the Coast Guard and INS to treat the inspection of Qin Shang Maritime ships entering our waters with the same courtesy offered to any other foreign shipping company."

Laird's brow was furrowed in disbelief. He sat quietly and did not immediately acknowledge the presidential order.

"Thank you, Mr. President," said Qin Shang courteously. "I speak for my board of directors when I say we are very honored by your friendship."

"You're not off the hook that easily, Qin Shang," said Wallace. "Please pass on my concern to Premier Wu Kwong regarding the continued use of slave labor to manufacture your trade goods. If we are to maintain close ties, his government must accept the use of decently paid workers in its manufacturing facilities and reject violation of human rights. Otherwise, I will cut off our export of phosphatic fertilizers to China."

Morton Laird smiled inwardly. At last the President struck a chord. Phosphatic fertilizers exceeded one billion dollars in sales by a chemical company in Texas that was a subsidiary of the vast global chemical corporation in Jiangsu Province with headquarters in Shanghai. Without threatening trade sanctions against Chinese exported cotton goods, shoes, toys, radios, television sets and related items that totaled over fifty billion dollars a year, Wallace had zeroed in on the most essential commodity of all.

Qin Shang's green eyes briefly flashed with uneasiness. "I will relate your counsel to Premier Wu Kwong."

Wallace stood, signaling an end to the discussion.

"Thank you, Mr. President. It was a privilege to meet with you again."

"I'll accompany you to the reception room," said Laird graciously, while diplomatically concealing his contempt for the financial criminal.

A few minutes later Laird returned to the Oval Office. Wallace did not look up as he signed a stack of bills sent over from Congress. "Well, Morton, it was obvious by the sour apple look on your face that you're not happy with my performance."

"No, sir, I am not. I am appalled that you even talk to that murderer."

"He's not the first ghoul from hell who has walked in this office since it was built. If not for Qin Shang and his influence with the Chinese government, I might not be sitting where I am."

"You are being conned, sir. Conned by Qin Shang and his government up and down Pennsylvania Avenue. In the interest of political expediency, Mr. President, you've dug yourself a grave too deep to climb out of."

"We're dealing with a country that has one-point-four billion people," Wallace persisted. "This presents an incredible opportunity to sell billions of dollars' worth of American goods. Whatever sin I've committed was in the interest of the country."

"There is no justification to stand by while the Chinese rip off the American public," said Laird earnestly. "The last combined CIA-FBI counterintelligence report named over a hundred Chinese agents who have penetrated every level of our government from NASA to the Pentagon. Several have achieved high-level staff jobs in the Congress and the Commerce and Interior departments."

"Come now, Morton. I browsed the report. I failed to see a critical threat to our security. China no longer harbors a fanatical desire to steal our nuclear technology and military secrets."

"Why should they?" Laird's voice was hard and low. "Their priority is now political and economic espionage. Besides obtaining our business and technology secrets, they're working every minute of the day to influence our trade policy as it relates to their economic expansion. They've already passed Japan as the trading partner with whom we have the greatest deficit. Economic forecasts put their economy ahead of ours before your term of office expires."

"So what? Even if China does pass us in the gross size of its economy, her people will still only have a per-capita income one quarter of the average American."

"I respectfully say to you, Mr. President, wake up and smell the coffee. Their forty-five-billion-dollar balance-of-trade surplus is poured back into building their military and worldwide criminal smuggling activities, all the while enhancing their mushrooming economic power."

"You've taken a pretty tough stand against me, Morton," said Wallace coldly. "I hope you know what you're doing."

"Yes, sir," said Morton inflexibly, "I do, because I honestly believe you have sold out the country for your own personal political gain. You are well aware how strongly I disagreed when you extended most-favored-nation trade status and at the same time said your decision was no longer contingent on progress in human rights."

"My only concern was for American jobs." Wallace was standing behind his desk now, his face turning red with anger.

"If that's the case, how do you explain the fact that in the last fifteen years a total of eight hundred thousand American workers have lost their jobs to cheap Chinese labor, much of it slave labor?"

"Do not push too far, Morton," Wallace snarled through clenched jaws. "I have done nothing that will not pay dividends for the American public."

Laird crossed a hand wearily over his eyes. "I've known you too many years not to know when you're distorting the truth."

"Are you calling me a liar?"

"That and more, sir. I'm calling you a traitor. And to back up my sentiments, you'll have my resignation as chief of staff on your desk within the hour. I don't want to be around when the chickens come home to roost."

With that, Morton Laird walked out of the Oval Office for the last time. Fully enlightened as to his former friend's vindictiveness, he and his wife soon dropped out of public view and moved to an island off the Great Barrier Reef of Australia, where he began to write the memoirs of his life and times in Washington with great insight into his long association with President Dean Cooper Wallace.

Su Zhong, Qin Shang's personal secretary, was sitting at a desk inside his large armored bus, which he entered after concluding his meeting with the President. As soon as he settled into a leather chair behind a desk covered with a battery of telephones and computer systems, she handed him several messages that had arrived by fax and satellite phone. Qin Shang had developed a code to frustrate any agents, government or commercial, who attempted to eavesdrop on his personal business. He ran the messages through a scanner that instantly translated them.

"Any word yet from Zhu Kwan?"

Su Zhong recited a synopsis of the reports as her boss scanned the translations. "Only that he is attempting to track down the location where it was rumored the *Princess Dou Wan* sank. He claims the pieces do not fit together as constructed."

"If anyone can find the whereabouts of the ship, Zhu Kwan can," Qin Shang said confidently. "What else do you have?"

"The purchase of four Russian oil tankers has been concluded. Our company crews are in flight to Sevastopol to take command of the ships. They are scheduled to reach your yard in Hong Kong for refitting by the middle of next month."

"Progress on the new cruise ship?"

"The *Evening Star?*" said Su Zhong. "Four months from comple-
tion. Our promotion department has produced preliminary art for her
introduction as the largest and most luxurious cruise ship in the world."

"And the *United States.* What is the latest on her status?"

"She has entered the Head of Passes at the mouth of the Mississippi
River and is in transit to New Orleans. That part of your operation is
going as planned."

"Anything else I should know about?" asked Qin Shang warily.
"Any incidents at Sungari, perhaps?"

Su Zhong shook her head. "Not Sungari."

He could tell from the way she avoided his eyes the news was bad.
"What is the story?"

"Federal agents have raided and closed down the staging depot at
Bartholomeaux, Louisiana. Three hundred and forty-two immigrants
were apprehended."

"Our people?"

"Ki Wong is dead. Jack Loo of the Dragon Triad is dead. His assistant, May Ching, is in the custody of INS agents."

Qin Shang merely shrugged. "No great loss, any of them. Jack Loo
was only one cog in the American-Chinese syndicate. His death and
the raid, no doubt brought about by his lax security and stupidity, offers
me an excellent opportunity to renegotiate my agreement with the
Dragon Triad."

"A more profitable agreement in your favor, of course," said Su
Zhong.

"Of course," Qin Shang said, smiling. "I would have ordered Bartholomeaux closed down in thirty-six hours anyway, once I realized my
goal of making Sungari the premier shipping port on the Gulf."

"The last report will not be to your liking," Su Zhong murmured
reluctantly.

"No review?"

"Perhaps you should absorb it with your own eyes, Qin Shang." She
nodded at the message containing a report detailing the destruction of
the security post on the Mystic Canal.

As Qin Shang scanned the report his eyes shifted from somber to
wrathful, especially when he reached the message from Pitt. "So Mr.
Pitt wonders if I still stoop to pick up bananas. He seems to take great
delight in taunting me."

"The accursed devil should have his tongue torn out," Su Zhong
said loyally.

"I have had many enemies in my time," Qin Shang said quietly. "Most were business competitors. But none were as challenging as Pitt. I must say, I relish his pathetic attempts at sarcastic wit. A worthy opponent?" Qin Shang shook his head wearily. "Not really. But an opponent to be savored, not like fine caviar, but more like an American hamburger—coarse, common and primitive."

"If he but knew where to look he would be able to view the pitiful remains of those who wished you ill and tried to obstruct your ambitions."

"Pitt will be eliminated," Qin Shang said in a cold voice. "So far he has merely thwarted a pair of minor projects that can be easily restored. My only concern with him now is why is he in Louisiana when my sources here in Washington informed me that NUMA was taken off all investigations involving immigrant smuggling? His dogged persistence in annoying me is a mystery."

"A misguided vendetta against you, perhaps?"

"Pitt is what the Americans call a righteous do-gooder," said Qin Shang with a rare flash of humor. "And therein lies his flaw. When he makes a mistake, as he surely will, his demise will come because he took a moral road. He has never learned that money and power, when arranged in appropriate designs, cannot lose." He paused to pat her on the knee. "Do not trouble yourself over Dirk Pitt, my little songbird. He will die very soon."

PART IV

OLD MAN RIVER

Mystic Canal

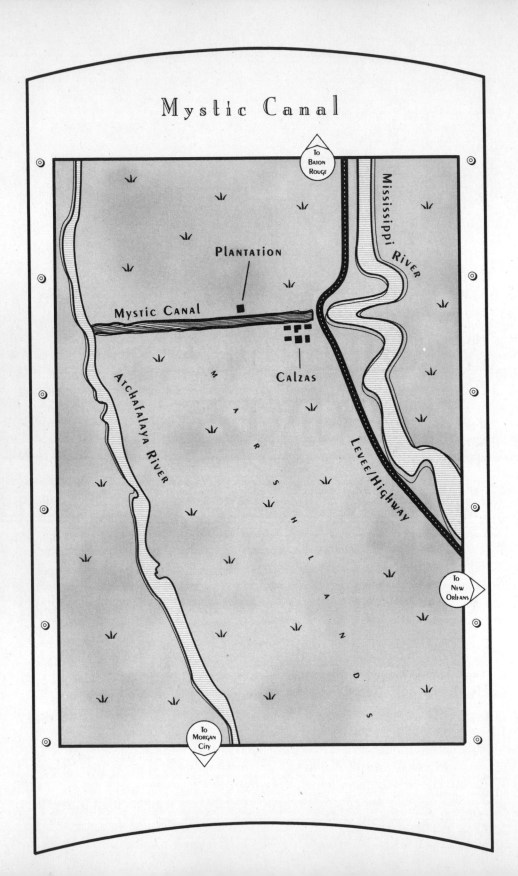

To
Baton
Rouge

Mississippi River

Plantation

Mystic Canal

Calzas

Atchafalaya River

Levee/Highway

M
A
R
S
H
L
A
N
D
S

To
New
Orleans

To
Morgan
City

39

April 29, 2000
The Lower Mississippi River

TWENTY MILES SOUTH of the Head of Passes, that part of the lower
Mississippi that branches into three major channels leading into the
Gulf of Mexico, two large helicopters took turns dropping onto the
open stern deck of the *United States* and discharging their cargo of men
and equipment. Then they lifted into the air again and flew west toward
the port of Sungari. The operation lasted little more than fifteen minutes
while the ship continued moving at a speed of twenty-five knots, as
dictated by her automated control systems.

A tight unit of heavily armed men from Qin Shang's private security
forces, led by a former colonel from the Chinese People's Liberation
Army, dressed in work clothes usually worn by the men who worked
the river, and carrying automatic weapons and portable missile launchers, dispersed throughout the decks as maritime crewmen went to the
engine room and wheelhouse, where they took manual command of the
ship's systems. Before reaching the Southwest Pass, the channel most
often used by oceangoing vessels entering the river, the great liner
slowed as it was met by the boat carrying the pilot who would navigate
the ship upriver to New Orleans.

The pilot was a heavy man with a beer belly. He was sweating
heavily and dabbing a red bandanna across his balding head after climbing the rope ladder when he stepped into the wheelhouse. He gave a
wave and walked up to Captain Li Hung-chang, who until two days
before had commanded the *Sung Lien Star.*

"Howdy, Captain, Sam Boone. I got lucky and won a lottery of river pilots for the honor of taking this here monstrosity up to New Orleans," he proclaimed, pronouncing Orleans as *Auwlans*.

"That won't be necessary," said Hung-chang without bothering to introduce himself. He pointed toward the short Chinese man standing at the helm who was the rudder master. "My first officer will do the job."

Boone looked at Hung-chang queerly. "You're funnin' me, right?"

"No," answered Hung-chang. "We are quite capable of running the ship to our destination under our own command." He nodded at two guards who were nearby. They took Boone by the arms and began leading him away.

"Now wait just a damned minute," snorted Boone, fighting off the guards. "You're violating maritime law. You're headin' for a calamity if you're dumb enough to try navigatin' it yourself. You don't know the river like an experienced pilot. We have rigorous standards. I've been taking ships up and down the delta for twenty-five years. It might look easy to you, but believe you me, it ain't."

Hung-chang nodded at the guards. "Lock him up. Knock him unconscious if you have to."

"You're crazy!" Boone shouted over his shoulder as he was dragged away. "You'll run her aground sure as hell!"

"Is he right, Ming Lin?" Hung-chang asked the rudder master. "Will you run us aground?"

Lin turned and smiled a narrow smile. "I've taken this ship upriver over two hundred times in computer-generated virtual reality in three dimensions."

"Have you ever run aground?" Hung-chang persisted.

"Twice," replied Ming Lin without taking his eyes off the river channel. "The first two times I tried it, but never after."

Hung-chang's dark amber eyes gleamed. "Please keep your speed within the limit. We can allow curiosity, but we cannot afford to arouse suspicion, not for the next several hours."

Hung-chang was chosen by Qin Shang's personal orders to captain the *United States* upriver to New Orleans. Not only did Qin Shang trust him explicitly, but his decision was also based on expediency. Having a captain at the helm who was experienced in ocean liners was not a necessity. By selecting a ship's captain and his crew who were already in America and within a short helicopter flight of the approaching liner, Qin Shang saved time and the expense of sending a crew from Hong Kong. His ulterior motive was that he did not believe more experienced cruise-ship chief officers were as expendable as the captain and crew of the *Sung Lien Star.*

Hung-chang's duties consisted of little more than greeting the customs inspectors and immigration officials and acting the conquering hero to the crowds of people lining the riverbanks. His true function was mostly for ornamentation. Besides twenty heavily armed security men on Qin Shang's payroll, his crew of fifteen was primarily made up of demolition experts mixed in with a few engineers to stand by in case there was a call for emergency repairs if the ship was attacked.

He turned a blind eye to the dangerous part of the journey. Twenty-four hours, that was all the time Qin Shang had requested of his services. His evacuation, when the moment came, was well timed and organized. Helicopters were standing by to swoop in and pick up the fighting men and crew once the charges were detonated and the ship was scuttled in precisely the right spot. Qin Shang had given his assurances that Hung-chang would be a rich man when he returned home, providing, of course, the operation went as conceived.

He sighed. All that troubled him now was navigating the sharp bends in the river, avoiding other ships and passing under the six bridges that faced him after New Orleans. The distance from the Head of Passes to the city was ninety-five miles. Although the navigation channel for oceangoing traffic in the lower reaches of the river averaged more than forty feet deep by one thousand feet wide, no ship the size of the *United States* had ever traveled on the Mississippi before. The narrow inland waterway channel was not dredged for a vessel of her huge bulk and restricted maneuverability.

After passing Venice, the last town on the west bank that was accessible by highway, the levees were lined with thousands of people who had turned out to see the grand spectacle of the great liner's passage up the river. Students had been temporarily let out of schools to witness an event that had never before taken place and would not again. Hundreds of small private boats trailed after the ship, tooting and honking their horns, and were kept a safe distance away from her churning wake by two escorting Coast Guard boats that had appeared after the *United States* had emerged from the Head of Passes.

They all stood, many in awed silence, others waving and cheering, as the *United States* negotiated the sharp bends of the river, her bow brushing the edge of the channel on the west bank, her stern and slowly turning propellers thrashing past the east bank that protruded around the bend. This was late April going on May, and the spring runoff far to the north that came flowing down from the Mississippi's tributaries had raised the water level above the base of the levees. Hung-chang was thankful for extra water between the keel and river bottom. It gave him an extra margin for success.

He readjusted the buckle on the strap of his binoculars, squared the cap on his head, then stepped out onto the bridge wing. He ignored the compass mounted on a stand that responded to the ship's every change of direction as it moved over the curling river. He was glad the waterway had been emptied of traffic in anticipation of the big ship's passage. It would be a different story after New Orleans, but he would deal with that problem when the time came.

He looked up at the sky and was relieved to see the weather had cooperated. The day was warm with only a whisper of a breeze. A twenty-mile-an-hour wind against the gigantic hull of the ship could have caused disaster by pushing her broadside into the bank during navigation of a sharp river bend. The azure-blue cloudless sky and the sunlight reflected off the water surface, giving it a green, almost clean, look. Because he was ascending the river the green channel buoys swayed aimlessly on his left while the red navigation buoys rolled to his right.

He waved back at the people standing on the levee amid a sea of parked cars and pickup trucks. From his height nine stories above the water he looked down on the horde and saw the flat marsh and farmlands beyond. Li Hung-chang felt like a spectator watching someone else play his role in a drama.

He began to speculate on the reception waiting along the waterfront in New Orleans, and he smiled to himself. Millions of Americans would remember this day, he mused, but not for the reasons they had expected.

40

RUDI GUNN WAS WAITING for Pitt and Giordino when they returned the shantyboat to Doug Wheeler's dock late the same afternoon. His eyes were red from lack of sleep caused by sitting up most of the night waiting for Pitt's sporadic reports. He wore khaki shorts and a white T-shirt with the words ST. MARY PARISH, GOOD OL' FASHION SOUTHERN HOSPITALITY printed across the back.

After replacing the fuel they had used and loading their equipment in the Marine Denizen's launch, Pitt and Giordino bade a fond farewell to Romberg, who raised his head from the deck and gave them a lethargic goodbye "Woof," before promptly falling back to sleep.

As they cleared the dock, Giordino stood beside Gunn at the helm. "I'd say we could all use some dinner and a good night's sleep."

"I'll second the motion," Pitt yawned.

"All you get is a thermos of coffee with chicory," said Gunn. "The admiral flew into town along with Peter Harper of the Immigration Service. Your presence has been requested on board the Coast Guard cutter Weehawken."

"Last I saw of her," said Pitt, "she was anchored just above Sungari."

"She's now tied up at the Coast Guard dock near Morgan City," Gunn enlightened him.

"No dinner?" asked Giordino sadly.

"No time," Gunn replied. "Maybe if you act like good little boys, you can get a fast bite from the Weehawken's galley."

"I promise to be good," Giordino said with a wily shift to his eyes.

Pitt and Gunn exchanged disbelieving looks. "Never happen," Gunn sighed.

"Not in our lifetime," Pitt agreed.

Peter Harper, Admiral Sandecker, Captain Lewis and Julia Lee were waiting for them in the wardroom of the *Weehawken* when they climbed on board. Also present were Major General Frank Montaigne of the Army Corps of Engineers and Frank Stewart, captain of the *Marine Denizen*. Lewis cordially asked if there was anything he could get them. Before Giordino could open his mouth, Gunn said, "We had coffee on the run from Wheeler's dock, thank you."

Pitt shook hands with Sandecker and Harper before giving Julia a light kiss on the cheek. "How long has it been since we've seen each other?"

"All of two hours."

"Seems like an eternity," he said with his devilish grin.

"Stop," she said, pushing him away. "Not here."

"I suggest we get on with it," said Sandecker restlessly. "We have a lot of ground to cover."

"Not the least of which is Duncan Monroe's humble apology that he asked me to convey," Harper said, making a show of penitence by pumping Pitt's and Giordino's hands. "I also wish to express my personal debt of gratitude to NUMA and to you gentlemen for ignoring our demands to disassociate yourselves from the investigation. Without your timely intervention at Bartholomeaux, our assault team would have found nothing but a dead INS agent and an empty sugar mill. The only unfortunate aspect was the killing of Ki Wong."

"I suppose in hindsight I should have kneecapped him," Giordino said without remorse. "But he was not a nice man."

"I fully realize your act was justified," admitted Harper, "but with Ki Wong dead, we lost a direct link to Qin Shang."

"Was he that essential to your case?" Captain Lewis queried Harper. "It seems to me you have more than enough proof to hang Qin Shang from the nearest tree. He was caught red-handed smuggling nearly four hundred illegal immigrants into Sungari and then up Bayou Teche to Bartholomeaux. All on vessels owned by his shipping company and by men on his payroll. What more could you want?"

"Proving the orders came directly from Qin Shang."

Sandecker seemed as puzzled as Lewis. "Surely you have all the evidence you need to indict him now."

"We can indict," acknowledged Harper, "but whether we can convict is another story. We're looking at a long, drawn-out legal fight that federal prosecutors are not certain they can win. Qin Shang will counterattack with a task force of highly paid and respected Washington attorneys. He has the Chinese government and certain ranking members of Congress on his side, and also, I'm sorry to say, possibly the White House. When we look at all the political IOUs that he will undoubtedly call due, you can see that we are not getting in the ring with a lightweight, but rather a very powerful and highly connected man."

"Wouldn't Chinese government leaders turn their backs on him if it meant a huge scandal?" inquired Frank Stewart.

Harper shook his head. "His services and influence in Washington cancel out any political liabilities that might result."

"Surely, you have enough on Qin Shang to close down Sungari and cut off all shipping by Qin Shang Maritime into the United States," probed General Montaigne, speaking for the first time.

"Yes, it's within our power," answered Harper. "But the billions of dollars' worth of Chinese goods that are pouring into the United States are carried on Qin Shang Maritime ships, subsidized by their government. They'd be cutting their own throat if they sat by and remained silent while we slammed the door on Qin Shang's shipping line." He paused to massage his temples. Harper was clearly a man who did not relish losing a battle to forces beyond his control. "At the moment all we can do is prevent his smuggling operations from succeeding and hope that he makes a colossal mistake."

A knock came at the door, and Lieutenant Stowe entered. He silently handed Captain Lewis a message and just as quietly departed. Lewis scanned the wording and looked over the table at Frank Stewart. "A communication from your first officer, Captain. He said you wished to be kept informed on any new developments concerning the old luxury liner the *United States*."

Stewart nodded at Pitt. "Dirk is the one who is monitoring the ship's passage up the Mississippi."

Lewis handed the message to Pitt. "Pardon me for reading it, but it simply says the *United States* has passed under the Crescent City Connection and greater New Orleans bridges and is approaching the city's commercial waterfront, where it will be docked as a permanently floating hotel and casino."

"Thank you, Captain. Another puzzling project with Qin Shang's tentacles wrapped around it."

"Quite a feat just sailing it up the river from the Gulf," said Montaigne. "You might compare it with dropping a pin through a straw without it touching the sides."

"I'm glad you're here, General," said Pitt. "I have nagging questions that only you, as an expert on the river, can answer."

"I'll be glad to try."

"I have a crazy theory that Qin Shang built Sungari where he did because he intends to destroy a section of the levee and divert the Mississippi into the Atchafalaya, making it the most important port on the Gulf of Mexico."

It would be an overstatement to say that the men and one woman seated in the wardroom all accepted Pitt's fanciful scenario—all, that is, except General Montaigne. He nodded his head like a professor who threw a trick question at a student and received the correct answer. "It may surprise you to learn, Mr. Pitt, that I've had the same notion bouncing around inside my own head for the past six months."

"Divert the Mississippi," Captain Lewis said in a careful sort of voice. "There are many, myself included, who would say that's unthinkable."

"Unthinkable, perhaps, but not unimaginable to a man with Qin Shang's diabolic mind," Giordino said evenly.

Sandecker looked thoughtfully into the distance. "You've hit upon a rationale that should have been obvious from the first day of Sungari's construction."

Every eye was drawn to General Montaigne when Harper asked the obvious question. "Is it possible, General?"

"The Army Corps has been fighting Nature for over a hundred and fifty years to keep her from accomplishing the same cataclysm," answered Montaigne. "We all live with the nightmare of a great flood, greater than ever recorded since the first explorers saw the river. When that happens, the Atchafalaya River will become the main stream of the Mississippi. And that section of 'Old Man River' that presently runs from the northern border of Louisiana to the Gulf will become a silted-in tidal estuary. It's happened in the ancient past and it will happen again. If the Mississippi wants to head west, we can't stop her. The event is only a matter of time."

"Are you telling us that the Mississippi changes course on a set schedule?" asked Stewart.

Montaigne rested his chin on the head of his cane. "Not predictable by the hour or year, but it *has* wandered back and forth across Louisiana seven times in the past six thousand years. Had it not been for man, and especially the Army Corps of Engineers, the Mississippi would probably be flowing down the Atchafalaya Valley, over the sunken ruins of Morgan City and into the Gulf as we speak."

"Let us suppose Qin Shang destroys the levee and opens a vast spillway from the Mississippi into the canal he's had dredged into the Atchafalaya," Pitt speculated. "What would be the result?"

"In one word, catastrophic," answered Montaigne. "Pushed by a spring runoff current of seven miles an hour, a turbulent flood tide twenty, maybe thirty feet high would explode down the Mystic Canal and rage across the valley. The lives of two hundred thousand residents living on three million acres will be endangered. Most of the marsh-lands will become permanently inundated. The wall of water will sweep away whole towns, causing a tremendous death toll. Hundreds of thou-sands of animals, cows, horses, deer, rabbits, family dogs and cats swept away as though they'd never been born. Oyster beds, shrimp nurseries and catfish farms will be destroyed by the sudden decrease in salinity due to the overpowering flow of fresh water. Most of the alliga-tor population and water life will vanish."

"You paint a grim picture, General," said Sandecker.

"That's only the pitiful part of the forecast," said Montaigne. "On the economic side, the surge would collapse the highway and railroad bridges that cross the valley, closing down all transportation from east to west. Generating plants and high-voltage lines will likely be under-mined and destroyed, disrupting electrical service for thousands of square miles. The fate of Morgan City would be sealed. It will cease to exist. Interstate gas pipelines will rupture, cutting off major portions of natural gas to every state from Rhode Island and Connecticut to the Carolinas and Florida.

"And then we have the unrepairable damage to what's left of the Mississippi," he continued. "Baton Rouge would become a ghost town. All barge and water traffic would cease. The Great American Ruhr Valley, with its industrial magnitude of oil refineries, petrochemical plants and grain elevators, could no longer operate efficiently beside a polluted creek. Without fresh water, without the river's ability to scour a channel, it would soon build a wasteland of silt. Isolated from interstate commerce, New Orleans would go the way of Babylon, Angkor Wat and Pueblo Bonito. And like it or not, all oceangoing shipping would be diverted from New Orleans to Sungari. The terrible loss to the economy alone would be measured in the tens of billions of dollars."

"There's a thought that brings on a migraine," muttered Giordino.

"Speaking of relief." Montaigne looked at Captain Lewis. "I don't suppose you have a bottle of whiskey on board?"

"Sorry, sir," replied Lewis with a slight shake of the head. "No alcohol allowed on a Coast Guard ship."

"It never hurts to ask."

"How would the new river compare to the old?" Pitt asked the general.

"At the present time we control the flow of the Mississippi at the Old River Control Structure located about forty-five miles upriver from Baton Rouge. Our purpose is to maintain a distribution of thirty percent into the Atchafalaya and seventy percent into the Mississippi. When the two rivers merge with their full potential of a hundred-percent flow along a straighter path at half the distance to the Gulf compared to the channel through New Orleans, you're going to have one hell of a big river with current flowing at a great rate of speed."

"Is there no way to plug the gap should it occur?" asked Stewart.

Montaigne thought for a moment. "With the right preparation, there are any number of responses the Corps can make, but the longer it takes to get our equipment in place, the more time the flood widens the hole in the levee. Our only salvation is that the dominant current of the Mississippi would continue in the channel until the levee erodes far enough to accept the entire flow."

"How long do you think that would take?"

"Difficult to project. Perhaps two hours, perhaps two days."

"Would the process be speeded up if Qin Shang sank barges diagonally across the Mississippi to divert the main flow?" queried Giordino.

Montaigne thought a moment, then said, "Even if a tow unit consisting of enough barges to block the entire width of the river could be pushed into the correct position and sunk—not an easy maneuver even by the best towboat pilots—the river's main current would still flow over the barges due to their low profile. Sitting on the riverbed, their upper cargo roofs would still have a good thirty to thirty-five feet of water flowing over them. As a diversionary dam, the concept would not prove practical."

"Is it possible for you to begin preparations for an all-out effort?" asked Captain Lewis. "And have your men and equipment in position ready to go if and when Qin Shang destroys the levee?"

"Yes, it's possible," answered Montaigne. "It won't come cheap to the taxpayers. The problem I face in issuing the order is that it's based simply on conjecture. We may suspect Qin Shang's motives, but without absolute proof of his intentions, my hands are tied."

Pitt said, "I do believe, ladies and gentlemen, we've fallen into the 'close the barn door after the horse has escaped' syndrome."

"Dirk is right," Sandecker said solidly. "We'd be far better off to stop Qin Shang's operation before it takes place."

"I'll contact the St. Mary Parish sheriff's department and explain the situation," volunteered Harper. "I'm sure they will cooperate and send deputies to guard the levee."

"A sound proposition," agreed Montaigne. "I'll go one step further. My West Point classmate, General Oskar Olson, commands the National Guard in Louisiana. He'll be glad to send a contingent of troops to back up the sheriff's deputies if I make it a personal request."

"The first men on the scene should search out and disarm the explosives," said Pitt.

"They'll need equipment to torch open the iron door to a tunnel that Dirk and I discovered that runs under the highway and levee," suggested Giordino. "Inside the tunnel is where the explosives are likely stored."

"If Qin Shang wants to cut a wide breach," said Montaigne, "he'd have to pack additional explosives into side tunnels that branch out for at least a hundred yards."

"I'm certain Qin Shang's engineers have figured out what it will take to blow a giant hole in the levee," said Pitt grimly.

"It feels good," Sandecker sighed, "to finally have a grip on Qin Shang's testicles."

"Now all we need to know is the scumbag's time schedule," said Giordino.

At that moment Lieutenant Stowe reentered the wardroom and handed Captain Lewis another communication. As he read the message, his eyes narrowed. Then he peered at Pitt. "It seems the pieces of the puzzle that were missing have appeared."

"If the message is for me," said Pitt, "please read it aloud for everyone."

Lewis nodded and began reading. " 'To Mr. Dirk Pitt, NUMA, on board Coast Guard ship *Weehawken*. Please be advised that the former passenger liner *United States* has not stopped at New Orleans. I repeat, has not stopped at New Orleans. With total disregard to scheduled docking procedures and welcoming ceremonies, the ship has continued upriver toward Baton Rouge. The captain has refused to answer all radio calls.' '' Lewis looked up. "What do you make of it?"

"Qin Shang never intended to make the *United States* into a New Orleans hotel and gambling casino," Pitt explained dryly. "He plans to use it as a diversionary dam. Once the ship's nine-hundred-ninety-foot hull with its height of ninety feet is scuttled diagonally across the river, it will block ninety percent of the Mississippi's flow, sending one enormous flood tide through the shattered levee into the Atchafalaya."

"Ingenious," murmured Montaigne. "Then there would be no stopping the full force of the surge once it broke through. Nothing in this world could stop it."

"You know the Mississippi better than anyone here, General," Sandecker said to Montaigne. "How long do you think it will take the *United States* to reach the Mystic Canal below Baton Rouge?"

"Depends," the general replied. "She'd have to slow to jockey her immense bulk around several sharp turns in the river, but she could use her top speed on the straighter reaches. From New Orleans to where the Mystic Canal stops, just short of the Bayou Goula bend of the Mississippi, is about a hundred miles."

"With her interior an empty steel shell," said Pitt, "she rides high in the water, adding to her potential speed. With all her boilers fired up, she can conceivably cut water at close to fifty miles an hour."

"A band of angels would be powerless to help any barge or pleasure-craft traffic that's caught in her wash," said Giordino.

Montaigne turned to Sandecker. "She could arrive on site in less than three hours."

"We haven't a minute to lose in alerting the state emergency services to spread the alarm and begin evacuating every resident of the Atchafalaya Valley," said Lewis, his face grave.

"Almost five-thirty," Sandecker said, studying his watch. "We have only until eight-thirty this evening to stop a disaster of incalculable magnitude." He paused to rub his eyes. "If we fail, hundreds, maybe thousands of innocent people will die and their bodies will be swept out into the Gulf and never found."

After the meeting was over and everyone had left the wardroom, Pitt and Julia stood alone.

"It seems we're always saying good-bye," she said, standing with her arms at her sides, her forehead pressed into Pitt's chest.

"A bad habit we have to break," he said softly.

"I wish I didn't have to return to Washington with Peter, but Commissioner Monroe has ordered me to serve on the task force to indict Qin Shang."

"You're an important lady for the government's case."

"Please come home soon," she whispered as the tears began to form.

He embraced and held her tightly. "You can stay at my hangar. Between my security system and the bodyguards to protect you from harm, you'll be safe until I get there."

A mischievous twinkle came into her eyes through the tears. "Can I drive your Duesenberg?"

He laughed. "When was the last time you drove a stick shift?"

"Never," she said, smiling. "I've always owned cars with automatic transmissions."

"I promise that as soon as I can get there, we'll take the Duesy and go on a picnic."

"Sounds wonderful."

He stood back and stared downward at her through his opaline-green eyes. "Try to be a good girl."

Then he kissed her and they both turned away, neither looking back as they walked apart.

41

THE RIVER SOUNDS were muted by a light mist that hung over the dark water like a diaphanous quilt. The egrets and herons that walked silently along the shorelines, their long, curved beaks dipping into the silt for food, were the first to sense something not of their world moving toward them out of the night. It began as a slight tremor through the water that increased to a sudden rush of air and a loud throb that sent the startled birds flapping into the air.

The few bystanders strolling the levees after dinner and watching the lights of the boats on the water were startled by the sudden appearance of the monstrous shadow. And then the leviathan materialized from the mist with her towering raked bows slicing through the water with incredible ease for an object of such massive proportions. Although her four bronze screws were throttled down to negotiate the sharp bend at Nine Mile Point, she still threw a massive wake that rolled up the levees nearly to the roads running along their crests, crushing small vessels anchored along the shore and sweeping a dozen people into the water. Only after she maneuvered into a straight reach did her engines go on full throttle and thrust her up the river at an incredible rate of speed.

Except for a white light on the stub of her once-tall foremast and the red and green running lights, the only other illumination was an eerie glow that came from her wheelhouse. No movement could be seen on her decks, and only the occasional flicker of silhouettes on the bridge wings offered any signs of life. For the brief minutes it took for her to pass she seemed like a colossal dinosaur charging across a shallow lake. Her white superstructure was a shadow in the gloom, her black hull all but invisible. She flew no flag, her only identification the raised letters of her name on the bows and stern.

Before the mist shrouded her again, her decks seemed to come to life as men scurried about setting up weapons stations and arming an array of portable missile launchers against possible attack by American law enforcement. These were not foreign mercenaries or amateur terrorists. Despite their casual clothing, they were an elite team of fighters— ruthless, trained and disciplined for this mission. If captured alive, they were prepared to commit suicide or die fighting. If the operation went according to plan without interference, they would all be evacuated by helicopters before the ship was scuttled.

Captain Hung-chang had been right about the surprise and shock shown by the thousands of spectators lining the waterfront of New Orleans waiting to welcome the *United States*. After racing past the all-steel, stern-wheel steamboat called the *Natchez IX,* he had ordered full speed, watching amused as the great liner left the city behind her stern while crushing a small cabin cruiser and its occupants that had happened to get in the path of her sharp bow. He had laughed when he viewed the faces of the official welcoming committee, consisting of the Louisiana governor, the mayor of New Orleans and other dignitaries, through his binoculars. They looked absolutely stricken when the *United States* failed to stop and raced on past the dock where she was to be moored and refurbished with plush rooms, restaurants, gift shops and gambling tables.

For the first thirty miles, a fleet of yachts, outboards and fishing boats followed in the liner's wake. A Coast Guard cutter also raced in pursuit up the river, along with sheriff and police patrol cars that tore along parallel highways with sirens screaming and red lights flashing. Helicopters from New Orleans television news channels swarmed around the ship, cameras aimed at the grand scene being enacted below. Hung-chang ignored all orders demanding the ship come to a stop. Unable to match the great ship's incredible speed on the straight runs of the river, the private craft and Coast Guard cutter soon fell back.

As darkness fell, the first real problem Hung-chang faced was not the narrowing of the shipping channel between New Orleans and Baton Rouge that decreased from one thousand to five hundred feet. He was reasonably safe with the forty-foot depth. Her hull was only 101 feet at its widest point, narrowing considerably toward the waterline. If she could pass through the Panama Canal, Hung-chang reasoned, the two-hundred-foot clearance on either side provided just enough leeway through the tight turns. It was clearing the six bridges that spanned the banks of the river that gave him his greatest concern. The spring runoff had added nearly fourteen feet to the height of the river, making for a tight passage.

The *United States* narrowly slipped under both the Crescent City Connection bridges, and the Huey P. Long Bridge, scraping the lower span with the tops of her towering funnels. The next two bridges, the Luling and Gramercy, provided a slim gap of less than twelve feet of space. Only the Sunshine Bridge at Donaldsonville remained, and Hung-chang had carefully calculated the *United States* could safely pass under with six feet to spare. After that, the liner was free of all obstructions on her dash to the Mystic Canal except for river traffic.

A myriad of uneasy thoughts began to fade from Hung-chang's mind. There was no strong wind to push the ship off course. Ming Lin guided the ship through the intricate river bends with practiced mastery. And, most important of all, surprise was on his side. Before the Americans realized what was happening, it would be too late. Hung-chang would have the ship in the precise spot to divert the water through the breach blasted in the levee before he and his crew scuttled the ship and were to be in the air and on their way back to the safety of Sungari and the *Sung Lien Star* which was prepared to cast off immediately and head out to sea. The closer the *United States* steamed to the scuttling point, the more distant such worries became.

He felt an unexpected shudder through the deck and tensed, looking quickly at Ming Lin, searching for a sign of an error, a tiny mistake in judgment. All he could detect was a few beads of sweat on the helm master's forehead and a tight set to the lips. Then the decks became placid again, except for the beat of the engines, as they again went to full speed up a straight reach of the river.

Hung-chang stood with both legs braced apart. He had never felt such incredible strength from a ship before: 240,000 horsepower, 60,000 each to drive her massive propellers, which in turn hurled her up the river at the incredible speed of fifty miles an hour, speed that Hung-chang could not imagine from a ship under his command. He studied his image in the front storm windows of the bridge and saw a face calm and poised with no stress lines. He smiled as the ship passed a large waterfront home with a tall pole flying the stars and bars of the Confederate flag. Soon, very soon, the flag would no longer be flapping in the wind over the mighty Mississippi, but over a muddy creek.

The bridge was strangely quiet. There was no need for Hung-chang to call out orders for course and speed changes. Ming Lin was in complete command of the ship's passage, his hands locked on the wheel, his eyes staring into a large monitor that displayed the vessel and its relation to the river in a three-dimensional image that was transmitted by infrared cameras mounted on the bow and funnels. Through the medium of digital science, a display across the bottom of the monitor also gave him recommended course deviations and velocity instructions, providing him with far better mastery over the ship's progress than if he had piloted by eye during daylight.

"We have a towboat pushing ten grain barges coming up ahead," announced Ming Lin.

Hung-chang picked up the ship's radiophone. "Captain of the towboat approaching St. James Landing. We are overtaking you. We are one-half mile behind and will overtake you on the Cantrelle Reach, passing on your starboard. We have a hundred-foot beam and suggest you give us a wide berth."

There was no response from the unknown towboat captain, but when the *United States* turned into Cantrelle Reach, Hung-chang could see through his night-vision glasses that the towboat was slowly turning to port, too slowly. The towboat captain had not followed the news from New Orleans and could never imagine that a giant behemoth the size of the *United States* was bearing down on him at unbelievable speed.

"He's not going to make it in time," Ming Lin certified calmly.

"Can we slow?" asked Hung-chang.

"If we don't pass him on a straight reach, it will be impossible after we enter the next series of bends."

"Then it's now or never."

Ming Lin nodded. "For us to deviate from our computer-programmed passage might very well imperil the operation."

Hung-chang picked up the radiophone. "Captain, please veer away quickly or we may run you down."

The towboat captain's voice came back angrily. "You don't own the river, Charlie Brown. Who the hell do you think you're threatening?"

Hung-chang shook his head wearily. "I think you had better look over your stern."

The reply came like a choked gasp. "Jeezez! Where did *you* come from?"

Then the towboat and her barges quickly veered to port. Although the move came in time, the great wash from the superliner, her hull displacing over forty thousand tons of water with her passing, cascaded over the towboat and barges, sweeping them sideways and depositing them high and dry on the bank of the levee.

In another ten minutes the ship rounded Point Houmas, named for a tribe of Indians who once lived there, before rushing past the town of Donaldsonville and successfully clearing the Sunshine Bridge. As the lights of the bridge faded around the last bend in the river, Hung-chang allowed himself the luxury of a cup of tea.

"Only twelve more miles until we're there," said Ming Lin. His words were not a report but came as casually as a statement that the weather was mild. "Twenty minutes, twenty-five at most."

Hung-chang was just finishing his tea when a crewman who was standing watch on the starboard bridge wing leaned through the door of the wheelhouse. "Aircraft, Captain. Approaching from the north. Sounds like helicopters."

He had hoped for a radar installation, but Qin Shang, knowing the *United States* was on her final voyage saw no reason for the added expense. "Can you tell how many?"

"I count two coming straight down the river," replied the crewman, staring through night-vision glasses."

No need for panic, thought Hung-chang. They were either state law-enforcement craft that could do little but issue warnings for the ship to stop, or those chartered by the news media. He raised his night-vision glasses and peered upriver. Then the veins in his neck became taut as he recognized the helicopters as belonging to the military.

In the same moment a long row of floodlights blinked on, illuminating the river as brightly as daylight, and he saw a convoy of armored tanks rise from the opposite side of the east levee and train their guns on the river channel where the ship was about to pass. Hung-chang was surprised to see no rocket launchers. Not trained in military weapons systems, he did not recognize the National Guard's older M1A1 tanks with their 105-millimeter guns. But he knew well the damage they were capable of against the unarmored superliner.

The two helicopters, Sikorsky H-76 Eagles, split apart and flew past the side of the ship on a height even with the upper deck. One slowed and hovered above the stern while the other circled, drew even with the wheelhouse and trained a bright spotlight on it.

A voice from a loudspeaker boomed above the thump of the rotor blades. "Bring your ship to a halt immediately!"

Hung-chang gave no orders to comply. The fates had suddenly turned against him. The Americans must have somehow been warned. They knew! Damn them! They knew that Qin Shang intended to destroy the levee and use the superliner as a diverting dam.

"Halt immediately!" the voice came again. "We are coming aboard to secure your ship!"

Hung-chang hesitated as he weighed his chances of running the gauntlet. He counted six tanks lined up on the levee ahead. Lacking missiles with powerful warheads, the enemy would find the great ship next to impossible to sink by tank gunfire alone. The big engines were well below the waterline and immune to destruction from the surface. He glanced at his watch. Bayou Goula and the Mystic Canal were only fifteen minutes away now. For a moment, he considered stopping the ship and surrendering to the American military. But he was committed. To quit now would mean a loss of face. He would do nothing to dishonor his family. He made the decision to keep going.

As if to bind his commitment, one of the Chinese special forces team fired an SA-7 Russian-made man-portable infrared homing antiaircraft missile at the helicopter hovering over the stern. At less than two hundred yards it was impossible to miss, even without the homing system. The missile struck the helicopter's boom behind the fuselage and blasted it off. Horizontal control was lost and the craft spun crazily in circles before falling into the river and sinking out of sight, but not before the two crewmen and ten troops inside managed to struggle clear.

The men in the second helicopter flying opposite the liner's bridge were not as lucky. The next missile blew it apart in an explosive burst of fire, sending flaming debris and bodies crashing into the dark current of the river, their grave swept clean by the seething wake from the ship's propellers.

During the death and destruction, Hung-chang and the Chinese fighting force were unaware of the low-pitched buzzing sound approaching from upriver. Nor did any of them see the two black parachutes that fleetingly hid the stars in the night sky. Every eye was turned toward the menacing guns of the tanks, every mind concentrating on running the gauntlet of devastating fire they knew was about to ravage them.

Captain Hung-chang spoke quietly into the ship's phone to the engine room. "Full ahead, all engines."

42

TEN MINUTES EARLIER, from a schoolyard a block from the river, Pitt and Giordino lifted into the night sky. After donning helmets and harnesses, they strapped small motors that were mounted on backpacks across their shoulders. Next, they hooked into a thirty-foot-wide canopy with over fifty suspension lines spread on the turf and started their little three-horsepower engines that were about the same size as those used on power mowers and chainsaws. For stealth, the exhaust manifolds were specially muffled, emitting only a soft popping sound. The propellers, looking more like the wide blades on a fan and encased behind a wire cage so as not to entangle their lines, bit the air. After Pitt and Giordino ran a few steps, the thrust of the motors took over, the 230-square-foot canopies inflated and the two men lifted into the sky.

Except for wearing a steel helmet and a body-armor vest, the only weapon Giordino carried was Pitt's 12-gauge Aserma Bulldog, which was slung across his chest. Pitt elected his battle-scarred Colt automatic. Heavier weapons would have made it difficult to keep the paraplanes and their tiny engines in the air. There were other considerations as well. Their mission was not to engage in combat but to reach the wheelhouse and gain control of the ship. The Army assault team was relied on to handle any fighting.

Too late, only after they were in the air, did they see the Army helicopters shot out of the sky.

Less than an hour after the *United States* bypassed New Orleans, Pitt and Giordino met with General Oskar Olson, General Montaigne's old army buddy and commander of the National Guard of Louisiana, at the Guard Headquarters in Baton Rouge, the state capital of Louisiana. He had strictly forbidden Pitt and Giordino to accompany his assault team, brushing aside their argument that they were the only marine engineers on the scene familiar with the deck plan of the *United States,* and knowledgeable enough to take control of the wheelhouse and stop the ship before it reached Bayou Goula.

"This is an Army show," Olson declared, rapping the knuckles of one hand into the palm of the other. For a man in his late fifties, he was youthful-looking, confident and buoyant. He was about the same size as Pitt but with a slight paunch at the waist that comes to most all men as they age. "There may be bloodshed. I can't allow civilians to get hurt, and certainly not you, Mr. Pitt, not the son of a United States senator. I don't need the hassle. If my men can't stop the ship, I'll order them to run it ashore."

"Is that your only plan after the ship is secured?" asked Pitt.

"How else do you stop a vessel the size of the Empire State Building?"

"The length of the *United States* is more than the width of the river below Baton Rouge. Unless someone stands at the helm who knows how to command the automated systems, the ship could easily go out of control and swing broadside across the channel before ramming both bow and stern into the riverbanks—a barrier that would effectively block all barge traffic for months."

"Sorry, gentlemen, I'm committed," said Olson, smiling, showing even but gapped white teeth. "Only after the ship has been secured will I allow you and Mr. Giordino to be airlifted aboard. Then you can do your thing and bring that monster to a quick halt and anchor her before she becomes a menace to river traffic."

"If it's all the same to you, General," said Pitt without warmth, "Al and I will make our own arrangements to come aboard."

Olson did not immediately absorb Pitt's words; his olive-brown eyes were far away. They were the eyes of an old warhorse whose nose had not sniffed the smells of combat for two decades but sensed one more battle was coming his way. "I warn you, Mr. Pitt, I will not tolerate any foolishness or interference. You *will* obey my orders."

"A question, General, if you please?" said Giordino.

"Shoot."

"If your team fails to take the ship, what then?"

"As insurance, I have a squadron of six M1A1 tanks, two self-propelled howitzers and a mobile one-hundred-six-millimeter mortar on their way to the levee a few miles downriver. More than enough firepower to blast the *United States* into scrap."

Pitt gave General Olson a very skeptical look indeed, but made no effort to reply.

"If that's it, gentlemen, I have an attack to carry out." Then, as if he was a school principal dismissing a pair of unruly boys, General Oskar Olson marched back to his office and closed the door.

The original plan of landing on the ship after it was seized by the Army assault team went down the toilet in less time than it takes to tell, Giordino mused ironically, as he flew less than fifty feet behind Pitt and slightly above. He didn't need a diagram on a blackboard to know their odds of being riddled with bullets or blasted into tiny molecules by heavy firearms were somewhere between ordained and a sure thing. And if those options weren't bad enough, there was still the onslaught from the Army to live through.

Dropping onto a rapidly moving ship in the dead of night without breaking several bones will not be a routine affair, thought Pitt. Faced with an inconceivable landing, their biggest difficulty would be the forty-mile-an-hour speed of the ship versus the barely twenty-five-mile crawl of the paraplanes. Only by coming in downwind of the ship could they increase their airspeed.

They could lower the odds slightly, he reasoned, by flying downriver, meeting the ship and circling in as it slowed while turning through the sharp bend at the old Evan Hall plantation.

Pitt wore yellow-lensed glasses to soften the darkness, and relied on the ambient illumination from the houses and cars traveling on the highways and roads on both sides of the river to guide his descent. Though he was in full control, he felt as if he was falling into a deep crevasse with some unspeakable minotaur rushing toward him out of the depths. He could see the giant ship now, more imagined than real, but materializing out of the night, the colossal funnels looming ominous and threatening.

There could be no error in judgment. He fought off an urge to pull a toggle and veer off to avoid crashing into the unyielding superstructure and smashing his body to pulp. Al, he knew with dead certainty, would follow him without an instant's hesitation whatever the consequence. He spoke into the radio attached inside his helmet.

"Al?"

"Here."

"Do you see the ship?"

"Like standing on railroad tracks inside a tunnel watching an express train come at you."

"She's slowing down through the bend. We'll get one chance and one chance only before she picks up speed again."

"Just in time for the buffet, I hope," he said, still hungry after not eating since breakfast.

"I'm going to make a left turn and land on the open deck behind the aft funnel."

"Right behind you," Giordino said laconically. "Mind the ventilators and don't forget to step aside for me."

Giordino's resolution conveyed the loyalty he felt toward his best friend. That he would have accompanied Pitt into the deepest reaches of hell went without saying. They acted as one, almost as if each read the other's mind. From now until they came down on the deck of the *United States,* no more conversation would pass between them. It wasn't necessary.

Not requiring power to land, Pitt and Giordino hit the kill switches to their little motors to cut off all sound of their final approach. Pitt set up for his circular course and firmly pulled on the left toggle in preparation for a sweeping hook turn. Under their canopies, like a pair of black flying reptiles out of the Mesozoic era about to attack a galloping Sphinx, they swung over the east levee and then made a tight corkscrew turn toward the approaching ship, timing their descent to come from astern for their landing, much like a hobo running from a field onto a railroad track to catch the last freight car of a train.

No gunfire erupted from the ship. No shells reached up and shredded their canopies. They were coming in unseen, undetected and unheard by the armed men defending the ship. With the helicopters down, the Chinese fighting force was no longer focusing on what it thought was an empty sky.

As the deck with its two rows of low ventilators came into view behind the huge funnel, Pitt expertly adjusted and buried both toggles, causing his canopy to stall as he gradually flared down in the clear space between the ventilators. His landing gear—his legs and feet— lightly touched down on the surface of the deck as his lifeless canopy collapsed with the barest of whispers behind him. Not waiting to congratulate himself for landing uninjured, he quickly pulled the canopy and caged motor off to one side. Three seconds later, Giordino dropped out of the sky and made a picture-perfect landing less than six feet away.

"Is this where one of us is supposed to say, 'So far, so good'?" said Giordino softly as he released his harness and engine pack.

"No gunshot holes and no broken bones," Pitt whispered. "Who could ask for anything more?"

They moved into the shadow of the funnel and, while Giordino searched the darkness for signs of life, Pitt set a new frequency on his helmet radio and hailed Rudi Gunn, who was with the sheriff's deputies and a team of Army demolition experts on the highway above the Mystic Canal.

"Rudi, this is Pitt. Do you read me?"

Before a reply came back, he stiffened as a blast from the Aserma Bulldog intermingled with the staccato fire of an automatic rifle. He spun around and saw Giordino crouched on one knee, aiming the shotgun at an unseen target on the aft end of the deck.

"The natives aren't at all friendly," Giordino said with glacial calm. "One of them must have heard our motors, and came to investigate."

"Rudi, please answer," Pitt said, an urgent tone in his voice. "Dammit, Rudi, talk to me."

"I hear you, Dirk." Gunn's voice came resonant and precise through the earphones inside Pitt's helmet. "Are you on the ship?"

Gunn's words ended just as Giordino unleashed another two rounds from his shotgun. "It's getting a bit warm," he said. "I don't think we should hang around."

"On board, safe and sound for the moment," Pitt answered Gunn.

"Is that gunfire?" the unmistakable voice of Admiral Sandecker came over the radio.

"Al is celebrating the Fourth of July early. Did you find and cut the detonators on the explosives?"

"Bad news on this end," replied Sandecker soberly. "The army used a small charge to blow the doors to the tunnel at the end of the canal. We gained entrance and found an empty chamber."

"You've lost me, Admiral."

"I hate to be the bearer of sad tidings, but there are no explosives. If Qin Shang means to blast a hole in the levee, it's not anywhere around here."

43

THERE WAS FAR MORE LIGHT on the highway levee above the Mystic Canal. Portable floodlights and flashing red and blue lights lit up the river and surrounding countryside. Eight Army vehicles in their camouflage paint schemes mingled with a dozen sheriff's cars from Iberville Parish. Highway barricades had north and southbound traffic backed up for nearly a mile.

The group of men standing beside an Army command vehicle wore expressions of grave concern. Admiral Sandecker, Rudi Gunn, Sheriff Louis Marchand of Iberville Parish and General Olson looked like men who had wandered into a maze with no exit. General Olson was especially exasperated.

"A fool's errand," he snarled angrily. After being informed his helicopters were shot down and a dozen of his men feared dead, he no longer put up a cocky front. "We were sent on a fool's errand. All this talk about blowing up the levee is a myth. We're dealing with a gang of international terrorists. That's our real problem."

"I'm forced to agree with the general," said Sheriff Marchand. No redneck, this man. He was trim and smartly dressed in a tailored uniform. He was polished, urbane and extremely street-smart. "The plan to blow up the levee to divert the river seems most implausible. The terrorists who stole the *United States* have a different goal in mind."

"They are not terrorists in the usual sense," said Sandecker. "We know for a fact who is behind the operation, and they did not steal the ship. This is an incredibly complex and well-financed operation to divert the flow of the Mississippi past the port of Sungari."

"Sounds like some kind of fantastic dream," retorted the sheriff.

"A nightmare," Sandecker said flatly. He looked at Marchand. "What's been done about evacuating residents from the Atchafalaya Valley?"

"Every sheriff's department and all military personnel are alerting the farms, towns and neighborhoods to the possible flood and ordering them to go to higher ground," replied the sheriff. "If there is a threat to lives, we hope to keep casualties to a minimum."

"Most residents will never get the word in time," Sandecker said seriously. "When that levee splits apart, every morgue between here and the Texas border will be working overtime."

"If your conclusion is correct," said Marchand, "and I pray to God you and Commander Gunn are wrong, we're already too late to conduct a search for explosives up and down the river before the ship arrives some time in the next hour—"

"Make that fifteen minutes," interrupted Sandecker.

"The *United States* will never reach here," Olson said emphatically. He paused to glance at his watch. "My battle group of national guardsmen under the able command of Colonel Bob Turner, a decorated veteran of the Gulf War, should be in place and ready to fire from the levee at point-blank range any minute."

"You might as well send bees after a grizzly bear," snorted Sandecker. "From the time she passes in front of your firepower until she passes out of sight around the next bend your men will have no more than eight or ten minutes. As a Navy man, I can tell you that fifty guns won't stop a ship the size of the *United States* in that length of time."

"Our high-velocity, armor-piercing rounds will make short work of her," persisted Olson.

"The liner is no battleship and carries no armor, sir. The superstructure is not steel but aluminum. Your armor-penetrating shells will dart through one side and out the other without detonating, unless a lucky shot strikes a support beam. You'd be far better off firing fragmentation shells."

"Should the ship survive the Army's blitz," said Marchand, "matters little. The bridge at Baton Rouge was designed and built low specifically to prevent oceangoing ships from continuing any farther up the Mississippi. The *United States* will have to stop or destroy herself."

"You people still don't get it," Sandecker said in frustration. "That ship is rated at over forty thousand tons. It will go through your bridge like an enraged elephant through a greenhouse."

"The *United States* will never reach Baton Rouge," Gunn maintained. "Where we stand is exactly where Qin Shang intends to blow the levee and scuttle the ship as a diversionary dam."

"Then where are the explosives?" asked Olson sarcastically.

"If what you say is true, gentlemen," said Marchand slowly, "why not simply ram the liner through the levee. Wouldn't it produce an opening with the same result as explosives?"

Sandecker shook his head. "It may breach the levee, Sheriff, but it would also plug its own hole."

The admiral had no sooner finished speaking than the sound of cannonfire began thundering a few short miles to the south. The highway quaked as the tank's guns roared out in unison, their flashes lighting up the horizon. Every man on the highway stopped and stared wordlessly downriver. The younger ones, not having served during a war, had never heard a cannon barrage before and stood enthralled. General Oskar Olson's eyes gleamed like a man looking at a beautiful woman.

"My men have opened up on her," he exclaimed excitedly. "Now we'll see what concentrated firepower at point-blank range can do."

A sergeant came rushing out of the command truck, snapped to attention in front of General Olson and saluted. "Sir, the troops and deputies manning the north highway barricade report that a pair of tractor trailers have crashed through at a high rate of speed and are heading this way."

They all spontaneously turned and stared north, seeing two large trucks speeding side by side down the southbound lanes of the highway, the sheriff patrol cars giving chase with sirens and flashing lights. A patrol car cut in front of one of the trucks and slowed in an attempt to pull it to a stop on the road shoulder, but the truck driver deliberately swerved into the patrol car and struck it in the rear, sending it spinning wildly off the highway.

"The idiot!" Marchand snapped. "He's going to jail for that."

Only Sandecker instantly recognized the threat. "Clear the road!" he shouted to Marchand and Olson. "For God's sake clear the road."

Then Gunn knew. "The explosives are in those trucks!" he yelled.

Olson stood shock-still in uncomprehending confusion. His first reaction, his instantaneous conclusion, was that both Sandecker and Gunn had gone mad. Not Marchand. He responded without hesitation and began ordering his deputies to evacuate the area. Finally, Olson came out of his trance and shouted orders to his subordinates to get all men and vehicles a safe distance away.

Crowded as the highway might have been, guardsmen and deputies scattered to their cars and trucks and accelerated away, leaving the stretch of road totally empty within sixty seconds. Their response was as immediate as it was instinctive once they became aware of the danger. The trucks could be seen clearly now as they sped closer. They were semitrucks and trailers, big eighteen-wheelers capable of carrying a load weighing over eighty thousand pounds. No markings or advertising was painted on their sides. They came on seemingly unstoppable, their drivers hunched over the steering wheels, acting as though they were bent on suicide.

Their intentions became unmistakable as they skidded to a stop adjacent to the Mystic Canal, one of them jackknifing across the center strip dividing the highway. Unseen and unnoticed during the bedlam, a helicopter appeared out of the darkness and dropped between the trucks. The drivers leaped from their cabs, ran to the aircraft and scrambled inside. Almost before the last driver's feet had left the ground, the helicopter's pilot lifted the craft into the sky, whipped it on a nearly ninety-degree bank and disappeared into the night toward the Atchafalaya River to the west.

As they raced south in the backseat of Sheriff Marchand's patrol car, Sandecker and Gunn twisted around and stared back through the rear window. Behind the wheel, Marchand kept darting his eyes from the highway and the vehicles speeding around him into the sideview mirror. "If only the Army's demolition men could have had time to defuse the explosives."

"It would have taken them an hour just to find and figure out the detonating mechanism," said Gunn.

"They won't blow the levee just yet," Sandecker said quietly. "Not before the *United States* arrives."

"The admiral is right," Gunn agreed. "If the levee is breached before the *United States* can be angled across the channel to divert the water, enough of the Mississippi's flow will gush into the canal to leave the liner with her keel in the mud."

"There is still a slight chance," said Sandecker. He tapped Marchand on the shoulder. "Can you raise General Olson on your radio?"

"I can if he's listening," replied the sheriff. He reached for the microphone and began asking for Olson to respond. After repeating the request several times, a voice answered. "Corporal Welch in the command truck. I read you, Sheriff. I'll patch in the general for you."

There was a pause punctuated by static, and then Olson answered. "Sheriff, what do you want? I'm busy getting battle reports from my tanks."

"One moment, sir, for Admiral Sandecker."

Sandecker leaned over the front seat and took the microphone. "General, do you have any aircraft in the air?"

"Why do you ask?"

"I believe they intend to set off the explosives by radio from the helicopter that snatched the drivers."

Olson's voice suddenly sounded old and very tired. "Sorry, Admiral, the only aircraft I had at my immediate command were two helicopters. And now they and the men inside are gone."

"You can't call up any jets from the nearest Air Force base?"

"I can try," Olson replied solemnly, "but there is no guarantee they could scramble and get here in time."

"I understand, thank you."

"Not to worry, Admiral," Olson said, his self-assurance all but gone. "She won't get past my tanks." But this time around he didn't sound entirely as if he meant it.

The gunfire downriver came like a death knell as the *United States* presented her broadside to the gunners inside the tanks. What General Olson did not yet know was that it wasn't a one-sided battle.

Sandecker passed the microphone back to Marchand and sagged into the rear seat, anxiety and defeat etched in his eyes. "That bastard Qin Shang has outsmarted us all, and there isn't a damned thing we can do about it except stand by helplessly and watch a lot of people die."

"And let us not forget Dirk and Al," he said grimly. "They must be taking it from the Chinese as well as Olson's tanks and howitzers."

"God help them," Sandecker murmured. "God help everybody who lives on or near the Atchafalaya River if the *United States* comes through the chaos."

44

THE *UNITED STATES* did not reel, she barely quivered as the guns on the turrets of the six tanks opened up on her, their flashes lighting up the sky. At less than two hundred yards it was impossible to miss. As if by witchcraft, black, jagged holes appeared in the funnels and upper decks that once housed the cocktail lounges, cinemas and libraries. As Admiral Sandecker had predicted, every round in the first salvo from the tanks' 120-millimeter guns was ineffective. The armor-penetrating rounds passed through the ship's aluminum bulkheads as if they were made of cardboard, buried themselves in the marshlands on the other side of the west-bank levee and exploded harmlessly. The 106-millimeter mortar rounds fired from the launchers of the M125 carriers arched high into the sky and rained down on the exposed decks, gouging craters in the decks below but causing little serious damage. The tried-and-true 155-millimeter high-explosive fragmentation shells that spat from the Paladin self-propelled howitzers were a different story. Their fire battered the superliner unmercifully, causing significant destruction but none that affected her vital machinery deep within the bowels of her hull.

One shell plowed into what had been the main dining room in the center of the hull and burst, shattering the bulkheads and the old stairway. The second exploded against the base of the foremast and toppled it over the side. The great ship shook off the onslaught. And then it was the turn of the Chinese weapons team of professional fighters who were geared to put up a tactical confrontation despite the odds. The battle was not about to be one-sided. There would be no turning the cheek after the first slap.

Their missile launchers, though armed for surface-to-air and not antitank, lashed out. One struck the lead tank without penetrating its armor but burst against the barrel of the 120-millimeter gun, effectively putting it out of action. It also killed the tank commander, who was standing in the hatch observing the results of the barrage and who never expected return fire. Another projectile struck the circular opening in the roof of the mortar carrier, killing two men, wounding three and setting the vehicle on fire.

Colonel Robert Turner, directing the fire from within his XM4 command-and-control vehicle, was slow to comprehend the magnitude of his mission. The last thing he would have predicted was for the old passenger liner to shoot back. It's downright outrageous, he thought. He immediately called Olson and said in a voice vague with shock, "We're taking hits, General. I just lost my mortar unit."

"What are they using?" Olson demanded.

"They're firing portable missiles at us from the ship! Fortunately, they don't appear to be armor-piercing. But I've taken casualties." As he spoke another missile blew the treads off a third tank, but its crew gamely kept up their rate of fire, hammering the rapidly passing liner.

"What is the effect of your fire?"

"Severe damage to the superstructure but no vital hits. It's like trying to stop a charging rhino with air-pellet guns."

"Don't let up!" Olson ordered. "I want that ship stopped."

Then, almost as suddenly as the hail of missiles from the ship was launched, their fire slackened off. Not until later was the reason known. Pitt and Giordino, risking their lives to halt the counterfire, had shot down the two Chinese missile-launching teams.

Scuttling across the deck on their stomachs to avoid the hurricane of shrapnel and to make aim difficult for the Chinese riflemen who had discovered their presence, they moved around the giant aft funnel and lay prone, peering cautiously down onto the lifeboat deck, whose davits were now empty. Almost directly below, four Chinese soldiers crouched behind a steel bulwark, busily loading and firing their portable missiles, completely disregarding the hail of explosions erupting around them.

"They're murdering our guys on the levee," Giordino shouted in Pitt's ear, his words barely heard over the bedlam.

"Take the two on the left," Pitt yelled back. "The others are mine."

Giordino took careful aim with the shotgun and fired two shots. The two men beneath him never knew what hit them. They fell to the deck like stuffed dolls in almost the same moment as Pitt's Colt dropped their comrades a few feet away. Now, but for a curtain of small-arms fire that was directed at any soldier who showed himself through a hatch in the armored vehicles, no missiles came from the ship.

Pitt grabbed Giordino's arm to get his attention. "We've got to get to the bridge—"

His voice was cut off in a painful gasp, his arms and legs suddenly thrust into the air as his body was catapulted against a ventilator, driving the air from his lungs. A tremendous blast rang in his ears as the deck beneath him was heaved up in an enormous explosion. A shell from a howitzer had smashed into the crew's cabins below and burst, leaving a jagged hole filled with tangled wreckage and shattered metal. Almost before the debris had settled, Pitt was fighting off the blackness that seeped into his vision. With agonizing slowness he forced himself to sit up. His first words muttered through a cut and bleeding lip were, "Damn the Army, damn their hides." But he knew they were just doing their job, fighting for their own lives, and doing it well.

The mist slowly cleared from his mind, but there were still blinding flashes of white and orange colors before his eyes. He looked down and saw that Giordino was lying across his legs. He reached out and shook his shoulder. "Al, are you hurt?"

Giordino blinked one of his dark brooding eyes open and stared up. "Hurt? I feel like I've had root canals all over my body."

As they lay recovering, another wave of shells pounded into the ship. The tanks had lowered their guns now and were firing into the steel hull. Now their high-explosive antitank armor began to score, burning through the steel hull plates before smashing into one of the thousands of the ship's bulkheads and exploding. One howitzer zeroed in on the bridge and soon the structure became a mass of jagged wreckage that looked as if a giant had chopped it with a cleaver. The great ship stubbornly bored through the exploding hell, looming huge in front of the gunners as they loaded and fired with incredible calm. The national guardsmen, often called weekend warriors, fought like seasoned veterans. But like a wounded whale that shook off a cloud of harpoons and swam on, the *United States* absorbed the punishment they dished out without so much as a fractional drop in speed.

The ship was almost past the gauntlet now. Desperately, the forces on the levee loosed one final wall of devastating fire that tore the night air apart. A crescendo of explosions rocked the battered, once-proud superliner. There was no fire, no mushrooming balls of flame or billowing clouds of smoke. Her designer William Francis Gibbs, would have been saddened by her mauling but pleased that his fetish for fireproofing had resisted any attempt to turn his achievement into a fiery shambles. In his command vehicle, Colonel Turner watched in utter frustration as the juggernaut showed her stern and disappeared into the night.

Without warning, three figures rushed out of the blackness toward Pitt and Giordino. A burst of gunfire cut across the deck. Giordino stumbled but regained his feet, firing off a blast from the 12-gauge Aserma that dropped the Chinese who had managed to squeeze the trigger of his Chinese-copied Kalashnikov AKM automatic rifle. Then the remaining four men fell on each other in a thrashing melee of bodies. Pitt felt the muzzle of a gun jam into his ribs, but he knocked it aside a millisecond before a stream of bullets whipped past his hip. He brought the Colt's barrel down on his opponent's head once, twice, three times and clubbed him to the deck. In icy disregard for his injury, Giordino thrust his shotgun against his assailant's chest at the same time he pulled the trigger. The Aserma's muzzle erupted with a muffled roar that knocked the Chinese fighter backward as if he had been jerked off his feet by a horse galloping in the opposite direction. Only then did the feisty little Italian crumple to the deck.

Pitt dropped to his friend's side. "Where are you hit?"

"The bastard got me in the leg above the knee," Giordino answered in a hoarse grunt. "I think it's broken."

"Let me take a look."

Giordino pushed Pitt away. "Never mind me. Get to the bridge and stop this tub before the levee blows." Then he forced a grin through the pain. "That's what we came for."

There were only two more miles left to go and five minutes to get there. And then Pitt was charging like a demon struggling through the shattered wreckage toward the remains of the wheelhouse. He fought his way through the maze of fallen wires left by the broken foremast and came to a shocked halt. The bridge structure hardly existed anymore. Nothing could be recognized of it. The walls of the wheelhouse looked to have collapsed outward. Miraculously, the interior console had survived with minor damage. The body of Captain Li Hung-chang lay on the floor covered with glass and debris. His fixed expression, his open, staring eyes and few spots of blood on his uniform almost made him seem as though he was looking up through the vanished roof, staring at the stars. Pitt instantly recognized that he had been killed by concussion.

The master helmsman still stood, his lifeless hands gripping the wheel. It seemed that a curse from the devil had refused to let him fall beside his captain. Pitt saw with blood-chilling horror that his head was gone, taken off cleanly at the shoulders.

Pitt glanced through the shattered remains of the bridge window. Mystic Canal was less than a mile away. Far below, the crew had abandoned the engine room and were rushing onto the outer decks in expectation of being evacuated by helicopter.

All gunfire had stopped now and the thunderous tumult became a hushed and unimaginable silence. Pitt's hands played over the levers and switches of the console, trying frantically to cut all power throughout the ship. But without a chief engineer to carry out the commands, the enormous turbines ignored any attempt to stop them. No power on earth could stop the *United States* now. Her massive bulk and incredible impetus drove her on. In his final moment of life Ming Lin had begun to turn the wheel and send the ship on an oblique angle, lining her up to be scuttled, as dictated by Qin Shang's master plan. Her bow was already coming around toward the east bank of the river.

Pitt knew the explosive charges far below in the ship's bilge were set and timed to go off and sink the ship at any second. He wasted no time in staring helplessly at the obscene apparition at the helm. He pushed the mutilated body off to one side and took the wheel at the exact instant the trucks on the highway, now only a few hundred yards away, exploded with a thunderous roar that shook the ground and churned the river. He felt the icy needles of disaster in his spine. Hopelessness swamped him in a fleeting rage. But his resolve, his infinite endurance, would never allow him to fail. He had developed a sixth sense after having survived death over the years. The fear of hopelessness came and went. He was oblivious to anything and everything, except for what he must do.

With unwavering concentration, he gripped the wheel and desperately spun it, turning the rudder to head the ship on a new course before her bottom was blown out.

Back on the deck beneath the colossal funnels where Pitt had left him, Al Giordino pulled himself up against the base of a ventilator. The pain in his leg had receded to little more than a dull ache. Running figures suddenly appeared, dressed head to toe in black night-fighting attire. Believing him to be among the dead scattered about the deck, they rushed past and ignored him. As he lay there a black helicopter abruptly shot out of the dark and darted over the east levee. The pilot did not waste moments hovering but dove right in, barely clearing the aft railing by less than two feet and dropping onto the same deck behind the rear funnel where Giordino and Pitt had landed their paraplanes. Almost before the helicopter's wheels slammed onto the deck, Qin Shang's men were diving inside through the open door in the fuselage.

Giordino checked the drum on his Aserma shotgun and counted seven 12-gauge rounds left. He leaned to one side, stretched out his hand and retrieved a Kalashnikov AKM rifle dropped by one of the dead ship defenders. He punched out the clip and noted that it was only a quarter empty before shoving it back in the magazine. Wincing from pain, he struggled to one knee and aimed the Aserma at the helicopter, keeping the AKM automatic rifle as a backup.

His eyes did not blink, his face was still. There was no sensation of coldness, no pitiless thoughts running through his mind, but more a perception of detachment. These men did not belong here. They came to kill and cause destruction. To Giordino's way of thinking, allowing them to escape unpunished was a crime in itself. He stared at the men inside the helicopter, who began to laugh with satisfaction in the belief they had won out over the stupid Americans. Giordino became mad, madder than he had ever been.

"How do I hate you," he muttered angrily. "Let me count the ways."

With the last man aboard, the pilot lifted the craft vertically into the air. Buffeted by its own downdraft, it hung for a few moments before slipping sideways and aiming its bow toward the east. At that instant, Giordino opened up, pumping round after round into the turbine engines mounted below the rotor. He could see the twelve-gauge magnum-charged pellets tearing holes in the cowlings but without seeming effect.

He pumped out his last casing, dropped the Aserma and snatched up the AKM. There was a thin wisp of smoke coming from the port turbine now, but the helicopter showed no other signs of vital damage. There was no infrared laser pointer on the rifle, and Giordino disregarded the night scope mounted on the barrel. A large target at this distance was hard to miss. He peered over the iron sights at the great bird about to disappear and pulled the trigger evenly on semiautomatic. After pounding the final shot home, Giordino could do no more that hope that he had at least wounded the bird to a condition where it could not reach its destination. The helicopter seemed to hang before falling backward in a tail-low attitude. It was clearly out of control now as flames shot out of both turbines. Then it was falling like a rock, crashing onto the stern deck before exploding in a solid wall of flame that shot straight up in the air. Within seconds, the stern became a raging inferno, radiating heat and fire with the energy of a blast furnace.

Giordino threw the gun aside as the shooting pain in his broken leg returned with a vengeance. He gazed approvingly at the blazing, twisted tongue of fire shooting into the sky. "Damn," he murmured softly. "I forgot the marshmallows."

45

THE EXPLOSION THUNDERED in the ears of the soldiers and sheriff's deputies who had stopped just half a mile from the two semitrucks and trailers. The sky tore apart in a violent, demented convulsion of compressed air as the horrendous detonation tore the heart out of the levee. Seconds later, the eruption of the pressure wave stunned them, followed by a blast of dirt from the levee and concrete from the highway. Then flaming metal from the shattered trucks rained down from a world in chaos. As if given a universal order, everyone ducked behind or under his vehicle to shield himself from the storm of debris.

Sandecker threw up an arm to protect his eyes from the blinding flash and flying fragments. The air felt thick and charged with electricity as a great roar pounded his ears. A huge ball of fire rose and mushroomed, spreading into the sky, transforming into a swirling black cloud that blotted out the stars.

And then all eyes turned back to where a hundred yards of highway, the levee and the two big trucks once stood. All had disintegrated. None of those standing there in shock were prepared for the horrific spectacle that avalanched through the vanished remains of the levee. To a man they stood numbed by the rumbling reverberation in their ears that slowly faded, only to be replaced with a far more ominous sound, an unbelievably loud hissing and sucking sound as a seething wall of water gushed catastrophically into the waiting arms of the Mystic Canal, dredged by Qin Shang for this very event.

For one long, terrible minute they stared bleakly through disbelieving eyes, hypnotically drawn to a cataract so violent that it could not be conceived unless witnessed. They watched impotently as millions of gallons of water poured through the breach in the highway and levee, dragged by the natural laws of gravity and impelled by the force of the river's mass and current. It exploded into a wall of boiling water with nothing to stop its great momentum as it began draining off the main flow of the Mississippi.

The great destroying flood tide was on its way, oblivion in the making.

Unlike ocean tidal waves, there was no trough. Behind the crest, the fluid mass moved without the slightest suggestion of distortion, its texture smooth and rolling, surging with immeasurable energy.

What was left of the abandoned town of Calzas was inundated and swept away. Nearly thirty feet high, the irresistible, seething mass engulfed the marshlands as it hurled toward the waiting arms of the Atchafalaya River. A small cabin cruiser, with its four occupants in the wrong part of the river, at the wrong time, was sucked into the breach, where it plunged dizzily through the wild maelstrom and vanished. No act of man could halt the raging wall of uncontrollable water as it rushed across the valley before advancing toward the Gulf, where its muddy flow would be absorbed by the sea.

Sandecker, Olson and the other men on the highway could do nothing but watch the nightmarish disaster like eyewitnesses at a train derailment, unable to fathom the unrelenting cataclysm that could penetrate and crush concrete, wood, steel and flesh. They watched silently in the face of what appeared to promise inevitable calamity, their faces tightened in expressionless masks. Gunn shivered and looked away toward the Mississippi.

"The ship!" he shouted above the rush of the flood. He pointed excitedly. "The ship!"

In almost the same terror-bred moment in time, the *United States* came rushing past. Mesmerized by the awesome spectacle of the unleashed flood tide, they had forgotten about her. Their eyes followed Gunn's outstretched hand and finger, seeing an unending black silhouette emerge from the night, a tangible monster from the darkness. Her superstructure, fore and aft, was blasted into a shell-torn, jagged mass of indescribable shambles. Her foremast was gone, her funnels raked and holed, great gaps of twisted steel ripped into the sides of her hull.

But still she came, propelled by her great engines, bent on adding her weight to the devastation. There was no stopping her. She passed them by at a tremendous rate of speed, her bows throwing up a great sheet of water as she drove against the current under full power. Despite the fact she had been used to cause death and destruction, she looked magnificent. No man who saw her that night would ever forget that they were seeing a legend die. No drama was ever played to a more climactic ending.

They stared enthralled, expecting to see her hull turn and slant across the river in preparation of her role of becoming a dam to cast the Mississippi away from her established channel forever. Their convictions seemed verified as waterspouts burst alongside her hull.

"Mother of God!" muttered Olson in shock. "They've blown the charges! She's going down!"

Any shred of misplaced hope any of them had of the Corps stemming the flow was gone now as the glorious superliner began to settle in the water.

But the *United States* was not headed on a course to bury her bows in the east bank with her stern slanted across the river toward the west. She was running straight up the center of the main channel, ever so slowly curving toward the Niagara-like falls roaring through the breach.

Pitt stood and clutched the wheel, now jammed against its stop. He had turned the rudder as far as it could go. His calculated determination could do no more. He felt the ship shudder as the explosive charges blew great holes in her bottom, and he cursed himself for not being able to control the speed or somehow reverse the port propellers and twist the ship in a tighter turn. But the automated control system had been shut down by damage from the Army's gunfire, making it impossible without a crew down in the engine room to carry out his course change. Then, with torturous slowness, almost miraculously, he watched as the bow began easing toward port.

Pitt felt his heart jump. Imperceptibly at first, but as the angle slowly increased, the river's current began nudging her starboard bow sideways. It was as though the *United States* refused to give up and was not about to pass from the ages with a black mark against her remarkable history. She had survived forty-eight long years of sailing the seas and being laid up, and unlike many of her sister ships who went quietly to the scrap yard, she was not going willingly to her death, but with her heart and soul resisting to the end.

Unerringly, as if Pitt had ordained it, the ship's bow stem cut into the steep slope on the edge of the channel and forged through the bottom mud on an oblique angle to the levee two hundred feet beyond the breach. On a sharper angle she might have driven straight through.

The power of the river's flow through the gash blown out by the explosion came into play and helped slew her massive hull laterally against the breach. And then as suddenly as the vast surge had burst into the marshlands, it was dying, falling off to a small torrent that curled around the liner's still-flailing propellers at the stern.

At last she came to a complete stop, her four great bronze screws beating against the riverbed, embedding their blades in the mud until they could turn no more. The *United States,* the once-grand superliner of America's shipping fleet, had finished her final voyage.

Pitt stood like a man who had run a triathlon, his head dropped over the wheel, his hands still locked on the rim. He was dead-tired, his body, never fully recovered from the injuries received on an island off the coast of Australia only a few weeks before, shrieking for a rest. He was so brain-weary he could not distinguish any separation of the bruises and abrasions suffered from the explosions or the fight with the Chinese defenders of the ship. They all blended into a growing sea of torment.

It took nearly a full minute before he became dimly aware that the ship was no longer moving. His legs could hardly keep him upright as he released the helm and turned to go search for Giordino. But his friend was already standing in the shattered doorway, leaning on the Kalashnikov AKM that he used to shoot down the helicopter, using it as a cane.

"I have to tell you," Giordino said with a slight grin, "your docking technique leaves much to be desired."

"Give me another hour of practice and I'll get the hang of it," Pitt replied in a tone barely above a whisper.

On shore, the sickening moment of panic had passed. They no longer looked out across a broken levee and saw a roaring, unstoppable flood. The flow had fallen off to that of a rushing stream. Every man on the highway cheered and shouted exultantly, all except Sandecker. He gazed at the *United States* through saddened eyes. His face was weary and haggard. "No seaman likes to see a ship die," he said somberly.

"But what a noble death," said Gunn.

"I suppose there is nothing left for her but to be scrapped."

"It would cost too many millions to restore her."

"Dirk and Al, bless their hides, prevented a major disaster."

"A lot of people will never know how much they owe those two characters," Gunn agreed.

Already, a long convoy of trucks and equipment was descending on both ends of the break. Towboats pushing barges loaded with huge stones were arriving from up and down the river. Directed by General Montaigne, the Army Corps of Engineers, seasoned veterans at making emergency repairs along the river, rapidly deployed. Every available man and piece of equipment from New Orleans to Vicksburg had been marshaled to restore the levee and put the highway back in serviceable order for auto and truck traffic.

Thanks to the massive hull of the *United States* acting as a barrier, the flood tide that hurtled toward the Atchafalaya was robbed of the immense power of the Mississippi. After spreading across the marshlands, the wild waters diminished to a wave less than three feet high when it reached Morgan City.

Not for the first time had the mighty Mississippi been prevented from forging her way into a new channel. The battle between men and nature would go on, and eventually there could be but one outcome.

PART V

THE PEKING MAN

Peking Man

46

April 30, 2000
Washington, D.C.

CHINA'S AMBASSADOR TO THE UNITED STATES, Qian Miang, was a portly man. Short, hair styled in a crewcut, face fixed in a constant little grin that almost never revealed teeth, he reminded those who first met him of a sculpture of a contented Buddha with its hands supporting a round stomach. Never behaving like a dogmatic Communist, Qian Miang was a very gracious man. Supremely confident, he cultivated many powerful friends in Washington and moved through the halls of the Capitol and White House with the ease of a Cheshire cat.

Preferring to do business capitalist-style, he met with Qin Shang in the private dining room of Washington's finest Chinese restaurant, where he often entertained the city's power elite. He greeted the shipping magnate with a warm two handed shake. "Qin Shang, my dear friend." The voice was jolly and congenial. Instead of Mandarin, he spoke perfect English with a trace of a British accent absorbed during three years of schooling at Cambridge. "You have neglected me during your stay in town."

"My humble apologies, Qian Miang," said Qin Shang. "I have experienced pressing problems. I was informed earlier this morning that my project to divert the Mississippi River past my port of Sungari has failed."

"I am quite aware of your problems," replied Qian Miang without loosening his smile. "I cannot suggest otherwise, but President Lin Loyang is not happy. Your smuggling ventures, it seems, have become a substantial embarrassment to our government. Our long-standing strategy to infiltrate high level government offices and influence American policy toward China is threatened."

Qin Shang was shown to a high-backed chair carved out of ebony before a large circular table and offered a choice of Chinese wines the ambassador kept stocked in the basement of the restaurant. Only after a waiter pulled the cord to a chime to announce his entrance, poured the wine and exited the room, did Qin Shang speak. "My carefully laid plans were somehow thwarted by the INS and NUMA."

"NUMA is not an investigative agency," Qian Miang reminded him.

"No, but their people were a direct cause of the raid on Orion Lake and the disaster at the Mystic Canal. Two men in particular."

Qian Miang nodded. "I have studied the reports. Your attempt to kill NUMA's special projects director and the female INS agent was not a wise judgment, certainly one not condoned by me. This is not our homeland, where such things can be carried out in secret. You cannot run—what do they call it in the West—roughshod over citizens within their own borders. I am instructed to tell you that any attempt to murder NUMA officials is strictly forbidden."

"Whatever I have done, old friend," said Qin Shang bluntly, "I have done for the People's Republic of China."

"And Qin Shang Maritime," added Qian Miang quietly. "We go back too far to delude each other. Until now, as you have profited, so has our country. But you have gone, not one but several steps too far. Like a bear that has knocked a nest of bees from a tree, you have maddened a swarm of Americans."

Qin Shang stared at the ambassador. "Am I to assume you have instructions from President Lin Loyang?"

"He wished me to convey his regrets, but I am to tell you that from this moment, all operations by Qin Shang Maritime will cease within North America, and all your personal ties to the American government are to be terminated."

Qin Shang's normally controlled demeanor cracked. "That would spell the end of our smuggling operations."

"I think not. The government's own shipping company, China Marine, will substitute for Qin Shang Maritime in all smuggling as well as the legal transportation of Chinese goods and materials into the United States and Canada."

"China Marine is not half as efficiently run as Qin Shang Maritime."

"Perhaps so, but since Congress is demanding public investigations into Orion Lake and the debacle on the Mississippi, and the United States Justice Department is in the process of building a case for your indictment, you should consider yourself fortunate that Lin Loyang hasn't given orders to surrender yourself to the FBI. Already, the news media is calling the destruction of the levee and the ocean liner the *United States* an act of terrorism. Unfortunately, lives were lost and the coming scandal is certain to expose many of our agents around the country."

The chime announced the arrival of the waiter, who entered the private room with a tray of steaming dishes. He artfully arranged the dishes around the table and retreated.

"I took the liberty of preordering to save time," said Qian Miang. "I hope you don't mind?"

"An excellent selection. I am especially fond of tomato-and-eggdrop soup and squab soong."

"So I've been told."

Qin Shang smiled as he tasted his soup with the traditional porcelain spoon. "The soup is every bit as good as your intelligence."

"Your gourmet preferences are well known."

"I shall never be indicted," Qin Shang said abruptly and indignantly. "I have too many powerful friends in Washington. Thirty senators and congressmen are in my debt. I contributed heavily to President Wallace's campaign. He considers me a loyal friend."

"Yes, yes," Qian Miang agreed with an airy wave of his chopsticks before attacking a dish of noodles with scallions and ginger prepared in the authentic manner. "But any influence you had has been drastically diminished. Because of unfortunate events, my dear Qin Shang, you have become a political liability to the People's Republic as well as to the Americans. I'm told there is great activity in the White House to disavow any relationship with you."

"The influence our government enjoys in Washington was due in a large part to me. I bought and paid for access and favors that benefited the People's Republic."

"No one denies your contribution," said Qian Miang amicably. "But mistakes were made, disastrous mistakes that must be swept away before irreparable damage is done. You must quietly vanish from America, never to return. Qin Shang Maritime will still have access to all other ports around the world. Your power base with the People's Republic in Hong Kong remains strong. You will survive, Qin Shang, and go on adding to your incalculable assets."

"And Sungari?" asked Qin Shang, picking at the squab soong with his chopsticks as his appetite rapidly waned. "What of Sungari?"

Qian Miang shrugged. "You write it off. Most of the money for its construction was subsidized by American business interests and in part by our government. Whatever it cost you, Qin Shang, will be recouped within six months. It is hardly a reverse that will affect your empire."

"It pains me deeply to simply walk away from it."

"If you don't, the American Justice Department will see that you go to prison."

Qin Shang stared at the ambassador. "If I refused to divorce myself from all White House and congressional contacts, you're saying President Lin Loyang would turn his back to me, or perhaps even order my execution?"

"If it was in the best interests of the country, he would not blink an eye."

"Is there no way to save Sungari?"

Qian Miang shook his head. "Your plan to divert the Mississippi River through your port facility on the Gulf was brilliant, but too complex. Better you should have built it on the West Coast."

"When I originally presented the plan to Yin Tsang, he approved it," Qin Shang protested. "We agreed that there was a dire need for our government to control a shipping port on the Atlantic side of the United States; a terminal to siphon illegal immigrants and goods throughout middle America and the eastern states."

Qian Miang gazed at Qin Shang queerly. "Unfortunately, Internal Affairs Minister Yin Tsang died an untimely death."

"A great tragedy," Qin Shang said with a straight face.

"A new directive has been approved, one that places our priorities along the West Coast for the purchase of existing facilities, such as our acquisitions of the United States naval bases in Seattle and San Diego."

"The new directive?"

Qian Miang paused before answering to taste a stew called curried beef. "President Lin Loyang has given Project Pacifica his total blessing," Qian Miang answered.

"Project Pacifica? I have not been informed of it."

"Because of your recent difficulties with the Americans, all concerned thought it best if you not be involved."

"Can you tell me its purpose, or do our nation's leaders feel I am no longer worthy of their trust?"

"Not at all," replied Qian Miang. "You are still held in high esteem.

Project Pacifica is a long-range plan to split the United States into three countries."

Qin Shang looked puzzled. "Forgive me, but I find that nothing more than an outlandish fantasy."

"Not fantasy, old friend, but a certainty. Pacifica may not become a reality in our lifetimes, but with the migration over the next forty to fifty years of millions of our countrymen, respected geographic scientists are predicting a new Pacific-rim nation stretching from Alaska to San Francisco."

"The United States went to war in eighteen sixty-one to prevent the Confederacy from secession. They could easily do it again to keep their house united."

"Not if the central government was struck from two sides instead of one. What may even come earlier than Pacifica," Qian Miang explained, "is Hispania, another new nation of Spanish-speaking people that will spread from Southern California across Arizona, New Mexico and the lower half of Texas."

"I find it all but impossible to think of the United States divided into three sovereign nations," said Qin Shang.

"Look how the borders of Europe have changed in the past hundred years. The United States can no more remain united for eternity than the Roman Empire. And the beauty of Project Pacifica is that when it comes to pass, the People's Republic of China will have the power to control the entire economy of the countries surrounding the Pacific Ocean, including Taiwan and Japan."

"As a loyal citizen of my country," said Qin Shang, "I would like to think I helped in some small way to make it a reality."

"You have, my friend, you have," Qian Miang assured him. "But first, you must leave the country by no later than two o'clock this afternoon. That's when, according to my sources at the Justice Department, you will be taken into custody."

"And accused of murder?"

"No, willful destruction of federal property."

"It sounds rather mundane."

"Only the first tier of the government's case. The murder conspiracy at Orion Lake comes later. They also intend to indict you for the smuggling of illegal immigrants, guns and drugs."

"I imagine the news media must be gathering like locusts."

"Make no mistake," said Qian Miang, "the fallout will be great. But if you quietly disappear and keep a low profile while conducting business from your offices in Hong Kong, I believe we can weather the storm. Congress and the White House are not about to throw a shroud over relations between our two governments because of the acts of one man. We will, of course, deny all knowledge of your activities while our Information Ministry creates a flood of misleading information by throwing all blame on Taiwanese capitalists."

"Then I am not to be thrown to the dogs."

"You will be protected. The Justice Department and State Department will demand your extradition, but you can rest assured it will never happen, certainly not to a man of your wealth and power. You have many years of service to the People's Republic left. I speak for our countrymen when I say that we do not want to lose you."

"I am honored," Qin Shang said solemnly. "Then this is good-bye."

"Until we meet in our homeland," said Qian Miang. "By the way, how did you find the date pancakes?"

"Please tell the chef that he should use sweet rice flour instead of cornstarch."

The Boeing 737 soared through a cloudless sapphire sky and made a sweeping bank to the west as it passed over the Mississippi Delta. The pilot glanced out his side window and down at the marshlands of Plaquemines Parish. Five short minutes later, the aircraft crossed over the green-brown waters of the Mississippi River at the little town of Myrtle Grove. At the instructions of his employer, the pilot had flown in a southwesterly direction from Washington to Louisiana before turning due west on a course that would take the plane over Sungari.

Qin Shang sat in a comfortable chair in his luxurious private jet and stared through the view port as the golden pyramids of his dockside warehouses and administration buildings grew on the horizon. The afternoon sun's rays flashed off the gold galvanized walls with blinding intensity, causing the precise effect Qin Shang had demanded from his architects and construction company.

At first, he tried to put the port from his mind. It was, after all, merely an investment gone bad. But Qin Shang had poured too much of himself into the project. The finest, most modern and efficient shipping port in the world, lying desolate and seemingly abandoned, haunted him. He gazed down and saw no ships at the docks. All Qin Shang Maritime ships arriving in the Gulf from overseas had been diverted to Tampico, Mexico.

He picked up the phone to the cockpit and ordered the pilot to make a circle over the port. He pressed his face against the window as the pilot banked to give him a good view. After a few moments Qin Shang's mind began to drift, and he gazed without really seeing the empty docks, the big, deserted cargo-loading cranes and the vacant buildings. That he had come within the snap of a finger from pulling off the greatest enterprise in history and achieving what no man had ever attempted before gave him little satisfaction. He was not a man who could block failure from his mind and go on to the next project without a backward glance.

"You will be back," came the musically soothing voice of his private secretary, Su Zhong.

The beginnings of anger stirred inside Qin Shang. "Not any time soon. If I so much as step foot on American shores again, I will be thrown into one of their federal prisons."

"Nothing is forever. American governments change with every election. Politicians come and go like migrating lemmings. New ones will have no personal memories of your affairs. Time will soften all condemnation. You will see, Qin Shang."

"You are good to say so, Su Zhong."

"Do you wish me to hire a crew to maintain the facility?" she asked.

"Yes," he said with a curt nod. "When I return in ten or twenty years from now, I want to see Sungari looking exactly as it does now."

"I am worried, Qin Shang."

He looked at her. "Why?"

"I do not trust the men in Beijing. There are many who have an envious hatred of you. I fear they may use your misfortune to take advantage."

"Like an excuse to assassinate me?" he said with a thin smile.

She dropped her head, unable to gaze into his eyes. "I ask forgiveness for my unseemly thoughts."

Qin Shang rose from his chair and took Su Zhong by the hand. "Do not worry, my little swallow. I have already conceived a plan to make me indispensable to the Chinese people. I shall give them a gift that will last two thousand years." Then he led her into the spacious bedroom in the aft section of the aircraft. "Now," he said softly, "you can help me forget my ill fortune."

47

AFTER HIS MEETING with Dirk and Julia, St. Julien Perlmutter rolled up his sleeves and went to work. Once he walked the trail leading to a lost ship, he became obsessed. No lead, no rumor, no matter how seemingly insignificant, was left unexplored. Though his diligence and persistence had paid off in ferreting out any number of answers and solutions that led searchers to successful shipwreck discoveries, he failed more often than he succeeded. Most ships that vanished into thin air left no thread to follow. They were simply swallowed up by the infinite sea that very rarely gave up her secrets.

On the surface, the *Princess Dou Wan* looked to be simply another one of the many dead ends Perlmutter had experienced during his decades as a marine historian. He launched the search by scouring his own immense collection of sea lore before expanding into the many marine archives around the United States and the rest of the world.

The more impossible the project, the more he tackled it with inflexible tenacity, laboring all hours of the day or night. He began by assembling every shred of known historical information concerning the *Princess Dou Wan,* from the time her keel was laid until she went missing. He obtained and studied plans and designs of her construction, including engine specifications, equipment, dimensions and deck plans. One particularly interesting bit of data he gleaned from the records was a description of her sailing qualities. She was revealed as a very stable ship, having survived the worst storms during her time in service that the seas around Asia could throw at her.

A team of fellow researchers was hired to dig through archives in England and Southeast Asia. By using the expertise of other marine historians, he saved himself considerable time and expense.

Perlmutter sorely wished he could consult his old friend and fellow marine historian Zhu Kwan in China, but it was his understanding that Pitt wanted no revelations making their way back to Qin Shang. He did, however, contact personal friends on Taiwan for leads to still living comrades of Chiang Kai-shek who might shed some light on the missing treasure trove.

In the early hours of the morning, when most of the world was asleep, he stared into a computer monitor the size of a home-entertainment video screen and analyzed the data as it accumulated. He peered at one of the six known photographs of the *Princess Dou Wan.* She was a stately-looking ship, he thought. Her superstructure was set far aft of the bow and appeared small in relation to her hull. He studied the colored image of her, magnifying the white band in the center of the green funnel, focusing on the emblem of the Canton Lines, a golden lion with its left paw raised. Her maze of loading cranes suggested a ship that could carry a substantial cargo besides her passengers.

He also found photos of her sister ship, the *Princess Yung T'ai,* which was launched and entered service the year after the *Princess Dou Wan.* According to the records the *Princess Yung T'ai* was broken up six months before the *Princess Dou Wan* was scheduled to be scrapped.

A tired old liner doomed for the scrappers at Singapore would not have made an ideal transport to move China's national treasures to a secret location, he thought. She was beyond her time and hardly in prime condition to weather heavy seas on an extended voyage across the Pacific. It also seemed to Perlmutter that Taiwan was the more sensible destination since it was where Chiang Kai-shek eventually set up the Chinese Nationalist government. It was not conceivable the last known report of the ship had come from a naval radio operator in Valparaiso, Chile. What possible purpose could the *Princess Dou Wan* have for being over six hundred miles south of the Tropic of Capricorn in an area of the Pacific Ocean far off the traditional shipping lanes?

Even if the liner was on a clandestine mission to hide China's art treasures somewhere on the other side of the world in either Europe or Africa, why go across the vast, empty region of the South Pacific and through the Strait of Magellan when it was shorter to steer west across the Indian Ocean and around the Cape of Good Hope? Was secrecy so

441

consuming that captain and crew could not risk going through the Panama Canal, or did Chiang Kai-shek have an unknown cavern or man-made structure hidden in the Andes to conceal the immense treasure, if indeed it could be proven the ship *was* carrying China's national historic wealth?

Perlmutter was a pragmatic man. He took nothing for granted. He went back to square one and restudied the photos of the ship. As he examined her outline, a vague notion began to form in his mind. He called a nautical archivist friend in Panama, waking him from a sound sleep, and charmed him into going through the records of ships passing west to east through the Canal between November 28 and December 5, 1948.

With that lead being pursued, he began reading through a list of names of the ship's officers last known to have sailed on the *Princess*. All were Chinese except for Captain Leigh Hunt and Chief Engineer Ian Gallagher.

He felt as if he was throwing chips on every number of a roulette table. What are the odds of losing? he mused. Thirty-six out of thirty-six? But then he had to consider the zero and double zero. Perlmutter was no old fool. He covered every bet, firmly believing that if only one number paid off, he'd win.

He punched the buttons on his speakerphone and waited for a sleepy voice to answer. "Hello, this better be good."

"Hiram, it's St. Julien Perlmutter."

"Julien, why in God's name are you calling me at four in the morning?" Hiram Yaeger's voice sounded as if he was talking through a pillow.

"I'm in the middle of a research project for Dirk, and I need your help."

Yaeger became marginally alert. "Anything for Dirk, but does it have to be four in the morning?"

"The data is important, and we need it as quickly as possible."

"What do you want me to investigate?"

Perlmutter sighed with relief, knowing from experience that the NUMA computer genius had never let anyone down. "Got a pencil and paper? I'm going to give you some names."

"Then what?" asked Yaeger, yawning.

"I'd like you to hack your way through government census, IRS and Social Security records for a match. Also, check them out through your vast file of maritime records."

"You don't want much."

"And while you're at it . . ." said Perlmutter, forging onward.

"Does it never end?"

"I also have a ship for you to trace."

"So?"

"If my intuition is working, I'd like you to find what port it arrived at between November twenty-eighth and December tenth, nineteen forty-eight."

"What's her name and owner?"

"The Canton Lines' *Princess Dou Wan,*" he replied, spelling it out.

"Okay, I'll start first thing after I arrive at NUMA headquarters."

"Leave for work now," urged Perlmutter. "Time is vital."

"You sure you're doing this for Dirk?" demanded Yaeger.

"Scout's honor."

"Can I ask what this is all about?"

"You may," replied Perlmutter, and then he hung up.

Within minutes after he began his probe of Captain Leigh Hunt of the *Princess Dou Wan,* Yaeger found the old seaman mentioned in various references in maritime journals listing ships and their crews that sailed the China Sea between 1925 and 1945, in Royal Navy historical documents and old newspaper accounts describing the rescue of eighty passengers and crew from a sinking tramp steamer off the Philippines by a ship captained by Hunt in 1936. Hunt's final mention came from a Hong Kong maritime register, a short paragraph stating that the *Princess Dou Wan* had failed to arrive at the scrappers in Singapore. After 1948 it was as if Hunt had vanished from the face of the earth.

Yaeger then concentrated on Ian Gallagher, smiling when his search ran across remarks in an Australian marine engineer's journal telling of Gallagher's colorful testimony during an investigation into a shipwreck he had survived that had gone aground near Darwin. "Hong Kong" Gallagher, as he was referred to, had little good to say about his captain and fellow crewmen, blaming them for the disaster and claiming he had never seen any of them sober during the entire voyage. The final mention of the Irishman was a brief account of his service with Canton Lines, with a footnote on the disappearance of the *Princess Dou Wan.*

Then, to cover all bases, Yaeger programmed his vast computer complex to conduct a search of all worldwide records pertaining to commercial engineering officers. This would take some time, so he wandered down to the NUMA building's cafeteria and had a light breakfast. Upon his return, he worked on two other marine geological projects for the agency before finally returning to see if anything turned up on his monitor.

He stared fascinated at what he saw, not willing to accept it. For several seconds the information did not register in his brain. Now suddenly out of the blue he had a hard hit. He spread the search in several different directions. Several hours later, he finally sat back in his chair, shaking his head. Feeling supremely self-satisfied, he called Perlmutter.

"St. Julien Perlmutter here," came the familiar voice.

"Hiram Yaeger here," the computer genius mimicked.

"Did you find anything of interest?"

"Nothing you can use on Captain Hunt."

"What about his chief engineer?

"Are you sitting down?"

"Why?" Perlmutter asked cautiously.

"Ian 'Hong Kong' Gallagher did not go down on the *Princess Dou Wan.*"

"What are you saying?" demanded Perlmutter.

"Ian Gallagher became a citizen of the United States in nineteen fifty."

"Not possible. It must be another Ian Gallagher."

"It's a fact," said Yaeger, enjoying his triumph. "As we speak, I'm looking at a copy of his engineering papers, which he renewed with the Maritime Administration of the U.S. Department of Transportation shortly after he became a citizen. He then hired on for the next twenty-seven years as chief engineer with the Ingram Line out of New York. He married one Katrina Garin in nineteen forty-nine and raised five kids."

"Is he still alive?" asked a dazed Perlmutter.

"According to the records, he draws his pension and Social Security checks."

"Can it be he survived the sinking of the *Princess?*"

"Providing Gallagher was on it when she went down," replied Yaeger. "Do you still want me to see if the *Princess Dou Wan* arrived in an eastern seaboard port during the dates you gave me?"

"By all means," answered Perlmutter. "And scan the shipping-port arrival records for a ship called the *Princess Yung T'ai,* also owned by the Canton Lines."

444

"You got something going?"

"Crazy intuition," replied Perlmutter. "Nothing more."

The border of the puzzle is in place, thought Perlmutter. Now he had to fit the inside pieces. Exhaustion finally caught up with him, and he allowed himself the extravagance of a short two-hour sleep. He awoke to the sound of his phone ringing. He allowed it to ring five times while his mind came back on track before answering.

"St. Julien, Juan Mercado from Panama."

"Juan, thank you for calling. Did you turn up anything?"

"Nothing, I'm afraid, on the *Princess Dou Wan.*"

"I'm sorry to hear it. I'd hoped by chance she might have made passage through the canal."

"I did, however, find an interesting coincidence."

"Oh?"

"A Canton Lines ship, the *Princess Yung T'ai,* passed through on December first, nineteen forty-eight."

Perlmutter's fingers and hands tightened around the receiver. "What direction was her passage?"

"West to east," answered Mercado. "From the Pacific into the Caribbean."

Perlmutter said nothing, soaking up a wave of jubilation. Several pieces were still missing in the puzzle, but a visible pattern was slowly emerging. "I owe you a great debt, Juan. You've just made my day."

"Happy to have been of service," said Mercado. "But do me a favor next time, will you?"

"Anything."

"Call me during daylight hours. Any time my wife thinks I'm awake after we've gone to bed, she gets amorous."

48

WHEN PITT RETURNED to his hangar in Washington, he was pleasantly surprised to find Julia waiting in his apartment above the car collection. After a hug and a kiss, she presented him with a margarita on the rocks made the right way—without the sweet mix and crushed ice popular in most restaurants.

"You are so nice to come home to," he said happily.

"I couldn't think of a more comfortable and secure place to stay," she said, smiling seductively. She was wearing a blue leather miniskirt with a tan nylon mesh one-shoulder top.

"I can see why. The grounds outside are crawling with security guards."

"Courtesy of the INS."

"I hope they're more alert than the last group," he said, sipping the margarita and giving an approving nod.

"Did you fly in from Louisiana alone?"

Pitt nodded. "Al is in a local hospital having a cast put on his broken leg. Admiral Sandecker and Rudi Gunn came in earlier to make a report directly to the President."

"Peter Harper filled me in about your heroics on the Mississippi. You prevented a national disaster and saved countless lives. The newspapers and TV news programs are filled with stories of terrorists blowing up the levee and the battle between the *United States* and the National Guard. The whole country was rocked by the event. Strangely, there was no mention of you or Al."

"Just the way we like it." He raised his head and sniffed the air. "What's that appetizing aroma I smell?"

"My Chinese dinner for the party tonight."

"What's the occasion?"

"St. Julien Perlmutter called just before you returned and said he thinks he and Hiram Yaeger have the inside track on a solution to the disappearance of Qin Shang's treasure ship. He said he intensely dislikes meeting in government buildings, so I invited him for dinner to hear his revelations. Peter Harper is coming, and I also sent invitations to Admiral Sandecker and Rudi Gunn. I hope they can find time to come."

"They're fans of St. Julien," said Pitt, smiling. "They'll be here."

"They'd better, or you'll be eating leftovers for two weeks."

"I couldn't have had a nicer homecoming," said Pitt, embracing Julia and squeezing the breath out of her.

"Phew!" she said, wrinkling her nose. "When was the last time you bathed?"

"It's been a few days. Except for diving in swamp water I haven't had the opportunity to jump in a shower since I last saw you on the *Weehawken.*"

Julia rubbed the reddish blush on one of her cheeks. "Your beard is like sandpaper. Hurry and pretty up. Everyone will be showing up in another hour."

"Your presentation is magnificent," said Perlmutter, eyeing the array of delectable dishes Julia had prepared buffet-style and set out on an antique credenza in Pitt's dining room.

"It looks absolutely scrumptious," said Sandecker.

"I couldn't have described it better," added Gunn.

"My mother took special pains to teach me to cook, and my father was a lover of fine Chinese food prepared with a French influence," said Julia, basking in the flattery. She had changed into a red Lycra jersey tube dress and looked stunning amid the room full of five men.

"I hope you don't leave INS to open a restaurant," joked Harper.

"Not much chance of that. I have a sister who owns a restaurant in San Francisco, and it's a hard job with long hours in a small, hot kitchen. I'd rather have freedom of movement."

Helping themselves and gathering around a table built from a cabin roof off a nineteenth-century sailing ship, they dug into Julia's feast with great anticipation. She didn't disappoint them. The compliments flowed and bubbled like fine champagne.

During dinner, the talk purposely skirted Perlmutter's findings and centered instead around the events on the Mystic Canal levee and the Army Corps efforts to repair the damage. All hated the idea of the *United States* being scrapped as she lay, and expressed the hope that necessary funding would be found to save and refit her, if not for voyaging then as a floating hotel and casino, as originally proposed. Harper filled them in on the indictments being handed down against Qin Shang. Despite his influence and the reluctance of the President and some congressmen, the charges of criminal conduct rolled over any opposition.

For dessert, Julia served fried apples with syrup. After dinner was finished and Pitt had helped Julia clear the dishes and load them in the dishwasher, everyone settled in his living room filled with nautical antiques, maritime paintings and ship models. Sandecker lit up one of his big cigars without asking permission while Pitt poured them all a glass of forty-year-old port.

"Well, St. Julien," said Sandecker, "what is this great discovery Pitt tells me you made?"

"I'm also interested in hearing how you think it concerns the INS," Harper said to Pitt.

Pitt held up his port and stared at the dark liquid as if it was a crystal ball. "If St. Julien puts us on the wreck of a ship called the *Princess Dou Wan,* it will alter the relationship between the U.S. and China for decades to come."

"Forgive me if I say that sounds wildly improbable," said Harper.

Pitt grinned. "Wait, and you shall see."

Perlmutter eased his bulk into a big chair and opened his briefcase, retrieving several files. "First, a little history to enlighten those of you who don't yet know exactly what it is we're talking about." He paused to open the first file and pull out several papers. "Let me begin by saying that rumors concerning the passenger ship *Princess Dou Wan* as leaving Shanghai with a vast cargo of historical Chinese art treasures in November of nineteen-forty-eight are true."

"What was your source?" asked Sandecker.

"Name is Hui Wiay, a former Nationalist Army colonel who served under Chiang Kai-shek. Wiay now lives in Taipei. He fought the Communists until forced to flee to Taiwan when it was called Formosa. He's ninety-two years old but with a memory sharp as a razor. He

vividly recalled following orders by Generalissimo Chiang Kai-shek
to empty the museums and palaces of every art treasure they could
lay their hands on. Private collections belonging to the rich were
also seized, along with any and all wealth found in bank vaults. All
of it was packed in wooden crates and trucked to the Shanghai docks.
There it was loaded on board an old passenger liner that was commandeered by one of Chiang Kai-shek's generals, whose name was Kung
Hui. He seems to have dropped off the face of the earth the same time
as the *Princess Dou Wan,* so there is every reason to believe he was
on her.

"More treasure was seized than the ship could ordinarily hold. But
since the *Princess Dou Wan* had been stripped of her furnishings and
fixtures in preparation for her final voyage to the scrappers in Singapore, Kung Hui managed to cram over a thousand crates into the cargo
holds and empty passenger staterooms. Most of the crates with large
sculptures were tied down on the open decks. Then on November
second, nineteen forty-eight, the *Princess Dou Wan* sailed from Shanghai into oblivion."

"Vanished?" said Gunn.

"Like a midnight ghost."

"When you say historical art treasures," said Rudi Gunn, "is it
known exactly what pieces were seized?"

"The ship's manifest, if there was one," answered Perlmutter,
"would make every curator in every museum of the world mad with
envy and desire. A brief catalog would include the monumental designs
of Shang-dynasty bronze weapons and vases. From sixteen hundred
until eleven hundred B.C., Shang artists were advanced in the carving
of stone, jade, marble, bone and ivory. There were the writings of
Confucius inscribed in wood in his own hand from the Chou dynasty
that reigned from eleven hundred to two hundred B.C.; magnificent
bronze sculptures, incense burners inlaid with rubies, sapphires and
gold, life-size chariots with drivers and six horses and beautifully lacquered dishes from the Han dynasty, two-oh-six B.C. to two twenty
A.D.; exotic ceramics, books from China's classical poets and paintings
by their masters living in the T'ang dynasty, six eighteen to nine-oh-
seven A.D.; beautifully created artifacts from the Sung, Yüan, and the
famous Ming dynasty, whose artisans were masters at sculptures and
carvings. Their workmanship is widely known for the decorative arts,
including cloisonné, furniture and pottery, and of course, we're all
familiar with their famous blue- and white-porcelain."

Sandecker studied the smoke that curled from his cigar. "You make it sound more valuable than the Inca treasure Dirk found in the Sonoran Desert."

"Like comparing a cup of rubies to a carload of emeralds," Perlmutter said, sipping his port. "Impossible to set a value on such a grand hoard. Moneywise, you're talking billions of dollars, but as historical treasure, the word *priceless* becomes inadequate."

"I can't imagine riches of such magnitude," said Julia wonderingly.

"There's more," Perlmutter said quietly, adding to the spell. "The icing on the cake. What the Chinese would consider as their crown jewels."

"More precious than rubies and sapphires," said Julia, "or diamonds and pearls?"

"Something far more rare than mere baubles," Perlmutter said softly. "The bones of Peking man."

"Good lord!" Sandecker expelled a breath. "You're not suggesting that the Peking man was on the *Princess Dou Wan.*"

"I am," Perlmutter nodded. "Colonel Hui Wiay swore that an iron box containing the long-lost remains were placed on board the *Princess Dou Wan* in the captain's cabin minutes before the ship sailed."

"My father often spoke of the missing bones," said Julia. "Chinese adoration of our ancestors made them more meaningful than tombs still containing early emperors."

Sandecker sat up and gazed at Perlmutter. "The saga behind the loss of the Peking man's fossilized bones remains one of the great unexplained enigmas of the twentieth century."

"You're familiar with the story, Admiral?" asked Gunn.

"I once wrote a paper on the missing bones of Peking man at the Naval Academy. I thought they vanished in nineteen forty-one and were never found. But St. Julien is now saying they were seen seven years later on the *Princess Dou Wan* before she set sail."

"Where did they come from?" asked Harper.

Perlmutter nodded at Sandecker and deferred. "You wrote the paper, Admiral."

"*Sinanthropus pekinensis,*" Sandecker spoke the words almost reverently. "Chinese man of Peking, a very ancient and primitive human who walked upright on two feet. In nineteen twenty-nine the discovery of his skull was announced by a Canadian anatomist, Dr. Davidson Black, who directed the excavation and was funded by the Rockefeller Foundation. Over the next several years, digging in a quarry that had once been a hill with limestone caves near the village of Choukoutien, Black found thousands of chipped-stone tools and evidence of hearths, which indicated Peking man had mastered fire. Excavations carried out over the next ten years found the partial remains of another forty individuals, both juveniles and adults, and what has been acknowledged as the largest hominid fossil collection ever assembled."

"Any relation to Java man, who was found thirty years sooner?" asked Gunn.

"When the Java and Peking skulls were compared in nineteen thirty-nine, they were seen to be very similar, with Java man arriving on the scene a shade earlier and not as sophisticated in toolmaking as Peking man."

"Since scientific dating techniques didn't come into play until much later," said Harper, "is there any idea as to how old Peking man is?"

"Because he cannot be scientifically dated until he's refound, the best guess to his age is between seven hundred thousand and one million years. New discoveries in China, however, indicate that *Homo erectus,* an early species of human, is now thought to have migrated out of Africa to Asia two million years ago. Naturally, Chinese paleoanthropologists hope to prove that early man evolved in Asia and migrated to Africa instead of the accepted other way around."

"How did the remains of Peking man disappear?" Julia asked Sandecker.

"In December of nineteen forty-one, invading Japanese troops were closing in on Peking," narrated Sandecker. "Officials at the Peking Union Medical College, where the irreplaceable bones of Peking man were stored and studied, decided they should be removed to a place of safety. It was also evident, more so in China than in the West, that war between Japan and the United States was imminent. American and Chinese scientists agreed that the fossils should be sent to the United States for safekeeping until after the war. After months of negotiation, the American ambassador in Peking finally arranged shipment by a detachment of U.S. marines that was under orders to sail for the Philippines.

"The ancient bones were carefully packed in two Marine Corps footlockers and, along with the marines, were put aboard a train bound for the port city of Tientsin, where both living and dead were to board the S.S. *President Harrison,* a passenger ship belonging to the American President Lines. The train never arrived in Tientsin. It was halted by Japanese troops who ransacked it. By now it was December the eighth, nineteen forty-one, and the marines, who had thought themselves neutrals, were then sent to Japanese prison camps to sit out the war. It can only be assumed that after lying underground for a million years, the remains of Peking man were scattered around the rice paddies beside the railroad track."

"That was the last word on their fate?" Harper inquired.

Sandecker shook his head and smiled. "Myths thrived after the war. One had the fossils secretly hidden in a vault under the Museum of Natural History in Washington. The marines who guarded the shipment and survived the war came up with at least ten different stories of their own. The footlockers went down on a Japanese hospital ship that in reality was loaded with weapons and troops. The marines buried the footlockers near an American consulate. They were hidden in a prisoner-of-war camp and then lost at the end of the war. They were stored in a Swiss warehouse, in a vault on Taiwan, in the closet of a marine who smuggled them home. Whatever the true story, Peking man is still lost in a fog of controversy. And how they somehow found their way into Chiang Kai-shek's hands and onto the *Princess Dou Wan* is anybody's guess."

"All very tantalizing," said Julia, setting a pot of tea and cups on the center table for anyone who wanted some. "But what good is all this if the *Princess* can't be found?"

Pitt smiled. "Leave it to a woman to cut to the heart of the matter."

"Any details surrounding her loss?" asked Sandecker.

"On November twenty-eighth, she sent out a Mayday signal that was picked up in Valparaiso, Chile, giving her position as two hundred miles west of the South American coast in the Pacific. Her radio operator claimed a fire was raging in her engine room and she was rapidly taking on water. Ships in the general area were diverted to the location given, but the only trace that was ever found were several empty life jackets. Repeated signals from Valparaiso brought no response, and no extensive search was undertaken."

Gunn shook his head thoughtfully. "You could look for years with the Navy's latest deep-sea-penetrating technology and not find anything. A vague position like that means a search grid of at least two thousand square miles."

Pitt poured himself a cup of tea. "Was her destination known?"

Perlmutter shrugged. "None was ever given nor determined." He opened another file and passed around several photos of the *Princess Dou Wan.*

"For her time, she was a pretty ship," observed Sandecker, admiring her lines.

Pitt's eyebrows raised in speculation. He rose from his chair, walked to a desk and picked up a magnifying glass. Then he studied two of the photos closely before looking up. "These two photos," he said slowly.

"Yes," Perlmutter murmured expectantly.

"They are not of the same ship."

"You're absolutely right. One photo shows the *Princess Dou Wan*'s sister ship, the *Princess Yung T'ai.*"

Pitt stared into Perlmutter's eyes. "You're hiding something from us, you old fox."

"I have no rock-hard proof," said the big history expert, "but I do have a theory."

"We'd all like to hear it," said Sandecker.

Out came another file from the briefcase. "I strongly suspect the distress signal received in Valparaiso was a fabrication that was probably sent by Chiang Kai-shek's agents either on land or from a fishing boat somewhere offshore. The *Princess Dou Wan,* while en route across the Pacific, was given a few minor modifications by her crew, including a name change. She became the *Princess Yung T'ai,* which had been broken up at the scrappers a short time before. Under her new disguise, she then continued toward her ultimate destination."

"Very canny of you to fathom the substitution," said Sandecker.

"Not at all," Perlmutter replied modestly. "A fellow researcher in Panama discovered that the *Princess Yung T'ai* passed through the Canal only three days after the *Princess Dou Wan* sent her Mayday signal."

"Were you able to trace her course from Panama?" asked Pitt.

Perlmutter nodded. "Thanks to Hiram Yaeger, who used his vast computer complex to trace ship arrivals at ports up and down the eastern seaboard during the first and second week of December, nineteen forty-eight. Bless his little heart, he struck gold. The records show a vessel passing through the Welland Canal listed as the *Princess Yung T'ai* on December the seventh."

Sandecker's face lit up. "The Welland Canal separates Lake Erie from Lake Ontario."

"It does indeed," agreed Perlmutter.

"My God," Gunn muttered. "That means the *Princess Dou Wan* didn't disappear in the ocean but sank in one of the Great Lakes."

"Who would have thought it?" Sandecker said more to himself than the others.

"Quite a feat of seamanship to navigate a ship her size down the St. Lawrence River before the seaway was built," said Pitt.

"The Great Lakes," Gunn echoed the words slowly. "Why would Chiang Kai-shek order a ship filled with priceless art treasures to go thousands of miles out of the way? If he wanted to hide the cargo in the United States, why not San Francisco or Los Angeles as a destination?"

"Colonel Hui Wiay claimed he was not told the ship's final destination. But he did know that Chiang Kai-shek flew agents into the U.S. to arrange for the cargo to be unloaded and stored with the utmost secrecy. According to him, it was at the direction of officials at the State Department in Washington, who set up the operation."

"Not a bad plan," said Pitt. "The main port terminals along the East and West coasts were too open. The dockworkers would have known what they were unloading in a second. Word would have spread like wildfire. The Communist leaders back in China would never have suspected their national treasures were to be smuggled into America's heartland and hidden."

"Seems to me a naval base would have been the obvious choice if they wanted secrecy," suggested Harper.

"That would have taken a direct order from the White House," said Sandecker. "They were already catching flak from Communist Romania and Hungary for keeping their royal jewels in a Washington vault after the American Army found them hidden in a salt mine in Austria immediately after the war."

Pitt said, "Not a bad plan when you think about it. Communist Chinese intelligence agents would have put their money on San Francisco. They probably had agents crawling over the dock terminals around the bay, waiting for the *Princess Dou Wan* to steam under the Golden Gate Bridge, never dreaming the ship was actually headed for a port in the Great Lakes."

"Yes, but what port?" said Gunn. "And on which lake?"

They all turned to Perlmutter. "I can't give you an exact location," he said candidly, "but I do have a lead who might direct us to a ballpark location containing the wreck."

"This person has information you don't?" asked Pitt unbelievingly.

"He does."

Sandecker looked steadily at Perlmutter. "You've questioned him?"

"Not yet. I thought I'd leave that up to you."

"How can you be sure he's reliable?" asked Julia.

"Because he was an eyewitness."

Everyone stared openly at Perlmutter. Finally, Pitt asked the obvious question in their minds. "He saw the *Princess Dou Wan* go down?"

"Better yet, Ian 'Hong Kong' Gallagher was the only survivor. He was the ship's chief engineer, so if anyone can provide details of the sinking, he can. Gallagher never went back to China but remained in the States, eventually becoming a citizen and shipping out again on an American line before retiring."

"Is he still living?"

"My very same question to Yaeger," answered Perlmutter with a smile wide with teeth. "He and his wife retired to a lakefront town called Manitowoc on the Wisconsin side of Lake Michigan. I have Gallagher's address and phone number right here. If he can't point the way to the wreck, nobody can."

Pitt came over and shook Perlmutter's hand and said warmly, "You do good work, St. Julien. My congratulations on an extraordinary piece of research."

"I'll drink to that," said a happy Perlmutter, ignoring the tea and pouring another glass of the forty-year-old port.

"Now, Peter," Pitt said, focusing his eyes on Harper. "My question to you is what if Qin Shang should return to the United States?"

"Unless he goes completely insane, he would never come back."

"But if he does?"

"He'd be arrested the minute he stepped off the plane and placed in a federal prison until his trial on at least forty different charges, including mass murder."

Pitt turned back to Perlmutter. "St. Julien, you once mentioned a respected Chinese researcher you've worked with in the past who was interested in the *Princess Dou Wan.*"

"Zhu Kwan. China's most renowned historian and the author of several classic books on the different dynasties. I'll have you know I followed your instructions and did not contact him for fear he might alert Qin Shang."

"Well, now you can feed him everything you've got except Ian Gallagher. And if Gallagher puts us in the ballpark, you can give that to Zhu Kwan too."

"None of this makes sense," said Julia, puzzled. "Why give away the art treasures by leading Qin Shang to them?"

"You and Peter, the INS, FBI and the entire Justice Department want Qin Shang. And Qin Shang wants what is on board the wreck of the *Princess Dou Wan*."

"I catch your drift," said Harper. "There is method to your madness. What you're saying is that Qin Shang is obsessed and will move heaven and earth to lay his hands on the missing art treasures, even risking arrest and exposure by sneaking back into the United States."

"Why should he risk everything when he could just as well direct a salvage expedition from his headquarters in Hong Kong?" questioned Gunn.

"I'd bet the bank the wreck haunts his dreams and he wouldn't trust his mother to run the operation. I checked the shipping registry. Qin Shang Maritime owns a salvage vessel. The minute he sniffs the *Princess Dou Wan*'s location, he'll send the ship and board it from Canada when it comes down the St. Lawrence River into the Great Lakes."

"Aren't you afraid of him finding it first?" asked Julia.

"Not to fear. We won't show our hand until we've salvaged the treasure first."

"Finding it is only the first step. Salvaging the treasure will take a year, maybe more."

Sandecker looked doubtful. "You may be placing too much confidence in Gallagher to lead you to the wreck. He might have jumped ship before it vanished."

"The admiral has a point," said Gunn. "If Gallagher knew the position of the sinking, he'd have tried to salvage it himself."

"But he hasn't," Pitt said firmly, "simply because the artifacts have never surfaced. St. Julien can tell you, no one can cover up a treasure find. Whatever his reason, Gallagher has kept the location to himself or St. Julien would have found a record of his attempt."

Sandecker looked mildly through the smoke of his cigar at Pitt. "How soon can you leave for Manitowoc?"

"I have your permission to go?"

The admiral winked at Harper. "I think the INS will let NUMA carry the ball until Qin Shang puts in an appearance."

"You'll get no argument out of me, Admiral," said Harper cheerfully. He smiled at Julia. "You're due for a long rest, Julia, but I suspect you'll be happy to act as liaison between our two agencies during the search and salvage."

"If you're asking me to volunteer," she said, restraining feelings of eagerness, "the answer is an unqualified yes."

"Any hint on what kind of guy Gallagher is?" Pitt asked Perlmutter.

"He must have been tough in his early days. His nickname of 'Hong Kong' came from all the bars he wiped butt in while his ship was in port."

"Then he's no pussycat?"

Perlmutter chuckled. "No, I don't guess he is."

49

DARK CLOUDS THREATENED but no rain fell as Pitt and Julia turned off Highway 43 and took a well-graded dirt road through fruit orchards common to the shore of Lake Michigan before entering a forest of pine and birch trees. Keeping one eye on the mailboxes perched beside the road, Pitt finally spotted the one he was looking for, a box built in the shape of an old steamship and elevated by welded anchor chain. The name GALLAGHER was lettered on the hull.

"This must be the place," said Pitt as he turned into the little grassy lane leading to a picturesque two-story log house.

He and Julia had flown into Green Bay, Wisconsin, where they rented a car for the thirty-mile drive south to Manitowoc, a port for the big ships sailing the Lakes. The Gallagher residence sat on the lakefront ten miles below the port.

Perlmutter had offered to call ahead and alert the Gallaghers to their coming, but Sandecker thought it best to arrive unexpected in case the *Princess Dou Wan* was not a subject the old ship's engineer wished to discuss and conveniently found a reason not to be at home.

The front of the Gallagher house faced the trees while the rear opened onto Lake Michigan. The logs had been rough-hewn into squared beams before they were fitted together and chinked. The entire lower third of the house was mortared river rock that gave it a rustic look. The peaked roof was sheathed in copper that had patinated to a dark turquoise green. The windows were high and trimmed with vertical shutters. The exterior wood was stained a partridge brown with a tint of gray to make it blend perfectly with the surrounding forest.

Pitt stopped the car on a lawn that ran around the house and parked next to a roofed-over carport that housed a Jeep Grand Cherokee and a small, eighteen-foot cabin cruiser with a big outboard motor on the transom. He and Julia walked up the steps to a narrow front porch where Pitt raised a door knocker and rapped three times.

Suddenly, they could hear the yapping of small dogs inside. After a few moments the door was opened by a tall, older woman with long gray hair tied in a bow. Her eyes were startlingly blue and her face untouched by the advance of wrinkles. Her body had rounded during the years, but she still carried herself like a woman forty years younger. It was obvious to Julia that she had once been very beautiful. She paused to shoo a pair of short-haired dachshunds into silence.

"Hello," she said sweetly. "The skies look like they might send us some rain."

"Perhaps not," replied Pitt. "The clouds appear to be passing to the west."

"Can I help you with anything?"

"My name is Dirk Pitt and this is Julia Lee. We're looking for Mr. Ian Gallagher."

"You found him," the lady said, smiling. "I'm Mrs. Gallagher. Won't you come in?"

"Yes, thank you," said Julia, passing through the doorway as Pitt stood aside. The dachshunds ran and sat obediently on the stairway leading up to the second floor of the house. Julia stopped and gazed in mild surprise through the entryway into the rooms beyond. She had expected to see the interior of the house decorated in Early American with a sprinkling of antiques. But this house was filled with exquisitely carved Chinese furniture and art objects. The wall hangings were embroidered with silk designs. Beautifully glazed vases stood in corners with dried floral arrangements rising from them. Delicate porcelain figurines perched on high shelves. One glass-enclosed cabinet held nearly thirty jade sculptures. The carpets lying on the wooden floors were all woven with Chinese designs.

"Oh my," Julia gasped. "I feel like I've just walked into my mother and father's house in San Francisco."

Mrs. Gallagher suddenly began speaking to Julia in Mandarin Chinese. "I thought you might appreciate things from the Orient."

"May I ask if your things are very old, Mrs. Gallagher?" inquired Julia, replying in Mandarin.

"Please call me Katie. Everyone else does. It's short for Katrina." She made a hand gesture around the house. "None go back more than fifty years. My husband and I accumulated what you see since we were married. I was born and raised in China, and we met there. We still have a great affection for its culture." She invited them into the living room and then returned to speaking English for Pitt's benefit. "Please make yourself comfortable. May I get you some tea?"

"Yes, thank you," said Julia.

Pitt walked over to a rock fireplace and stared up at a painting of a ship that hung over the mantel. Without turning, he said, "The *Princess Dou Wan.*"

Mrs. Gallagher pressed both hands to her breast and let out a deep sigh. "Ian always said someone would come someday."

"Who did you think would come?"

"Someone from the government."

Pitt gave her a warm smile. "Your husband is very perceptive. I'm from the National Underwater and Marine Agency and Julia is an agent with the Immigration and Naturalization Service."

She looked at Julia sadly. "I suppose you'll be wanting to deport us because we came into the country illegally."

Pitt and Julia exchanged puzzled glances. "Why no," he said. "We're here on a completely different matter."

Julia walked over and put her arm around the taller woman. "You do not have to worry about the past," she said softly. "That was a long time ago and, according to the records, both you and your husband are solid, taxpaying citizens."

"But we did some shenanigans with the paperwork."

"The less said, the better," Julia laughed. "If you won't tell, neither will I."

Pitt looked at Katie Gallagher curiously. "You talk as if you both entered the United States at the same time."

"We did," she said, nodding at the painting. "On the *Princess Dou Wan.*"

"*You* were on the ship when she sank?" asked Pitt incredulously.

"It's a strange story."

"We'd love to hear it."

"Please sit down and I'll bring the tea." She smiled at Julia. "I think you'll enjoy the taste. I order it from Shanghai from the same store I used to buy it at sixty years ago."

A few minutes later, as she poured a dark green tea, Katie told the story about how she met Ian "Hong Kong" Gallagher when they both worked for the Canton Lines Shipping Company. She told of visiting her future husband on board the *Princess* while the ship was being stripped for the voyage to the scrappers and how hundreds of crates were delivered to the dock and loaded aboard in the dead of night.

"One of Chiang Kai-shek's generals, a man by the name of Kung Hui—"

"We're familiar with the name," Pitt interrupted her. "It was he who seized the ship and loaded it with a stolen cargo."

"All done in great secrecy," Katie agreed. "After General Hui commandeered the *Princess,* he refused to allow me and my little dog, Fritz, to go ashore. I was a virtual prisoner in Ian's cabin from then until the ship sank in a violent storm a month later. Ian knew the ship was about to break up and he made me dress in several layers of warm clothes. Then he literally dragged me to the upper boat deck, where he threw me in a life raft. General Hui joined us just before the ship floundered and we floated free."

"General Hui left the ship with you?"

"Yes, but he froze to death a few hours later. The cold was unbearable. The waves tall as houses. It was a miracle we survived."

"You and Ian were picked up?"

"No, we drifted ashore. I was within an inch of death from hypothermia, but he broke into a vacation cabin, started a fire and brought me back to life. Several days later, we made our way across the country to the house of a cousin of Ian's who lived in New York. He took us in until we could stand on our own feet. We knew we couldn't go back to China after it had been taken over by the Communists, so we decided to remain in the United States, where we were married. After obtaining the proper documents, I won't say how, Ian went back to sea while I raised our family. Most of those years we lived on Long Island, New York, but we vacationed every summer around the Great Lakes when the children were young and grew to love the west coast of Lake Michigan. When Ian retired, we built this house. It's a good life, and we enjoy boating on the lake."

"You were both very lucky people," said Julia.

Katie looked longingly at a photograph of her with their children and grandchildren taken during their last Christmas reunion. There were other photos. One of a young Ian standing on a dock in the Orient next to a tramp steamer was in a frame next to a beautiful blond Katrina holding a small dachshund under her arm. She wiped a tear that formed in one eye. "You know," she said, "every time I look at that picture I feel sad. Ian and I had to abandon the ship so quickly that I left my little dachshund Fritz behind in the cabin. The poor little thing went down with the ship."

Julia looked at the two little dogs that followed Katie everywhere, tails wagging. "It looks as if Fritz is still with you, at least in spirit."

"Do you mind if I talk to Mr. Gallagher?" asked Pitt.

"Not at all. Just go through the kitchen to the back door. You'll find him down on the boat dock."

Pitt stepped from the kitchen door onto a long porch overlooking the lake. He walked across a lawn that sloped toward the shore and ended at a small pier that jutted out about thirty feet into the lake. He found Ian "Hong Kong" Gallagher sitting on a canvas stool at the end of the pier, a fishing pole propped on a small handrail. An old, weathered slouch hat was pulled down over his eyes, and he appeared to be dozing.

The gentle movement of the pier and the sound of footsteps awakened him to Pitt's approach. "That you, Katie?" he asked in a rumbling voice.

"Afraid not," Pitt answered.

Gallagher turned, peered at the stranger a moment from under the brim of his hat, and then refaced the lake. "I thought you might be my wife." The words came with a soft Irish accent.

"Doing any good?"

The old Irishman reached down and pulled up a chain from the water with six good-sized fish dangling from it. "They're hungry today."

"What do you use for bait?"

"I've tried them all, but chicken livers and worms still work the best." Then he asked, "Do I know you?"

"No, sir. My name is Dirk Pitt. I'm with NUMA."

"I've heard of NUMA. You conducting research on the lake?"

"No, I've come to talk to 'Hong Kong' Gallagher about the *Princess Dou Wan.*"

There it was. No fireworks, no drumroll, just the plain simple fact. Gallagher sat immobile. Neither the twitch of a muscle nor the tic of an eye gave away what Pitt knew had to be a shocking surprise. Finally, Gallagher sat up stiffly on his canvas stool, pulled the hat to the back of his head and fixed Pitt with a melancholy gaze. "I always knew you'd come someday, asking questions about the *Princess.* Who'd you say you were with again, Mr. Pitt?"

"The National Underwater and Marine Agency."

"How did you track me down after all these years?"

"It's almost impossible to hide from computers nowadays."

Pitt moved closer and observed that Gallagher was a big man, weighing close to 230 pounds and every bit as tall as Pitt at six feet, three inches. His face was surprisingly smooth for an old seaman, but then most all his time at sea had been spent in the engine room where it was warm and the air heavy with the smell of oil. Only the red skin and bulbous nose gave away the effects of a love for alcohol. The stomach was round and hung over his belt but the shoulders were still strong and broad. He had kept most of his hair and let it go white along with a mustache that hid his upper lip.

The fishing pole gave a jerk, and Gallagher grabbed the grip and reeled in a nice three-pound coho salmon. "They stock the lake with trout and salmon, but I miss the old days when you could pull in a big pike or muskie."

"I talked to your wife," said Pitt. "She told me how the two of you survived the storm and the sinking."

"A bit of a wonder, that one."

"She said General Hui died on the raft."

"The scum got what he deserved," Gallagher said, smiling tightly. "You must be aware of Hui's role in the last voyage of the *Princess* or you wouldn't be here."

"I know General Hui and Chiang Kai-shek stole China's historic heritage and seized the *Princess Dou Wan* with the intention of secretly smuggling the treasure to the United States, where it was to be hidden."

"That was their plan until Mother Nature stepped in."

"It took a team of dedicated people to dig through the subterfuge," Pitt informed him. "The fake distress signal about the ship sinking off Valparaiso, salting the water with the ship's life vests, altering the *Princess Dou Wan* to pass for her sister ship the *Princess Yung T'ai* during her passage through the Panama Canal and down the St. Lawrence into the Great Lakes. The only missing piece of the puzzle was your destination."

Gallagher cocked an eyebrow. "Chicago. Hui had arranged through the American State Department to unload the treasures at the terminal facilities at the Port of Chicago. Where they were to be sent from there, I haven't the foggiest idea. But foul weather swept in from the north. As a man familiar with the oceans, I had no conception that the Great Lakes in North America could brew up worse storms than any at sea.

By God, man, since then I've seen saltwater sailors get seasick and heave their guts out during an inland-water storm."

"They say there are over fifty-five thousand recorded shipwrecks in the Great Lakes alone," said Pitt. "And Lake Michigan wins the prize for having swallowed more ships than all the other lakes combined."

"The waves on the Lakes can be deadlier than those on any ocean," Gallagher maintained. "They pile up thirty feet and come at you much faster. Ocean waves swell and roll from only one direction. Great Lakes waves are more treacherous and relentless. They seethe and gyrate like a maelstrom from every direction at once. No sir, I've seen cyclones in the Indian Ocean, typhoons in the Pacific and hurricanes in the Atlantic, but I'm telling you, there is nothing more terrible than a winter tempest on the Great Lakes. And the night the *Princess* went down was one of the worst."

"Unlike the sea, there is almost no room to maneuver a ship on the Lakes," said Pitt.

"That's a fact. A ship can run before the storm at sea. Here she must continue on course or founder." Gallagher then told of the night the *Princess Dou Wan* broke up and sank. He spoke of it as though it was a recurring dream. The fifty-two years since had not dimmed his memory of the tragedy. Every detail seemed as fresh as if it happened the day before. He told of the suffering he and Katie had endured, and how General Hui froze to death in the raft. "After we came ashore, I pushed the raft with Hui still in it back into the raging waters of the lake. I never saw him again and often wondered if his body was found."

"Can I ask you where the ship foundered? In which Great Lake?"

Gallagher hooked the fish through the gill on the chain and dropped it in the water beside the pier before answering. Then he raised his hand and pointed toward the east. "Right out there."

At first Pitt didn't get it. He thought Gallagher was referring to any one of the four Great Lakes that lay to the east. Then it hit him. "Lake Michigan? The *Princess Dou Wan* sank here in Lake Michigan, not far from where we stand?"

"I'd guess about twenty-five miles slightly south of east from here."

Pitt was elated and numb at the same time. This revelation was too good to be true: The wreck of the *Princess Dou Wan* and its priceless treasure were lying only twenty-five miles away. He turned and stared at Gallagher. "You and Mrs. Gallagher must have been cast ashore nearby."

"Not close by," Gallagher said, smiling. "This exact spot where the pier sits. We tried for years to buy this property for sentimental reasons, but the owners wouldn't sell. Only after they died did their kids let us have it. We tore down the old cabin they used for family vacations on the lake, the same cabin that saved Katie and me from freezin' to death. It was in poor shape, so we tore it down and built the house you see. We figured we was given a second chance in life and it would be a good idea to spend our remaining years at the very spot we were reborn."

"Why didn't you look for the wreck and salvage the artifacts yourself?"

Gallagher gave a short laugh and slowly shook his head. "What good would it do? The Communists still run China. They would claim it as theirs. I'd be lucky to keep a nail out of one of them packing crates they rest in."

"You might have filed a claim for yourself and become a very rich man."

"The Communists wouldn't be the only vultures to come gatherin' around. The minute I'd begin pulling up them antiques, the bureaucrats from the states of Wisconsin, Michigan and the federal government would have come down all over me. I'd have ended up spending more time in court than salvaging the wreck and paying attorneys more than I'd make out of it."

"You're probably right," said Pitt.

"You bet I'm right," snorted Gallagher. "I did a bit of treasure-hunting myself when I was young. It never paid off. You make a strike and, besides having to fight the government, other treasure hunters appear like locusts to rape your wreck. No, Mr. Pitt, my family was my riches. I figured, leave well enough alone. The treasure ain't goin' anywhere. When the proper time comes, I always thought, somebody will salvage it for the good of the people. In the meantime, I've been perfectly content without it."

"There aren't many men who think like you do, Mr. Gallagher," said Pitt with respect.

"Son, when you're as old as I am, you see there are a lot more things in life than owning a fancy yacht and a jet plane."

Pitt smiled at the old man on the canvas stool. "Mr. Gallagher, I like your style."

Ian cleaned his catch of fish, and Katie insisted Dirk and Julia stay for dinner. They also offered to put them up for the night, but Pitt was anxious to return to Manitowoc, find a place to use as a headquarters for the search-and-salvage project, and call Sandecker with the news. During dinner, the two women happily chatted away in Mandarin Chinese while the men swapped sea stories.

"Was Captain Hunt a good man?"

"No better seaman ever trod a deck." Gallagher stared sadly through the window out onto the lake. "He's still out there. He went down with the ship. I saw him standin' in the wheelhouse as calm as if he was waitin' for a table at a restaurant." He turned back to Pitt. "I hear the cold fresh water preserves things, unlike salt water and sea creatures that eat bodies and ships until there's nothing left."

Pitt nodded. "Not long ago, divers brought up an automobile from a car ferry that had been on the bottom of this same lake for nearly seventy years. The upholstery was still sound, the tires still held air, and after drying out the engine and carburetor, and changing the oil, they charged the original battery and started the car. It was then driven to an auto museum in Detroit."

"Then the Chinese treasures should be in good shape."

"Most of it, I should imagine, especially the bronze and porcelain artworks."

"Wouldn't that be a sight," Gallagher said wistfully, "seeing all them antiques lying there on the bottom of the lake." Then he shook his head and rubbed eyes that were beginning to moisten. "But it would tear my heart out to look at the poor old *Princess.*"

"Perhaps," said Pitt, "but she found a more noble death than if she was torn apart by the scrappers in Singapore."

"You're right," Gallagher said solemnly. "She did find a noble death."

50

IN THE MORNING Pitt and Julia bade the Gallaghers a fond good-bye and checked into an attractive bed and breakfast in Manitowoc. While she unpacked, Pitt called Sandecker and filled him in on their meeting with the Gallaghers.

"You mean to tell me," Sandecker said in amazement, "that one of the world's greatest treasures has been sitting under everyone's nose for the past half century, and Gallagher told no one?"

"The Gallaghers are your kind of people, Admiral. Unlike Qin Shang, they were never driven by greed. They felt it was best not to disturb the wreck until the proper time."

"They should receive a fat reward as a finders' fee."

"A grateful government may make the offer, but I doubt if they'll accept it."

"Incredible," said Sandecker quietly. "The Gallaghers have restored my faith in the human race."

"Now that we have a ballpark, we're going to require a proper search-and-survey vessel."

"I'm way ahead of you," Sandecker said smoothly. "Rudi has already hired a fully equipped search boat. The crew is on its way to Manitowoc from Kenosha. The boat's name is *Divercity*. Because we have a requirement for secrecy to consider, I felt you'd attract less attention with a smaller vessel. Not wise to advertise a hunt for a treasure of inestimable value. If word leaked, a thousand treasure seekers would flood onto Lake Michigan like a school of piranha in a pond stocked with catfish."

"A phenomenon that takes place with every treasure find," Pitt concurred.

"And in the hope and anticipation that you'll make a successful discovery, I've also ordered the *Ocean Retriever* off a project on the Maine coast and directed her to Lake Michigan."

"The perfect choice. She's ideally equipped for intricate salvage work."

"She should arrive on site and be in position over the wreck within four days."

"You planned and arranged all this before you knew if Gallagher could lead us to the wreck?" Pitt asked incredulously.

"Again, anticipation."

Pitt's admiration of Sandecker never ceased. "You're a tough man to keep up with, Admiral."

"I always hedge my bets."

"I can see that."

"Good luck, and let me know how it goes."

With Julia in tow, Pitt spent the day talking to local divers about water conditions and studying charts of the lake bed in the general location of the *Princess Dou Wan.* The following morning at the crack of dawn, they parked the car at Manitowoc's yacht basin and walked along the dock until they found the *Divercity* and her crew waiting for them.

The boat, a twenty-five-foot Parker with a cabin, was powered by a 250 Yamaha outboard. Functional and electronically well equipped with a NavStar differential global-positioning system interfaced with a 486 computer and Geometerics 866 marine magnetometer, the *Divercity* also mounted a Klein side-scan sonar that would play a key role in seeking out the remains of the *Princess Dou Wan.* For a close-up identification, the boat carried a Benthos MiniRover MK II underwater robotic vehicle.

The experienced crew consisted of Ralph Wilbanks, a big, jolly man in his early forties with expansive brown eyes and a bristling mustache; and his partner, Wes Hall, easygoing, soft-spoken and smoothly handsome, who could have doubled for Mel Gibson.

Wilbanks and Hall greeted Pitt and Julia warmly and introduced themselves. "We didn't expect you this early," said Hall.

"Up with the birds, that's us," Pitt said, nodding humorously. "How was your trip from Kenosha?"

"Calm water all the way," answered Wilbanks.

Both men spoke in a soft Southern accent. Pitt liked them almost immediately. He didn't need a drawing to see they were a professional, job-dedicated pair. They watched amused as Julia jumped from the dock, landing on the deck with the finesse of a limber cat. She was dressed in jeans and a sweater under a nylon windbreaker.

"She's a fine, no-nonsense boat," said Pitt, admiring the *Divercity*.

Wilbanks nodded in agreement. "She does the job." He turned to Julia. "I hope you don't mind roughing it, ma'am. We're not equipped with a head."

"Don't worry about me," Julia said, smiling. "I've got an iron bladder."

Pitt looked across the water of the little harbor at the seemingly endless lake. "Light breeze, one- to two-foot waves, conditions look good. Are we ready to cast off?"

Hall nodded and unwound the mooring lines from the dock's cleats. Just as he was about to climb on board, he pointed down the dock at a figure awkwardly approaching and waving wildly. "Is he with you?"

Pitt found himself staring at Al Giordino, who was stomping across the wooden planks on a pair of crutches, his wounded leg encased in a plaster cast from ankle to crotch. Giordino flashed his celebrated smile and said, "A pox on your house for thinking you could leave me onshore while you got all the glory."

Happy to see his old friend, Pitt said, "You can't say I didn't try."

Wilbanks and Hall gently lifted Giordino over the side and sat him on a long cushion that lay on a raised hump in the middle of the boat. Pitt introduced him to the crew as Julia fussed over him and pressed a cup of coffee in his hand from a thermos she carried in a picnic basket.

"Shouldn't you be in a hospital?" she asked.

"I hate hospitals," Giordino grumbled. "Too many people die in them."

"Is everyone aboard who's coming aboard?" Wilbanks inquired.

"All present and accounted for," replied Pitt.

Wilbanks grinned and said, "Then let's do it."

As soon as they cleared the harbor, Wilbanks pushed the throttle forward and the *Divercity* leaped ahead, bow clear of the water, until she was skimming the waves at nearly thirty miles an hour. While Julia and Giordino sat aft, enjoying the view and the beginning of a spectacular day under a sky decorated with clouds drifting overhead like a grazing herd of white buffalo, Pitt gave Wilbanks his chart with an X marked twenty-five miles just south of east from the Gallagher's house. He had enclosed the X within a five-mile-by-five-mile search grid. Wilbanks then programmed the coordinates into the computer and watched as the numbers came up on the monitor. Hall busied himself studying the photos and dimensions of the *Princess Dou Wan.*

It seemed hardly any time had passed before Wilbanks slowed the boat and announced, "Coming up on lane one in eight hundred meters." He used the metric system, since the equipment was set up for it.

Pitt helped Hall drop over the magnetometer sensor and the side-scan sonar towfish, trailing them behind the stern of the boat on tethered cables. After tying off the cables, they returned to the cabin.

Wilbanks steered the boat toward the end of a line displayed on the monitor that led to a search grid with parallel lanes. "Four hundred meters to go."

"I feel like I'm taking part in an adventure," said Julia.

"You're going to be sadly disappointed," Pitt laughed. "Running search lanes for a shipwreck is downright tedious. You might compare it to mowing grass on an endless lawn. You can go hours, weeks or even months without finding so much as an old tire."

Pitt took over the magnetometer duties as Hall set up the Klein & Associates Systems 2000 sonar. He sat on a stool in front of the high-resolution color video display unit that was mounted in the same console as a thermal printer that recorded the floor of the lake in 256 shades of gray.

"Three hundred meters," Wilbanks droned.

"What range are we set for?" Pitt asked Hall.

"Since we're hunting for a large target five hundred feet in length, we'll run thousand-meter lanes." He pointed to the lake-bed detail that was beginning to unreel from the printer. "The bottom looks flat and undisturbed, and since we're operating in fresh water, we should have no problem spotting an anomaly that fits the target's dimensions."

"Speed?"

"The water's pretty calm. I think we can run at ten miles an hour and still get a sharp recording."

"Can I watch?" asked Julia from the cabin doorway.

"Be my guest," said Hall, making room for her in the cramped quarters.

"The detail is amazing," she said, staring at the image from the printer. "You can clearly see ripples in the sand."

"The resolution is good," Hall lectured her, "but nowhere near the definition of a photograph. The sonar image translates similar to a photo that's been duplicated and then run through a copy machine three or four times."

Pitt and Hall exchanged grins. Observers always became addicted to watching the sonar data. Julia would be no different. They knew that she would gaze entranced for hours, enthusiastically waiting for the image of a ship to materialize.

"Starting lane one," Wilbanks proclaimed.

"What's our depth, Ralph?" Pitt asked.

Wilbanks glanced up at his depth sounder, which hung from the roof on one side of the helm. "About four hundred ten feet."

An old hand at search-and-survey, Giordino shouted from his comfortable position on the cushion where he lay with his cast propped up on a railing. "I'm going to take a siesta. Yell out if you spot anything."

The hours passed slowly as the *Divercity* plowed through the low waves at ten miles an hour mowing the lawn, the magnetometer ticking away, the recording line trailing down the center of the graph paper until swinging off to the sides when it detected the presence of iron. In unison, the side-scan sonar emitted a soft clack as the thermal plastic film unreeled from the printer. It revealed a lake bed cold and desolate and free of human debris.

"It's a desert down there," said Julia, rubbing tired eyes.

"No place to build your dream house," said Hall with a little grin.

"That finishes lane twenty-two," Wilbanks broadcast. "Coming around on lane twenty-three."

Julia looked at her watch. "Lunchtime," she announced, opening the picnic basket she had packed at the bed and breakfast. "Anybody besides me hungry?"

"I'm always hungry," Giordino called out from the back of the boat.

"Amazing." Pitt shook his head incredulously. "At twelve feet away, outside in a breeze with the roar of the outboard motor, he can still hear the mere mention of food."

"What delicacies have you prepared?" Giordino asked Julia, having dragged himself to the cabin doorway.

"Apples, granola bars, carrots and herbal ice tea. You have your choice between hummus and avocado sandwiches. It's what I call a healthy lunch."

Every man on the boat looked at each of the others with utter horror. She couldn't have received a more unpalatable reaction if she had said she was volunteering their services as diaper changers at a day-care center. Out of deference to Julia none of the men said anything negative, since she went to the bother of fixing lunch. The fact that she was a woman and their mothers had raised them all as gentlemen added to the dilemma. Giordino, however, did not come from the old school. He complained vociferously.

"Hummus and avocado sandwiches," he said disgustedly. "I'm going to throw myself off the boat and swim to the nearest Burger King—"

"I have a reading on the mag!" Pitt interrupted. "Anything on the sonar?"

"My sonar towfish is trailing farther astern than your mag sensor," said Hall, "so my reading will lag behind yours."

Julia leaned closer to the sonar's printer in anticipation of seeing an object appear from the printer. Slowly, the image of a hard target began to move across the video display and the printer simultaneously.

"A ship!" Julia shouted excitedly. "It's a ship!"

"But not the one we're after," Pitt said flatly. "She's an old sailing ship sitting straight up off the bottom."

Wilbanks leaned around the others to peer at the sunken ship. "Look at that detail. The cabins, the hatch covers, the bowsprit, they all show clearly."

"Her masts are gone," observed Hall.

"Probably swept away by the same storm that sank her," said Pitt.

The ship had passed behind the range of the towfish now, but Hall recalled its image on the video screen before zooming in, freezing the target, and comparing synchronous magnifications. "Good size," Hall said, studying the image. "At least a hundred and fifty feet."

"I can't help wondering about her crew," said Julia. "I hope they were saved."

"Since she's relatively intact," said Wilbanks, "she must have gone down pretty fast."

The moment of fascination quickly passed, and the search for the *Princess Dou Wan* continued. The breeze had slowly veered from north to west and dropped until it barely fluttered the flag on the stern of the boat. An ore ship passed a few hundred yards away and rocked the *Divercity* in its wake. At four o'clock in the afternoon, Wilbanks turned and looked at Pitt.

"We've got two hours of daylight left. What time do you want to pack it in and head back to the dock?"

"You never know when the lake will turn ugly," Pitt answered. "I suggest we keep going and finish as much of the grid as we can while the water is calm."

"Gotta make hay while the sun shines," Hall agreed.

The mood of anticipation had not diminished. Pitt had requested that Wilbanks begin the search through the center of the grid and work east. That half had been completed, and now they were working west with over thirty lanes to go. The sun was lingering over the western shore of the lake when Pitt called out again.

"A target on the mag," he said with a tinge of excitement in his voice. "A big one."

"Here she comes," said Julia, electrified.

"We've got a modern steel ship," Hall acknowledged.

"How big?" asked Wilbanks.

"Can't tell. She's still showing on the edge of the screen."

"She's huge," Julia muttered in awe.

Pitt grinned like a gambler who hit a jackpot. "I think we've got her." He checked his X on the chart. The wreck was three miles closer inshore than Gallagher had estimated. Actually, an incredibly close guess, all things considered, Pitt thought.

"She's broken in two," Hall said, pointing at the blue-black image on the video screen as everyone, including Giordino, pushed in for a closer look. "About two hundred feet of her stern lies a good hundred and fifty feet away with a large debris field in between."

"The forward section looks to be sitting upright," added Pitt.

"Do you really think it's the *Princess Dou Wan?*" asked Julia.

"We'll know for certain after we get the ROV down on her." He stared at Wilbanks. "Do you want to wait until tomorrow?"

"We're here, ain't we?" Wilbanks retorted with a smile. "Anybody have any objections against working at night?"

No one objected. Pitt and Hall quickly retrieved the sonar towfish and magnetometer sensor, and soon they had the Benthos MiniRover MK II robotic vehicle tethered up to the control handbox and a video monitor. At seventy-five pounds, it only took two of the men to lift it over the side and lower it into the water. The bright halogen underwater lights of the ROV slowly vanished in the deep as she began her journey downward into the dark void of Lake Michigan. She was attached to the *Divercity* and the control console by an umbilical cable. Wilbanks aimed an eye on the computer screen of the global positioning system and adroitly kept the *Divercity* floating motionless above the wreck.

The descent to four hundred feet took only a few minutes. All light from the setting sun vanished at 360 feet. Hall stopped the MiniRover when the bottom came into sight. It looked like a lumpy blanket of gray silt.

"The depth here is four hundred thirty feet," he said as he swung the ROV in a tight circle. Suddenly, the lights illuminated a large shaft that looked like a giant tentacle reaching out from a sea monster.

"What in hell is that?" muttered Wilbanks, turning from his computer positioning screen.

"Move toward it," Pitt ordered Hall. "I think we've come down on the forward cargo section of the hull, and we're looking at the overhead boom of a loading crane on the forward deck."

Working the controls of the MiniRover's handbox, Hall slowly sent the ROV along one side of the crane until the camera revealed a clear video image of a hull belonging to a large ship. He worked the ROV along the sides of the hull toward the bow, which still stood perfectly upright, as if the ship had refused to die and still dreamed of sailing the seas. Soon the outline of the ship's name became visible. It looked to have been painted crudely on the raised white gunwale atop the black bow slightly aft of the anchor, which still fit snug in its hawsehole. One by one the letters slid past the screen.

A doctor will tell you that if your heart stops, you're dead. But it seemed everyone's heart paused for several seconds as the name of the sunken ship passed under the MiniRover's cameras.

"*Princess Yung T'ai,*" Giordino shouted. "We got her!"

"The queen of the China Sea," Julia murmured as if she was in a trance. "She looks so cold and isolated. It's almost as if she was praying we'd come."

"I thought you wanted a ship called the *Princess Dou Wan,*" said Wilbanks.

"It's a long story," Pitt replied with a big grin, "but they're one and the same." He laid one hand on Hall's shoulder. "Move aft, keeping at least ten feet from the side of the ship so we don't entangle our tether and lose the ROV."

Hall silently nodded and worked the little joysticks on the handbox that controlled the camera and vehicle movement. Visibility was nearly fifty feet under the vehicle's halogen lights and showed that the exterior of the *Princess Dou Wan* had changed very little after fifty-two years. The frigid fresh water and deep depth had inhibited marine growth and corrosion.

The superstructure came into view, looking surprisingly fresh. None of it had collapsed. Only a light coat of silt adhered to the paint, which had dulled somewhat but still appeared surprisingly fresh. The *Princess Dou Wan* looked like the interior of a haunted, abandoned house that had not been dusted for half a century.

Hall maneuvered the MiniRover around the bridge. Most of the windows had been smashed from the force of the waves and the pressure of the deep. They could see the engine-room telegraph standing inside, its pointer still set on FULL AHEAD. Only a few fish lived in her now. The crew was no more, most all swept away by frenzied waves when she went down. The MiniRover crept alongside the ship on a horizontal course a short distance from the main promenade deck. The lifeboat davits were empty and twisted out, grim evidence of the chaos and terror that occurred that violent night in 1948. Wooden crates, still intact, were lashed down on every square foot of open deck. Her funnel was missing aft of the bridge, but could be seen where it had fallen beside the hull when the ship drove herself into the soft bottom.

"I'd give anything to see what's inside those packing boxes," said Julia.

"Maybe we'll find one that's broken open," said Pitt without taking his eyes off the screen.

The hull aft of the superstructure had been ruptured and spread open, the steel twisted and jagged from when she had broken up from the battering of the giant waves. The stern section was completely torn away when the ship plunged under the water. It was as if a giant had squeezed the ship apart and then tossed her broken pieces aside.

"Looks like mementos from the ship are scattered in a debris field that leads from one part of the wreck to the other," observed Giordino.

"Can't be," said Pitt. "Every nonessential piece was stripped off before she was to go to the scrappers. At the risk of sounding like an irrepressible optimist, I'm betting we're looking at an acre or more of fabulous works of art."

On closer inspection the cameras on the MiniRover revealed a sea of wooden crates that had been spilled between the broken sections of the ship when she sank. Pitt's prediction was confirmed when the ROV soared over the debris field and homed in on a strange shape materializing out of the murk. They all stared astonished as a poignant artifact from the distant past slowly rose and met the camera lens. The walls of a large crate had burst open like petals of a rose, exposing a strange shape standing in eerie solitude.

"What is it?" queried Wilbanks.

"A bronze life-size horse and rider," Pitt muttered in awe. "I'm not enough of an expert, but it must be the sculpture of an ancient Chinese emperor from the Han dynasty."

"How old do you reckon it is?" asked Hall.

"Close to two thousand years."

The effect of the horse and rider standing proud on the bottom was so profound, they all gazed solemnly at its image on the screen for the next two minutes without speaking. To Julia it was as if she had been carried back in time. The horse's head was turned slightly in the direction of the MiniRover, its nostrils flared. The rider sat stiffly upright, his sightless eyes staring into nothingness.

"The treasure," whispered Julia. "It's everywhere."

"Steer toward the stern," Pitt said to Hall.

"I've got the tether at its maximum length now," Hall replied. "Ralph will have to move the boat."

Wilbanks nodded, measured the distance and direction on the computer, and moved the *Divercity,* dragging the MiniRover until it was sitting atop the detached stern section. Then Hall deftly steered the ROV past the ship's propellers, whose upper blades rose from the silt. The huge rudder was still set on a direct course ahead. The lettering across the stern could be distinctly seen to identify the vessel's home port as Shanghai. The story was the same—the bent and shredded hull plates, the disemboweled engines, the scattered art treasures.

Midnight came and went as the first humans to lay eyes on the *Princess Dou Wan* in fifty-two years studied the two broken hulks and their priceless cargo from every angle. When they finally decided that there was no more to see, Hall began reeling in the MiniRover.

No one tore his gaze away from the screen until long after the MiniRover ascended toward the surface and the *Princess Dou Wan* was lost to view in the black void. The ship was once again alone on the bottom of the lake, her only companion an unknown sailing ship that rested only a mile away. But the solitude was temporary. Soon men, ships and equipment would be probing her bones and removing the precious cargo she had carried so far across the world and jealously guarded through the years since she steamed from Shanghai.

The ill-fated voyage of the *Princess Dou Wan* had not ended, not quite yet. Her epilogue was still to be written.

51

HISTORIAN ZHU KWAN sat at a desk on a stage in the middle of a huge office and studied reports gathered by an international army of researchers hired by Qin Shang. The *Princess Dou Wan* project took up half of one floor in the Qin Shang Maritime office building in Hong Kong. No expense was spared. And yet, despite the massive effort, nothing of substance had been found. To Zhu Kwan, the loss of the ship remained a mystery.

Zhu Kwan and his team scouted every maritime source for leads while Qin Shang's survey-and-salvage ship kept up its search of the waters off the coast of Chile for the elusive passenger liner. Built in his Hong Kong shipyard, the vessel was a marvel of undersea technology and the envy of every maritime nation's oceanographic science and research institutions. Named the *Jade Adventurer* rather than a Chinese name to make documentation simpler when operating in foreign waters, the ship and its crew had previously discovered the wreck of a sixteenth-century junk in the China Sea and salvaged its cargo of Ming-dynasty porcelain.

Zhu Kwan examined a description of works of art from a private collection of Chinese art owned by a wealthy merchant in Peking that had disappeared in 1948. The merchant had been murdered, and Zhu Kwan had tracked down his heirs in what turned out to be a successful hunt for an inventory of the lost art. He was studying a drawing of a rare wine vessel when his assistant's voice came over the speakerphone.

"Sir, you have a call from the United States. A Mr. St. Julien Perlmutter."

Zhu Kwan laid aside the drawing. "Please put him on."

"Hello, Zhu Kwan, are you there?" came the jovial voice of Perlmutter.

"St. Julien. What an unexpected surprise. I am honored to hear from my old friend and colleague."

"You'll be more than honored when you hear what I have to tell you."

The Chinese historian was bewildered. "I am always happy to hear of your archival discoveries."

"Tell me, Zhu Kwan, are you still interested in finding a ship called the *Princess Dou Wan?*"

Zhu Kwan sucked in his breath, a fear rising inside him. "You are also searching for her?"

"Oh, no, no, no," Perlmutter said carelessly. "I have no interest in the ship whatsoever. But while researching another lost ship, a missing Great Lakes car ferry, I ran across a document by a ship's engineer, since deceased, that told of a harrowing experience while he served on board the *Princess Dou Wan.*"

"You found a survivor?" asked Zhu Kwan, unable to believe his luck.

"His name is Ian Gallagher. His friends called him 'Hong Kong.' He was the chief engineer on the *Princess* when she went down."

"Yes, yes, I have a file on him."

"Gallagher was the only survivor. He never went back to China for obvious reasons and dropped out of sight in the United States."

"The *Princess,*" gasped Zhu Kwan, unable to contain his growing expectation. "Did Gallagher give an approximate position off Chile where the ship sank?"

"Brace yourself, my Oriental friend," said Perlmutter. "The *Princess Dou Wan* did not go to the bottom of the South Pacific."

"But her final distress call?" muttered a confused Zhu Kwan.

"She lies under Lake Michigan in North America."

"Impossible!" Zhu Kwan gasped.

"Believe me, it's true. The distress signal was a fake. The captain and crew, under the direction of a General Kung Hui, altered the name to that of her sister ship, the *Princess Yung T'ai.* Then they sailed through the Panama Canal up the East Coast of the United States and down the St. Lawrence River into the Great Lakes. She was overtaken by a horrendous storm and went down two hundred miles north of Chicago, her ultimate destination."

"This is incredible. Are you sure of your facts?"

"I'll fax you Gallagher's report of the voyage and sinking."

A sick feeling began to spread in the pit of Zhu Kwan's stomach. "Did Gallagher make mention of the ship's cargo?"

"He made only one reference," replied Perlmutter. "Gallagher said that General Hui told him the numerous wooden cases and crates loaded on board in Shanghai were filled with personal furnishings and clothes of high-ranking Nationalist Chinese officials and military leaders who were fleeing mainland China ahead of the Communists."

A wave of great relief settled over Zhu Kwan. The secret appeared safe. "Then it seems the rumors of a great treasure are not true. There was no cargo of great value on board the *Princess Dou Wan.*"

"Perhaps some jewelry, but certainly nothing that would excite a professional salvage hunter. The only artifacts that will ever be retrieved will probably surface in the hands of local sport divers."

"Have you given out this information to anyone besides me?" asked Zhu Kwan warily.

"Not a soul," Perlmutter answered. "You're the only one I know who had any interest in the wreck."

"I would be grateful to you, St. Julien, if you did not reveal your discovery. At least not for the next few months."

"From this moment on, I promise not to disclose a word."

"Also, as a personal favor—"

"You have but to name it."

"Please do not fax Gallagher's report. I think it would be better if you sent it by private courier. I will, of course, take care of any expense."

"Whatever you wish," said Perlmutter agreeably. "I'll hire the services of a courier the minute I lay down the phone."

"Thank you, my friend," Zhu Kwan said sincerely. "You have done me a great service. Though the *Princess Dou Wan* is of no great historical or economic value, it has been a mosquito in my ear for many years."

"Believe me, I've been there. Some lost shipwrecks, no matter how insignificant, captivate and consume a researcher's imagination. They're never forgotten until answers behind their disappearance are finally found."

"Thank you, St. Julien, thank you."

"My best wishes to you Zhu Kwan. Good-bye."

The Chinese historian could not believe his luck. What had seemed

479

an impossible enigma only minutes ago had suddenly been solved and dropped in his lap. Though exhilarated, he decided to put off informing Qin Shang until the courier arrived with Ian Gallagher's narrative of the final moments of the *Princess Dou Wan* and he had an hour or two to study it.

Qin Shang would be highly pleased to learn that the fabulous art treasure stolen from the country had been lying safe and preserved in the fresh water of a lake all these years and was now within reach. Zhu Kwan fervently hoped that he would live long enough to see the artifacts on display in a national gallery and museum.

"You do nice work, St. Julien," said Sandecker as Perlmutter put down the phone. "You missed your calling as a used-car salesman."

"Or a politician running for election," Giordino muttered.

"I feel like a low-down skunk, misleading that nice old man," said Perlmutter. He paused and looked around Sandecker's office at the four NUMA men seated around him. "Zhu Kwan and I go back many years. We've always had the highest respect for each other. I hated lying to him."

"Fair is fair," said Pitt. "He conned you, too. All this time he's claimed his only interest in the *Princess Dou Wan* was strictly academic. He knows damned well the ship sank with a fantastic fortune in art on board. A fax line can be eavesdropped on. Why else would he insist you send Gallagher's story by courier? You can bet he's itching to give the news to Qin Shang."

Perlmutter shook his head. "Zhu Kwan is a hard-nosed scholar. He won't make any announcement to his boss until he's analyzed the document." He looked into the other faces one by one. "Out of curiosity, *who* did write the report I'm sending him?"

Rudi Gunn raised his hand almost sheepishly. "I volunteered for the chore. And a rather good job, if I may say so. Naturally, I took writer's liberty with the text. A footnote makes mention of Ian Gallagher's death from a heart attack in nineteen ninety-two. So he and Katie's tracks are covered."

Sandecker looked at his special projects director. "Will we have enough time to properly bring up the art treasures before Qin Shang's salvage ship arrives?"

Pitt shrugged. "Not if the *Ocean Retriever* is the only ship working the wreck."

"Not to worry," said Gunn. "We've already chartered two more salvage vessels. One is from a private company in Montreal and the other is on loan from the U.S. Navy."

"Speed is essential," said Sandecker. "I want the treasure raised before word leaks out. I want no interference from any quarter, including our own government."

"And when the salvage work is completed?" inquired Perlmutter.

"Then the artifacts will be quickly turned over to facilities equipped to preserve them from damage after so many years of immersion. At that time we'll announce the discovery and stand back while the bureaucrats from Washington and Beijing fight over it."

"And Qin Shang?" Perlmutter probed deeper. "What happens when he shows up on site with his own salvage ship?"

Pitt grinned deviously. "We'll give him a reception fitting for a man of his sterling qualities."

52

THE *OCEAN RETRIEVER,* with Pitt, Giordino, Gunn and Julia on board, was the first to arrive and position herself over the wreck of the *Princess Dou Wan.* The Canadian salvage ship from Deep Abyss Systems Limited out of Montreal, *Hudson Bay,* arrived only four hours later. She was an older vessel converted from a powerful oceangoing salvage and tugboat. Aided by clear weather and smooth water, the salvage of the art treasures commenced immediately.

The underwater part of the project was handled by submersibles using articulated arms in cooperation with divers encased in deep-water atmospheric diving systems called Newtsuits that were similar in appearance to the Michelin tire man. Bulbous, constructed of fiberglass and magnesium, and self-propelled, the suit enabled a diver inside to work for long periods of time at the four-hundred-foot-plus depth without concern over decompression.

The artifacts were beginning to come up systematically and with rapid regularity once a routine was established. The operation continued at an even more rapid pace when the U.S. Navy salvage vessel *Dean Hawes* came charging down from the north end of the lake two days earlier than expected and took up station beside the other two ships. She was considered new, only two years from her launch date, and was constructed especially for deep-water work, the recovery of submarines in particular.

An immense open barge with long ballast tanks attached along its hull was parked in place by use of the global positioning system and sunk, falling to the lake bed a short distance from the forward section of the *Princess Dou Wan.* Then crane operators, working from the ships on the surface and employing underwater cameras, manipulated the clamshell claws on the end of their winch cables, deftly recovering the crates exposed on the outer decks of the ship, those deep inside the cargo holds and the artifacts littering the bottom between the two sections of the broken hull. The crates, together with their contents, were then lifted onto the sunken barge. When it was fully loaded, the ballast tanks were filled with pressurized air and the barge rose to the surface. A tugboat then took it in tow for the trip to the Port of Chicago, where it was met by a team of NUMA archaeologists who took charge of the art treasures. They very carefully removed them from the waterlogged packing cases and immediately immersed them in temporary conservation tanks until they could be transported to a more permanent preservation facility.

No sooner was one fully loaded barge towed off site than another one was maneuvered into position and sunk, repeating the process.

Six submersibles, three owned by NUMA, one by the Canadians and two by the Navy worked in harmony, meticulously lifting the crates with their invaluable contents into the specially designed cargo compartment of the sunken barge.

To facilitate the removal of the artwork from inside the hull, the divers in the Newtsuits cut through the steel plates with state-of-the-art torch systems that melted metal underwater at an incredible rate. Once an opening was made, the submersibles moved in and lifted out the treasures, aided by the clamshell claws from the cranes on the surface.

The entire operation was observed and directed from a control room on board the *Ocean Retriever.* Video screens linked to cameras set at strategic locations around the wreck revealed every stage of the recovery project. The high-resolution video systems were carefully monitored by Pitt and Gunn, who managed the intricate deployment of men and equipment. They worked twelve-hour shifts, as did the crews of all three vessels. The around-the-clock project never stopped bringing up the seemingly endless mountain of artifacts on the bottom below.

Pitt would have given his right arm to have worked on the wreck in one of the submersibles or Newtsuits, but as project director his experience was required to coordinate and guide the operation from the surface. He watched one of the monitors with envy as it showed Giordino being lifted into the *Sappho IV* submersible, broken leg and all. Giordino had over seven hundred hours in submersibles, and the one he was piloting was his favorite. On this shift, the wily little Italian planned to take his sub deep into the *Princess Dou Wan*'s superstructure after the bulkheads were cut away by the divers inside the Newtsuits.

Pitt turned as Rudi Gunn stepped into the control room. The early sun flashed through the doorway, momentarily illuminating the compartment, which had no ports or windows. "You here already? I'd swear you just walked out."

"It's that time," Gunn answered, smiling. He was carrying a large, rolled mosaic photograph under one arm that had been shot above the wreck before the start of the salvage operation. The mosaic was invaluable in detecting artifacts that had been scattered in the debris field and for directing the submersibles and divers to different sections of the wreck. "How do we stand?" he asked.

"The barge has been filled and is on its way to the surface," replied Pitt, his nose catching the smell of coffee from the galley and yearning for a cup.

"I never cease to be amazed by the sheer numbers of it all," said Gunn, taking his place in front of the communications console and array of video screens.

"The *Princess Dou Wan* was incredibly overloaded," said Pitt. "It's no small wonder she broke up and sank in heavy weather."

"How close are we to wrapping it up?"

"Most all the loose packing crates have been recovered from the lake bed. The stern section is about cleaned out. The cargo holds should be emptied before the end of the next shift. Now it's down to ferreting out all the smaller cases that were stowed in the passageways and staterooms in the center part of the ship. The deeper they penetrate, the more difficult it is for the men in the Newtsuits to cut through the bulkheads."

"Any word on when Qin Shang's salvage ship is due to arrive?" Gunn asked.

"The *Jade Adventurer?*" Pitt looked down on a chart of the Great Lakes spread out on a table. "At last report she passed Quebec on her way down the St. Lawrence."

"That should put her here in a little under three days."

"She didn't waste any time coming off her search operation off Chile. She was on her way north less than an hour after Zhu Kwan received your phony report from Perlmutter."

"It's going to be close," said Gunn as he watched a submersible's articulated fingers delicately pick up a porcelain vase protruding from the muck. "We'll be lucky to finish up and get out of the neighborhood before the *Jade Adventurer* and our friend come charging onto the scene."

"We've been lucky Qin Shang didn't send any of his agents ahead to scout out the environment."

"The Coast Guard cutter that patrols our search area has yet to report an encounter with a suspicious vessel."

"When I came on my shift last night, Al said a reporter from a local newspaper somehow got a call through to the *Ocean Retriever.* Al strung him along when the reporter asked what we were doing out here."

"What did Al tell him?"

"He said we were drilling cores in the bottom of the lake, looking for signs of dinosaurs."

"And the reporter bought it?" Gunn asked skeptically.

"Probably not, but he got excited when Al promised to bring him on board over the weekend."

Gunn looked puzzled. "But we should be gone by then."

"You get the picture," Pitt laughed.

"We should consider ourselves lucky that rumors of treasure haven't brought out swarms of salvors."

"They come as soon as they get the word and rush out to pick over the scraps."

Julia came into the control room balancing a tray on one hand. "Breakfast," she announced gaily. "Isn't it a beautiful morning?"

Pitt rubbed the stubble of a beard on his chin. "I hadn't noticed."

"What are you so happy about?" Gunn asked her.

"I just received a message from Peter Harper. Qin Shang came off a Japanese airliner at the Quebec airport disguised as a crew member. The Canadian Royal Mounted Police followed him to the waterfront, where he boarded a small boat and rendezvoused with the *Jade Adventurer.*"

"Hallelujah!" exclaimed Gunn. "He took the bait."

"Hook, line and sinker," said Julia, flashing her teeth. She set the tray on the chart table and removed a tablecloth, revealing plates of eggs and bacon, toast, grapefruit and coffee.

"That is good news," said Pitt, pulling a chair up to the table without being told. "Did Harper say when he plans to take Qin Shang into custody?"

"He's meeting with the INS legal staff to formulate a plan. I must tell you, there is great fear the State Department and White House may intervene."

"I was afraid of that," said Gunn.

"Peter and Commissioner Monroe are very afraid Qin Shang will slip through the net because of his political connections."

"Why not board the *Jade Adventurer* and haul his ass off now?" Gunn asked.

"We can't legally apprehend him if his ship skirts the Canadian shoreline while sailing through Lakes Ontario, Erie and Huron," explained Julia. "Only after the *Jade Adventurer* has passed through the Straits of Mackinac into Lake Michigan will Qin Shang be on American waters."

Pitt slowly ate his grapefruit. "I'd like to see his face when his crew lays a camera on the *Princess* and finds her guts ripped out and her cupboards bare."

"Did you know that he's filed a claim on the ship and its cargo through one of his subsidiary corporations in state and federal district courts?"

"No," said Pitt. "But I'm not surprised. That's the way he operates."

Gunn rapped a knife on the table. "If any of us were to stake a claim on a treasure ship through legal channels, we'd be laughed out onto the street. And whatever artifacts we found would have to be turned over to the government."

"People who search for treasure," Pitt said philosophically, "believe their problems are over when they make the big strike, never realizing their troubles are only beginning."

"How true," Gunn assented. "I've yet to hear of a treasure discovery that wasn't contested in court by a parasite or government bureaucrat."

Julia shrugged. "Maybe so, but Qin Shang has too much influence to have the door slammed in his face. If anything, he's bought off all opposition."

Pitt looked at her as though his fatigued mind had suddenly thought of something. "Aren't you eating?" he asked.

She shook her head. "I had a bite in the galley earlier."

The ship's first officer leaned in the doorway and motioned to Pitt. "The barge has surfaced, sir. You said you wanted to take a look at her payload before she was towed away."

"Yes, thank you," Pitt acknowledged. He turned back to Gunn. "She's all yours, Rudi. I'll see you, same time, same place tomorrow."

Gunn waved without taking his eyes from the monitors. "Sleep tight."

Julia hung on Pitt's arm as they stepped out onto the bridge wing and gazed down at the big barge that had risen from the depths. The interior cargo hold was filled with crates of all sizes containing incredible treasures from China's past. All had been neatly spaced by the cranes and submersibles. In a divided compartment with extra-thick padding, the artworks whose packing crates had been either damaged or destroyed sat open and exposed. Some were musical instruments—tuned chimes of stone, bronze bells and drums. There was a three-legged cooking stove with a hideous face molded on the door, large jade ceremonial carvings of half-size men, women and children, and animal sculptures in marble.

"Oh, look," she said, pointing. "They brought up the emperor on the horse."

Standing under the sun for the first time in over half a century, the water glistening on the bronze armor of the rider and streaming from his horse, the two-thousand-year-old sculpture looked little the worse for wear than the day it came out of the mold. The unknown emperor now stared over a limitless horizon, as if in search of new lands to conquer.

"It's all so incredibly beautiful," said Julia, staring at the ancient wonder. Then she gestured at the other crates, their contents still hidden. "I'm amazed the wooden containers did not rot away after being submerged all these years."

"General Hui was a thorough man," Pitt said. "Not only did he insist that the crates be built with an outer wall and an inner lining, he specified teak instead of a more common wood. It was probably transported to Shanghai from Burma by freighter for use in the shipyards. Hui knew that teak is extraordinarily strong and durable, and he undoubtedly seized the shipment to construct the crates. What he couldn't have predicted at the time was that his foresight paid off in protecting the treasures for the fifty years they were resting underwater."

Julia raised a hand to shield her eyes from the glare of the sun on the water. "A pity he couldn't have made them watertight. The lacquerware, wooden carvings and paintings cannot have survived without some damage or disintegration."

"The archaeologists will know soon enough. Hopefully, the icy, fresh water will have preserved many of the more delicate objects."

As the tugboat maneuvered into position to tow the barge to the receiving dock in Chicago, a crewman stepped from the wheelhouse with a paper in his hand. "Another message for you, Ms. Lee, from Washington."

"Must be another message from Peter," she said, taking the communication. She studied the wording for a long time, her facial expression turning from surprise to utter frustration to downright anger. "Oh, good God," she muttered.

"What is it?"

Julia held out the message to Pitt. "The INS operation to apprehend Qin Shang has been called off by order of the White House. We are not to molest or harass him in any way. Any and all treasure recovered from the *Princess Dou Wan* is to be turned over to Qin Shang as acting representative of the Chinese government."

"That's crazy," Pitt said wearily, too tired to display outrage. "The man is a proven mass murderer. Give him the treasure? The President must have a brain hemorrhage."

"I've never felt so helpless in my life," Julia said, furious.

Suddenly, unpredictably, Pitt's lips spread in a crazy grin. "I wouldn't take it too badly if I were you. There's always a bright side."

She stared at him as if he was certifiably insane. "What are you talking about? Where do you see a bright side in allowing that scum to roam free and steal the art masterpieces for himself?"

"The orders from the White House definitely state that the INS is not to molest or harass Qin Shang."

"So?"

"The orders," Pitt said, still grinning but with a hard edge to his voice, "make no mention of what NUMA can or cannot do—"

He broke off as Gunn ran excitedly from the control room onto the bridge wing. "Al thinks he's got them," the words rushed out. "He's coming to the surface now and wants to know how you want them handled."

"Very carefully," said Pitt. "Tell him to rise slowly and maintain a good grip. When he surfaces, we'll lift the *Sappho IV* aboard with them."

"Who is *them?*" asked Julia.

Pitt gave her a quick glance before he rushed down a ladder to the submersible recovery deck. "The bones of Peking man, that's who."

Word quickly spread throughout the salvage fleet, and the *Ocean Retriever*'s crew began assembling on the stern work deck. The crews of the other vessels crowded their railings, watching the activity aboard the NUMA ship. There was a strange silence as the turquoise *Sappho IV* broke the surface and rolled slightly from the low waves of the lake. Divers waited in the water to attach the crane's cable hook to the lifting ring on top of the submersible. Every eye was on the large wire-mesh basket between the twin articulated arms. Two wooden boxes sat in the basket. They all held their breath as the submersible was slowly lifted from the lake. The crane operator used great caution in swinging the underwater craft over the stern before lowering it gently into its cradle.

The crowd on deck gathered around the sub as the ship's archaeologist directed the unloading of the crates on the deck. While the archaeologist, a blond lady in her forties by the name of Pat O'Connell, was engaged in exposing the interior of the crates, Giordino threw back the hatch from inside the submersible and pushed his head and shoulders into the open air.

"Where did you find them?" Pitt shouted up at him.

"Using a diagram of the deck plans I managed to force entry into the captain's cabin."

"The location sounds right," said Gunn, peering through his eyeglasses.

With the help of four eager pairs of hands, archaeologist O'Connell pried off the top of the crate and peered inside. "Oh my, oh me, oh my," she muttered in awe.

"What is it?" Pitt demanded. "What do you see?"

"Military footlockers with U.S.M.C. stenciled on the top."

"Well, don't stand there. Open it up."

"It really should be opened in a laboratory," O'Connell protested. "Proper methodology, you know."

"No!" Pitt said flatly. "Proper methodology be damned. These people worked long and hard. And by God they deserve to see the fruits of their labor. Open the footlocker."

Seeing that Pitt was not to be denied, and glancing at the sea of faces around her reflecting expressions of hostility, O'Connell knelt down and began working open the latch on the front of the footlocker with a small crowbar. The wall around the latch quickly fell away as if it were made of clay, and she lifted the lid open very, very slowly.

Inside the footlocker the upper tray held several objects neatly wrapped in sodden gauze and exactingly placed in little individual compartments. As if she was unwrapping the Holy Grail, O'Connell delicately removed the covering from the largest object. When the last piece of gauze fell away, she held up what looked like a yellow-brown circular bowl.

"A skullcap," she said in a hushed voice, "from Peking man."

53

THE CAPTAIN of the *Jade Adventurer*, Chen Jiang, had served Qin Shang Maritime Limited for twenty of his thirty years at sea. Tall and thin with straight white hair, he was quiet and efficient in the operation of his ship. He forced back a smile and spoke to his employer.

"There is your ship, Qin Shang."

"I can't believe after all these years I'm seeing her at last," said Qin Shang, his eyes locked on the video monitor receiving images from an ROV that was moving over the sunken wreck.

"We are very lucky the depth is only four hundred and thirty feet. If the ship had, indeed, foundered off the coast of Chile, we'd have found ourselves working in ten thousand feet."

"It appears the hull is separated in two parts."

"Not unusual for ships caught in storms on the Great Lakes to break up," explained Chen Jiang. "The *Edmund Fitzgerald*, a legendary ore carrier, was twisted apart when *she* sank."

During the search, Qin Shang had paced the deck of the wheelhouse restlessly. He appeared impassive to the captain and officers of the ship, but beneath the cold exterior, his adrenaline was pumping madly. Qin Shang was not a patient man. He hated doing nothing but waiting while the ship swept back and forth before finally striking the wreck he hoped was the *Princess Dou Wan*. The tedious search was a torment he could have happily done without.

The *Jade Adventurer* did not look like the usual businesslike survey-and-salvage ship. Her sleek superstructure and twin catamaran hulls gave her more the look of an expensive yacht. Only the stylized, contemporary A-frame crane on her stern suggested that she was anything but a pleasure cruiser. Her hulls were painted blue with a red stripe running around the leading edges. The upperworks gleamed white.

A big ship with a length of 325 feet, elegant and brutishly powered, she was a marvel of engineering, loaded from the keel with the latest and most sophisticated equipment and instrumentation. She was Qin Shang's pride and joy, expressly designed and constructed to his specifications for this moment, the salvage of the *Princess Dou Wan.*

The ship had arrived on site early in the morning, relying on the approximate position Zhu Kwan had received from St. Julien Perlmutter. Qin Shang was relieved to see only two ships within twenty miles. One was an ore carrier heading toward Chicago, the other Chen Jiang identified as a research vessel only three miles away, showing her starboard broadside as she moved on an opposite course with uncommon lethargy.

Using the same basic techniques and equipment as Pitt and the crew of the *Divercity,* the *Jade Adventurer* was only in the third hour of the search when the sonar operator announced a target. After four more passes to improve the quality of the recording, the sonar operator could safely say they had a ship on the bottom that, although broken up, matched the dimensions of the *Princess Dou Wan.* Then a Chinese-manufactured ROV was lowered over the side and descended to the wreck.

After another hour of passionately staring at the monitor, Qin Shang snapped angrily. "This cannot be the *Princess Dou Wan!* Where is her cargo? I see nothing that confirms the report of wooden crates protecting the art treasures."

"Odd," murmured Chen Jiang. "The steel plates of the hull and superstructure look scattered around the wreck. It looks as if the ship was burst apart."

Qin Shang's face went pale. "This wreck cannot be the *Princess Dou Wan,*" he repeated.

"Move the ROV around the stern," Chen Jiang ordered the operator.

In a few minutes the little underwater prowler stopped and the operator zoomed the camera in on the lettering across the stern of the hulk. There was no mistaking the name, PRINCESS YUNG T'AI, SHANGHAI.

"It *is* my ship!" Qin Shang's eyes were stricken as he stared into the monitor.

"Could it have been salvaged without your knowledge?" asked Chen Jiang.

"Not possible. No treasure that immense could have remained hidden all these years. Pieces of it would have most certainly surfaced."

"Shall I order the crew to prepare the submersible?"

"Yes, yes," Qin Shang said anxiously. "I must have a closer look."

Qin Shang hired his own engineers to design the submersible he named *Sea Lotus*. She was built at a company in France that specialized in deep-undersea vehicles. He had watched over every aspect of her construction. Unlike most submersibles, where the requirements of the equipment came before the comfort of the crew, the *Sea Lotus* was built more like an office than a Spartan chamber for scientific study. She was a pleasure craft to Qin Shang. He trained himself in her operation and often piloted her around the Hong Kong harbor shortly after she was built, making suggestions for modifications to suit his personal demands.

He also ordered a second submersible built, called *Sea Jasmine*. Her purpose was to act as backup in case *Sea Lotus* suffered mechanical problems while on the seabed.

An hour later, Shang's private submersible was rolled out of her compartment onto the stern of the salvage vessel and stationed beneath the modernistic A-frame that would lift her out and into the water. When all systems were checked, the copilot stood at the hatch, waiting for Qin Shang to enter.

"I will pilot the craft alone," he said imperiously.

Captain Chen Jiang looked up at him from the deck. "Do you think that wise, sir? You are unfamiliar with these waters."

"I am quite familiar with the operation of the *Sea Lotus*. You forget, Captain, I created her. I will go down alone. It is for me to be the first to see the treasures stolen from our country all these years. I have dreamed too long of this moment to share it."

Chen Jiang shrugged and said nothing. He merely nodded for the submersible's copilot to stand aside as Qin Shang descended the ladder down through the tower that prevented rough water from cascading into the open hatch leading to the control and pressure chamber. He pulled the hatch closed and sealed it, then turned on the life-support systems.

Diving to 430 feet was child's play for a vessel built to withstand the immense squeeze that water exerted at depths of 25,000 feet. He sat in a comfortable chair of his own design, facing the control console and a large viewing window on the bow of the submersible.

Sea Lotus was swung out over the water by the A-frame away from the ship's fantail, where she hung for a few moments until her rocking motion ceased. Then she was lowered into Lake Michigan. Divers released the lift hook and made a final check of the exterior before Qin Shang took her into the frigid depths.

"You are free of the lift line and cleared to descend," Chen Jiang's voice came over the communications speaker.

"Flooding ballast tanks," Qin Shang replied.

Chen Jiang was too experienced an officer to allow his employer to override his responsibilities as captain of the *Jade Adventurer.* He turned to an officer and issued an order unheard by Qin Shang. "Have the *Sea Jasmine* prepared to launch as a safety precaution."

"Do you expect trouble, sir?"

"No, but we cannot allow harm to come to Qin Shang."

The *Sea Lotus* quickly slipped out of sight beneath the waves and began her slow fall to the bottom of the lake. Qin Shang stared through the viewing window into the dark green water as it magically went black and he saw his reflection inside the pressure chamber. His eyes were cold, his mouth was in a tight line, unsmiling. Within the brief span of an hour he had gone from a man of supreme confidence to someone who looked sick and tired and baffled. He did not like what he saw in the nebulous face staring back at him, seemingly outside in the depths. For the only time in his life that he could remember, he felt a growing surge of anxiety. The treasures had to be somewhere inside the broken hulks, he told himself over and over as the submersible sank ever deeper into the cold waters of the lake. They had to be. It was inconceivable that someone had come before.

The descent took less than ten minutes, but to Qin Shang the seconds passed like hours. He gazed into pure blackness before switching on the exterior lights. It was also becoming cold inside the chamber, and he set a small heating unit to seventy degrees. The echo sounder indicated the bottom was coming up fast. He allowed a small amount of pressurized air to flow into the ballast tanks to slow his descent. On deep-water dives beyond one thousand feet, he would have dropped weights attached to the keel of the submersible.

The flat, barren lake bed emerged under the lights. He adjusted the ballast and stopped five feet from the bottom. Then Qin Shang turned on the electric thrusters and began banking in a wide circle. "I am on the bottom," he called to his support crew above. "Can you see where I am in relation to the wreck?"

"The sonar shows you only forty yards west of the starboard side of the main wreckage," Jiang answered.

Qin Shang's heartbeat raced in anticipation. He banked the *Sea Lotus* until it was moving parallel to the hull, and then brought the sub upward until it passed over the railing along the edge of the forward cargo deck. He saw the cranes looming out of the black void and banked to miss them. Now he was over one of the cargo holds. Hovering the submersible and tilting its stern upward so the lights beamed down, his eyes strained into the darkness as he stared into the gaping cavern.

With indescribable dread, he saw that it was empty.

Then something moved in the shadows. At first he merely thought it was a fish, but then it moved up from the black of the cargo hold and materialized into an unspeakable monstrosity, an apparition that belonged in another world. Slowly it rose, as if levitated in air, like some hideous creature from the murky abyss, and moved toward the submersible.

On the surface, Captain Chen Jiang stared with mounting apprehension as the research vessel he'd sighted earlier had turned on a ninety-degree course and was now facing the *Jade Adventurer.* Abruptly presenting its bows after having showed its starboard broadside, the research vessel now revealed a United States Coast Guard cutter that it had shielded from view. Now both vessels were traveling at full speed directly toward the Chinese salvage ship.

54

QIN SHANG LOOKED like a man who had seen the deepest pit in hell and wanted no part of it. His face was as white and rigid as hardened putty. Sweat streamed from his forehead, his eyes glazed with shock. For a man totally in control of his emotions during his entire life, he was suddenly paralyzed. He stared awestruck at the face inside the bubble-shaped head of the yellow and black monster as it broke into a ghastly grin. And then he recognized the familiar features.

"Pitt!" he gasped in a rasping whisper.

"Yes, it's me," Pitt answered over his underwater communications system inside the Newtsuit. "You do hear me, don't you, Qin Shang?"

The trauma of disbelief, then revulsion at who the apparition was, released a flow of venom in Qin Shang's veins as shock turned into crazed wrath. "I hear you," he said slowly, his thoughts coming back under his iron control. He did not demand to know where Pitt came from or what he was doing here. There was only one question in Qin Shang's mind.

"Where is the treasure?"

"Treasure," Pitt said, his face taking on a witless expression behind the transparent bubble on the globular helmet of the Newtsuit. "I ain't got no treasure."

"What has happened to it?" Qin Shang demanded, his eyes sick with the cold realization of defeat. "What have you done with the historical masterworks of my country?"

"Put it all in a place where it's safe from scum like you who want it all to themselves."

"How?" he asked simply.

"With much luck and many good people," Pitt said impassively. "After my researcher discovered a survivor who pointed the way, I put together a salvage project combining NUMA, the U.S. Navy and the Canadians. Together, they completed the salvage in ten days before leaking the *Princess Dou Wan*'s position to your researcher. I believe his name is Zhu Kwan. Then it was merely a matter of sitting back and waiting for you to show up. I knew you were obsessed by the treasure, Qin Shang. I read you like a book. Now it's payoff time. By coming back into the U.S. you've forfeited any chance you had of a long life. Unfortunately, because there is a great lack of ethics and morality in the world these days, your money and political influence has undoubtedly kept you out of prison. But the final entry in your ledger, Qin Shang, is that you are going to die. You are going to die as retribution for all those innocent people you murdered."

"You create amusing plots, Pitt." There was a sneer in Qin Shang's voice, but it was contradicted by a deep uneasiness in his eyes. "And who is going to see that I die?"

"I've been waiting for you," Pitt said, hate mirrored in his green eyes. "There was never a doubt that you would come and come alone."

"Are you quite finished? Or do you wish to bore me to death?"

Qin Shang knew his life was hanging by a thread, but he had yet to figure by what means he was supposed to die. Although Pitt's casualness made him uncomfortable, all fear was slowly replaced by an inner self-defense mechanism. His conspiring mind began to concentrate on a plan to save himself. His hopes rose when he comprehended that Pitt had no support from a surface ship. A diver inside a Newtsuit did not make descents and ascents without an umbilical cable. He had to be lowered and raised by winch from a mother ship on the surface. The cable also served as a communications link. Pitt was breathing self-contained air that could not last much longer than an hour. Without life support on the surface, Pitt was on borrowed time and totally defenseless.

"You're not as clever as you think," Qin Shang said, a faint pallor on his face. "From my side of the viewing port, it looks like you are the one who is going to die, Mr. Pitt. Your ingenious diving apparatus against my submersible? You stand about as much chance as a sloth against a bear."

"I'm willing to give it a try."

"Where is your support ship?"

"I don't need one," Pitt said with unnerving nonchalance. "I walked from shore."

"You are very humorous for a man who will never see the sun again." As Qin Shang spoke, his hands moved furtively toward the controls of the submersible's manipulator arms and their claws. "I can either drop my weights and float to the surface, leaving you alone to your fate. Or, I can call my crew and order them to send down my backup submersible."

"Not fair. That would make it two bears against one sloth."

The man's imperturbable composure is inhuman, thought Qin Shang. Something is not as it seems. "You act sure of yourself," he said, as he measured his options.

Pitt raised one of the Newtsuit's manipulator arms and displayed a small, watertight box with an antenna. "In case you're wondering why you haven't heard from your friends topside, this little device scrambles all communications within five hundred feet."

That explained why he had received no calls from the *Jade Adventurer.* But that piece of news did nothing to deter Qin Shang's determination to wreak punishment on Pitt.

"You have meddled in my affairs for the last time." Qin Shang's fingers slowly curled around the throttle of the thrusters and the manipulator controls. "I can not waste another minute with you. I must seek out where you've hidden the treasure. Farewell, Mr. Pitt. I'm dropping my ballast weights and returning to the surface."

Pitt knew full well what was coming. Even through the murky water that separated them, he detected the sudden shift in Qin Shang's eyes. He threw up his manipulator arms to protect his vulnerable bubble mask and reversed the two small motors mounted on each side of the Newtsuit's waist. His reaction came at almost the same instant as the submersible lurched forward.

It was a battle Pitt could not win. One second the *Sea Lotus* was hovering level, the next it was relentlessly coming toward him. His much smaller manipulator pincers were no match for the larger claws on the arms of the submersible. Qin Shang's vehicle could also move at twice the speed of the Newtsuit. If the submersible's mechanical claws cut through the Newtsuit, it would be all over.

Pitt could do nothing but helplessly watch as the big ugly manipulator arms spread in preparation of encircling him in a death grip, squeezing until the integrity of the Newtsuit was gashed open to the water waiting to rush inside. When that happened, Pitt would die an agonizing death.

He had no wish to wait for the water to gush down his open throat into his lungs. The burst of sudden pressure alone would make his final moments unbearable. He had come close to drowning on at least two occasions, and he had no desire to repeat the events. Tormented, struggling and dying with no one near him to see except his most vicious enemy was not what Pitt had in mind.

Pitt longed to drive the Newtsuit forward, using his own manipulator pincers to smash Qin Shang's viewing window of the submersible, but they were too short and would have easily been knocked away by the arms on the submersible. Also, an aggressive attack was not part of his plan. He looked into the twin jaws of death, saw the evil leer on Qin Shang's face and maneuvered his cumbersome pressure suit backward in a losing effort to stall for time.

Directing the articulated joints of the Newtsuit, he leaned over and used the manipulator pincers to pick up a short length of pipe that was lying on the deck. Then he swung the pipe to ward off the deadly arms of the submersible. It was almost a laughable gesture. Qin Shang guided his claws toward Pitt from two sides. Almost as if he was snatching candy from a baby, he seized the pipe and tore it from the Newtsuit's pincers. If spectators could have seen the fight through the murk, it would have looked like a ballet between two huge animals in slow motion. All movement at that depth was hindered by the surrounding water pressure.

Then Pitt felt the Newtsuit come to an abrupt halt as he backed it against the forward bulkhead of the *Princess Dou Wan*'s superstructure. Now there was no room to escape the onslaught. The uneven fight had only lasted eight or nine minutes. Pitt could see the satanic grin on Qin Shang's face as his sadistic opponent closed in for the kill.

Then, unexpectedly, without warning, a vague shape came gliding silently out of the gloom like a great incarnate vulture.

Stretched prone inside a submersible with the configuration of a small airplane with stubby wings and a tail assembly, Giordino angled the *Sappho IV* from above and dropped behind the *Sea Lotus*. With grim concentration he operated the controls to a viselike talon that protruded from beneath the craft. Clutched in the talon was a small round ball less than three inches in diameter that was attached to a small suction device. Completely oblivious, Qin Shang's attention was focused on murdering Pitt. Then Giordino pressed the ball and suction device against the pressure hull of the *Sea Lotus* until it adhered. After that he tilted the *Sappho IV*'s bow sharply upward and banked away, quickly disappearing into the watery void.

Twenty seconds later a sharp thump sounded through the water. At first Qin Shang was mystified as he felt the *Sea Lotus* shudder. Too late he realized that Pitt's brave defiance against overwhelming odds was a diversion for an attack from another source. And then he watched in growing horror as a spiderweb of tiny fractures spread across the upper wall of the pressure chamber. Suddenly water burst inside as if shot from a small cannon. The pressure chamber maintained its integrity and did not implode, but the incoming flood spelled its doom.

Qin Shang froze in cold fright as the water rose higher and higher, rapidly filling the small interior of the submersible. He frantically switched on the pumps to drain the ballast tanks and hit the lever to drop the heavy weights beneath the keel. The *Sea Lotus* sluggishly ascended for several feet and then hung there as the flooding water neutralized its buoyancy. Then it slowly began to fall, settling into the bottom and throwing up a thin cloud of silt.

Now in mindless panic, Qin Shang desperately tried to open the outer hatch in an insane attempt to reach the surface 430 feet above, an impossible gesture because of the immense water pressure outside.

Pitt moved the Newtsuit through the cloud of silt and gazed through the submersible's viewing window, remembering the sight of the bodies strewn in the depths of Orion Lake as the Chinese arch-criminal pulled himself up into a rapidly compressing air pocket for one last breath before the icy water of the lake filled his nose and open, screaming mouth. The screams were soon choked off until the only sound coming from the *Sea Lotus* was the gurgling of escaping bubbles. Then, as if set on a timer, the halogen lights blinked out, throwing the submersible into total darkness.

Pitt was sweating heavily inside the Newtsuit. He stood on the bottom, staring with grim satisfaction at the underwater tomb of Qin Shang. The billionaire shipping magnate, who had dominated and exploited and slain thousands of innocent people, would spend eternity in the deep next to the empty treasure ship that had obsessed most of his waking life. It was a fitting end, Pitt thought without the slightest sense of pity.

He glanced up as Giordino reappeared in the *Sappho IV.* "You took your sweet time. I might have been killed."

Giordino hovered the sub until their faces behind the protective transparent shields were no more than two feet apart. "I can't tell you how much I enjoyed the show," he laughed. "If you could have only seen yourself in that Pillsbury Doughboy suit playing Errol Flynn with a pipe as a sword."

"Next time, you do the hard part."

"Qin Shang?" asked Giordino.

Pitt pointed a pincer at the inert submersible. "Where he belongs."

"How are you fixed for air?"

"Down to twenty minutes."

"No time to waste. Stand still until I can connect up my cable to the lift ring on top of your helmet. Then I'll tow you to the surface."

"Not just yet," said Pitt. "I've got a little task to perform."

He activated the little thrusters on the Newtsuit and moved up the sides of the superstructure until he came to the wheelhouse. The bulkheads had been torched away for entry and for the removal of the treasures packed in the passageways and former passenger staterooms. He quickly studied a diagram of the ship's interior that he had taped to the globular view plate and began propelling the pressurized suit past the captain's cabin next to the wheelhouse to the next cabin beyond. Amazingly, the furnishings were still relatively intact and jumbled about the small compartment. After only a few minutes' search, Pitt found what he was looking for and removed a small pouch from the utility belt on the Newtsuit and filled it with objects from one corner of the cabin.

"You'd better get a move on," came Giordino's worried voice.

"On my way," Pitt complied.

With three minutes to spare, the *Sappho IV* and the Newtsuit surfaced one behind the other and were lifted on board the *Ocean Retriever.* As the technicians worked to remove Pitt from the big dive suit, he looked across the water at Qin Shang's *Jade Adventurer.* A boarding party from the Coast Guard cutter was routinely examining the ship's papers before ordering it out of American waters.

When he was finally free of the ponderous suit, Pitt leaned wearily over the railing and gazed down into the water as Julia came up behind him and ran her arms around his waist, clasping her hands across his stomach. "I was worried about you," she said softly.

"I put my trust in Al and Rudi, knowing they would never fail."

"Is Qin Shang dead?" she asked, certain of the answer.

He held her head between his hands and looked down into her gray eyes. "He's only a bad memory it pays to forget."

She pulled back, her face suddenly disturbed. "When word leaks out that you killed him, you're going to be in big trouble with the government."

Despite the exhaustion, Pitt threw back his head and laughed. "Dearheart, I'm *always* in big trouble with the government."

EPILOGUE

FRITZ

55

July 31, 2000
Washington, D.C.

PRESIDENT DEAN COOPER WALLACE worked late hours in his office in his secret living quarters at Fort McNair and thought nothing of inconveniencing his staff and visitors for meetings in the middle of the night. He did not rise from behind his desk as Commissioner Duncan Monroe, Admiral Sandecker and Peter Harper were escorted into the office by his newly appointed chief of staff, Harold Pecorelli. Nor did he invite his visitors to sit down.

Wallace was not a happy man.

The news media was crucifying him for his relations with Qin Shang, now accused of conspiracy for the destruction and deaths along the Mississippi River. To make matters worse, the Chinese leaders had thrown Qin Shang on their sacrificial altar and denied any association with him. The head of Qin Shang Maritime Limited had disappeared, and even the Chinese government was at a loss as to his whereabouts. The *Jade Adventurer* was still at sea on its way back to China. Throughout the voyage from Lake Michigan, Captain Chen Jiang had maintained radio silence, not wanting to be the one to announce Qin Shang's death at the hands of the Americans.

At the same time, Wallace took great delight in pretending that he played a key role in the discovery and salvage of the Chinese art treasures. Negotiations were already under way for their return to mainland China. Photojournalists and television news cameras had a field day recording the incredible display of artifacts as they were removed from the original teak packing crates and prepared for preservation.

The bones of Peking man by themselves caused an international sensation.

Advised that it was not in his best interests to interfere, Wallace remained quiet as the INS and FBI, working hand in hand, rounded up nearly three hundred Chinese gang leaders and members around the country and arraigned them for trial. Thousands of illegal immigrants working in virtual slavery were taken into custody for later deportation back to China. The flow of illegal aliens coming in from Asia may not have been plugged completely, but the smuggling operations were cut back drastically.

The President's closest advisers, having observed the recklessness of the previous chief executive in conducting coverups, strongly advised Wallace simply to admit that mistakes were made and make no excuses. Any errors of judgment were made for what he thought was the good of the country. Damage control was already in high gear to sidestep any criticism encountered along his way for election to a second term.

"You stepped far beyond the bounds of your office," Wallace said, directing his wrath toward Monroe. "And you did it without briefing anyone in my office regarding your intent."

"Sir, I did nothing but the job I was appointed to do," Duncan replied resolutely.

"China is a magnificent stage for the future of the American economy, and you jeopardized the close relationship I have worked to build between our two countries. The future of the United States lies in a universal world-trading system, and China is a vital step toward that goal."

"But not, Mr. President," said Sandecker with his usual testiness, "if it means flooding the country with illegal immigrants."

"You people are not foreign-policy experts, nor are you economists," Wallace said coldly. "Your business, Duncan, is to properly conduct immigration procedures. And yours, Admiral, is to conduct ocean-science projects. Neither of you were appointed to run amok."

Sandecker shrugged and then dropped his bomb. "I admit NUMA scientists and engineers are not in the business of executing criminals, but—"

"What was that you said?" Wallace demanded. "What are you insinuating?"

With feigned innocence Sandecker replied. "No one briefed you?"

"Briefed me on what?"

"The unfortunate accident that took the life of Qin Shang."

"He's dead?" Wallace gasped.

Sandecker nodded solemnly. "Yes, he suffered a temporary fit of insanity and attacked my special projects director on the wreck of the *Princess Dou Wan,* who in self-defense was forced to kill Qin Shang."

Wallace was stunned. "Do you have any idea of what you've done?"

"If ever a monster deserved to be terminated," Sandecker came back caustically, "it was Qin Shang. And I might add that I'm proud it was my people who were responsible."

Before the President could censure the admiral, Peter Harper jumped into the debate. "I received a report from the CIA revealing that certain members of the Chinese government were themselves plotting to assassinate Qin Shang. Their plan was to appropriate Qin Shang Maritime Limited and merge it with their government-owned shipping line, China Marine. There is no reason to believe they will curtail illegal smuggling operations, but without Qin Shang they won't be able to operate as efficiently or on the same scale. This is all to our advantage."

"You must realize, gentlemen," said Pecorelli diplomatically, "the President has policies to protect and interests to defend no matter how unpopular they might seem."

Sandecker gave Pecorelli a stern look. "It's no longer a secret, Harold, that Qin Shang acted as a middleman between the White House and illegal Chinese interests."

"Purely a misinformed judgment call," Pecorelli said, shrugging indifferently.

Sandecker turned to President Wallace. "Rather than bring Duncan and me in here to chew our asses, we should be awarded medals for getting rid of a scourge to national security and laying one of the greatest treasures of all time in your lap."

"You will certainly score a vast number of points with the Chinese when you return it to them," added Monroe.

"Yes, yes, an amazing feat," Wallace acknowledged unresponsively. He pulled a handkerchief from his suit coat pocket and dabbed his upper lip, and then blandly continued to defend his decisions. "You have to look at the international situation through my eyes. I am currently balancing a hundred different trade deals with China worth billions of dollars to the American economy and hundreds of thousands of jobs for American workers."

"But why should American taxpayers help build China into a global power?" asked Harper.

"If nothing else," said Monroe, changing the subject, "allow the

INS more powers to halt illegal immigration. At last estimate over six million illegals are in the United States. We've established solid programs for reducing the flow over the border with Mexico, but the smuggling of Chinese across our shorelines is far more sophisticated and calls for stronger measures."

"Maybe it's better to issue them all amnesty," suggested Wallace, "and be done with it."

"I don't think you realize the seriousness of the situation for our grandchildren, Mr. President," said Monroe gravely. "By the year twenty fifty the American population will stand at over three hundred sixty million. Fifty years after that, with the present birth rate and flow of new immigrants, legal or illegal, the count will be half a billion. From there, the numbers become downright horrifying."

"Short of a devastating war or plague," argued Wallace, "nothing can stand in the way of the coming worldwide population explosion. As long as we have the capacity to feed ourselves, I fail to see the consequences."

"Have you seen the predictions by CIA analysts and geographers?" asked Sandecker.

Wallace shook his head. "I'm not sure what predictions you're talking about."

"The outlook for the future forecasts a breakup of the United States as we know it."

"Ridiculous."

"The Chinese in time will control the West Coast from San Francisco to Alaska and the Hispanics will govern the lands east from Los Angeles to Houston."

"It's happening before our eyes," said Harper. "Enough Chinese have poured into British Columbia alone to take over its politics."

"I can't conceive of a divided America," said Wallace.

Sandecker stared at him for a moment. "No nation or civilization lasts forever."

The President's new chief of staff, who replaced Morton Laird, cleared his throat. "I'm sorry for interrupting, Mr. President, but you're late for the next appointment."

Wallace shrugged. "That's it, then. I'm sorry I can't carry this discussion further, gentlemen. However, since you do not agree with my positions on policy, I have no choice but to ask for your resignations."

Sandecker's eyes hardened. "You'll not get mine, Mr. President. I know where too many bodies are buried, literally. And if you fire me,

I'll throw so much dirt on the White House your advisers will still be digging out by the next election."

"My sentiments go with the admiral's," said Monroe. "The INS and I have come too far together to hand it over to some bureaucratic stooge. My agents and I have worked closely together for the last six years to see light at the end of the tunnel. No, Mr. President, I'm sorry, but I won't resign without a fight either."

Strangely, in the light of such mutinous opposition, Wallace did not become angry. He looked at both men and recognized their grim determination. He realized they were no ordinary officials afraid of their jobs, but dedicated patriots. They were not men he wished to engage in what would prove a messy fight, certainly not now when he needed all the good press and TV coverage he could get to weather the storm. Then he smiled disarmingly.

"It's a free country, gentlemen. You are entitled to express your dissatisfaction even to the president of the nation. I take back my request for your resignations and shall stand back and allow you to run your respective agencies with a free hand. But I warn you. If either of you cause me any political embarrassment in the future, you'll both be out on the street without a moment's hesitation. Do I make myself clear?"

"Very," said Sandecker.

"Quite clear," Monroe conceded.

"Thank you for coming and clearing the air," said Wallace. "I wish I could say I enjoyed the company, but it wouldn't be true."

Sandecker paused in the doorway. "One question, Mr. President."

"Yes, Admiral."

"The Chinese historical treasures we recovered out of Lake Michigan. When do you plan to turn them over to the Chinese?"

"After I've milked every political compensation out of them I can get." Then Wallace smiled self-righteously. "But they won't receive any of the artifacts until they're displayed at the National Gallery of Art and then taken on the road throughout America and placed for a time on exhibit in every major city. I owe that much to the people."

"Thank you, sir. My compliments on your astute judgment."

"You see," said Wallace, grinning, "I'm not the ogre you thought I was."

After Sandecker, Monroe and Harper departed through the tunnel back to the White House, Wallace told his chief of staff he wanted a few moments alone. He sat there lost in his thoughts, wondering how history would treat him. If only he was clairvoyant and could read the future. No doubt a talent every president since Washington wished he'd possessed. Finally he sighed and called in Pecorelli.

"Who am I scheduled to see now?"

"Your speech writers would like a few minutes of your time to put the finishing touches on your speech to the Hispanic American College Association."

"Yes, that is an important speech," said the President, his thoughts coming back on line. "It's an excellent opportunity to announce my new plan for a cultural-arts agency."

It was business as usual in the executive office.

"HOW NICE TO SEE YOU AGAIN," said Katie, standing in the open front door. "Please come in. Ian is out on the porch, reading his morning newspaper."

"We can't stay long," said Julia as she passed into the entryway. "Dirk and I have to be on a plane back to Washington by noon."

Pitt followed the two women into the house. He carried a small wooden box under one arm. They passed into the kitchen and out onto the porch overlooking the lake. There was a brisk breeze and a good chop on the waves. A sailboat was running with the wind about a mile offshore. Gallagher rose to his feet, his newspaper in one hand.

"Dirk, Julia, thank you for stopping by," he boomed.

"Let me bring you some tea," said Katie.

Pitt would have preferred coffee this early in the morning, but he simply smiled and said, "I'd love some."

"I hope you've come to tell us about the salvage project," said Gallagher.

Pitt nodded. "The very purpose of our visit."

Gallagher motioned for them to sit around a picnic table set up on the porch. "Take a load off your feet."

As they gathered around the table, Pitt placed the box at his feet. After Katie returned with a pot of tea, Pitt and Julia talked about the salvage project and described some of the art treasures they had actually seen because of broken packing crates. Their only omission was any reference to Qin Shang, whom Ian and Katie were not aware of anyway. Pitt told of Giordino's discovery of the bones of Peking man.

"Peking man," Katie repeated slowly. "The Chinese people revere him as an honored ancestor."

"Are we keeping any of the treasure?" asked Gallagher.

Pitt shook his head. "I don't think so. I've been told that President Wallace intends on turning the entire treasure over to the Chinese people after it has gone on exhibit around the United States. Peking man's bones are already on their way home."

"Just think, Ian," said Katie, gazing fondly at her husband, "it might have been all ours."

Gallagher patted her on one knee and gave a hearty laugh. "Where would we have put it? We've got enough Chinese junk sitting around the house to start a museum as it is."

Katie rolled her eyes and gave Gallagher a hard slap on the shoulder. "You big mick, you love those objects as much as I do." She turned to Julia. "You have to excuse Ian. Once a roughneck always a roughneck."

"We really should be moving along," said Julia, reluctant to leave.

Pitt leaned down, picked up the box from the floor and presented it to Katie. "A gift from the *Princess Dou Wan* that I thought you should have."

"I hope it's not a piece of the treasure," she said, surprised. "That would be stealing."

"Oh, but it belongs to you," Julia assured her.

Katie slowly, somewhat apprehensively, opened the lid on the box. "I don't understand," she said, bewildered. "It looks like the bones of some kind of animal." Then she saw the little golden dragon that was attached to a faded red leather collar. "Ian! Ian!" she cried in sudden comprehension. "Look, they've brought me Fritz."

"He's come back to his mistress," said Gallagher, his eyes beginning to mist.

Tears instantly formed in Katie's eyes as she came around the table and embraced Pitt. "Thank you, thank you. You don't know how much this means to me."

"If he didn't," said Julia, gazing at Pitt tenderly, "he does now."

Gallagher put an arm around his wife's shoulders. "I'll bury him with the others." He looked at Pitt and Julia. "We have a little cemetery that holds the pets we've owned over the years who've died."

As they drove away, Ian "Hong Kong" Gallagher stood next to Katie, who smiled and smiled and smiled as she waved goodbye. Pitt found himself envying the big Irishman. Gallagher had been right, he *had* found riches without salvaging the *Princess Dou Wan*'s treasure.

"They're a wonderful couple," said Julia, waving back.

"It must be nice to grow old with someone you love."

Julia stared at Pitt, her eyes narrowing in wonder. "I didn't know you were a sentimental guy."

"I have my dark moments," he answered, smiling.

She sat back in the seat and stared out the windshield at the passing trees pensively. "I wish we could keep right on going and not fly back to Washington."

"What's to stop us?"

"Are you mad? I have my job at INS. You have yours at NUMA. Our superiors are waiting for lengthy reports on the treasure recovery and all the other harrowing experiences we've had cutting the flow of illegal immigrants. They'll keep us so busy for the next few weeks, we'll be lucky if we get to see each other for a few hours on Sundays. And Lord only knows what the Justice Department will do to you when they learn you entombed Qin Shang on the wreck of the *Princess Dou Wan*."

Pitt said nothing. He took one hand off the wheel, reached in the inside pocket of his jacket and passed two envelopes to Julia.

"What's this?" she asked.

"Two airline tickets to Mexico. I forgot to tell you, we're not going back to Washington."

Her mouth dropped open. "You get crazier by the minute."

"Sometimes I scare myself." Then he grinned. "Don't worry your little head. I cleared it with both Commissioner Monroe and Admiral Sandecker. We have their blessings for a ten-day vacation. They admitted it was the least they could do. The reports can wait. The federal government isn't going anywhere."

"But I didn't bring any proper clothes."

"I'll buy you an entire new wardrobe."

"But where are we going in Mexico?" she asked, suddenly becoming excited. "What are we going to do?"

"We," he said with emphasis, "are going to lie on the beach at Mazatlán, drink margaritas and watch the sunset over the Sea of Cortez."

"I think I'm going to love that," she said, nestling against him.

He looked down and smiled. "Somehow, I thought you would."

CYCLOPS

To the eight hundred American men
who were lost with the *Leopoldville*
Christmas Eve 1944 near Cherbourg, France.
Forgotten by many, remembered by few.

Prologue

The *Cyclops* had less than one hour to live. In forty-eight minutes she would become a mass tomb for her 309 passengers and crew—a tragedy unforeseen and unheralded by ominous premonitions, mocked by an empty sea and a diamond-clear sky. Even the seagulls that had haunted her wake for the past week darted and soared in languid indifference, their keen instincts dulled by the mild weather.

There was a slight breeze from the southeast that barely curled the American flag on her stern. At three-thirty in the morning, most of the off-duty crewmen and passengers were asleep. A few, unable to drift off under the oppressive heat of the trade winds, stood around on the upper deck, leaning over the railing and watching the ship's bow hiss and lift over the high rolling swells. The main surge of the sea seemed to be moving beneath the smooth surface, while massive forces were building in the depths below.

Inside the *Cyclops'* wheelhouse, Lieutenant John Church stared vacantly through one of the large circular ports. He had the midnight to 4 A.M. dog watch, and it was all he could do to stay awake. He vaguely noticed the increasing height of the waves, but as long as they remained wide-spaced and their slopes gentle he saw no reason to reduce speed.

Nudged by a friendly current, the heavily loaded collier was plodding along at only nine knots. Her machinery was badly in need of overhaul and even now she was steaming on just her port engine. Shortly after departing Rio de Janeiro, the starboard engine broke down and the chief engineer reported it could not be repaired until they reached port in Baltimore.

Lieutenant Church had worked his way up through the ranks to commissioned officer. He was a thin, prematurely gray-haired man a few months shy of thirty. He had been assigned to many different ships and had sailed around the world four times. But the *Cyclops* was the strangest vessel he'd ever encountered during his twelve years in the Navy. This was his first voyage on the eight-year-old vessel and it was not without its odd events.

Since leaving home port, a seaman who fell overboard was battered into pulp by the port propeller. Next came a collision with the cruiser *Raleigh* that caused minor damage to both ships. The brig was filled with five prisoners. One of them, convicted in the brutal murder of a shipmate, was being transported to the naval prison at Portsmouth, New Hampshire. Outside the entrance to Rio Harbor, the ship came within a hair of running onto a reef, and when the executive officer accused the captain of endangering the ship by altering course, he was placed under arrest and confined to quarters. Finally, there was a malcontent crew, a problem-plagued starboard engine, and a captain who was drinking himself into oblivion. When Church summed up the luckless incidents, he felt as if he were standing watch over a disaster waiting to happen.

His gloomy reverie was interrupted by the sound of heavy footsteps behind him. He turned and stiffened as the captain came through the door of the wheelhouse.

Lieutenant Commander George Worley was a character straight out of *Treasure Island*. All that was missing was an eye patch and a pegleg. He was a bull of a man. His neck was almost nonexistent, his massive head seemed to erupt from his shoulders. The hands that hung at his sides were the largest Church had ever seen. They were as long and thick as a volume out of an encyclopedia. Never a stickler for Navy regulations, Worley's uniform aboard ship usually consisted of bedroom slippers, derby hat, and long-john underwear. Church had never seen the captain in a dress uniform except when the *Cyclops* was in port and Worley went ashore on official business.

With merely a grunt of a greeting, Worley walked over and rapped the barometer with a beefy knuckle. He studied the needle and nodded.

"Not too bad," he said with a slight German accent. "Looks good for the next twenty-four hours. With luck it'll be a smooth sail, at least until we catch hell passing Cape Hatteras."

"Every ship catches hell off Cape Hatteras," said Church flatly.

Worley walked into the chart room and peered at the penciled line showing the *Cyclops'* course and approximate position.

"Alter course five degrees north," he said as he returned to the wheelhouse. "We'll skirt the Great Bahama Bank."

"We're already twenty miles west of the main channel," said Church.

"I have my reasons for avoiding the shipping lanes," Worley responded gruffly.

Church simply nodded at the helmsman, and the *Cyclops* came around. The slight alteration brought the swells running against her port bow and her motion changed. She began to roll heavily.

"I don't much care for the look of the sea," said Church. "The waves are getting a bit steep."

"Not uncommon in these waters," replied Worley. "We're nearing the area where the North Equatorial Current meets the Gulf Stream. I've seen the surface as flat as a desert dry lake, other times I've seen waves twenty feet high, nice easy rollers that slide under the keel."

Church started to say something, but paused, listening. The sound of metal scraping against metal rasped through the wheelhouse. Worley acted as though he hadn't heard anything, but Church walked to the rear bulkhead and looked out over the long cargo deck of the *Cyclops.*

She was a large ship for her day, with an overall length of 542 feet and a 65-foot beam. Built in Philadelphia in 1910, she operated with the Naval Auxiliary Service, Atlantic Fleet. Her seven cavernous holds could handle 10,500 tons of coal, but this trip she was carrying 11,000 tons of manganese. Her hull was settled deep in the water a good foot over her Plimsoll mark. To Church's mind the ship was dangerously overloaded.

Staring astern, Church could see the twenty-four coaling derricks looming through the darkness, their giant clamshell buckets secured for rough weather. He could also make out something else.

The deck amidships appeared to be lifting and dropping in unison with the swells as they passed under the keel.

"My God," he muttered, "the hull is bending with the sea."

Worley didn't bother to look. "Nothing to concern yourself over, son. She's used to a little stress."

"I've never seen a ship twist like this," Church persisted.

Worley dropped into a large wicker chair he kept on the bridge and propped his feet on the binnacle. "Son, no need to worry about the old *Cyclops*. She'll be sailing the seas long after you and me are gone."

Church's apprehension was not soothed by the captain's unconcern. If anything, his sense of foreboding deepened.

After Church turned over the next watch to a fellow officer, he left the bridge and stopped by the radio room to have a cup of coffee with the operator on duty. Sparks, as every wireless man aboard every ship at sea was called, looked up as he entered.

"Mornin', Lieutenant."

"Any interesting news from nearby vessels?"

Sparks lifted his headset from one ear. "Sorry?"

Church repeated the question.

"Only a couple of radiomen on a pair of merchant ships exchanging chess moves."

"You should join in to avoid the monotony."

"Checkers is my game," said Sparks.

"How close are those two merchantmen?"

"Their signals are pretty weak... probably a good hundred miles away."

Church straddled a chair and leaned his arms and chin on the backrest. "Give them a call and ask what sort of sea they're encountering."

Sparks gave a helpless shrug. "I can't."

"Your transmitter acting up?"

"She's fit as a sixteen-year-old Havana whore."

"I don't understand."

"Captain Worley's orders," answered Sparks. "When we left Rio, he called me to his quarters and said not to transmit any messages without his direct order before we dock in Baltimore."

"He give a reason?"

"No, sir."

"Damned odd."

"My hunch is it has something to do with that bigwig we took on as a passenger in Rio."

"The consul general?"

"I received my orders right after he came on board—"

Sparks broke off and pressed the headset to his ears. Then he began scribbling an incoming message on a pad of paper. After a few moments he turned, his face grim.

"A distress signal."

Church stood up. "What position?"

"Twenty miles southeast of the Anguilla Cays."

Church mentally calculated. "That puts them about fifty miles off our bow. What else?"

"Name of vessel, *Crogan Castle*. Prow stove in. Superstructure heavily damaged. Taking on water. Require immediate assistance."

"Prow stove in?" Church repeated in a puzzled tone. "From what?"

"They didn't say, Lieutenant."

Church started for the door. "I'll inform the captain. Tell the *Crogan Castle* we're coming at full steam."

Sparks's face took on a pained look. "Please, sir, I can't."

"Do it!" Church commanded. "I'll take full responsibility."

He turned and ran down the alleyway and up the ladder to the wheelhouse. Worley was still sitting in the wicker chair, swaying with the roll of the ship. His spectacles were dipped low on his nose and he was reading a dog-eared *Liberty* magazine.

"Sparks has picked up an SOS," Church announced. "Less than fifty miles away. I ordered him to acknowledge the call and say we were altering course to assist."

Worley's eyes went wide and he launched himself out of the chair and clutched a startled Church by the upper arms. "Are you crazy?" he roared. "Who in hell gave you the authority to countermand my orders?"

Pain erupted in Church's arms. The viselike pressure from those huge hands felt as if it were squeezing his biceps into pulp. "Good God, Captain, we can't ignore another vessel in distress."

"We damn well can if I say so!"

Church was stunned at Worley's outburst. He could see the reddened, unfocused eyes and smell the breath reeking of whisky. "A basic rule of the sea," Church persisted. "We must render assistance."

"Are they sinking?"

"The message said 'taking on water.'"

Worley shoved Church away. "The hell you say. Let the bastards man the pumps until their ass is saved by any ship but the *Cyclops*."

The helmsman and the duty officer looked on in amazed silence as Church and Worley faced each other with unblinking eyes, the atmosphere in the wheelhouse charged with tension. Any rift that was between them in the past weeks was hurled wide open.

The duty officer made a move as if to intervene. Worley twisted his head and snarled, "Keep to your business and mind the helm."

Church rubbed his bruised arms and glared at the captain. "I protest your refusal to respond to an SOS and I insist it be entered in the ship's log."

"I warn you—"

"I also wish it noted that you ordered the radio operator not to transmit."

"You're out of bounds, mister." Worley spoke coldly, his lips compressed in a tight line, his face bathed in sweat. "Consider yourself under arrest and confined to quarters."

"You arrest any more of your officers," Church snapped, his anger out of control, "and you'll have to run this jinx ship by yourself."

Suddenly, before Worley could reply, the *Cyclops* lurched downward into a deep trough between the swells. From instinct, honed by years at sea, everyone in the wheelhouse automatically grabbed at the nearest secure object to keep his footing. The hull plates groaned under the stress and they could hear several cracking noises.

"Mother of God," muttered the helmsman, his voice edged with panic.

"Shut up!" Worley growled as the *Cyclops* righted herself. "She's seen worse seas than this."

A sickening realization struck Church. "The *Crogan Castle*, the ship that sent the distress signal, said her prow was stove in and her superstructure damaged."

Worley stared at him. "So what?"

"Don't you see, she must have been struck by a giant, rogue wave."

"You talk like a crazy man. Go to your cabin, mister. I don't want to see your face until we reach port."

Church hesitated, his fists clenched. Then slowly his hands relaxed as he realized any further argument with Worley was a waste of breath. He turned without a word and left the wheelhouse.

He stepped onto the deck and stared out over the bow. The sea appeared deceptively mild. The waves had diminished to ten feet and no water was coming over the deck. He made his way aft and saw that the steam lines that ran the winches and auxiliary equipment were scraping against the bulwarks as the ship rose and fell with the long, slow swells.

Then Church went below and checked two of the ore holds, probing his flashlight at the heavy shorings and stanchions installed to keep the manganese cargo from shifting. They groaned and creaked under the stress, but they seemed firm and secure. He could not see any sign of trickling grit from the ship's motion.

Still, he felt uneasy, and he was tired. It took all his willpower to keep from heading to the snug confines of his bunk and gratefully closing his eyes to the grim set of problems surrounding the ship. One more inspection tour down to the engine room to see if any water was reported rising in the bilges. A trip that proved negative, seeming to confirm Worley's faith in the *Cyclops*.

As he was walking down a passageway toward the wardroom for a cup of coffee a cabin door opened and the American consul general to Brazil, Alfred Gottschalk, hesitated on the threshold, talking to someone inside. Church peered over Gottschalk's shoulder and saw the ship's doctor bent over a man lying in a bunk. The patient's face looked tired and yellow-skinned, a youngish face that belied the thick forest of white hair above. The eyes were open and reflected fear mingled with suffering and hardship, eyes that had seen too much. The scene was only one more strange element to be added to the voyage of the *Cyclops*.

As officer of the deck before the ship departed Rio de Janeiro, Church had observed a motor caravan arrive on the dock. The consul general had stepped out of a chauffeur-driven town car and directed the loading of his steamer trunks and suitcases. Then he looked up, taking in every detail of the *Cyclops* from her ungainly straight-up-and-down bow to the graceful curve of her champagne-glass stern. Despite his short, rotund, and almost comical frame, he radiated that indefinable air of someone accustomed to the upper rungs of authority. He wore his silver-yellow hair cropped excessively short, Prussian style. His narrow eyebrows very nearly matched his clipped moustache.

The second vehicle in the caravan was an ambulance. Church watched as a figure on a stretcher was lifted out and carried on board, but he failed to discern any features because of heavy mosquito netting that covered the face. Though the person on the stretcher was obviously part of his entourage, Gottschalk took little notice, turning his attention instead to the chain-drive Mack truck that brought up the rear.

He gazed anxiously as a large oblong crate was hoisted in the air by one of the ship's loading booms and swung into the forward cargo compartment. As if on cue, Worley appeared and personally supervised the battening down of the hatch. Then he greeted Gottschalk and escorted him to his quarters. Almost immediately, the mooring lines were cast off and the ship got under way and was heading out to sea through the harbor entrance.

Gottschalk turned and noticed Church standing in the passageway. He stepped from the cabin and closed the door behind him, his eyes narrowed with suspicion. "Something I can help you with, Lieutenant..."

"Church, sir. I was just finishing an inspection of the ship and heading for the wardroom for a cup of coffee. Would you care to join me?"

A faint expression of relief passed over the consul general's face and he smiled. "Might as well. I can never sleep more than a few hours at a stretch. Drives my wife crazy."

"She remain in Rio this trip?"

"No, I sent her on ahead to our home in Maryland. I terminated my assignment in Brazil. I hope to spend the rest of my State Department service in Washington."

Gottschalk appeared unduly nervous to Church. His eyes darted up and down the passageway, and he constantly dabbed a linen handkerchief at his small mouth. He took Church by the arm.

"Before we have coffee, would you be so kind, Lieutenant, as to escort me to the baggage cargo hold?"

Church stared at him. "Yes, sir, if you wish."

"Thank you," said Gottschalk. "I need something from one of my trunks."

If Church thought the request unusual, he said nothing, simply nodded and started off toward the forward part of the ship with the fat little consul general huffing in his wake. They made their way topside and walked along the runway leading from the aft deckhouses toward the forecastle, passing under the bridge superstructure awkwardly suspended on steel stiltlike stanchions. The steaming light, suspended between the two forward masts that formed a support for the skeletal grid connecting the coaling derricks, cast a weird glow that was reflected by the eerie radiance of the approaching swells.

Stopping at a hatch, Church undogged the latches and motioned Gottschalk down a ladder, illuminating the way with his flashlight. When they reached the bottom deck of the cargo hold, Church found the switch and flicked on the overhead lights, which lit the area with an unearthly yellow glow.

Gottschalk shouldered past Church and walked directly to the crate, which was secured by chains whose end links were padlocked into eyebolts protruding from the deck. He stood there for a few moments, a reverent expression on his face as he stared at it, his thoughts wandering in another place, another time.

Church studied the crate up close for the first time. There were no markings on the stout wooden sides. He judged its measurements at nine feet long by three feet high by four feet wide. He couldn't begin to guess the weight, but knew the contents were heavy. He recalled how the winch had strained when it hoisted the crate on board. Curiosity overcame his mask of unconcern.

"Mind if I ask what's inside?"

Gottschalk's gaze remained on the crate. "An archeological artifact on its way to a museum," he said vaguely.

"Must be valuable," Church probed.

Gottschalk did not answer. Something along the edge of the lid struck his eye. He pulled out a pair of reading spectacles and peered through the lenses. His hands trembled and his body stiffened.

"It's been opened!" he gasped.

"Not possible," said Church. "The top is so tightly secured by chains that the links have made indentations on the edges of the wood."

"But look here," he said, pointing. "You can see the pry marks where the lid was forced up."

"Those scratches were probably caused when the crate was sealed."

"They were not there when I checked the crate two days ago," said Gottschalk firmly. "Someone in your crew had tampered with it."

"You're unduly concerned. What crew member would have any interest in an old artifact that must weigh at least two tons? Besides, who else but you has the key to the padlocks?"

Gottschalk dropped to his knees and jerked one of the locks. The shackle came off in his hand. Instead of steel, it was carved from wood. He looked frightened now. As if hypnotized, he slowly rose, looked wildly about the cargo compartment, and uttered one word.

"Zanona."

It was as if he triggered a nightmare. The next sixty seconds were locked in horror. The murder of the consul general happened so quickly that Church could only stand frozen in shock, his mind uncomprehending of what his eyes witnessed.

A figure leaped from the shadows onto the top of the crate. He was dressed in the uniform of a Navy seaman, but there was no denying the racial characteristics of his coarse, straight black hair, the prominent cheekbones, the unusually dark, expressionless eyes.

Without uttering a sound, the South American Indian plunged a spearlike shaft through Gottschalk's chest until the barbed point protruded nearly a foot beyond the shoulder blades. The consul general did not immediately fall. He slowly turned his head and stared at Church, his eyes wide and devoid of recognition. He tried to say something, but no words came out, only a sickening, gurgling kind of cough that turned his lips and chin red. As he began to sag the Indian put a foot on his chest and yanked out the spear.

Church had never seen the assassin before. The Indian was not one of the *Cyclops'* crew and could only be a stowaway. There was no malevolence in the brown face, no anger or hate, only an inscrutable expression of total blankness. He grasped the spear almost negligently and silently jumped from the crate.

Church braced himself for the onslaught. He deftly sidestepped the spear's thrust and hurled the flashlight at the Indian's face. There was a soft thud as the metal tube smashed into the right jaw, breaking the bone and loosening several teeth. Then he lashed out with his fist and struck the Indian's throat. The spear dropped onto the deck and Church snatched up the wooden shaft and lifted it above his head.

Suddenly, the world inside the cargo compartment went mad and Church found himself fighting to keep his balance as the deck canted nearly sixty degrees. He somehow kept his footing, running downhill with gravity until he reached the slanting forward bulkhead. The Indian's inert body rolled after him, coming to rest at his feet. Then he watched in helpless terror as the crate, unbound by its locks, hurtled across the deck, crushing the Indian and pinning Church's legs against the steel wall. The impact caused the lid to twist half off the crate, revealing the contents.

Church dazedly stared inside. The incredible sight that met his eyes under the flickering overhead lights was the final image burned into his mind during the fractional seconds that separated him from death.

In the wheelhouse, Captain Worley was witnessing an even more awesome sight. It was as though the *Cyclops* had abruptly dropped into a fathomless hole. Her bow pitched sharply into an immense trough and her stern rose steeply into the air until her propellers came clear of the water. Through the gloom ahead, the *Cyclops'* steaming lights reflected on a seething black wall that rose up and blotted out the stars.

Deep in the bowels of the cargo holds came a dreadful rumbling that felt and sounded like an earthquake, causing the entire ship to shudder from stem to stern. Worley never had time to voice the alarm that flashed through his mind. The shorings had given way and the shifting manganese ore increased the *Cyclops'* downward momentum.

The helmsman stared out the bridge port in mute astonishment as the towering column, the height of a ten-story building, roared toward them with the speed of an avalanche. The top half crested and curled under. A million tons of water crashed savagely into the forward part of the ship, completely inundating the bow and superstructure. The doors to the bridge wings shattered and water shot into the wheelhouse. Worley gripped the counter railing, his paralyzed mind unable to visualize the inevitable.

The wave swept over the ship. The entire bow section twisted away as steel beams snapped and the keel buckled. The heavy riveted hull plates were ripped away as if they were paper. The *Cyclops* plunged deeper under the immense pressure of the wave. Her propellers bit the water again and helped impel her into the waiting depths. The *Cyclops* could not come back.

She kept on going, down, down, until her shattered hull and the people it imprisoned fell against the restless sands of the sea floor below, leaving only a flight of bewildered seagulls to mark her fateful passage.

PART I

The Prosperteer

1

THE BLIMP HUNG MOTIONLESS in the tropical air, poised and tranquil, like a fish suspended in an aquarium. Her bow nudged against a yellow mooring mast as she balanced daintily on a single landing wheel. She was a tired-looking old airship; her once silver skin had wrinkled and turned white and was spotted by numerous patches. The gondola, the control car that hung beneath her belly, wore an antique boat—like look, and its glass windows were yellowed with age. Only her two 200-horsepower Wright Whirlwind engines appeared new, having been carefully restored to pristine condition.

Unlike her younger sister ships that plied the skies above football stadiums, her gas-tight envelope was made from aluminum with riveted seams instead of rubber-coated polyester and was supported by twelve circular frames like the back of a fish. Her cigar shape was 149 feet in length and held 200,000 cubic feet of helium, and if no headwinds attacked her rotund nose, she could barrel through the clouds at sixty-two miles an hour. Her original designation was ZMC-2, Zeppelin Metal Clad Number Two, and she had been constructed in Detroit and turned over to the United States Navy in 1929. Unlike most airships with four massive stabilizing fins, she sported eight small fins on her tapered tail. Very advanced for her era, she had given solid and dependable service until 1942, when she was dismantled and forgotten.

For forty-seven years the ZMC-2 languished in an abandoned hangar along the runway of a deserted naval air station near Key West, Florida. Then in 1988, the property was sold by the government to a financial conglomerate headed by a wealthy publisher, Raymond LeBaron, who intended to develop it as a resort.

Shortly after arriving from his corporate headquarters in Chicago to inspect the newly purchased naval base, LeBaron stumbled onto the dusty and corroded remains of the ZMC-2 and became intrigued. Charging it off to promotion, he had the old lighter-than-air craft reassembled and the engines rebuilt, calling her the *Prosperteer* after the business magazine that was the base of his financial empire, and emblazoning the name in huge red letters on the side of the envelope.

LeBaron learned to fly the *Prosperteer,* mastering the fickle moods of the craft and the constant adjustments required to maintain steady flight under the capricious nature of the wind. There was no autopilot to relieve the chore of dipping the bow against a sudden gust and lifting it when the breeze slackened. The near-neutral buoyancy varied greatly with the atmosphere. Residue from a light rain could add hundreds of pounds to the blimp's vast skin, decreasing her ability to lift, while dry air blowing down from the northwest forced the pilot to fight the craft's insistence on rising to an undesired altitude.

LeBaron reveled in the challenge. The exhilaration of second-guessing the moods of the antique gas bag and wrestling with her aerodynamic whims far exceeded any enjoyment he received from flying any of the five jet aircraft belonging to his corporate holdings. He sneaked away from the boardroom at every opportunity to travel to Key West so he could island-hop around the Caribbean. The *Prosperteer* soon became a familiar sight over the Bahama Islands. A native worker, laboring in a sugarcane field, looked up at the blimp and promptly described her as a "little pig running backwards."

LeBaron, however, like most entrepreneurs of the power elite, suffered from a restless mind and a driving urge to tackle a new project lying over the next hill. After nearly a year his interest in the old blimp began to wane.

Then one evening in a waterfront saloon he met an old beach rat by the name of Buck Caesar, who operated a backwater salvage company with the grandiloquent title "Exotic Artifact Ventures, Inc."

During a conversation over several rounds of iced rum, Caesar spoke the magic word that has fired the human mind into insanity for five thousand years and probably caused more grief than half the wars: *treasure.*

After listening to Caesar spin tales of Spanish galleons littering the waters of the Caribbean, their cargoes of gold and silver mingled with the coral, even a shrewd financial manipulator with the acute business sense of LeBaron was hooked. With a handshake they formed a partnership.

LeBaron's interest in the *Prosperteer* was revived. The blimp made a perfect platform for spotting potential shipwreck sites from the air. Airplanes moved too fast for aerial survey, while helicopters had a limited flying time and churned up the surface of the water with wash from their rotor blades. The blimp could remain airborne for two days and cruise at a walk. From an altitude of 400 feet, the straight lines of a man-made object could be detected by a sharp eye a hundred feet beneath a calm and clear sea.

Dawn was crawling over the Florida Straits as the ten-man ground crew assembled around the *Prosperteer* and began a preflight inspection. The new sun caught the huge envelope covered by morning dew, giving off an iridescent effect like that from a soap bubble. The blimp stood in the center of a concrete runway whose expansion cracks were lined with weeds. A slight breeze blew in from the straits and she swung around the mooring mast until her bulbous nose faced into it.

Most of the ground crew were young, deeply tanned, and casually dressed in an assortment of shorts, bathing suits, and denim cutoffs. They took scant notice as a Cadillac stretch limousine drove across the runway and stopped at the large truck that served as the blimp's repair shop, crew chief's office, and communications room.

The chauffeur opened the door and LeBaron unlimbered from the rear seat, followed by Buck Caesar, who immediately made for the blimp's gondola with a roll of nautical charts tucked under one arm. LeBaron, looking a very trim and healthy sixty-five, towered above everyone at six foot seven. His eyes were the color of light oak, the graying hair combed just so, and he possessed the distant, preoccupied gaze of a man whose thoughts were several hours in the future.

He bent down and spoke for a few moments to an attractive woman who leaned from the car. He kissed her lightly on the cheek, closed the car door, and began walking toward the *Prosperteer.*

The crew chief, a studious-looking man wearing a spotless white shop coat, came over and shook LeBaron's outstretched hand. "Fuel tanks are topped off, Mr. LeBaron. The preflight check list is completed."

"How's the buoyancy?"

"You'll have to adjust for an extra five hundred pounds from the dampness."

LeBaron nodded thoughtfully. "She'll lighten in the heat of the day."

"The controls should feel more responsive. The elevator cables were showing signs of rust, so I had them replaced."

"What's the weather look like?"

"Low scattered clouds most of the day. Little chance of rain. You'll be bucking a five-mile-an-hour head wind from the southeast on the way out."

"And a tail wind on the return trip. I prefer that."

"Same radio frequency as the last trip?"

"Yes, we'll report our position and condition, using normal voice communication, every half hour. If we spot a promising target we'll transmit in code."

The crew chief nodded. "Understood."

Without further conversation LeBaron climbed the ladder to the gondola and settled in the pilot's seat. He was joined by his copilot, Joe Cavilla, a sixty-year-old, sad-eyed, dour individual who seldom opened his mouth except to yawn or sneeze. His family had immigrated to America from Brazil when he was sixteen and he had joined the Navy, flying blimps until the last airship unit was formally disbanded in 1964. Cavilla had simply showed up one day, impressed LeBaron with his expertise in lighter-than-air craft, and was hired.

The third member of the crew was Buck Caesar. He wore a constant smile on a gentle, middle-aged face that had the texture of cowhide, but his gaze was shrewd, and the body held the firmness of boxer. He sat hunched over a small table contemplating his charts, drawing a series of squares near a sector of the Bahama Channel.

Blue smoke burst from the exhaust stacks as LeBaron turned over the engines. The ground crew untied a number of canvas sacks containing ballast shot from the gondola. One crewman, the "butterfly catcher," held up a windsock on a long pole so LeBaron could note the exact direction of the wind.

LeBaron gave a hand signal to the crew chief. A wooden chock was pulled from the landing wheel, the nose coupling was released from the mooring mast, and the men holding the bow ropes heaved to one side and let go. When the airship was free and clear of the mast, LeBaron eased the throttles forward and spun the large elevator wheel next to his seat. The Prosperteer pointed her comic-opera snout upward at a fifty-degree angle and slowly drove into the sky.

The ground crew watched until the huge airship gradually faded from view over the blue-green waters of the straits. Then their interest turned briefly to the limousine and the vague feminine shape behind the tinted windows.

Jessie LeBaron shared her husband's passion for outdoor adventure, but she was an orderly woman, who preferred organizing charity balls and political fund raisers over a time-wasting hunt for dubious treasure. Vibrant and bouncy, with a mouth that had a repertory of a dozen different smiles, she was six months past fifty but looked closer to thirty-seven. Jessie was slightly heavy-bodied but firm, her facial skin was creamy smooth, and she had allowed her hair to turn a natural salt-and-pepper. The eyes were large and dark and bore no trace of the blank look usually left by plastic surgery.

When she could no longer see the blimp, Jessie spoke into the limousine's intercom. "Angelo, please drive back to the hotel."

The chauffeur, a somber Cuban with the etched face of a postage stamp engraving, touched two fingers to the brim of his cap and nodded.

The ground crew watched the long Cadillac turn and head through the deserted front gate of the former naval base. Then someone produced a volleyball. Quickly they drew out the boundaries and set up a net. After choosing up sides, they began batting the ball back and forth to fight the boredom of waiting.

Inside the air-conditioned truck, the crew chief and a radio operator acknowledged and recorded the reports from the blimp. LeBaron religiously transmitted every thirty minutes, never varying more than a few seconds, describing his approximate position, any changes in weather, and vessels passing below.

Then, at half past two in the afternoon, the reports stopped. The radio operator tried to raise the *Prosperteer,* but there was no response. Five o'clock came and went with still no word. Outside, the ground crew wearily ceased their play and crowded around the door to the radio compartment as the uneasiness inside began to grow. At six o'clock, with no sign of the blimp over the sea, the crew chief put in a call to the Coast Guard.

What no one knew, or possibly suspected, was that Raymond LeBaron and his friends on board the *Prosperteer* had vanished in a mystery that went far beyond any mere treasure hunt.

2

TEN DAYS LATER, the President of the United States stared pensively out the window of his limousine at the passing landscape and idly drummed his fingers on one knee. His eyes didn't see the picturesque estates amid the horse country of Potomac, Maryland. He took scant notice of the sun gleaming on the coats of the Thoroughbreds roaming the rolling pastures. The images that reflected in his mind coursed around the strange events that had literally hurled him into the White House.

As the Vice President he was sworn into the nation's highest office when his predecessor was forced to resign after admitting to a mental illness. Mercifully, the news media did not launch a full-blown investigation. Of course there were the routine interviews with White House aides, congressional leaders, and noted psychiatrists, but nothing smelling of intrigue or conspiracy emerged. The former President left Washington and retired to his farm in New Mexico, still respected with great sympathy from the public, and the truth remained locked in the minds of a very few.

The new Chief Executive was an energetic man who stood slightly over six feet and weighed a solid two hundred pounds. His face was square-jawed, with firm features and a brow that was usually furrowed in a thoughtful frown, yet his intense gray eyes could be deceptively limpid. The silver hair was always neatly trimmed and parted on the right side in the homespun style of a Kansas banker.

He was not handsome or flamboyant in the eyes of the public, but emitted an appealing style and charm. Though he was a professional politician, he somewhat naïvely viewed the government as a giant team with himself as the coach who sent in plays during the game. Highly regarded as a mover and shaker, he surrounded himself with a cabinet and staff of gifted men and women who made every effort to work in harmony with Congress rather than enlisting a band of cronies who were more concerned with fortifying their personal power base.

His thoughts slowly focused on the local scenery as his Secret Service driver slowed down and turned off River Road North through a large stone gate bordered by a white rail fence. A uniformed security guard and a Secret Service agent wearing the standard dark sunglasses and business suit stepped from the gatehouse. They simply peered in the car and nodded in recognition. The agent spoke into a small radio transmitter strapped to his wrist like a watch.

"The Boss is on his way."

The limousine rolled up the tree-lined circular drive of the Congressional Country Club, past the tennis courts on the left teeming with the staring wives of the members, and eased to a stop under the portico of the clubhouse.

Elmer Hoskins, the advance man, stepped forward and opened the rear door. "Looks like a good day for golf, Mr. President."

"My game couldn't get worse if we were standing in snow," the President said, smiling.

"I wish I could shoot in the low eighties."

"So do I," said the President as he followed Hoskins around the side of the clubhouse and down to the pro shop. "I've added five strokes to my score since taking over the Oval Office."

"Still, not bad for someone who only plays once a week."

"That and the fact it becomes increasingly difficult to keep my mind on the game."

The club pro came over and shook his hand. "Reggie has your clubs and is waiting on the first tee."

The President nodded and they climbed into a golf cart and set off over a path that curved around a large pond and onto one of the longest golf courses in the nation. Reggie Salazar, a short, wiry Hispanic, stood leaning on a huge leather bag packed with golf clubs that came up to his chest.

Salazar's appearance was deceiving. Like a small Andes Mountains burro, he could lug a fifty-pound bag of irons around eighteen holes without losing a breath or showing a drop of sweat. When he was only a boy of thirteen he had carried his ailing mother in his arms with a three-year-old sister strapped to his back across the California/Baja border thirty miles to San Diego. After the illegal alien amnesty was granted in 1985 he worked around golf courses, becoming a top caddy on the professional tour. He was a genius at learning the rhythm of a course, claiming it spoke to him, and unerringly picking the right club for a difficult shot. Salazar was also a wit and a philosopher, blurting adages that would have made Casey Stengel envious. The President had drawn him in a congressional tournament five years before and they became good friends.

Salazar always dressed like a field laborer—denim jeans, western shirt, GI boots, and a rancher's wide-brimmed straw hat. It was his trademark.

"*Saludos,* Mr. President," he greeted in border English, his dark coffee-brown eyes glistening. "Do you wish to walk or ride the cart?"

The President pressed Salazar's outstretched hand. "I could use the exercise, so let's walk for a while and maybe ride the back nine."

He teed off and hit a lofting ball with a slight hook that stopped rolling 180 yards up and near the border of the fairway. As he strolled from the tee the problems of running the country melted away and his mind began planning the next shot.

He played in silence until he dropped his putt in the cup for a par. Then he relaxed and handed his putter to Salazar. "Well, Reggie, any suggestions for dealing with Capitol Hill?"

"Too many black ants," Salazar replied with an elastic grin.

"Black ants?"

"Everyone wear dark suits and run crazy. All they make is paper and wave tongues. Me, I'd write law saying congresspeople could only meet every other year. That way they'd cause less trouble."

The President laughed. "I can think of at least two hundred million voters who would applaud your idea."

They continued along the course, followed at a discreet distance by two Secret Service agents in a golf cart while at least a dozen others prowled the course grounds. The banter remained cheerful as the President's game went smoothly. After he retrieved the ball from the cup on the ninth green, his score tallied thirty-nine. He considered it a minor triumph.

"Let's take a break before we attack the back nine," said the President. "I'm going to celebrate with a beer. Care to join me?"

"No, thank you, sir. I'll use the time to clean grass and dirt from your clubs."

The President handed him the putter. "Suit yourself. But I must insist you join me for a drink after we finish the eighteenth."

Salazar beamed like a lighthouse. "An honor, Mr. President." Then he trotted off toward the caddy shack.

Twenty minutes later, after returning a call from his chief of staff and downing a bottle of Coors, the President left the clubhouse and joined Salazar, who was sitting slouched in a golf cart on the tenth tee, the wide brim of his straw hat pulled low over his forehead. His hands hung loosely draped on the steering wheel and were now encased in a pair of leather work gloves.

"Well, let's see if I can break eighty," said the President, his eyes glistening in anticipation of a good game.

Salazar said nothing and simply held out a driver.

The President took the club and looked at it, puzzled. "This is a short hole. Don't you think a number three wood should do the job?"

Staring at the ground, the hat hiding any facial expression, Salazar silently shook his head.

"You know best," the President said agreeably. He approached the ball, flexed his hands on the club, arched into a back swing, and brought the head down gracefully but entered into a rather awkward follow-through. The ball sailed straight over the fairway and landed a considerable distance beyond the green.

A perplexed expression spread across the President's face as he retrieved his tee and climbed in the seat of the electric cart. "That's the first time I've ever see you call the wrong club."

The caddy did not reply. He pressed the battery pedal and steered the cart toward the tenth green. About halfway down the fairway he reached over and placed a small package on the dashboard shelf directly in front of the President.

"Bringing along a snack in case you get hungry?" asked the President good-naturedly.

"No, sir, it's a bomb."

The President's eyebrows pinched a fraction in irritation. "Not a funny joke, Reggie—"

His words suddenly choked off as the straw hat rose and he found himself staring into the indigo-blue eyes of a total stranger.

3

"PLEASE KEEP YOUR ARMS in their present position," said the stranger conversationally. "I am aware of the hand signal you were advised to give your Secret Service people if you thought your life was endangered."

The President sat like a dead tree, disbelieving, more curious than afraid. He couldn't trust himself to speak at first, to assemble the right words. His eyes remained locked on the package.

"A stupid act," he said finally. "You won't live to enjoy it."

"This is not an assassination. You will not be harmed if you follow my instructions. Do you accept that?"

"You've got guts, mister."

The stranger ignored the remark and kept talking in the tone of a schoolteacher reciting class rules of conduct. "The bomb is a fragmentation type that will shred any flesh and bone within twenty yards. If you attempt to alert your bodyguards I will detonate it with an electronic control strapped to my wrist. Please continue your golf game as if nothing is out of the ordinary."

He stopped the cart several feet from the ball, stepped to the grass, and glanced warily at the Secret Service agents, satisfying himself that they appeared more intent on scanning the woods around the course. Then he reached in the bag and pulled out a six iron.

"It's obvious you don't know crap about golf," said the President, mildly pleased at gaining a small measure of control. "This calls for a chip shot. Hand me a nine iron."

The intruder obliged and stood by while the President chipped onto the green and putted into the cup. When they set off for the next tee, he studied the man seated beside him.

The few strands of gray hair that strayed beneath the straw hat and the lines bordering the eyes revealed an age in the late fifties. The body was slender, almost frail, the hips slim, a good match for Reggie Salazar except this man was a good three inches taller. The facial features were narrow and vaguely Scandinavian. The voice was educated, the cool manner and the squared shoulders suggested someone who was used to authority, yet there was no hint of viciousness or evil.

"I get the crazy impression," said the President calmly, "that you staged this intrusion to make a point."

"Not so crazy. You're very astute. But I would expect no less from a man with your power."

"Who the hell *are* you?"

"For the sake of conversation call me Joe. And I'll save you asking what this is all about as soon as we reach the tee. There is a restroom there." He paused and removed a folder from inside his shirt, sliding it across the seat to the President. "Enter and quickly scan the contents. Take no more than eight minutes. Linger beyond that time and you might arouse the suspicions of your bodyguards. I needn't describe the consequences."

The electric cart slowly eased to a halt. Without a word the President entered the restroom, sat down on the john, and began reading. Precisely eight minutes later he came out, his face a mask of confusion.

"What kind of insane trick have you hatched?"

"No trick."

"I don't understand why you went to such elaborate lengths to force me to read comic-book science fiction."

"Not fiction."

"Then it has to be some sort of con job."

"The Jersey Colony exists," said Joe patiently.

"Yes, and so does Atlantis."

Joe smiled wryly. "You've just been inducted into a very exclusive club. You're only the second President ever to be briefed on the project. Now I suggest you tee off and I'll flesh out the picture as you continue playing around the course. It won't be a complete picture because there is too little time. Also, some details are not necessary for you to know."

"First, one question. You owe me that."

"All right."

"Reggie Salazar?"

"Sleeping soundly in the caddy shack."

"God help you if you're lying."

"Which club?" Joe asked blithely.

"A short hole. Give me a four iron."

The President swung mechanically, but the ball flew straight and true, landing and rolling to within ten feet of the cup. He tossed the club at Joe and sat heavily in the cart, waiting.

"Well, then..." Joe began as he accelerated toward the green. "In 1963, only two months before his death, President Kennedy met with a group of nine men at his home in Hyannis Port who proposed a highly secret leapfrog project to be developed behind the scenes of the fledgling man-in-space program. They were an 'inner core' of brilliant young scientists, corporate businessmen, engineers, and politicians who had achieved extraordinary success in their respective fields. Kennedy bought their idea and went so far as to launch a government agency that acted as a front to siphon federal tax money for what was to be code-named Jersey Colony. The pot was also sweetened by the businessmen, who set up a fund to match the government dollar for dollar. Research facilities were created in existing buildings, usually old warehouses, scattered around the country. Millions were saved in start-up costs, while eliminating questions by the curious over new construction of one vast development center."

"How was the operation kept secret?" the President asked. "Surely there were leaks."

Joe shrugged. "A simple technique. The research teams had their own pet projects. Each worked at a different location. The old act of one hand not knowing what the other was doing. The hardware was farmed out to small manufacturers. It was that elementary. The difficult part was coordinating the efforts under NASA's nose without letting their people know what was going on. So phony military officers were moved into the space centers at Cape Canaveral and Houston, also one at the Pentagon to backstop any embarrassing probes."

"Are you saying the Defense Department knows nothing of this?"

Joe smiled. "The easiest part. One member of the 'inner core' was a high-ranking staff officer, whose name is of no importance to you. He had no problem burying another military mission in the labyrinth of the Pentagon."

Joe paused as they pulled up beside the ball. The President played another shot as if he were sleepwalking. He returned to the cart and stared at Joe.

"Doesn't seem possible NASA could be so completely hoodwinked."

"Again, one of the Space Administration's key directors belonged to the 'inner core.' His vision was also that of a permanent base with limitless opportunity instead of focusing on a few temporary manned landings on the lunar surface. But he realized NASA couldn't do two complicated and expensive programs at the same time, so he became a member of the Jersey Colony. The project was kept secret so there would be no interference from the Executive Office, Congress, or the military. As things turned out, it was a wise decision."

"And the bottom line is that the United States has a solid foot on the moon."

Joe nodded solemnly. "Yes, Mr. President, that is correct."

The President could not fully comprehend the enormity of the concept. "Incredible that a project so vast could be carried off behind an impenetrable curtain of security, unknown and undiscovered for twenty-six years."

Joe stared down the fairway. "It would take me a month to describe the problems, the setbacks, and the tragedies that were suffered. The scientific and engineering breakthroughs in developing a hydrogen-reduction process for making water, an oxygen-extraction apparatus, and a power-generating plant whose turbine is driven by liquid nitrogen. The accumulation of materials and equipment launched into designated orbit by a private space agency sponsored by the 'inner core.' The construction of a lunar transfer vehicle designed to ferry it all from earth orbit to the Jersey Colony."

"And this was done under the nose of our entire space program?"

"What was advertised as large communication satellites were disguised sections of the lunar transfer vehicle, each containing a man in an internal capsule. I won't go into the ten years of planning for that moment or the remarkable complexity of their linkup with each other and one of our abandoned space laboratories that was used as a base for the vehicle's assembly. Or the breakthrough in designing a lightweight, efficient solar electric engine using oxygen as the propulsion fuel. But the job was accomplished."

Joe stopped to allow the President to hit another shot. "Then it was a matter of gathering up the life-support systems and supplies already sent into orbit and transporting all of it, actually towing it like a tugboat, to the predetermined site on the moon. Even an old Soviet orbiting laboratory and any useful piece of space junk were pulled to the Jersey Colony. From the beginning, it's been a no-frills operation, the pioneering trek of man from his home on earth, the most important evolutionary step since the first fish struggled onto land over 300 million years ago. But by God, we did it. As we sit here and talk ten men are living and working in a hostile environment 240,000 miles away."

As Joe spoke his eyes took on the look of a messiah. Then the vision faded and he glanced at his watch. "We'd better hurry along before the Secret Service wonders why we're lagging. Anyway, that's the gist of it. I'll try to answer your questions while you play."

The President stared at him in awe. "Jesus," he groaned. "I don't think I can absorb all this."

"My apologies for throwing so much at you in so short a time," said Joe swiftly. "But it was necessary."

"Where exactly on the moon is this Jersey Colony?"

"After studying the photographs from the Lunar Orbiter probes and Apollo missions, we detected a geyser of vapor issuing from a volcanic region in the southern hemisphere of the moon's far side. Closer examination showed it to be a large cavern, perfect shelter for locating the initial installation."

"You said ten men are up there?"

"Yes."

"What about rotation, replacements?"

"No rotation."

"God, that means the original crew who assembled the lunar transport have been in space six years."

"That's true," acknowledged Joe. "One died and seven were added as the base was expanded to support more life."

"What about their families?"

"All bachelors. All knew and accepted the hardship and risk."

"You say I'm only the second President to learn of the project?"

"That's correct."

"Not allowing the nation's Chief Executive to share in the project is an insult to the office."

Joe's dark blue eyes deepened even more; he stared at the President with stern malice. "Presidents are political animals. Votes become more precious than treasure. Nixon might have used the Jersey Colony as a smokescreen to bail himself out of Watergate. Same with Carter and the Iranian hostage fiasco. Reagan to enhance his image while lording it over the Russians. What's even more deplorable is the thought of what Congress would do with the project, the partisan politics that would come into play as debate raged to no good purpose over whether the money would be better spent on defense or feeding the poor. I love my country, Mr. President, and consider myself a better patriot than most, but I no longer have any faith in the government."

"You took the people's tax dollars."

"Which will be repaid with interest from scientific benefits. But do not forget, private individuals and their corporations contributed half the money, and, I might add, without any thought of profit or personal gain. Defense and space contractors cannot make that claim."

The President did not argue. He quietly set his ball on a tee and socked the ball toward the eighteenth green.

"If you distrust Presidents so much," he said bitterly, "why did you drop out of the heavens to tell *me* all this?"

"We may have a problem." Joe slipped a photograph from the back of the folder and held it up. "Through our connections I've obtained a picture taken from an Air Force stealth aircraft making surveillance flights over Cuba."

The President knew better than to ask how it came to be in Joe's hands. "So what am I looking for?"

"Please study the area above the northern coast of the island and below the Florida Keys."

The President took a pair of glasses from his shirt pocket and peered at the image in the photo. "Looks like the Goodyear blimp."

"No, it's the *Prosperteer*, an old airship belonging to Raymond LeBaron."

"I thought he was lost over the Caribbean two weeks ago."

"Ten days to be exact, along with the blimp and two crewmen."

"Then this photo was taken before he disappeared."

"No, the film came off the aircraft only eight hours ago."

"Then LeBaron must be alive."

"I'd like to think so, but all attempts to raise the *Prosperteer* by radio have gone unanswered."

"What's LeBaron's connection with the Jersey Colony?"

"He was a member of the 'inner core.'"

The President leaned close. "And you, Joe, are you one of the original nine men who conceived the project?"

Joe didn't answer. He didn't have to. The President, staring at him, knew without a doubt.

Satisfied, he sat back and relaxed. "Okay, so what's your problem?"

"In ten days the Soviets will take their newest heavy-lift launch vehicle out of the barn and send it into space with a manned lunar lander that's six times the size and weight of the module used by our astronauts during the Apollo program. You know the details from CIA intelligence reports."

"I've been briefed on their lunar mission," the President agreed.

"And you're also aware that over the past two years they've sent three unmanned probes in orbit around the moon to survey and photograph landing sites. The third and last crashed onto the moon's surface. The second had an engine malfunction and its fuel exploded. The first probe, however, performed successfully, at least in the beginning. It circled the moon twelve times. Then something went wrong. After returning to earth orbit prior to reentry it suddenly refused all commands from the ground. For the next eighteen months, Soviet space controllers worked at bringing the craft down intact. Whether or not they were able to retrieve its visual data, we have no way of knowing. Finally, they managed to fire the retro-rockets. But instead of Siberia, their lunar probe, Selenos 4, landed in the Caribbean Sea."

"What has this to do with LeBaron?"

"He went searching for the Soviet moon probe."

A doubtful look crossed the President's face. "According to CIA reports, the Russians retrieved the craft in deep water off Cuba."

"A smokescreen. They even put on a good show of raising the craft. But in reality, they were never able to find it."

"And your people think they know where it lies?"

"We have a site pinpointed, yes."

"Why would you want to beat the Russians out of a few pictures of the moon? There are thousands of photos available to anybody who wants to study them."

"Those were all taken before Jersey Colony was established. The new Russian survey will no doubt reveal the location."

"What harm could it do?"

"I believe that if the Kremlin discovers the truth, the USSR's first mission to the moon will be to attack, capture our colony, and use it for their own purposes."

"I don't buy that. The Kremlin would be laying their entire space program open for retaliation by our side."

"You forget, Mr. President, our lunar project is blanketed in secrecy. No one can charge the Russians with stealing something that isn't supposed to exist."

"You're stabbing in the dark," the President said sharply.

Joe's eyes hardened. "No matter. Our astronauts were the first to step on the lunar surface. We were the first to colonize it. The moon belongs to the United States and we shall fight any intrusion."

"This isn't the fourteenth century," said the President, shocked. "We can't take up arms and keep the Soviets or anyone else off the moon. Besides, the United Nations ruled that no country had jurisdiction over the moon and planets."

"Would the Kremlin heed U.N. policy if they were in our shoes? I think not." Joe twisted in the seat and extracted a putter from the bag. "The eighteenth green. Your final play, Mr. President."

Dazedly, the President lined up the lay of the green and sank a twenty-foot putt. "I could stop you," he said coldly.

"How? NASA has no ready hardware to land a platoon of Marines on the lunar surface. Thanks to the shortsightedness of you and your predecessors, their efforts are wrapped up in the orbiting space station."

"I can't stand by and allow you to start a war in space that might spill over on earth."

"Your hands are tied."

"You could be wrong about the Russians."

"Let us hope so," said Joe. "But I suspect they may have already killed Raymond LeBaron."

"And this is why you've taken me into your confidence?"

"If the worst happens, at least you have been alerted to the facts and can prepare your strategy for the bedlam to follow."

"Suppose I have my bodyguards arrest you as a crackpot assassin, and then blow the lid off Jersey Colony?"

"Arrest me and Reggie Salazar dies. Expose the project and all the behind-the-scenes double-dealing, the backstabbing, the fraud and the lies, and, yes, the deaths that took place to accomplish what has been achieved, will be laid on your political doorstep, beginning when you were sworn into the Senate. You'll get bounced out of the White House under a bigger cloud than Nixon, providing, of course, you live that long."

"You're threatening me with blackmail?" So far the President had kept his anger under control but now he was seething with fury. "Salazar's life would be a small price to pay to preserve the integrity of the presidency."

"Two weeks, then you can announce the existence of the Jersey Colony to the world. With trumpets sounding and drums beating you can play the big political hero. Two weeks, and you can demonstrate proof of this century's greatest scientific achievement."

"After all this time, why then?"

"Because that's when we've scheduled the original crew to leave Jersey Colony and return to earth with the accumulation of two decades of space research—reports on meteorological and lunar probes; the scientific results on thousands of biological, chemical, and atmospheric experiments; uncountable photographs and miles of video records of the first human establishment of a planetary civilization. The first phase of the project is completed. The dream of the 'inner core' is finished. Jersey Colony now belongs to the American people."

The President toyed with his putter thoughtfully. Then he asked, "Who are you?"

"Look to your memory. We knew each other many years ago."

"How am I to contact you?"

"I'll arrange another meeting when I feel it's required." Joe lifted the clubs from the cart's rack and began walking along a narrow path toward the clubhouse. Then he stopped and came back.

"By the way, I lied. That's not a bomb, but a present from the 'inner core'—a new box of golf balls."

The President gazed at him in frustration. "Burn in hell, Joe."

"Oh, and one more thing...congratulations."

"Congratulations?"

Joe handed him the scorecard. "I kept track of your play. You hit a seventy-nine."

4

THE SLEEK HULL of the sailboard skimmed the choppy water with the graceful elegance of an arrow shot through mist. Its slick and delicately curved shape was as visually pleasing to the eye as it was efficient in achieving great speed over the waves. Perhaps the simplest of all sailing systems, the board was built with a polyethylene shell molded over an inner core of rigid plastic foam to give it lightness and flexibility. A small skeg or fin protruded from below the stern for lateral control, while a daggerboard hung down near the middle to prevent the board from being swept sideways by the wind.

A triangular sail, dyed purple with a broad turquoise stripe, clung to an aluminum mast that was mounted onto the board by a universal joint. An oval tubular wishbone or boom circled the mast and sail, and was tightly gripped by long, slender hands that were coarse-skinned and callused.

Dirk Pitt was tired, more tired than his dulled mind could accept. The muscles of his arms and legs felt as though they were sheathed in lead and the ache in his back and shoulders grew more intense with each maneuver of the sailboard. For at least the third time in the last hour he fought off a growing urge to head for the nearest beach and stretch out in the sand.

Through the clear window of the sail he studied the orange buoy marking the final windward leg of the thirty-mile boardsailing marathon race around Biscayne Bay to the Cape Florida lighthouse on Key Biscayne. Carefully, he chose his position to arc around the buoy. Deciding on a jibe, the most graceful maneuver in windsurfing, he threaded his way through the heavy traffic, weighted down the stern of his board, and aimed the bow on the new course. Then, gripping the mast with one hand, he swung the rigging to windward, shifted his feet, and released the boom with his other hand. Next he pulled the fluttering sail against the wind and caught the boom at the precise moment. Propelled by a fresh twenty-knot breeze from the north, the sailboard sped through the choppy sea and soon gained a speed of nearly thirty miles an hour.

Pitt was mildly surprised to see that out of a field of forty-one racers, most of them at least fifteen years younger, he was in third place, only twenty yards behind the leaders.

The multicolored sails from the fleet of windsurfers flashed across the blue-green water like a prism gone mad. The finish at the lighthouse was in sight now. Pitt closely watched the boardsailer ahead of him, waiting for the right moment to attack. But before he attempted to pass, his opponent miscalculated a wave and fell. Now Pitt was second, with only half a mile to go.

Then, ominously, a dark shadow in a cloudless sky passed overhead and he heard the exhaust of propeller-driven aircraft engines above and slightly to his left. He stared upward and his eyes widened in disbelief.

No more than a hundred yards away, shielding the sun like an eclipse, a blimp was descending from the sky, her great bow set on a collision course with the sailboard fleet. She appeared to be drifting out of control. Her two engines were barely turning over at idle speed, but she was swept through the air by the strong breeze. The sailboarders watched helplessly as the giant intruder crossed their path.

The gondola struck the crest of a wave and the blimp bounced back into the air, leveling off five feet above the water in front of the lead boardsailer. Unable to turn in time, the young boy, no more than seventeen, dove from his board an instant before his mast and sail were minced to shreds under the blimp's starboard propeller.

Pitt nimbly carved a sharp tack and swung on a parallel course with the rampaging airship. From the corner of his eye he noted the name, *Prosperteer*, in huge red letters on her side. The gondola door was open, but he couldn't make out any movement inside. He shouted, but his voice was lost in the exhaust of the engines and rush of the wind. The ungainly craft skidded across the sea as though it had a mind of its own.

Suddenly, Pitt felt the prickle of disaster in the small of his back. The *Prosperteer* was moving toward the beach, only a quarter mile away, and headed directly at the broad terraced side of the Sonesta Beach Hotel. Though the impact of a lighter-than-air ship against a solid structure would cause little damage, there was the ugly certainty of fire from ruptured fuel tanks spilling into the rooms of dozing guests or falling onto the diners on the patio below.

Ignoring the numbing drain of exhaustion, Pitt angled his sailboard on a course that would cross under the great rounded nose. The gondola danced into another swell and a spinning propeller whipped a cloud of salt spray into his eyes. His vision blurred momentarily and he came within inches of losing his balance. He settled in a squatting stance and steadied his tiny craft as he narrowed the distance. Crowds of sunbathers gestured excitedly at the strange sight rapidly approaching the hotel's sloping beach.

Pitt's timing would have to be near perfect; there would be no second attempt. If he missed, there was every chance his body would end up in pieces behind the propellers. He was beginning to feel lightheaded. His strength was nearly sapped. He sensed that his muscles were taking longer to respond to the demands of his brain. He braced himself as his sailboard streaked under the blimp's nose.

Then he leaped.

His hands grasped one of the *Prosperteer*'s bow ropes but slipped on the wet surface, scraping the skin from his fingers and palms. Desperately he swung a leg around the line and held on with every scrap of energy he had left. His weight pulled down the bow and he was dragged under the surface. He clawed up the rope until his head broke free. Then he was gulping air and spitting out seawater. The pursuer had become the captive.

The drag from Pitt's body wasn't nearly enough to stop the air monster, much less slow its momentum from the wind. He was about to release his precarious hold when his feet touched bottom. The blimp carried him through the surge of the surf and he felt like he was riding a roller coaster. Then he was hurtled onto the warm sands of the beach. He looked up and saw the low seawall of the hotel looming a scant hundred feet away.

My God! he thought, this is it—in a few seconds the *Prosperteer* would crash into the hotel and possibly explode. And there was something else. The whirling propellers would shatter on impact, their metal fragments spraying the awestruck crowds with a force as deadly as shrapnel.

"For God's sake, help me!" Pitt shouted.

The mass of people on the beach stood frozen, their mouths gaping, held stupefied in childlike fascination by the strange spectacle. Suddenly two teenage girls and a boy sprang forward and grabbed one of the other tow ropes. Next came a lifeguard, followed by an elderly heavyset woman. Then the dam broke and twenty onlookers surged forward and gathered in the trailing lines. It was as though a tribe of half-naked natives had challenged a maddened brontosaurus to a tug-of-war.

Bare feet dug into the sand, plowing furrows as the stubborn mass above their heads tugged them across the beach. The drag on the bow lines caused the hull to pivot, and the huge finned tail swung around in a 180-degree arc until it was pointing at the hotel, the wheel on the bottom of the gondola scraping through the bushes growing from the top of the seawall, the propellers missing the concrete by inches and chopping through the branches and leaves.

A strong gust of wind blew in from the sea, shoving the *Prosperteer* over the patio, smashing umbrellas and tables, driving her stern toward the fifth story of the hotel. Lines were torn from hands and a wave of helplessness swept over the beach. The battle seemed lost.

Pitt struggled to his feet and half ran, half staggered to a nearby palm tree. In a final desperate act he coiled his line around the slender trunk, feverishly praying it wouldn't snap from the strain.

The line took up the slack and stretched taut. The fifty-foot palm shuddered, swayed, and bent for several seconds. The crowd collectively held its breath. Then with agonizing slowness, the tree gradually straightened into its former upright position. The shallow roots held firm and the blimp stopped, its fins less than six feet from the east wall of the hotel.

Two hundred people gave out a rousing cheer and began applauding. The women jumped up and down and laughed while the men roared and thrust out their hands in the thumbs-up position. No winning team ever received a more spontaneous ovation. The hotel security guards materialized and kept stray onlookers away from the still-turning propellers.

Sand coated Pitt's wet body as he stood there catching his breath, becoming conscious of the pain from his rope-burned hands. Staring up at the *Prosperteer*, he had his first solid look at the airship and was fascinated by the antiquated design. It was obvious she predated the modern Goodyear blimps.

He made his way around the scattered tables and chairs on the patio and climbed into the gondola. The crew were still strapped in their seats, unmoving, unspeaking. Pitt leaned over the pilot, found the ignition switches, and turned them off. The engines popped softly once or twice and went silent as their propellers gave a final twitch and came to rest.

The quiet was tomblike.

Pitt grimaced and scanned the interior of the gondola. There was no sign of damage, the instruments and controls appeared to be in operating order. But it was the extensive electronics that amazed him. Gradiometers for detecting iron, side-scan sonar and sub-bottom profiler to sweep the sea floor, everything for an underwater search expedition.

He wasn't aware of the sea of faces peering up into the open door of the gondola, nor did he hear the pulsating scream of approaching sirens. He felt detached and momentarily disoriented. The hot, humid atmosphere was heavy with a morbid eeriness and the sickening stench of human decay.

One of the crewmen was slouched over a small table, head resting on arms as if he were asleep. His clothes were damp and stained. Pitt placed his hand on a shoulder and gave a slight shake. There was no firmness to the flesh. It felt soft and pulpy. An icy shroud fell over him that lifted goose bumps on every inch of his skin, yet the sweat was trickling down his body in streams.

He turned his attention to the ghastly apparitions seated at the controls. Their faces were covered by a blanket of flies, and decomposition was eating away all traces of life. The skin was slipping from the flesh like broken blisters on burns. Jaws hung slack with mouths agape, the lips and tongues swollen and parched. Eyes were open and staring into nothingness, eyeballs opaque and clouded over. Hands still hung on the controls, their fingernails turned blue. Unchecked by enzymes, bacteria had formed gases that grotesquely bloated the stomachs. The damp air and the high temperatures of the tropics were greatly speeding the process of putrefaction.

The rotting corpses inside the *Prosperteer* had flown from some unknown grave, a macabre crew in a charnel airship on a ghostly mission.

5

THE NAKED CORPSE of an adult black woman lay stretched on an examining table under the glaring lights of the autopsy room. Preservation was excellent, no visible injuries due to violence. To the trained eye the state of rigor mortis indicated she had been dead less than seven hours. Her age appeared to be somewhere between twenty-five and thirty. The body might have drawn male stares once, but now it lay undernourished, wasted, and ravaged by a decade of drug intake.

The Dade County coroner, Dr. Calvin Rooney, wasn't too pleased about doing the autopsy. There were enough deaths in Miami to keep his staff working around the clock, and he preferred to spend his time on the more dramatic and puzzling postmortem examinations. A garden-variety drug overdose held little interest for him. But this one was found dumped on a county commissioner's front lawn, and it wouldn't do to send in a third-string quarterback.

Wearing a blue lab coat because he detested the standard white issue, Rooney, a home-grown Floridian, U.S. Army veteran, and Harvard Medical School graduate, slipped a new cassette in a portable tape recorder and dryly commented on the general condition of the body.

He picked up a scalpel and bent over for the dissection, starting a few inches under the chin and slicing downward toward the pubic bone. Suddenly Rooney halted the incision over the chest cavity and leaned closer, squinting through a pair of wide-lensed, horn-rimmed glasses. In the next fifteen minutes, he removed and examined the heart while delivering a running monologue into the tape recorder.

Rooney was in the midst of making a last-minute observation when Sheriff Tyler Sweat entered the autopsy room. He was a medium-built, brooding man, slightly round-shouldered, his face a blend of melancholy and brutish determination. Methodical and shrewdly earnest, he enjoyed great respect from the men and women under him.

He threw an expressionless glance at the opened cadaver and then nodded a greeting to Rooney. "New piece of meat?"

"The woman from the commissioner's yard," answered Rooney.

"Another OD?"

"No such luck. More work for homicide. She was murdered. I found three punctures in the heart."

"Ice pick?"

"From all indications.".

Sweat peered at the balding little chief medical examiner, whose benign appearance seemed better suited to a parish priest. "They can't fool you, Doc."

"What brings the master scourge of evildoers to the forensic palace?" Rooney asked amiably. "You slumming?"

"No, an identification by VIPs. I'd like you in on it."

"The bodies from the blimp," Rooney deduced.

Sweat nodded. "Mrs. LeBaron is here to view the remains."

"I don't recommend it. What's left of her husband isn't a pretty sight to someone who doesn't see death every day."

"I tried to tell her that identification of his effects would satisfy legal requirements, but she persisted. Even brought along an aide from the governor's office to grease the way."

"Where are they?"

"Waiting in the morgue office."

"News media?"

"An entire regiment of TV and press reporters running around like crazy people. I've ordered my deputies to keep them confined to the lobby."

"Strange how the world works," said Rooney in one of his philosophical moods. "The renowned Raymond LeBaron gets front-page headlines while this poor baggage gets a column inch next to classified advertising." Then he sighed, removed his lab coat, and threw it over a chair. "Let's get it over with. I've got two more postmortems to conduct this afternoon."

As he spoke a tropical storm passed over and the sound of thunder rumbled through the walls. Rooney slipped on a sports jacket and straightened his tie. They fell into step, Sweat staring down pensively at the design in the hallway carpet.

"Any idea on the cause of LeBaron's death?" asked the sheriff.

"Too soon to tell. The lab results were inconclusive. I want to run some more tests. Too many things don't add up. I don't mind admitting, this one is a puzzler."

"No guesses?"

"Nothing I'd put on paper. Problem is the incredibly rapid rate of decomposition. I've seldom seen tissue disintegrate so fast, except maybe once back in 1974."

Before Sweat could prod Rooney's recollection, they reached the morgue office and entered. The governor's aide, a slippery type in a three-piece suit, jumped up. Even before he opened his mouth, Rooney classified him as a jerk.

"Can we please get the show on the road, Sheriff. Mrs. LeBaron is most uncomfortable and would like to return to her hotel as soon as possible."

"I sympathize with her," the sheriff drawled. "But I shouldn't have to remind a public servant that there are certain laws we must follow."

"And I needn't remind you, the governor expects your department to extend every courtesy to ease her grief."

Rooney marveled at Sweat's stony patience. The sheriff simply brushed by the aide as though he were walking past trash on a sidewalk.

"This is our chief medical examiner, Dr. Rooney. He will assist with the identification."

Jessie LeBaron didn't look the least bit uncomfortable. She sat in an orange plastic contour chair, poised, cool, head held high. And yet Rooney sensed a fragility that was held together by discipline and nerve. He was an old hand at presiding over corpse identification by relatives. He'd suffered through the ordeal hundreds of times in his career and instinctively spoke softly and in a gentle manner.

"Mrs. LeBaron, I understand what you're going through and will make this as painless as possible. But first, I wish to make it clear that by simply identifying the effects found on the bodies you will satisfy the laws set down by the state and county. Second, any physical characteristics you can recall, such as scars, dental work, bone fractures, or surgical incisions, will be of great help in my own identification. And third, I respectfully beg you not to view the remains. Though facial features are still recognizable, decomposition has done its work. I think you'd be happier remembering Mr. LeBaron as he was in life rather than how he looks in a morgue."

"Thank you, Dr. Rooney," said Jessie. "I'm grateful for your concern. But I must be certain my husband is truly dead."

Rooney nodded miserably, and then gestured at a worktable containing several pieces of clothing, wallets, wristwatches, and other personal articles. "You've identified Mr. LeBaron's effects?"

"Yes, I have sorted through them."

"And you're satisfied they belonged to him?"

"There can be no doubt about the wallet and its contents. The watch was a gift from me on our first anniversary."

Rooney walked over and held it up. "A gold Cartier with matching band and roman numerals marked in . . . am I correct in saying they're diamonds?"

"Yes, a rare form of black diamond. It was his birthstone."

"April, I believe."

She merely nodded.

"Besides your husband's personal articles, Mrs. LeBaron, do you recognize anything belonging to Buck Caesar or Joseph Cavilla?"

"I don't recall the jewelry they wore, but I'm certain the other clothing items are what Buck and Joe were wearing when I last saw them."

"Our investigators can find no next of kin of Caesar and Cavilla," said Sweat. "It would be most helpful if you can point out which articles of clothing belonged to whom."

For the first time Jessie LeBaron faltered. "I'm not sure . . . I think the denim shorts and flowered shirt are Buck's. The other things probably belonged to Joe Cavilla." She paused. "May we view my husband's body now?"

"I can't change your mind?" Rooney asked in a sympathetic voice.

"No, I must insist."

"You'd best do what Mrs. LeBaron asks," said the governor's aide, who had yet to introduce himself.

Rooney looked at Sweat and shrugged in resignation. "If you will please follow me. The remains are kept in the refrigeration room."

Obediently, everyone trailed him to a thick door with a small window set at eye level and stood in silence as he yanked on a heavy latch. Cold air spilled over the threshold and Jessie involuntarily shivered as Rooney motioned them inside. A morgue attendant appeared and led the way to one of the square doors along the wall. He swung it open, pulled out a sliding stainless steel table, and stood aside.

Rooney took one corner of the sheet covering the corpse and hesitated. This was the only part of his job he hated. The reaction to viewing the dead usually fell into four categories. Those who vomited, those who passed out cold, those who broke into hysterics. But it was the last type that intrigued Rooney. The ones who stood as if turned to stone and showed no emotion at all. He would have given a month's salary to know the thoughts circulating through their minds.

He lifted the sheet.

The governor's aide took one look, made a pathetic groaning sound, and passed out into the arms of the sheriff. The grisly work of decay was revealed in all its horror.

Rooney was astonished by Jessie's response. She stared long and hard at the grotesque thing that lay rotting on the table. She sucked in her breath and her whole body went taut. Then she raised her eyes, not blinking, and spoke in a calm, controlled voice.

"*That* is not my husband!"

"Are you positive?" Rooney asked softly.

"Look for yourself," she said in a flat monotone. "The hairline is wrong. So is the bone structure. Raymond had an angular face. This one is more round."

"Decomposition of the flesh distorts facial features," Rooney explained.

"Please study the teeth."

Rooney looked down. "What about them?"

"They have silver fillings."

"I don't follow."

"My husband's fillings were gold."

There was no arguing with her on that score, thought Rooney. A man of Raymond LeBaron's wealth wouldn't have settled for cheap dental work.

"But the watch, the clothing, you identified them as his."

"I don't give a damn what I said!" she cried. "This loathsome thing is not Raymond LeBaron."

Rooney was stunned at her fury. He stood dazed and unable to speak as she stormed from the icy room. The sheriff handed the limp aide to the morgue attendant and turned to the coroner.

"What in hell do you make of that?"

Rooney shook his head. "I don't know."

"My guess is, she went into shock. Probably fell over the edge and began raving. You know better than I, most people can't accept the death of a loved one. She closed her mind and refused to accept the truth."

"She wasn't raving."

Sweat looked at him. "What do you call it?"

"Shrewd acting."

"How did you pick that out of the air?"

"The wristwatch," answered Rooney. "One of my staff worked nights as a jeweler to put himself through medical school. He spotted it right off. The expensive Cartier watch Mrs. LeBaron gave her husband on their anniversary is a fake, one of those inexpensive reproductions that are illegally manufactured in Taiwan or Mexico."

"Why would a woman who could write a check for a million dollars give her husband a cheap imitation?"

"Raymond LeBaron was no slouch when it came to style and taste. He must have recognized it for what it was. Better to ask the question, Why did he stoop to wearing it?"

"So you think she put on an act and lied about the body ID?"

"My gut reaction is that she prepared herself for what to expect," Rooney replied. "And I'd go so far as to bet my new Mercedes-Benz that genetic tracing, the dental report, and the results of the rubber casts I made from what remained of the fingerprints and sent to the FBI lab will prove she was right." He turned and peered at the corpse. "That *isn't* Raymond LeBaron lying there on the slab."

6

DETECTIVE LIEUTENANT HARRY VICTOR, a lead investigator for the Metro Dade County Police Department, sat back in a swivel chair and studied several photographs taken inside the *Prosperteer's* control cabin. After several minutes, he raised a pair of rimless glasses over a forehead that slipped under a blond hairpiece and rubbed his eyes.

Victor was a tidy man, everything in its correct pigeonhole, neatly alphabetized and consecutively numbered, the only cop in the memory of the department who actually enjoyed making out reports. When most men watched sports on television on weekends or relaxed around a resort swimming pool on vacations, reading Rex Burns detective novels, Victor reviewed files on unsolved cases. A diehard, he was more fanatical about tying up loose ends than obtaining a conviction.

The *Prosperteer* case was unlike any he'd faced in his eighteen years on the force. Three dead men falling out of the sky in an antique blimp didn't exactly lend itself to routine police investigation. Leads were nonexistent. The three bodies in the morgue revealed no clues to where they had been hiding for a week and a half.

He lowered his glasses and was attacking the photographs again when the desk phone buzzed. He lifted the receiver and said pensively, "Yes?"

"You have a witness to see you about a statement," answered the receptionist.

"Send him on back," said Victor.

He closed the file containing the photographs and laid it on the metal desk, whose surface was antiseptic except for a small sign with his name and the telephone. He held the receiver to his ear as though receiving a call and swiveled sideways, looking across the spacious homicide office, keeping his eyes focused at an angle toward the door leading to the corridor.

A uniformed receptionist appeared at the threshold and pointed in Victor's direction. A tall man nodded, eased past her, and approached. Victor gestured to a chair opposite the desk and began muttering in a one-way conversation with the dial tone. It was an old interrogation ploy that gave him an uninterrupted minute to inspect a witness or suspect and mentally construct a profile. Most important, it was an opportunity to observe habits and odd mannerisms that could be used for leverage later.

The male seated across from Victor was about thirty-seven or thirty-eight, approximately six foot three, weight 185, give or take five pounds, black hair tending to be a bit wavy, with no indication of gray. Skin darkened from year-round exposure to the sun. Eyebrows dark and slightly bushy. Straight, narrow nose, lips firm with corners turned up in a slight but fixed grin. Wearing light blue sports coat and off-white slacks, pale yellow polo shirt with collar open. Good taste, casual but not ultraexpensive, probably purchased at Saks rather than a plush men's store. Nonsmoker, as there was no evidence of cigarette package bulge in coat or shirt. Arms were folded, suggesting calm and indifference, and the hands were narrow, long and weathered. No rings or other jewelry, only an old orange-faced diver's watch with a heavy stainless steel band.

This one didn't follow the general pattern. The others who had sat in that chair turned fidgety after a while. Some masked nervousness with arrogance, most restlessly stared around the office, through the windows, at pictures on the walls, at the other officers working their cases, changing position, crossing and recrossing their legs. For the first time Victor could recall, he felt uncomfortable and at a disadvantage. His routine was sidetracked, his act rapidly washing out.

The visitor wasn't the least bit ruffled. He stared at Victor with bemused interest through opaline green eyes that possessed a mesmeric quality. They seemed to pass right through the detective, and finding nothing of interest, examined the paint on the wall behind. Then they dropped to the telephone.

"Most police departments use the Horizon Communications System," he said in an even tone. "If you wish to speak to someone on the other end, I suggest you push a button for an open line."

Victor looked down. One of his four buttons was lit but not punched. "You're very astute, Mr...."

"Pitt, Dirk Pitt. If you're Lieutenant Victor, we had an appointment."

"I'm Victor." He paused to replace the receiver in its cradle. "You were the first person inside the control car of the *Prosperteer* blimp?"

"That's right."

"Thank you for coming in, especially so early on a Sunday. I'd appreciate your cooperation in clearing up a few questions."

"Not at all. Will it take long?"

"Twenty minutes, maybe half an hour. Do you have to be somewhere?"

"I'm booked on a plane for Washington in two hours."

Victor nodded. "I'll get you on your way in plenty of time." He pulled open a drawer and took out a portable tape recorder. "Let's go somewhere more private."

He led Pitt down a long hallway to a small interview room. The interior was spartan, only a desk, two chairs, and an ashtray. Victor sat down and fed a new cassette into the recorder.

"Mind if I put our conversation on tape? I'm a terrible note taker. None of the secretaries can decipher my handwriting."

Pitt shrugged agreeably.

Victor moved the machine to the center of the desk and pressed the red Record button.

"Your name?"

"Dirk Pitt."

"Middle initial?"

"E for Eric."

"Address?"

"266 Airport Place, Washington, D.C. 20001."

"Telephone where you can be reached?"

Pitt gave Victor the phone number of his office.

"Occupation?"

"Special projects director for the National Underwater and Marine Agency."

"Can you describe the event you witnessed on the afternoon of Saturday, October 20?"

Pitt told Victor of his sighting the out-of-control blimp during the sailboard marathon race, the mad ride while clinging to the mooring line, and the last-second capture only a few feet away from potential disaster, ending with his entry into the gondola.

"Did you touch anything?"

"Only the ignition and battery switches. And I laid my hand on the shoulder of the corpse seated at the navigator's table."

"Nothing else?"

"The only other place I might have left a fingerprint was on the boarding ladder."

"And the backrest of the copilot's seat," said Victor with a smug smile. "No doubt when you leaned over and turned off the switches."

"Fast work. Next time I'll wear surgical gloves."

"The FBI was most cooperative."

"I admire competence."

"Did you take anything?"

Pitt shot Victor a sharp look. "No."

"Could anyone else have entered and removed any objects?"

Pitt shook his head. "After I left, the hotel security guards sealed off the gondola. The next person inside was a uniformed police officer."

"Then what did you do?"

"I paid one of the hotel lifeguards to swim out and retrieve my sailboard. He owned a small pickup truck and was kind enough to run me back to the house where I was staying with friends."

"In Miami?"

"Coral Gables."

"Mind if I ask what you were doing in town?"

"I wound up an offshore exploration project for NUMA and decided to take a week's vacation."

"Did you recognize any of the bodies?"

"Not damned likely. I couldn't identify my own father in that condition."

"Any idea who they might be?"

"I assume one of them was Raymond LeBaron."

"You're familiar with the disappearance of the *Prosperteer?*"

"The news media covered the disappearance in great depth. Only a backwoods recluse could have missed it."

"Any pet theories on where the blimp and its crew were buried for ten days?"

"I haven't a clue."

"Not even a wild idea?" Victor persisted.

"Could be a colossal publicity stunt, a media campaign to promote LeBaron's publishing empire."

Interest grew in Victor's eyes. "Go on."

"Or maybe an ingenious scheme to manipulate LeBaron conglomerate stock prices. Sell large blocks before he disappears and buy when prices tumble afterward. And sell again when they rise during his resurrection."

"How do you explain their deaths?"

"The plot backfired."

"Why?"

"Ask your coroner."

"I'm asking you."

"They probably ate tainted fish on whatever deserted island they hung out on," said Pitt, tiring of the game. "How would I know? If you want a scenario, hire a screenwriter."

The interest in Victor's eyes blinked out. He relaxed in his chair and sighed dejectedly. "I thought for a second you might have something, a gimmick that could get me and the department off the hook. But your theory went down the drain like all the others."

"I'm not surprised," said Pitt with an indifferent grin.

"How were you able to switch off the power within seconds of entering the control car?" Victor asked, bringing the interrogation back on track.

"After piloting twenty different aircraft during service in the Air Force and civilian life, I knew where to look."

Victor appeared satisfied. "One more question, Mr. Pitt. When you first spotted the blimp, from what direction was she flying?"

"She was drifting with the wind out of the northeast."

Victor reached over and turned off the recorder. "That should do it. Can I reach you at your office number during the day?"

"If I'm not there, my secretary can track me down."

"Thank you for your help."

"Nothing substantial, I'm afraid," said Pitt.

"We have to pull on every thread. Lots of pressure with LeBaron being the bigshot that he was. This has to be the weirdest case the department's ever encountered."

"I don't envy you finding a solution." Pitt glanced at his watch and rose from his chair. "I'd better get a move on for the airport."

Victor stood and reached across the desk to shake hands. "If you should dream up another plot line, Mr. Pitt, please give me a call. I'm always interested in a good fantasy."

Pitt paused in the doorway and turned, a foxlike expression on his face. "You want a lead, Lieutenant? Run this one up the flagpole. Airships need helium for their lift. An old antique like the *Prosperteer* must have required a couple hundred thousand cubic feet of gas to get her in the air. After a week, enough would have leaked out to keep her grounded. Do you follow?"

"Depends on where you're heading."

"There is no way the blimp could have materialized off Miami unless an experienced crew with the necessary supplies reinflated the hull forty-eight hours before."

Victor had the look of a man about to be baptized. "What are you suggesting?"

"That you look for a friendly neighborhood service station that can pump two hundred thousand cubic feet of helium."

Then Pitt turned into the hallway and was gone.

7

"I HATE BOATS," Rooney grumbled. "I can't swim, can't float, and get seasick looking through the window of a washing machine."

Sheriff Sweat handed him a double martini. "Here, this will cure your hangups."

Rooney ruefully eyed the waters of the bay and drained half his drink. "You're not going out in the ocean, I hope."

"No, just a leisurely cruise around the bay." Sweat ducked into the forward cabin of his gleaming white fishing boat and turned over the engine. The single 260-horsepower turbocharged diesel knocked into life. Exhaust rumbled from the stern and the deck throbbed beneath their feet. Then Sweat cast off the lines and eased the boat away from the dock, threading through a maze of moored yachts to Biscayne Bay.

By the time the bow skipped past the channel buoys, Rooney was looking for a second drink. "Where do you keep the courage?"

"Down in the forward cabin. Help yourself. There's ice in the brass diver's helmet."

When Rooney resurfaced he asked, "What's this all about, Tyler? This is Sunday. You didn't drag me away from my season box in the middle of a good football game to show me Miami Beach from the water."

"Truth is, I heard you finished your report on the bodies from the blimp last night."

"Three o'clock this morning, to be exact."

"I thought you might want to tell me something."

"For God's sake, Tyler, what's so damned earthshaking that you couldn't have waited until tomorrow morning?"

"About an hour ago, I got a call from some Fed in Washington." Sweat paused to ease the throttle up a notch. "Said he was with a domestic intelligence agency I'd never heard of. I won't bore you with his downright belligerent talk. Never can understand why everybody up North thinks they can blindside a Southern boy. The upshot was he demanded we turn over the dead from the blimp to federal authorities."

"Which federal authorities?"

"Refused to name them. Got vague as hell when I pushed."

Rooney was suddenly intensely interested. "He give any hint why they wanted the bodies?"

"Claimed it was a security matter."

"You told him no, of course."

"I told him I'd think about it."

The turn of events and the gin combined to make Rooney forget his fear of water. He began to notice the trim lines of the fiberglass craft. It was Sheriff Sweat's second office, occasionally pressed into service as a backup police cruiser, but more often used to entertain county and state officials on weekend fishing trips.

"What do you call her?" Rooney asked.

"Call who?"

"The boat."

"Oh, the *Southern Comfort*. She's a thirty-five-footer, cruises at fifteen knots. Built in Australia by an outfit caled Stebercraft."

"To get back to the LeBaron case," Rooney said, sipping at his martini, "are you going to give in?"

"I'm tempted," said Sweat, smiling. "Homicide has yet to turn up lead one. The news media are making a circus out of it. Everybody from the governor on down is pressuring my ass. And to top it off, there's every likelihood the crime wasn't committed in my jurisdiction. Hell, yes, I'm tempted to pass the buck to Washington. Only I'm just stubborn enough to think we might pull a solution out of this mess."

"All right, what do you want from me?"

The sheriff turned from the helm and looked at him steadily. "I want you to tell me what's in your report."

"My findings made the puzzle worse."

A small sailboat with four teenagers slipped across their bow and Sweat slowed down and gave way. "Tell me about it."

"Let's start at the end and work backwards. Okay with you?"

"Go ahead."

"Threw the hell out of me at first. Mostly because I wasn't looking for it. I had a similar case fifteen years ago. A female body was discovered sitting in a patio chair in her backyard. Her husband claimed they'd been drinking the night before and he'd gone to bed alone, thinking she would follow. When he awoke in the morning and looked around, he found her right where he left her, sitting on the patio, only now she was dead. She had all the appearances of a natural death, no marks of violence, no sign of poison, just a generous amount of alcohol. The organs seemed healthy enough. There were no indications of previous disease or disorder. For a woman of forty she had the body of a twenty-five-year-old. It bugged the hell out of me. Then the pieces began to come together. The postmortem lividity—that's the discoloration of the skin caused by the sinking of blood due to gravity—is usually purplish. Her lividity was cherry pink, which pointed to death from either cyanide or carbon monoxide poisoning or hypothermia. I also discovered hemorrhaging of the pancreas. Through a process of elimination the first two were discarded. The final nail in the coffin was the husband's occupation. The evidence wasn't exactly hard core, but it was enough for the judge to put him away for fifty years."

"What was the husband's line of work?" asked Sweat.

"He drove a truck for a frozen-food company. A neat plan. He pumped booze in her until she passed out. Set her inside his truck, which he always took home nights and weekends, turned up the refrigeration unit, and waited for her to harden. After the poor woman expired, he put her back in the patio chair and went to bed."

Sweat stared blankly. "You're not saying the corpses found in the blimp froze to death."

"I'm saying exactly that."

"No mistake?"

"On a certainty scale from one to ten, I can promise an eight."

"Do you realize how that sounds?"

"Crazy, I would imagine."

"Three men disappear over the Caribbean in ninety-degree weather and freeze to death?" Sweat asked no one in particular. "We'll never make this one stick, Doc. Not without a handy frozen-food truck."

"You've got nothing to stick it to anyway."

"Meaning?"

"The FBI report came in. Jessie LeBaron's ID was on the money. That isn't her husband in the morgue. The other two aren't Buck Caesar or Joseph Cavilla either."

"God, what next," Sweat moaned. "Who are they?"

"There's no record of them in the FBI's fingerprint files. Best guess is they were foreign nationals."

"Did you find anything at all that might give a clue to their identity?"

"I can give you their height and weight. I can show you X rays of their teeth and previous bone fractures. Their livers suggested all three favored generous amounts of hard liquor. The lungs gave away their heavy smoking, teeth and fingertips the fact they smoked unfiltered cigarettes. They were also big eaters. Their last meal consisted of dark bread and various fruits and beets. Two were in their early thirties. One was forty or over. They were in above-average physical condition. Beyond that I can tell you very little that might pin an ID on them."

"It's a start."

"But it still leaves us with LeBaron, Caesar, and Cavilla among the missing."

Before Sweat could reply a female voice rasped out his boat's call sign over the radio speaker. He answered and turned to another channel frequency as instructed.

"Sorry for the interruption," he said to Rooney. "I've got an emergency call over the ship-to-shore phone."

Rooney nodded, went into the forward cabin, and poured himself another drink. A delicious glow coursed through his body. He took a few moments to go to the head. When he returned topside to the wheelhouse, Sweat was hanging up the phone, his face red with anger.

"The rotten bastards!" he hissed.

"What's the problem?" Rooney asked.

"They seized them," Sweat said, pounding the helm with his fist. "The damned Feds walked into the morgue and seized the bodies from the blimp."

"But there are legal procedures to follow," Rooney protested.

"Six men in plainclothes and two federal marshals showed up with the necessary paperwork, stuffed the corpses into three aluminum canisters filled with ice, and took off in a U.S. Navy helicopter."

"When did this happen?"

"Not ten minutes ago. Harry Victor, the lead investigator on the case, says they also rifled his desk in the homicide office when he was in the john and ripped off his files."

"What about my autopsy report?"

"They lifted that too."

The gin had put Rooney in a euphoric mood. "Oh, well, look at it this way. They took you and the department off the hook."

Sweat's anger slowly subsided. "I can't deny they did me a favor, but it's their method that pisses me off."

"There's one small consolation," mumbled Rooney. He was beginning to have trouble standing. "Uncle Sam didn't get everything."

"Like what?"

"Something omitted from my report. One lab result that was too controversial to put on paper, too wild to mention outside a looney house."

"What are you talking about?" Sweat demanded.

"The cause of death."

"You said hypothermia."

"True, but I left out the best part. You see, I neglected to state the time of death." Rooney's speech was becoming slurred.

"Could only be within the last few days."

"Oh, no. Those poor guys froze their guts a long time ago."

"How long?"

"Anywhere from one to two years ago."

Sheriff Sweat stared at Rooney, incredulous. But the coroner stood there grinning like a hyena. He was still grinning when he sagged over the side of the boat and threw up.

8

THE HOME OF DIRK PITT was not on a suburban street or in a high-rise condominium overlooking the jungled treetops of Washington. There was no landscaped yard or next-door neighbors with squealing children and barking dogs. The house was not a house but an old aircraft hangar that stood on the edge of the capital's International Airport.

From the outside it appeared deserted. Weeds surrounded the building and its corrugated walls were weathered and devoid of paint. The only clue remotely suggesting any occupancy was a row of windows running beneath the huge curved roof. Though they were stained and layered with dust, none were shattered like those of an abandoned warehouse.

Pitt thanked the airport maintenance man who had given him a lift from the terminal area. Glancing around to see that he wasn't observed, he took a small transmitter from his coat pocket and issued a series of voice commands that closed down the security systems and opened a side door that looked as if it hadn't swung on its hinges for thirty years.

He entered and stepped onto a polished concrete floor that held nearly three dozen gleaming, classic automobiles, an antique airplane, and a turn-of-the-century railroad car. He paused and stared fondly at the chassis of a French Talbot-Lago sports coupé that was in an early stage of reconstruction. The car had been nearly destroyed in an explosion, and he was determined to restore the twisted remains to their previous elegance and beauty.

He hauled his suitcase and garment bag up a circular staircase to his apartment, elevated against the far wall of the hangar. His watch read 2:15 P.M., but his mind and body felt as though it was closer to midnight. After unpacking his luggage, he decided to spend a few hours working on the Talbot-Lago and take a shower later. He had already donned a pair of old coveralls and his hand was pulling open the drawer of a toolbox, when a loud chime echoed through the hangar. He pulled a cordless phone from a deep pocket.

"Hello."

"Mr. Pitt, please," said a female voice.

"Speaking."

"One moment."

After waiting for nearly two minutes, Pitt cut the connection and began rebuilding the Talbot's distributor. Another five minutes passed before the chime sounded again. He opened the line and said nothing.

"Are you still there, sir?" asked the same voice.

"Yes," Pitt replied indifferently, tucking the phone between his shoulder and ear as he kept working with his hands.

"This is Sandra Cabot, Mrs. Jessie LeBaron's personal secretary. Am I talking to Dirk Pitt?"

Pitt took an instant dislike to people who couldn't dial their own phone calls. "You are."

"Mrs. LeBaron wishes to meet with you. Can you come to the house at four o'clock?"

"Pretty fast off the mark, aren't you?"

"I beg your pardon?"

"Sorry, Miss Cabot, but I have to doctor a sick car. Maybe if Mrs. LeBaron cares to drop by my place, we could talk."

"I'm afraid that won't do. She's holding a formal cocktail party in the greenhouse later in the evening that will be attended by the Secretary of State. She can't possibly break away."

"Some other time then."

There was an icy silence, then Miss Cabot said, "You don't understand."

"You're right, I don't understand."

"Doesn't the name LeBaron mean anything to you?"

"No more than Shagnasty, Quagmire, or Smith," Pitt lied fiendishly.

She seemed lost for a moment. "Mr. LeBaron—"

"We can cut the fun and games," Pitt interrupted. "I'm quite aware of Raymond LeBaron's reputation. And I can save us both time by saying I have nothing to add to the mystery surrounding his disappearance and death. Tell Mrs. LeBaron she has my condolences. That's all I can offer."

Cabot took a deep breath and exhaled. "Please, Mr. Pitt, I know she would be most grateful if you could see her."

Pitt could almost see her speaking the word "please" through clenched teeth. "All right," he said. "I guess I can make it. What's the address?"

The arrogance quickly returned to her tone. "I'll send the chauffeur to pick you up."

"If it's all the same to you, I'd prefer to drive my own car. I get claustrophobic in limousines."

"If you insist," she said stiffly. "You'll find the house at the end of Beacon Drive in Great Falls Estates."

"I'll check a street map."

"By the way, what kind of car do you drive?"

"Why do you want to know?"

"To inform the guard at the gate."

Pitt hesitated and looked across the hangar floor at a car parked by the main door. "An old convertible."

"Old?"

"Yes, a 1951."

"Then would you be so kind to park in the lot by the servants' house. It's to the right as you come up the drive."

"Aren't you ever ashamed of the way you dictate to people?"

"I don't have to be ashamed of anything, Mr. Pitt. We'll expect you at four."

"Will you be through with me before the guests arrive?" asked Pitt, his voice heavy with sarcasm. "I wouldn't want to embarrass anyone by having them see my old junk car littering the grounds."

"Not to worry," she replied testily. "The party doesn't begin until eight. Goodbye."

After Sandra Cabot hung up, Pitt walked over to the convertible, staring at it for several moments. He removed the floorboards under the rear seat and clipped on the cables of a battery charger. Then he returned to the Talbot-Lago and calmly took up where he left off.

At precisely eight-thirty, the security guard at the LeBaron estate's front gate greeted a young couple driving a yellow Ferrari, checked their names on the party list, and waved them through. Next came a Chrysler limousine carrying the President's chief adviser, Daniel Fawcett, and his wife.

The guard was immune to the exotic cars and their celebrity occupants. He raised his hands over his head in a bored stretch and yawned. Then his hands froze in midair and his mouth snapped shut as he found himself staring at the largest car he'd ever seen.

The car was a veritable monster, measuring nearly twenty-two feet from bumper to bumper and weighing well over three tons. The hood and doors were silver-gray and the fenders a metallic maroon. A convertible, its top was completely hidden from view when folded down. The body lines were smooth and elegant in the grand manner, an example of flawless craftsmanship seldom equaled.

"That's some kind of car," the guard finally said. "What is it?"

"A Daimler," replied Pitt.

"Sounds British."

"It is."

The guard shook his head in admiration and looked at his guest list. "Your name, please."

"Pitt."

"I can't seem to find your name. Do you have an invitation?"

"Mrs. LeBaron and I had an earlier appointment."

The guard went into the gatehouse and checked a clipboard. "Yes, sir, your appointment was for four o'clock."

"When I phoned to say I was running late, she said to join the party."

"Well, since she expected you," the guard said, still soaking in the Daimler's lines, "I guess it's all right. Have a good evening."

Pitt nodded a thank-you and eased the immense car silently up the winding drive to the LeBaron residence. The main building sat on a low hill above a tennis court and a swimming pool. The architecture was common to the area, a three-story brick colonial with a series of white columns holding up the roof over a long front porch, the wings extending to each side. To the right a clump of pine trees shielded a carriage house with a garage below, what Pitt assumed were the servants' living quarters. Opposite and to the left of the manor sat a huge glass-enclosed structure, lit by crystal chandeliers hanging from the roof. Exotic flowers and shrubs blossomed around twenty or more dinner tables while a small orchestra played on a stage beneath a waterfall. Pitt was properly impressed. The perfect setting for a party on a brisk October evening. Raymond LeBaron got high marks for originality. He pulled the Daimler up to the front of the greenhouse where a liveried parking valet stood with the awed expression of a carpenter gazing at redwoods.

As he slid from behind the wheel and straightened the jacket of his tuxedo Pitt noticed a crowd beginning to gather behind the transparent wall of the greenhouse, pointing and gesturing at the car. He gave the valet instructions on how to shift the transmission and then passed through the glass doors. The orchestra was playing themes from John Barry scores, light on the brass and heavy on the strings. A woman, elegantly dressed in the latest designer fashion, was standing just inside the entrance, greeting the guests.

He had no doubt she was Jessie LeBaron. Cool composure, the embodiment of grace and style, the living proof women can be beautiful after fifty. She wore a glittery beaded green and silver tunic over a long, slim velvet skirt.

Pitt approached and gave a brief bow. "Good evening," he said, flashing his best gate crasher's smile.

"What is that sensational car?" Jessie asked, peering through the doorway.

"A Daimler powered by a 5.4 liter, straight-eight engine with Hooper coachwork."

She smiled graciously and extended her hand. "Thank you for coming, Mr...." She hesitated, gazing at him curiously. "Forgive me, but I don't seem to recall meeting you before."

"That's because we've never laid eyes on each other," he said, marveling at her throaty voice, almost husky, with a sensual coarseness about it. "My name is Pitt, Dirk Pitt."

Jessie's dark eyes looked at Pitt in a most peculiar way. "You're four and a half hours late, Mr. Pitt. Did you suffer some sort of accidental delay?"

"No accident, Mrs. LeBaron. I planned my arrival most carefully."

"You weren't invited to the party," she said smoothly. "So you'll have to leave."

"A pity," said Pitt mournfully. "I seldom get a chance to wear my tux."

Jessie's face registered scorn. She turned to a prim woman wearing large-lensed glasses and standing slightly to her rear, who Pitt guessed was her secretary, Sandra Cabot.

"Find Angelo and tell him to show this gentleman out."

Pitt's green eyes glinted mischievously. "I seem to have a talent for spreading ill will. Do you wish me to go peacefully or cause a nasty scene?"

"I think peacefully would be best."

"Then why did you ask to meet with me?"

"A matter concerning my husband."

"He was a perfect stranger to me. I can't tell you anything about his death that you don't already know."

"Raymond is not dead," she said adamantly.

"When I saw him in the blimp he gave a damn good imitation of it."

"That wasn't him."

Pitt stared at her skeptically, saying nothing.

"You don't believe me, do you?"

"I don't really care."

"I was hoping you'd help me."

"You have a strange way of asking for favors."

"This a formal charity dinner, Mr. Pitt. You don't fit in. We'll set a time to meet tomorrow."

Pitt decided his anger wasn't important, so he shoved it aside. "What was your husband doing when he disappeared?" he asked abruptly.

"Searching for the El Dorado treasure," she replied, looking nervously around the greenhouse at her guests. "He believed it sank on a ship called the *Cyclops*."

Before Pitt could make a comment, Cabot returned with Angelo, the Cuban chauffeur.

"Goodbye, Mr. Pitt," said Jessie, dismissing him and greeting a pair of new arrivals.

Pitt shrugged and offered his arm to Angelo. "Let's make it official. You lead me out." Then he turned to Jessie. "One last thing, Mrs. LeBaron. I don't respond to shabby treatment. You needn't bother to contact me again, ever."

Then Pitt allowed Angelo to escort him from the greenhouse to the driveway where the Daimler was waiting. Jessie watched as the great car disappeared into the night. Then she began mingling with her guests.

Douglas Oates, the Secretary of State, looked over from a conversation he was having with presidential adviser Daniel Fawcett as she approached. "Splendid affair, Jessie."

"Yes indeed," echoed Fawcett. "Nobody in Washington puts on a finer spread."

Jessie's eyes flashed and her full lips curved in a warm smile. "Thank you, gentlemen."

Oates nodded toward the doorway. "Was I imagining things, or did I see Dirk Pitt bounced out the door?"

Jessie looked at Oates blankly. "You know him?" she asked, surprised.

"Of course. Pitt is the number two man over at NUMA. He's the guy who raised the *Titanic* for the Defense Department."

"And saved the President's life in Louisiana," added Fawcett.

Jessie noticeably paled. "I had no idea."

"I hope you didn't make him mad," said Oates.

"Perhaps I *was* a bit rude," she conceded.

"Aren't you interested in drilling for offshore oil below San Diego?"

"Yes. Seismic surveys indicate a vast untapped field. One of our companies has the inside track for the drilling rights. Why do you ask?"

"Don't you know who heads up the Senate committee for oil exploration on government lands?"

"Certainly, it's..." Jessie's voice trailed off and her composure melted away.

"Dirk's father," Oates finished. "Senator George Pitt of California. Without his backing and the blessing of NUMA on environmental issues, you don't stand a prayer of winning the drilling rights."

"It would appear," Fawcett said sardonically, "your inside track just washed out."

9

THIRTY MINUTES LATER, Pitt rolled the Daimler into his parking stall in front of the tall, solar-glassed building that housed NUMA headquarters. He signed in at the security desk and took the elevator to the tenth floor. When the doors opened, he stepped into a vast electronic maze, comprising the communications and information network of the marine agency.

Hiram Yaeger looked up from behind a horseshoe-shaped desk, whose surface lay unseen beneath a jungle of computer hardware, and smiled. "Hullo, Dirk. All dressed up and no place to go?"

"The party's hostess decided I was persona non grata and made me walk the plank."

"Anybody I know?"

It was Pitt's turn to smile. He looked down at Yaeger. The computer wizard was a throwback to the hippie days of the early seventies. He wore his blond hair long and tied in a ponytail. His beard was untrimmed and kinky with uncontrolled curls. And his standard uniform for work and play was Levi jacket and pants stuffed into scruffy cowboy boots.

Pitt said, "I can't picture you and Jessie LeBaron traveling in the same social circles."

Yaeger gave out a low whistle. "You got booted from a Jessie LeBaron bash? Man, you're some kind of hero to the downtrodden."

"Are you in the mood for an excavation?"

"On her?"

"On him."

"Her husband? The one who's missing?"

"Raymond LeBaron."

"Another moonlight operation?"

"Whatever you want to call it."

"Dirk," Yaeger said, peering over the rims of his granny glasses, "you are a nosy bastard, but I love you just the same. I'm hired to build a world-class computer network and amass an archive on marine science and history, but every time I belch you turn up, wanting to use my creation for shady purposes. Why do I go along? Okay, I'll tell you why. Larceny flows faster in my veins than yours. Now, how deep do you want me to dig?"

"To the bottom of his past. Where he came from. What was the money base for his empire."

"Raymond LeBaron was pretty secretive about his private life. He may have covered his trail."

"I realize that, but you've pulled skeletons out of the closet before."

Yaeger nodded thoughtfully. "Yes, the Bougainville shipping family a few months ago. A neat little caper, if I do say so."

"One more thing."

"Lay it on me."

"A ship called the *Cyclops*. Could you pull her history for me?"

"No sweat. Anything else?"

"That should do it," Pitt answered.

Yaeger stared at him. "What's going down this time, old friend? I can't believe you're going after the LeBarons because you were dumped at a society party. Take me, I've been thrown out of the worst sleaze joints in town. And I just accept it."

Pitt laughed. "No revenge. I'm just curious. Jessie LeBaron said something that struck me odd about her husband's disappearance."

"I read about it in the *Washington Post*. There was a paragraph mentioning you as the hero of the hour, saving LeBaron's blimp with your rope and palm tree trick. So what's the catch?"

"She claimed that her husband wasn't among the dead I found inside the control cabin."

Yaeger paused, his eyes uncomprehending. "Doesn't make sense. If old man LeBaron flew off in that gas bag, it stands to reason he'd still be inside when it turned up."

"Not according to the bereaved wife."

"Think she's got an angle, insurance or financial?"

"Maybe, maybe not. But there is a chance that because the mystery occurred over water, NUMA will be called in to assist in the investigation."

"And we'll already be on first base."

"Something like that."

"Where does the *Cyclops* fit in the picture?"

"She told me LeBaron was looking for it when he vanished."

Yaeger rose from his chair. "All right then, let's get off the mark. While I design a search program, you study what we have on the ship in our data files."

He led Pitt into a small viewing theater with a large monitor mounted on the far wall and motioned for him to sit behind a console containing a computer keyboard. Then he leaned over Pitt and pressed a series of commands on the keyboard.

"We installed a new system last week. The terminal is hooked into a voice synthesizer."

"A talking computer," said Pitt.

"Yes, it can comprehend over ten thousand verbal commands, make the appropriate reply, and actually carry on a conversation. The voice sounds a little weird, sort of like Hal, the giant computer in the movie *2001*. But you get used to it. We call her Hope."

"Hope?"

"Yeah, we *hope* she'll come up with the right answers."

"Funny."

"I'll be at the main terminal desk if you need help. Just pick up the phone and dial four-seven."

Pitt looked up at the screen. It had a bluish-gray cast. He warily picked up a microphone and spoke into it.

"Hope, my name is Dirk. Are you ready to conduct a search for me?"

God, he felt like an idiot. It was like talking to a tree and expecting a reply.

"Hello, Dirk," replied a vaguely female voice that sounded as if it was coming out of a harmonica. "Ready when you are."

Pitt took a deep breath and made the plunge. "Hope, I'd like you to tell me about a ship named *Cyclops*."

There was a five-second pause, then the computer said, "You will have to be more specific. My memory disks contain data on five different vessels called *Cyclops*."

"This one had treasure on board."

"Sorry, none show any treasure in their cargo manifest."

Sorry? Pitt still couldn't believe he was conversing with a machine. "If I may digress for a moment, Hope, allow me to say you're a very bright and most congenial computer."

"Thank you for the compliment, Dirk. In case you're interested, I can also do sound effects, imitate animals, sing—though not too well—and pronounce 'supercalifragilisticexpialidocious,' even if I haven't been programmed to its exact definition. Would you like me to say it backwards?"

Pitt laughed. "Some other time. Getting back to the *Cyclops*, the one I'm interested in probably sank in the Caribbean."

"That narrows it down to two. A small steamer that ran aground in Montego Bay, Jamaica, 5 May 1968, and a U.S. Navy collier—an ore or coal transport—lost without a trace, between 5 and 10 February 1918."

Raymond LeBaron wouldn't be flying around searching for a ship stranded in a busy harbor only twenty years ago, Pitt reasoned. The tale of the Navy collier came back to him. The loss was touted as one of the great mysteries of the mythical Bermuda Triangle.

"We'll go with the Navy collier," said Pitt.

"If you wish me to print out the data for you, Dirk, press the control button on your keyboard and the letters PT. Also, if you watch the screen I can project whatever photos are available."

Pitt did as he was told and the printer began pounding away. True to her word, Hope flashed a picture of the *Cyclops* lying at anchor in an unnamed port.

Although her hull was slender with its old-fashioned straight-up-and-down bow and graceful champagne-glass stern, her superstructure had the look of a child's erector set gone wild. A maze of derricks, spiderwebbed by cables and laced by overhead supports, rose amidships like a dead forest. A long deckhouse ran along the aft part of the ship above the engine room, its roof festooned with towering twin smokestacks and several tall ventilators. Forward, the wheelhouse perched above the main deck like a vanity table on four legs, spotted with a single row of portholes and open beneath. Two high masts with a crossbar protruded from a bridge that could have passed for a football goalpost. She seemed ungainly, an ugly duckling that never made it to swan.

There was also a ghostly quality about her. At first Pitt couldn't put his finger on it, and then it struck him: oddly, no crew member was visible anywhere on her decks. It was if she were deserted.

Pitt turned from the monitor and scanned the printout of the ship's statistics:

Launched:	7 May 1910 by William Cramp & Sons Shipbuilders, Philadelphia
Tonnage:	19,360 displaced

Length:	542 feet (actually longer than the battleships of her time)
Beam:	65 feet
Draft:	27 feet 8 inches
Speed:	15 knots (3 knots faster than the Liberty ships of World War II)
Armament:	Four 4-inch guns
Crew:	246
Master:	G. W. Worley, Naval Auxiliary Service

Pitt noted that Worley was the *Cyclops'* captain from the time she was placed in service until she disappeared. He sat back, his mind drifting as he studied the picture of the ship.

"Do you have any other photographs of her?" he asked Hope.

"Three from the same angle, one stern shot, and four of the crew."

"Let's have a look at the crew."

The monitor went black for a moment and soon an image of a man, standing at a ship's railing and holding a little girl's hand, came into view.

"Captain Worley with his daughter," explained Hope.

A huge man with thinning hair, neatly trimmed moustache, and massive hands stood in a dark suit, necktie casually askew outside the jacket, shoes highly shined, staring into a camera that froze his image seventy-five years ago. The little blond girl at his side wore a knee-length jumper and a little hat, and gripped what looked to be a very rigid doll in the shape of a bottle.

"Real name was Johann Wichman," Hope briefed without command. "He was born in Germany and illegally entered the United States when he jumped a merchant ship in San Francisco during the year 1878. How he falsified his records is not known. While commanding the *Cyclops*, he lived in Norfolk, Virginia, with his wife and daughter."

"Any possibility he was working for the Germans in 1918?"

"Nothing was ever proven. Would you like the reports from naval investigations of the tragedy?"

"Just print them out. I'll study them later."

"The next photo is of Lieutenant David Forbes, the executive officer," said Hope.

The camera had caught Forbes in dress uniform standing beside what Pitt guessed to be a 1916 Cadillac touring car. He had the face of a greyhound, long, narrow nose, pale eyes whose color could not be determined from the black-and-white photograph. His face was clean-shaven, the eyebrows arched, and he had slightly protruding teeth.

"What sort of man was he?" asked Pitt.

"His naval record was unblemished until Worley put him under ship's arrest for insubordination."

"Reason?"

"Captain Worley altered course from one plotted by Lieutenant Forbes and almost wrecked the ship entering Rio. When Forbes demanded to know why, Worley blew up and confined him to quarters."

"Was Forbes still under arrest during the last voyage?"

"Yes."

"Who's next?"

"Lieutenant John Church, second officer."

The photo showed a small, almost frail-looking man in civilian clothes sitting at a table in a restaurant. His face wore the tired look of a farmer after a long day in the fields, yet his dark eyes seemed to advertise a humorous disposition. The graying hair above a large forehead was brushed back over small ears.

"He seems older than the others," observed Pitt.

"Actually only twenty-nine," said Hope. "Joined the Navy when he was sixteen and worked his way up through the ranks."

"Did he have problems with Worley?"

"Nothing in the file."

The final photograph was of two men standing at attention in a courtroom. There was no sign of apprehension in their faces; if anything, they appeared sullen and defiant. The one on the left was tall and rangy with heavily muscled arms. The other one had the size and shape of a grizzly bear.

"This picture was taken at the court-martial of Fireman First Class James Coker and Fireman Second Class Barney DeVoe for the murder of Fireman Third Class Oscar Stewart. All three men were stationed aboard the U.S. cruiser *Pittsburgh*. Coker, on the left, was sentenced to death by hanging, which was carried out in Brazil. DeVoe, on the right, was sentenced to fifty to ninety-nine years in the naval prison at Portsmouth, New Hampshire."

"What's their connection with the *Cyclops*?" Pitt inquired.

"The *Pittsburgh* was in Rio de Janeiro when the murder occurred.

When Captain Worley reached port, he was instructed to transport DeVoe and four other prisoners in the *Cyclops'* brig to the United States."

"And they were on board at the end."

"Yes."

"No other pictures of the crew?"

"They are probably available in family albums and other private sources, but this is all I have in my library."

"Tell me about the events leading to the disappearance."

"Verbal or print?"

"Can you print it out and talk at the same time?"

"Sorry, I can only perform such functions in sequence. Which do you prefer first?"

"Verbal."

"Very well. One moment while I assemble the data."

Pitt was beginning to feel drowsy. It had been a long day. He used the pause to dial Yaeger and ask for a cup of coffee.

"How are you and Hope getting along?"

"I'm almost beginning to think she's real," Pitt answered.

"Just so long you don't start fantasizing about her nonexistent body."

"I'm not at that stage yet."

"To know her is to love her."

"How are you doing on LeBaron?"

"What I was afraid of," said Yaeger. "He pretty much buried his past. No insight, only statistics up to the time he became the Wall Street whiz."

"Anything interesting?"

"Not really. He came from a fairly affluent family. His father owned a chain of hardware stores. I get the idea Raymond and his father didn't get along. There's no mention of his family in any newspaper biographies after he became the financial whiz."

"Did you find out how he made his first big bucks?"

"That area is pretty vague. He and a partner by the name of Kronberg had a marine salvage company in the middle nineteen-fifties. Seems they scratched along for a few years and then went broke. Two years later, Raymond launched his publication."

"The *Prosperteer.*"

"Right."

"Is there any mention of where his backing came from?"

"None," replied Yaeger. "By the way, Jessie is his second wife. His first was named Hillary. She died a few years ago. Nothing on her at all."

"Keep hunting."

Pitt hung up as Hope said, "I'm ready with the data on the ill-fated final voyage of the *Cyclops*."

"Let's hear it."

"She put to sea from Rio de Janeiro on 16 February 1918, bound for Baltimore, Maryland. On board were her regular crew of 15 officers and 231 men, 57 men from the cruiser *Pittsburgh*, who were being rotated to the Norfolk Naval Base for reassignment, the 5 prisoners including DeVoe, and the American consul general at Rio, Alfred L. Morean Gottschalk, who was returning to Washington. Her cargo was 11,000 tons of manganese ore.

"After a brief call at the port of Bahia to pick up mail, the ship made an unscheduled stop on 4 March, when she entered Carlisle Bay on the island of Barbados and dropped anchor. Here, Worley took on extra coal and provisions, which he claimed were necessary to continue the voyage to Baltimore, but was later considered to be quite excessive. After the ship was lost at sea, the American consul in Barbados reported a number of suspicious rumors regarding Worley's unusual action, strange events on board, and a possible mutiny. The last anyone saw of the *Cyclops* and the men on board was 4 March 1918, when she steamed away from Barbados."

"There was no further contact?" asked Pitt.

"Twenty-four hours later, a lumber freighter called the *Crogan Castle* reported her bow crushed by an immense freak wave. Her radio signals for assistance were answered by the *Cyclops*. The final words from the collier were her call number and the message, 'We are fifty miles due south of you and coming at full steam.'"

"Nothing else?"

"That was it."

"Did the *Crogan Castle* give her position?"

"Yes, it was reported as latitude twenty-three degrees, thirty minutes north by longitude seventy-nine degrees, twenty-one minutes west, which put her about twenty miles southeast from a bank of shallow reefs called the Anguilla Cays."

"Was the *Crogan Castle* lost also?"

"No, the records say she limped into Havana."

"Any wreckage of the *Cyclops* turn up?"

"An extensive search by the Navy found nothing."

Pitt hesitated as Yaeger entered the viewing room, set a cup of coffee by the console, and silently retreated. He took a few sips and asked Hope to reshow the photo of the *Cyclops*. The ship materialized on the monitor's screen and he stared at it thoughtfully.

He picked up the phone, punched a number, and waited. A digital clock on the console read 11:55, but the voice that answered sounded bright and cheerful.

"Dirk!" boomed Dr. Raphael O'Meara. "What the hell is going down? You caught me at a good time. I just came home this morning from a dig in Costa Rica."

"Find another truckload of potsherds?"

"Only the richest cache of pre-Columbian art discovered to date. Amazing pieces, some dating back to three hundred B.C."

"Too bad you can't keep them."

"All my finds go to the Museo Nacional de Costa Rica."

"You're a generous man, Raphael."

"I don't donate them, Dirk. The governments where my finds are made preserve the artifacts as part of their national heritage. But why bore an old waterlogged relic like you. To what do I owe the pleasure of your call?"

"I need your expertise on a piece of treasure."

"You know, of course," O'Meara said, his tone edged with a touch of seriousness, "treasure is an unspeakable word to a respected archeologist."

"We all carry an albatross," said Pitt. "Can you meet me for a drink?"

"Now? Do you realize what time it is?"

"I happen to know you're a night owl. Make it easy on yourself. Someplace close to your house."

"How about the Old Angler's Inn on MacArthur Boulevard? Say in half an hour."

"Sounds good."

"Can you tell me what treasure you're interested in?"

"The one everyone dreams about."

"Oh? And which one is that?"

"Tell you when I see you."

Pitt hung up and gazed at the *Cyclops*. There was an eerie loneliness about her. He could not help wondering what secrets she took with her to a watery grave.

"Can I provide any further data?" asked Hope, interrupting his morbid reverie. "Or do you wish to terminate?"

"I think we can call it quits," he replied. "Thank you, Hope. I wish I could give you a big kiss."

"I am grateful for the compliment, Dirk. But I am not physiologically capable of receiving a kiss."

"You're still a sweetheart in my book."

"Come up and use me anytime."

Pitt laughed. "Goodnight, Hope."

"Goodnight, Dirk."

If only she was real, he thought with a dreamy sigh.

10

"JACK DANIEL'S NEAT," Raphael O'Meara said cheerfully. "Make that a double. Best medicine I know to clear the brain of jungle rot."

"How long were you in Costa Rica?" asked Pitt.

"Three months. Rained the whole time."

"Bombay gin on the rocks with a twist," Pitt said to the barmaid.

"So you're joining the greedy ranks of the sea scavengers," O'Meara said, the words emanating through a thick Gabby Hayes beard that hid his face from the nose down. "Dirk Pitt a treasure hunter. I never thought I'd see the day."

"My interest is purely academic."

"Sure, that's what they all say. Take my advice and forget it. More loot has been poured into underwater treasure hunts than was ever found. I can count on one hand the number of lucky discoveries that paid a profit in the last eighty years. The adventure, excitement, and riches, nothing but hype and all myth."

"I agree."

O'Meara's barbed-wire eyebrows narrowed. "So what is it you want to know?"

"You familiar with Raymond LeBaron?"

"Old rich and reckless Raymond, the financial genius who publishes the *Prosperteer?*"

"The same. He disappeared a couple of weeks ago on a blimp flight near the Bahamas."

"How could anybody disappear in a blimp?"

"Somehow he managed. You must have heard or read something about it."

O'Meara shook his head. "I haven't watched TV or seen a newspaper in ninety days."

The drinks were brought, and Pitt briefly explained the strange circumstances surrounding the mystery. The crowd was beginning to thin and they had the bar mostly to themselves.

"And you think LeBaron was flying around in an old gas bag looking for a shipwreck loaded to the gills with the mother lode."

"According to his wife, Jessie."

"What ship?"

"The *Cyclops*."

"I know about the *Cyclops*. A Navy collier that vanished seventy-one years ago. I don't recall any report of riches on board."

"Apparently LeBaron thought so."

"What sort of treasure?"

"The El Dorado."

"You've got to be kidding."

"I'm only repeating what I was told."

O'Meara went quiet for a long moment, his eyes taking on a faraway look. *"El hombre dorado,"* he said at last. "Spanish for the golden man or the gilded one. The legend—some call it a curse—has fired imaginations for four hundred and fifty years."

"Is there any truth to it?" asked Pitt.

"Every legend is based on fact, but like all the others before and since, this one has been distorted and embellished into a fairy tale. El Dorado has inspired the longest continuing treasure hunt on record. Thousands of men have died searching for a glimpse of it."

"Tell me how the tale originated."

Another Jack Daniel's and Bombay gin arrived. Pitt laughed as O'Meara downed the water chaser first. Then the archeologist made himself comfortable and stared into another time.

"The Spanish conquistadores were the first to hear of a gilded man who ruled an incredibly wealthy kingdom somewhere in the mountainous jungles east of the Andes. Rumors described him as living in a secluded city built of gold with streets paved in emeralds and guarded by a fierce army of beautiful Amazons. Made Oz sound like a slum. Extremely overvalued, of course. But in reality there were a number of El Dorados—a long line of kings who worshiped a demon god who lived in Lake Guatavita, Colombia. When a new monarch took command of the tribal empire, his body was painted with resinous gums and then coated with gold dust, thus the gilded man. Then he was placed on a ceremonial raft, piled high with gold and precious stones, and rowed into the middle of the lake, where he proceeded to pitch the riches into the water as an offering to the god, whose name escapes me."

"Was the treasure ever raised?"

"There were any number of attempts to drain the lake, but they all failed. In 1965 the government of Colombia declared Guatavita an area of cultural interest and banned all salvage operations. A pity, when you consider that estimates of the wealth on the bottom of the lake run between one hundred and three hundred million dollars."

"And the golden city?"

"Never found," said O'Meara, signaling the barmaid for another round. "Many looked and many died. Nikolaus Federmann, Ambrosius Dalfinger, Sebastián de Belalcázar, Gonzalo and Hernán Jiménez de Quesada, all sought El Dorado but only found the curse. So did Sir Walter Raleigh. After his second fruitless expedition, King James put his head on the block, literally. The fabulous city of El Dorado and the greatest treasure of them all remained lost."

"Let's back up a minute," said Pitt. "The treasure at the bottom of the lake is not lost."

"That's in scattered pieces," explained O'Meara. "The second one, the grand prize, the bonanza at the end of the rainbow, remains hidden to this day. With maybe two exceptions, no outsider has ever laid eyes on it. The only description came from a monk who wandered out of the jungle into a Spanish settlement on the Orinoco River in 1675. Before dying a week later, he told of being on a Portuguese expedition looking for diamond mines. Out of eighty men, he was the only survivor. He claimed they'd stumbled into a deserted city surrounded by high cliffs and guarded by a tribe who called themselves Zanonas. The party lived in the city for three months, but one by one the men began to die off. Too late they discovered the Zanonas were not as friendly as they made out, but were cannibals, poisoning the Portuguese and eating them. The monk alone managed to escape. He described massive temples and buildings, strange inscriptions, and the legendary treasure that sent so many of its hunters to their graves."

"A true golden man," Pitt speculated. "A statue."

"You're close," said O'Meara. "Damned close, but you missed on the sex.'

"Sex?"

"*La mujer dorada,* the golden woman," O'Meara replied. "Or more commonly, La Dorada. You see, the name first applied to a man and a ceremony, later to a city, and finally to an empire. Over the years it became a term for any place where riches could be found on the ground. Like so many descriptions the feminists hate, the masculine myth became generic, while the feminine was forgotten. Ready for another drink?"

"No, thanks. I'll nurse this one."

O'Meara ordered another Jack Daniel's. "Anyway, you know the story behind the Taj Mahal. A Mogul ruler erected the ornate tomb as a monument to his wife. Same with a pre-Columbian, South American king. His name is not recorded, but, so the legend goes, she was the most beloved of the hundreds of women at his court. Then an event occurred in the sky. Probably either an eclipse or Halley's comet. And the priests called on him to sacrifice her to appease the angry gods. Life was no fun in those days. So she was killed, heart torn out in an elaborate ceremony."

"I thought only the Aztecs went in for heart removal."

"The Aztecs didn't have a monopoly on human sacrifice. The upshot was the king called together his artisans and ordered them to build a statue of her likeness so he could elevate her to a god."

"Did the monk describe it?"

"In vivid detail, if his story can be believed. She stands nude, nearly six feet tall, on a pedestal of rose quartz. Her body is solid gold. God, it must weigh at least a ton. Imbedded in the chest, where the heart should be, is a great ruby, judged to be in the neighborhood of twelve hundred carats."

"I don't profess to be an expert," said Pitt, "but I know that rubies are the most valuable of all the gemstones, and one of thirty carats is a rarity. Twelve hundred carats is unbelievable."

"That's not even the half of it," O'Meara continued. "The entire head of the statue is one gigantic carved emerald, deep blue-green and flawless. I can't begin to guess the carat weight, but it would have to hit the scales around thirty pounds."

"More like forty if you include a likeness of the hair."

"What's the largest known emerald?"

Pitt thought a moment. "Certainly no more than ten pounds."

"Can't you just see her standing under spotlights in the main lobby of Washington's Museum of Natural History," O'Meara said wistfully.

"I can only wonder at the value on today's market."

"You could safely say it's priceless."

"There was another man who saw the statue?" Pitt asked.

"Colonel Ralph Morehouse Sigler, a real character from the old explorer school. An engineer in the English army, he tramped around the empire, surveying boundaries and building forts throughout Africa and India. He was also a trained geologist and spent his leave time prospecting. He was either damned lucky or damned good, discovering an extensive chromite deposit in South Africa and several precious gemstone veins in Indochina. He became wealthy but didn't have time to enjoy it. The Kaiser marched into France and he was ordered to the Western Front to build fortifications."

"So he didn't enter South America until after the war."

"No, in the summer of 1916, he stepped off the boat at Georgetown, in what was then British Guiana. It seems some hotshot in the British treasury got the bright idea of sending out expeditions around the world to find and open gold mines to finance the war. Sigler was recalled from the front and ordered into the South American interior."

"You think he knew the monk's story?" Pitt asked.

"Nothing in his diaries or papers indicates he ever believed in a lost city. The guy was no wild-eyed treasure hunter. He was after raw minerals. Historic artifacts never interested him. Are you hungry, Dirk?"

"Yes, come to think of it. I was cheated out of dinner."

"We're long past the dinner hour, but if we ask nice I'm sure the kitchen can rustle up some appetizers."

O'Meara gestured for the barmaid and after pleading his case persuaded her to serve them a platter of shrimp with cocktail sauce.

"Hits the spot," said Pitt.

"I could eat these little devils all day long," O'Meara agreed. "Now, where were we?"

"Sigler was about to find La Dorada."

"Oh, yes. After forming a party of twenty men, mostly British soldiers, Sigler plunged into the uncharted wilds. For months, nothing was heard of them. The British began to sense disaster and sent out several search parties, but none found a trace of the missing men. At last, nearly two years later, an American expedition, surveying for a railroad, stumbled upon Sigler five hundred miles northeast of Rio de Janeiro. He was alone, the only survivor."

"Seems like an incredible distance from British Guiana."

"Almost two thousand miles from his jump-off point as the crow flies."

"What kind of shape was he in?"

"More dead than alive, according to the engineers who found him. They carried Sigler to a village that had a small hospital and sent off a message to the nearest American consulate. A few weeks later a relief party arrived from Rio."

"American or British?"

"An odd twist there," answered O'Meara. "The British consulate claimed they were never notified of Sigler's reappearance. Gossip had it that the American consul general himself showed up to question him. Whatever happened, Sigler dropped from sight. The story is he escaped from the hospital and wandered back into the jungle."

"Doesn't figure that he'd turn his back on civilization after two years of hell," said Pitt.

O'Meara shrugged. "Who can say?"

"Did Sigler give an account of his expedition before he disappeared?"

"Raved in delirium most of the time. Witnesses said afterward that he babbled about finding a huge city surrounded by steep cliffs and overgrown by jungle. His description pretty much matched the Portuguese monk's. He also drew a rough sketch of the golden woman that was saved by a nurse and now lies in Brazil's national library. I had a look at it while researching another project. The real thing must be an awesome sight."

"So it remains buried in the jungle."

"Ah, there's the rub," sighed O'Meara. "Sigler claimed he and his men stole the statue and dragged it twenty miles to a river, fighting off the Zanona Indians the whole trip. By the time they built a raft, heaved La Dorada on board, and pushed off, there were only three of them left. Later one died of his injuries and the other was lost in a stretch of rapids."

Pitt was fascinated by what O'Meara was telling him, but he was having a hard time keeping his eyes open. "The obvious question is, Where did Sigler stash the golden woman?"

"If I only knew," replied O'Meara.

"Didn't he give a clue?"

"The nurse thought he said the raft came apart and the statue dropped into the river a few hundred yards from where the surveyors' party found him. But don't get your hopes up. He was muttering nonsense. Treasure hunters have been dragging metal detectors up and down that river for years without a reading a tick."

Pitt swirled the ice cubes around inside his glass. He knew, he *knew* what happened to Ralph Morehouse Sigler and La Dorada.

"The American consul general," Pitt said slowly, "he was the last person to see Sigler alive?"

"The puzzle gets cloudy at this point, but as near as anyone can tell, the answer is yes."

"Let me see if I can fill in the pieces. This took place in January and February of 1918. Right?"

O'Meara nodded, and then he gave Pitt a queer stare.

"And the consul general's name was Alfred Gottschalk, who died a few weeks later on the *Cyclops*. Right?"

"You know this?" said O'Meara, his eyes uncomprehending.

"Gottschalk probably heard of Sigler's mission through his counterpart at the British consulate. When he received the message from the railroad surveyors that Sigler was alive, he kept the news to himself and headed into the interior, hoping to interview the explorer and steal a jump on the British by turning over any valuable information to his own government. What he learned must have shattered any code of ethics he still retained. Gottschalk decided to grab the bonanza for himself.

"He found and raised the golden statue from the river and then transported it, along with Sigler, to Rio de Janeiro. He covered his tracks by buying off anyone who might talk about Sigler, and, if my guess is correct, killing off the men who helped him recover the statue. Then, using his influence with the Navy, he smuggled them both on board the *Cyclops*. The ship was lost and the secret died with her."

O'Meara's eyes deepened in curious interest. "Now *that*," he said, "you can't possibly know."

"Why else would LeBaron be looking for what he thought was La Dorada?"

"You make a good case," O'Meara admitted. "But you left the door open to a moot question. Why didn't Gottschalk simply kill Sigler after he found the statue? Why keep the Englishman alive?"

"Elementary. The consul general was consumed by gold fever. He wanted La Dorada and the emerald city too. Sigler was the only person alive who could give him directions or lead him there."

"I like the way you think, Dirk. Your wild-assed theory calls for another drink."

"Too late, the bar's closed. I think they'd like us to leave so the help can get home to bed."

O'Meara mimicked a crestfallen expression. "That's one nice thing about primitive living. No hours, no curfew." He took a final swallow from his glass. "Well, what are your plans?"

"Nothing complicated," said Pitt, smiling. "I'm going to find the *Cyclops*."

11

THE PRESIDENT WAS AN EARLY RISER, awakening at about 6 A.M. and exercising for thirty minutes before showering and eating a light breakfast. In a ritual going back to the days soon after his honeymoon, he gently eased out of bed and quietly dressed while his wife slept on. She was a night person and could not force herself to rise before 7:30.

He slipped on a sweatsuit and then removed a small leather briefcase from a closet in the adjoining sitting room. After giving his wife a tender kiss on the cheek, he took the back stairway down to the White House gym beneath the west terrace.

The spacious room, containing a variety of exercise equipment, was empty except for a thick-bodied man who lay on his back bench-pressing a set of weights. With each lift he grunted like a woman in childbirth. The sweat beaded from a round head that sprouted a thick mat of ivory hair styled in a short crewcut. The stomach was immense and hairy, the arms and legs protruding like heavy tree limbs. He had the look of a carnival wrestler long past his prime.

"Good morning, Ira," said the President. "I'm glad you could make it."

The fat man set the weight bar on a pair of hooks above his head, rose from the bench, and squeezed the President's hand. "Good to see you, Vince."

The President smiled. No bowing, no scraping, no greeting of "Mr. President." Tough, stoical Ira Hagen, he mused. The gritty old undercover agent never gave an inch to anybody.

"I hope you don't mind meeting like this."

Hagen uttered a coarse laugh that echoed off the gym walls. "I've been briefed in worse places."

"How's the restaurant business?"

"Showing a nice profit since we switched from continental gourmet to downhome American food. Food costs were eating us alive. Twenty entrées with expensive sauces and herbs didn't cut it. So now we specialize in only five menu items the higher-class restaurants don't serve—ham, chicken, fish casserole, stew, and meatloaf."

"You may have something," said the President. "I haven't bitten into a good meatloaf since I was a kid."

"Our customers go for it, especially since we retained the fancy service and intimate atmosphere. My waiters all wear tuxedos, candles on tables, stylish settings, food presented in a continental manner. And the best part is the diners eat faster, so there's a quicker turnover on tables."

"And you're breaking even on the food while taking a profit on the booze and wine, right?"

Hagen laughed again. "Vince, you're okay. I don't care what the news media say about you. When you're an old has-been politician look me up, and we'll open a chain of beaneries together."

"Do you miss criminal investigation, Ira?"

"Sometimes."

"You were the best undercover operative the Justice Department ever had," the President said, "until Martha died."

"Gathering evidence on slime for the government didn't seem to matter anymore. Besides, I had three daughters to raise, and the demands of the job kept me away from home for weeks at a time."

"The girls doing all right?"

"Just fine. As you well know, all three of your nieces have happy marriages and presented me with five grandchildren."

"A pity Martha couldn't have seen them. Of my four sisters and two brothers, she was my favorite."

"You didn't fly me here from Denver on an Air Force jet just to talk old times," said Hagen. "What's going down?"

"Have you lost your touch?"

"Have you forgotten how to ride a bicycle?"

It was the President's turn to laugh. "Ask a stupid question..."

"The reflexes are a mite slower, but the gray matter still turns at a hundred percent."

The President tossed him the briefcase. "Digest this while I hike a couple of miles on the treadmill."

Hagen wiped his sweating brow with a towel and sat on a stationary bicycle, his bulk threatening to bend the frame. He opened the leather case and didn't look up from reading the contents until the President had walked 1.6 miles.

"What do you think?" the President asked finally.

Hagen shrugged, still reading. "Make a great pilot for a TV show. Closet funding, an impenetrable security veil, covert activity on an immense scale, an undetected moon base. The stuff H. G. Wells would have loved."

"Do you figure it's a hoax?"

"Let's say I want to believe it. What flag-waving taxpayer wouldn't? Makes our intelligence community look like deaf and blind mutants. But if it is a hoax, where's the motive?"

"Other than a grand scheme to defraud the government, I can't think of any."

"Let me finish reading. This last file is in longhand."

"My recollection of what was said on the golf course. Sorry about the chicken scratch, but I never learned to type."

Hagen stared at him questioningly. "You've told no one about this, not even your security council?"

"Perhaps I'm paranoid, but this 'Joe' character slipped through my Secret Service cordon like a fox through a barnyard. And he claimed members of the 'inner core' were highly placed at NASA and the Pentagon. It stands to reason they've also penetrated the intelligence agencies and my White House staff as well."

Hagen studied the President's report of the golf course meeting intently, going back occasionally to check the Jersey Colony file. Finally he hoisted his body off the bicycle and sat on a bench, looking at the President.

"This photo blowup of a man sitting next to you in a golf cart. Is that Joe?"

"Yes. When returning to the clubhouse, I spotted a reporter from the *Washington Post* who had been photographing my golf game through a telescopic lens. I asked him to do me a favor and send an enlargement over to the White House so I could autograph it for my caddy."

"Good thinking." Hagen peered closely at the picture and then set it aside. "What do you want me to do, Vince?"

"Dig out the names of the 'inner core.'"

"Nothing else? No information or evidence on the Jersey Colony project?"

"When I know who they are," the President said in a dead voice, "they'll be rounded up and interrogated. Then we'll see how deep their tentacles reach."

"If you want my opinion, I'd pin a medal on every one of those guys."

"I may just do that," the President replied with a cold smile. "But not before I stop them from kicking off a bloody battle for the moon."

"So it adds up to a presidential cutout situation. You can't trust anyone in normal intelligence circles and you're hiring me to be your private field intelligence agent."

"Yes."

"What's my deadline?"

"The Russian spacecraft is set to land on the moon nine days from now. I need every hour I can steal to prevent a fight between their cosmonauts and our moon colonists that might spread into a space conflict that none of us could stop. The 'inner core' must be convinced to back off. I've got to have them under wraps, Ira, at least twenty-four hours before the Russians touch down."

"Eight days isn't much to find nine men."

The President gave a helpless shrug. "Nothing comes easy."

"A certificate saying I'm your brother-in-law won't be enough to pass me through legal and bureaucratic roadblocks. I'll require a concrete cover."

"I leave it to you to create one. An Alpha Two clearance should get you through most doors."

"Not bad," said Hagen. "The Vice President only carries a Three."

"I'll give you the number of a safe phone line. Report to me day or night. Understood?"

"Understood."

"Questions?"

"Raymond LeBaron, dead or alive?"

"Undecided. The wife refused to identify the body found in the blimp as his. She was right. I asked the FBI director, Sam Emmett, to take possession of the remains from Dade County, Florida. They're over at Walter Reed Army Hospital now, undergoing examination."

"Can I see the county coroner's report?"

The President shook his head in wonderment. "You never miss a trick, do you, Ira?"

"Obviously there had to be one."

"I'll see you get a copy."

"And the lab results at Walter Reed."

"That too."

Hagen stuffed the files back into the briefcase, but left out the photo from the golf course. He studied the images for perhaps the fourth time. "You realize, of course, Raymond LeBaron may never be found."

"I've considered that possibility."

"Nine little Indians. And then there were eight...make that seven."

"Seven?"

Hagen held up the photo in front of the President's eyes. "Don't you recognize him?"

"Frankly, no. But he did say we knew each other many years ago."

"Our high school baseball team. You played first base. I was left field and Leonard Hudson caught."

"Hudson!" The President gasped incredulously. "Joe is Leo Hudson. But Leo was a fat kid. Weighed at least two hundred pounds."

"He became a health nut. Lost sixty pounds and ran marathons. You were never sentimental about the old gang. I still keep track of them. Don't you remember? Leo was the school brain. Won all sorts of awards for his science projects. Later he graduated with honors at Stanford and became director of the Harvey Pattenden National Physics Laboratory in Oregon. Invented and pioneered rocket and space systems before anyone else was working in the field."

"Bring him in, Ira. Hudson is the key to the others."

"I'll need a shovel."

"You saying he's buried?"

"Like in dead and buried."

"When?"

"Back in 1965. A light-plane crash in the Columbia River."

"Then who is Joe?"

"Leonard Hudson."

"But you said—"

"His body was never found. Convenient, huh?"

"He faked his death," the President said as if beholding a revelation. "The son of a bitch faked his death so he could go underground to ramrod the Jersey Colony project."

"A brilliant idea when you think about it. No one to answer to. No way he could be tied to a clandestine program. Disguise himself as any character who could be used to his advantage. A nonperson can accomplish far more than the average taxpayer whose name, birthmarks, and nasty habits are stored in a thousand computers."

There was a silence, then the President's grim voice: "Find him, Ira. Find and bring Leonard Hudson to me before all hell breaks loose."

Secretary of State Douglas Oates peered through his reading glasses at the last page of a thirty-page letter. He closely examined the structure of each paragraph, trying to read between the lines. At last he looked up at his deputy secretary, Victor Wykoff.

"Looks genuine to me."

"Our experts on the subject think so too," said Wykoff. "The semantics, the rambling flow, the disjointed sentences, all fit the usual pattern."

"No denying it sounds like Fidel all right," Oates said quietly. "However, it's the tone of the letter that bothers me. You almost get the impression he's begging."

"I don't think so. More like he's trying to stress utmost secrecy with a healthy dose of urgency thrown in."

"The consequences of his proposal are staggering."

"My staff has studied it from every angle," said Wykoff. "Castro has nothing to gain from creating a hoax."

"You say he went through devious lengths to get the document into our hands."

Wykoff nodded. "Crazy as it sounds, the two couriers, who delivered it to our field office in Miami, claim they sneaked from Cuba to the United States on board a blimp."

12

THE BARREN MOUNTAINS and the shadowy ridges on the moon's craters leaped out at Anastas Rykov as he peered through the twin lenses of a stereoscope. Beneath the eyes of the Soviet geophysicist the desolate lunar landscape unreeled in three dimensions and vivid color. Taken from thirty-four miles up, the details were strikingly sharp. Solitary pebbles, measuring less than one inch across, were visually distinct.

Rykov lay face downward on a pad, studying the photographic montage that slowly rolled beneath to the stereoscope on two wide reels. The process was similar to a motion picture director editing film, only more comfortable. His hand rested on a small control unit that could stop the reels and magnify whatever area he was scrutinizing.

The images had been received from sophisticated devices on a Russian spacecraft that had circumnavigated the moon. Mirrorlike scanners reflected the lunar surface into a prism that broke it down into spectrum wavelengths that were digitized into 263 different shades of gray: black beginning at 263 and fading to white at zero. Next, the spacecraft's computer converted them into a quiltwork of picture elements on high-density tape. After the data was retrieved from the orbiting spacecraft, it was printed in black-and-white on a negative by laser and filtered with blue, red, and green wavelengths. Then it was computer enhanced in color on two continuous sheets of photographic paper that were overlapped for stereoscopic interpretation.

Rykov raised his glasses and rubbed his bloodshot eyes. He glanced at his wristwatch. It was 11:57 P.M. He'd been analyzing the peaks and valleys of the moon with only a few catnaps for nine days and nights. He readjusted his glasses and ran both hands through a dense carpet of oily black hair, dully realizing he hadn't bathed or changed his clothes since beginning the project.

He shook away the exhaustion and dutifully returned to his work, examining a small area on the far side of the moon that was volcanic in origin. Only two inches of the photo roll remained before it mysteriously ended. He had not been informed by his superiors of the reason for the sudden cutoff, but assumed it was a malfunction of the scanning gear.

The surface was pockmarked and wrinkled, like pimpled skin under a strong magnifying glass, and appeared more beechnut brown than gray in color. The steady bombardment of meteorites through the ages had left crater gouged on crater, scar crossing scar.

Rykov almost missed it. His eyes detected an unnatural oddity, but his tired mind nearly ignored the signal. Wearily he backed the image and magnified a grid on the edge of a steep ridge soaring from the floor of a small crater. Three tiny objects came into crisp focus.

What he saw was unbelievable. Rykov pulled back from the stereoscope and took a deep breath, clearing the creeping fog from his brain. Then he looked again.

They were still there, but one object was a rock. The other two were human figures.

Rykov was transfixed by what he saw. Then the shock set in and his hands began to tremble and his stomach felt as though it had been twisted in a knot. Shaken, he climbed off the pad, walked over to a desk, and opened a small booklet containing private phone numbers of the Soviet Military Space Command. He misdialed twice before he connected with the correct number.

A voice slurred from vodka answered. "What is it?"

"General Maxim Yasenin?"

"Yes, who's this?"

"We've never met. My name is Anastas Rykov. I'm a geophysicist on the Cosmos Lunar Project."

The commander of Soviet military space missions made no attempt to hide his irritation over Rykov's intrusion on his privacy. "Why in hell are you calling me this time of night?"

Rykov fully realized he was overstepping his bounds, but he didn't hesitate. "While analyzing pictures taken by Selenos 4, I've stumbled on something that defies belief. I thought you should be first to be informed."

"Are you drunk, Rykov?"

"No, General. Tired but Siberian sober."

"Unless you are a complete fool, you must know you are in deep trouble for going over the heads of your superiors."

"This is too important to share with anyone beneath your level of authority."

"Sleep on it and you won't be so brash in the morning," said Yasenin. "I'll do you a favor and forget the whole matter. Goodnight."

"Wait!" Rykov demanded, throwing caution aside. "If you dismiss my call, I will have no choice but to turn my discovery over to Vladimir Polevoi."

Rykov's statement was greeted by an icy silence. Finally Yasenin said, "What makes you think the chief of state security would listen to a crazy man?"

"When he checked my dossier, he would find I am a respected party member and a scientist who is far from lunacy."

"Oh?" Yasenin asked, his irritation turning to curiosity. He decided to pin Rykov down. "All right. I'll hear you out. What's so vital to the interest of Mother Russia that it can't go through prescribed channels?"

Rykov spoke very calmly. "I have proof that someone is on the moon."

Forty-five minutes later, General Yasenin strode into the photo analysis laboratory of the Geophysical Space Center. Big, beefy, and red of face, he wore a rumpled uniform that was ablaze with decorations. The hair was smoke-gray, the eyes steady and hard. He walked quietly, his head thrust out as if stalking a prey.

"You Rykov?" he asked without prelude.

"Yes," Rykov said simply but firmly.

They stared at each other a moment, neither making any attempt at shaking hands. Finally, Rykov cleared his throat and motioned toward the stereoscope.

"This way, General," he said. "Please lie prone on the leather cushion and look through the eyepiece."

As Yasenin positioned himself over the photo montage he asked, "What am I searching for?"

"Focus on the small area I've circled," replied Rykov.

The general adjusted the lenses to his vision and peered downward, his face impassive. After a full minute, he looked up strangely, then bent over the stereoscope again. At last he slowly rose and stared at Rykov, eyes stark in open astonishment.

"This is not a photographic trick?" he asked dumbly.

"No, General. What you see is real. Two human forms, wearing encapsulated suits, are aiming some sort of device at Selenos 4."

Yasenin's mind could not accept what his eyes saw to be true. "It's not impossible. Where do they come from?"

Rykov shrugged helplessly. "I don't know. If they're not United States astronauts, they can only be aliens."

"I do not believe in supernatural fairy tales."

"But how could the Americans launch men to the moon without the event leaking to the world news media or our intelligence people?"

"Suppose they left men behind and stockpiled material during the Apollo program. Such an effort might be possible."

"Their last known lunar landing was by Apollo 17 in 1972," Rykov recalled. "No human could survive the harsh lunar conditions for seventeen years without being resupplied."

"I can think of no one else," Yasenin insisted.

He returned to the stereoscope and intently studied the human forms standing in the crater. The sun's glare was coming from the right, throwing their shadows to the left. Their suits were white, and he could make out the dark green viewports on the helmets. They were of a design unfamiliar to him. Yasenin could clearly distinguish footprints leading into a pitch-black shadow cast by the crater's rim.

"I know what you're looking for, General," said Rykov, "but I've already examined the landscape on the floor of the crater and cannot find any sign of their spacecraft."

"Perhaps they climbed down from the top?"

"That's a sheer drop of over a thousand feet."

"I'm at a loss to explain any of this," Yasenin admitted quietly.

"Please look closely at the device they're both holding and pointing at Selenos 4. It seems to be a large camera with an extremely long telephoto lens."

"No," said Yasenin. "You're treading in my territory now. Not a camera but a weapon."

"A laser?"

"Nothing so advanced. Strikes me as a hand-held surface-to-air missile system of American manufacture. A Lariat type 40, I should say. Homes in with a guidance beam, ten-mile range on earth, probably much more in the moon's rarefied atmosphere. Became operational with NATO forces about six years ago. So much for your alien theory."

Rykov was awed. "Every ounce of weight is precious in space

flight. Why carry something so heavy and useless as a rocket launcher?"

"The men in the crater found a purpose. They used it against Selenos 4."

Rykov thought a moment. "That would explain why the scanners stopped operating a minute later. They were damaged—"

"By a hit from a rocket," Yasenin finished.

"We were fortunate the scanners finally relayed the digitized data before it crashed."

"A pity the crew were not so lucky."

Rykov stared at the general, not sure he'd heard right. "Selenos 4 was unmanned."

Yasenin pulled a slim gold case from his coat, selected a cigarette, and lit it with a lighter embedded in the top. Then he slid the case back into a breast pocket.

"Yes, of course, Selenos 4 *was* unmanned."

"But you said—"

Yasenin smiled coldly. "I said nothing."

The message was clear. Rykov valued his position too much to pursue the subject. He simply nodded.

"Do you wish a report on what we've seen here tonight?" Rykov asked.

"The original, no copies, on my desk by ten o'clock tomorrow. And, Rykov, consider this a state secret of the highest priority."

"I will confide in no one but you, General."

"Good man. There may be party honor in this for you."

Rykov wasn't going to hold his breath waiting for the award, yet he could not suppress a glow of pride in his work.

Yasenin returned to the stereoscope, drawn to the image of the intruders on the moon. "So the fabled star wars have begun," he murmured to himself. "And the Americans have launched the first blow."

13

PITT REJECTED ANY THOUGHT of lunch, and opened one of several granola bars he kept in his desk. Fumbling with the wrapper, held over a wastebasket to catch the crumbs, he kept his concentration locked on a large nautical chart spread across the desk. The chart's tendency to curl was held down by a memo pad and two books on historic shipwrecks that were opened to chapters on the *Cyclops*. The chart covered a large area of the Old Bahama Channel, flanked on the south by the Archipelago de Camagüey, a group of scattered islands off the coast of Cuba, and the shallow waters of the Great Bahama Bank to the north. The upper left corner of the chart took in the Cay Sal Bank, whose southeastern tip included the Anguilla Cays.

He sat back and took a bite out of the granola bar. Then he bent over the chart again, sharpened a pencil, and picked up a pair of dividers. Setting the needle tips of the dividers on the scale printed on the bottom of the chart, he measured off twenty nautical miles and carefully marked the distance from the tip of the Anguilla Cays with a penciled dot. Next, he described a short arc another fifty miles to the southeast. He labeled the top dot *Crogan Castle* and the lower arc *Cyclops* with a question mark.

Somewhere above the arc is where the *Cyclops* sank, he reasoned. A logical assumption given the fact of the lumber freighter's position at the time of her distress signal and the *Cyclops'* distance as given in her reply.

The only problem was that Raymond LeBaron's piece of the puzzle didn't fit.

From his experience in searching for shipwrecks, Pitt was convinced LeBaron had performed the same exercise a hundred times, only delving deeper into currents, known weather conditions at the time of the loss, and the projected speed of the Navy collier. But one conclusion always came out the same. The *Cyclops* should have gone down in the middle of the channel under 260 fathoms of water, over 1,500 feet to the bottom. Far too deep to be visible to anything other than a fish.

Pitt relaxed in his chair and stared at the markings on the chart. Unless LeBaron dredged up information nobody else knew about, what was he searching for? Certainly not the *Cyclops,* and certainly not from a blimp. A side-scan survey from a surface craft or a deep-diving submersible would have been better suited for the job.

In addition, the prime search area was only twenty miles off Cuba. Hardly a comfortable place to cruise around in a slow-flying gas bag. Castro's gunboats would have declared open season on such an easy target.

He was sitting lost in contemplation, nibbling on the granola bar, trying to see a probability in Raymond LeBaron's scheme that he had missed, when his desk speaker beeped. He pressed the Talk switch.

"Yes?"

"Sandecker. Can you come up to my office?"

"Five minutes, Admiral."

"Try for two."

Admiral James Sandecker was the director of the National Underwater and Marine Agency. A man in his late fifties, he was of short stature, his body thin and stringy but hard as armor plating. The straight hair and Vandyke beard were blaze red. A fitness freak, he adhered to a strict exercise regimen. His naval career was distinguished more by hard-nosed efficiency than sea combat tactics. And though he wasn't popular in Washington social circles, politicians respected him for his integrity and organizational ability.

The admiral greeted Pitt's entry into his office with nothing more than a curt nod, then gestured to a woman sitting in a leather chair across the room.

"Dirk, I understand you've met Mrs. Jessie LeBaron."

She looked up and smiled, but it was an ingratiating smile. Pitt bowed slightly and pressed her hand.

"Sorry," he said indifferently. "I'd rather forget I know Mrs. LeBaron."

Sandecker's eyebrows pinched together. "Am I missing something?"

"My fault," said Jessie, staring into Pitt's eyes but seeing only green ice. "I was very rude to Mr. Pitt last night. I hope he accepts my apology and forgives my bad manners."

"You needn't act so formal, Mrs. LeBaron. Since we're old pals, I won't throw a tantrum if you call me Dirk. As to forgiving you, how much is it going to cost me?"

"My intent was to hire *you*," she replied, ignoring the gibe.

He gave Sandecker a bemused look. "Strange, I had this funny idea I worked for NUMA."

"Admiral Sandecker has kindly consented to release you for a few days, providing, of course, you're agreeable," she added.

"To do what?"

"To look for my husband."

"No deal."

"May I ask why?"

"I have other projects."

"You won't work for me because I'm a woman. Is that it?"

"Sex has no bearing on my decision. Let's just say I don't work for someone I can't respect."

There was an embarrassed silence. Pitt looked at the admiral. The lips were turned down in a grimace, but the eyes fairly twinkled. The old bastard was enjoying this, he thought.

"You've misjudged me, Dirk." Jessie's face was flushed in confusion, but her eyes were hard as crystal.

"Please." Sandecker raised both hands. "Let's call a truce. I suggest you two get together some evening and have it out over dinner."

Pitt and Jessie stared at each other for a long moment. Then Pitt's mouth slowly spread in a wide infectious smile. "I'm willing, providing I pay."

Despite herself Jessie had to smile too. "Allow me some self-respect. Let's split the bill?"

"Done."

"Now we can get on with the business at hand," Sandecker said in his no-nonsense way. "Before you arrived, Dirk, we were discussing theories on Mr. LeBaron's disappearance."

Pitt looked at Jessie. "There is no doubt in your mind that the bodies in the blimp were not those of Mr. LeBaron and his crew?"

Jessie shook her head. "None."

"I saw them. There wasn't much left to identify."

"The corpse lying in the morgue was more muscular than Raymond," explained Jessie. "Also, he'd been wearing an imitation of a Cartier wristwatch. One of those cheap replicas made in Taiwan. I'd given my husband an expensive original on our first anniversary."

"I've made a few calls on my own," added Sandecker. "The Miami coroner backed Jessie's judgment. Physical characteristics of the bodies in the morgue didn't match the three men who took off in the *Prosperteer.*"

Pitt looked from Sandecker to Jessie LeBaron, realizing he was getting involved in something he had wished to avoid: the emotional entanglements complicating any project that depended on solid research, practical engineering, and razor-sharp organization.

"Bodies and clothes switched," said Pitt. "Personal jewelry replaced with fakes. Any thoughts on a motive, Mrs. LeBaron?"

"I don't know what to think."

"Did you know that between the time the blimp vanished and when it reappeared in Key Biscayne the gas bags inside the hull would have had to be reinflated with helium?"

She opened her purse, took out a Kleenex, and daintily dabbed at her nose, to give her something to do with her hands. "After the police released the *Prosperteer,* my husband's crew chief inspected every inch of her. I have his report, if you care to see it. You're very perceptive. He found that the gas bags had been refilled. Not with helium, but with hydrogen."

Pitt looked up in surprise. "Hydrogen? That hasn't been used in airships since the *Hindenburg* burned."

"Not to worry," said Sandecker. "The *Prosperteer*'s gas bags have been refilled with helium."

"So what's going down?" Pitt asked cautiously.

Sandecker gave him a hard look. "I hear you want to go after the *Cyclops.*"

"It's no secret," answered Pitt.

"You'd have to do it on your own time without NUMA personnel and equipment. Congress would eat me alive if they learned I sanctioned a treasure hunt with government funds."

"I'm aware of that."

"Will you listen to another proposal?"

"I'll listen."

"I'm not going to hand you a lot of double-talk about doing me a great service by keeping this conversation to yourself. If it gets out I go down the drain, but that's my problem. True?"

"If you say so, yes."

"You were scheduled to direct a survey of the sea floor in the Bering Sea off the Aleutians next month. I'll bring in Jack Harris from the deep-ocean mining project to replace you. To head off any questions or later investigations or bureaucratic wrongdoing, we'll sever your connections with NUMA. As of now, you're on leave of absence until you find Raymond LeBaron."

"Find Raymond LeBaron," Pitt repeated sarcastically. "A piece of cake. The trail is two weeks cold and getting colder by the hour. No motive, no leads, not one clue to why he vanished, who did it, and how. Impossible is an understatement."

"Will you at least give it a try?" asked Sandecker.

Pitt stared at the teakwood planking that made up the floor of the admiral's office, his eyes seeing a tropical sea two thousand miles away. He disliked becoming linked with a riddle without being able to calculate at the very least an approximate solution. He knew Sandecker knew that he would accept the challenge. Chasing after an unknown over the next horizon was a lure Pitt could never resist.

"If I take this on, I'd need NUMA's best scientific team to man a first-rate research vessel. The resources and political clout to back me up. Military support in case of trouble."

"Dirk, my hands are tied. I can offer you nothing."

"What?"

"You heard me. The situation requires the search be conducted as quietly as possible. You'll have to make do without any help from NUMA."

"Have you got both oars in the water?" Pitt demanded. "You expect me, one man working alone, to accomplish what half the Navy, Air Force, and Coast Guard failed to do? Why, hell, they couldn't find a one-hundred-and-fifty-foot airship until it showed up on its own. What am I supposed to use, a dowser and a canoe?"

"The idea," Sandecker explained patiently, "is to fly LeBaron's last known course in the *Prosperteer.*"

Pitt slowly sank into an office sofa. "This is the craziest scheme I've ever heard," he said, unbelieving. He turned to Jessie. "Do you go along with this?"

"I'll do whatever it takes to find my husband," she said evenly.

"A cuckoo's nest," Pitt said gravely. He stood and began to pace the room, clasping and unclasping his hands. "Why the secrecy? Your husband was an important man, a celebrity, a confidant of the rich and famous, closely connected with high government officials, a financial guru to executives of major corporations. Why in God's name am I the only man in the country who can search for him?"

"Dirk," Sandecker said softly. "Raymond LeBaron's financial empire touches hundreds of thousands of people. Right now, it's hanging in limbo because he's still among the missing. It can't be proven whether he's alive or dead. The government has called off any further hunt, because over five million dollars have been spent by military search and rescue teams without a sighting, without a hint of where he might have disappeared. Budget-conscious congressmen will howl for scalps if more government money is spent on another fruitless effort."

"What about the private sector and LeBaron's own business associates?"

"Many business leaders respected LeBaron, but at one time or another most of them were burned by him in his editorials. They won't spend a dime or go out of their way to look for him. As to the men around him, they have more to gain by his death."

"So does Jessie here," said Pitt, gazing at her.

She smiled thinly. "I can't deny it. But the bulk of his estate goes to charities and other family members. I do, however, receive a substantial inheritance."

"You must own a yacht, Mrs. LeBaron. Why don't you assemble your own crew of investigators and look for your husband?"

"There are reasons, Dirk, why I can't conduct a large publicized effort. Reasons you needn't know. The admiral and I think there is a chance, a very slight chance, that three people can quietly retrace the flight of the *Prosperteer* under the same conditions and discover what happened to Raymond."

"Why bother?" asked Pitt. "All islands and reefs within the blimp's fuel range were covered by the initial search. I'd only be covering the same trail."

"They might have missed something."

"Like maybe Cuba?"

Sandecker shook his head. "Castro would have claimed LeBaron overflew Cuban territory under instructions from the CIA and flaunted the blimp's capture to the world. No, there has to be another answer."

Pitt walked over to the corner windows and gazed longingly down at a fleet of small sailboats that were holding a regatta on the Anacostia River. The white sails gleamed against the dark green water as they raced toward the buoy markers.

"How do we know where to concentrate?" he asked without turning. "We're looking at a search grid as large as a thousand square miles. It would take weeks to cover it properly."

"I have all my husband's records and charts," said Jessie.

"He left them behind?"

"No, they were found in the blimp."

Pitt silently watched the sailboats, his arms crossed in front of him. He tried to probe the motives, penetrate the intrigue, lay out the safeguards. He tried to segregate each into an orderly niche.

"When do we go?" he asked finally.

"Sunrise tomorrow morning," Sandecker replied.

"You both still insist I lead the fishing expedition?"

"We do," Jessie said flatly.

"I want two old hands for my crew. They're both on NUMA's payroll. Either I get them or I'll walk."

Sandecker's face clouded. "I've already explained—"

"You've got the moon, Admiral, and you're asking for Mars. We've been friends long enough for you to know I don't operate on a half-assed basis. Put the two men I need on leaves of absence too. I don't care how you do it."

Sandecker wasn't angry, wasn't even annoyed. If there was one man in the country who could pull off the unthinkable, it was Pitt. The admiral had no more cards to play, so he folded.

"All right," he said quietly. "You've got them."

"There's one more thing."

"Which is?" Sandecker demanded.

Pitt turned around with a bleak smile. His gaze went from Jessie to the admiral. Then he shrugged and said, "I've never flown a blimp."

14

"APPEARS TO ME YOU'RE MAKING an end run behind my back," said Sam Emmett, the outspoken chief of the Federal Bureau of Investigation.

The President looked across his desk in the Oval Office and smiled benignly. "You're absolutely right, Sam. I'm doing exactly that."

"I give you credit for laying it on the line."

"Don't get upset, Sam. This in no way reflects any displeasure with you or the FBI."

"Then why can't you tell me what this is all about?" Emmett asked, holding his indignation in check.

"In the first place, it's primarily a foreign affairs matter."

"Has Martin Brogan at CIA been consulted?"

"Martin has not been called in. You have my word on it."

"And in the second place?"

The President was not about to be pushed. "That's my business."

Emmett stiffened. "If the President wishes my resignation—"

"I don't wish anything of the sort," the President cut in. "You're the ablest and best-qualified man to head up the bureau. You've done a magnificent job, and I've always been one of your biggest boosters. However, if you want to pick up your marbles and go home because you think your vanity has been dented, then go right ahead. Prove me wrong about you."

"But if you don't trust—"

"Wait just a damned minute, Sam. Let's not say anything we'll be sorry about tomorrow. I'm not questioning your loyalty or integrity. No one is stabbing you in the back. We aren't talking crime or espionage. This matter doesn't directly concern the FBI or any of the intelligence agencies. The bottom line is that it's you who has to trust me, at least for the next week. Will you do that?"

Emmett's ego was temporarily soothed. He shrugged and then relented. "You win, Mr. President. Status quo. I'll follow your lead."

The President sighed heavily. "I promise I won't let you down, Sam."

"I appreciate that."

"Good. Now let's start at the beginning. What have you got on the dead bodies from Florida?"

The tight uneasiness went out of Emmett's expression, and he noticeably relaxed. He opened his attaché case and handed the President a leather-bound folder.

"Here is a detailed report from the Walter Reed pathology lab. Their examination was most helpful in giving us a lead for identification."

The President looked at him in surprise. "You identified them?"

"It was the analysis of the borscht paste that opened the door."

"Borscht what?"

"You recall that the Dade County coroner fixed death by hypothermia, or freezing?"

"Yes."

"Well, borscht paste is a god-awful food supplement given to Russian cosmonauts. The stomachs of the three corpses were loaded with the stuff."

"You're telling me that Raymond LeBaron and his crew were exchanged for three dead Soviet cosmonauts?"

Emmett nodded. "We were even able to put a name on them through a defector, a former flight surgeon with the Russian space program. He'd examined each of them on several occasions."

"When did he defect?"

"He came over to our side in August of '87."

"A little over two years ago."

"That's correct," Emmett acknowledged. "The names of the cosmonauts found in LeBaron's blimp are Sergei Zochenko, Alexander Yudenich, and Ivan Ronsky. Yudenich was a rookie, but Zochenko and Ronsky were both veterans with two space flights apiece."

"I'd give my next year's salary to know how they came to be inside that damned blimp."

"Regrettably, we turned up nothing concerning that part of the mystery. At the moment, the only Russians circling the earth are four cosmonauts on board the Salyut 9 space station. But the NASA people, who are monitoring the flight, say they're all in good health."

The President nodded. "So that eliminates any Soviet cosmonaut on a space flight and leaves only those on the ground."

"That's the odd twist," Emmett continued. "According to the forensic pathology people at Walter Reed, the three men they examined probably froze to death while in space."

The President's eyebrows raised. "Can they prove it?"

"No, but they say several factors point in that direction, starting with the borscht paste and the analysis of other condensed foods the Soviets are known to consume during space travel. Also evident were physiological signs the men had breathed air of a high oxygen constant and spent considerable time in a weightless environment."

"Wouldn't be the first time the Soviets have launched men into space and failed to retrieve them. They could have been up there for years, and fell to earth only a few weeks ago after their orbit decayed."

"I'm only aware of two instances where the Soviets suffered fatalities," said Emmett. "The cosmonaut whose craft became tangled in the shrouds of its reentry parachute and slammed into Siberia at five hundred miles an hour. And the three Soyuz crewmen who died after a faulty hatch leaked away their oxygen."

"The disasters they couldn't cover up," said the President. "The CIA has recorded at least thirty cosmonaut deaths since the beginning of their space missions. Nine of them are still up there, drifting around in space. We can't advertise the fact on our end because it would jeopardize our intelligence sources."

"We-know-but-they-don't-know-we-know kind of affair."

"Precisely."

"Which brings us back to the three cosmonauts we've got lying here in Washington," said Emmett, clutching his briefcase on his lap.

"And a hundred questions, beginning with, Where did they come from?"

"I did some checking with the Aerospace Defense Command Center. Their technicians say the only spacecraft the Russians have sent aloft large enough to support a manned crew—besides their orbiting station shuttles—were the Selenos lunar probes."

At the word "lunar" something clicked in the President's mind. "What about the Selenos probes?"

"Three went up and none came back. The Defense Command boys thought it highly unusual for the Soviets to screw-up three times in a row on simple moon orbiting flights."

"You think they were manned?"

"I do indeed," said Emmett. "The Soviets wallow in deception.

As you suggested, they almost never admit to a space failure. And keeping the buildup for their coming moon landing clouded in secrecy was strictly routine."

"Okay, if we accept the theory the three bodies came from one of the Selenos spacecraft, where did it land? Certainly not through their normal reentry path over the steppes of Kazakhstan."

"My guess is somewhere in or around Cuba."

"Cuba." The President slowly rolled the two syllables from his lips. Then he shook his head. "The Russians would never allow their national heroes, living or dead, to be used for some kind of crazy intelligence scheme."

"Maybe they don't know."

The President looked at Emmett. "Don't know?"

"Let's say for the sake of argument that their spacecraft had a malfunction and fell in or near Cuba during reentry. About the same time, Raymond LeBaron and his blimp show up searching for a treasure ship and are captured. Then, for some unfathomable reason, the Cubans switch the cosmonauts' bodies for LeBaron and his crew and send the blimp back to Florida."

"Do you have any idea how ridiculous that sounds?"

Emmett laughed. "Of course, but considering the known facts, it's the best I can come up with."

The President leaned back and stared at the ornate ceiling. "You know, you just might have struck a vein."

A quizzical look crossed Emmett's face. "How so?"

"Try this on for size. Suppose, just suppose, Fidel Castro is trying to tell us something."

"He picked a strange way to send out a signal."

The President picked up a pen and began doodling on a pad. "Fidel has never been a stickler for diplomatic niceties."

"Do you want me to continue the investigation?" Emmett asked.

"No," the President answered tersely.

"You still insist on keeping the bureau in the dark?"

"This is not a domestic matter for the Justice Department, Sam. I'm grateful for your help, but you've taken it about as far as you can go."

Emmett snapped his attaché case shut and rose to his feet. "Can I ask a touchy question?"

"Shoot."

"Now that we've established a link, regardless of how weak, to a possible abduction of Raymond LeBaron by the Cubans, why is the

President of the United States keeping it to himself and forbidding his investigative agencies to follow up?"

"A good question, Sam. Perhaps in a few days we'll both know the answer."

Moments after Emmett left the Oval Office, the President turned in his swivel chair and stared out the window. His mouth went dry and sweat soaked his armpits. He was gripped by foreboding that there was a tie between the Jersey Colony and the Soviet lunar probe disasters.

15

IRA HAGEN STOPPED his rental car at the security gate and displayed a government ID card. The guard made a phone call to the visitors center of the Harvey Pattenden National Physics Laboratory, then waved Hagen through.

He drove up the drive and found an empty space in a sprawling parking lot crowded by a sea of multicolored cars. The grounds surrounding the laboratory were landscaped with clusters of pine trees and moss rock planted amid rolling mounds of grass. The building was typical of tech centers that had mushroomed around the country. Contemporary architecture with heavy use of bronze glass and brick walls curving at the corners.

An attractive receptionist, sitting behind a horseshoe-shaped desk, looked up and smiled as he walked through the lobby. "May I help you?"

"Thomas Judge to see Dr. Mooney."

She went through the phone routine again and nodded. "Yes, Mr. Judge. Please enter the security center to my rear. They'll direct you from there."

"Before I go in, can I borrow your men's room?"

"Certainly," she said, pointing. "The door on the right beneath the mural."

Hagen thanked her and passed under a massive painting of a futuristic starship soaring between a pair of spectral blue-green planets. He went into a stall, closed the door, and sat down on the toilet. Opening a briefcase, he removed a yellow legal pad and turned to the middle. Then, writing on the upper back of the page, he made a series of tiny cryptic notes and diagrams on the security systems he'd observed since entering the building. A good undercover operative would never put anything down on paper, but Hagen could afford to run fast and loose, knowing the President would bail him out if his cover was blown.

A few minutes later he strolled out of the restroom and entered a glass-enclosed room manned by four uniformed security guards, who eyeballed an array of twenty television monitors mounted against one wall. One of the guards rose from a console and approached the counter.

"Sir?"

"I have an appointment with Dr. Mooney."

The guard scanned a visitor list. "Yes, sir, you must be Thomas Judge. May I see some identification, please?"

Hagen showed him his driver's license and government ID. Then he was politely asked to open the briefcase. After a cursory search the guard silently gestured for Hagen to close it, asked him to sign a "time in and out" sheet, and gave him a plastic badge to clip on his breast pocket.

"Dr. Mooney's office is straight down the corridor through the double doors at the end."

In the corridor, Hagen paused to put on his reading glasses and peer at two bronze plaques on the wall. Each bore the raised profile of a man. One was dedicated to Dr. Harvey Pattenden, founder of the laboratory, and gave a brief description of his accomplishments in the field of physics. But it was the other plaque that intriqued Hagen. It read:

In memory of
Dr. Leonard Hudson
1926–1965
Whose creative genius is an
inspiration for all who follow.

Not very original, Hagen thought. But he had to give Hudson credit for playing the dead-man game down to the last detail.

He entered the anteroom and smiled warmly at the secretary, a demure older woman in a mannish navy-blue suit. "Mr. Judge," she said, "please go right in. Dr. Mooney is expecting you."

"Thank you."

Earl J. Mooney was thirty-six, younger than Hagen had expected when he studied a file on the doctor's history. His background was surprisingly similar to Hudson's; same brilliant mind, same high academic record, even the same university. A fat kid who went thin and became director of Pattenden Lab. He stared through pine-green eyes under thunderous eyebrows and above a Pancho Villa moustache. Dressed casually in a white sweater and blue jeans, he seemed remote from intellectual rigor.

He came from behind the desk, scattered with papers, notebooks, and empty Pepsi bottles, and pumped Hagen's hand. "Sit down, Mr. Judge, and tell me what I can do for you."

Hagen lowered his bulk into a straight-back chair and said, "As I mentioned over the phone, I'm with the General Accounting Office, and we've had a legislative request to review your accounting systems and audit research funding expenditures."

"Who was the legislator who made the request?"

"Senator Henry Kaltenbach."

"I hope he doesn't think Pattenden Lab is mixed up in fraud," said Mooney defensively.

"Not at all. You know the senator's reputation for smelling out misuse in government funding. His witch-hunts make good publicity for his election campaign. Just between you and me, there're many of us at GAO who wish he'd fall through an open manhole and stop sending us out chasing moonbeams. However, I must admit in all fairness to the senator, we *have* turned up discrepancies at other think tanks."

Mooney was quick to correct him. "We prefer to think of ourselves as a research facility."

"Of course. Anyway, we're making spot checks."

"You must understand, our work here is highly classified."

"The design of nuclear rocketry and third-generation nuclear weapons whose power is focused into narrow radiation beams that travel at the speed of light and can destroy targets deep in space."

Mooney looked at Hagen queerly. "You're very well informed."

Hagen shrugged it off. "A very general description given to me by my superior. I'm an accountant, Doctor, not a physicist. My mind can't function in the abstract. I flunked high school calculus. Your secrets are safe. My job is to help see the taxpayer gets his money's worth out of government-funded programs."

"How can I help you?"

"I'd like to talk to your controller and administration officials. Also, the staff that handles the financial records. My auditing team will arrive from Washington in two weeks. I'd appreciate it if we could set up someplace out of your way, preferably close to where the records are kept."

"You'll have our fullest cooperation. Naturally, I must have security clearances for you and your team."

"Naturally."

"I'll take you around personally and introduce you to our controller and accounting staff."

"One more thing," said Hagen. "Do you permit after-hours work?"

Mooney smiled. "Unlike nine-to-five office people, physicists and engineers have no set hours. Many of us work around the clock. I've often put in thirty hours at a stretch. It also helps to stagger the time on our computers."

"Would it be possible for me to do a little preliminary checking from now until, say, about ten o'clock this evening?"

"I don't see why not," Mooney said agreeably. "We have an all-night cafeteria on the lower level if you want to grab a bite. And a security guard is always nearby to point out directions."

"And keep me out of the secret areas." Hagen laughed.

"I'm sure you're familiar with facility security."

"True," Hagen admitted. "I'd be a rich man if I had a dime for every hour I put in auditing different departments of the Pentagon."

"If you'll come this way," said Mooney, heading for the door.

"Just out of curiosity," Hagen said, remaining in his chair. "I've heard of Harvey Pattenden. He worked with Robert Goddard, I believe."

"Yes, Dr. Pattenden invented several of our early rocket engines."

"But Leonard Hudson is unfamiliar to me."

"A pretty bright guy," said Mooney. "He paved the way by design-engineering most of our spacecraft years before they were actually built and sent aloft. If he hadn't died in his prime, there's no telling what he might have achieved."

"How did he die?"

"Light-plane crash. He was flying to a seminar in Seattle with Dr. Gunnar Eriksen when their plane exploded in midair and dropped into the Columbia River."

"Who was Eriksen?"

"A heavy thinker. Perhaps the most brilliant astrophysicist the country ever produced."

A tiny alarm went off in Hagen's mind. "Did he have any particular pursuit?"

"Yes, it was geolunar synoptic morphology for industrialized peoplement."

"Could you translate?"

"Of course." Mooney laughed. "Eriksen was obsessed with the idea of building a colony on the moon."

16

TEN HOURS AHEAD IN TIME, 2 A.M. in Moscow, four men were grouped around a fireplace that warmed a small sitting room inside the Kremlin. The room was poorly lit and had a morbid feel about it. Cigarette smoke mingled with that of a single cigar.

Soviet President Georgi Antonov stared thoughtfully at the undulating flames. He had removed his coat after a light dinner and replaced it with an old fisherman's sweater. His shoes were off and his stocking feet casually propped on an embroidered ottoman.

Vladimir Polevoi, head of the Committee for State Security, and Sergei Kornilov, chief of the Soviet space program, wore dark wool suits, custom-tailored in London, while General Yasenin sat in full bemedaled uniform.

Polevoi threw the report and photographs on a low table and shook his head in amazement. "I don't see how they accomplished it without a breach of secrecy."

"Such an extraordinary advance seems inconceivable," Kornilov agreed. "I won't believe it until I see more proof."

"The proof is evident in the photographs," said Yasenin. "Rykov's report leaves no room for doubt. Study the detail. The two figures standing on the moon are real. They're not an illusion cast by shadows or created by a flaw in the scanning system. They exist."

"The space suits do not match those of American astronauts," Kornilov retorted. "The helmets are also designed differently."

"I won't argue over trivials," said Yasenin. "But there is no mistaking the weapon in their hands. I can positively identify it as a surface-to-air missile launcher of American manufacture."

"Then where is their spacecraft?" Kornilov persisted. "Where is their lunar rover? They couldn't just materialize out of nowhere."

"I share your doubts," said Polevoi. "An absolute impossibility for the Americans to put men and supplies on the moon without our intelligence network monitoring the progress. Our tracking stations would have detected any strange movement entering or coming from space."

"Even stranger yet," said Antonov, "is why the Americans have never announced such a momentous achievement. What do they gain by keeping it a secret?"

Kornilov gave a slight nod. "All the more reason to challenge Rykov's report."

"You're all overlooking one important fact," said Yasenin in a level tone. "Selenos 4 went missing immediately after its scanners recorded the figures in the photographs. I say our space probe was damaged by rocket fire which penetrated the hull, drained away the capsule's pressure, and killed our cosmonauts."

Polevoi looked at him, startled. "What cosmonauts?"

Yasenin and Kornilov exchanged bemused looks. "There are some things even the KGB doesn't know," said the general.

Polevoi looked squarely at Kornilov. "Selenos 4 was a manned probe?"

"As were Selenos 5 and 6. Each craft carried three men."

He turned to Antonov, who was calmly puffing on a Havana cigar. "You knew about this?"

Antonov nodded. "Yes, I was briefed. But you must remember, Vladimir, not all matters concerning space fall under state security."

"None of you wasted any time running to me when your precious moon probe fell and vanished in the West Indies," Polevoi said angrily.

"An unforeseen circumstance," Yasenin patiently explained. "After its return from the moon, control could not be established for Selenos 4's earth reentry. The engineers at our space command wrote it off as a dead lunar probe. After orbiting for nearly a year and a half, another attempt was made to establish command. This time the guidance systems responded, but the reentry manuever was only partially successful. Selenos 4 fell ten thousand miles short of its touchdown area. It was imperative we keep the deaths of our cosmonaut heroes secret. Naturally the services of the KGB were required."

"How many lost cosmonauts does that make?" asked Polevoi.

"Sacrifices must be made to ensure Soviet destiny," Antonov murmured philosophically.

"And to cover up blunders in our space program," Polevoi said bitterly.

"Let's not argue," cautioned Antonov. "Selenos 4 made a great contribution before it impacted in the Caribbean Sea."

"Where it has yet to be found," Polevoi added.

"True," said Yasenin. "But we retrieved the lunar surface data. That was the main purpose of the mission."

"Don't you think American space surveillance systems tracked its descent and pinpointed the landing position? If they had set their minds on salvaging Selenos 4, they'd already have it sitting hidden away inside a secure facility."

"Of course they tracked the descent trajectory," said Yasenin. "But their intelligence analysts had no reason to believe Selenos 4 was anything but a scientific deep-space probe that was programmed to land in Cuban waters."

"There is a crack in your carefully laid plot," Polevoi argued. "The United States rescue forces made an exhaustive air and sea search for the missing capitalist Raymond LeBaron in the same general area only a few days after Selenos 4 dropped from orbit. I have strong suspicions their search was a decoy to find and retrieve our spacecraft."

"I read your report and analysis of the LeBaron disappearance," said Kornilov. "I disagree with your conclusion. Nowhere did I see that they conducted an underwater search. The rescue mission was soon called off. LeBaron and his crew are still listed as missing in the American press and presumed dead. That event was merely a coincidence, nothing more."

"Then we all agree that Selenos 4 and her cosmonauts lie somewhere on the bottom of the sea." Antonov paused to blow a smoke ring. "The questions we still face are, Do we concede the probability the Americans may have a base on the moon, and if so, What do we do about it?"

"I believe it exists," Yasenin said with conviction.

"We cannot ignore the possibility," Polevoi granted.

Antonov stared narrowly at Kornilov. "And you, Sergei?"

"Selenos 8, our first manned lunar landing mission, is scheduled for launch in seven days," he answered slowly. "We cannot scrap the mission as we did when the Americans upstaged us with their Apollo program. Because our leaders saw no glory in being the second nation to set men on the moon we tucked our tail between our legs and quit. It was a great mistake to place political ideology above scientific achievement. Now we have a proven heavy-lift launch vehicle capable of placing an entire space station with a crew of eight men on lunar soil. The benefits in terms of propaganda and military rewards are immeasurable. If our ultimate goal is to obtain permanent preeminence in space and beat the Americans to Mars, we must follow through. I vote we program the guidance systems of Selenos 8 to land the crew within walking distance of where the astronauts stood in the crater and eliminate them."

"I am in complete agreement with Kornilov," said Yasenin. "The facts speak for themselves. The Americans are actively engaged in imperialistic aggression in space. The photographs we've studied prove they've already destroyed one of our spacecraft and murdered the crew. And I believe the cosmonauts in Selenos 5 and 6 met the same fate. They have taken their colonialistic designs to the moon and claimed it for their own. The evidence is unequivocal. Our cosmonauts will be attacked and murdered when they attempt to plant the red star on lunar soil."

There was a prolonged hush. No one spoke his thoughts.

Polevoi was the first to break the pensive silence. "So you and Kornilov propose we attack them first."

"Yes," said Yasenin, warming to the subject. "Think of the windfall. By capturing the American moon base and its scientific technology intact, we'd be advancing our own space program by ten years."

"The White House would surely mount a propaganda campaign and condemn us before the world as they did with the KAL Flight 007 incident," protested Polevoi.

"They will remain quiet," Yasenin assured him. "How can they announce the seizure of something that isn't known to exist?"

"The general has a point," said Antonov.

"You realize we could be guilty of launching a war in space," cautioned Polevoi.

"The United States struck first. It is our sacred duty to retaliate." Yasenin turned to Antonov. "The decision must be yours."

The President of the Soviet Union again turned his gaze to the fire. Then he laid the Havana in an ashtray and looked down in wonder at his trembling hands. His face, ordinarily ruddy, was gray. The omen was plain. The demons outnumbered the forces of good. Once the course was set in motion, it would hurtle forward outside his control. Yet he could not allow the country to be slapped in the face by the imperialists. At last he turned back to the other men in the room and wearily nodded.

"For Mother Russia and the party," he said solemnly. "Arm the cosmonauts and order them to strike the Americans."

17

EIGHT INTRODUCTIONS and three tiresome conversations after his introduction to Dr. Mooney, Hagen was seated in a small office feverishly pounding an adding machine. Scientists dote on computers and engineers fondle digital calculators, but accountants are a Victorian lot. They still prefer traditional adding machines with thumb-size buttons and paper tapes that spit out printed totals.

The controller was a CPA, a graduate of the University of Texas School of Business, and an ex-Navy man. And he had the engraved degrees and photographs of the ships he'd served on displayed on the oak-paneled wall of his office to prove it. Hagen had detected an uneasiness in the man's eyes, but no more than he'd expect from any corporate finance director who had a government auditor snooping around his private territory.

There had been no suspicious look, no hesitation, when he asked to spot-check the telephone records for the last three years. Though his accounting experience with the Justice Department was limited to photographing ledgers in the dead of night, he knew enough of the jargon to talk a good line. Anyone who happened to glance in his office and saw him scribbling notes and intently examining the tape on the adding machine would have thought he was an old pro.

The numbers on the tape were exactly that, numbers. But the note scribbling consisted of a methodical diagram of the placement and view angles of the security TV cameras between his office and Mooney's. He also wrote out two names and added several notations beside each one. The first was Raymond LeBaron and the second was Leonard Hudson. But now he had a third: Gunnar Eriksen.

He was certain that Eriksen had faked his death along with Hudson and dropped from the living to work on the Jersey Colony project. He also knew Hudson and Eriksen would never completely cut their ties with Pattenden Laboratory. The facility and its high-powered crop of young scientists were too great an asset to ignore. There had to be an underground channel to the "inner core."

The telephone records for a facility with three thousand employees filled several cardboard cartons. Control had been tight. Everyone who used a phone for any purpose, business or personal, had to keep a diary of the calls. Hagen wasn't about to attempt an examintion of each one. That chore would take weeks. He was concerned only with the entries in Mooney's monthly diaries, especially those involving long distance.

Hagen was not psychic, nor was he as exact as some men he knew who had a talent for detecting an irregularity, but he had an eye and a gut instinct for the hidden that seldom failed him.

He copied down six numbers that Mooney had phoned more than once in the past ninety days. Two were itemized as personal calls, four as company calls. Long shots all. Still, it was the only way he might trace a lead to another member of the "inner core."

Playing by the rules, he picked up the phone and punched the Pattenden Lab operator, requesting an open line and promising to record all his calls. The hour was late, and most of the list showed area codes of numbers in the Middle West or in the East Coast. Their time zones were two or three hours ahead and they had likely shut down for the day, but he doggedly began calling anyway.

"Centennial Supply," announced a male in a bored tone.

"Yes, hello, is anyone in this evening?"

"The office is closed. This is the twenty-four-hour order desk."

"My name is Judge, and I'm with the federal government," said Hagen, using his cover in case the phone was tapped. "We're doing an audit of the Pattenden Physics Laboratory in Bend, Oregon."

"You'll have to call back tomorrow morning after the office opens."

"Yes, I'll do that. But can you tell me exactly what kind of business Centennial Supply conducts?"

"We supply specialized parts and electronics for recording systems."

"For what applications?"

"Mostly business. Video for recording executive meetings, laboratory experiments, security systems. And executive audio for secretaries. Stuff like that, you know."

"How many employees do you have?"

"Around twelve."

"Thank you very much," said Hagen. "You've been most helpful.

Oh, one more thing. Do you get many orders from Pattenden?"

"Not really. Every couple of months they'll order a part to update or modify their video systems."

"Thanks again. Goodbye."

Hagen scratched that one and tried again. His next two calls reached answering machines. One was a chemical lab at Brandeis University in Waltham and the other an unidentified office at the National Science Foundation in Washington. He checked the latter for a follow-up in the morning and tried an individual's number.

"Hello?"

Hagen looked at the name in Mooney's diary. "Dr. Donald Fremont?"

"Yes."

Hagen went through his routine.

"What do you wish to know, Mr. Judge?" Fremont's voice sounded elderly.

"I'm making a spot check of long-distance telephone calls. Has anyone from Pattenden called you in the last ninety days?" Hagen asked, looking at the dates of the calls and playing dumb.

"Why, yes, Dr. Earl Mooney. He was a student of mine at Stanford. I retired five years ago, but we still keep in touch."

"Did you by chance also have a student by the name of Leonard Hudson?"

"Leonard Hudson," he repeated as if trying to recall. "I met him on two occasions. He wasn't in my class, though. Before my time, or I should say before my tenure at Stanford. I was teaching at USC when he was a student."

"Thank you, Doctor. I won't trouble you further."

"Not at all. Glad to help."

Scratch four. The next name from the diary was an Anson Jones. He tried again, well aware it never came easy and that making a gold strike was 99 percent luck.

"Hello?"

"Mr. Jones, my name is Judge."

"Who?"

"Thomas Judge. I'm with the federal government, and we're running an audit on Pattenden Physics Laboratory."

"I don't know any Pattenden. You must have the wrong number."

"Does the name Dr. Earl Mooney ring a bell?"

"Never heard of him."

"He's called your number three times in the last sixty days."

"Must be a phone company foulup."

"You *are* Anson Jones, area code three-zero-three, number five-four-seven—"

"Wrong name, wrong number."

"Before you hang up, I have a message."

"What message?"

Hagen paused, and then leaped. "Tell Leo that Gunnar wants him to pay for the airplane. You got that?"

There was silence on the other end for several moments. Then finally, "Is this a crank call?"

"Goodbye, Mr. Jones."

Pay dirt.

He called the sixth listing just to be on the safe side. An answering service for a stock brokerage firm answered. A dry hole.

Elation, that was what he felt. He became even more elated as he added to his notes. Mooney was not one of the "inner core," but he was connected—one of the subordinate officers under the high command.

Hagen tapped out a number in Chicago and waited. After four rings, a woman answered sweetly. "Drake Hotel."

"Ny name is Thomas Judge and I'd like to confirm a room reservation for tomorrow night."

"One moment and I'll connect you with reservations."

Hagen repeated the request for confirmation with the desk clerk. When asked for a credit card number to hold the room for late arrival, he gave Anson Jones's phone number in reverse

"Your room is confirmed, sir."

"Thank you."

What time was it? A glance at his watch told him it was eight, minutes to midnight. He closed the briefcase and wiggled into his coat. Taking a cigarette lighter from one pocket, he slid the interior workings from its case. Next, he removed a thin metal shaft with a dental mirror on one end from a slit in his rear coat flap.

Hagen moved to the doorway. Clutching the briefcase between his knees, he stopped short of the threshold and tilted the tiny mirror up and down the corridor. It was empty. He turned the mirror until it reflected the television monitor above the far end of the corridor. Then he positioned the lighter until it barely protruded around the doorframe and pressed the flint lever.

Inside the security booth behind the main lobby, a screen on one of the TV monitors suddenly turned to snow. The guard at the console quickly began checking the circuit lights.

"I've got a problem with number twelve," he announced.

His supervisor came over from a desk and stared at the monitor. "Interference. The eggheads in the electrophysics lab must be at it again."

Suddenly the interference stopped, only to begin again on another monitor.

"That's funny," said the supervisor. "I've never seen it happen in sequence before."

After a few seconds, the screen cleared, showing nothing but an empty corridor. The two security guards simply looked at each other and shrugged.

Hagen turned off the miniature electrical impulse jammer as soon as he stepped inside and closed the door to Mooney's office. He walked softly over to the window and closed the drapes. He slipped on a pair of thin plastic gloves and turned on the overhead lights.

Hagen was a master at the technique of tossing a room. He didn't bother with the obvious, the drawers, files, address and telephone lists. He went directly to a bookshelf and found what he had hoped to find in less than seven minutes.

Mooney might have been one of the leading physicists in the nation, but Hagen had read him like a pictorial magazine. The small notebook was hidden inside a book entitled *Celestial Mechanics in True Perspective* by Horace DeLiso. The contents were in a code employing equations. It was Greek to Hagen but he wasn't fooled by the significance. Normally he would have photographed the pages and put them back, but this time he simply pocketed them, fully realizing he could never have them deciphered in time.

The guards were still struggling with the monitors when he stepped up to the counter.

"Would you like me to sign out?" he said with a smile.

The head security guard came over, a quizzical expression on his face. "Did you just come from finance?"

"Yes."

"We didn't see you on the security TV."

"I can't help that," said Hagen innocently. "I walked out the door and through the hallways until I came here. I don't know what else to tell you."

"Did you see anyone? Anything unusual?"

"No one. But the lights flickered and dimmed a couple of times."

The guard nodded. "Electrical interference from the electrophysics lab. That's what I thought it was."

Hagen signed out and walked into a cloudless night, humming softly to himself.

PART II

The Cyclops

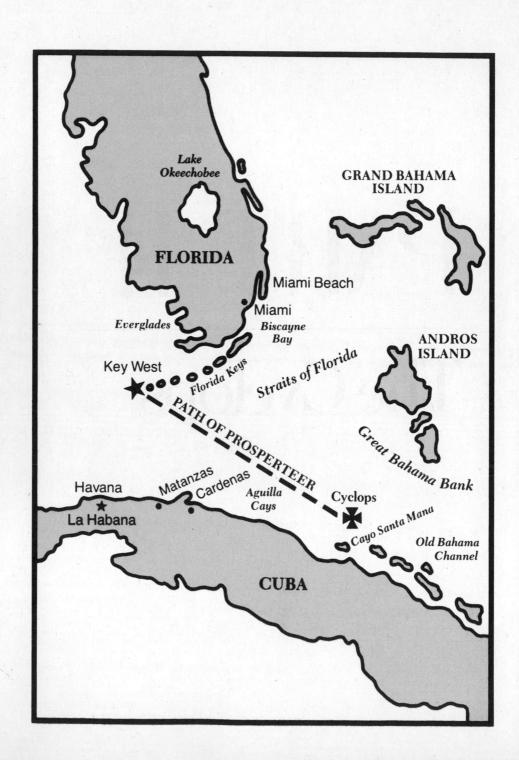

18

October 25, 1989
Key West, Florida

PITT LAY with his back pressed against the cool concrete of the airstrip, looking up at the *Prosperteer*. The sun pushed over the horizon and slowly covered her worn hull in a shroud of pastel orange. The blimp had an eerie quality about it, or so it seemed in Pitt's imagination, an aluminum ghost unsure of where it was supposed to haunt.

He'd been awake most of the time during the flight from Washington to Key West, poring over Buck Caesar's charts of the Old Bahama Channel and retracing Raymond LeBaron's carefully marked flight path. He closed his eyes, trying to get a clear picture of the *Prosperteer*'s spectral wanderings. Unless the gas bags inside the blimp were reinflated from a ship, an extremely unlikely event, the only answer to Raymond LeBaron's whereabouts lay in Cuba.

Something nagged at his mind, a thought that kept returning after he unconsciously brushed it aside, a piece of the picture that became increasingly lucid as he began dwelling on it. And then suddenly it crystallized.

The flight to trace LeBaron's trail was a setup.

A rational and logical conclusion remained a dim outline in a thick mist. The trick was to try to fit it into a pattern. His mind was casting about for directions to explore when he sensed a shadow fall over him.

"Well, well," said a familiar voice, "looks as though Snow White fell for the old apple routine again."

"Either that or he's hibernating," came another voice Pitt recognized.

He opened his eyes, shielded them from the sun with one hand, and looked up at a pair of grinning individuals who stared down. The shorter of the two, a barrel-chested, muscled character with black curly hair and the ironbound look of a man who enjoyed eating bricks for breakfast, was Pitt's old friend and assistant projects director at NUMA, Al Giordino.

Al reached down, grabbed an outstretched hand, and pulled Pitt to his feet as effortlessly as a sanitation worker picking up an empty beer can from park grass.

"Departure time in twelve minutes."

"Our unnamed pilot arrive yet?" Pitt asked.

The other man, slightly taller and much thinner than Giordino, shook his head. "No sign of one."

Rudi Gunn peered through a pair of blue eyes that were magnified by thick-lensed glasses. He had the appearance of an undernourished assistant bookkeeper toiling for a gold watch. The impression was deceptive. Gunn was the overseer of NUMA's oceanographic projects. While Admiral Sandecker waged pitched battles with Congress and the federal bureaucracy, Gunn watched over the agency's day-to-day operation. For Pitt, prying Gunn and Giordino from under Sandecker had been a major victory.

"If we want to match LeBaron's departure time, we'll have to wrestle it aloft ourselves," said Giordino, unconcerned.

"I guess we can manage," said Pitt. "You study the flight manuals?"

Giordino nodded. "Requires fifty hours of instruction and flying time to qualify for a license. The basic control isn't difficult, but the art of keeping that pneumatic scrotum stable in a stiff breeze takes practice."

Pitt couldn't help grinning at Giordino's colorful description. "The equipment loaded on board?"

"Loaded and secured," Gunn assured him.

"Then I guess we might as well shove off."

As they approached the *Prosperteer*, LeBaron's crew chief climbed down the ladder from the control car. He spoke a few words to one of the ground crew and then waved a friendly greeting.

"She's all ready to go, gentlemen."

"How close are we to the actual weather conditions of the previous flight?" asked Pitt.

"Mr. LeBaron was flying against a five-mile-an-hour head wind out of the southeast. You'll buck eight, so figure on compensating. There's a late-season hurricane moving in over the Turks and Caicos

Islands. The meteorological guys christened her Little Eva because she's a small blow with a diameter no more than sixty miles wide. The forecasters think she'll swing north toward the Carolinas. If you turn back no later than 1400 hours, Little Eva's outer breeze should provide you with a nice fat tail wind to nudge you home."

"And if we don't?"

"Don't what?"

"Swing back by 1400 hours."

The crew chief smiled thinly. "I don't recommend getting caught in a tropical storm with fifty-mile-an-hour winds, at least not in an airship that's sixty years old."

"You make a strong case," Pitt admitted.

"Allowing for the head wind," said Gunn, "we won't reach the search area until 1030 hours. That doesn't leave us much time to look around."

"Yes," Giordino said, "but LeBaron's known flight path should put us right in the ballpark."

"A tidy package," Pitt mused to no one in particular. "Too tidy."

The three NUMA men were about to climb on board when the LeBaron limousine pulled up beside the blimp. Angelo got out and smartly opened the passenger door. Jessie stepped into the sun and walked over, looking outdoorsy in a designer safari suit with her hair tied in a bright scarf, nineteen-thirties style. She was carrying a suede flight bag.

"Are we ready?" she said brightly, slipping past them and nimbly hustling up the ladder to the control car.

Gunn gave Pitt a grim look. "You didn't tell us we were going on a picnic."

"Nobody told me either," Pitt said, gazing up at Jessie, who had turned and was framed in the doorway.

"My fault," said Jessie. "I forgot to mention that I'm your pilot."

Giordino and Gunn looked as if they had swallowed live squid. Pitt's face wore an amused expression.

He said, "No kidding."

"Raymond taught me to fly the *Prosperteer,*" she said. "I've logged over eighty hours at the controls and have a license."

"No kidding," Pitt repeated, becoming intrigued.

Giordino failed to see the humor. "Do you also know how to dive, Mrs. LeBaron?"

"Sky or scuba? I'm certified for both."

"We can't take a woman," said Gunn resolutely.

"Please, Mrs. LeBaron," pleaded the crew chief. "We don't know what happened to your husband. The flight might be dangerous."

"We'll use the same communication plan as Raymond's flight," she said, ignoring him. "If we find anything interesting we'll transmit in normal voice. No code this time."

"This is ridiculous," snapped Gunn.

Pitt shrugged. "Oh, I don't know. I'll vote for her."

"You don't really mean it!"

"Why not?" replied Pitt with a sardonic grin. "I firmly believe in equal rights. She has just as much right to get herself killed as we do."

The ground crew stood as silent as pallbearers, their eyes following the old blimp as she lifted into the sunrise. Suddenly she began dropping. They held their breath as the landing wheel touched the crest of a wave. Then she slowly bounced back into the air and struggled to rise.

Someone muttered anxiously, "Lift, baby, lift!"

The *Prosperteer* agonizingly rose a few feet at a time until she finally leveled out at a safe altitude. The ground crew watched motionless, staring until the blimp became a tiny dark speck above the silent horizon. They stood there when she was no longer in view, instinctively quiet, a sense of dread in their hearts. There would be no volleyball game this day. They all herded inside the maintenance truck, overburdening the air conditioning system, clustering around the radio.

The first message came in at 0700 hours. Pitt explained away the shaky liftoff. Jessie had undercompensated for the lack of buoyancy caused by the extra payload Giordino and Gunn had placed on board.

From then on until 1400 hours, Pitt kept the frequency open and maintained a running dialogue, matching his observations with the transcribed report that was recorded during LeBaron's flight.

The crew chief picked up the microphone. "*Prosperteer,* this is Grandma's house. Over."

"Go ahead, Grandma."

"Can you give me your latest VIKOR satellite position."

"Roger. VIKOR reading H3608 by T8090."

The crew chief quickly plotted the position on a chart. "*Prosper-*

teer, you're looking good. I have you five miles due south of Guinchos Cay on the Bahama Bank. Over."

"I read the same, Grandma."

"How are the winds?"

"Judging from the wave crests, I'd say the breeze has picked up to about Force 6 on the Beaufort scale."

"Listen to me, *Prosperteer.* The Coast Guard has issued a new update on Little Eva. She has doubled her speed and swung east. Hurricane warnings are up throughout the southern Bahamas. If she sticks to her present course, she'll strike the east coast of Cuba some-time this evening. I repeat, Little Eva has swung east and is heading in your direction. Call it a day, *Prosperteer,* and beat a course for home."

"Will do, Grandma. Turning onto new course for the Keys."

Pitt was silent for the next half hour. At 1435 hours, the crew chief hailed again.

"Prosperteer, come in, please. Over."

No reply.

"Come in, *Prosperteer.* This is Grandma's house. Do you read?"
Still nothing.

The stifling air inside the truck seemed suddenly to turn cold as fear and apprehension gripped the crew. The seconds crawled past and took forever to become minutes as the crew chief tried desper-ately to raise the blimp.

But the *Prosperteer* did not respond.

The crew chief slammed down the microphone and pushed his way outside the truck through the stunned ground crew. He ran over to the parked limousine and feverishly jerked open a rear door.

"They're gone! We've lost them, the same as the last time!"

The man sitting alone in the rear seat simply nodded. "Keep trying to raise them," he said quietly.

As the crew chief hurried back to the radio, Admiral James San-decker lifted a telephone receiver from a varnished cabinet and placed a call.

"Mr. President."

"Yes, Admiral."

"They're missing."

"Understood. I've briefed Admiral Clyde Monfort of the Caribbean Joint Task Force. He's already put ships and planes on alert around the Bahamas. As soon as we hang up I'll order him to launch a search and rescue operation."

"Please impress upon Monfort the need for speed. I've also been informed the *Prosperteer* disappeared in the predicted path of a hurricane."

"Return to Washington, Admiral, and do not worry. Your people and Mrs. LeBaron should be sighted and picked up within a few hours."

"I'll try to share your optimism, Mr. President. Thank you."

If there was one doctrine Sandecker believed in with all his heart, it was "Never trust a politician's word." He placed another call on the limousine's phone.

"Admiral James Sandecker. I'd like to speak with Admiral Monfort."

"Right away, sir."

"Jim, is that really you?"

"Hello, Clyde. Good to hear your voice."

"Damn, it's been nearly two years. What's on your mind?"

"Tell me, Clyde, have you been alerted for a rescue mission in the Bahamas?"

"Where did you hear that?"

"The rumor mill."

"News to me. Most of our Caribbean forces are conducting an amphibious landing exercise on Jamaica."

"Jamaica?"

"A little muscle-flexing display of military capability to shake up the Soviets and Cubans. Keeps Castro off balance, thinking we're going to invade one of these days."

"Are we?"

"What in hell for? Cuba is the best advertising campaign we've got running that promotes communism as a big economic bust. Besides, better the Soviet Union throws twelve million dollars a day down Castro's toilet than us."

"You've received no orders to keep an eye on a blimp that left on a flight from the Keys this morning?"

There was an ominous silence on the other end of the line.

"I probably shouldn't be telling you this, Jim, but I did receive a verbal order concerning the blimp. I was told to keep our ships and aircraft out of the Bahama Banks and to put a blackout on all communications coming from the area."

"The order come direct from the White House?"

"Don't press your luck, Jim."

"Thanks for setting me straight, Clyde."

"Any time. Let's get together next time I'm in Washington."

"I'll look forward to it."

Sandecker hung up, his face red with anger, his eyes fired with fury.

"God help them," he muttered through clenched teeth. "We've all been had."

19

JESSIE'S SMOOTH, HIGH-CHEEKBONED FACE was tense from the strain of fighting the wind gusts and rain squalls that pounded against the skin of the blimp. Her arms and wrists were turning numb as she orchestrated the throttles and the big elevator pitch control. With the added weight from the rain it was becoming nearly impossible to keep the wallowing airship level and steady. She began to feel the icy caress of fear.

"We'll have to head for the nearest land," she said, her voice uneven. "I can't keep her aloft much longer in this turbulence."

Pitt looked at her. "The nearest land is Cuba."

"Better arrested than dead."

"Not yet," Pitt replied from his seat to the right and slightly behind her. "Hang on a little longer. The storm will sweep us back to Key West."

"With the radio out, they won't know where to look if we're forced to ditch in the sea."

"You should have thought of that before you spilled coffee on the transmitter and shorted its circuitry."

She stole a glance at him. God, she thought, it was maddening. He was leaning out the starboard window, nonchalantly peering through a pair of binoculars at the sea below. Giordino was observing out the port side, while Gunn was taking readings off the VIKOR navigating computer and laying out their course on a chart. Every so often, Gunn calmly examined the stylus markings on the recorder of a Schonstedt gradiometer, an instrument for detecting iron by measuring magnetic intensity. All three men looked at though they didn't have a care in the world.

"Didn't you hear what I said?" she asked in exasperation.

"We heard," Pitt replied.

"I can't control her in this wind. She's too heavy. We've got to drop ballast or touch down."

"The last of the ballast was dumped an hour ago."

"Then get rid of that junk you brought on board," she ordered, gesturing to a small mountain of aluminum boxes strapped to the deck.

"Sorry. That junk, as you call it, may come in handy."

"But we're losing lift."

"Do the best you can."

Jessie pointed through the windshield. "The island off to our starboard is Cayo Santa María. The landmass beyond is Cuba. I'm going to bring the blimp around on a southerly course and take our chances with the Cubans."

Pitt swung from the window, his green eyes set and purposeful. "You volunteered for this mission," he said roughly. "You wanted to be one of the boys. Now hang in there."

"Use your head, Pitt," she snapped. "If we wait another half hour the hurricane will tear us to pieces."

"I think I have something," Giordino called.

Pitt moved from his seat over to the port side. "What direction?"

Giordino pointed. "We just passed over it. About two hundred yards off our stern."

"A big one," Gunn said excitedly. "The markings are going off the scale."

"Come about to port," Pitt ordered Jessie. "Take us back over the same course."

Jessie didn't argue. Suddenly caught up in the fervor of the discovery, she felt her exhaustion fall away. She slammed the throttles forward and rolled the blimp to port, using the wind to crab around on a reverse course. A gust slammed into the aluminum envelope, causing a shudder to run through the ship and rocking the control car. Then the buffeting eased and the flight smoothed as the eight tail fins came around and the wind beat from astern.

The interior of the control car was as hushed as the crypt of a cathedral. Gunn unreeled the line from the gradiometer's sensing unit until it dangled four hundred feet below the belly of the blimp and skimmed the rolling swells. Then he turned his attention back to the recorder and waited for the stylus to make a horizontal swing across the graph paper. Soon it began to waver and scratch back and forth.

"Coming up on target," Gunn announced.

Giordino and Pitt ignored the wind stream and leaned farther out the windows. The sea was building and foam was spraying from the wave crests, making it difficult to see into the transparent depths. Jessie was having a tougher time of it now, struggling with the controls, trying to reduce the violent shaking and swaying of the blimp, which behaved like a whale fighting its way up the Colorado River rapids.

"I've got her!" Pitt suddenly shouted. "She's lying north and south, about a hundred yards to starboard."

Giordino moved to the opposite side of the control car and gazed down. "Okay, I have her in sight too."

"Can you detect any sign of derricks?" Gunn asked.

"Her outline is distinct, but I can't make out any detail. I'd say she's about eighty feet under the surface."

"More like ninety," said Pitt.

"Is it the *Cyclops?*" Jessie asked anxiously.

"Too early to tell." He turned to Gunn. "Mark the position from the VIKOR."

"Position marked," Gunn acknowledged.

Pitt nodded at Jessie. "All right, pilot, let's make another pass. And this time, as we come about into the wind, try to hover over the target."

"Why don't you ask me to turn lead into gold," she snapped back.

Pitt came over and kissed her lightly on the cheek. "You're doing great. Stick in a little longer and I'll spell you at the controls."

"Don't patronize me," she said testily, but her eyes took on a warm glow and the tension lines around her lips softened. "Just tell me when to stop the bus."

Very self-willed she was, thought Pitt. For the first time he felt himself envying Raymond LeBaron. He returned aft and put a hand on Gunn's shoulder.

"Use the clinometer and see if you can get a rough measurement of her dimensions."

Gunn nodded. "Will do."

"If that's the *Cyclops,*" said Giordino happily, "you made a damned good guess."

"A lot of luck mixed with a small amount of hindsight," Pitt admitted. "That, and the fact Raymond LeBaron and Buck Caesar aimed us toward the ballpark. The puzzle is why the *Cyclops* lies outside the main shipping lane."

Giordino gave a helpless tilt to his head. "We'll probably never know."

"Coming back on target," Jessie reported.

Gunn set the distance on the clinometer and then sighted through the eyepiece, measuring the length of the shadowy object under the water. He managed to hold the instrument steady as Jessie fought a masterful battle against the wind.

"No way of accurately measuring her beam because it's impossible to see if she lies straight up or on her side," he said, studying the calibrations.

"And the overall length?" asked Pitt.

"Between five hundred thirty and five hundred fifty feet."

"Looking good," Pitt said, visibly relieved. "The *Cyclops* was five hundred and forty-two feet."

"If we drop down closer, I might be able to get a more precise reading," said Gunn.

"One more time, Jessie," Pitt called out.

"I don't think so." She lifted a hand from the controls and pointed out the forward window. "A welcoming committee."

Her expression appeared calm, almost too calm, while the men watched in mild fascination as a helicopter materialized out of the clouds a thousand feet above the blimp. For several seconds it seemed to hang there, fastened in the sky like a hawk eyeing a pigeon. Then it swelled in size as it approached and banked around on a parallel course with the *Prosperteer*. Through the binoculars they could clearly see the grim faces of the pilots and the two pairs of hands grasping the automatic guns that poked through the open side door.

"They brought friends," Gunn said succinctly. He was aiming his binoculars at a Cuban gunboat about four miles away that was planing through the swells, throwing up great wings of sea spray.

Giordino said nothing. He tore the holding straps from the boxes and began throwing the contents on the deck as fast as his hands could move. Gunn joined him as Pitt began assembling a strange-looking screen.

"They're holding up a sign in English," Jessie announced.

"What does it say?" Pitt asked without looking up.

"'Follow us and do not use your radio,'" she read aloud. "What should I do?"

"Obviously we can't use the radio, so smile and wave to them. Let's hope they won't shoot if they see you're a woman."

"I wouldn't count on it," grunted Giordino.

"And keep hovering over the shipwreck," Pitt added.

Jessie didn't like what was going on inside the control car. Her face noticeably paled. She said, "We'd better do what they want."

"Screw them," Pitt said coldly. He unbuckled her seat belt and lifted her away from the controls. Giordino held up a pair of air tanks and Pitt quickly adjusted the straps over her shoulders. Gunn handed her a face mask, swim fins, and a buoyancy compensator vest.

"Quickly," he ordered. "Put these on."

She stood there baffled. "What are you doing?"

"I thought you knew," said Pitt. "We're going for a swim."

"We're what?" The dark gypsy eyes were wide, not so much from alarm as astonishment.

"No time for the defense to make a closing argument," Pitt said calmly. "Call it a wild plan for staying alive and let it go at that. Now do as you're told and lie down on the deck behind the screeen."

Giordino stared dubiously at the inch-thick screen. "Let's hope it does the job. I'd hate to be around if a bullet finds an air tank."

"Fear not," Pitt replied, as the three men hurriedly strapped on their diving gear. "High-tensile plastic. Guaranteed to stop anything up to a twenty-millimeter shell."

With no hands at the controls, the blimp lurched sideways under the onslaught of a fresh gust and pitched downward. Everyone instinctively dropped to the deck and snatched at the nearest handgrip. The boxes that held the equipment skidded madly across the deck and crashed into the pilots' seats.

There was no hesitation, no further attempt at communication. The Cuban commander of the helicopter, thinking the sudden erratic movement of the blimp meant it was trying to escape, ordered his crew to open fire. A storm of bullets struck the starboard side of the *Prosperteer* from no more than thirty yards away. The control car was immediately turned into a shambles. The old yellowed windows melted away in a shower of fragments that splashed cross the deck. The controls and the instrument panel were blasted into twisted junk, filling the shattered cabin with smoke from shorted circuitry.

Pitt lay prone on top of Jessie, Gunn and Giordino blanketing him, listening to the steel-nosed shells thump against the bulletproof screen. Then the gunmen in the helicopter altered their aim and concentrated on the engines. The aluminum cowlings were torn and mangled by the devastating fire until they shredded and blew away in the air stream. The engines coughed and sputtered into silence, their cylinder heads shot away, oil spewing out amid torrents of black smoke.

"The fuel tanks!" Jessie heard herself shouting above the mad din. "They'll explode!"

"The least of our worries," Pitt yelled back in her ear. "The Cubans aren't using incendiary bullets, and the tanks are made out of self-sealing neoprene rubber."

Giordino crawled over to the ripped and jumbled pile of equipment boxes and retrieved what looked to Jessie like some kind of tubular container. He pushed it ahead of him up the steeply tilted deck.

"Need any help?" Pitt yelled.

"If Rudi can brace my legs..." His voice trailed off.

Gunn didn't require a lecture on instructions. He jammed his feet against a bulkhead for support and clutched Giordino around the knees in a vise grip.

The blimp was totally out of control, dead in the sky, the nose pointing at a forty-degree angle toward the sea. All lift was gone and it began to sink from the sky as the Cubans sprayed the plump, exposed envelope. The stabilizer fins still reached for the clouds, but the old *Prosperteer* was in her death throes.

She would not die alone.

Giordino wrestled the tube open, pulled out an M-72 missile launcher, and loaded the 66-millimeter rocket. Slowly, moving with great caution, he eased the snout of the bazookalike weapon over the jagged glass left in the frame of the window and took aim.

To the astonished men in the patrol boat, less than one mile away, the helicopter appeared to disintegrate in a huge mushroom of fire. The sound of the explosion burst through the air like thunder, followed by a flaming rain of twisted metal that hissed and steamed when it hit the water.

The blimp still hung there, pivoting slowly on its axis. Helium surged through gaping rents in the hull. The circular supports inside began snapping like dried sticks. As if heaving out her final breath the *Prosperteer* caved in on herself, collapsing like an eggshell, and fell into the seething whitecaps.

The raging devastation all happened so quickly. In less than twenty seconds both engines were torn from their mounts, and the support beams holding the control car twisted apart, accompanied by a banshee screeching sound. Like a fragile toy thrown on the sidewalk by a destructive child, the rivets burst and the internal structure shrieked in agony as it disintegrated.

The control car kept sinking into the deep, the water flooding through the shattered windows. It was as if a giant hand was pressing the blimp downward until at last she slipped into the depths and disappeared. Then the control car broke free and dropped like a falling leaf, trailed by a confused maze of wire and cable. The remains of the duraluminum envelope followed, flapping wildly like a drunken bat in flight.

A school of yellowtail snappers darted from under the plunging mass an instant before it struck the sea floor, the impact throwing up billowing clouds of fine sand.

Then all was as quiet as a grave, the deathly stillness broken only by the gentle gurgle of escaping air.

On the turbulent surface the stunned crew of the gunboat began sweeping back and forth over the crash sites, searching for any sign of survivors. They only found spreading pools of fuel and oil.

The winds from the approaching hurricane increased to Force 8. The waves reached a height of eighteen feet, making any further search impossible. The boat's captain had no choice but to turn about on a course toward a safe harbor in Cuba, leaving behind a swirling and malignant sea.

20

THE OPAQUE CLOUD OF SILT that hid the shredded remains of the *Prosperteer* was slowly carried away by a weak bottom current. Pitt rose to his hands and knees and looked around the shambles that had been the control car. Gunn was sitting upright on the deck, his back pressed against a buckled bulkhead. His left ankle was swelling into the shape of a coconut, but he sucked on his mouthpiece and raised one hand with the fingers formed in a V.

Giordino doggedly pulled himself upright and tenderly pressed the right side of his chest. One broken ankle and probably a few ribs between them, thought Pitt. It could be worse. He bent over Jessie and lifted her head. Her eyes appeared blank through the lens of the face mask. The hollow hiss of her regulator and the rise and fall of her chest indicated her breathing was normal, if a bit on the rapid side. He ran his fingers over her arms and legs but found no sign of a fracture. Except for a rash of black-and-blue marks that would bloom in the next twenty-four hours, she seemed whole. As if to assure him, she reached out for his arm and gave it a firm squeeze.

Satisfied, Pitt turned his attention to himself. All the joints swiveled properly, the muscles functioned, nothing seemed distorted. Yet he didn't escape unscathed. A purplish lump was rising on his forehead, and he noticed a strange stiffening sensation in his neck. Pitt canceled out the discomfort with the consolation that no one appeared to be bleeding. One hairline brush with death was enough for one day, he mused. The last thing they needed now was a shark attack.

Pitt focused on the next problem: getting out of the control car. The door was jammed, small wonder after the beating it had taken. He sat on his buttocks, grasped both hands on the bent frame, and lashed out with his feet. Lashed out was an exaggeration. The water pressure impeded the thrust of his legs. He felt as though he was trying to kick out the bottom of a huge jar of glue. On the sixth attempt, when the balls and heels of his feet could take no more, the metal seal gave and the door swung outward in slow motion.

Giordino emerged first, his head swathed by a surge of bubbles from his breathing regulator. He reached back inside, dug his feet into the sand, braced himself for the chest pain that was sure to come, and gave a mighty heave. With Pitt and Gunn shoving from the inside, a large, unwieldy bundle slowly squeezed through the door and dropped to the sand. Then eight steel tanks containing 104 cubic feet of air were passed out to the waiting hands of Giordino.

Inside the mangled control car Jessie fought to equalize her ears with the water pressure. The blood roared and a stabbing pain burst in her head, blanking out the trauma of the crash. She pinched her nose and snorted furiously. On the fifth try her ears finally popped, and the relief was so marvelous that tears came to her eyes. She clamped her teeth on the regulator's mouthpiece and sucked in a lungful of air. How beautiful it would be to wake up in her own bed, she thought. Something touched her hand. It was another hand, firm and rough-skinned. She looked up to see Pitt's eyes staring at her through his mask; they seemed crinkled in a smile. He nodded for her to follow him.

He led her outside into the vast liquid void. She gazed up, watching her air bubbles hiss and swirl toward the restless surface. Despite the turbulence above, visibility on the bottom was nearly two hundred feet and she could clearly see the entire length of the airship's main carcass lying a short distance from the control car. Gunn and Giordino were nowhere in sight.

Pitt gestured for her to wait by the air tanks and the strange bundle. He checked the compass on his left wrist and swam off into the blue haze. Jessie drifted, weightless, her head feeling light from a touch of nitrogen narcosis. An overwhelming sense of loneliness closed over her, but quickly evaporated when she saw Pitt retuning. He made a sign for her to follow, and then he turned and slowly paddled away. Pounding her feet against the water resistance, she quickly caught up with him.

The white sandy bottom gave way to clumps of coral inhabited by a variety of oddly shaped fish. Their natural bright colors were deadened to a soft gray by the scattering and absorption of the water particles that filtered out the reds, oranges, and yellows, leaving only dull greens and blues. They pedaled their fins, moving only an arm's length above the weird and exotically molded underwater jungle, observed queerly by a crowd of small angelfish, pufferfish, and trumpetfish. The amusing scene reminded Pitt of children watching the huge ballooned cartoon characters that float down Broadway in Macy's Thanksgiving Day parade.

Suddenly Jessie dug her fingers into Pitt's leg and pointed above and behind. There, swimming in lazy apathy, only twenty feet away, was a school of barracuda. There must have been two hundred of them, none measuring less than four feet in length. They turned as one and began circling the divers while displaying a beady-eyed curiosity. Then, deciding that Pitt and Jessie were not worth lingering over, they flashed away in the wink of an eye and were lost to view.

When Pitt turned back he saw Rudi Gunn materializing out of the smoky blue curtain. Gunn came to a stop and beckoned for them to hurry in his direction. Then he made the V sign of success.

The meaning was clear. Gunn vigorously kicked with one fin, rapidly rising at an angle until he was about thirty feet above the coral landscape, Pitt and Jessie trailing immediately in his wake.

They had traveled nearly a hundred yards when Gunn abruptly slowed and curved his body into a vertical position, one whitened hand held out, slightly bent finger pointing like the grim reaper.

Like a haunted castle looming from the mists of a Yorkshire moor, the phantom shape of the *Cyclops* rose up through the watery gloom, evil and sinister, as though some unspeakable force lurked within her bowels.

21

PITT HAD DIVED on many shipwrecks and he was the first man to view the *Titanic,* but staring at the lost ghost ship of legend left him numb with an almost superstitious awe. The knowledge that she was the tomb for over three hundred men only deepened her malignant aura.

The sunken ship was lying on her port side with a list of about twenty-five degrees, her bow set toward the north. She did not have the look of anything that was supposed to rest on the sea floor, and mother nature had gone to work laying a veil of sediment and marine organisms over the steel intruder.

The entire hull and superstructure were encrusted with sea growth of every imaginable description—sponges, barnacles, flowery anemones, feathery sea ferns, and slender weeds that gracefully swayed with the current like the arms of dancers. Except for the distorted bow and three fallen derricks, the ship was suprisingly intact.

They found Giordino busily scraping the growth from a small section below the stern railing. He turned at their approach and showed off his handiwork. He had exposed the raised letters that spelled out *Cyclops.*

Pitt glanced at his orange-faced Doxa diver's watch. It seemed an eternity since the blimp crashed, but only nine minutes had passed from the moment they swam out of the control car. It was imperative that they conserve their air. They still had to search the wreck and have enough left in the spare tanks for decompression. The safety margin would be cut dangerously thin.

He checked Jessie's air gauge and studied her eyes. They looked clear and bright. She was breathing slowly in a comfortable rhythm. She gave him a thumbs-up sign and then threw him a coquettish wink. Her brush with death in the *Prosperteer* was forgotten for the moment.

Pitt winked back. She's actually enjoying this, he thought.

Using hand signals for communication, the four of them fanned out in a line above the fantail and began prowling her length. The doors of the aft deckhouse had rotted away and the teak deck was heavily worm-eaten. Any flat surface was coated by sediment that gave the appearance of a dusty shroud.

The jackstaff stood bare, the United States ensign having rotted away long ago. The two stern guns pointed aft, mute and deserted. The twin smokestacks stood like sentries over the decaying wreckage of ventilators, bollards and railings, rotting coils of wire and cable still hugging rusting winches. Like a shantytown, each piece of debris offered a nesting place for spiny urchins, arrow crabs, and other creatures of the sea.

Pitt knew from studying a diagram of the *Cyclops'* interior that searching the stern section was a waste of time. The smokestacks stood over the engine room and its crew quarters. If they were to find the La Dorada statue it would most likely be in the general cargo compartment beneath the bridge and forecastle. He motioned the others to continue their probe toward the bow.

They swam slowly, carefully along the catwalk that stretched over the sprawling coal hatches, skirting around the great clamshell loading buckets and under the corroded derricks that reached forlornly toward the refracted rays from above. It became apparent to them that the *Cyclops* had died a quick and violent death. The rotting remains of the lifeboats were forever frozen in their davits and much of the superstructure looked as if it had been crushed by a monstrous fist.

The odd boxlike form of the bridge slowly took form out of the blue-green dusk. The two support legs on the starboard side had buckled, but the hull's tilt to port had compensated for the angle. Peculiarly out of kilter with the rest of the ship, the bridge stood on a perfect horizontal plane.

The dark on the other side of the wheelhouse door looked ominous. Pitt switched on his dive light and drifted slowly inside, taking care not to stir up the silt on the deck with his fins. Dim light filtered through the slime-coated portholes on the forward bulkhead. He brushed away the muck from the glass covering the ship's clock. The tarnished hands were frozen at 12:21. He also examined the big upright compass stand. The interior was still watertight and the needle floated free in kerosene, pointing faithfully toward magnetic north. Pitt noted that the ship's heading was 340 degrees.

On opposite sides of the compass, covered over by a colony of sponges that turned vivid red under Pitt's light, were two postlike objects that rose from the deck and fanned out at the top. Curious, Pitt wiped the growth from the port one, revealing a glass face, through which he could barely make out the words AHEAD FULL, HALF, SLOW, DEAD SLOW, STOP, and FINISHED WITH ENGINES. It was the bridge telegraph to the engine room. He noted that the brass arrow was pointing to FULL. He floated over and cleaned the glass on the starboard telegraph. The pointer was locked on FINISHED WITH ENGINES.

Jessie was about eight feet behind Pitt when she let out a garbled scream that lifted the hair on the nape of his neck. He spun around, half thinking she was being dragged away by a shark, but she was gesturing frantically at a pair of objects protruding from the silt.

Two human skulls, muck up to their nose openings, stared through empty eye sockets. They give Pitt the disconcerting feeling he was being watched. The bones of another crewman rested against the base of the helm, one skeletal arm still wedged between the spokes of the wheel. Pitt wondered if one of them might be the pitiful remains of Captain Worley.

There was nothing else to see, so Pitt led Jessie outside the wheelhouse and down a companionway to the crew and passenger quarters. At almost the same time, Gunn and Giordino disappeared down a hatch leading to a small cargo hold.

The layer of silt was shallow in this section of the ship, no more than an inch deep. The companionway led to a long passageway with small compartments off to the sides. Each one contained bunks, porcelain sinks, scattered personal effects, and the skeletal relics of their occupants. Pitt soon lost count of the dead. He paused and added air to his buoyancy compensator to keep his body balanced in a free-floating, horizontal position. The slightest touch from his fins would stir up large clouds of blinding silt.

Pitt tapped Jessie on the shoulder and shone his light into a small head with a bathtub and two toilets. He made a questioning gesture. She grinned around her mouthpiece and made a comical but negative reply.

He accidentally struck his dive light against a steampipe running along the ceiling and momentarily knocked the switch into the Off position. The sudden realm of utter darkness was as total and stifling as if they were dropped into a coffin and the lid slammed shut. Pitt had no wish to remain surrounded by eternal black within the grave of the *Cyclops*, and he quickly flicked on the light again, exposing a brilliant yellow and red sponge colony that clung to the bulkheads of the passageway.

It soon became obvious they would find no evidence of the La Dorada statue here. They made their way back through the passageway of death and resurfaced on the forecastle deck. Giordino was waiting and motioned toward a hatch that was frozen half open. Pitt squeezed through, clanging his air tanks on the frame, and dropped down a badly eroded ladder.

He swam through what looked like a baggage cargo hold, twisting around the jumbled and decayed rubbish, heading toward the unearthly glow of Gunn's dive light. A pile of unhinged bones passed under him, the jaw of the skull gaping in what seemed in Pitt's imagination a ghastly scream of terror.

He found Gunn intently examining the rotting interior of a large shipping crate. The grisly skeletal remains of two men were wedged between the crate and a bulkhead.

For a brief instant Pitt's heart pounded with excitement and anticipation, his mind certain they had found the most priceless treasure of the sea. Then Gunn looked up, and Pitt saw the bitter disappointment reflected in his eyes.

The crate was empty.

A frustrating search of the cargo hold turned up a startling revelation. Lying in the dark shadows like a collapsed rubber doll was a deep-sea diving suit. The arms were outstretched, the feet encased in Frankenstein-style weighted boots. A tarnished brass diving helmet and breastplate covered the head and neck. Curled off to the side like a dead gray snake was the umbilical line that contained the air hose and lifeline cable. They were severed about six feet from the helmet couplings.

The layer of silt and slime on the diving outfit indicated it had lain there for many years. Pitt removed a knife strapped to his right calf and used it to pry loose the wing nut clamping the helmet's faceplate. It gave slowly at first and then loosened enough to be removed by his fingers. He pulled the faceplate open and aimed the beam of the dive light inside. Protected from the ravages of destructive sea life by the rubber suit and the helmet's safety valves, the head still retained hair and remnants of flesh.

Pitt and his party were not the first to have probed the gruesome secrets of the *Cyclops*. Someone else had already come and gone with the La Dorada treasure.

22

PITT CHECKED HIS OLD DOXA WATCH and calculated their decompression stops. He added an extra minute to each stop as a safety margin to eliminate the gas bubbles from their blood and tissues and prevent the agony of diver's bends.

After leaving the *Cyclops,* they had exchanged the nearly empty air cylinders for their reserve supply stashed beside the control car and began their slow rise to the surface. A few feet away, Gunn and Giordino added air to their buoyancy compensators to maintain the required depth while handling the cumbersome bundle.

Below them in the watery gloom, the *Cyclops* lay desolate and cursed to oblivion. Before another decade passed, her rusting walls would begin to collapse inward, and a century later the restless sea floor would cover her pitiful remains under a shroud of silt, leaving only a few pieces of coral-encrusted debris to mark her grave.

Above them, the surface was a turmoil of quicksilver. At the next decompression stop, they began to feel the crushing momentum from the mountainous swells and fought to hang in the void together. There was no thought of a stop at the twenty-foot level. Their air supply was almost exhausted and only death by drowning waited in the depths. They had no alternative but to surface and take their chances in the tempest above.

Jessie seemed composed and unshaken. Pitt realized that she didn't suspect the danger on the surface. Her only thoughts were of seeing the sky again.

Pitt made one final check of the time and motioned upward with his thumb. They began to ascend as one, Jessie hanging on to Pitt's leg, Gunn and Giordino dragging the bundle. The light increased and when Pitt looked up he was surprised to see a whorl of foam only a few feet above his head.

He surfaced in a trough and was lifted by a vast sloping wall of green that carried him up and over the crest of a high wave as lightly as a bathtub toy. The wind shrieked in his ears and sea spray lashed his cheeks. He pulled up his mask and blinked his eyes. The sky to the east was filled with dark swirling clouds, dark as charcoal as they soared over the gray-green sea. The speed of the approaching storm was uncanny. It seemed to be leaping from one horizon to the next.

Jessie popped up beside him and stared through wide stricken eyes at the blackening overcast bearing down on them. She spit out her mouthpiece. "What is it?"

"The hurricane," Pitt shouted over the wind. "It's coming faster than anyone thought."

"Oh, God!" she gasped.

"Release your weight belt and unstrap your air tanks," he said.

Nothing needed to be said to the others. They had already dropped their gear and were tearing open the bundle. The clouds swept overhead and they were hurled into a twilight world drained of all color. They were stunned at the violent display of atmospheric power. The wind suddenly doubled in strength, filling the air with foam and driving spray and shattering the wave crests into froth.

Abruptly, the bundle that they had so doggedly hauled with them from the *Prosperteer* burst open into an inflatable boat, complete with a compact twenty-horsepower outboard motor encased in a waterproof plastic cover. Giordino rolled over the side, followed by Gunn, and they frantically tore at the motor covering. The savage winds quickly drove the boat away from Pitt and Jessie. The gap began widening at an alarming rate.

"The sea anchor!" Pitt bellowed. "Throw out the sea anchor!"

Gunn barely heard Pitt over the wail of the wind. He heaved a canvas cone-shaped sack over the side that was held open by an iron hoop at the mouth. He then paid it out on a line which he made fast to the bitt on the bow. As the drag on the anchor took hold, the boat's head came around into the wind and slowed its drift.

While Giordino labored over the motor, Gunn threw out a line to Pitt, who tied it under Jessie's arms. As she was towed toward the boat Pitt swam after her, the waves breaking over his head. The mask was torn from his head and the salt spray whipped his eyes. He doubled his effort when he saw that the running sea was carrying away the boat faster than he could swim.

Giordino's muscled arms thrust into the water, closed on Jessie's wrists, and yanked her into the boat as effortlessly as if she were a ten-pound sea bass. Pitt squinted his eyes until they were almost slits. He felt rather than saw the line fall over his shoulder. He could just make out Giordino's grinning face leaning over the side, his great hands winding in the line. Then Pitt was lying in the bottom of the wildly rocking boat, panting and blinking the salt from his eyes.

"Another minute and you'd have been beyond reach of the line," Giordino yelled.

"Time sure flies when you're having fun," Pitt yelled back.

Giordino rolled his eyes at Pitt's cocky reply and went back to laboring over the motor.

The immediate danger facing them now was overturning. Until the motor could be started to provide a small degree of stability, a thrashing wave could flip them upside down. Pitt and Gunn threw over trailing ballast bags, which temporarily reduced the threat.

The strength of the wind was ungodly. It tore at their hair and bodies, the spray felt as abrasive to their skin as if it came from a sand blaster. The little inflatable boat flexed under the stress of the mad sea and reeled in the grip of the gale, but she somehow refused to be tipped over.

Pitt knelt on the hard rubber floorboards, clasping the lifeline with his right hand, and turned his back to the wind. Then he extended his left arm. It was an old seaman's trick that always worked in the Northern Hemisphere. His left hand would be pointing to the center of the storm.

They were slightly outside the center, he judged. There would be no breathing spell from the relative calm of the hurricane's eye. Its main path lay a good forty miles to the northwest. The worst was yet to come.

A wave crashed over them, and then another; two in quick succession that would have broken the back of a larger, more rigid vessel. But the tough, runty inflatable shook off the water and struggled back to the surface like a playful seal. Everyone managed to keep a firm grip and no one was washed overboard.

At last Giordino signaled that he had the motor running. No one could hear it over the howl of the wind. Quickly Pitt and Gunn pulled in the sea anchor and the ballast bags.

Pitt cupped one hand and yelled in Giordino's ear, "Run with the storm!"

To sheer on a sideways course was impossible. The combined force of wind and water would have flung them over. To head into the thrust of the storm bows-on meant a sure battering they could never survive. Their only hope was to ride in the path of the least resistance.

Giordino grimly nodded and pushed the throttle lever. The boat banked around sharply in a trough and surged forward across a sea that had turned completely white from the driving spray. They all flattened themselves against the floorboards except Giordino. He sat with one arm wrapped around a lifeline and gripped the outboard motor's steering lever with his free hand.

The daylight was fading slowly away and night would fall in another hour. The air was hot and stifling, making it difficult to breathe. The almost solid wall of wind-stripped water decreased visibility to less than three hundred yards. Pitt borrowed Gunn's diver's mask and raised his head over the bow. It was like standing under Niagara Falls and staring upward.

Giordino felt icy despair as the hurricane unleashed its full wrath around them. That they had survived this long was just short of a miracle. He was fighting the tumbling sea in a kind of restrained frenzy, struggling desperately to keep their puny oasis from being overwhelmed by a wave. He constantly changed throttle settings, trying to ride just behind the towering crests, warily glancing over his shoulder every few seconds at the gaping trough chasing their stern thirty feet below and behind.

Giordino knew the end was only minutes away, certainly no more than an hour with enormous luck. It would be so easy to swing the boat abeam of the sea and finish it now. He allowed himself a quick look down at the others and saw a broad smile of encouragement on Pitt's lips. If his friend of nearly thirty years felt close to death, he gave no hint of it. Pitt threw a jaunty wave and returned to peering over the bow. Giordino couldn't help wondering what he was looking at.

Pitt was studying the waves. They were piling up higher and more steeply, the wind hurling the foaming white horse at the peaks into the next trough. He estimated the distance between crests and judged that they were packing together like the forward lines of a marching column that was slowing its pace.

The bottom was coming up. The surge was flinging them into shallower water.

Pitt's eyes strained to penetrate the chaotic wall of water. Slowly, as if a black-and-white photograph were being developed, shadowy images began taking shape. The first image that flashed through his mind was that of stained teeth, blackened molars being scrubbed by white toothpaste. The image sharpened into dark rocks with the waves smashing against them in great unending explosions of white. He watched the water shoot skyward as the backwash struck an incoming surge. Then, as the surf momentarily settled, he spotted a low reef extending parallel to the rocks that formed a natural wall in front of a wide, sweeping beach. It had to be the Cuban island of Cayo Santa María, he reckoned.

Pitt had no problem visualizing the probabilities of the new nightmare: bodies torn to shreds on the coral reef or crushed on the jagged rocks. He wiped the salt from the mask lens and stared again. Then he saw it, a thousand-in-one chance to survive the vortex.

Giordino had seen it too—a small inlet between the rocks. He steered for it, knowing he stood a better chance of threading a needle in a thrashing washing machine.

In the next thirty seconds the churning outboard and the storm had carried them a hundred yards. The sea over the reef boiled in a dirty foam and the wind velocity increased to where the driving spray and the darkness made vision almost impossible. Jessie's face went white, her body rigid. Her eyes met Pitt's for an instant, fearful yet trusting. His arm circled her waist and squeezed tight.

A breaker caught and struck them like an avalanche down a mountain. The screw of the outboard raced as it lifted clear of the crest, but its protesting whirr was drowned by the deafening noise of the surf. Gunn opened his mouth to shout a warning, but no sound came. The plunging breaker curled over the boat and smashed down on them with fantastic force. It tore Gunn's hold on the lifeline, and Pitt saw him gyrate through the air like a kite with a broken string.

The boat was driven over the reef, buried in foam. The coral sliced through the rubberized fabric into the air chambers; a field of razor blades couldn't have done it more efficiently. The thickly encrusted bottom swirled past. For several moments they were completely submerged. Then at last the faithful little inflatable wallowed to the surface and they were clear of the reef with only fifty yards of open water separating them from the craggy ramparts, looming dark and wet.

Gunn bobbed up only a few feet away, gasping for breath. Pitt reached way out, grabbed him by the shoulder strap of his buoyancy compensator, and hauled him on board. The rescue didn't come a second too soon. The next breaker came roaring over the reef like a herd of crazed animals running before a forest fire.

Giordino grimly hung on to the motor, which was unfalteringly purring away with every bit of horsepower her pistons could punch out. It didn't take a psychic to know the frail craft was being torn to bits. She was only buoyed up by air still trapped in her chambers.

They were almost within reach of the gap between the rocks when they were caught by the wave. The preceding trough slipped under the base of the breaker, causing it to steepen to twice its height. Its speed increased as it rushed toward the rocky shoreline.

Pitt glanced up. The menacing pinnacles towered above them, water boiling around their foundations like a seething caldron. The boat was thrust up the front of the breaker, and for a brief instant Pitt thought they might be carried over the peak before it broke. But it curled suddenly and toppled forward, striking the rocks opposite the inlet with the shattering crash of thunder, throwing the shredded boat and its occupants into the air, spilling them into the maelstrom.

Pitt heard Jessie scream from far in the distance. It barely pierced his numbed mind, and he struggled to reply, but then everything blurred. The boat fell with such jarring force the motor was ripped from the transom and slung onto the beach.

Pitt remembered nothing after that. A black whirlpool opened up and he was sucked into it.

23

THE MAN WHO WAS THE DRIVING FORCE behind the Jersey Colony lay on an office couch inside the concealed headquarters of the project. He rested his eyes and concentrated on his meeting with the President on the golf course.

Leonard Hudson knew damn well the President wasn't about to sit still and wait patiently for another surprise contact. The Chief Executive was a pusher who never left anything to luck. Although Hudson's sources inside the White House and the intelligence agencies reported no indication of an investigation, he was certain the President was figuring a way to penetrate the curtain around the "inner core."

He could almost feel the net being thrown.

His secretary rapped softly on the door and then opened it. "Excuse me for intruding, but Mr. Steinmetz is on the viewer and wishes to talk to you."

"I'll be there in a minute."

Hudson rearranged his thoughts as he laced his shoes. Like a computer, he logged out of one problem and called up another. He didn't look forward to battling with Steinmetz even if the man *was* a quarter of a million miles away.

Eli Steinmetz was the kind of engineer who overcame an obstacle by designing a mechanical solution and then building it with his own hands. His talent for improvisation was the reason Hudson had chosen him as the leader of the Jersey Colony. A graduate of Caltech with a master's degree from MIT, he had supervised construction projects in half the countries of the world, even Russia.

When approached by the "inner core" to build the first human habitat on lunar soil, Steinmetz had taken nearly a week to make a decision while his mind wrestled with the awesome concept and staggering logistics of such a project. Finally, he accepted, but only on his own terms.

He and only he would select the crew to live on the moon. There would be no pilots or prima donna astronauts in residence. All space flight would be directed by ground control or computers. Only men whose special qualifications were vital in the construction of the base would be included. Besides Steinmetz, the first three to launch the colony were solar and structural engineers. Months later a biologist-doctor, a geochemical engineer, and a horticulturist arrived. Other scientists and technicians followed as their special skills and knowledge were required.

At first Steinmetz had been considered too old. He was fifty-three when he set foot on the moon, and he was fifty-nine now. But Hudson and the other "inner core" members weighed experience over age and never once regretted their selection.

Now Hudson stared into the video monitor at Steinmetz, who was holding up a bottle with a hand-drawn label. Unlike the other colonists', Steinmetz's face sprouted no beard and his head was clean-shaven. His skin had a dusky tint that complemented his slate-black eyes. Steinmetz was a fifth-generation American Jew, but he could have walked unnoticed in a Moslem mosque.

"How's that for self-sufficiency?" said Steinmetz. "Château Lunar Chardonnay, 1989. Not exactly a premier vintage. Only had enough grapes to make four bottles. Should have allowed the vines in the greenhouses to mature another year, but we got impatient."

"I see you even made your own bottle," observed Hudson.

"Yes, our pilot chemical plant is in full operation now. We've increased our output to where we can process almost two tons of lunar-soil materials into two hundred pounds of a bastard metal or five hundred pounds of glass in fifteen days."

Steinmetz appeared to be sitting at a long flat table in the center of a small cave. He was wearing a thin cotton shirt and a pair of jogger's shorts.

"You look cool and comfortable," said Hudson.

"Our first priority when we landed," Steinmetz said, smiling. "Remember?"

"Seal the entrance to the cavern and pressurize its interior so you could work in a comfortable atmosphere without the handicap of encapsulated suits."

"After living in those damned things for eight months, you can't imagine what a relief it was to get back into normal clothing."

"Murphy has been closely monitoring your temperatures and he says the walls of the cavern are increasing their rate of heat absorption. He suggests that you send a man out and lower the angle on the solar collectors by half a degree."

"I'll see to it."

Hudson paused. "It won't be long now, Eli."

"Much changed on earth since I left?"

"About the same, only more smog, more traffic, more people."

Steinmetz laughed. "You trying to talk me into another tour of duty, Leo?"

"Wouldn't dream of it. You're going to be the biggest-man-on-campus since Lindbergh when you drop out of the blue."

"I'll have all our records packed and secured in the lunar transfer vehicle twenty-four hours before liftoff."

"I hope you don't have a mind to uncork your lunar vino on the trip home."

"No, we'll hold our farewell party in plenty of time to purge all alcoholic residue."

Hudson had been trying to approach his point sideways, but decided it was better to come right out with it. "You'll have to deal with the Russians shortly before you leave," he said in a monotone.

"We've been through this," Steinmetz replied firmly. "There is no reason to believe they'll land within two thousand miles of the Jersey Colony."

"Then seek them out and destroy them. You have the weapons and equipment for such a hunting expedition. Their scientists won't be armed. The last thing they'd expect is an attack from men already on the moon."

"The boys and I will gladly defend the homestead, but we're not about to go out and shoot down unarmed men who are innocent of any threat."

"Listen to me, Eli," Hudson implored. "There is a threat, a very real one. If the Soviets somehow discover the existence of Jersey Colony, they can move right in. With you and your people returning to earth less than twenty-four hours after the cosmonauts land, the colony will be deserted and everything in it fair game."

"I realize that as well as you," said Steinmetz roughly, "and hate it even worse. But the sad fact is we can't postpone our departure. We've pushed ourselves to the limit and beyond up here. I can't order these men to hang on another six months or a year, or until your friends can whistle up another craft to take us from space to a soft landing on earth. Cross it off to bad luck and the Russians, who leaked their lunar landing schedule after it was too late for us to alter our return flight."

"The moon belongs to us by right of possession," Hudson argued angrily. "Men of the United States were the first to walk on its soil, and we were the first to colonize it. For God's sake, Eli, don't turn it over to a bunch of thieving Communists."

"Dammit, Leo, there's enough moon for everybody. Besides, this isn't exactly a Garden of Eden. Outside this cavern, day and night temperatures can vary as much as two hundred and fifty degrees Celsius. I doubt if even casino gambling could make a go of it here. Look, even if the cosmonauts fall into our colony, they won't strike a gold vein of information. The accumulation of all our data will go back to earth with us. What we leave behind we can destroy."

"Don't be a fool. Why destroy what can be used by the next colonists, permanent colonists, who will need every advantage they can get?"

Viewing the monitor in front of him, Steinmetz could see the flush on Hudson's face 240,000 miles away. "I've made my position clear, Leo. We'll defend Jersey Colony if need be, but don't expect us to form a posse to kill innocent cosmonauts. It's one thing to shoot at an unmanned space probe, but quite another to murder a fellow human being for trespassing on land he has every right to walk on."

There was an uneasy silence after this statement, but it was no less than what Hudson expected from Steinmetz. The man was no coward. Far from it. Hudson had heard reports of many fights and brawls. Steinmetz could be pushed and clubbed to the floor, but when he came to his feet and his rage seethed to a boil, he could fight like ten devils incarnate. Purveyors of his legend had lost count of the backcountry saloon patrons he had mauled.

Hudson broke the spell. "Suppose the Soviet cosmonauts land within fifty miles? Will that prove to you they intend to occupy Jersey Colony?"

Steinmetz shifted in his stone-carved chair, reluctant to make a concession. "We'll have to wait and see."

"Nobody ever won a battle by going on the defensive," Hudson lectured him. "If their landing site is within striking distance and they show every indication of advancing on the colony, will you accept a compromise and attack?"

Steinmetz bowed his shaven head in assent. "Since you insist on putting my back to the wall, you don't leave me much choice."

"The stakes are too high," said Hudson. "You have no choice at all."

24

THE FOG IN PITT'S BRAIN LIFTED, and one by one his senses flickered back to life like lights across a circuitboard. He struggled to raise his eyelids and focus on the nearest object. For a good half minute he stared at the water-wrinkled skin of his left hand, then at the orange face of his diver's watch as if it were the first time he had ever laid eyes on it.

In the dim twilight the luminescent hands read 6:34. Only two hours since they had escaped from the wrecked control car. It seemed more like a lifetime, and none of it real.

The wind was still roaring off the sea with the speed of an express train and the sea spray combined with rain to beat against his back. He tried to lift himself to his hands and knees, but his legs felt trapped in concrete. He turned and looked down. They were half buried under the sand by the burrowing action of the ebbing surf line.

Pitt lay there for a few more moments, recharging his strength, an exhausted and battered piece of flotsam thrown on the beach. Boulders rose up on either side of him like tenements overlooking an alley. His first really conscious thought was that Giordino had done it, he had steered them through the needle's eye of the rock barrier.

Then somewhere through the howling wind, he could hear Jessie calling faintly. He dug out his legs and forced himself to his knees, staggering under the gale, retching out the saltwater that had been forced into his nose, mouth, and down his throat.

Half crawling, half stumbling across the stinging sand, he found Jessie sitting dazed, her hair limp and stringy on her shoulders, Gunn's head resting in her lap. She looked up at him through lost eyes that suddenly widened in vast relief.

"Oh, thank God," she murmured, her words drowned out by the storm.

Pitt put his arms around her shoulders and gave her a reassuring hug. Then he turned his attention to Gunn.

He was semiconscious. The broken ankle had swelled like a soccer ball. There was an ugly gash above the hairline, and his body was cut in a dozen places from the coral, but he was alive and his breathing was deep and steady.

Pitt shielded his eyes and scanned the beach. Giordino was nowhere in sight. At first Pitt refused to believe it. The seconds passed and he stood rooted, his body leaning into the offshore gale, eyes peering desperately through the torrential dark. He caught a glimpse of orange in the swirl of a dying breaker, and immediately recognized it as the shredded carcass of the inflatable boat. It was caught in the grip of the backwash, drifting out and then swept in again by the next wave.

Pitt lurched into the water up to his hips, oblivious to the spent breakers that rolled around him. He dove under the tattered boat and extended his hands, feeling around like a blind man. His groping fingers found only torn fabric. Moved by some deep urgency to make absolutely sure, he pulled the boat toward the beach.

A large wave caught him unawares and smashed into his back. Somehow he managed to keep his feet under him and drag the boat into shallow water. As the blanket of foam dissolved and was blown away, he saw a pair of legs protruding from under the collapsed boat. Shock, disbelief, and a fanatical refusal to accept Giordino's death flooded through his mind. Frantically, oblivious to the battering of the hurricane, he tore away the sliced remains of the inflatable, revealing Giordino's body floating upright, his head buried inside a buoyancy chamber. Hope came first to Pitt, then optimism that struck him like a punch in the stomach.

Giordino might still be alive.

Pitt stripped away the interior liner and bent over Giordino's face, afraid deep down it would be a lifeless blue. But there was color, and there was breath—ragged and shallow, but there was breath. The brawny little Italian had incredibly survived on air that was trapped inside the buoyancy chamber.

Pitt felt suddenly drained to his bones. Physically and emotionally he was spent. He swayed wearily, the wind trying to beat him flat. Only a firm resolve to save everyone drove him on. Slowly, stiffly from a myriad of cuts and bruises, he slid his arms under Giordino and picked him up. The dead weight of Giordino's solid hundred and seventy-five pounds felt like a ton.

Gunn had come around and was huddled with Jessie. He looked up questioningly at Pitt, who was struggling across the windswept beach under Giordino's inert body.

"We've got to find shelter from the wind," Pitt yelled, his voice rasped by the intake of saltwater. "Can you walk?"

"I'll help him," Jessie yelled in reply. She circled both arms around Gunn's waist, braced her feet in the sand, and shoved him upright.

Panting under his load, Pitt made for a line of palm trees bordering the beach. Every twenty feet he glanced back. Jessie had somehow retained her dive mask, so she was the only one who could keep her eyes open and see straight ahead. She was supporting nearly half of Gunn's weight while he gamely hobbled beside her, eyes shut against the stinging sand, dragging his badly swollen foot.

They made it into the trees but received no mercy from the hurricane. The gale bent the tops of the palms almost to the ground, their fronds splitting like paper in a shredding machine. Coconuts were ripped from their clusters, striking the ground with the velocity of cannonballs and just as deadly. One grazed Pitt's shoulder, its husk tearing his exposed skin. It was as though they were running through the no-man's-land of a battlefield.

Pitt kept his head bent down and squinted sideways, watching the ground directly in front of him. Before he knew it he had walked into a chain link fence. Jessie and Gunn drew up beside him and stopped. He stared to the right and then the left, but found no sign of a break. Trying to climb it was out of the question. The fence was at least ten feet high with a thick angle of barbed wire at the top. Pitt also spotted a small porcelain insulator and realized the chain links were wired for electricity.

"Which way?" Jessie cried.

"You lead," Pitt shouted in her ear. "I can hardly see."

She nodded to the left and set off with Gunn limping along at her side. They staggered onward, beaten every step by the unrelenting force of the wind.

Ten minutes later they had covered only fifty yards. Pitt couldn't push on much longer. His arms were going numb and he was losing his grip on Giordino. He closed his eyes and blindly began to count the steps, staying in a straight line by brushing his right shoulder against the fence, certain the hurricane must have cut off the power source.

He heard Jessie shouting something, and he opened one eye in a narrow slit. She was pointing vigorously ahead. Pitt sank to his knees, gently lowered Giordino to the ground, and looked past Jessie. A palm tree had been uprooted by the insane wind and hurled through the air like some monstrous javelin, landing on the fence and crushing it against the sand.

With appalling abruptness, night closed in and the sky went pitch black. Blindly, they stepped over the flattened fence like sightless drones, reeling and falling, driven on by instinct and some inner discipline that wouldn't allow them to lie down and give up. Jessie gamely kept the lead. Pitt had slung Giordino over a shoulder and held on to the waistband of Gunn's swim trunks, not so much for support as to prevent them from becoming separated.

A hundred yards, then another hundred yards, and suddenly Gunn and Jessie seemed to drop into the ground as if they were swallowed up. Pitt released his grip on Gunn and fell backward, grunting as Giordino's full weight fell across his chest, forcing the air from his lungs. He scrambled from under Giordino and stretched his hand gropingly forward into the dark until he felt nothing there.

Jessie and Gunn had fallen down a steep, eight-foot slope into a sunken road. He could just make out their vague outlines huddled in a heap below.

"Are you injured?" he called.

"We already hurt so much we can't tell." Gunn's voice was muffled by the gale, but not so muffled Pitt couldn't tell it came through clenched teeth.

"Jessie?"

"I'm all right...I think."

"Can you give me a hand with Giordino?"

"I'll try."

"Send him down," said Gunn. "We can manage it."

Pitt eased Giordino's limp figure over the edge of the slope and lowered him gently by the arms. The others held him by the legs until Pitt could scramble down beside them and take up the heavy bulk. Once Giordino was stretched comfortably on the ground, Pitt looked around and took stock.

The sunken road provided a shelter from the gale-force wind. The blowing sand had dropped off and Pitt could finally open his eyes. The road's surface was made up of crushed seashells and appeared hard packed and little used. No sign of light was visible in either direction, which wasn't too surprising when Pitt considered that any local inhabitants would have evacuated the shoreline before the full energy of the hurricane struck.

Both Jessie and Gunn were very nearly played out, their breath coming in short, tortured rasps. Pitt was aware his own breathing was fast and labored, and his heart pounding like a steam engine under full load. Exhausted and battered as they were, Pitt reflected, it still felt like paradise to lie behind a barrier that reduced by half the main drive of the gale.

Two minutes later Giordino began to groan. Then he slowly sat up and looked around, seeing nothing.

"Jesus, it's dark," he muttered to himself, his mind crawling from a woolly mist.

Pitt knelt beside him and said, "Welcome back to the land of the walking dead."

Giordino raised his hand and touched Pitt's face in the darkness. "Dirk?"

"In the flesh."

"Jessie and Rudi?"

"Both right here."

"Where is here?"

"About a mile from the beach." Pitt didn't bother to explain how they survived the landing or how they arrived at the road. That could come later. "Where are you hurt?"

"All over. My rib cage feels like it's on fire. I think my left shoulder is dislocated, one leg feels like it was twisted off at the knee, and the base of my skull where it meets the neck throbs like hell." He swore disgustedly. "Damn, I blew it. I thought I could bring us through the rocks. Forgive me for screwing up."

"Would you believe me if I told you we'd all be fish food if it wasn't for you?" Pitt smiled and then gently probed Giordino's knee, guessing that the injury was a torn tendon. Then he turned his attention to the shoulder. "I can't do anything about your ribs, knee, or thick skull, but your shoulder is out of place, and if you're in the mood I think I can manipulate it back where it belongs."

"Seems I recall you doing that to me when we played football in high school. The team doctor raised holy hell. Said you should have let him do it."

"That's because he was a sadist," Pitt said, grasping Giordino's arm. "Ready?"

"Go on, tear it off."

Pitt yanked and the joint snapped into place with an audible *pop*. Giordino let out a gasp that died into a relieved sigh. Pitt felt around in the dark beside the road until he found a stout branch that had been torn off a small scrub pine, and gave it to Gunn to use as a staff in place of a crutch. Jessie clutched one of Gunn's arms to steady him, while Pitt hoisted Giordino onto his sound leg and supported him with an arm around his waist.

This time Pitt led the way, mentally flipping a coin and heading up the road to their right, plodding close to the high embankment to shelter their progress from the unabating onslaught of the storm. Now the going was easier. No deep sand to wade through, no fallen trees to stumble over, not even the wind-propelled rain to torture them, for the edge of the slope caused it to fly over their heads. Just the graded flat of the road leading off into the stricken darkness.

After an hour had passed, Pitt figured they had hobbled about a mile. He was about to call a rest stop when Giordino suddenly stiffened and stopped so unexpectantly that he lost Pitt's support and toppled to the road.

"Barbecue!" he yelled. "Smell it? Somebody's barbecuing beef."

Pitt sniffed the air. The aroma was faint, but it was there. He lifted Giordino and pushed ahead. The smell of steaks broiling over charcoal grew stronger with every step. In another fifty yards they met with a massive iron gate whose bars were welded in the shape of dolphins. A wall topped by broken glass stretched into the darkness on either side and stood astride a guardhouse. Not surprisingly, in light of the hurricane, it was vacant.

The gate, reaching a good twelve feet toward the ebony sky, was locked, but the outer and inner doors of the guardhouse were open, so they walked through. A short distance beyond, the road ended in a circular drive that passed in front of what seemed in the stormy dark to be a large mound. As they approached, it became a castlelike structure whose roof and three sides were covered over with sandy soil and planted with palmetto trees and native scrub brush. Only the front of the building lay exposed, starkly barren with no windows and only one huge, mahogany door artistically carved with lifelike fish.

"Reminds me of a buried Egyptian temple," said Gunn.

"If it wasn't for the ornate door," said Pitt, "I'd guess it was some kind of military supply depot."

Jessie set them straight. "A subinsulator house. Soil is an ideal insulation against temperatures and weather. Same principle as the sod houses on the early American prairie. I know an architect who specializes in designing them."

"Looks deserted," observed Giordino.

Pitt tried the doorknob. It turned. He eased the door open. The aroma of food wafted out from somewhere within the darkened interior.

"Doesn't smell deserted," said Pitt.

The foyer was paved in tile with a Spanish motif and was lit by several large candles set on a tall stand. The walls were carved blocks of black lava rock and their only decoration was a gruesome painting of a man hanging from the fanged mouth of a snakelike sea monster. They entered and Pitt pulled the door closed behind them.

For some strange reason, the howl of the tempest outside and everyone's weary breathing seemed to add to the deathly stillness of the house.

"Anyone home?" Pitt called out.

He repeated the question twice more, but his only reply was a ghostly silence. A dim corridor beckoned, but Pitt hesitated. Another smell invaded his nostrils. Tobacco smoke. Stronger than the near-lethal gas emitted by Admiral Sandecker's cigars. Pitt was no expert, but he knew that expensive cigars smelled more rotten than the cheap ones. He guessed the smoke must be coming from prime Havanas.

He turned to the others. "What do you think?"

"Do we have a choice?" Giordino asked dumbly.

"Two," replied Pitt. "We can either get out of here while we can and take our chances in the hurricane. Then, when it begins to die down, we can try to steal a boat and head back to Florida—"

"Or throw ourselves on the mercy of the Cubans," Gunn interrupted.

"That's how it boils down."

Jessie shook her head and stared at him through soft, tender eyes. "We can't go back," she said quietly with no trace of fear. "The storm will take days to die, and none of us is in any condition to survive out there another four hours. I vote we take our chances with Castro's government. The very worst they can do is throw us in jail while the State Department negotiates our release."

Pitt looked at Gunn. "Rudi, how say you?"

"We're done in, Dirk. Logic is on Jessie's side."

"Al, how do you see it?"

Giordino shrugged. "Say the word, pal, and I'll swim back to the States." And Pitt knew he meant it too. "But the honest truth is we can't take much more. It pains me to say this, but I think we'd better throw in the towel."

Pitt looked at them and reflected that he couldn't have been blessed with a better team of people to face an unpleasant situation, and it didn't take a visionary to see things were going to become very unpleasant indeed.

"Okay," he said with a grim smile. "Let's crash the party."

They set off down the corridor and soon passed under an archway that opened onto a vast living room decorated in early Spanish antiques. Giant tapestries hung on the walls, depicting galleons sailing sunset seas or being driven helplessly onto reefs by thrashing storms. The furnishings seemed to have a nautical flair; the room was illuminated by ancient ship's lanterns of copper and colored glass. The fireplace was glowing with a crackling fire that warmed the room to hothouse temperatures.

There wasn't a soul to be seen anywhere.

"Ghastly," murmured Jessie. "Our host has simply dreadful taste in decor."

Pitt held up his hand for quiet. "Voices," he said softly. "Coming from that other archway between those two suits of armor."

They moved into another corridor that was dimly lit by candle holders every ten feet. The sounds of laughter and obscure words, from both male and female, became louder. A light loomed from under a curtain ahead. They paused for a second, and then swung it aside and passed through.

They had entered a long dining hall filled with nearly forty people, who stopped in midconversation and stared at Pitt and the others with the awed expression of a group of villagers meeting their first aliens from space.

The women were elegantly dressed in evening gowns, while half the men wore tuxedos and the other half were attired in military uniforms. Several servants waiting on the table stood stock-still like images on motion picture film that was suddenly freeze-framed. The stunned silence was as thick as a wool blanket. A scene straight out of an early thirties Hollywood melodrama.

Pitt realized he and the rest must have made a shocking picture. Soaking wet, their clothing torn and ragged, bruised and gashed skin, torn muscles, broken bones. Hair plastered down around their heads, they must have looked like drowned rats rejected from a polluted river.

Pitt looked at Gunn and said, "How do you say 'Pardon the intrusion' in Spanish?"

"Haven't the vaguest idea. I took French in school."

Then it struck Pitt. Most of the uniformed men were high-ranking

Soviet officers. Only one appeared to be from the Cuban military.

Jessie was in her element. To Pitt she couldn't have looked more regal, even if the designer safari suit hung on her body in tatters.

"Is there a gentleman among you who will offer a lady a chair?" she demanded.

Before she received an answer, ten men with Russian-type machine pistols burst into the room and surrounded them in a loose circle, sphinx-faced men whose weapons were aimed at all four stomachs. Their eyes were icy and their lips set in tight lines. There was little doubt in Pitt's mind that they were highly trained to kill on command.

Giordino, with the appearance of a man run over by a garbage truck, painfully pulled himself to his full height and stared back. "Did you ever see so many smiling faces?" he asked conversationally.

"No," said Pitt with the beginning of a to-hell-with-you grin. "Not since Little Big Horn."

Jessie didn't hear them. As if in a trance she shouldered her way through the armed guards and stopped near the head of the table, staring down at a tall, gray-haired man attired in formal evening wear, who stared back at her in shocked disbelief.

She brushed back her wet, tangled hair and struck a sophisticated, feline pose. Then she spoke in a soft, commanding voice. "Be a dear, Raymond, and pour your wife a glass of wine."

25

HAGEN DROVE NINETEEN MILES east of downtown Colorado Springs on Highway 94 until he came to Enoch Road. Then he turned right and arrived at the main entrance of the Unified Space Operations Center.

The two-billion-dollar project, constructed on 640 acres of land and manned by 5,000 uniformed and civilian personnel, controlled all military space vehicle and shuttle flights as well as satellite monitoring programs. An entire aerospace community mushroomed around the center, covering thousands of acres with residential developments, scientific and industrial parks, high-tech research and manufacturing plants, and Air Force test facilities. In ten short years, what had once been sparse grazing land inhabited by small herds of cattle had become the "Space Capital of the World."

Hagen flashed his security clearance, drove into the parking lot, and stopped opposite a side entrance to the massive building. He did not get out of the car but opened his briefcase and removed his worn legal pad. He turned to a page with three names and added a fourth.

> Raymond LeBaron...............Whereabouts unknown.
> Leonard Hudson...................Same.
> Gunnar Eriksen....................Same.
> General Clark Fisher............Colorado Springs.

Hagen's call to the Drake Hotel from Pattenden Lab had alerted an old friend at the FBI, who traced the number of Anson Jones to a classified line at an officer's residence on Peterson Air Force Base outside of Colorado Springs. The house was occupied by four-star General Clark Fisher, head of the Joint Military Space Command.

Posing as a pest control inspector, Hagen had been given the run of the house by the general's wife. Fortunately for him, she considered his unexpected arrival as a heaven-sent opportunity to complain about an army of spiders that had invaded the premises. He listened attentively and promised to attack the insects with every weapon in his arsenal. Then, while she fussed around in the kitchen with the hired cook, experimenting with a new recipe for apricot sautéd prawns, Hagen tossed the general's study.

His search revealed only that Fisher was a stickler for security. Hagen found nothing in desk drawers, files, or hidden recesses that could prove beneficial to a Soviet agent or himself. He decided to wait it out until the general left for the evening and then search his office at the space center. As he left by the rear door Mrs. Fisher was talking on the telephone and simply waved goodbye. Hagen paused for a moment and overheard her telling the general to stop off on his way home and pick up a bottle of sherry.

Hagen put the legal pad back in the briefcase and took out a can of diet cola and a thick salami sandwich with sliced dill pickle, wrapped in wax paper with a delicatessen's advertising printed on both sides. The Colorado temperature had cooled considerably once the sun had dropped over the Rocky Mountains. The shadow of Pike's Peak stretched out over the plains, casting a dark veil over the treeless landscape.

Hagen didn't notice the scenic beauty unfolding through the windshield. What disturbed him was that he did not have a firm grip on any member of the "inner core." Three of the names on his list remained hidden, God only knew where, and the fourth was still innocent until proven guilty. No hard facts, only a phone number and a gut instinct that Fisher was part of the Jersey Colony conspiracy. He had to be absolutely certain, and most important, he desperately needed to pick up a thread to the next man.

Hagen stopped his mental wanderings, his eyes focused on the rearview mirror. A man in a blue officer's uniform was passing through the side entrance, the door held open by a five-stripe sergeant, or whatever specialist rating the Air Force gave its enlisted men these days. The officer was tall, athletically built, wore four stars on his shoulders, and was quite handsome in a Gregory Peck way. The sergeant accompanied him across a sidewalk to a waiting Air Force blue sedan and smartly opened the rear door.

Something about the scene snapped a string in Hagen's mind. He sat up straight and turned around to stare boldly out the side window. Fisher was in the act of bending over to enter the backseat of his car, holding a briefcase. That was it. The briefcase wasn't held by the handle as it would normally be carried. Fisher was clutching it like a football, under his arm and against the side of his chest.

Hagen had no qualms against changing his carefully laid out plan in midstream. He improvised on the spot, quickly forgetting about searching Fisher's command office. If his sudden creative spark didn't pan out, he could always go back. He started the engine and moved off across the parking lot behind the general's car.

Fisher's driver pulled across the intersection and turned onto Highway 94 under a yellow light. Hagen hung back until the traffic thinned. Then he ran the red light and accelerated until he was close enough behind the Air Force blue car to make out the driver's face in its rearview mirror. He held that position, watching to see if there was any eye contact. There was none. The sergeant was not a suspicious sort and never checked his tail. Hagen rightly assumed the man had no training in defensive driving tactics against possible terrorist attack.

After a slight bend in the highway the lights of a shopping center came into view. Hagen glanced at his speedometer. The sergeant was cruising along five miles an hour below the posted speed limit. Hagen pulled into the outer lane and passed. He speeded up slightly and then slowed down to turn into the driveway of the shopping center, gambling that one of the stores sold liquor, gambling that General Fisher hadn't forgotten his wife's instructions to buy the bottle of sherry.

The Air Force car drove on past.

"Damn!" Hagen muttered to himself. It struck him that any serviceman would have purchased liquor at his base post exchange, where it was sold for much less than at a retail store.

Hagen was stalled for a few seconds behind a woman trying to back out of a parking slot. When he finally broke free, he burned rubber swinging from the driveway onto the road. Luckily, Fisher's driver had caught a red light at the next intersection and Hagen was able to catch and pass him again.

He pressed the accelerator to the floor, trying to put as much distance as he could between them. In two miles he turned into the narrow road leading to the main gate of Peterson Air Force Base. He showed his security clearance to the Air Policeman standing stiffly, wearing a white helmet, matching silk scarf at the neck, and a black leather side holster that contained a pearl-handled revolver.

"Where can I find the PX?" Hagen asked.

The AP pointed up the road. "Straight ahead to the second stop sign. Then left toward the water tower. A large gray building. You can't miss it."

Hagen thanked him and moved away just as Fisher's car pulled up behind and was smartly waved on through the gate. Taking his time, he stayed within the base speed limit and eased into the post exchange parking area only fifty feet ahead of Fisher. He stopped between a Jeep Wagoneer and a Dodge pickup truck with a camper that effectively hid most of his car from view. He slipped from behind the wheel, turning off the lights but keeping the engine running.

The general's car had stopped, and Hagen unhurriedly approached it in a direct line, wondering if Fisher would get out and buy the sherry or send the sergeant to run the errand.

Hagen smiled to himself. He should have known it was a pre-ordained conclusion. The general, of course, sent the sergeant.

Hagen reached the car at nearly the same moment as the sergeant walked through the door into the PX. One quick scan to see if some bored soul waiting in a parked car might be idly staring in his direction or a shopper from the PX pushing a grocery cart close by. The old cliché "The coast is clear" ran through his mind.

Without the slightest hesitation or wasted movement, Hagen slipped a weighted rubber sap from a specially sewn pocket under one arm of his windbreaker, jerked open the rear car door, and swung his arm in a short arc. No words of greeting, no trivial conversation. The sap caught Fisher precisely on the point of his jaw.

Hagen snatched the briefcase from the general's lap, slammed the door, and walked casually back to his car. From start to finish the action had taken no more than four seconds.

As he drove away from the PX toward the main gate he ticked off the timing sequence in his mind. Fisher would be unconscious for twenty minutes, maybe an hour. Give the sergeant four to six minutes to find the shelf with the sherry, pay for it, and return to the car. Another five minutes before an alert was sounded, providing the sergeant even noticed the general had been mugged in the backseat.

Hagen felt pleased with himself. He would be through the main gate and halfway to the Colorado Springs airport before the Air Police realized what had happened.

• • •

An early snow started to fall over southern Colorado shortly after midnight. At first it melted when it met the ground, but soon an icy sheet formed, and then a white blanket began to build. Farther east the winds kicked up, and the Colorado Highway Patrol closed off the smaller county roads due to blizzard conditions.

Inside a small, unmarked Lear jet parked at the far end of the airport terminal, Hagen sat at a desk and studied the contents of General Fisher's briefcase. Most of it was highly classified material concerning day-to-day operations of the space center. One file of papers concerned the flight of the space shuttle *Gettysburg*, which had been launched from Vandenberg Air Force Base in California only two days before. He was amused to find amid the slots of the briefcase a pornographic magazine. But the champion prize was a black leather book that contained a total of thirty-nine names and phone numbers. No addresses or notations, only names and numbers segregated in three sections. The first section gave fourteen; the second, seventeen; and the third, eight.

None of them struck a chord with Hagen. It was possible they were simply friends and associates of Fisher's. He stared at the third list, the printing beginning to blur before his eyes from weariness.

Abruptly the top name leaped out at him. Not the surname, but the first name.

Startled, shocked that he had missed something so simple, a code so obvious that no one would consider it, he copied the list on his legal pad and matched up three of the names by adding the correct ones.

Gunnar Monroe/Eriksen
Irwin Dupuy
Leonard Murphy/Hudson
Daniel Klein
Steve Larson
Ray Sampson/LeBaron
Dean Beagle
Clyde Ward

Eight names instead of nine. Then Hagen shook his head, marveling at his slow grasp of the conspicuous fact that General Clark Fisher would hardly have included his own name on a telephone list.

He was almost home, but his elation was muted by fatigue; he'd had no sleep in the past twenty-two hours. The gamble to snatch General Fisher's briefcase had paid off with unexpected dividends. Instead of one thread, he held five, all the remaining members of the "inner core." Now all he had to do was match up the first names with the phone numbers and he would have a neat and tidy package.

All this was wishful thinking. He had made an amateur's error by mouthing off to General Clark Fisher, alias Anson Jones, over the telephone from Pattenden Lab. He'd tried to write it off as a shrewd move designed to goad the conspirators into making a mistake and give him an opening. But now he realized it was nothing but cockiness mixed with a healthy dose of stupidity.

Fisher would alert the "inner core," if he hadn't already done so. There was nothing Hagen could do now. The damage was done. He was left with no choice but to plunge ahead.

He was staring blankly into the distance when the aircraft pilot entered the main compartment from the cockpit. "Excuse me for interrupting, Mr. Hagen, but the snowstorm is expected to get worse. The control tower just informed me they're going to close down the airport. If we don't take off now, we may not get clearance till tomorrow afternoon."

Hagen nodded. "No sense in hanging around."

"Can you give me a destination?"

There was a short pause as Hagen looked down at his handwritten notes on the legal pad. He decided to leave Hudson until last. Besides, Eriksen, Hudson, and Daniel Klein or whoever, all had the same telephone area code. He recognized the code after Clyde Ward's name and settled on it simply because the location was only a few hundred miles south of Colorado Springs.

"Albuquerque," he said finally.

"Yes, sir," replied the pilot. "If you'll strap yourself in, I'll have us off the ground in five minutes."

As soon as the pilot disappeared into the control cabin, Hagen stripped to his shorts and dropped into a soft berth. He was dead asleep before the wheels left the snow-carpeted runway.

26

THE FEAR THAT the President's chief of staff, Dan Fawcett, inspired inside the White House was immense. His was one of the most powerful positions in Washington. He was the keeper of the sanctum sanctorum. Virtually every document or memo sent to the President had to go through him. And no one, including members of the cabinet and the leaders of Congress, gained entry to the Oval Office unless Fawcett approved it.

The times that someone, high-ranking or low, refused to take no for an answer were nonexistent. So he was uncertain how to react as he looked up from his desk into the smoldering eyes of Admiral Sandecker. Fawcett couldn't remember when he had seen a man seething with so much anger, and he sensed that the admiral was exerting every disciplined resource to hold it under control.

"I'm sorry, Admiral," said Fawcett, "but the President's schedule is airtight. There is no way I can squeeze you in."

"Get me in," Sandecker demanded through tight lips.

"Not possible," replied Fawcett firmly.

Sandecker slowly braced his arms and hands sacrilegiously on the paperwork strewn on Fawcett's desk and leaned over until only a few inches separated their noses.

"You tell the son of a bitch," he snarled, "that he just killed three of my best friends. And unless he gives me a damned good reason why, I'm going to walk out of here, hold a press conference, and reveal enough dirty secrets to scar his precious administration for the rest of his term. Am I getting through to you, Dan?"

Fawcett sat there, rising anger unable to overcome shock. "You'll only destroy your own career. What would be the sense?"

"You're not paying attention. I'll run it by you again. The President is responsible for the deaths of three of my dearest friends. One of them you knew. His name was Dirk Pitt. If it wasn't for Pitt, the President would be resting on the bottom of the sea instead of sitting in the White House. Now, I demand to know for what purpose Pitt died. And if it costs me my career as chief of NUMA, then you can damn well let it."

Sandecker's face was so close that Fawcett could have sworn the admiral's red beard had a life force all its own. "Pitt's dead?" he said dumbly. "I haven't heard—"

"Just tell the President I'm here," Sandecker cut in, his voice turned to steel. "He'll see me."

The news came so abruptly, so coldly, that Fawcett was startled. "I'll inform the President about Pitt," he said slowly.

"Don't bother. If I know, he knows. We're tuned into the same intelligence sources."

"I need time to find out what this is all about," Fawcett said.

"You don't have time," said Sandecker stonily. "The President's nuclear energy bill is coming up for a vote before the Senate tomorrow. Think what might happen if Senator George Pitt is told the President had a hand in murdering his son. I don't have to paint you a picture of what will happen when the senator stops throwing his weight in support of presidential policies and starts opposing them."

Fawcett was shrewd enough to recognize an ambush looming in the distance. He pushed himself back from the desk, clasped his hands and stared at them for a few moments. Then he stood and walked toward the hallway.

"Come with me, Admiral. The President is in a meeting with Defense Secretary Jess Simmons. They should be wrapping up about now."

Sandecker waited outside the Oval Office while Fawcett entered, pardoned himself, and spoke a few whispered words to the President. Two minutes later Jess Simmons came out and exchanged a friendly greeting with the admiral, followed by Fawcett, who motioned for him to come in.

The President came from behind his desk and shook Sandecker's hand. His face was expressionless, his body loose and composed, and his intelligent eyes locked on the hard, burning stare of his visitor.

He turned to Fawcett. "Would you please excuse us, Dan? I'd like to speak with Admiral Sandecker privately."

Wordlessly Fawcett stepped out and closed the door behind him.

The President gestured toward a chair and smiled. "Why don't we sit down and relax."

"I'd rather stand," Sandecker said flatly.

"As you wish." The President eased into an overstuffed armchair and crossed his legs. "I'm sorry about Pitt and the others," he said without preamble. "No one meant for it to happen."

"May I respectfully ask what in hell is going on?"

"Tell me something, Admiral. Would you believe that when I asked for your cooperation in sending out a crew on the blimp it went far beyond a mere hunt for a missing person?"

"Only if there was a solid explanation to back you up."

"And would you also believe that besides looking for her husband, Mrs. LeBaron was part of an elaborate deception to open a direct line of communication between myself and Fidel Castro?"

Sandecker stared at the President, his anger momentarily placed on hold. The admiral was not awed in the least by the nation's leader. He had seen too many Presidents come and go, seen too many of their human frailties. He could not think of one he'd have set on a pedestal.

"No, Mr. President, I can't buy that," he said, his tone sarcastic. "If my memory serves me, you have a very capable Secretary of State in Douglas Oates, who is backed by an occasionally efficient State Department. I'd have to say they're better equipped to communicate with Castro through existing diplomatic channels."

The President smiled wryly. "There are times negotiations between unfriendly countries must deviate from normal standards of statesmanship. Surely, you must believe that."

"I do."

"You don't involve yourself with politics, matters of state, Washington social parties, cronies or cliques, do you, Admiral?"

"That's right."

"But if I gave you an order, you'd obey it."

"Yes, sir, I would," Sandecker replied without hesitation. "Unless, of course, it was illegal, immoral, or unconstitutional."

The President considered that. Then he nodded and held out his hand toward a chair. "Please, Admiral. My time is limited, but I'll briefly explain what's going down." He paused until Sandecker was seated. "Now then...

"Five days ago a highly classified document written by Fidel Castro was smuggled out of Havana to our State Department. Basically it was a proposal for paving the way for positive and constructive relations between Cuba and America."

"What's so startling about that?" Sandecker asked. "He's been angling for closer ties since President Reagan kicked his ass out of Grenada."

"True," the President acknowledged. "Until now the only agreement we've reached over the bargaining table was a deal raising immigration quotas for dissident Cubans coming to America. This new stance, however, went way beyond. Castro wants our help in throwing off the Russian yoke."

Sandecker looked at him, skeptical. "Castro's hatred of the U.S. is an obsession. Why, hell, he still holds rehearsals for an invasion. The Russians aren't about to be shoved out. Cuba represents their only toehold in the Western Hemisphere. Even if they suffered from a moment of madness and yanked their support, the island would sink in an economic quagmire. Cuba can't possibly stand on its own feet, it doesn't have the resources. I wouldn't buy Fidel's act if Christ himself applauded."

"The man is mercurial," admitted the President. "But don't underestimate his intentions. The Soviets are buried in their own economic quagmire. The Kremlin's paranoia against the outside world has driven their military budget to astronomical heights they can no longer afford. Their citizens' standard of living is the worst of any industrialized nation. Their agricultural harvests, industrial goals, and oil exports have all fallen into the cellar. They've lost the means to continue pumping massive aid to the Eastern bloc countries. And in Cuba's situation, the Russians have reached a point where they're demanding more while supplying less. The days of the billion-dollar aid grants, soft loans, and cheap arms supplies have passed. The free ride is over."

Sandecker shook his head. "Still, if I were in Castro's shoes, I'd consider it a bad trade. There is no way Congress would vote billions of dollars to subsidize Cuba, and the island's twelve million people could barely exist without imported goods."

The President glanced at the clock on the mantel. "I've only got another couple of minutes. Anyway, Castro's greatest fear doesn't come from economic chaos or a counterrevolution. It comes from the slow, steady creep of Soviet influence into every corner of his government. The people from Moscow chip off a little here, steal a little there, waiting patiently to make the right moves until they can dominate the government and control the country's resources. Only now has Castro awakened to the fact that his friends in the Kremlin are attempting to steal the country out from under him. His brother, Raúl, was stunned when he became alerted to the heavy infiltration of his officer corps by fellow Cubans who had shifted their loyalty to the Soviet Union."

"I find that surprising. The Cubans detest the Russians. Their viewpoints on life don't mix at all."

"Certainly Cuba never intended to become a Kremlin pawn, but since the revolution thousands of Cuban students have studied in Russian universities. Many, rather than return home and work in a job dictated by the state, a job they might hate or which could lead to a dead end, were swayed by subtle Russian offerings of prestige and money. The canny ones, who placed their future above patriotism, secretly renounced Castro and swore allegiance to the Soviet Union. You have to give the Russians credit. They kept their promises. Using their influence over the Cuban government, they wove their new subjects into positions of power."

"Castro is still revered by the Cuban people," said Sandecker. "I can't see how they could stand by and watch him totally subjugated by Moscow."

The President's expression turned grave. "The very real threat is that the Russians will assassinate the Castro brothers and throw the blame on the CIA. Easy enough to do since the agency is known to have made several attempts on his life back in the sixties."

"And the Kremlin walks through the open door and installs a puppet government."

The President nodded. "Which brings us to his proposed U.S.–Cuban pact. Castro doesn't want to scare the Russians into making their move before we've agreed to back his play to boot them out of the Caribbean. Unfortunately, after making the opening gambit, he has stonewalled all replies from myself and Doug Oates."

"Sounds like the old stick-and-carrot routine to whet your appetite."

"The way I see it too."

"So where do the LeBarons fit into all this?"

"They fell into it," the President said with a touch of irony. "You know the story. Raymond LeBaron flew off in his antique blimp in search of a treasure ship. Actually, he had another target in mind, but that needn't concern NUMA or you personally. As fate would have it, Raúl Castro was on an inspection tour of the island's defense command complex outside of Havana when LeBaron was spotted by their offshore detection systems. The thought struck him that the contact might prove useful. So he ordered his guard forces to intercept the blimp and escort it to an airfield near the city of Cárdenas."

"I can guess the rest," said Sandecker. "The Cubans reinflated the blimp, hid an envoy on board, who was carrying the U.S.–Cuban document, and sent it aloft, figuring prevailing winds would nudge it toward the States."

"You're close," the President acknowledged, smiling. "But they didn't take any chances on fickle winds. A close friend of Fidel's and a pilot sneaked on board with the document. They flew the blimp to Miami, where they jumped into the water a few miles offshore and were picked up by a waiting yacht."

"I'd be curious to learn where the three bodies in the control cabin came from," Sandecker probed.

"A melodramatic display by Castro to prove his good intentions that I haven't got time to go into."

"The Russians haven't become suspicious?"

"Not yet. Their superior attitude over the Cubans prevents them from seeing anything resembling Latin ingenuity."

"So Raymond LeBaron is alive and well somewhere in Cuba."

The President made an open gesture with his hands. "I can only assume that's his situation. CIA sources report that Soviet intelligence demanded to interrogate LeBaron. The Cubans obliged and LeBaron hasn't been seen since."

"Aren't you going to even try to negotiate LeBaron's release?" asked Sandecker.

"The situation is delicate as it is without throwing him on the bargaining table. When we can nail down and sign the U.S.–Cuban pact, I have no doubt that Castro will take custody of LeBaron from the Russians and turn him over to us."

The President paused and stared at the mantel clock. "I'm late for a conference with my budget people." He stood up and started for the door. Then he turned to Sandecker. "I'll wrap this up quickly. Jessie LeBaron was briefed on the situation and memorized our response to Castro. The plan was to have the blimp return with a LeBaron on board. A signal to Castro that my reply was being sent in the same way his proposal was sent out. Something went wrong. You passed Jess Simmons on your way in. He briefed me on the photos taken by our aerial reconnaissance. Instead of stopping the blimp and escorting it to Cárdenas, the Cuban patrol helicopter fired upon it. Then for some unexplained reason the helicopter exploded, and they both crashed into the sea. You must realize, Admiral, I couldn't send rescue forces because of the sensitive nature of the mission. I'm truly sorry about Pitt. I owed him a debt I could never repay. We can only pray that he, Jessie LeBaron, and your other friends somehow survived."

"Nobody could survive a crash in the path of hurricane," Sandecker said caustically. "You'll have to pardon me, Mr. President, but even Mickey Mouse could have put together a better operation."

A pained expression lined the President's face. He started to say something, thought better of it, and pulled open the door. "I'm sorry, Admiral, I'm late for the conference."

The President spoke no more. He walked from the Oval Office and left Sandecker standing confused and alone.

27

THE WORST OF HURRICANE Little Eva skirted the island and turned northeast into the Gulf of Mexico. The winds dropped off to forty miles an hour, but another two days would pass before they were replaced by the gentle trade winds from the south.

Cayo Santa María seemed empty of any life, animal or human. Ten years earlier, in a moment of generous comradeship, Fidel Castro had deeded the island over to his Communist allies as a gesture of goodwill. He then slapped the face of the White House by proclaiming it as a territory of Russia.

The natives were quietly but forcefully relocated onto the mainland, and engineering units of the GRU (Glavnoye Razvedyvatelnoye Upravleniye, or Chief Intelligence Directorate of the Soviet General Staff), the military arm of the KGB, moved in and began building a highly secret underground installation. Working in stages and only under cover of darkness, the complex slowly took shape beneath the sand and palm trees. CIA spy planes monitored the island, but intelligence analysis failed to detect any defense installations or heavy shipment of supplies by sea or air. Enhanced photo examination showed little except a few eroding roads that seemingly went nowhere. Only as a matter of routine was the island studied, but nothing ever turned up that indicated a threat to United States security.

Somewhere beneath the wind-beaten island, Pitt awoke in a small sterile room on a bed with a goosedown mattress under a fluorescent light that blazed continuously. He could not recall if he had ever slept in a feather bed, but he found it most comfortable and made a mental note to look around for one, if and when he ever got back to Washington.

Apart from bruises, sore joints, and a slight throb in his head he felt reasonably fit. He lay there and stared at the gray-painted ceiling, recalling the night before: Jessie's discovery of her husband; the guards escorting Pitt, Giordino, and Gunn to an infirmary, where a female Russian doctor, who was built like a bowling pin, tended to their injuries; a meal of mutton stew in a mess hall that Pitt rated six points below an east Texas truck stop; and finally being locked in a room with a toilet and washbasin, a bed, and a narrow wooden wardrobe.

Slipping his hands under the sheet, he explored his body. Except for several yards of tape and gauze, he was naked. He marveled at the homely doctor's fetish for bandages. He swung his bare feet onto the concrete floor and sat there, pondering his next move. A signal from his bladder reminded him he was still human, so he moved over to the commode and wished he had a cup of coffee. They, whoever they were, had left him his Doxa watch. The dial read 11:55. Since he had never slept more than nine hours in his life, he rightly assumed that it was the following morning.

A minute later he leaned over the basin and splashed cold water on his face. The single towel was coarse and hardly absorbed the moisture. He went over to the wardrobe, pulled it open, and found a khaki shirt and pants on a hanger and a pair of sandals. Before he put them on he removed several bandages over wounds that were already beginning to scab, and flexed the newfound freedom of movement. After he dressed, he tried the heavy iron door. The latch was still locked, so he pounded on the thick metal panel, causing a hollow boom to reverberate around the concrete walls.

A boy who looked no older than nineteen and wearing Soviet army fatigues opened the door and stood back, aiming a machine pistol, no larger than an ordinary household hammer, at Pitt's midsection. He motioned down a long hall to the left, and Pitt obliged. They passed several other iron doors, and Pitt wondered if Gunn and Giordino were behind any of them.

They stopped at an elevator whose doors were held open by another guard. They entered and Pitt felt the slight pressure against his feet as the car rose. He glanced at the indicator above the door and noticed that it showed lights for five levels. A good-sized layout, he thought. The elevator came to a stop and the automatic doors glided open.

Pitt and his guard stepped out into a carpeted room with a vaulted ceiling. The two side walls held shelves stacked with hundreds of books. Most of the books were in English and many of them were by current bestselling American authors. A vast map of North America covered the entire far wall. The room looked to Pitt to be a private study. There was a big, antique carved desk whose marble top was strewn with current issues of the *Washington Post*, the *New York Times*, the *Wall Street Journal*, and *USA Today*. Stacked atop tables on each side of the doorway were piles of technical magazines, including *Computer Technology, Science Digest*, and the *Air Force Journal*. The carpet was burgundy red with six green leather chairs spaced evenly about its thick pile.

Maintaining his silence, the guard reentered the elevator and left Pitt standing alone in the empty room.

Must be time to observe the monkey, he mused. Pitt didn't bother to probe the walls for the lens to the video camera. There was little doubt in his mind that it was concealed in the room somewhere, recording his actions. He decided to try for a reaction. He swayed drunkenly for a moment, rolled his eyes upward, and then crumpled onto the carpet.

Within fifteen seconds a hidden door, whose edges perfectly matched latitude and longitude lines of the giant wall map, swung open and a short, trim man in an elegantly tailored Soviet military uniform walked into the room. He knelt down and peered into Pitt's half-open eyes.

"Can you hear me?" he asked in English.

"Yes," Pitt mumbled.

The Russian went over to a table and tilted a crystal decanter over a matching glass. He returned and lifted Pitt's head.

"Drink this," he ordered.

"What is it?"

"Courvoisier cognac with a sharp, biting taste," the Russian officer answered in a flawless American accent. "Good for what ails you."

"I prefer a richer, smoother Rémy Martin," said Pitt, holding up the glass. "Cheers."

He sipped the cognac until it was gone, then rose lightly to his feet, found a chair, and sat down.

The officer smiled with amusement. "You seem to have made a quick recovery, Mr...."

"Snodgrass, Elmer Snodgrass, from Moline, Illinois."

"A nice Midwestern touch," the Russian said, coming around and sitting behind the desk. "I am Peter Velikov."

"General Velikov, if my memory of Russian military insignia is correct."

"Quite correct," Velikov acknowledged. "Would you care for another cognac?"

Pitt shook his head and studied the man across the desk. He judged Velikov to be no taller than five foot seven, weighing about a hundred and thirty pounds, and somewhere in his late forties. There was a comfortable friendliness about him, and yet Pitt sensed an underlying coldness. His hair was short and black with only a touch of gray at the sideburns and receding around a peak above the forehead. His eyes were as blue as an alpine lake, and the light-skinned face seemed sculptured more by classic Roman influence than Slavic. Dress him in a toga and set a wreath on his head, Pitt imagined, and Velikov could have posed for a marble bust of Julius Caesar.

"I hope you don't mind if I ask you a few questions," said Velikov politely.

"Not at all. I have no pressing engagements for the rest of the day. My time is yours."

A look of ice glinted in Velikov's eyes for an instant and then quickly faded. "Suppose you tell me how you came to be on Cayo Santa María."

Pitt held out his hands in a helpless gesture. "No sense in wasting your time. I might as well make a clean breast of it. I'm president of the Central Intelligence Agency. My board of directors and I thought it would be a great promotional idea to charter a blimp and drop redeemable coupons for toilet paper over the length of Cuba. I'm told there's an acute shortage down here. Unfortunately, the Cubans didn't agree with our marketing strategy and shot us down."

General Velikov gave Pitt a tolerant but irritated look. He perched a pair of reading glasses on his nose and opened a file on his desk.

"I see by your dossier, Mr. Pitt—Dirk Pitt, if I read it right—that your character profile mentions a drift toward dry wit."

"Does it also tell you I'm a pathological liar?"

"No, but it seems you have a most fascinating history. A pity you aren't on our side."

"Come now, General, what future could a nonconformist possibly have in Moscow?"

"A short one, I'm afraid."

"I compliment your honesty."

"Why not tell me the truth?"

"Only if you're willing to believe it."

"You don't think I can?"

"Not if you adhere to the Communist mania of seeing a CIA plot under every rock."

"Seems you have a high disregard for the Soviet Union."

"Name one thing you people have ever done in the last seventy years to earn a humanity award. What is baffling as hell is why the Russians have never wised up to the fact they're the laughing stock of the world. Your empire is history's most pathetic joke. The twenty-first century is just around the corner and your government operates as though it never advanced past the nineteen-thirties."

Velikov didn't bat an eyelid, but Pitt detected a slight redness in his face. It was clear the general wasn't used to being lectured by a man he looked down upon as an enemy of the state. His eyes examined Pitt with the unmistakable gaze of a judge who was weighing a convicted murderer's life in the balance. Then his gaze turned speculative.

"I'll see that your comments are passed on to the Politburo," he said dryly. "Now if you're through with the speech, Mr. Pitt, I'd be interested in hearing how you came to be here."

Pitt nodded toward the table with the decanter. "I think I'd like that cognac now."

"Help yourself."

Pitt half filled his glass and returned to the chair. "What I'm about to tell you is the straight truth. I want you to understand I have no reason to lie. To the best of my knowledge I am not on any sort of intelligence mission for my government. Do you understand me so far, General?"

"I do."

"Is your hidden tape recorder running?"

Velikov had the courtesy to nod. "It is."

Pitt then related in detail his discovery of the runaway blimp, the meeting with Jessie LeBaron in Admiral Sandecker's office, the final flight of the *Prosperteer,* and finally the narrow escape from the hurricane, omitting any mention of Giordino's downing of the patrol helicopter or the dive on the *Cyclops.*

Velikov did not look up when Pitt finished speaking. He sifted through the dossier without a flicker of change in his expression. The general acted as if his mind were light-years away and he hadn't heard a word.

Pitt could play the game too. He took his cognac glass and rose from his chair. Picking up a copy of the *Washington Post,* he noted with mild surprise that the masthead carried that day's date.

"You must have an efficient courier system," he said.

"Sorry?"

"Your newspapers are only a few hours old."

"Five hours, to be exact."

The cognac fairly glowed on Pitt's empty stomach. The awkward consequences of his predicament mellowed after his third drink. He went on the attack.

"Why are you holding Raymond LeBaron?" he asked.

"At the moment he is a house guest."

"That doesn't explain why his existence has been kept quiet for two weeks."

"I don't have to explain anything to you, Mr. Pitt."

"How is it LeBaron receives gourmet dinners in formal dress, while my friends and I are forced to eat and dress like common prisoners."

"Because that is precisely what you all are, Mr. Pitt, common prisoners. Mr. LeBaron is a very wealthy and powerful man whose dialogue is most enlightening. You, on the other hand, are merely an inconvenience. Does that satisfy your curiosity?"

"It doesn't satisfy a thing," Pitt said, yawning.

"How did you destroy the patrol helicopter?" Velikov asked suddenly.

"We threw our shoes at it," Pitt fired back testily. "What did you expect from four civilians, one of whom was a woman, flying in a forty-year-old gas bag?"

"Helicopters don't blow up in midair for no reason."

"Maybe it was struck by lightning."

"Well, then, Mr. Pitt, if you were on a simple search mission to locate a clue to Mr. LeBaron's disappearance and hunt for treasure, how do you explain the report from the captain of the patrol boat, who stated that the blimp's control car was so shattered by shellfire that no one could have survived, and that a streak of light issued from the blimp an instant before the helicopter exploded, and that a thorough search over the crash site showed no signs of survivors? Yet you all appear like magic on this island in the middle of a hurricane, when the security patrols were taking shelter from the winds. Most opportune, wouldn't you say?"

"How do you read it?"

"The blimp was either remote controlled or another crew was killed by the gunners on board the helicopter. You and Mrs. LeBaron were brought close to shore by submarine, but during the landing everyone was thrown onto the rocks and injured."

"You get a passing grade for creativity, General, but you fail accuracy. Only the landing part is correct. You forgot the most important ingredient, a motive. Why would four unarmed castaways attack whatever it is you've got here?"

"I don't have the answers yet," said Velikov with a disarming smile.

"But you intend to get them."

"I'm not a man who accepts failure, Mr. Pitt. Your story, though imaginative, does not wash." He pressed a button on the desk intercom. "We'll talk again soon."

"When can we expect you to contact our government so they can begin negotiations for our release?"

Velikov gave Pitt a patronizing look. "My apologies. I neglected to mention that your government was notified only an hour ago."

"Of our rescue?"

"No, of your deaths."

For a long second it didn't dawn on Pitt. Then it slowly began to register. His jaw stiffened and his eyes bored into Velikov.

"Spell it out, General."

"Very simple," said Velikov in a manner as friendly as if he were passing the time of day with a mailman. "Whether by accident or by design, you have stumbled onto our most sensitive military installation outside the Soviet Union. You cannot be permitted to leave. After I learn the true facts, you will all have to die."

28

INDULGING IN HIS FAVORITE PASTIME—eating—Hagen stole an hour to enjoy a Mexican lunch of flat enchiladas topped with an egg followed by sopaipillas and washed down with a tequila sour. He paid the check, left the restaurant, and drove to the address assigned to Clyde Ward. His source with the telephone company had traced the number in General Fisher's black book to a public phone in a gas station. He marked the time. In another six minutes his pilot would call the number from the parked jet.

He found the gas station in an industrial area near the rail yards. It was self-serve, selling an unknown independent brand. He pulled up to a pump whose red paint was heavily coated by grime and inserted the nozzle into the car's fuel spout, careful to avoid looking toward the pay phone inside the station's office.

Shortly after landing at the Albuquerque airport, Hagen had rented a car and siphoned ten gallons of fuel from the tank so his pit stop would appear genuine. The trapped air pockets inside the tank gurgled and he screwed on the cap and replaced the nozzle. He entered the office and was fumbling with his wallet when the pay phone mounted on the wall began to ring.

The only attendant on duty, who was in the act of repairing a flat tire, wiped his hands on a rag and picked up the receiver. Hagen tuned in on the one-way conversation.

"Mel's Service.... Who?... There ain't no Clyde here.... Yeah, I'm sure. You got the wrong number.... That's the right number, but I've worked here for six years and I ain't never heard of no Clyde."

He hung up and stepped up to the cash register and smiled at Hagen. "How much you get?"

"Ten point two gallons. Thirteen dollars and fifty-seven cents."

While the attendant made change for a twenty, Hagen scanned the station. He couldn't help admiring the professionalism that went into setting up the stage, because that's what it was, a stage setting. The office and lube bay floors hadn't seen a mop in years. Cobwebs hung from the ceilings, the tools had more rust than oil on them, and the attendant's palms and fingernails didn't look as if they had ever seen grease. But it was the surveillance system that astounded him. His trained eye picked out subtly placed electrical wiring that didn't belong in a run-of-the-mill service station. He sensed rather spotted the bugs and cameras.

"Could you do me a favor?" Hagen ask the attendant as he received his change.

"Whatta you need?"

"I've got a funny noise in the engine. Could you take a look under the hood and tell me what might be wrong?"

"Sure, why not. Ain't got much else to do."

Hagen noticed the attendant's designer hair style and doubted if it had ever been touched by the neighborhood barber. He also caught the slight bulge in the pants leg, on the outer right calf just above the ankle.

Hagen had parked the car on the opposite side of the second gas-pump island away from the station building. He started the engine and pulled the hood latch. The attendant put his foot on the front bumper and peered over the radiator.

"I don't hear nothin'."

"Come around on this side," said Hagen. "It's louder over here." He stood with his back to the street, shielded from any electronic observation by the pumps, the car, and its raised hood.

As the attendant leaned over the fender and poked his head into the engine compartment, Hagen slipped a gun from a belt holster behind his back and pushed the muzzle between the man's buttocks.

"This is a two-and-a-half-inch-barreled combat magnum .357 shoved up your ass and it's loaded with wad cutters. Do you understand?"

The attendant tensed, but he did not show fear. "Yes, I read you, friend."

"And do you know what a wad cutter can do at close range?"

"I'm aware of what a wad cutter is."

"Good, then you know it'll make a nice tunnel from your asshole to your brain if I pull the trigger."

"What are you after, friend?"

"What happened to your phony jerkwater accent?" Hagen asked.

"It comes and goes."

Hagen reached down with his free hand and removed a small Beretta .38-caliber automatic from under the attendant's pants leg. "Okay, *friend,* where can I find Clyde?"

"Never heard of him."

Hagen rammed the muzzle of the magnum up against the base of the spine with such force the fabric on the seat of the attendant's pants split and he grunted in agony.

"Who are you working for?" he gasped.

"The 'inner core,'" answered Hagen.

"You can't be."

Hagen gave an upward thrust with the snub-nosed gun barrel again. The attendant's face contorted and he moaned as his lower body burned with the jarring pain.

"Who is Clyde?" Hagen demanded.

"Clyde Booth," the attendant muttered through clenched teeth.

"I can't hear you, friend."

"His name is Clyde Booth."

"Tell me about him."

"He's supposed to be some kind of genius. Invents and manufactures scientific gadgets used in space. Secret systems for the government. I don't know exactly, I'm only a member of the security staff."

"Location?"

'The plant is ten miles west of Santa Fe. It's called QB-Tech."

"What's the QB stand for?"

"Quarter Back," the attendant answered. "Booth was an all-American football player for Arizona State."

"You knew I would show up?"

"We were told to be on the lookout for a fat man."

"How many others positioned around the station?" asked Hagen.

"Three. One down the street in the tow truck, one on the roof of the warehouse behind the station, one in the red van parked beside the western bar and diner next door."

"Why haven't they made their move?"

"Our orders were only to follow you."

Hagen eased the pressure and reholstered his revolver. Then he removed the shells from the attendant's automatic, dropped it on the ground, and kicked it under the car.

"Okay," said Hagen. "Now walk, don't run, back inside the station."

Before the attendant was halfway across the station drive, Hagen had turned the corner a block away. He made four more quick turns to lose the tow truck and the van, and then sped toward the airport.

29

LEONARD HUDSON STEPPED OUT of the elevator that lowered him into the heart of the Jersey Colony headquarters. He carried an umbrella that was dripping from the rain outside, and a fancy briefcase of highly polished walnut.

He looked neither right nor left and acknowledged the greetings from his staff with a curt wave. Hudson was not the nervous type, nor was he a worrier, but he was concerned. The reports coming in from other members of the "inner core" spelled danger. Someone was methodically tracking each of them down. An outsider had breached their carefully devised cover operations.

Now the whole lunar base effort—the ingenuity, the planning, the lives, the money, and the manpower that had gone into the Jersey Colony—was in jeopardy because of an unknown intruder.

He walked into his large but austere office and found Gunnar Eriksen waiting for him.

Eriksen was sitting on a couch, sipping a cup of hot coffee and smoking a curved pipe. His round, unlined face wore a somber look and his eyes had a benign glow. He was dressed casually, but unrumpled, in an expensive cashmere sports jacket and a tan V-neck sweater over matching woolen slacks. He would not look out of place selling Jaguars or Ferraris.

"You talked to Fisher and Booth," said Hudson, hanging up the umbrella and setting the briefcase beside the desk.

"I have."

"Any idea who it might be?"

"None."

"Strange that he never leaves fingerprints," said Hudson, sitting on the couch with Eriksen and pouring himself a cup of coffee from a glass pot.

Eriksen sent a puff of smoke toward the ceiling. "Stranger yet that every image we have of him on videotape is a blur."

"He must carry some sort of electronic erasing device."

"Obviously not your ordinary private investigator," Eriksen mused. "A top-of-the-line professional with heavy backing."

"He knows his way around, produces all the correct identification papers and security clearances. The story he handed Mooney about being an auditor with the General Accounting Office was first-rate. I'd have swallowed it myself."

"What have we got on him?"

"Only a stack of descriptions that don't agree on anything except his size. They're unanimous in referring to him as a fat man."

"Could be the President has turned an intelligence agency loose on us."

"If that were the case," said Hudson doubtfully, "we'd be looking at an army of undercover agents. This man appears to work alone."

"Did you consider the possibility the President might have quietly hired an agent outside the government?" asked Eriksen.

"The thought crossed my mind, but I'm not completely sold on it. Our friend in the White House is tapped into the Oval Office. Everyone who calls or walks in and out of the executive wing is accounted for. Of course, there's always the President's private line, but I don't think this is the sort of mission he could instigate over the telephone."

"Interesting," said Eriksen. "The fat man started his probe at the facility where we first created the idea of the Jersey Colony."

"That's right," Hudson acknowledged. "He rifled Earl Mooney's office at Pattenden Lab and traced a phone call to General Fisher, even made some remark about you wanting me to pay for the airplane."

"An obvious reference to our advertised deaths," Eriksen said thoughtfully. "That means he's tied us together."

"Then he turned up in Colorado and mugged Fisher, stealing a notebook with the names and numbers of the top people on the Jersey Colony project, including those of the 'inner core.' Then he must have seen through the trap we laid to trail him from New Mexico and escaped. We got a small break when one our security men who was watching the Albuquerque airport spotted a fat man arrive in an unmarked private jet and take off again only two hours later."

"He must have rented a car, used some sort of identification."

Hudson shook his head. "Nothing of any use. He showed a driver's license and a credit card from a George Goodfly of New Orleans, who doesn't exist."

Eriksen tapped the ashes from his pipe into a glass dish. "Seems odd he didn't drive to Santa Fe and attempt to penetrate Clyde Booth's operation."

"My guess is he's only on a fact-finding hunt."

"But who is paying him? The Russians?"

"Certainly not the KGB," said Hudson. "They don't send subtle messages over the phone or move around the country in a private jet. No, this man moves fast. I'd say he's running on a tight deadline."

Eriksen stared into his coffee cup. "The Soviet lunar mission is scheduled to set down on the moon in five days. That has to be his deadline."

"I believe you may be right."

Eriksen stared at him. "You realize now that the power behind the intruder has to be the President," he said quietly.

Hudson nodded slowly. "I blinded myself to the possibility," he said in a distant voice. "I wanted to believe he would back the security of the Jersey Colony from Russian penetration."

"From what you told me of your meeting, he wasn't about to condone a battle on the moon between our people and Soviet cosmonauts. Nor would he be overjoyed to learn Steinmetz destroyed three Soviet spacecraft."

"The point that bothers me," said Hudson, "is if we accept the President's interference, why, with all of his resources, would he send only one man?"

"Because once he accepted the Jersey Colony as a reality, he realized our supporters cover his every move, and he rightly assumed we could throw a school of red herrings across our trail to mislead any investigation. A wise man, the President. He brought in a ringer from left field who cracked our walls before we knew what was happening."

"There may still be time to send him on the wrong scent."

"Too late. The fat man has Fisher's notebook," said Eriksen. "He knows who we are and where to find us. He is a very real threat. He started at the tail and now he's working toward the head. When the fat man comes through this door, Leo, the President will surely move to stop any confrontation between the Soviet cosmonauts and our people in the Jersey Colony."

"Are you hinting we eliminate the fat man?" asked Hudson.

"No," Eriksen replied. "Better not to antagonize the President. We'll merely put him on ice for a few days."

"I wonder where he'll turn up next," Hudson pondered.

Eriksen methodically reloaded his pipe. "He began his witch-hunt in Oregon and from there to Colorado and then New Mexico. My guess is his next stop will be Texas, at the office of our man with NASA in Houston."

Hudson punched a number on his desk phone. "A pity I can't be there when we snare the bastard."

30

PITT SPENT THE NEXT TWO HOURS on his back in bed, listening to the sounds of metal doors being opened and closed, tuning in on the footsteps heard outside his cell. The youthful guard brought lunch and waited while Pitt ate, making sure all the utensils were accounted for when he left. This time the guard seemed in a better humor and was unarmed. He also left the door open during the meal, giving Pitt a chance to study the latch.

He was surprised to see that it was an ordinary doorknob lock instead of a heavy-security or mortice throw bolt. His cell was never meant to serve as a jail. It was mostly likely intended as a storeroom.

Pitt stirred a spoon over a bowl of foul-smelling fish stew and handed it back, more interested in the closing of the door than eating slop that he knew was the first step of a psychological ploy to lower his mental defense mechanisms. The guard stepped back and yanked the iron door shut. Pitt cocked his ear and caught a single, decisive click immediately after the slam.

He knelt and closely examined the crack between the door and the strike. The gap was ⅙ inch across. Then he scoured the cell, searching for an object thin enough to slip between the crack so he could jimmy the latch.

The bunk supporting the down mattress was made of wood with grooved joints. No metal or hard, flat surface there. The faucets and spouts on the sink were ceramic and the plumbing underneath and in the toilet tank offered nothing he could mold with his hands. He got lucky with the wardrobe. Any one of the hinges would work perfectly, except he could not remove the screws with his fingernails.

He was pondering this problem when the door swung open and the guard stood in the entrance. His eyes cautiously scanned the cell for a moment. Then he brusquely motioned Pitt outside, led him through a maze of gray concrete corridors, stopping finally outside a door marked with the numeral 6.

Pitt was roughly shoved into a small boxlike room with a sickly stench about it. The floor was cement with a drain in its center. The walls were painted a dreary shade of red that ominously matched the pattern of stains that were splattered on them. The only illumination came from a dull yellow bulb hanging by a cord from the ceiling. It was the most depressing room Pitt had ever entered.

The only furniture was a cheap, deeply scarred wooden chair. But it was the man seated in the chair that Pitt's eyes focused on. The eyes that stared back were as expressionless as ice cubes. Pitt could not tell the stranger's height, but his chest and shoulders were so ponderous they seemed deformed, the look of a body builder who had spent thousands of hours of sweat and effort. The head was completely shaven, and the face might have been considered almost handsome but for the large misshapen nose that was totally out of place with its surroundings. He was wearing only a pair of rubber boots and tropical shorts. Except for a Bismarck moustache, he looked strangely familiar to Pitt.

Without looking up he began reading off a list of crimes Pitt was accused of. They began with violating Cuban air space, shooting down a helicopter, murdering its crew, working as an agent for the Central Intelligence Agency, entering the country illegally. The accusations droned on until they ended at last with unlawful entry into a forbidden military zone. The voice spoke in pure American with a trace of a Western accent.

"How do you respond?"

"Guilty as sin."

A piece of paper and a pen were held out by an enormous hand. "Please sign the confession."

Pitt took the pen and signed the paper against a wall without reading the wording.

The interrogator stared at the signature broodingly. "I think you've made a mistake."

"How so?"

"Your name is not Benedict Arnold."

Pitt snapped his fingers. "By God, you're right. That was last week. This week I'm Millard Fillmore."

"Very amusing."

"Since General Velikov has already informed American officials of my death," said Pitt seriously, "I fail to see any good of a confession.

Seems to me it's like injecting penicillin into a skeleton. What purpose can it possibly serve?"

"Insurance against an incident, propaganda reasons, even a bargaining position," answered the interrogator amiably. "There could be any number of reasons." He paused and read from a file on the desk. "I see from the dossier General Velikov gave me that you directed a salvage project on the *Empress of Ireland* shipwreck in the Saint Lawrence River."

"That is correct."

"I believe I was on the same project."

Pitt stared at him. There was a familiarity, but it wouldn't frame in his mind. He shook his head. "I don't recall you working on my team. What's your name?"

"Foss Gly," he said slowly. "I worked with the Canadians to disrupt your operations."

A scene burst within Pitt's mind of a tugboat tied to a dock in Rimouski, Quebec. He had saved the life of a British secret agent by braining Gly on the head with a wrench. He also remembered with great relief that Gly's back had been turned and he had not seen Pitt's approach.

"Then we've never met face to face," Pitt said calmly. He watched for a faint sign of recognition from Gly, but he didn't bat an eye.

"Probably not."

"You're a long way from home."

Gly shrugged his great shoulders. "I work for whoever pays top dollar for my special services."

"In this case the money machine spits out rubles."

"Converted into gold," Gly added. He sighed and pulled himself to a standing position and stretched. The skin was so taut, the veins so pronounced, they actually looked grotesque. He rose from the chair and looked up, the smooth dome of his head on a level with Pitt's chin. "I'd like to continue the small talk about past events, Mr. Pitt, but I must have the answers to several questions and your signature on the confession."

"I'll discuss whatever subject that interests you when I'm assured the LeBarons and my friends will not be harmed."

Gly did not reply, only stared with a look that bordered on indifference.

Pitt sensed a blow was coming and tensed his body to roll with it. But Gly did not cooperate. Instead, he slowly reached out with one hand and gripped Pitt at the base of the neck on the soft part of the shoulder. At first the pressure was light, a squeeze, and then a gradual tightening until the pain erupted like fire.

Pitt clutched Gly's wrist with both hands and tried to wrench away the ironlike claw, but he might as well have tried to pull a twenty-foot oak out of the ground by the roots. He ground his teeth together until he thought they would crack. Dimly through the bursting fireworks in his brain, he could hear Gly's voice.

"Okay, Pitt, you don't have to go through this. Just tell me who masterminded your intrusion on this island and why. No need to suffer unless you're a professional masochist. Believe me, you won't find the experience enjoyable. Tell the general what he wants to know. Whatever you're hiding won't change the course of history. Thousands of lives won't hang in the balance. Why feel your body being pulped day after day until all bones are crushed, all joints are cracked, your sinews reduced to the consistency of mashed potatoes. Because that is exactly what will happen if you don't play ball. You understand?"

The ungodly agony eased as Gly released his grip. Pitt swayed on his feet and stared through half-open eyes at his tormentor, one hand massaging the ugly bruise that was spreading on his shoulder. He realized that whatever story he told, true or fabricated, would never be accepted. The torture would continue until his physical resources finally gave in and numbed to it.

He asked politely, "Do you get a bonus for every confession?"

"I do not work on commission," said Gly with friendly humor.

"You win," said Pitt easily. "I have a low threshold of pain. What do you want me to confess to, attempting to assassinate Fidel Castro or plotting to convert Russian advisers to democrats?"

"Merely the truth, Mr. Pitt."

"I've already told General Velikov."

"Yes, I have your recorded words."

"Then you know that Mrs. LeBaron, Al Giordino, Rudi Gunn, and I were trying to find a clue to the disappearance of Raymond LeBaron while searching for a shipwreck supposedly containing treasure. What's so sinister about that?"

"General Velikov sees it as a front for a more classified mission."

"For instance?"

"An attempt to communicate with the Castros."

"Ridiculous is the first word that comes to mind. There must be easier ways for our governments to negotiate with each other."

"Gunn has told us everything," said Gly. "You were to head the operation to stray into Cuban waters, where you were to be captured by their patrol craft and escorted to the mainland. Once there, you were to turn over vital information dealing with secret U.S.–Cuban relations."

Pitt was genuinely at a loss. This was all Greek to him. "That has to be the dumbest cock-and-bull tale I've ever heard."

"Then why were you armed and able to destroy the Cuban patrol helicopter?"

"We carried no arms," Pitt lied. "The helicopter suddenly exploded in our faces. I can't give you a reason."

"Then explain why the Cuban patrol boat could find no survivors at the crash site."

"We were in the water. It was dark and the seas were rough. They didn't spot us."

"Yet you were able to swim six miles through the violent water of a hurricane, all four of you keeping together as a group, and landing intact on Cayo Santa María. How was it possible?"

"Just lucky, I guess."

"Now who's telling a dumb cock-and-bull tale?"

Pitt never got a chance to answer. Without a flicker of warning, Gly swung and rammed a fist into the side of Pitt's body near the left kidney.

The pain and the sudden understanding burst within him at the same time. As he sank into the black pool of unconsciousness he reached out for Jessie, but she laughed and made no effort to reach back.

31

A DEEP, RESONANT VOICE was saying something, almost in his ear. The words were vague and distant. An army of scorpions crept over the edge of the bed and began thrusting their poisoned tails in his side. He opened his eyes. The bright fluorescent light above blinded him, so he closed them again. His face felt wet and he thought he might be swimming and threw out his arms. Then the voice beside him spoke more distinctly.

"Lie easy, partner. I'm just sponging off your face."

Pitt reopened his eyes and focused them on the face of an older, gray-haired man with soft, concerned eyes in a warm, scholarly face. The eyes met his and he smiled.

"Are you in much pain?"

"It smarts a bit."

"Would you like some water?"

"Yes, please."

When the man stood up, the hair on his head nearly touched the ceiling. He produced a cup from a small canvas bag and filled it from the washbasin.

Pitt clutched his side and eased very slowly to a sitting position. He felt rotten and realized he was ravenously hungry. When was the last time he'd eaten? His drowsy mind couldn't recall. He accepted the water thankfully and quickly downed it. Then he looked up at his benefactor.

"Old rich and reckless Raymond, I presume."

LeBaron smiled tightly. "Not a title I'm fond of."

"You're not an easy man to locate."

"My wife has told me how you saved her life. I wish to thank you."

"According to General Velikov, the rescue is only temporary."

LeBaron's smile vanished. "What did he tell you?"

"He said, and I quote, 'You all have to die.'"

"Did he give you a reason?"

"The story he handed me was that we had stumbled into a most sensitive Soviet military installation."

A pensive look crossed LeBaron's face. Then he said, "Velikov was lying. Originally this place was built to gather communications data from microwave transmissions around the U.S., but the rapid development of eavesdropping satellites made it obsolete before it was completed."

"How do you know that?"

"They've allowed me the run of the island. Something impossible if the area was highly secret. I've seen no evidence of sophisticated communications equipment or antennas anywhere. I've also become friendly with a number of Cuban visitors who let slip bits and pieces of information. The best I can figure is that this place is like a businessmen's retreat, a hideaway where corporate executives go to discuss and plan marketing strategy for the coming year. Only here, high-ranking Soviet and Cuban officials meet to create political and military policy."

It was difficult for Pitt to concentrate. His left kidney hurt like hell and he felt drowsy. He staggered over to the commode. His urine was pink with blood, but not very much, and he didn't feel the damage was serious.

"We had best not continue this conversation," said Pitt. "My cell is probably bugged."

LeBaron shook his head. "No, I don't think so. This level of the compound wasn't constructed for maximum security detention because there is no way out. It's like the old French penal colony at Devil's Island; impossible to escape from. The Cuban mainland is over twenty miles away. The water teems with sharks, and the currents sweep out to sea. In the other direction the nearest landfall is in the Bahamas, a hundred and ten miles to the northeast. If you're thinking of escape, my advice is to forget it."

Pitt gingerly settled back on his bed. "Have you seen the others?"

"Yes."

"Their condition?"

"Giordino and Gunn are together in a room thirty feet down the corridor. Because of their injuries they've been spared a visit to room number six. Until now, they've been treated quite well."

"Jessie?"

LeBaron's face tensed very slightly. "General Velikov has graciously allowed us a VIP room to ourselves. We're even permitted to dine with the officers."

"I'm glad to hear you've both been spared a trip to room six."

"Yes, Jessie and I are lucky our treatment is humanly decent."

LeBaron's tone seemed unconvincing, his words spoken in a flat monotone. There was no light in his eyes. This wasn't the man who was famous for his audacious and freewheeling adventures and flamboyant fiascos in and out of the business world. He seemed completely out of character with the prodigious dynamo whose advice was sought by financiers and world leaders. He struck Pitt as a beaten farmer, forced off his land by an unscrupulous banker.

"And the status of Buck Caesar and Joe Cavilla?" Pitt asked.

LeBaron shrugged sadly. "Buck eluded his guards during an exercise period outside the compound and tried to swim for it, using the trunk of a fallen palm tree as a raft. His body, or what was left after the sharks were through with it, drifted onto the beach three days later. As for Joe, after several sessions in room six, he went into a coma and died. A great pity. There was no reason for him not to cooperate with General Velikov."

"You've never paid a visit to Foss Gly?"

"No, I've been spared the experience. Why, I can't say. Perhaps General Velikov thinks I'm too valuable as a bargaining tool."

"So I've been elected," said Pitt grimly.

"I wish I could help you, but General Velikov ignored all my pleas to save Joe. He is equally cold in your case."

Pitt idly found himself wondering why LeBaron always referred to Velikov with due respect to the Russian's military rank. "I don't understand the brutal interrogation. What was to be gained by killing Cavilla? What do they hope to get out of me?"

"The truth," LeBaron said simply.

Pitt gave him a sharp look. "The truth as I know it is, you and your team searched for the *Cyclops* and vanished. Your wife and the rest of us went after the shipwreck in hopes we could get a clue as to what happened to you. Tell me where it rings false."

LeBaron wiped newly formed sweat from his forehead with his sleeve. "No use in arguing with me, Dirk, I'm not the one who doesn't believe you. The Russian mentality thinks there is a lie behind every truth."

"You've talked with Jessie. Surely she explained how we happened to find the *Cyclops* and land on the island."

LeBaron visibly winced at Pitt's mention of the *Cyclops*. He suddenly seemed to recoil from Pitt. He picked up his canvas bag and pounded on the door. It swung open almost immediately and he was gone.

Foss Gly was waiting when LeBaron entered room six. He sat there, a brooding evil, a human murder machine immune to suffering or death. He smelled of decayed meat.

LeBaron stood trembling and silently handed over the canvas bag. Gly rummaged inside and drew out a small recorder and rewound the tape. He listened for a few seconds to satisfy himself that the voices were distinct.

"Did he confide in you?" asked Gly.

"Yes, he made no attempt to hide anything."

"Is he working for the CIA?"

"I don't believe so. His landing on the island was merely an accident."

Gly came from behind the desk and grabbed the loose skin on the side of LeBaron's waist, squeezing and twisting in the same motion. The publisher's eyes bulged, gasping as the agony pierced his body. He slowly sank to his knees on the concrete.

Gly bent down until he stared with frozen malignancy scant inches from LeBaron's eyes. "Do not screw with me, scum," he said menacingly, "or your sweet wife will be the next one who pays with a mutilated body."

32

IRA HAGEN THREW Hudson and Eriksen a curve and bypassed Houston. There was no need for the trip. The computer on board his jet told him all he needed to know. A trace of the Texas phone number in General Fisher's black book led to the office of the director of NASA's Flight Operations, Irwin Mitchell, alias Irwin Dupuy. A check of another name on the list, Steve Larson, turned up Steve Busche, who was director of NASA's Flight Research Center in California.

Nine little Indians, and then there were four...

Hagen's tally of the "inner core" now read:

Raymond LeBaron.............Last reported in Cuba.
General Mark Fisher.........Colorado Springs.
Clyde Booth...................Albuquerque.
Irwin Mitchell ....Houston.
Steve Busche..................California.
Dean Beagle (?)..............Philadelphia. (ID and location
                             not proven)
Daniel Klein (?)...............Washington, D.C. (ditto)
Leonard Hudson..............Maryland. (location not
                             proven)
Gunnar Eriksen...............Maryland. (ditto)

His deadline was only sixty-six hours away. He had kept the President advised of his progress and warned him that his investigation would be cutting it thin. Already, the President was putting together a trusted team to gather up members of the "inner core" and transport them to a location the President had yet to specify. Hagen's ace card was the proximity of the last three names on the list. He was gambling they were all sitting in the same basket.

Hagen altered his routine and did not waste time renting a car when his plane landed at Philadelphia International Airport. His pilot had called ahead, and a Lincoln limousine was waiting when he stepped down the stairway. During the twenty-four-mile drive along the Schuylkill River to Valley Forge State Park, he worked on his report to the President and formulated a plan to speed the discovery of Hudson and Eriksen, whose joint phone number turned out to be a disconnected number in an empty house near Washington.

He closed his briefcase as the car rolled past the park where George Washington's army had camped during the winter of 1777–78. Many of the trees still bore golden leaves and the rolling hills had yet to turn brown. The driver turned onto a road that wound around a hill overlooking the park and was bordered on both sides by old stone walls.

The historic Horse and Artillery Inn was built in 1790 as a stagecoach stop and tavern for colonial travelers and sat amid sweeping lawns and a grove of shade trees. It was a picturesque three-story building with blue shutters and a stately front porch. The inn was an original example of early limestone farm architecture and bore a plaque designating it as listed on the National Register of Historic Places.

Hagen left the limousine, climbed the steps to the porch furnished with old-fashioned rockers, and passed into a lobby filled with antique furniture clustered around a cozy fireplace containing a crackling log. In the dining room he was shown to a table by a girl dressed in colonial costume.

"Is Dean around?" he asked casually.

"Yes, sir," answered the girl brightly. "The Senator is in the kitchen. Would you like to see him?"

"I'd be grateful if he could spare me a few minutes."

"Would you like to see a menu in the meantime?"

"Yes, please."

Hagen scanned the menu and found the list of early American dishes to be quite tempting. But his mind didn't really dwell on food. Was it possible, he thought, that Dean Beagle was Senator Dean Porter, who once chaired the powerful Foreign Relations Committee and narrowly lost a presidential primary race to George McGovern? A member of the Senate for nearly thirty years, Porter had left an indelible mark on American politics before he had retired two years ago.

A baldheaded man in his late seventies walked through a swinging door from the kitchen, wiping his hands on the lower edge of an

715

apron. An unimpressive figure with a grandfatherly face. He stopped at Hagen's table and looked down without expression. "You wish to see me?"

Hagen came to his feet. "Senator Porter."

"Yes."

"My name is Ira Hagen. I'm a restaurateur myself, specializing in American dishes, but not nearly as creative as your recipes."

"Leo told me you might walk through my door," Porter said bluntly. "Won't you please sit down."

"You staying for dinner, Mr. Hagen?"

"That was my plan."

"Then permit me to offer you a bottle of local wine on the house."

"Thank you."

Porter called over his waitress and gave the order. Then he turned back to Hagen and looked him solidly in the eye. "How many of us have you tagged?"

"You make six," Hagen answered.

"You're lucky you didn't go to Houston. Leo had a reception committee waiting for you."

"Were you a member of the 'inner core' from the beginning, Senator?"

"I came on board in 1964 and helped set up the undercover financing."

"I compliment you on a first-rate job."

"You're working for the President, I take it."

"Correct."

"What does he intend to do with us?"

"Eventually hand out the honors you all so richly deserve. But his main concern is stopping your people on the moon from starting a war."

Porter paused when the waitress brought over a bottle of chilled white wine. He expertly pulled the cork and poured one glass. He took a large sip and swished the wine around in his mouth and nodded. "Quite good." Then he filled Hagen's glass.

"Fifteen years ago, Mr. Hagen, our government made a stupid mistake and gave away our space technology in a sucker play that was heralded as a 'handshake in space.' If you remember, it was a much publicized joint venture between American and Russian space programs that called for our Apollo astronauts to team up and meet with the Soyuz cosmonauts in orbit. I was against it from the beginning, but the event occurred during the détente years and my voice was only a cry in the wilderness. I didn't trust the Russians then and I don't trust them now. Their whole space program was built on political propaganda and damned little technical achievement. We exposed the Russians to American technology that was twenty years ahead of theirs. After all this time Soviet space hardware is still crap next to anything we've created. We blew four hundred million dollars on a scientific giveaway. The fact we kissed the Russians' asses while they reamed ours only proves Barnum's moral about 'one born every minute.' I made up my mind to never let it happen again. That's why I won't stand dumb and let the Russians steal the fruits of the Jersey Colony. If they were technically superior to us, there is no doubt in my mind they would bar us from the moon."

"So you agree with Leo that the first Russians to land on the moon must be eliminated."

"They'll do everything in their power to grab every scientific windfall from our moon base they can touch. Face reality, Mr. Hagen. You don't see our secret agents buying Russian high technology and smuggling it to the West. The Soviets have to rely on our progress because they're too stupid and nearsighted to create it on their own."

"You don't have a very high regard for the Russians," said Hagen.

"When the Kremlin decides to build a better world rather than divide and dictate to it, I might change my mind."

"Will you help me find Leo?"

"No," the senator said simply.

"The least the 'inner core' can do is listen while the President pleads his case."

"Is that why he sent you?"

"He hoped I could find all of you while there is still time."

"Time for what?"

"In less than four days the first Soviet cosmonauts land on the moon. If your Jersey Colony people murder them their government might feel justified in shooting down a space shuttle or the space lab."

The senator looked at Hagen, his eyes turning to ice. "An interesting conjecture. I guess we'll just have to wait and see, won't we?"

33

PITT USED THE CATCH from his watchband as a screwdriver to remove
the screws holding the hinges to the wardrobe. He then slid the flat
side of one hinge between the door latch and the strike. It was a
near perfect fit. Now all he had to do was wait until the guard showed
up with his dinner.

He yawned and lay on the bed, his thoughts turning to Raymond
LeBaron. His image of the famous publisher-tycoon was chipped and
cracked. LeBaron did not measure up to his hard reputation. He gave
the appearance of a man who was running scared. Not once did he
quote Jessie, Al, or Rudi. Surely they would have relayed a message
of encouragement. There was something very fishy about LeBaron's
actions.

He sat up at the sound of the door latch turning. The guard entered,
holding a tray in one hand. He held it out to Pitt, who set it on his
lap.

"What gourmet delight have you brought this evening?" Pitt inquired cheerfully.

The guard gave a distasteful twist of his lips and shrugged indifferently. Pitt couldn't blame him. The tray held a small loaf of doughy,
tasteless bread and a bowl of god-awful chicken stew.

Pitt was hungry, but more important he needed to keep his strength.
He forced the slop down, somehow managing to keep from gagging.
Finally he passed the tray back to the guard, who silently took it and
then pulled the door closed as he stepped into the corridor.

Pitt leaped from the bed, dropped to his knees, and slipped one
of the wardrobe hinges between the latch and the doorjamb, preventing the bolt from passing through the strike into the catch. In
almost the same motion he pressed his shoulder against the door and

tapped the second hinge on it to imitate the click of the latch snapping into place.

As soon as he heard the guard's footsteps fade down the corridor he eased open the door slightly, peeled a piece of tape from a bandage covering a cut on his arm, and stuck it over the latch shaft so the door would remain unlocked.

Removing his sandals and stuffing them into his waistband, he eased the door closed, taped a hair across the crack, and soundlessly padded down the empty corridor, pressing his body close against the wall. There was no sign of any guards or security equipment.

Pitt's first goal was to find his friends and plan an escape, but twenty yards down the corridor he discovered a narrow, circular emergency shaft with a ladder that led upward into darkness. He decided to see where it went. The climb seemed endless and he realized it was taking him past the upper levels of the underground facility. At last his groping hands touched a wooden cover above his head. He leaned his upper back against it and slowly applied pressure. The cover creaked loudly as it lifted.

Pitt sucked in his breath and froze. Five minutes came and went and nothing happened, nobody shouted, and when he finally eased the cover high enough, he found himself looking out across the concrete floor of a garage containing several military and construction vehicles. The structure was large, eighty by a hundred feet and perhaps fifteen feet to a ceiling supported by row of steel girders. The parking area was dark, but there was an office at one end whose interior was brightly lit. Two Russians in Army fatigues were sitting at a table playing chess.

Pitt snaked from the exit shaft, skirted behind the parked vehicles, and crawled under the windows of the office until he reached the main entry door. Coming this far from his cell was surprisingly easy but now defeat had arrived where he least expected it. The door was electric. There was no way he could activate it without alerting the chess players.

Staying in the shadows, he moved along the walls searching for another entrance. In his mind he knew it was a lost cause. If this building was on the surface it was probably another covered mound with the large vehicle entry door as the only means of getting in and out.

He made a complete circuit of the walls and returned to the spot where he started. Disheartened, he was about to give up when he looked upward and spotted an air vent mounted on the roof. It appeared large enough to squeeze through.

Pitt quietly climbed on top of a truck, reached over his head, and pulled himself onto a support girder. Then he inched his way about thirty feet to the vent and squirmed his way to the outside. The rush of fresh, humid air felt invigorating. He guessed that the dying wind of the hurricane was only blowing at about twenty miles an hour. The sky was only partially overcast and there was a quarter moon that provided enough visibility to vaguely make out objects within a hundred feet.

His next problem was to get beyond the high wall enclosing the compound. The guardhouse by the gate was manned, so there would be no repeat of his entry two nights ago.

In the end, luck came to his aid once again. He walked along a small drainage culvert that passed under the wall. He ducked under but was brought up short by a row of iron bars. Fortunately they were badly rusted from the tropical salt air and he easily bent them apart.

Three minutes later Pitt was well clear of the installation, jogging through the palm trees lining the sunken road. There were no signs of guards or electronic surveillance cameras and the low shrubs helped conceal his silhouette against the light-colored sand. He ran at an angle toward the beach until he was up against the electrified fence.

Eventually, he came to the section damaged by the hurricane. It had been repaired, but he knew it was the correct spot because the fallen palm tree that had caused the break was lying nearby. He dropped to his knees and began scooping the sand from under the fence. The deeper he dug the more the walls of his trench kept sliding and filling in the bottom. Nearly an hour passed before he formed a crater deep enough for him to wiggle on his back through to the other side.

His shoulder and kidney ached and he was sweating like a soaked sponge. He tried to retrace his steps to the landing site by the rocks on the beach. None of the landscape seemed the same under the dim light of the moon, not that he could recall how it looked when beaten flat by hurricane winds and with his eyes mostly closed.

Pitt wandered up and down the beach, probing between the rock formations. He was almost ready to give up and quit when his eye caught the moon's glint on an object in the sand. His hands reached out and touched the fuel tank of the inflatable boat's outboard motor. The shaft and propeller were buried in the sand about thirty feet from the high-tide line. He dug away the damp sand until he could pull the motor free. Then he hoisted it over his shoulder and began walking down the beach away from the Russian compound.

Pitt had no idea where he was going or where he was going to hide the motor. His feet dug into the sand and the burden of sixty pounds made it tough going. He had to stop every few hundred yards and rest.

He had walked about two miles when he met a weed-covered road that passed through several rows of deserted and decaying houses. Most of them were little more than shacks and they nestled around a small lagoon. It must have once been a fishing village, Pitt thought. He could not know it was one of the settlements whose residents had been forcefully uprooted to the mainland during the Soviet take-over.

He gratefully shrugged off the motor and began rummaging in the houses. The walls and roofing were made from corrugated iron sheets and scrap wood. Little of the furnishings remained. He found a boat pulled up on the beach, but any hope of using it was crushed. The bottom was rotted away.

Pitt considered building a raft, but it would take too long, and he couldn't run the risk of putting together something under the double handicap of working in darkness with no tools. The end result would not offer much peace of mind in rough water.

The luminous dial on his watch read 1:30. If he wanted to find and talk to Giordino and Gunn, he'd have to get a move on. He wondered what to do about fuel for the outboard motor, but there was no time to search now. He calculated it would take him a good hour to regain his cell.

He found an old cast-iron bathtub lying outside a collapsed shed. He placed the outboard motor on the ground and turned the tub upside down over it. Then he threw some tires and a rotting mattress on top and walked backward, brushing sand over his footprints with a palm frond until he stood a good seventy-five feet away.

Sneaking back in went more smoothly than sneaking out. All he had to remember was to restraighten the bars in the culvert. Belat-edly, he wondered why the island compound wasn't crawling with security guards, but then it came to him that the area was constantly overflown by American spy planes whose cameras had the uncanny ability to produce photographs that could read the name on a golf ball from ninety thousand feet.

The Soviets must have figured it was better to trade heavy security for the appearance of a lifeless, abandoned island. Cuban dissidents fleeing Castro's government would ignore it and any Cuban exile commandos would certainly bypass it for the mainland. With no one landing and no one escaping, the Russians had nothing to guard against.

Pitt dropped through the air ventilator and stealthily made his way back across the garage and down the exit shaft. The corridor was still quiet. He checked his door and saw the hair was still in place.

His plan now was to find Gunn and Giordino. But he didn't want to crowd his luck. Although their imprisonment was lax, there was always the problem of a chance discovery. If Pitt was caught outside his cell now, it would spell the end. Velikov and Gly were sure to keep him tightly locked away if they didn't outright execute him.

He felt he had to risk it. There might not be another opportunity. Any sound echoed throughout the concrete corridor. He would be able to hear footsteps in plenty of time to regain his cell if he didn't probe too far.

The room next to his was a paint locker. He searched it for a few minutes but found nothing useful. Two rooms across the corridor were empty. The third held plumbing supplies. Then he unlatched another door and found himself staring into the surprised faces of Gunn and Giordino. He quickly slipped inside, careful to keep the door's bolt from engaging.

"Dirk!" Giordino cried.

"Keep it down," Pitt whispered.

"Good to see you, buddy."

"Have you checked this place for ears?" Pitt asked.

"Thirty seconds after they pitched us in," answered Gunn. "The room is clean."

It was then Pitt saw the dark shades of purple around Giordino's eyes. "I see you've met with Foss Gly in room six."

"We had an interesting conversation. Pretty much one-sided, though."

Pitt looked at Gunn but saw no marks. "What about you?"

"He's too smart to beat my brains out," said Gunn with a taut smile. He pointed to his broken ankle. The cast was gone. "He gets his kicks by twisting my foot."

"What about Jessie?"

Gunn and Giordino exchanged grim looks. "We fear the worst," said Gunn. "Al and I heard a woman's screams late in the afternoon as we stepped out of the elevator."

"We were coming from an interrogation by that slimy bastard Velikov."

"Their system," explained Pitt. "The general uses the velvet glove and then turns you over to Gly for the iron fist treatment." He angrily paced the tiny room. "We've got to find Jessie and get the hell out of here."

"How?" asked Giordino. "LeBaron has paid a visit and made a point of stressing the hopelessness of escaping the island."

"I don't trust rich and reckless Raymond as far as I can throw this building," said Pitt acidly. "I think Gly has beaten him into jelly."

"Agreed."

Gunn twisted to his side in his bunk, favoring the broken ankle. "How do you intend on leaving the island?"

"I found and stashed the outboard motor for insurance if I can't steal a boat."

"What?" Giordino stared at Pitt increduously. "You walked out of here?"

"Not exactly a garden stroll," Pitt replied. "But I scouted an escape route to the beach."

"Stealing a boat is impossible," Gunn said flatly.

"You know something I don't."

"My smattering of Russian came in handy. I've begun developing a prison grapevine through the guards. I was also able to glean a few details from Velikov's papers in his office. One item of interesting information is that the island is supplied at night by submarine."

"Why so complicated?" muttered Giordino. "Seems to me surface transportation would be more efficient."

"That calls for docking facilities that can be seen from the air," explained Gunn. "Whatever is going on around here, they want to keep it damned quiet."

"I'll second that," said Pitt. "The Russians have gone to a lot of work to make the island look deserted."

"No wonder it shook them up when we walked through the front door," Giordino said thoughtfully. "That explains the interrogation and torture."

"All the more reason to make a break and save our lives."

"And alert our intelligence agencies," Gunn added.

"When do you plan to cut out?" asked Giordino.

"Tomorrow night, right after the guard brings dinner."

Gun gave Pitt a long, hard stare. "You'll have to go it alone, Dirk."

"We came together, we'll leave together."

Giordino shook his head. "You can't carry Jessie and us on your back too."

"He's right," said Gunn. "Al and I are in no condition to crawl fifty feet. Better we stay than foul your chances. Take the LeBarons and swim like hell for the States."

"I can't risk taking Raymond LeBaron into our confidence. I'm positive he would inform on us. He lied up a storm claiming the island is nothing but a businessmen's retreat."

Gunn shook his head in disbelief. "Whoever heard of a retreat run by the military that tortured its guests."

"Forget LeBaron." Giordino's eyes went black with fury. "But for God's sake, save Jessie before that son of a bitch Gly kills her."

Pitt stood there confused. "I can't go off and leave you two behind to die."

"If you don't," said Gunn gravely, "you'll die too, and no one will be left alive to tell what's happening here."

34

THE MOOD WAS SOMBER but softened by the long gap in time. No more than one hundred people had assembled for the early morning ceremony. In spite of the President's presence, only one network bothered to send a television crew. The small crowd stood quietly in a secluded corner of Rock Creek Park and listened to the conclusion of the President's brief address.

"...and so we have gathered this morning to pay belated tribute to the eight hundred American men who died when their troopship, the *Leopoldville*, was torpedoed off the port of Cherbourg, France, on Christmas Eve of 1944.

"Never has such a wartime tragedy been denied the honor it deserved. Never has such a tragedy been so completely ignored."

He paused and nodded toward a veiled statue. The shroud was pulled away, revealing a solitary figure of a soldier, standing brave with grim determination in the eyes, wearing a GI overcoat and full field gear with an M-1 carbine slung over one shoulder. There was a pained dignity about the life-sized bronze fighting man, heightened by the wave of water that lapped around his ankles.

After a minute of applause, the President, who had served in Korea as a lieutenant in an artillery company of the Marine Corps, began pumping hands with survivors of the *Leopoldville* and other veterans of the Panther Division. As he worked his way toward the White House limousine he suddenly stiffened when he shook the hand of the tenth man in line.

"A moving speech, Mr. President," said a recognizable voice. "May we talk in private?"

Leonard Hudson's lips were spread in an ironic smile. He bore no resemblance to Reggie Salazar the caddy. His hair was thick and gray and matched a Satan-style beard. He wore a wool turtleneck sweater under a tweed jacket. The flannel slacks were a dark coffee color and the English leather shoes were highly polished. He looked as though he had stepped out of a cognac ad in *Town & Country* magazine.

The President turned and spoke to a Secret Service agent who stood less than a foot from his elbow. "This man will be accompanying me back to the White House."

"A great honor, sir," said Hudson.

The President stared at him for a moment and decided to carry on the charade. His face broke into a friendly grin. "I can't miss an opportunity to swap war stories with an old buddy, can I, *Joe?*"

The presidential motorcade turned onto Massachusetts Avenue, red lights flashing, sirens cutting the rush-hour traffic sounds. Neither man spoke for nearly two minutes. At last Hudson made the opening play.

"Have you recalled where we first knew each other?"

"No," the President lied. "You don't look the least bit familiar to me."

"I suppose you meet so many people..."

"Frankly, I've had more important matters on my mind."

Hudson brushed aside the President's seeming hostility. "Like throwing me in prison?"

"I thought something more along the lines of a sewer."

"You're not the spider, Mr. President, and I'm not the fly. It may look like I've walked into a trap, in this case a car surrounded by an army of Secret Service bodyguards, but my peaceful exit is guaranteed."

"The old phony bomb trick again?"

"A different twist. A plastic explosive is attached to the bottom of a table in one of the city's four-star restaurants. Precisely eight minutes ago Senator Adrian Gorman and Secretary of State Douglas Oates sat down at that table for a breakfast meeting."

"You're bluffing."

"Maybe, but if I'm not, my capture would hardly be worth the carnage inside a crowded restaurant."

"What do you want this time?"

"Call off your bloodhound."

"Make sense, for Christ's sake."

"Get Ira Hagen off my back while he can still breathe."

"Who?"

"Ira Hagen, an old school chum of yours who used to be with the Justice Department."

The President stared unseeing out the window as if recalling. "Seems like a lifetime since I've talked to Ira."

"No need to lie, Mr. President. You hired him to track down the 'inner core.'"

"I what?" The President acted genuinely surprised. Then he laughed. "You forget who I am. With one phone call I could have the entire capabilities of the FBI, CIA, and at least five other intelligence services on your ass."

"Then why haven't you?"

"Because I've questioned my science advisers and some pretty respected people in our space program. They agreed unanimously. The Jersey Colony is a pipedream. You talk a good scheme, Joe, but you're nothing but a fraud who sells hallucinations."

Hudson was caught off base. "I swear to God, Jersey Colony is a reality."

"Yes, it sits midway between Oz and Shangri-la."

"Believe me, Vince, when our first colonists return from the moon, your announcement will fire the imagination of the world."

The President ignored the presumptuous use of his first name. "What you'd really like me to announce is a make-believe battle with the Russians over the moon. Just what is your angle? Are you some kind of Hollywood publicity flack who's trying to hype a space movie, or are you an escaped mental patient?"

Hudson could not suppress a flash of fury. "You idiot!" he snapped. "You can't turn your back on the greatest scientific achievement in history."

"Watch me." The President picked up the car phone. "Roger, pull up and stop. My guest is getting out."

On the other side of the glass divider, the Secret Service chauffeur raised one hand from the wheel and nodded in understanding. Then he notified the other vehicles of the President's order. A minute later the motorcade turned onto a quiet residential side street and stopped at the curb.

The President reached over and opened the door. "The end of the line, Joe. I don't know what your fantasy is with Ira Hagen, but if I hear of his death, I'll be the first to testify at your trial that you threatened his life. That is, of course, if your execution hasn't already been carried out for committing mass murder in a swank restaurant."

In an angry daze, Hudson slowly climbed from the limousine. He hesitated, bent half in, half out of the car. "You're making a terrible mistake," he said accusingly.

"It won't be a new experience," the President said, dismissing him.

The President leaned back in his seat and smiled smugly to himself. A masterful performance, he thought. Hudson was off balance and building barricades on the wrong streets. Moving up the unveiling of the *Leopoldville* memorial by a week was a shrewd move. An inconvenience to the veterans who attended perhaps, but a boon to an old spook like Hagen.

Hudson stood on a grassy parkway and watched the motorcade grow smaller before turning on the next cross street, his mind confused and disoriented. "Goddamned mud-brained bureaucrat!" he shouted in frustration.

A woman walking her dog on the sidewalk gave him a distasteful look indeed.

An unmarked Ford van eased to a stop, and Hudson climbed inside. The interior was plush with leather captain's chairs spaced around a highly polished redwood table. Two men, impeccably dressed in business suits, looked at him expectantly as he slipped tiredly into a chair.

"How did it go?" asked one.

"The dumb bastard threw me out," he said in exasperation. "Claims he hasn't seen Ira Hagen in years and couldn't care less if we killed him and blew up the restaurant."

"I'm not surprised," said an intense-looking man with a square red face and a condor nose. "The guy is pragmatic as hell."

Gunnar Eriksen sat with a dead pipe stuck between his lips. "What else?" he asked.

"Said he believed the Jersey Colony was a hoax."

"Did he recognize you?"

"I don't think so. He still called me Joe."

"Could be an act."

"He was pretty convincing."

Eriksen turned to the other man. "How do you read it?"

"Hagen is a puzzle. I've closely monitored the President and haven't detected any contact between them."

"You don't think Hagen was brought in by any of the intelligence directors?" asked Eriksen.

"Certainly not through ordinary channels. The only meeting the

President has had with any intelligence people was a briefing by Sam Emmett of the FBI. I couldn't get my hands on the report, but it had to do with the three bodies found in LeBaron's blimp. Beyond that, he's done nothing."

"No, he's most certainly done something." Hudson's voice was quiet but positive. "I fear we've underestimated his shrewdness."

"In what way?"

"He knew I would make contact again and warn him to call off Hagen."

"What brought you to that conclusion?" asked Condor Nose.

"Hagen," replied Hudson. "No good undercover operative calls attention to himself. And Hagen was one of the best. He had to have a good reason for advertising his presence by that phone call to General Fisher and his little face-to-face chat with Senator Porter."

"But what was the President's purpose in forcing our hand if he made no demands, no requests?" asked Eriksen.

Hudson shook his head. "That's what scares me, Gunnar. I can't see for the life of me what he had to gain."

Unnoticed in the downtown traffic, an old dusty camper with Georgia license plates kept a discreet distance behind the van. In the back, Ira Hagen sat at a small dining table with earphones and a microphone clamped to his head and uncorked a bottle of Martin Ray Cabernet Sauvignon. He let the opened bottle sit while he made an adjustment with the voice-tone knob on a microwave receiving set that was plugged into reel-to-reel tape decks.

Then he raised his headset to expose one ear. "They're fading. Close up a bit."

The driver, wearing a fake scraggly beard and an Atlanta Braves baseball cap, replied without looking back. "I had to drop off when a taxi cut in front of me. I'll make up the distance in the next block."

"Keep them in sight until they park."

"What's going down, a drug bust?"

"Nothing that exotic," replied Hagen. "They're suspected of working a traveling poker game."

"Big deal," grunted the driver without realizing the pun.

"Gambling is still illegal."

"So is prostitution and it's a helluva lot more fun."

"Just keep your eyes glued on the van," Hagen said in an official tone. "And don't let it get more than a block away."

The radio crackled. "T-bone, this is Porterhouse."

"I hear you, Porterhouse."

"We have Sirloin in visual but would prefer a lower altitude. If he should happen to merge with another similar-colored vehicle under trees or behind a building, we could lose him."

Hagen turned and stared upward from the camper's rear window at the helicopter above. "What's your height?"

"The limit for aircraft over this section of the city is thirteen hundred feet. But that's only half the problem. Sirloin is heading for the Capitol mall. We're not allowed to fly over that area."

"Stand by, Porterhouse. I'll get you an exemption."

Hagen made a call over a cellular telephone and was back to the helicopter pilot in less than a minute. "This is T-bone, Porterhouse. You are cleared for any altitude over the city so long as you do not endanger lives. Do you read?"

"Man, you must carry some kind of heavy weight."

"My boss knows all the right people. Don't take your eyes off Sirloin."

Hagen lifted the lid of an expensive picnic basket from Abercrombie & Fitch and pried open a can of goose liver pâté. Then he poured the wine and returned to listening in on the conversation ahead.

There was no doubt that Leonard Hudson was one of the men in the van. And Gunnar Eriksen was mentioned by his first name. But the identity of the third man remained a mystery.

Hagen was dogged by an unknown. Eight men of the "inner core" were accounted for, but number nine was still lost in the fog. The men in the van were heading... where? What kind of facility housed the headquarters for the Jersey Colony project? A dumb name, the Jersey Colony. What was the significance? Some connection with the state of New Jersey? There must be something that could be comprehended, that might explain how none of the information on the establishment of the moon base ever came to the attention of a high government official. Someone with more power than Hudson or Eriksen had to be the key. The last name on the "inner core" list perhaps.

"This is Porterhouse. Sirloin has turned northeast onto Rhode Island Avenue."

"I copy," answered Hagen.

He spread a map of the District of Columbia on the table and unfolded a map of Maryland. He began tracing a line with a red grease pencil, extending it as they crossed from the District into

Prince Georges County. Rhode Island Avenue became U.S. Highway 1 and swung north toward Baltimore.

"Got any idea where they're heading?" asked the driver.

"Not the slightest," replied Hagen. "Unless..." he muttered under his breath. The University of Maryland. Not twelve miles from downtown Washington. Hudson and Eriksen would hang close to an academic institution to take advantage of the research facilities.

Hagen spoke into the mike. "Porterhouse, keep a sharp eye. Sirloin may be heading for the university."

"Understood, T-bone."

Five minutes later the van turned off the highway and passed through the small city of College Park. Then after about a mile it pulled into a large shopping center, anchored on both ends by well-known department stores. The several acres of parking space were filled with shoppers' cars. All conversation had died inside the van, and Hagen was caught off guard.

"Damn!" Hagen swore.

"Porterhouse," came the voice of the helicopter pilot.

"I read you."

"Sirloin just pulled under a big projection in front of the main entrance. I have no visual contact."

"Wait until he appears again," ordered Hagen, "and then stay on his tail." He rose from the table and stepped behind the driver. "Pull up on his ass."

"I can't. There are at least six cars between him and me."

"Did anybody get out and enter the stores?"

"Hard to tell in the crush of people. But it looked like two, maybe three heads ducked out of the van."

"Did you get a good look at the guy who was picked up in town?" asked Hagen.

"Gray hair and beard. Thin, about five nine. Turtleneck, tweed coat, brown pants. Yeah, I'd recognize him."

"Circle the parking lot and watch for him. He and his pals may be switching cars. I'm going inside the shopping mall."

"Sirloin is moving," announced the helicopter pilot.

"Stick with him, Porterhouse," said Hagen. "I'm going off the air for a while."

"I read you."

Hagen jumped out of the camper and rushed through the crowd of shoppers into the interior mall. It was like looking for three needles hidden inside a straw in a haystack. He knew what Hudson looked like, and he had obtained photographs of Gunnar Eriksen, but either one or both might still be in the van.

Frantically he rushed from store to store, searching the faces, staring at any male head that showed above the mob of female shoppers. Why did it have to be a weekend, he thought. He could have shot a cannon through the mall at this early hour on a weekday and not hit anybody. After nearly an hour of fruitless searching, he went outside and stopped the camper.

"Spot them?" he questioned, knowing the answer.

The driver shook his head. "Takes me almost ten minutes to make a full circuit. The traffic is too thick and most of them drive like zombies when they're looking for a parking space. Your suspects could have easily come out another exit and driven off while I was on the opposite side of the building."

Hagen pounded his fist against the camper in frustration. He had come so close, so damned close, only to stumble at the finish line.

35

PITT SOLVED THE PROBLEM of sleeping without the constant glare from the fluorescent light by simply climbing on top of the wardrobe and disconnecting the tubes. He did not wake up until the guard brought him breakfast. He felt refreshed and dug into the thick gruel as if it were his favorite dish. The guard seemed upset at finding the light fixture dark, but Pitt simply held up his hands in a helpless gesture of ignorance and finished his gruel.

Two hours later he was escorted to General Velikov's office. There was the expected interminable wait to crack his emotional barriers. God, but the Russians were transparent. He played along by pacing the floor and acting nervous.

The next twenty-four hours were, to say the least, critical. He was confident that he could escape the compound again, but he could not predict any new obstacles that might be thrown in his way, or whether he would be capable of physical exertion after another interview with Foss Gly.

There could be no postponement, no falling back. He had to somehow leave the island tonight.

Velikov finally entered the room and studied Pitt for several moments before addressing him. There was a noticeable coldness about the general, an unmistakable toughness in his eyes. He nodded for Pitt to sit on a hard chair that hadn't been in the room during the last meeting. When he spoke, his tone was menacing.

"Will you sign a valid confession to being a spy?"

"If it will make you happy."

"It will not pay you to act clever with me, Mr. Pitt."

Pitt could not contain his anger and it overpowered his common sense. "I do not take kindly to scum who torture women."

Velikov's eyebrows raised. "Explain."

Pitt repeated Gunn's and Giordino's words as though they were his. "Sound carries in concrete hallways. I've heard Jessie LeBaron's screams."

"Have you now?" Velikov brushed at his hair in a practiced gesture. "It seems to me you should see the advantages of cooperating. If you tell me the truth, I might see my way clear to relax the discomfort of your friends."

"You know the truth. That's why you've reached a dead end. Four people have given you identical stories. Doesn't that seem odd to a professional interrogator like yourself? Four people who have been physically tortured in separate sessions, and yet give the same answers to the same questions. The utter lack of depth in the Russian mentality equals your fossilized infatuation with confessions. If I signed a confession for espionage, you'd demand another for crimes against your precious state, followed up with one for spitting on a public sidewalk. Your tactics are as unsophisticated as your architecture and gourmet recipes. One demand comes on the heels of another. The truth? You wouldn't accept the truth if it rose up out of the ground and bit you in the balls."

Velikov sat silent and examined Pitt with the contempt only a Slav could show to a Mongol. "I'll ask you again to cooperate."

"I'm only a marine engineer. I don't know any military secrets."

"My only interest is what your superiors told you about this island and how you came to be here."

"What are the percentages? You've already made it clear my friends and I are to die."

"Perhaps your future can be extended."

"Makes no difference. We've already told you all we know."

Velikov drummed his fingers on the desktop. "You still claim you landed on Cayo Santa María purely by chance?"

"I do."

"And you expect me to believe that of all the islands and all the beaches in Cuba Mrs. LeBaron came ashore at the exact spot—without any prior knowledge, I might add—where her husband was residing?"

"Frankly, I'd have a tough time believing it too. But that's exactly how it happened."

Velikov glared at Pitt, but he seemed to sense an integrity that he could not bring himself to approve. "I have all the time in the world, Mr. Pitt. I'm convinced you're withholding vital information. We'll talk again when you're not so arrogant." He pushed a button on his desk that summoned the guard. There was a smile on his face, but there was no satisfaction, no hint of pleasure. If anything, the smile was sad.

"You must excuse me for being so abrupt," said Foss Gly. "Experience has taught me that the unexpected produces more effective results than lengthy anticipation."

No word had been spoken when Pitt entered room six. He had taken only one step over the threshold when Gly, who was standing behind the half-opened door, struck him in the small of his back just above the kidney. He gasped in agony and nearly blacked out but somehow remained standing.

"So, Mr. Pitt, now that I have your attention, perhaps there is something you wish to say to me."

"Did anybody ever tell you you're a psycho case?" Pitt muttered through pressed lips.

He saw the fist lashing out, expected it, and rolled with the punch, reeling backward into a wall and melting to the floor, feigning unconsciousness. He tasted the blood inside his mouth and felt a numbness creeping over the left side of his face. He kept his eyes closed and lay limp. He had to feel his way with this sadistic hulk of slime, assess Gly's reaction to answers and attitude, and predict when and where the next blow would strike. There would be no stopping the brutality. His only objective was to survive the interrogation without a crippling injury.

Gly went over to a dirty washbasin, filled a bucket of water, and splashed it on Pitt. "Come now, Mr. Pitt. If I'm any judge of men, you can take a punch better than that."

Pitt struggled to his hands and knees, spit blood on the cement floor, and groaned convincingly, almost pitiable. "I can't tell you any more than I already have," he mumbled.

Gly picked him up as if he were a small child and dropped him in a chair. Out of the corner of one eye Pitt caught Gly's right fist coming at him in a vicious swing. He rode the impact as best he could, catching the blow just above the cheekbone under the temple. For a few seconds he absorbed the stunning pain and then pretended to pass out again.

Another bucket of water and he went through his moaning routine. Gly leaned down until they were face to face. "Who are you working for?"

Pitt raised his hands and clutched his throbbing head. "I was hired by Jessie LeBaron to find out what happened to her husband."

"You landed from a submarine."

"We left the Florida Keys in a blimp."

"Your purpose in coming here was to gather information on the transfer of power in Cuba."

Pitt furrowed his brow in confusion. "Transfer of power? I don't know what you're talking about."

This time Gly struck Pitt in the upper stomach, knocking every cubic inch of wind from him. Then he calmly sat down and watched the reaction.

Pitt went rigid as he fought for breath. He felt as if his heart had stopped. He could taste the bile in his throat, feel the sweat seep from his forehead, and his lungs seemed to be twisted in knots. The walls of the room wavered and swam before his eyes. Gly looked to be smiling wickedly at the end of a long tunnel.

"What were your orders once you arrived on Cayo Santa María?"

"No orders," Pitt rasped.

Gly rose and approached to strike again. Pitt drunkenly came to his feet, swayed for a moment, and began to sag, his head drooping to one side. He had Gly's measure now. He recognized a weak point. Like most sadists, Gly was basically a coward. He would flinch and be thrown off his track if he was evenly matched.

Gly flexed his body to swing, but suddenly froze in stunned astonishment. Bringing up his fist from the floor and pivoting his shoulder, Pitt threw a right-hand cross that carried every ounce of power he could muster. He connected with Gly's nose, mashing the cartilage and breaking the bone. Then he followed up with two left jabs and a solid hook to the body. He might as well have attacked the cornerstone of the Empire State Building.

Any other man would have fallen flat on his back. Gly staggered back a few feet and stood there with his face slowly reddening in rage. The blood streamed from his nose but he took no notice of it. He raised one fist and shook it at Pitt. "I'll kill you for that," he said.

"Stick it in your ear," Pitt replied sullenly. He grabbed the chair and threw it across the room. Gly merely smashed it aside with his arm. Pitt caught the shift of the eyes and realized his whiplash speed was about to lose out to brute strength.

Gly tore the washbasin from the wall, literally ripped it from its plumbing, and lifted it over his head. He took three steps and heaved it in Pitt's direction. Pitt jumped sideways and ducked around in one convulsive motion. As the sink sailed toward him like a safe falling from a high building, he knew his reaction came a split second too late. He threw up his hands instinctively in a hopeless gesture to ward off the flying mass of iron and porcelain.

Pitt's salvation came from the door. The latch caught the main crush from one corner of the washbasin and was smashed out of its catch. The door burst open and Pitt was knocked backward into the hallway, crashing in a heap at the feet of the startled guard. A shooting pain in his groin and right arm compounded the agonies already piercing his side and head. Gray-faced, waves of nausea sweeping over him, he shook away the beckoning unconsciousness and came to his feet, his hands spread on the wall for support.

Gly tore the sink from the doorway where it had become jammed and stared at Pitt with a look that could only be described as murderous. "You're a dead man, Pitt. You're going to die slowly, an inch at a time, begging to be put out of your agony. The next time we meet I'll snap every bone in your body and tear your heart out."

There was no fear in Pitt's eyes. The pain was draining away, to be replaced with elation. He had survived. He hurt, but the way was clear.

"The next time we meet," he said vengefully, "I'll carry a big club."

36

PITT SLEPT after the guard helped him back to his cell. When he woke up it was three hours later. He lay there for several minutes until his mind slowly shifted into gear. His body and face were an unending sea of contusions, but no bones were broken. He had survived.

He sat up and swung his feet to the floor, waiting for a few moments of dizziness to pass. He pushed himself to his feet and began doing stretching exercises to ease the stiffness. A wave of weakness swept over him, but he willed himself to reject it, continuing the drill until his muscles and joints became limber.

The guard came and went with dinner, and Pitt adroitly jammed the latch again, a maneuver he had honed so there would be no fumbling, no last-minute bungle. He paused, and hearing no footsteps or voices, stepped into the corridor.

Time was a luxury. There was too much to accomplish and too few hours of darkness to manage it. He regretfully wished he could say his farewells to Giordino and Gunn, but every minute he lingered in the compound depleted his odds of success. The first order of business was to find Jessie and take her with him.

She was behind the fifth door he tried, lying on the concrete floor with nothing under her but a dirty blanket. Her naked body was completely unmarked, but her once lovely face was grotesquely swollen with purplish bruises. Gly had shrewdly worked his evil by humiliating her virtue and brutalizing a beautiful woman's most valued asset—her face.

Pitt bent over and cradled her head in his arms, his expression tender, but his eyes insane with rage. He was consumed with revenge. He shook with a madness for savage vengeance that went far beyond anything he had experienced before. He gritted his teeth and gently shook her awake.

"Jessie. Jessie, can you hear me?"

Her mouth trembled open as her eyes focused on him. "Dirk," she moaned. "Is it you?"

"Yes, I'm taking you out of here."

"Taking...how?"

"I've found a way for us to escape the compound."

"But the island. Raymond said it's impossible to escape from the island."

"I've hidden the outboard motor from the inflatable boat. If I can build a small raft—"

"No!" she whispered adamantly.

She struggled to sit up, a look of concentration crossing the swollen mask that was her face. He lightly gripped her by the shoulders and held her down.

"Don't move," he said.

"You must go alone," she said.

"I won't leave you like this."

She shook her head weakly. "No. I would only increase your chances of getting caught."

"Sorry," Pitt said flatly. "Like it or not, you're coming."

"Don't you understand," she pleaded. "You're the only hope for saving all of us. If you make it back to the States and tell the President what's happening here, Velikov will have to keep us alive."

"What does the President have to do with this?"

"More than you know."

"Then Velikov was right. There is a conspiracy."

"Don't waste time conjecturing. Go, please go. By saving yourself you can save all of us."

Pitt felt an overwhelming surge of admiration for Jessie. She looked like a discarded doll now, battered and helpless, but he realized her outer beauty was matched by an inner one that was brave and resolute. He leaned over and kissed her lightly on puffed and split lips.

"I'll make it," he said confidently. "Promise me you'll hang on till I get back."

She tried to smile, but her mouth couldn't respond. "You crazy clown. You can't return to Cuba."

"Watch me."

"Good luck," she murmured softly. "Forgive me for messing up your life."

Pitt grinned, but the tears were welling in his eyes. "That's what men like about women. They never let us get bored."

739

He kissed her again on the forehead and turned away, his tanned fists white-knuckled by his side.

The climb up the emergency-shaft ladder made Pitt's arms ache, and when he reached the top he rested for a minute before pushing the lid aside and crouching in the darkness of the garage. The two soldiers were still engaged in a game of chess. It seemed to be a nightly routine to pass the boring hours of standby duty. They seldom bothered to glance at the vehicles parked outside their office. There was no reason to anticipate trouble. They were probably mechanics, Pitt reasoned, not security guards.

He reconnoitered the garage area: tool benches, lubrication racks, oil and parts storage, trucks, and construction equipment. The trucks had spare five-gallon fuel cans attached to their beds. Pitt lightly tapped the cans until he found one that was full. The rest were all half empty or less. He groped around a tool bench until he found a rubber tube and used it to siphon gas from one of the truck's tanks. Two cans containing ten gallons were all he could carry. The problem he faced now was getting them through the vent in the roof.

Pitt took a towrope that was hanging from one wall and tied the ends to the handles on the gas cans. Holding the middle in a loop, he climbed to the support girders. Slowly, watching to see that the mechanics kept their attention on the chess game, he pulled the cans to the roof one at a time and pushed them ahead of him into the vent.

In another two minutes he was lugging them across the yard into the culvert that ran under the wall. He quickly spread the bars apart and hurried outside.

The sky was clear and the quarter-moon floated in a sea of stars. There was only a whisper of wind and the night air was cool. He fervently hoped the sea was calm.

For no particular reason he skirted the opposite side of the road this time. It was slow going. The heavy cans soon made his arms feel as though they were separating at the joints. His feet sank into the soft sand, and he had to stop every two hundred yards to catch his breath and allow the growing ache in his hands and arms to subside.

Pitt tripped and sprawled on the edge of a wide clearing surrounded by a thick grove of palm trees, so thick their trunks almost touched each other. He reached out and swept around with his hands. They touched a metal network that blended into the sand and became nearly invisible.

Curious, he left the gas cans and crawled cautiously around the edge of the clearing. The metal grid rose two inches off the ground and extended across the entire diameter. The center dropped away until it became concave like a bowl. He ran his hands over the trunks of the palm trees circling the rim.

They were fake. The trunks and fronds were constructed out of aluminum tubes and covered with realistic sheathing made from sanded plastic. There were over fifty of them, painted with camouflage to deceive American spy planes and their penetrating cameras.

The bowl was a giant dish-shaped radio and television antenna and the bogus palm trees were hydraulic arms that raised and lowered it. Pitt was stunned at the implication of what he had accidentally discovered. He knew now that buried under the sands of the island was a vast communications center.

But for exactly what purpose?

Pitt had no time to reflect. But he was determined more than ever to get free. He continued walking in the shadows. The village was farther than he remembered. He was a mass of sweat and panted heavily from exhaustion when he finally stumbled into the yard where he'd hidden the outboard motor under the bathtub. He thankfully dropped the gas cans and lay down on the old mattress and dozed for an hour.

Although he could not afford the time, the short rest refreshed him considerably. It also allowed his mind to create. An idea crystallized that was so incredibly simple in concept he couldn't believe he hadn't thought of it before.

He carried the gas cans down to the lagoon. Then he returned for the outboard. Looking through piles of trash, he located a short plank that showed no rot. The last chore was the hardest. Necessity was the mother of invention, Pitt kept telling himself.

Forty-five minutes later, he had dragged the old bathtub from its resting place in the yard down the road to the water's edge.

Using the plank as a transom, Pitt bolted the outboard to the rear of the tub. Next he cleaned out the fuel filter and blew out the lines. A piece of tin bent in a cone served as a funnel to fill the outboard's tank. By holding his thumb over the bottom hole he could also use it for a bailing can. His final act before stuffing a rag plug in the drain was to knock off the bathtub's four webbed feet with an iron bar.

He pulled at the starter cord twelve times before the motor sputtered, caught, and began to purr. He shoved the tub into deeper water until it floated. Then he climbed in. The ballast weight of his body and the two full gas cans made it surprisingly stable. He lowered the propeller shaft into the water and pushed the gear lever to Forward.

The oddball craft slowly moved out into the lagoon and headed for the main channel. A shaft of moonlight showed the sea was calm, the swells no more than two feet. Pitt concentrated on the surf. He had to pass through the breaking waves and place as much distance between himself and the island by sunrise as possible.

He slowed the motor and timed the breakers, counting them. Nine heavies crashed one behind the other, leaving a long trough separating the tenth. Pitt pushed the throttle to Full and settled in the stern of the tub. The next wave was low and crashed immediately in front of him. He took the impact of the churning foam bow-on and plowed through. The tub staggered, then the propeller bit the water and it surged over the crest of the following wave before it curled.

Pitt let out a hoarse shout as he broke free. The worst was over. He knew he could only be discovered by sheer accident. The bathtub was too small to be picked up by radar. He eased up on the throttle to conserve the motor and the fuel. Dragging his hand in the water, he guessed his speed at about four knots. He should be well clear of Cuban waters by morning.

He looked up at the heavens, took his bearings, picked out a star to steer by, and set a course for the Bahama Channel.

PART III

Selenos 8

37

WITH A FIREBALL BRIGHTER than the Siberian sun, Selenos 8 rose into a chilly blue sky carrying the 110-ton manned lunar station. The super rocket and four strap-on boosters, generating 14 million pounds of thrust, threw out a tail of orange-yellow flame 1,000 feet long and 300 feet wide. White smoke burst around the launch pad and the rumble from the engines rattled glass twelve miles away. At first it lifted so ponderously that it hardly seemed to be moving at all. Then it picked up speed and thundered skyward.

Soviet President Antonov observed the liftoff from an armored glass bunker through a pair of large binoculars mounted on a tripod. Sergei Kornilov and General Yasenin stood beside him, intently monitoring voice communications between the cosmonauts and the space control center.

"An inspiring sight," Antonov muttered in awe.

"A textbook launch," Kornilov said. "They'll reach escape velocity in four minutes."

"Does all go well?"

"Yes, Comrade President. All systems are functioning normally. And they are exactly on track."

Antonov gazed at the long tongue of flame until it finally vanished. Only then did he sigh and step away from the binoculars. "Well, gentlemen, this space spectacular should take the world's eyes off the next American shuttle flight to their new orbital station."

Yasenin nodded in agreement and gripped Kornilov's shoulder.

"My congratulations, Sergei. You stole the Yankee triumph for the Soviet Union."

"No brilliance on my part," said Kornilov. "Because of orbital mechanics, our lunar launch window happened to be open for an advantageous shot several hours ahead of their scheduled launch."

Antonov stared into the sky as if mesmerized. "I assume American intelligence isn't privy to the fact our cosmonauts are not what they seem."

"A flawless deception," Yasenin said without reservation. "The switch of five space scientists for specially trained soldiers shortly before liftoff went smoothly."

"I hope we can say the same about the crash program to replace test equipment with weapons," said Kornilov. "The scientists whose experiments were canceled nearly caused a riot. And the engineers, who were ordered to redesign the interior of the station to accommodate new weight factors and weapon storage requirements, became angry at not being told the reason behind the last-minute changes. Their displeasure will most certainly be leaked."

"Don't lose any sleep over it," Yasenin laughed. "The American space authorities will suspect nothing until communication with their precious moon base goes dead."

"Who is in command of our assault team?" asked Antonov.

"Major Grigory Leuchenko. An expert on guerrilla warfare. The major won many victories against the rebels in Afghanistan. I can personally vouch for his qualities as a loyal and outstanding soldier."

Antonov nodded thoughtfully. "A good choice, General. He should find the lunar surface little different from that of Afghanistan."

"There is no question that Major Leuchenko will conduct a successful operation."

"You forget the American astronauts, General," said Kornilov.

"What about them?"

"The photographs demonstrate they have weapons too. I pray they are not fanatics who will wage a strong fight to protect their facility."

Yasenin smiled indulgently. "Pray, Sergei? Pray to whom? Certainly not to any God. He won't help the Americans once Leuchenko and his men begin their attack. The outcome is a foregone conclusion. Scientists cannot stand up against professional soldiers trained to kill."

"Do not underrate them. That's all I have to say."

"Enough!" Antonov said loudly. "I'll hear no more of this defeatist talk. Major Leuchenko has the double advantage of surprise and superior weaponry. Less than sixty hours from now the first real battle for space will begin. And I do not expect the Soviet Union to lose it."

In Moscow, Vladimir Polevoi sat at his desk in the KGB center on Dzerzhinski Square, reading a report from General Velikov. He did not glance up as Lyev Maisky strode into the room and sat down without an invitation. Maisky's face was common, blank and one-dimensional like his personality. He was Polevoi's deputy head of the First Chief Directorate, the foreign operations arm of the KGB. Maisky's relations with Polevoi were restrained, but they complemented each other.

Finally, Polevoi's eyes bored through Maisky. "I'd like an explanation."

"The LeBarons' presence was unforeseen," Maisky said tersely.

"Mrs. LeBaron and her crew of treasure hunters, perhaps, but certainly not her husband. Why did Velikov take him from the Cubans?"

"The general thought Raymond LeBaron might be a useful pawn in negotiations with the U.S. State Department after the Castros were removed."

"His good intentions have made for a dangerous game," said Polevoi.

"Velikov assures me that LeBaron is kept under strict security and fed false information."

"Still, there is always a small chance LeBaron might discover the true function of Cayo Santa María."

"Then he would simply be erased."

"And Jessie LeBaron?"

"My personal thoughts are that she and her friends will prove useful dupes in laying the blame for our projected disaster on the CIA's doorstep."

"Has Velikov or our resident agents in Washington uncovered any plans by American intelligence to infiltrate the island?"

"Negative," Maisky answered. "A check on the blimp's crew showed none have current ties with the CIA or the military."

"I want no screw-ups," said Polevoi firmly. "We're too close to success. You pass my words on to Velikov."

"He shall be instructed."

There was a knock on the door and Polevoi's secretary entered. Without a word she handed him a paper and left the room.

Sudden anger reddened Polevoi's face. "Damn! Speak of a threat, and it becomes a reality."

"Sir?"

"A priority signal from Velikov. One of the prisoners has escaped."

Maisky made a nervous movement with his hands. "It is impossible. There are no boats on Cayo Santa María, and if he is foolish enough to swim, he'll either drown or be eaten by sharks. Whoever it is won't get far."

"His name is Dirk Pitt, and according to Velikov he's the most dangerous of the lot."

"Dangerous or not—"

Polevoi waved him to silence and began pacing the carpet, his face reflecting deep agitation. "We cannot afford the unexpected. The deadline for our Cuban adventure must be moved up a week."

Maisky shook his head in disagreement. "The ships would never reach Havana in time. Also, we can't change the dates of the celebration. Fidel and every high-ranking member of his government will be on hand for the speechmaking. The wheels of the explosion are set in motion. Nothing can be done to alter the timing. Rum and Cola must either be called off or continue as scheduled."

Polevoi clasped and unclasped his hands in an agony of indecision. "Rum and Cola, a stupid name for an operation of such magnitude."

"Another reason to push on. Our disinformation program has already begun spreading rumors of a CIA plot to launch devastation in Cuba. The phrase 'Rum and Cola' is patently American. No foreign government would suspect it as being hatched in Moscow."

Polevoi shrugged in assent. "Very well, but I don't want to think about the consequences if this Pitt fellow by some miracle survives and makes it back to the United States."

"He is already dead," Maisky announced boldly. "I am sure of it."

38

THE PRESIDENT LEANED into Daniel Fawcett's office and waved. "Don't get up. Just wanted you to know I'm going upstairs for a quiet lunch with my wife."

"Don't forget we have a meeting with the intelligence chiefs and Doug Oates in forty-five minutes," Fawcett reminded him.

"I promise to be on time."

The President turned and took the elevator to his living quarters on the second floor of the White House. Ira Hagen was waiting for him in the Lincoln suite.

"You look tired, Ira."

Hagen smiled. "I'm behind on my sack time."

"How do we stand?"

"I've accounted for the identities of all nine members of the 'inner core.' Seven are pinpointed. Only Leonard Hudson and Gunnar Eriksen remain outside the net."

"You haven't picked up their trail from the shopping center?"

Hagen hesitated. "Nothing that panned out."

"The Soviet moon station was launched eight hours ago," said the President. "I can't delay any longer. Orders will go out this afternoon to round up as many of the 'inner core' as we can."

"Army or FBI?"

"Neither. An old buddy in the Marine Corps has the honors. I've already supplied him with your list of names and locations." The President paused and stared at Hagen. "You said you accounted for the identities of all nine men, Ira, but your report only gave eight names."

Hagen seemed reluctant, but he reached inside his coat and withdrew a sheet of folded paper. "I was saving the last man until I could be absolutely certain. A voice analyzer confirmed my suspicions."

The President took the paper from Hagen's hand, unfolded it, and read the single hand-printed name. He removed his glasses and wearily wiped the lenses as if he didn't trust his eyes. Then he slipped the paper into his pocket.

"I suppose I knew all along but couldn't bring myself to believe his complicity."

"Do not judge harshly, Vince. These men are patriots, not traitors. Their only crime is silence. Take the case of Hudson and Eriksen. Pretending to be dead all these years. Think of the agony that must have caused their friends and families. The nation can never compensate them for their sacrifices or fully comprehend the rewards of their accomplishment."

"Are you lecturing me, Ira?"

"Yes, sir, I am."

The President suddenly became aware of Hagen's inner struggle. He understood that his friend's heart wasn't in the final confrontation. Hagen's loyalty was balanced on a razor's edge.

"You're holding out on me, Ira."

"I won't lie to you, Vince."

"You know where Hudson and Eriksen are hiding."

"Let's say I have a damned solid hunch."

"Can I trust you to bring them in?"

"Yes."

"You're a good scout, Ira."

"Where do you want them delivered, and when?"

"Camp David," the President replied. "Eight o'clock tomorrow morning."

"We'll be there."

"I can't include you, Ira."

"The decent thing to do on your part, Vince. Call it a repayment of sorts. You owe it to me to be in on the finish."

The President considered that. "You're right. It's the very least I can do."

Martin Brogan, director of the CIA, Sam Emmett of the FBI, and Secretary of State Douglas Oates came to their feet as the President entered the conference room with Dan Fawcett on his heels.

"Please be seated, gentlemen," the President said, smiling.

There were a few minutes of small talk until Alan Mercier, the national security adviser, entered. "Sorry for being late," he said, quickly sliding into a chair. "I haven't even had time to think of a good excuse."

"An honest man," Brogan said, laughing. "How disgusting."

The President poised a pen above a note pad. "Where do we stand on the Cuban pact?" he asked, looking at Oates.

"Until we can open a secret dialogue with Castro, it's pretty much on the back burner."

"Is there a remote possibility Jessie LeBaron might have gotten through with our latest reply?"

Brogan shook his head. "I feel it's very doubtful she made contact. Our sources have had no word since the blimp was shot down. The consensus is she's dead."

"Any word at all from the Castros?"

"None."

"What do you hear from the Kremlin?"

"The internal struggle going on between Castro and Antonov is about to break out in the open," said Mercier. "Our people inside the Cuban war ministry say that Castro is going to pull his troops out of Afghanistan."

"That clinches it," said Fawcett. "Antonov won't stand idle and allow that to happen."

Emmett leaned forward and folded his hands on the table. "It all goes back to four years ago when Castro begged off making even a token payment on the ten billion dollars owned to the Soviet Union on loans constantly 'rolled over' since the nineteen-sixties. He painted himself into an economic corner and had to knuckle under when Antonov demanded he send troops to fight in Afghanistan. Not simply a few small companies, but nearly twenty thousand men."

"What estimate does the CIA have of casualties?" asked the President, turning to Brogan.

"Our figures show approximately sixteen hundred dead, two thousand wounded, and over five hundred missing."

"Good lord, that's better than twenty percent."

"Another reason the Cuban people detest the Russians," Brogan continued. "Castro is like a drowning man, sinking between a leaking rowboat whose crew is pointing a gun at him and a luxury yacht whose passengers are waving champagne bottles. If we throw him the rope, the crew in the Kremlin will blast him."

"Actually, they're planning on blasting him anyway," Emmett added.

"Do we have any idea how or when the assassination will take place?" asked the President.

Brogan shifted in his chair uneasily. "Our sources have been unable to turn up a timetable."

"Their security on the subject is as tight as anything I've ever seen," said Mercier. "Our computers have failed to decode any data from our space listening systems tuned to the operation. Only a few bits and pieces that fail to give us a concrete fix on their plans."

"Do you know who is in charge of it?" the President persisted.

"General Peter Velikov, GRU, considered something of a wizard at third-world government infiltration and manipulation. He was the architect of the Nigerian overthrow two years ago. Fortunately, the Marxist government he set up didn't last."

"Is he operating out of Havana?"

"He's secretive as hell," replied Brogan. "The perfect image of the man who isn't there. Velikov hasn't been seen in public in the past four years. We're dead certain he's directing the show from a hidden location."

The President's eyes seemed to darken. "All we have here is a vague theory that the Kremlin plans to assassinate Fidel and Raúl Castro, fix the blame on us, then take over the government using Cuban stooges who receive their orders straight from Moscow. Come now, gentlemen, I can't act on what-ifs. I need facts."

"It's a projection based on known facts," Brogan explained heavily. "We have the names of the Cubans who are on the Soviet payroll and waiting on the sidelines to assume power. Our information fully supports the Kremlin's intent to murder the Castros. The CIA makes the perfect scapegoat because the Cuban people have not forgotten the Bay of Pigs or the agency's fumbling plots to assassinate Fidel by the Mafia during the Kennedy administration. I assure you, Mr. President, I have given this every priority. Sixty agents on every level in and out of Cuba are concentrating on penetrating Velikov's wall of secrecy."

"And yet we can't reach Castro for an open dialogue to help each other."

"No, sir," said Oates. "He's resisting any contact through official channels."

"Doesn't he realize his time may be running out?" asked the President.

"He's wandering in a vacuum," Oates replied. "On one hand he feels secure in knowing the great mass of Cubans idolize him. Few national leaders can command the awe and affection he enjoys from his people. And yet on the other, he cannot fully comprehend the dead seriousness of the Soviet threat on his life and government."

"So what you're telling me," said the President gravely, "is that unless we can make an intelligence breakthrough or get someone into Castro's hideout who can make him listen to reason, we can only sit back and watch Cuba sink under total Soviet domination."

"Yes, Mr. President," said Brogan. "That is exactly what we're telling you."

39

HAGEN WAS DOING some browsing. He wandered through the mall of the shopping center, casually eyeing the merchandise in the stores. The smell of roasted peanuts reminded him that he was hungry. He stopped at a gaily painted wagon and bought a bag of roasted cashews.

Resting his feet for a few minutes, Hagen sat on a couch in an appliance store and watched an entire wall of twenty television sets all tuned to the same channel. The pictures showed an hour-old rerun of the space shuttle *Gettysburg* as it lifted off from California. Over three hundred people had been launched into space since the shuttle's first flight in 1981, and except for the news media, nobody paid much attention anymore.

Hagen wandered up and down, pausing to gawk through a large window at a disk jockey spinning records for a radio station that was located in the mall. He rubbed shoulders with the crowds of female shoppers, but he concentrated on the occasional man. Most seemed to be on their lunch break, probing the counters and racks, usually buying the first thing they saw, in contrast to the women, who preferred to keep searching in the forlorn hope they could find something better at a cheaper price.

He spotted two men eating submarine sandwiches at a fast-food restaurant. They were not carrying any purchase bags, nor were they dressed like store clerks. They wore the same casual style as Dr. Mooney at the Pattenden Lab.

Hagen followed them into a large department store. They took the escalator down to the basement, passed through the shopping area, and entered a rear hallway marked with a sign that read "Employees Only."

A warning bell went off inside Hagen's head. He returned to a counter stacked with bed sheets, removed his coat, and stuck a pencil behind one ear. Then he waited until the clerk was busy with a customer before picking up a pile of sheets and heading back into the hallway.

Three doors led to stock rooms, two to restrooms, and one was marked "Danger—High Voltage." He yanked open the latter door and rushed inside. A startled security guard sitting at a desk looked up. "Hey, you're not supposed to be—"

That was as far as he got before Hagen threw the sheets in his face and judo-chopped him on the side of the neck. There were two security guards behind a second door, and Hagen put them both down in less than four seconds. He crouched and whipped around in anticipation of another threat.

A hundred pairs of eyes stared at him in blank astonishment.

Hagen was confronted by a room that seemed to stretch into infinity. From wall to wall it was filled with people, offices, computer and communications equipment. For a long second, he stood stunned by the vastness of it all. Then he took a step forward and grabbed a terrified secretary by the arms and lifted her out of a chair.

"Leonard Hudson!" he snapped. "Where can I find him?"

Fear shone from her eyes like twin spotlights. She tilted her head to the right. "Th-the office w-with the blue d-door," she stammered.

"Thank you very much," he said with a broad smile.

Hagen released the girl and walked swiftly through the hushed complex. His face was twisted with malevolence, as if daring anyone to stop him.

No one made the slightest attempt. The growing crowd of people parted like the Red Sea as he passed down a main aisle.

When he came to the blue door, Hagen stopped and turned around, surveying the brain trust and communications center of the Jersey Colony program. He had to admire Hudson. It was an imaginative cover. Excavated during the construction of the shopping center, it would have attracted little or no suspicion. The scientists, engineers, and secretaries could come and go amid the shoppers, and their cars simply melted into hundreds of others in the parking lot. The radio station was also a work of genius. Who would suspect they were transmitting and receiving messages from the moon while broadcasting Top 40 records to the surrounding college community.

Hagen pushed inside the door and entered what seemed to be a studio control booth.

Hudson and Eriksen sat with their backs to him, staring up at a large video monitor that reflected the face and shaven head of a man who stopped speaking in midsentence and then said, "Who is that man behind you?"

Hudson made a cursory glance over his shoulder. "Hello, Ira." The voice mirrored the eyes; Hagen could almost hear the cracking of ice cubes. "I wondered when you'd show up."

"Come in," said Eriksen in an equally frigid tone. "You're just in time to talk to our man on the moon."

40

PITT HAD CLEARED Cuban waters and was well into the main shipping lane of the Bahama Channel. But his luck was running out. The only ships that came within sight failed to spot him. A large tanker flying the Panamanian flag steamed by no more than a mile away. He stood as high as he dared without tipping over the tub and waved his shirt, but his little vessel went unnoticed by the crew.

For a watch officer on the bridge to aim his binoculars at the precise spot at the precise instant when the bathtub rose out of a trough and climbed the crest of a swell before dropping from sight again was a bet no self-respecting bookie would make. The awful truth plagued Pitt: he made too small a target.

Pitt's movements were becoming mechanical. His legs had gone numb after rolling around the sea in the cramped bathtub for nearly twenty hours, and the constant friction of his buttocks against the hard surface had raised painful blisters. The tropical sun beat on him, but he wore a good tan and the least of his problems was sunburn.

The sea remained calm, but still it was a continuous effort to keep the bow of the tub straight into the swells and bail out the water at the same time. He had emptied the final drops from the fuel cans into the outboard motor before refilling them with seawater for ballast.

Another fifteen or twenty minutes, that was all he could expect the motor to keep running before it starved for gas. Then it would be all over. Without control, the tub would soon swamp and sink.

His mind began to slip away; he hadn't slept in thirty-six hours. He fought to stay awake, steering and bailing with leaden arms and water-wrinkled hands. For hour after endless hour his eyes swept the horizon, seeing nothing that was traveling toward his tiny area of the sea. A few sharks had bumped the bottom of the slow-moving tub; one made the mistake of coming too close to the spinning propeller and got his fin chewed up. Pitt eyed them with a detached air. He dumbly planned to beat them out of a meal by opening his mouth and drowning, before realizing it was a stupid thought and brushing it aside.

The wind gently began to rise. A squall passed overhead and deposited an inch of water in the tub. It wasn't the cleanest, but it was better than nothing. He scooped up a few handfuls and gratefully gulped it down, feeling refreshed.

Pitt looked up at the shimmering horizon to the west. Night would fall in another hour. His last spark of hope was dying with the setting sun. Even if he somehow kept afloat, he could never be seen in the darkness.

Hindsight, he mused. If only he'd stolen a flashlight.

Suddenly, the outboard sputtered and then caught again. He slowed the throttle as much as he dared, knowing he was only pushing off the inevitable by a minute or two.

Pitt fought off the cloud of morale collapse and steeled himself to bail until his arms gave out or a wave struck the drifting, helpless little tub on the beam and swamped her. He emptied one of the gas cans of seawater. When the tub sank, he reasoned, he would use the can as a float. So long as he could move a muscle, he wasn't about to give up.

The faithful little outboard coughed once, twice, and then died. After hearing the beat of the exhaust since the night before, Pitt felt smothered by the abrupt silence. He sat there in a doomed little craft on a vast and indifferent sea under a clear and cloudless sky.

He kept her afloat for another hour into the twilight. He was so tired, so physically exhausted that he missed a small movement five hundred yards away.

Commander Kermit Fulton pulled back from the periscope eyepiece, his face wearing a questioning expression. He looked across the control room of the attack submarine *Denver* at his executive officer. "Any contact on our sensors?"

The exec spoke into one of the control room phones. "Nothing on radar, skipper. Sonar reports a small contact, but it stopped about a minute ago."

"What do they make of it?"

The answer was slow in coming and the question was repeated.

"Sonar says it sounded like a small outboard motor, no more than twenty horsepower."

"There's something mighty peculiar out there," said Fulton. "I want to check it out. Slow speed to one-third and come left five degrees."

He pressed his forehead against the periscope eyepiece again and increased the magnification. Slowly, wonderingly, he pulled back. "Give the order to surface."

"You see something?" asked the executive officer.

He nodded silently.

Everyone in the control room stared at Fulton expectantly. The exec took the initiative. "Mind letting us in on it, skipper?"

"Twenty-three years at sea," said Fulton, "and I thought I'd seen almost everything. But damned if there isn't a man up there, almost a hundred miles from the nearest land, floating in a bathtub."

41

SINCE THE BLIMP'S DISAPPEARANCE, Admiral Sandecker had rarely left his office. He buried himself in work that soon lost all meaning. His parents, though quite elderly, were still alive, and so were his brother and sister. Sandecker had never really tasted personal tragedy before.

During his years in the Navy, he was infected with dedication. There was little time for a deep relationship with a woman, and he counted few good friends, mostly Navy acquaintances. He built a wall around him between superiors and subordinates and walked the middle ground. He made flag rank before he was fifty, but he was stagnating.

When Congress approved his appointment as chief of the National Underwater and Marine Agency, he came back to life. He formed warm friendships with three unlikely people, who looked up to him with respect but treated him no differently than the man on the next bar stool.

The challenges facing NUMA had drawn them together. Al Giordino, an extrovert who took a strange glee in volunteering for the dirtiest projects and stealing Sandecker's expensive cigars. Rudi Gunn, driven to accomplish nothing less than perfection, a natural at organizing programs, who couldn't make an enemy if he tried. And then there was Pitt, who had done more than anyone to revive Sandecker's creative spirit. They soon became as close as father and son.

Pitt's freewheeling attitude toward life and his sarcastic wit trailed behind him like a comet's tail. He couldn't enter a room without livening it up. Sandecker tried but failed to blot out the memories, to unchain himself from the past. He leaned back in the desk chair and closed his eyes and gave in to the sorrow. To lose all three of them at one time stunned him beyond comprehension.

While Pitt was in his thoughts, the light blinked and a muted chime came from his private phone line. He massaged his temples briefly and picked up the receiver.

"Yes?"

"Jim, is that you? I got your private number from a mutual friend at the Pentagon."

"I'm sorry. My mind was wandering. I don't recognize the voice."

"This is Clyde. Clyde Monfort."

Sandecker tensed. "Clyde, what's up?"

"A signal from one of our attack subs returning from the Jamaican landing exercise just came across my desk."

"How does that concern me?"

"The sub's commander reports picking up a castaway no more than twenty minutes ago. Not exactly standard procedure for our nuclear sub forces to take strangers on board, but his guy claimed he worked for you and got pretty nasty when the skipper refused to allow him to send a message."

"Pitt!"

"You got it," answered Monfort. "That's the name he gave. Dirk Pitt. How'd you know?"

"Thank God!"

"Does he check out?"

"Yes, yes, he's bona fide," Sandecker said impatiently. "What about the others?"

"No others. Pitt was alone in a bathtub."

"Say again."

"The skipper swears it was a bathtub with an outboard motor."

Knowing Pitt, Sandecker didn't doubt the story for a second. "How soon can you have him picked up by helicopter and dropped at the nearest airfield for transport to Washington?"

"You know that's not possible, Jim. I can't have him cleared and released until after the sub docks at its base in Charleston."

"Hang on, Clyde. I'll call the White House on another line and get the authorization."

"You got that kind of clout?" Monfort asked incredulously.

"That and more."

"Can you tell me what's going down, Jim?"

"Take my word for it. You don't want to get involved."

• • •

They gathered at a White House dinner party to honor the Prime Minister of India, Rajiv Gandhi, who was on a goodwill tour of the United States. Actors and labor leaders, athletes and billionaires, they all shed their opinions, their differences, and mingled like neighbors at a Sunday social.

Former Presidents Ronald Reagan and Jimmy Carter conversed and acted as though they had never left the West Wing. Standing in a corner filled with flowers, Secretary of State Douglas Oates swapped war stories with Henry Kissinger, while the Super Bowl champion quarterback of the Houston Oilers stood in front of the fireplace and peered openly at the breasts of ABC news anchor Sandra Malone.

The President shared a toast with Prime Minister Gandhi and then introduced him to Charles Murphy, who had recently flown over Antarctica in a hot-air balloon. The President's wife came over, took her husband's arm, and pulled him toward the dance floor of the state dining room.

A White House aide caught Dan Fawcett's eye and nodded toward the doorway. Fawcett went over, heard him out, then approached the President. The chain of command was well oiled.

"My apologies, Mr. President, but a courier has just arrived with a congressional bill that requires your signature before midnight."

The President nodded in understanding. There was no bill to sign. It was a code for an urgent message. He excused himself to his wife and went across the hall to a small private office. He paused until Fawcett closed the door before picking up the phone.

"This is the President."

"Admiral Sandecker, sir."

"Yes, Admiral, what is it?"

"I have the Chief of Naval Forces in the Caribbean on another line. He has just informed me that one of my people, who vanished with Jessie LeBaron, has been rescued by one of our submarines."

"Has he been identified?"

"It's Dirk Pitt."

"The man must be either indestructible or very lucky," the President said with a touch of relief in his voice. "How soon can we get him here?"

"Admiral Clyde Monfort is holding on the line for authorization to provide priority transport."

"Can you connect me to him?"

"Hold on, sir." There was a second's pause followed by a click.

The President said, "Admiral Monfort, can you hear me?"

"I hear you."

"This is the President. Do you recognize my voice?"

"Yes, sir, I do."

"I want Pitt in Washington as fast as you can possibly get him here. Understood?"

"I read you, Mr. President. I'll see that a Navy jet lands him at Andrews Air Force Base before daybreak."

"Spread a security net on this affair, Admiral. Keep the submarine at sea and place the pilots, or anyone else who comes within a hundred yards of Pitt, under confinement for three days."

There was a slight hesitation. "Your orders will be carried out."

"Thank you. Now please let me speak to Admiral Sandecker."

"I'm here, Mr. President."

"You heard? Admiral Monfort will have Pitt at Andrews before dawn."

"I'll personally be on hand to meet him."

"Good. Take him by helicopter to CIA headquarters in Langley. Martin Brogan and representatives from my office and the State Department will be waiting to debrief him."

"He may not be able to shed light on anything."

"You're probably right," said the President wearily. "I'm expecting too much. I guess I always expect too much."

He hung up and sighed heavily. He collected his thoughts for a moment and then shelved them in a mental niche for later retrieval, a technique mastered sooner or later by every President. Shifting the mind from crisis to trivial routine and back again to crisis like the flick of a light switch was a requirement that went with the job.

Fawcett knew the President's every mood and patiently waited. Finally he said, "It might not be a bad idea if I attended the debriefing."

The President looked up at him sadly. "You'll be going with me to Camp David at sunup."

Fawcett looked blank. "I have nothing on your schedule that includes a trip to Camp David. Most of the morning is taken up by meetings with congressional leaders over the proposed budget."

"They will have to wait. I have a more important conference tomorrow."

"As your chief of staff may I ask who you're conferring with?"

"A group of men who call themselves the 'inner core.'"

Fawcett stared at the President, his mouth slowly tightening. "I don't understand."

"You should, Dan. You're one of them."

Before a dazed Fawcett could reply, the President left the office and rejoined the dinner party.

42

THE THUMP OF THE LANDING WHEELS woke Pitt up. Outside the twin-engined Navy jet the sky was still dark. Through a small window he could see the first streaks of orange spearheading the new day.

The blisters caused by the friction from the bathtub made sitting almost impossible, and he had slept in a cramped position on his side. He felt generally awful, and he was thirsty for something besides the fruit juices forced down his stomach in endless quantities by an overly concerned doctor on the submarine.

He wondered what he would do if he ever met up with Foss Gly again. Whatever fiendish punishment he created in his mind didn't seem excessive enough. The thought of the agony Gly was inflicting on Jessie, Giordino, and Gunn haunted him. He felt guilty for having escaped.

The whine of the jet engines faded and the door was opened. He walked stiffly down the stairs and was embraced by Sandecker. The admiral rarely shook hands, and the unexpected display of affection surprised Pitt.

"I guess what they say about a bad penny is true," said Sandecker hoarsely, groping for words.

"Better to turn up than not," Pitt replied, smiling.

Sandecker took him by the arm and led him over to a waiting car. "They're waiting at CIA headquarters in Langley to question you."

Pitt suddenly stopped. "They're alive," he announced briefly.

"Alive?" said Sandecker, stunned. "All of them?"

"Imprisoned by the Russians and tortured by a defector."

Incomprehension showed on Sandecker's face. "You were in Cuba?"

"On one of the outer islands," Pitt explained. "We've got to apprise the Russians of my rescue as quickly as possible to stop them from—"

"Slow down," Sandecker interrupted. "I'm losing you. Better yet, wait and tell the whole story when we get to Langley. I suspect you may have fallen in the creek and come up with a pocketful of trout."

On the flight across the city it began to rain. Pitt gazed through the plexiglass windshield at the 219 wooded acres surrounding the sprawling gray marble and concrete structure that was the home of America's cloak-and-dagger army. From the air it seemed deserted, no people were visible on the grounds. Even the parking lot was only one quarter full. The only human shape Pitt could detect was a statue of the nation's most famous spy, Nathan Hale, who had made the mistake of getting caught and was hanged.

Two senior officials were waiting at the helipad with umbrellas. Everyone hurried into the building, and Pitt and Sandecker were shown into a large conference room. There were six men and one woman present. Martin Brogan came over and shook Pitt's hand and introduced the others. Pitt simply nodded and promptly forgot their names.

Brogan said, "I hear you've had a rough trip."

"Not one I'd recommend to tourists," Pitt replied.

"Can I get you something to eat or drink?" Brogan offered graciously. "A cup of coffee or breakfast maybe?"

"If you could find a bottle of cold beer..."

"Of course." Brogan picked up the phone and said something. "Be here in a minute."

The conference room was plain by business-office standards. The walls were a neutral beige color, the carpet the same, and the furniture looked as though it came from a discount store. No pictures, no decorations of any kind gave it life. A room whose only function was to serve as a place to work.

Pitt was offered a chair at one end of the table, but declined. His rear end did not feel up to sitting just yet. Every eye in the room stared at him, and he began to feel like an inmate at the zoo on a Sunday afternoon.

Brogan gave him a relaxed smile. "Please tell us everything you've heard and observed from the beginning. Your account will be recorded and transcribed. Afterward, we'll go for questions and answers. All right with you?"

The beer came. Pitt took a long pull, relaxed, and then started relating the events from the takeoff in Key West to elatedly seeing the submarine rise out of the water a few yards from his sinking tub. He left out nothing and took his time, going into every detail, no matter how minor, he could recall. It took him nearly an hour and a half, but they listened attentively without question or interruption. When he finally finished, he gently eased his aching body into a chair and calmly watched everyone check over their notes.

Brogan declared a short break while aerial photographs of Cayo Santa María, files on Velikov and Gly, and the copies of the transcription were brought in. After forty minutes of study, Brogan kicked off the questioning.

"You carried weapons in the blimp. Why?"

"Projections of the *Cyclops'* wreck site indicated it lay in Cuban waters. It seemed appropriate to carry a bulletproof shield and a missile launcher for protective insurance."

"You realize, of course, your unwarranted attack on the Cuban patrol helicopter was a breach of government policy." This from a man Pitt remembered as working for the State Department.

"I followed a higher law," said Pitt with a sardonic grin.

"And what law, may I ask, is that?"

"Comes from the Old West, something they called self-preservation. The Cubans fired first, about a thousand rounds, I would judge, before Al Giordino blew it away."

Brogan smiled. He could see Pitt was a man after his own heart. "Our main concern here is with your description of the Russians' installation on the island. You say the island is unguarded."

"Above ground the only guards I saw were stationed at the gate of the compound. None were patrolling the roads or the beaches. The only security measure was an electrified fence."

"That explains why infrared photography hasn't detected any signs of human activity," said an analyst eyeballing the photos.

"Unlike the Russians to step out of character," mused another CIA official. "They almost always give away a secret base by going overboard on security."

"Not this time," said Pitt. "They've gone to opposite extremes and it's paid off for them. General Velikov stated that it was the most sensitive military installation outside the Soviet Union. And I gather that no one in your agency was aware of it until now."

"I admit, we may have been taken in," said Brogan. "Providing what you've described to us is true."

Pitt gave Brogan a cold stare. Then he painfully rose from his chair and started for the door. "All right, have it your way. I lied. Thanks for the beer."

"May I ask where you're going?"

"To call a press conference," Pitt said, addressing Brogan directly. "I'm wasting precious time for your benefit. The sooner I announce my escape and demand the release of the LeBarons, Giordino, and Gunn, the sooner Velikov will be forced to halt their torture and execution."

There was a shocked quiet. None of the people at the conference table could believe Pitt was walking out, none except Sandecker. He sat there and smiled like the owner of a winning ball club. "You'd better pull your act together, Martin. You've just been presented with a top-of-the-line intelligence coup, and if no one in this room can recognize it, I suggest you all find another line of work."

Brogan may have been a brusque egotist, but he was no fool. He quickly rose and stopped Pitt at the doorway. "Forgive an old Irishman who's been burned more times than he can count. Thirty years in this business and you just naturally become a doubting Thomas. Please help us to fit the puzzle together. Then we'll discuss what's to be done for your friends and the LeBarons."

"It'll cost you another beer," Pitt said.

Brogan and the others laughed then. The ice was broken, and the questioning was resumed from all sides of the table.

"Is this Velikov?" asked an analyst, holding up a photograph.

"Yes, General Peter Velikov. His American-accented English was letter perfect. I almost forgot, he had my dossier, including a personality profile."

Sandecker looked at Brogan. "Sounds like Sam Emmett has a mole in his FBI records department."

Brogan smiled sarcastically. "Sam won't be happy to learn of it."

"We could write a book on Velikov's exploits," said a heavy man facing Pitt. "At a later time I'd like you to give me a profile of his mannerisms."

"Glad to," said Pitt.

"And this is the interrogator with the heavy hand, Foss Gly?"

Pitt nodded at the second photograph. "He's a good ten years older than the face in the picture, but that's him."

"An American mercenary, born in Arizona," said the analyst. "You say you two met before?"

"Yes, during the *Empress of Ireland* project in search of the North American Treaty. I think you may recall it."

Brogan nodded. "Indeed I do."

"Getting back to the layout of the installation," said the woman. "Levels of the compound?"

"According to the elevator indicator, five, all underground."

"Idea as to extent?"

"All I saw was my cell, the hallway, Velikov's office, and a motor pool. Oh, yes, and the entry to the upper living quarters, which was decorated like a Spanish castle."

"Wall thickness?"

"About two feet."

"Quality of construction?"

"Good. No leakage or noticeable cracking of the concrete."

"Type of vehicles in the motor pool?"

"Two military trucks. The rest construction—a bulldozer, a back hoe, and a cherry picker."

The woman looked up from her notes. "Excuse me. The last one?"

"Cherry picker," Pitt explained. "A special truck with a telescoping platform to work at heights. You see them used by tree trimmers and telephone linemen."

"Approximate dimensions of the antenna dish?"

"Difficult to measure in the dark. Approximately three hundred yards long by two hundred yards wide. It lifts into position by hydraulic arms camouflaged as palm trees."

"Solid or grid?"

"Grid."

"Circuitry, junction boxes, relays?"

"Didn't see any, which doesn't mean they weren't there."

Brogan had followed the questions without intruding. Now he held up a hand and stared at a studious-looking man seated halfway down the table. "What do you make of it, Charlie?"

"Not enough technical detail to pinpoint an exact purpose. But there are three possibilities. One is that it's a listening station capable of intercepting telephone, radio, and radar signals across the United States. Two, a powerful jamming facility, just sitting there waiting for a crucial moment, like a nuclear first strike when it is suddenly activated, scrambling all our vital military and commercial communications. The third prospect is that it might have the capability to transmit and feed false information throughout our communications systems. Most worrisome, the size and elaborate antenna design suggests the ability to perform the functions of all three."

The muscles in Brogan's face went taut. The fact that such a supersecret spy operation had been constructed less than two hundred miles from the shores of the United States did not exactly thrill the chief of the Central Intelligence Agency.

"If worse comes to worse, what are we looking at?"

"What I'm afraid we're looking at," answered Charlie, "is an electronically advanced and powerful facility capable of intercepting radio or phone communications and then using time-lag technology to allow a new-generation computerized synthesizer to imitate the callers' voices and alter the conversation. You'd be amazed how your words can be manipulated over a telephone to another party without your detecting the change. As a matter of fact, the National Security Agency has the same type of equipment on board a ship."

"So the Russians have caught up with us," said Brogan.

"Their technology is probably cruder than ours, but it seems they've gone a step further and expanded it on a grander scale."

The woman intelligence official looked at Pitt. "You said the island is supplied by submarine."

"So Raymond LeBaron informed me," said Pitt. "And what little I saw of the shoreline didn't include a docking area."

Sandecker played with one of his cigars but didn't light it. He pointed one end at Brogan. "Appears the Soviets have gone to unusual lengths to throw your Cuban surveillence off the track, Martin."

"The fear of exposure came out during the interrogation," said Pitt. "Velikov insisted we were agents on your payroll."

"Can't really blame the bastard," said Brogan. "Your entrance must have shocked the hell out of him."

"Mr. Pitt, could you describe the people at the dinner party when you entered?" asked a scholarly-looking man in an argyle sweater.

"Roughly I'd say there were sixteen women and two dozen men—"

"You did say women?"

"I did."

"What type?" asked the only woman in the room.

Pitt had to ask. "Define type."

"You know," she answered seriously. "Wives, nice single ladies, or hookers?"

"Definitely not hookers. Most were in uniform, probably part of Velikov's staff. The ones wearing wedding rings appeared to be wives of the Cuban civilians and military officers who were present."

"What in hell is Velikov thinking?" Brogan asked no one in particular. "Cubans and their wives at a top-secret installation? None of this makes any sense."

Sandecker stared pensively at the tabletop. "Makes sense to me, if Velikov is using Cayo Santa María for something besides electronic espionage."

"What are you hinting at, Jim?" asked Brogan.

"The island would make a perfect base of operations for the overthrow of the Castro government."

Brogan looked at him in astonishment. "How do you know about that?"

"The President briefed me," Sandecker replied loftily.

"I see." But it was clear Brogan didn't see.

"Look, I realize this is all highly important," said Pitt, "but every minute we spend speculating puts Jessie, Al, and Rudi that much closer to death. I expect you people to pull out all the stops to save them. You can begin by notifying the Russians that you're aware of their captivity because of my rescue."

Pitt's demand was met with an odd quiet. Nobody except Sandecker looked at him. The CIA people, especially, avoided his eyes.

"Forgive me," said Brogan stonily. "I don't think that would be a smart move."

Sandecker's eyes suddenly flashed with anger. "Watch what you say, Martin. I know there's a Machiavellian plot jelling in your mind. But take warning, my friend. You've got me to deal with, and I'm not about to let my friends be literally thrown to the sharks."

"We're looking at a high-stakes game," said Brogan. "Keeping Velikov in the dark may prove most advantageous."

"And sacrifice several lives for an intelligence gamble?" said Pitt bitterly. "No way."

"Please bear with me a moment," Brogan pleaded. "I'll agree to leak a story saying we know the LeBarons and your NUMA people are alive. Next, we'll accuse the Cubans of imprisoning them in Havana."

"How can Velikov be expected to fall for something he knows is crap?"

"I don't expect him to fall for it. He's no cretin. He'll smell a rat and wonder how much we know about his island. And that's all he can do—wonder. We'll also muddy the waters by claiming our knowledge comes from photographic evidence showing your inflatable boat washed up on the main island of Cuba. That should take the pressure off our captives and keep Velikov guessing. The *pièce de résistance* will be the discovery of Pitt's body by a Bahamian fisherman."

"What in hell are you proposing?" Sandecker demanded.

"I haven't thought it through yet," Brogan admitted. "But the basic idea is to sneak Pitt back on the island."

As soon as Pitt's debriefing had concluded, Brogan returned to his office and picked up the phone. His call went through the usual batting order of buffers before the President came on.

"Please make it quick, Martin. I'm about to leave for Camp David."

"We've just finished interrogating Dirk Pitt."

"Could he fill in any pieces?"

"Pitt gave us the intelligence breakthrough we discussed."

"Velikov's headquarters?"

"He led us straight to the mother lode."

"Nice work. Now your people can launch an infiltration operation."

"I think a more permanent solution would be in order."

"You mean offset its threat by exposing its existence to the world press?"

"No. I mean go in and destroy it."

43

THE PRESIDENT HAD A LIGHT BREAKFAST after reaching Camp David. The weather was unseasonably warm, there was Indian summer in the air, and he was dressed in cotton slacks and short-sleeved sweater.

He sat in a large wing chair with several file folders in his lap and studied the personal histories of the "inner core." After reading the last file he closed his eyes, pondering his options, wondering what he would say to the men who were waiting in the camp's main dining room.

Hagen entered the study and stood quietly until the President opened his eyes.

"Ready when you are, Vince."

The President slowly pushed himself from the chair. "Might as well get on with it then."

They were waiting around the long dining table as the President had arranged. No guards were present, none were required. These were honorable men who had no intent to commit crime. They respectfully rose to their feet as he entered the room, but he waved them down.

Eight were present and accounted for: General Fisher, Booth, Mitchell, and Busche sat on one side of the table opposite Eriksen, Senator Porter, and Dan Fawcett. Hudson was seated by himself at the far end. Only Raymond LeBaron was missing.

They were dressed casually, sitting comfortably like golfers in a clubhouse, relaxed, supremely confident and showing no signs of tension.

"Good morning, Mr. President," greeted Senator Porter cheerfully. "To what do we owe the honor of this mysterious summons?"

The President cleared his throat. "You all know why I've brought you here. So we don't have to play games."

"You don't want to congratulate us?" asked Clyde Booth sarcastically.

"Tributes may or may not be offered," said the President coldly. "That will depend."

"Depend on what?" Gunnar Eriksen demanded rudely.

"I believe what the President is fishing for," said Hudson, "is our blessing for allowing the Russians to claim a share of the moon."

"That and a confession of mass murder."

The tables were turned. They just sat there, eyes with the look of fish in a freezer, staring at the President.

Senator Porter, a fast thinker, launched his attack first. "Execution gangland style or *Arsenic and Old Lace* poison in the tea? If I may ask, Mr. President, what in hell are you talking about?"

"A small matter of nine dead Soviet cosmonauts."

"Those lost during the early Soyuz missions?" asked Dan Fawcett.

"No," answered the President. "The nine Russians who were killed on the Selenos lunar probes."

Hudson gripped the edge of the table and stared as if he had been electrocuted. "The Selenos spacecraft were unmanned."

"The Russians wanted the world to think so, but in reality they each carried three men. We have one of the crews on ice in the Walter Reed hospital morgue, if you care to examine the remains."

No one would have thought it to look at them. They considered themselves moral-minded citizens doing a job for their country. The last thing any of them expected to see in a mirror was the reflection of a cold-blooded killer. To say that the President had his audience in the palm of his hand would be an understatement.

Hagen sat fascinated. This was all news to him.

"If you'll bear with me," the President continued, "I'll indulge in mixing facts with speculation. To begin with, you and your moon colonists have accomplished an incredible achievement. I compliment you on your perseverance and genius, as will the world in the coming weeks. However, you have unwittingly made a terrible error that could easily stain your accomplishment.

"In your zeal to wave the Stars and Stripes you have ignored the international space law treaty governing activities on the moon, which was ratified by the United States, the Soviet Union, and three other countries in 1984. Then you took it upon yourselves to claim the moon as a sovereign possession and, figuratively speaking, posted 'Trespassers Will Be Shot' signs. Only you backed it up by somehow destroying three Soviet lunar probes. One of them, Selenos 4, managed to return to earth, where it orbited for eighteen months before control was reestablished. Soviet space engineers attempted to bring it down in the steppes of Kazakhstan, but the craft was damaged and it fell near Cuba instead.

"Under the guise of a treasure hunt, you sent Raymond LeBaron to find it before the Russians. Telltale marks of damage inflicted by your colonists had to be obliterated. But the Cubans beat you both to the downed craft and retrieved it. You weren't aware of that until now, and the Russians still don't know. Unless..."

The President hung on the word. "Unless Raymond LeBaron has spilled his knowledge of the Jersey Colony under torture. I have it on good authority he was captured by the Cubans and turned over to Soviet military intelligence, the GRU."

"Raymond won't talk," Hudson said wrathfully.

"He may not have to," the President replied. "A few hours ago intelligence analysts, whom I asked to reexamine Soviet space signals received during Selenos 4's reentry orbits, have discovered that its data on the lunar surface were transmitted to a ground tracking station on the island of Socotra, near Yemen. Do you comprehend the consequences, gentlemen?"

"We comprehend what you're driving at." It was General Fisher who spoke, his voice reflective. "The Soviets may have visual proof of the Jersey Colony."

"Yes, and they've probably put two and two together and figured your people up there had something to do with the Selenos disasters. You can be sure they will retaliate. No calls on the hot line, no messages slipped through diplomatic channels, no announcements in TASS or *Pravda*. The battle for the moon will be kept secret by both sides. When you total the score, gentlemen, the result is you have launched a war that may prove impossible to stop."

The men seated around the table were shocked and confused, dazed and angry. But they were angry only because of a miscalculation of an event that was beyond their knowledge. The awful truth took several moments to register.

"You speak of Soviet retaliation, Mr. President," said Fawcett. "Do you have any insight on the possibility?"

"Put yourself in Soviet shoes. They were on to you a good week before their Selenos 8 lunar station was launched. If I were President Antonov, I'd have ordered the mission converted from scientific exploration to a military operation. There is little doubt in my mind that when Selenos 8 touches down on the moon twenty hours from now, a special team of Soviet commandos will encircle and attack the Jersey Colony. Now you tell me, can the base defend itself?"

General Fisher looked at Hudson, then turned to the President and shrugged his shoulders. "I can't say. We've never made contingency plans for an armed assault on the colony. As I recall, their only weapons are two handguns and a missile launcher."

"Incidentally, when were your colonists scheduled to leave the moon?"

"They should lift off in about thirty-six hours," answered Hudson.

"I'm curious," said the President. "How do they intend to return through earth's atmosphere? Certainly their lunar transport vehicle doesn't have the capability."

Hudson smiled. "They'll return to the Kennedy spaceport at Cape Canaveral on the shuttle."

The President sighed. "The *Gettysburg*. Stupid of me not to think of it. She's already docked at our space station."

"Her crew hasn't been advised yet," said Steve Busche of NASA, "but once they get over the shock of seeing the colonists suddenly show up on the transport vehicle, they'll be more than willing to take on extra passengers."

The President paused and stared at the members of the "inner core," his expression suddenly bleak. "The burning question we all have to face, gentlemen, is whether the Jersey colonists will survive to make the trip."

44

"Do you really expect to get away with it?" Pitt asked.

Colonel Ramon Kleist, U.S. Marine Corps, Retired, rocked on his heels and scratched an itch on his back with a swagger stick. "So long as we can withdraw as a unit with our casualties, yes, I believe the mission can be pulled off successfully."

"Nothing this complicated can go letter perfect," said Pitt. "Destroying the compound and the antenna, plus killing off Velikov and his entire staff, sound to me like you're biting off more than you can chew."

"Your eyewitness observation and our stealth aircraft photos corroborate the light defensive measures."

"How many men make up your team?" asked Pitt.

"Thirty-one including yourself."

"The Russians are bound to find out who trashed their secret base. You'll be kicking a hornet's nest."

"All part of the plan," Kleist said airily.

Kleist stood ramrod straight, his chest threatening to burst from a flowered shirt. Pitt guessed his age as late fifties. He was a medium-skinned black, born in Argentina, the only child of a former SS officer who had fled Germany after the war and the daughter of a Liberian diplomat. Sent to a private school in New York, he decided to drop out and make a career in the Marines.

"I thought there was an unwritten agreement between the CIA and the KGB: we won't waste your agents if you don't waste ours."

The colonel gave Pitt an innocent look. "Whatever gave you the idea our side will do the dirty work?"

Pitt did not reply, only stared at Kleist, waiting.

"The mission will be conducted by Cuban Special Security Forces," he explained. "Their equivalent to our SEALS. Or to be honest, expertly trained exiles dressed in genuine Cuban battle fatigues. Even their underwear and socks will be standard Cuban military issue. Weapons, wristwatches, and other equipment will be of Soviet manufacture. And, just so we keep up appearances, the landing will come from the Cuban side of the island."

"All neat and tidy."

"We try to be efficient."

"Are you leading the mission?"

Kleist smiled. "No, I'm getting too old to leap out of the surf onto beaches. The assault team will be led by Major Angelo Quintana. You'll meet him at our camp in San Salvador. I'll be standing by on the SPUT."

"Say again."

"Special-purpose undersea transport," answered Kleist, "a vessel constructed expressly for missions of this kind. Most people don't know they exist. You'll find it most interesting."

"I'm not what you'd call trained for combat."

"Your job is purely to guide the team into the compound and show them the ventilator access to the garage area. Then you're to return to the beach and stay under cover until the mission is completed."

"Do you have a timetable for the raid?"

Kleist had a pained expression. "We prefer to call it a covert operation."

"Sorry, I've never read your bureaucratic manual on semantics."

"In answer to your question, the landing is set for 0200 four days from now."

"Four days may be too late to save my friends."

Kleist looked genuinely concerned. "We're already working on short notice and cutting our practice exercises razor thin. We need time to cover every uncertainty, every freak event. The plan has to be as airtight as our computer's tactical programs can make it."

"And if there's a human flaw in your plan?"

Any expression of friendly warmth left Kleist's face and was replaced with a cold, hard look. "If there is a human flaw, Mr. Pitt, it is you. Barring divine intervention, the success or failure of this mission will rest heaviest on *your* shoulders,"

The CIA people were thorough. Pitt was shuffled from office to office, interview to interview, with stopwatch precision. The plans to neutralize Cayo Santa María progressed with prairie-fire swiftness.

His briefing by Colonel Kleist took place less than three hours after he was interrogated by Martin Brogan. He came to realize there were thousands of contingency plans to invade every island in the Caribbean and every nation in Central and South America. Computerized war games created a series of options. All the covert-operation experts had to do was select the program that came closest to fitting the objective, and then refine it.

Pitt endured a thorough physical examination before he was allowed lunch. The physician pronounced him fit, pumped him full of high-potency vitamins, and prescribed an early bedtime before Pitt's drowsy mind turned to mush.

A tall, high-cheekboned woman with braided hair was assigned as his nursemaid, escorting him to the proper room at the proper time. She introduced herself as Alice, no surname, no title. She wore a soft tan suit over a lace blouse. Pitt thought her rather pretty and found himself wondering what she would look like curled up on satin sheets.

"Mr. Brogan has arranged for you to eat in the executive dining room," she said in perfect tour-guide fashion. "We'll take the elevator."

Pitt suddenly remembered something. "I'd like the use of a telephone."

"Sorry, not possible."

"Mind if I ask why?"

"Have you forgotten you're supposed to be dead?" Alice asked matter-of-factly. "One phone call to a friend or a lover and you could blow the entire operation."

"Yes, 'The slip of a lip may sink a ship,'" Pitt said cynically. "Look, I need some information from a total stranger. I'll hand him a phony name."

"Sorry, not possible."

A scratched phonograph record came to Pitt's mind. "Give me a phone or I'll do something nasty."

She looked at him quizzically. "Like what?"

"Go home," he said simply.

"Mr. Brogan's orders. You're not to leave the building until your flight to our camp in San Salvador. He'd have you in a straitjacket before you reached the front door."

Pitt hung back as they walked down a hallway. Then he suddenly turned and entered an anteroom whose door was unmarked. He calmly walked past a startled secretary and entered the inner office. A short man with cropped white hair, a cigarette dangling from his lips, and making strange markings on a graph, looked up in amused surprise.

Pitt flashed his best politician's smile and said, "I beg your pardon, may I borrow your phone?"

"If you work here, you know that using an unauthorized phone is against agency regulations."

"Then I'm safe," said Pitt. "I don't work here."

"You'll never get an outside line," said old White Hair.

"Watch me."

Pitt picked up the phone and asked the operator for Martin Brogan's office. In a few seconds Brogan's private secretary came on the line.

"My name is Dirk Pitt. Please inform Mr. Brogan that if I don't get the use of a telephone in one minute I'm going to cause a terrible scene."

"Who is this?"

"I told you."

Pitt was obstinate. Stoutly refusing to take no for an answer, it took him another twenty minutes of cursing, shouting, and generally being obnoxious before Brogan consented to a call outside the building, but only if Alice stood by and monitored the conversation.

She showed him to a small private office and pointed to the phone. "We have an internal operator standing by. Give her your number and she'll put it through."

Pitt spoke into the receiver. "Operator, what's your name?"

"Jennie Murphy," replied a sexy voice.

"Jennie, let's start with Baltimore information. I'd like the number of Weehawken Marine Products."

"Just a sec. I'll get it for you."

Jennie got the number from the Baltimore information operator and placed the call.

After explaining his problem to four different people, Pitt was finally connected to the executive chairman of the board—a title generally bestowed on old company heads who were eased out of the corporate mainstream.

"I'm Bob Conde. What can I do for you?"

Pitt looked at Alice and winked. "Jack Farmer, Mr. Conde. I'm with a federal archeological survey and I've discovered an old diving helmet in a shipwreck I hope you might identify."

"I'll do my best. My grandfather started the business nearly eighty years ago. We've kept fairly tight records. Have you got a serial number?"

"Yes, it was on a data plate attached to the front of the breastplate." Pitt closed his eyes and visualized the helmet on the corpse inside the *Cyclops*. "It read, 'Weehawken Products, Inc., Mark V, Serial Number 58-67-C.'"

"The Navy standard diving helmet," Conde said without hesitation. "We've been making them since 1916. Constructed of spun copper with bronze fittings. Has four sealed glass viewports."

"You sold it to the Navy?"

"Most of our orders came from the Navy. Still do, as a matter of fact. The Mark V, Mod 1 is still popular for certain types of surface-supplied-air diving operations. But this helmet was sold to a commercial customer."

"If you'll forgive me for asking, how do you know?"

"The serial number. Fifty-eight is the year it was manufactured. Sixty-seven is the number produced, and C stands for commercial sale. In other words, it was the sixty-seventh helmet to come out of our factory in 1958 and was sold to a commercial salvage company."

"Any chance of digging back and finding who bought it?"

"Might take a good half hour. We haven't bothered putting the old records on computer disks. I'd better call you back."

Alice shook her head.

"The government can afford the phone service, Mr. Conde. I'll hang on the line."

"Suit yourself."

Conde was as good as his word. He came back in thirty-one minutes. "Mr. Farmer, one of the bookkeepers found what you were looking for."

"I'm ready."

"The helmet along with a diving suit and hose equipment were sold to a private individual. Coincidentally, I knew him. Name was Hans Kronberg. A diver from the old school. Caught the bends more than anybody I ever knew. Hans was badly crippled, but it never stopped him from diving."

"Do you know what became of him?"

"As I recall, he purchased the equipment for a salvage job somewhere around Cuba. Rumor was the bends finally put him away for good."

"You don't remember who hired him?"

"No, it was too long ago," said Conde. "I think he found himself a partner who had a few bucks. Hans's regular diving gear was old and worn. His suit must have had fifty patches on it. He worked hand to mouth, barely earned enough to make a decent living. Then one day he walks in here, buys all new equipment, and pays cash."

"I appreciate your help," said Pitt.

"Not at all. Glad you called. Interesting you should call. May I ask where you found his helmet?"

"Inside an old steel wreck near the Bahamas."

Conde got the picture. He was quiet for a moment. Then he said, "So old Hans never surfaced. Well, I guess he would have preferred it to passing away in bed."

"Can you think of anyone else who might remember Hans?"

"Not really. All the hard-hat divers from the old days are gone now. The only lead I can think of is Hans's widow. She still sends me Christmas cards. She lives in a rest home."

"Do you know the name of the rest home or where it's located?"

"I believe it's in Leesburg, Virginia. Haven't a clue to the name. Speaking of names, hers is Hilda."

"Thank you, Mr. Conde. You've been a great help."

"If you're ever in Baltimore, Mr. Farmer, drop in and say hello. Got plenty of time to talk about the old days since my sons aced me out of the company helm."

"I'd like that," said Pitt. "Goodbye."

Pitt cut the connection and rang Jennie Murphy. He asked her to call senior citizen rest homes around the Leesburg area until she hit on the one that housed Hilda Kronberg.

"What are you after?" demanded Alice.

Pitt smiled. "I'm looking for El Dorado."

"Very funny."

"That's the trouble with CIA types," said Pitt. "They can't take a joke."

45

THE FORD DELIVERY TRUCK rolled up the driveway of the Winthrop Manor Nursing Home and stopped at the service entrance. The truck was painted a bright blue with illustrations of floral arrangements on the sides. Gold lettering advertised Mother's House of Flowers.

"Please don't dally," said Alice impatiently. "You have to be in San Salvador four hours from now."

"Do my best," Pitt said as he jumped from the truck, wearing a driver's uniform and carrying a bouquet of roses.

"A mystery to me how you talked Mr. Brogan into this private excursion."

Pitt smiled as he closed the door. "A simple matter of extortion."

The Winthrop Manor Nursing Home was an idyllic setting for the sunset years. There was a nine-hole golf course, tropical indoor swimming pool, an elegant dining room, and lush landscaped gardens. The main building was designed more along the lines of a five-star hotel than a drab sanatorium.

No ramshackle home for the aged poor, thought Pitt. Winthrop Manor radiated first-class taste for wealthy senior citizens. He began to wonder how the widow of a diver who struggled to make ends meet could afford to live in such luxury.

He came through a side door, walked up to a reception desk, and held up the flowers. "I have a delivery for Mrs. Hilda Kronberg."

The receptionist gave him a direct gaze and smiled. Pitt found her quite attractive, dark red hair, long and gleaming, gray-blue eyes set in a narrow face.

"Just leave them on the counter," she said sweetly. "I'll have an attendant give them to her."

"I have to deliver them personally," Pitt said. "They come with a verbal message."

She nodded and pointed to a side door. "You'll probably find Mrs. Kronberg out by the pool. Don't expect her to be lucid, she drifts in and out of reality."

Pitt thanked her and felt remiss for not making a try for a dinner date. He walked through the door and down a ramp. The glassed-in pool was designed like a Hawaiian garden with black lava rock and a waterfall.

After asking two elderly women for Hilda Kronberg, he found her sitting in a wheelchair, her eyes staring into the water, her mind elsewhere.

"Mrs. Kronberg?"

She shaded her eyes with one hand and looked up. "Yes?"

"My name is Dirk Pitt, and I wonder if I might ask you a few questions?"

"Mr. Pitt, is it?" she asked in a soft voice. She studied his uniform and the flowers. "Why would a florist's delivery boy want to ask me questions?"

Pitt smiled at her use of "boy" and handed her the flowers. "It concerns your late husband, Hans."

"Are you with *him?*" she asked suspiciously.

"No, I'm quite alone."

Hilda was sickly thin and her skin was as transparent as tissue paper. Her face was heavily made up and her hair skillfully dyed. Her diamond rings would have bought a small fleet of Rolls-Royces. Pitt guessed her age was a good fifteen years younger than the seventy-five she appeared. Hilda Kronberg was a woman waiting to die. Yet when she smiled at the mention of her husband's name, her eyes seemed to smile too.

"You look too young to have known Hans," she said.

"Mr. Conde of Weehawken Marine told me about him."

"Bob Conde, of course. He and Hans were old poker pals."

"You never remarried after his death?"

"Yes, I remarried."

"Yet you still use his name?"

"A long story that wouldn't interest you."

"When was the last time you saw Hans?"

"It was a Thursday. I saw him off on the steamship *Monterey*, bound for Havana, on December 10, 1958. Hans was always chasing rainbows. He and his partner were off on another treasure hunt. He swore they would find enough gold to buy me the dream house I always wanted. Sadly, he never came back."

"Do you recall who his partner was?"

Her gentle features suddenly turned hard. "What are you after, Mr. Pitt? Who do you represent?"

"I'm a special projects director for the National Underwater and Marine Agency," he replied. "During a survey on a sunken ship called the *Cyclops*, I discovered what I believe to be the remains of your husband."

"You found Hans?" she asked, surprised.

"I didn't make positive identification, but the diver's helmet on the body was traced to him."

"Hans was a good man," she said wistfully. "Not a good provider, perhaps, but we had a good life together until... well, until he died."

"You asked me if I was with *him?*" he prompted gently.

"A family skeleton, Mr. Pitt. I'm taken good care of. He watches over me. I've no complaints. My retreat from the real world is my own choosing..." Her voice trailed off and her stare grew distant.

Pitt had to catch her before she retreated into a self-induced shell. "Did *he* tell you Hans was murdered?"

Hilda's eyes flickered for an instant, and then she shook her head silently.

Pitt knelt beside her and held her hand. "His lifeline and air hose were cut while he was working underwater."

She noticeably trembled. "Why are you telling me this?"

"Because it's the truth, Mrs. Kronberg. I give you my word. Whoever worked with Hans probably killed him so he could steal Hans's share of the treasure."

Hilda sat there in trancelike confusion for nearly a minute. "You know about the La Dorada treasure," she said at last.

"Yes," Pitt answered. "I know how it came to be on the *Cyclops*. I also know Hans and his partner salvaged it."

Hilda began toying with one of the diamond rings on her hand. "Deep down I always suspected that Ray killed Hans."

The delayed shock of understanding slowly fell over Pitt's face. He cautiously played a wild card. "You think that Hans was murdered by Ray LeBaron?"

She nodded.

The unexpected revelation caught Pitt unawares, and it took him a few moments to come back on track. "The motive was the treasure?" he asked softly.

"No. The motive was me." She shook her head.

Pitt did not reply, only waited quietly.

"Things happen," she began in a whisper. "I was young and pretty in those days. Can you believe I was once pretty, Mr. Pitt?"

"You're still very pretty."

"I think you may need glasses, but thank you for the compliment."

"You also have a quick mind."

She gestured toward the main building. "Did they tell you I was a bit balmy?"

"The receptionist insinuated you weren't quite together."

"A little act I love to put on. Keeps everyone guessing." Her eyes sparkled briefly and then they took on a faraway look. "Hans was a nice man who was seventeen years older than me. My love for him was mixed with compassion because of his crippled body. We had been married about three years when he brought Ray home for dinner one evening. The three of us soon became close friends, the men forming a partnership to salvage artifacts from old shipwrecks and sell them to antique dealers and marine collectors. Ray was handsome and dashing in those days, and it wasn't long before he and I entered into an affair." She hesitated and stared at Pitt. "Have you ever deeply loved two women at the same time, Mr. Pitt?"

"I'm afraid the experience has eluded me."

"The strange part was that I didn't feel any guilt. Deceiving Hans became an exciting adventure. It was not that I was a dishonest person. It was just that I had never lied to somebody close to me before and remorse never entered my mind. Now I thank God that Hans didn't find out before he died."

"Can you tell me about the La Dorada treasure?"

"After graduating from Stanford, Ray spent a couple years tramping through the jungles of Brazil, hunting for gold. He first heard of the La Dorada from an American surveyor. I don't remember the details, but he was sure it was on board the *Cyclops* when it disappeared. He and Hans spent two years dragging some sort of instrument that detected iron up and down the Caribbean. Finally, they found the wreck. Ray borrowed some money from his mother to buy diving equipment and a small salvage boat. He sailed ahead to Cuba to set up a base of operations while Hans was finishing up a job off New Jersey."

"Did you ever receive a letter or a phone call from Hans after he sailed on the *Monterey*?"

"He called once from Cuba. All he said was that he and Ray were leaving for the wreck site the next day. Two weeks later, Ray returned and told me Hans had died from the bends and was buried at sea."

"And the treasure?"

"Ray described it as a huge golden statue," she replied. "He somehow raised it onto the salvage boat and took it to Cuba."

Pitt stood, stretched, and knelt beside Hilda again. "Odd that he didn't bring the statue back to the States."

"He was afraid that Brazil, the state of Florida, the federal government, other treasure hunters and marine archeologists would confiscate or tie up the La Dorada in court claims and eventually leave him nothing. Then, of course, there was always the Internal Revenue Service. Ray couldn't see giving away millions of dollars in taxes if he could get around it. So he told no one but me of the discovery."

"What ever became of it?"

"Ray removed a giant ruby from the statue's heart, cut it up into small stones, and sold them piecemeal."

"And that was the beginning of the LeBaron financial empire," said Pitt.

"Yes, but before Ray could cut up the emerald head or melt down the gold, Castro came to power and he was forced to hide the statue. He never told me where he hid it."

"Then the La Dorada is still buried somewhere in Cuba."

"I'm certain Ray was never able to return and retrieve it."

"Did you see Mr. LeBaron after that?"

"Oh my, yes," she said brightly. "We were married."

"You were the first Mrs. LeBaron?" Pitt asked, astonished.

"For thirty-three years."

"But the records say his first wife's name was Hillary and she died some years ago."

"Ray preferred Hillary over Hilda when he became wealthy. Thought it had more class. My death was a convenient arrangement for him when I became ill—divorcing an invalid was abhorrent to him. So he buried Hillary LeBaron, while Hilda Kronberg withers away here."

"That strikes me as inhumanly cruel."

"My husband was generous if not compassionate. We lived two different lives. But I don't mind. Jessie comes to see me occasionally."

"The second Mrs. LeBaron?"

"A very charming and thoughtful person."

"How can she be married to him if you're still alive?"

She smiled brightly. "The one time Ray made a bad deal. The doctors told him I had only a few months to live. But I fooled them all and have hung on for seven years."

"That makes him a bigamist as well as a murderer and a thief."

Hilda did not argue. "Ray is a complicated man. He takes far more than he gives."

"If I were you I'd nail him to the nearest cross."

"Too late for me, Mr. Pitt." She looked up at him, a sudden twinkle in her eyes. "But you could do something in my place."

"Name it."

"Find the La Dorada," she said fervently. "Find the statue and give it to the world. See that it's displayed to the public. That would hurt Ray more than losing his magazine. But more important, it's what Hans would have wanted."

Pitt took her hand and held it. "Hilda," he said softly, "I'll do my damnedest."

46

HUDSON ADJUSTED THE CLARITY of the image and nodded a greeting at the face staring back. "Eli, I have someone who has asked to talk to you."

"Always happy to see a new face," Steinmetz replied cheerfully.

Another man took Hudson's place beneath the video camera and monitor. He gazed in fascination for a few moments before speaking.

"Are you really on the moon?" he asked finally.

"Show time," Steinmetz said with an agreeable smile. He moved offscreen and lifted the portable camera from its tripod and panned it through a quartz window at the lunar landscape. "Sorry I can't show you earth, but we're on the wrong side of the ball."

"I believe you."

Steinmetz replaced the camera and moved in front of it again. He leaned forward and stared into his monitor. His smile slowly faded and his eyes took on a questioning look. "Are you who I think you are?"

"Do you recognize me?"

"You look and sound like the President."

It was the President's turn to smile. "I wasn't sure you were aware, knowing that I was a senator when you left earth, and newspapers aren't delivered in your neighborhood."

"When the moon's orbit around the earth is in the proper position we can tap into most communication satellites. During the crew's last rest break, they watched the latest Paul Newman movie on Home Box Office. We also devour the Cable News Network programs like starving dogs."

"The Jersey Colony is an incredible achievement. A grateful nation will forever be in your debt."

"Thank you, Mr. President, though it comes as a surprise that Leo jumped the gun and announced the success of the project before our return to earth. That wasn't part of the plan."

"There has been no public announcement," said the President, becoming serious. "Next to you and your colony people, I am the only one outside the 'inner core' who is aware of your existence, except maybe the Russians."

Steinmetz stared at him across 240,000 miles of space. "How could they know about the Jersey Colony?"

The President paused to look at Hudson, who was standing out of camera range. Hudson shook his head.

"The Selenos lunar photo probes," answered the President, omitting any reference to them being manned. "One managed to send its data back to the Soviet Union. We think it showed the Jersey Colony. We also have reason to believe the Russians suspect you destroyed the probes from the lunar surface."

An uneasy apprehension showed in Steinmetz's eyes. "You think they plan to attack us, is that it?"

"Yes, Eli, I do," said the President. "Selenos 8, the Soviet lunar station, entered orbit around the moon three hours ago. NASA computers project it to pass up a safe landing site on the face and come down on the dark side in your block of the neighborhood. A risky gamble unless they have a definite objective."

"The Jersey Colony."

"Their lunar landing vehicle holds seven men," the President continued. "The craft requires two pilot-engineers to direct its flight. That leaves five for combat."

"There are ten of us," said Steinmetz. "Two to one, not bad odds."

"Except they'll have firepower and training on their side. These men will be the deadliest team the Russians can field."

"You paint a grim picture, Mr. President. What would you have us do?"

"You've accomplished far more than any of us had any right to expect. But the deck is stacked against you. Destroy the colony and get out before there's any bloodshed. I want you and your people safely back on earth to receive the honors you deserve."

"I don't think you quite realize what we've busted our asses to build here."

"Whatever you've done isn't worth your lives."

"We've all lived with death for six years," said Steinmetz slowly. "A few more hours won't matter."

"Don't throw it all away on an impossible fight," the President argued.

"Sorry, Mr. President, but you're talking to a man who lost his daddy at a little sand spit called Wake Island. I'll put it to a vote, but I already know the outcome. The other guys won't cut and run any more than I will. We'll stay and fight."

The President felt proud and defeated at the same time. "What weapons do you have?" he asked wearily.

"Our arsenal consists of one used rocket launcher, which is down to its last shell, an M-14 National Match rifle, and a twenty-two-caliber target pistol. We brought them for a series of gravity experiments."

"You're outclassed, Eli," the President said miserably. "Can't you realize that?"

"No, sir. I refuse to quit on a technicality."

"What technicality?"

"The Russians are the visitors."

"So what?"

"That makes us the home team," said Steinmetz slyly. "And the home team always has the advantage."

"They've landed!" exclaimed Sergei Kornilov, smashing a fist into one hand. "Selenos 8 is on the moon!"

Below the VIP observation room, on the floor of the Soviet Mission Control Center, the engineers and space scientists burst into wild cheering and applause.

President Antonov held up a glass of champagne. "To the glory of the Soviet Union and the party."

The toast was repeated by the Kremlin officials and high-ranking military officers crowded in the room.

"To our first stepping-stone on our quest of Mars," toasted General Yasenin.

"Here, here!" replied a chorus of deep voices. "To Mars."

Antonov set his empty glass on a tray and turned to Yasenin, his face abruptly serious. "How soon before Major Leuchenko makes contact with the moon base?" he asked.

"Allowing for time to secure the spacecraft systems, make a reconnaissance of the terrain, and position his men for the assault, I would say four hours."

"How far away is the landing site?"

"Selenos 8 was programmed to touch down behind a low range of hills less than three kilometers from where Selenos 4 detected the astronauts," answered the general.

"That seems quite close," said Antonov. "If the Americans tracked our descent, Leuchenko has lost all opportunity for surprise."

"There is little doubt they have realized what we're up to."

"You're not concerned?"

"Our advantage lies in Leuchenko's experience and superior fire-power, Comrade President." Yasenin's face wore the expression of a boxing manager who had just sent his fighter into the ring against a one-armed man. "The Americans are faced with a no-win situation."

47

MAJOR GRIGORY LEUCHENKO LAY STRETCHED in the fine, gray dust of the moon's surface and stared at the desolate wasteland spread beneath the pitch-black sky. He found the silent and ghostly land-scape similar to the arid desert of Afghanistan's Seistan Basin. The gravel plains and rolling mound-shaped hills gave little definition. It reminded him of a great sea of plaster of paris, yet it seemed strangely familiar to him.

He fought off an urge to vomit. He and his men were all suffering from nausea. There had been no time to train for the weightless environment during the journey from earth, no weeks or months to adjust as had the cosmonauts of the Soyuz missions. They were given only a few hours' instruction on how to operate the life-support sys-tems of their lunar suits, a brief lecture on conditions they could expect to find on the moon, and a briefing on the location of the American colony.

He felt a hand squeeze his shoulder through his lunar suit. He spoke into his helmet's internal transmitter without turning.

"What have you got?"

Lieutenant Dmitri Petrov pointed toward a flat valley running be-tween the sloping walls of two craters about a thousand meters to the left. "Vehicle tracks and footprints, converging into that shadow below the left crater's rim. I make out three, maybe four small build-ings."

"Pressurized greenhouses," said Leuchenko. He set a pair of box-like binoculars on a small tripod and settled the wide viewing piece around the faceplate of his helmet. "Looks like vapor issuing out of the crater's sloping side." He paused to adjust the focus. "Yes, I can see it clearly now. There's an entrance into the rock, probably an airlock with access to their interior facility. No sign of life. The outer perimeter appears deserted."

"They could be hiding in ambush," said Petrov.

"Hide where?" asked Leuchenko, sweeping the open panorama. "The scattered rocks are too small to shield a man. There are no breaks in the terrain, no indication of defense works. An astronaut in a bulky white lunar suit would stand out like a snowman in a field of cinders. No, they must be barricaded inside the cave."

"Not a wise defensive position. All to our advantage."

"They still have a rocket launcher."

"That has little effect against men spread in a loose formation."

"True, but we'll have no cover and we can't be sure they don't have other weapons."

"A heavy concentration of fire inside the cave entrance might force their hand," suggested Petrov.

"Our orders are not to cause any unnecessary destruction to the facility," said Leuchenko. "We'll have to move in—"

"Something is moving out there!" Petrov cried.

Leuchenko stared through the binoculars. An odd-looking open vehicle had appeared from behind one of the greenhouses and was traveling in their direction. A white flag, attached to an antenna, hung limply in the airless atmosphere. He watched until it stopped fifty meters away and a figure stepped out onto the lunar soil.

"Interesting," said Leuchenko thoughtfully. "The Americans want to parley."

"Might be a trick. A ruse to study our force."

"I don't think so. They wouldn't make contact under a flag of truce if they were acting from a position of strength. Their intelligence people and tracking systems on earth warned them of our arrival, and they must realize they're outgunned. Americans are capitalists. They look at everything from a business viewpoint. If they can't make a fight for it, they'll try to strike a deal."

"You going out?" asked Petrov.

"No harm in talking. He doesn't appear armed. Perhaps they can be persuaded to bargain their lives for an intact colony."

"Our orders were to take no prisoners."

"I haven't forgotten," said Leuchenko tensely. "We'll cross that bridge when we've achieved our objective. Tell the men to keep the American in their sights. If I raise my left hand, give the order to fire."

He handed his automatic weapon to Petrov and rose lightly to his feet. His lunar suit, rifle, and life-support backpack, containing an oxygen recharger and water recharger for cooling, added 194 pounds to Leuchenko's body weight for a total of almost 360 earth pounds. But his lunar weight was only 60 pounds.

He moved toward the lunar vehicle in the half-walking, half-hopping gait typical when moving under the light gravitational pull of the moon. He quickly approached the lunar vehicle and halted about five meters away.

The American moon colonist was leaning unconcernedly against a front wheel. He straightened, knelt on one knee, and wrote a number in the lead-colored dust.

Leuchenko understood and turned his radio receiver to the frequency indicated. Then he nodded.

"Are you receiving me?" the American asked in badly mispronounced Russian.

"I speak English," replied Leuchenko.

"Good. That will save any misunderstanding. My name is Eli Steinmetz."

"You are the United States moon base leader?"

"I head up the project, yes."

"Major Grigory Leuchenko, Soviet Union."

Steinmetz moved closer and they stiffly shook hands. "It seems we have a problem, Major."

"One neither of us can avoid."

"You could turn around and hike back to your lunar lander," said Steinmetz.

"I have my orders," Leuchenko stated in a firm tone.

"You're to attack and capture my colony."

"Yes."

"Is there no way we can prevent bloodshed?"

"You could surrender."

"Funny," said Steinmetz. "I was about to ask the same of you."

Leuchenko was certain Steinmetz was bluffing, but the face behind the gold-tinted visor remained unreadable. All Leuchenko could see was his own reflection.

"You must realize that your people are no match for mine."

"In a knock-down, drag-out firefight you'd win," agreed Steinmetz. "But you can remain outside your landing craft only for a few hours before you must go back and replenish your breathing systems. I reckon you've already used up two."

"We have enough left to accomplish the job," Leuchenko said confidently.

"I must warn you, Major. We have a secret weapon. You and your men will surely die."

"A crude bluff, Mr. Steinmetz. I would have expected better from an American scientist."

Steinmetz corrected him. "Engineer, there's a difference."

"Whatever," said Leuchenko impatiently. As a soldier, he was out of his element in wordy negotiations. He was anxious for action. "It's senseless to carry this conversation any further. You would be wise to send your men out and turn over the facility. I'll guarantee your safety until you can be returned to earth."

"You're lying, Major. Either your people or mine will have to be erased. There can be no losers left to tell the world what happened here."

"You're wrong, Mr. Steinmetz. Surrender and you will be treated fairly."

"Sorry, no deal."

"Then there can be no quarter."

"I expected none," said Steinmetz, his tone grim. "You attack and the waste of human lives will be on your shoulders."

Anger rose within Leuchenko. "For one who is responsible for the deaths of nine Soviet cosmonauts, Mr. Steinmetz, you're hardly in a position to lecture me on human life."

Leuchenko couldn't be certain, but he swore Steinmetz tensed. Without waiting for a reply, he turned on his heels and loped away. He looked over his shoulder and saw that Steinmetz stood there for several seconds before slowly reentering the lunar vehicle and driving back to the colony, trailing a small cloud of gray dust behind the rear wheels.

Leuchenko smiled to himself. In two more hours, three at the most, his mission would be successfully achieved. When he reached his men, he studied the layout of the craggy surface in front of the moon base through the binoculars again. Finally, when he was satisfied there were no American colonists lurking amid the rocks, Leuchenko gave the order to spread out in loose formation and advance. The elite Soviet fighting team moved forward without an inkling that Steinmetz's inventive trap was set and waiting.

48

AFTER STEINMETZ RETURNED to the entrance of Jersey Colony's subterranean headquarters, he leisurely parked the lunar vehicle and shuffled slowly inside. He took his time, almost feeling Leuchenko's eyes probing his every movement. Once out of view of the Russians, he stopped short of the airlock and quickly stepped through a small side tunnel that gradually rose through the crater's interior slope. His passage raised small clouds of dust that filled the narrow shaft, and he had to continually wipe his visor to see.

Fifty steps and a minute later he crouched and crawled into an opening that led to a small shelf camouflaged by a large gray cloth perfectly matched to the surrounding surface. Another suited figure was lying on his stomach, gazing through the telescopic sight of a rifle.

Willie Shea, the colony's geophysicist, did not notice another presence until Steinmetz eased down beside him. "I don't think you made much of an impression," he said with a bare hint of a Boston twang. "The Slavs are about to attack the homestead."

From the elevated vantage point Steinmetz could clearly see Major Leuchenko and his men advancing across the valley. They came on like hunters stalking their prey, making no attempt to use the high ground of the crater's sides. The loose shale would have made the going too slow. Instead, they jumped across the flat ground in zigzag patterns, throwing themselves prone every thirty or forty feet, taking advantage of every boulder, every broken contour of the land. An expert marksman would have found the twisting and dodging figures nearly impossible to hit.

"Put a shot about ten feet in front of the point man," said Steinmetz. "I want to observe their reaction."

"If they're monitoring our frequency, we'll give away our every move," protested Shea.

"They haven't got time to hunt for our frequency. Shut up and shoot."

Shea shrugged inside his lunar suit, peered through the crosshairs of his scope, and squeezed off a round. The gunshot was strangely silent because there was no air on the moon to carry the sound waves.

A puff of dust kicked up ahead of Leuchenko and he immediately dropped to the ground. His men followed suit and stared over the sights of their automatic weapons, waiting expectantly for more fire. But nothing happened.

"Did anyone see where it came from?" Leuchenko demanded.

The replies were negative.

"They're sighting for range," said Sergeant Ivan Ostrovski. A hardened veteran of the Afghanistan fighting, he could not believe he was actually in combat on the moon. He swept a pointed finger over the ground about two hundred meters ahead. "What do you make of those colored rocks, Major?"

For the first time Leuchenko spied several boulders scattered in a ragged line across the valley, stained with bright orange paint. "I doubt if it has anything to do with us," he said. "Probably put there for some sort of experiment."

"I think the fire came on a downward angle," said Petrov.

Leuchenko took the binoculars from his hip pack, set them on the tripod, and carefully scanned the side and rim of the crater. The sun was a blazing white but with no air to spread the light an astronaut standing in the shadows of a rock formation would be almost invisible.

"Nothing shows," he said finally.

"If they're waiting for us to close the gap, they must be conserving a small supply of ammunition."

"We'll know in another three hundred meters what kind of reception they've planned," muttered Leuchenko. "Once we come under cover of the greenhouses we'll be out of sight of the cave entrance." He rose to one knee and waved his arm forward. "Fan out and keep alert."

The five Soviet fighters leaped to their feet and scrambled on. As they reached the orange rocks another shot struck the fine sand in front of them and they flung themselves prone, a jagged line of white figures, face visors flashing in the intense rays of the sun.

Only a hundred meters separated them from the greenhouses, but nausea was draining their energy. They were as tough as any fighting men in the world, but they were combating space sickness in tandem with an alien environment. Leuchenko knew he could count on them to go far beyond their limits of endurance. But if they didn't force their way into the safe atmosphere of the colony within the next hour, there was little chance of them making it back to their landing craft before their life-support systems gave out. He gave them a minute to rest while he made another examination of the ground ahead.

Leuchenko was an old hand at sniffing out traps. He had come within a hair of being killed on three different patrols in ambushes laid by the Afghan rebels, and he had learned the fine art of scenting danger the hard way.

It wasn't what his eyes could see; it was what they couldn't see that rang a warning bell in his head. The two shots didn't fit a wild pattern. They struck him as deliberately placed. A crude warning? No, it had to mean something else, he speculated. A signal perhaps?

The confining pressure suit and helmet irritated him. He longed for his comfortable and efficient combat gear, but fully realizing they could not protect his body from the frying heat and the cosmic rays. For at least the fourth time the bile rose in his throat and he gagged as he forced himself to swallow it.

The situation was hellish, he thought angrily. Nothing was to his liking. His men were exposed in the open. He'd been given no intelligence on the Americans' weapons except the reported rocket launcher. Now they were under attack by small-arms fire. Leuchenko's only consolation was that the colonists seemed to be using a rifle or maybe even a pistol. If they possessed a full automatic firearm, they could have cut down the Soviets a hundred meters back. And the rocket launcher. Why hadn't they tried it before now? What were they waiting for?

What bothered him most was the total lack of movement by the colonists. The greenhouses, equipment, and small laboratory modules sitting around the entrance to the cave appeared deserted.

"Unless you see a target," he ordered, "hold your fire until we reach cover. Then we'll regroup and storm the main quarters inside the hill."

Leuchenko waited until each of his four men acknowledged and then he motioned them on.

Corporal Mikhail Yushchuk was about thirty meters behind and to one side of the man on his left. He stood and began running in a crouching position. He had taken only a few steps when he felt a stinging sensation in his kidney. Then the sudden thrust of pain was repeated. He reached around and grasped the small of his back just below his support system pack. His vision began to blur and his breath came in gasps as his pressurized suit began to leak. He sank to his knees and stared dumbly at his hand. The glove was drenched in blood that was already steaming and coagulating under the roasting heat from the sun.

Yushchuk tried to warn Leuchenko, but his voice failed. He crumbled into the gray dust, his eyes dimly recognizing a figure in a strange space suit standing over him with a knife. Then his world went black.

Steinmetz witnessed Yushchuk's death from his vantage point and issued a series of sharp commands into his helmet's transmitter. "Okay, Dawson, your man is ten feet left and eight feet ahead of you. Gallagher, he's twenty feet to your right and moving forward. Steady, steady, he's cutting right into Dawson. Okay, nail him."

He watched two of the colonists materialize as if by magic and attack one of the Soviets who was lagging slightly behind his comrades.

"Two down, three to go," Steinmetz muttered softly to himself.

"I've got my sights set on the point man," said Shea. "But I can't promise a clean hit unless he freezes for a second."

"Lay another shot, only closer this time to get them on the ground again. Then stay on him. If he gets wise, he could cut our guys down before they could close on him. Blast his ass if he so much as turns his head."

Shea silently aimed his M-14 and pulled off another shot, which struck less than three feet in front of the lead man's boots.

"Cooper! Snyder!" Steinmetz barked. "Your man is flat on the ground twenty feet ahead and to your left. Take him, now!" He paused to scan the position of the second remaining Russian. "Same goes for Russell and Perry, thirty feet directly in front. Go!"

The third member of the Soviet combat team never knew what hit him. He died while hugging the ground for cover. Eight of the colonists were now closing the pincers from the rear of the Russians, whose concentration was focused on the colony.

Suddenly Steinmetz froze. The man behind the leader swung around just as Russell and Perry leaped at him like offensive tackles charging a quarterback.

Lieutenant Petrov spotted the converging shadows as he rose to his feet for the final dash to the greenhouses. He instinctively twisted around in an abrupt corkscrew motion as Russell and Perry crashed into him. A cold professional, he should have fired and brought them down. But he hesitated a split second too long out of astonishment. It was as if the Americans had risen up out of the moon's surface like spectral demons. He managed to snap off a shot that drilled one of his assailant's upper arms. Then a knife flashed.

Leuchenko's eyes were trained toward the colony ahead. He was unaware of the slaughter going on behind him until he heard Petrov gasp out a warning. He spun around and stood rooted in shocked awe.

His four men were stretched out in a lifeless sprawl on the lunar gravel. Eight American colonists had appeared out of nowhere and were rapidly encircling him. Sudden hatred burst within him, and he thrust his weapon into firing position.

A bullet thumped into his thigh and he tilted sideways. Tensed in sudden pain, he squeezed off twenty rounds. Most of them flew wide into the lunar desert, but two found their mark. One of the colonists fell backward and another dropped to his knees clutching his shoulder.

Then another bullet tore into his neck. He held on to the trigger, spewing rounds until the clip ran dry, his shots flying wild.

He cursed as he crumpled limply to the ground. "Damn the Americans!" he shouted inside his helmet. He thought of them as devils who didn't play the game according to the rules. He lay on his back, staring up at the faceless forms standing above him.

They parted as another member of the colonists approached and knelt down beside Leuchenko.

"Steinmetz?" Leuchenko asked weakly. "Can you hear me?"

"Yes, I'm on your frequency," answered Steinmetz. "I can hear you."

"Your secret weapon . . . how did you make your people appear from nothing?"

Steinmetz knew he would be talking to a dead man within seconds.

"An ordinary shovel," he replied. "Since we all have to wear pressurized lunar suits with self-contained life supports, it was a simple matter to bury the men in the soft soil."

"They were marked by the orange rocks?"

"Yes, from a hidden platform on the crater's side I could direct when and where to attack you from the rear."

"I do not wish to be buried here," Leuchenko murmured. "Tell my nation...tell them to bring us home someday."

It was close, but Steinmetz got it in. "You'll all go home," he said. "That's a promise."

In Russia a grim-faced Yasenin turned to President Antonov. "You heard," he said through clenched lips. "They're gone."

"They're gone," Antonov repeated mechanically. "It was as though Leuchenko's last words came from across the room."

"His communications were relayed by the two crewmen on the lunar landing craft direct to our space communications center," explained Kornilov.

Antonov moved away from the window overlooking the mission control room and sat down heavily in a chair. For such a large bear of a man he seemed shrunken and withered. He looked down at his hands and shook his head sadly.

"Poor planning," he said quietly. "We threw Major Leuchenko and his men's lives away and achieved nothing."

"There was no time to plan a proper mission," Yasenin offered lamely.

"Under the circumstances, we did all that was possible," added Kornilov. "We still have the glory of the first Soviet men to walk on the moon."

"The luster has already faded." Antonov's voice was leaden with defeat. "The Americans' incredible accomplishment will bury any propaganda value of our achievement."

"Perhaps we can still stop them," Yasenin said bitterly.

Kornilov stared at the general. "By sending up a better prepared fighting force?"

"Exactly."

"Better yet, why not wait until they return?"

Antonov looked at Kornilov with curious eyes. "What are you suggesting?"

"I've been speaking to Vladimir Polevoi. He's informed me that the GRU's listening center in Cuba has intercepted and identified the voice and video transmissions from the American moon colony to a location outside of Washington. He's sending copies of the communications by courier. One of them reveals the scheduled departure of the colonists for earth."

"They're returning?" asked Antonov.

"Yes," replied Kornilov. "According to Polevoi, they intend to link up with the American space station in forty-six hours, then return to the Kennedy spaceport at Cape Canaveral on the shuttle *Gettysburg*."

Antonov's face brightened. "Then we still have a chance to stop them?"

Yasenin nodded. "They can be destroyed in deep space before they dock at the space station. The Americans wouldn't dare retaliate after we confront them with the crimes they've committed against us."

"Better to reserve our retribution as leverage," said Kornilov thoughtfully.

"Leverage?"

Kornilov smiled enigmatically. "The Americans have a saying, 'The ball is in our court.' It is they who are on the defensive. The White House and the State Department are probably drafting a reply to our expected protest this minute. I propose we sidestep the accepted routine and remain silent. Do not play the role of a victimized nation. Instead, we use our leverage and cause an event."

"What kind of event?" asked Antonov, straightening with interest.

"The seizure of the vast amount of data carried by the returning moon colonists."

"By what means?" Yasenin demanded.

The smile left Kornilov's face and his expression went dead serious. "We force the *Gettysburg* to crash-land in Cuba."

PART IV

The Gettysburg

49

November 3, 1989
San Salvador Island

PITT WAS GOING MAD. The two days of inactivity were the most agonizing he had ever known. There was little for him to do but eat, exercise, and sleep. He had yet to be called on to participate in the training exercises. Hourly, he cursed Colonel Kleist, who bore Pitt's onslaughts with stoic indifference, explaining with tight-lipped patience that his Cuban Special Forces team could not assault Cayo Santa María until he pronounced them fit and ready. And no, he would not speed up the timetable.

Pitt worked off his frustration by taking long swims to the outer reef and climbing a steep rock face whose summit looked out over the surrounding sea.

San Salvador, the smallest of the Bahamas, was known to old mariners as Watling Island, after a zealot buccaneer who flogged members of his crew who did not observe the Sabbath. It is also believed to be the island where Columbus first stepped ashore in the New World. With a picturesque harbor and a lush interior blued by freshwater lakes, few tourists gazing at its beauty would have guessed it contained a huge military training complex and missile observation installation.

The CIA staked out its claim on a remote beach called French Bay at the southern tip of the island. There was no road linking the covert training center with Cockburn Town and the main airport. The only way in or out was by small boat through the surrounding reefs or by helicopter.

Pitt rose shortly before sunrise on the morning of his third day on the island and swam strongly for half a mile, and then worked his way back to shore, free-diving among the coral formations. Two hours later, he walked from the warm water and stretched out on the beach, overwhelmed by a surge of helplessness as he stared over the sea toward Cuba.

A shadow fell across his body, and he sat up. A dark-skinned man stood over him, dressed comfortably in a loose-fitting cotton shirt and shorts. His slick, night-black hair matched an enormous moustache. Sad eyes stared from a face wrinkled from long exposure to wind and sun, and when he smiled his lips barely moved.

"Mr. Pitt?"

"Yes."

"We haven't been formally introduced, but I'm Major Angelo Quintana."

Pitt came to his feet and they shook hands. "You're leading the mission."

Quintana nodded. "Colonel Kleist tells me you've been riding him pretty hard."

"I left friends who may be fighting to stay alive."

"I also left friends in Cuba, Mr. Pitt. Only they lost their battle to live. My brother and father died in prison merely because a member of their local block committee, who owed my family money, accused them of counterrevolutionary activities. I sympathize with your problem, but you do not have a monopoly on grief."

Pitt did not offer condolences. Quintana struck him as a man who didn't dwell on sorrow. "As long as I believe there is still hope," he said firmly, "I'm not about to stop pushing."

Quintana gave him an easy smile. He liked what he saw in Pitt's eyes. This was a man who could be trusted when things got tight. A hardnose who did not know the definition of failure.

"So you're the one who made the ingenious escape from Velikov's headquarters."

"A ton of luck played a heavy role."

"How would you describe the morale of the troops guarding the compound?"

"If you mean mental condition, I'd have to say they were bored to the gills. Russians aren't used to the draining humidity of the tropics. Overall they seemed sluggish."

"How many patrolling the island?"

"None that I could see."

"And the guardhouse at the front gate?"

"Only two."

"A canny man, Velikov."

"I gather you respect him for making the island appear deserted."

"You gather right. I would have expected a small army of guards and the usual Soviet security measures. But Velikov doesn't think like a Russian. He designs like an American, refines like a Japanese, and expedites like a German. The man is one shrewd operator."

"So I've heard."

"I'm told you met him."

"We've had a couple of conversations."

"What was your impression of him?"

"He reads the *Wall Street Journal*."

"That all?"

"He speaks better English than I do. His nails are clean and trimmed. And if he's read half the books and magazines in his library he knows more about the United States and its taxpayers than half the politicians in Washington."

"You're probably the only Westerner running around loose who's ever seen him face to face."

"It was no treat, believe me."

Quintana thoughtfully scraped one toe in the sand. "Leaving such a vital installation so lightly guarded is an open invitation for infiltration."

"Not if Velikov knows you're coming," said Pitt.

"Okay, the Cuban radar network and the Russian spy satellites can spot every plane and boat within fifty miles. An air drop or a landing from the sea would be impossible. But an underwater approach could squeeze under their detection grids with ease." Quintana paused and grinned. "In your case the vessel was too tiny to show up on a radarscope."

"My inventory of oceangoing yachts was marginal," Pitt said lightly. Then he turned serious. "You've overlooked something."

"Overlooked what?"

"Velikov's brain. You said he was a shrewd operator. He didn't build a fortress bristling with landmines and concrete bunkers for one simple reason: he didn't have to. You and Colonel Kleist are bleeding optimists if you think a submarine or your SPUD, or whatever you call it, can penetrate his security net."

Quintana's eyebrows narrowed. "Go on."

"Underwater sensors," explained Pitt. "Velikov must have ringed the island with sensors on the sea floor that can detect the movement of a submarine's hull against a water mass and the cavitation of its propellers."

"Our SPUT was designed to slip through such a system."

"Not if Velikov's marine engineers bunched the sensing units a hundred yards apart. Nothing but a school of fish could swim past. I saw the trucks in the compound's garage. With ten minutes' warning Velikov could put a security force on the beach that would slaughter your men before they stepped foot out of the surf. I suggest you and Kleist reprogram your electronic war games."

Quintana subsided into silence. His precisely conceived landing plan began to crack and shatter before his eyes. "Our computers should have thought of that," he said bitterly.

"They don't create what they're not taught," Pitt replied philosophically.

"You realize, of course, this means we have to scrub the mission. Without the element of surprise there isn't the slightest hope of destroying the installation and rescuing Mrs. LeBaron and the others."

"I disagree."

"You think you're smarter than our mission computers?"

"I escaped Cayo Santa María without detection. I can get your people in the same way."

"With a fleet of bathtubs?" Quintana said sarcastically.

"A more modern variation comes to mind."

Quintana looked at Pitt in deep speculation. "You've got an idea that might turn the trick?"

"I most certainly have."

"And still meet the timetable?"

"Yes."

"And succeed?"

"You feel safer if I underwrote an insurance policy?"

Quintana sensed utter conviction in Pitt's tone. He turned and began walking toward the main camp. "Come along, Mr. Pitt. It's time we put you to work."

50

FIDEL CASTRO SAT slouched in the fighting chair and gazed pensively over the stern of a forty-foot cabin cruiser. His shoulders were harnessed and his gloved hands loosely clutched the heavy fiberglass rod, whose line trailed from a huge reel into the sparkling wake. The dolphin bait was snatched by a passing barracuda, but Castro didn't seem to mind. His thoughts were not on marlin.

The muscular body that once earned him the title "Cuba's best school athlete" had softened and expanded with age. The curly hair and the barbed-wire beard were gray now, but the revolutionary fire in his dark eyes still burned as brightly as it did when he came down from the mountains of the Sierra Maestra thirty years ago.

He wore only a baseball cap, swimming trunks, old sneakers, and sunglasses. The stub of an unlit Havana drooped from one corner of his lips. He turned and shielded his eyes from the brilliant tropical sunlight.

"You want me to cease *internacionalismo?*" he demanded above the muffled roar of the twin diesels. "Renounce our policy of spreading Cuba's influence abroad? Is that what you want?"

Raúl Castro sat in a deckchair, holding a bottle of beer. "Not renounce but quietly bring down the curtain on our commitments abroad."

"My brother the hardline revolutionary. What brought on your about-face?"

"Times change," Raúl said simply.

Cold and aloof in public, Fidel's younger brother was witty and congenial in private. His hair was black, slick, and closely trimmed above the ears. Raúl viewed the world from a pixie face through dark, beady eyes. A narrow moustache stretched across his upper lip, the pointed tips ending precisely above the corners of his mouth.

Fidel rubbed the back of one hand against a few drops of sweat that clung to his eyebrows. "I cannot write off the enormous cost in money and the blood of our soldiers. And what of our friends in Africa and the Americas? Do I write them off like our dead in Afghanistan?"

"The price Cuba was paid for our involvement in revolutionary movements outweighs the gains. So we made friends in Angola and Ethiopia. What will they ever do for us in return? We both know the answer is nothing. We have to face it, Fidel, we made mistakes. I'll be the first to admit mine. But for God's sake, let's cut our losses and return to building Cuba into a great socialist nation to be envied by the third world. We'll achieve far more by having them copy our example than by giving them our people's blood."

"You're asking me to turn my back on our honor and our principles."

Raúl rolled the cool bottle across his perspiring forehead. "Let's look at the truth, Fidel. We've thrown principles overboard before when it was in the best interests of the revolution. If we don't shift gears soon and vitalize our stagnating economy, the people's discontent might turn to unrest, despite their love for you."

Fidel spat the cigar stub over the boat's transom and motioned to a deckhand for another. "The U.S. Congress would love to see the people turn against me."

"The Congress doesn't bother me half as much as the Kremlin," said Raúl. "Everywhere I look I find a traitor in Antonov's pocket. I can't even trust my own security people anymore."

"Once the President and I agree to the U.S.–Cuban pact and sign it, our Soviet fair-weather friends will be forced to release their tentacles from around our necks."

"How can you finalize anything when you refuse to sit down and negotiate with him?"

Fidel paused to light a fresh cigar brought by the deckhand. "By now he's probably made up his mind that my offer to sever our links with the Soviet Union in return for United States economic aid and open trade agreements is genuine. If I appear too eager for a meeting, he'll only set impossible preconditions. Let him stew for a while. When he realizes I'm not crawling over the White House doormat, he'll lower his sights."

"The President will be even more eager to come to terms when he learns of the reckless encroachment by Antonov's cronies into our government."

Fidel held up the cigar to make his point. "Exactly why I have sat back and allowed it to happen. Playing on American fears of a Soviet stooge figureheading a puppet regime is all to our advantage."

Raúl emptied the beer bottle and tossed it over the side. "Just don't wait too long, big brother, or we'll find ourselves out of a job."

"Never happen." Fidel's face creased in a cocksure smile. "I am the glue that holds the revolution together. All I have to do is go before the people and expose the traitors and the Soviet plot to undermine our sacred sovereignty. And then, as President of the Council of Ministers, you will announce the cutting of all ties to the Kremlin. Any discontent will be replaced with national rejoicing. With one swing of the ax I'll have cut the massive debt to Moscow and removed the U.S. trade embargo."

"Better be soon."

"In my speech during the Education Day celebration."

Raúl checked the calendar on his watch. "Five days from now."

"A perfect opportunity."

"I'd feel better if we could test the President's mood toward your proposal."

"I'll leave it to you to contact the White House and arrange for a meeting with his representatives during the Education Day festivities."

"Before your speech, I hope."

"Of course."

"Aren't you tempting fate, waiting until the last moment?"

"He'll take me up on it," said Fidel through a cloud of smoke. "Make no mistake. My gift of those three Soviet cosmonauts should have shown him my good intentions."

Raúl scowled. "Could be he has already sent us his reply."

Fidel turned and glared at him. "That is news to me."

"I didn't come to you because it was only a blind guess," said Raúl nervously. "But I suspect the President used Raymond LeBaron's airship to smuggle in an envoy behind the back of Soviet intelligence."

"Good Christ, wasn't it destroyed by one of our patrol helicopters?"

"A stupid blunder," confessed Raúl. "There were no survivors."

Fidel's face mirrored confusion. "Then why is the State Department accusing us of imprisoning Mrs. LeBaron and her crew?"

"I've no idea."

"Why am I kept in the dark on these matters?"

"The report was sent but not read, like so many others. You have become a difficult man to reach, big brother. Your attention to detail is not what it used to be."

Fidel furiously reeled in the line and undid the harness to the fighting chair. "Tell the captain to turn the boat toward the harbor."

"What do you intend to do?"

Fidel cut a wide smile around the cigar. "Go duck hunting."

"Now? Today?"

"As soon as we get to shore I'm going to hole up at my country retreat outside Havana, and you're coming with me. We'll remain secluded, taking no calls and meeting with no one until Education Day."

"Do you think that wise, leaving the President hanging, shutting ourselves off from the Soviet internal threat?"

"What harm can it do? The wheels of American foreign relations turn like the wheels of an ox cart. With his envoy dead, he can only stare at a wall and wait for my next exchange. As for the Russians, the opportunity isn't ripe for them to make their move." He lightly punched Raúl on the shoulder. "Cheer up, little brother. What could possibly happen in the next five days that you and I can't control?"

Raúl vaguely wondered too. He also wondered how he could feel as chilled as a tomb under a blazing Caribbean sun.

Shortly after midnight, General Velikov stood stiffly beside his desk as the elevator doors spread and Lyev Maisky strode into the study.

Velikov greeted him coolly. "Comrade Maisky. An unexpected pleasure."

"Comrade General."

"Can I offer you any refreshments?"

"This damnable humidity is a curse," replied Maisky, wiping a hand over his brow and studying the sweat on his fingers. "I could use a glass of iced vodka."

Velikov picked up a phone and issued a curt order. Then he gestured toward a chair. "Please, make yourself comfortable."

Maisky fell wearily into a soft leather chair and yawned from jet lag. "I'm sorry you weren't warned of my coming, General, but Comrade Polevoi thought it best not to risk interception and decoding of your new instructions by the U.S. National Security Agency's listening facilities."

Velikov raised his eyebrow in a practiced motion and gave Maisky a wary stare. "New instructions?"

"Yes, a most complicated operation."

"I hope the chief of the KGB isn't ordering me to postpone the Castro assassination project."

"Not at all. In fact, I've been asked to tell you the ships with the required cargoes for the job will arrive in Havana Harbor half a day ahead of schedule."

Velikov nodded gratefully. "We can use the extra time."

"Have you encountered any problems?" asked Maisky.

"Everything is running smoothly."

"Everything?" Maisky repeated. "Comrade Polevoi was not happy about the escape of one of your prisoners."

"He need not worry. A fisherman found the missing man's body in his nets. The secret of this installation is still secure."

"And what of the others? You must know the State Department is demanding their release from Cuban officials."

"A crude bluff," Velikov replied. "The CIA hasn't a shred of proof the intruders are still alive. The fact that Washington is demanding their release from the Cubans instead of us proves they're shooting in the dark."

"The question is, What are they shooting at?" Maisky paused and removed a platinum cigarette holder from his breast pocket. He lit a long, unfiltered cigarette and exhaled the smoke toward the ceiling. "Nothing must delay Rum and Cola."

"Castro will speak as promised."

"Can you be sure he won't suddenly change his mind?"

"If history repeats itself, we're on firm ground. *El jefe máximo,* the big boss, hasn't turned down a chance to make a speech yet."

"Barring accident, sickness, or hurricane."

"Some things are beyond human control, but I don't intend to fail."

A uniformed guard appeared with a chilled bottle of vodka and a glass resting in a bed of ice. "Only one glass, General? You're not joining me?"

"Perhaps a brandy later."

Velikov waited patiently until Maisky had consumed a third of the bottle. Then he took the leap.

"May I ask the deputy of the First Chief Directorate to enlighten me on this new operation?"

"Of course," Maisky said sociably. "You are to use whatever electronic capability under your command to force the United

States space shuttle down in Cuban territory."

"Did I hear you correctly?" asked Velikov, stunned.

"Your orders, which come from Comrade President Antonov, are to break into the computerized guidance control sensors of the space shuttle *Gettysburg* between its earth reentry and approach to Cape Canaveral and direct it to land on our military airfield at Santa Clara."

Frowning, baffled, Velikov openly stared at Maisky as if the KGB deputy were mad. "If I may say so, that's the craziest scheme the directorate has ever conceived."

"Nevertheless, it has all been worked out by our space scientists," Maisky said airily. He rested his foot on a large accountant's-type briefcase. "The data are all here for programming your computers and training your staff."

"My people are communications engineers." Velikov looked totally lost and sounded the same way. "They don't know anything about space dynamics."

"They don't have to. The computers will do it for them. What is most important is that your equipment here on the island have the capability to override the Houston Space Control Center and take command of the shuttle."

"When is this act supposed to take place?"

"According to NASA, the *Gettysburg* begins her earth reentry roughly twenty-nine hours from now."

Velikov simply nodded his head. The shock had quickly melted away and he regained total control, calm, mind clicking, the complete professional. "Of course, I'll give you every cooperation, but I don't mind saying it will take more than an ordinary miracle to accomplish the unbelievable."

Maisky downed another glass of vodka and dismissed Velikov's pessimism with a wave of the hand. "Faith, General, not in miracles, but in the brains of Soviet scientists and engineers. That's what will put America's most advanced spacecraft on the runway in Cuba."

Giordino stared dubiously at the plate sitting on his lap. "First they feed us slop and now it's sirloin steak and eggs. I don't trust these bastards. They probably spiced it with arsenic."

"A cheap shot to build us up before they tear us down again," said Gunn, ravenously digging into the meat. "But I'm going to ignore it."

"This is the third day the goon in room six has left us alone. Something smells."

"You'd prefer having another rib broken?" Gunn muttered between mouthfuls.

Giordino probed the eggs with his fork, gave in, and tried them. "They're probably fattening us up for the kill."

"I hope to God they've laid off Jessie too."

"Sadists like Gly get turned on beating women."

"Have you ever wondered why Velikov is never present during Gly's punch parties?"

"Typical of the Russians to let a foreigner do their dirty work, or maybe he can't stand the sight of blood. How should I know?"

Suddenly the door was flung open and Foss Gly stepped into the cell. The thick, protruding lips parted in a smile, and the pupils of his eyes were deep, black, and empty.

"Enjoying your dinner, gentlemen?"

"You forgot the wine," Giordino said contemptuously. "And I like my steak medium rare."

Gly stepped closer and, before Giordino could guess his intentions, swung his fist in a vicious backhand against Giordino's rib cage.

Giordino gasped, and his entire body jerked in a convulsive spasm. His face went ashen, and yet, incredibly, he gave a lopsided grin, blood rolling through the hairs of his stubbled chin from where his teeth had bitten his lower lip.

Gunn rose up from his cot on one arm and heaved his plate of food at Gly's head, the eggs spattering the side of the torturer's face, the half-eaten meat scoring a bull's-eye across the mouth.

"A stupid reaction," Gly said, his voice a furious whisper. "One you'll regret." He reached down, grabbed Gunn's shattered ankle, and gave it a sickening twist.

Gunn clenched his fists, eyes glazed in pain, but uttered no sound. Gly stepped back and studied him, seemingly fascinated. "You're tough, very tough, for a little man."

"Crawl back in your hole, slime," Giordino gasped, still catching his breath.

"Stubborn, stubborn," Gly sighed wearily. For a quick second his eyes took on a pensive look, then the black emptiness returned, as cold and evil as if chiseled on a statue. "Ah, yes, you distracted me. I came to deliver news of your friend Dirk Pitt."

"What about him?"

"He tried to escape and was drowned."

"You're lying," said Gunn.

"A Bahamian fisherman found him. The American consulate has already identified the body, or what was left after the sharks were finished with it." Then Gly wiped the egg from his face, removed the steak from Giordino's plate, dropped it on the floor, and ground his boot in it. *"Bon appétit,* gentlemen."

He walked from the cell and locked the door behind him.

Giordino and Gunn looked at each other in long silence, a sudden realization growing within them. Then their faces lit up with broad grins that quickly turned into laughter.

"He did it!" Giordino cried, his elation overcoming his pain. "Dirk made it home free!"

51

THE GLAMOUR EXPERIMENTS on the space station *Columbus* centered on the manufacture of exotic medicines, the growth of pure crystals for computer semiconductor chips, and gamma ray observation. But the bread-and-butter activity of the forty-ton settlement on the fringe of the last frontier was the repair and service of satellites.

Jack Sherman, commander of the station, was in the cylinder-shaped maintenance module helping a team of engineers jockey a satellite into a repair cradle when a voice came through the central speaker. "You available, Jack?"

"I'm here."

"Can you come to the command module?"

"What's up?"

"We've got some joker breaking into our communications channel."

"Pipe it down here."

"Better you should come up."

"Give me a couple of minutes."

The satellite secured and the airlock closed, Sherman peeled off his pressure suit and slipped his boots into a pair of slotted rails. Then he walked in a sliding motion through the weightless environment to the brain center of the station.

His chief communications and electronics engineer simply nodded at his approach. "Listen to this." He spoke into a microphone mounted in a control panel. "Please identify yourself again."

There was a slight pause and then: "*Columbus*, this is Jersey Colony. We request permission to dock at your station."

The engineer turned and looked up at Sherman. "What do you think? Must be some weirdo on earth."

Sherman leaned over the panel. "Jersey Colony, or whatever you call yourself, this is a closed NASA channel. You are interfering with space communications procedures. Please break off."

"No way," came the strange voice. "Our lunar transfer vehicle will rendezvous with you in two hours. Please advise us on docking procedures."

"Lunar what?" Sherman's face tightened in anger. "Houston Control, do you copy?"

"We copy," came a voice from the Houston Space Control Center. "What do you make of it?"

"We're trying to get a fix on it, *Columbus*. Please stand by."

"I don't know who you are, fella," snapped Sherman, "but you're in deep trouble."

"The name is Eli Steinmetz. Please have medical assistance standing by. I have two injured men on board."

Sherman pounded a fist on the back of the engineer's chair. "This is crazy."

"Who am I communicating with?" asked Steinmetz.

"This is Jack Sherman, commander of the *Columbus*."

"Sorry about the abrupt intrustion, Sherman, but I thought you'd been informed of our arrival."

Before Sherman could reply, Houston Control returned. "*Columbus*, his signals are not coming from earth, repeat, not coming from earth. They originate in space beyond you."

"All right, you guys, what's the gag?"

The voice of NASA's director of Flight Operations broke in. "No gag. Jack, this is Irwin Mitchell. Prepare your crew to receive Steinmetz and his colonists."

"What colonists?"

"About time someone from the 'inner core' showed up," said Steinmetz. "For a minute there, I thought we'd have to crash the front gate."

"Sorry, Eli. The President thought it best to keep things quiet until you reached *Columbus*."

"Will someone please tell me what's going on?" Sherman demanded in exasperation.

"Eli will explain when you meet him," answered Mitchell. Then he addressed Steinmetz. "How are the wounded?"

"Resting comfortably, but one will require major surgery. A bullet is lodged near the base of the brain."

"You heard, Jack," said Mitchell. "Alert the crew of the shuttle. They may have to advance their departure."

"I'll take care of it," Sherman said. His voice settled and the tone was calm, but he was far too intelligent not to be bewildered. "Just where in hell does this...this Jersey Colony come from?"

"Would you believe the moon?" Mitchell replied.

"No," said Sherman flatly. "I damned well wouldn't."

The Theodore Roosevelt Room in the West Wing of the White House was once called the Fish Room because it contained aquariums and fishing trophies of Franklin Delano Roosevelt. Under Richard Nixon it was furnished in Queen Anne and Chippendale style and used for staff meetings and occasional press conferences.

The walls and carpet were in light and dark shades of terra-cotta. A painting of the Declaration of Independence hung on the east wall over a carved wooden mantel. Sternly surveying the room from the south wall, Teddy Roosevelt sat astride a horse in a portrait painted in Paris by Tade Styka. The President preferred this intimate room over the more formal Cabinet Room for important discussions partly because there were no windows.

He sat at the head of the conference table and scribbled on a note pad. On his left sat Secretary of Defense Jess Simmons. Next to him came CIA Director Martin Brogan, Dan Fawcett, and Leonard Hudson. Douglas Oates, the Secretary of State, sat immediately to his right, followed by National Security Adviser Alan Mercier and Air Force General Allan Post, who headed up the military space program.

Hudson had spent over an hour briefing the President's men on the history of the Jersey Colony. At first they sat there stunned and silent. Then the excitement set in and they fired a barrage of questions that Hudson fielded until the President ordered lunch served in the room.

The utter astonishment gave way to enthusiastic compliments for Hudson and his "inner core," which slowly faded to grim reality at the report on the conflict with the Soviet cosmonauts.

"Once the Jersey colonists return safely to Cape Canaveral," said the President, "perhaps I can appease Antonov by offering to share some of the immense data accumulated by Steinmetz and his team."

"Why should we give away anything?" demanded Simmons. "They've stolen enough of our technology as it is."

"No denying their thievery," replied the President. "But if our positions were reversed, I wouldn't allow them to get away with killing fourteen of our astronauts."

"I'm on your side, Mr. President," said Secretary of State Oates.

"But if the shoe was indeed on your foot, what course of retribution could you take?"

"Simple," said General Post. "If I were Antonov, I'd order the *Columbus* blasted out of the sky."

"An abhorrent thought, but one we have to take seriously," said Brogan. "The Soviet leaders must feel they have a divine right to destroy the station and everyone on board."

"Or the shuttle and its crew," Post added.

The President stared at the general. "Can *Columbus* and *Gettysburg* be shielded?"

Post gave a slight shake of his head. "Our X-ray laser defense system won't be operational for another fourteen months. While in space, both the station and the shuttle are vulnerable to the Soviet Union's Cosmos 1400 killer satellites. We can provide solid protection for the *Gettysburg* only after she passes through earth's atmosphere."

The President turned to Brogan. "How do you see it, Martin?"

"I don't think they'll target *Columbus*. They'd be leaving themselves wide open for us to retaliate against their new Salyut 10 station. I say they'll try for the shuttle."

An icy silence settled over the Roosevelt Room as every man present struggled with his own thoughts. Then Hudson's face took on an enlightened expression, and he rapped his pen against the table surface.

"We've overlooked something," he said in a level tone.

"Like what?" asked Fawcett.

"The true purpose behind their attack on Jersey Colony."

Brogan took the lead. "To save face by destroying all trace of our breakthrough in space."

"Not destroy but steal," Hudson said fervently. "Murdering the colonists wasn't an eye-for-an-eye punishment. Jess Simmons hit on it. To the Kremlin's way of thinking it was vital to seize the base intact in order to help themselves to the technology, the data, and the results of billions of dollars and twenty-five years of work. That was their goal. Revenge was secondary."

"He makes a valid point," said Oates. "Except that with the colonists on their way to earth, Jersey Colony is up for grabs."

"By using our lunar transfer vehicle we can have another crew on site within two weeks," said Hudson.

"The two cosmonauts who are sitting in Selenos 8," Simmons said.

"What's to stop them from simply walking in and taking over the abandoned colony?"

"I'm sorry," Hudson answered. "I forgot to mention that Steinmetz transported the five dead Russians back to the lunar lander and loaded them on board. Then he forced the surviving crew to lift off and return to earth by threatening to scatter them over the moon's surface with the last rocket in his launcher."

"The sheriff cleaning up the town," Brogan said admiringly. "I can't wait to meet this guy."

"Not without cost," said Hudson quietly. "Steinmetz is bringing back two seriously wounded men and one body."

"What is the name of the dead man?" asked the President.

"Dr. Kurt Perry, a brilliant biochemist."

The President nodded at Fawcett. "Let's see that he receives a proper ceremony."

There was a slight pause, and then Post brought the discussion back on track. "Okay, if the Soviets didn't get Jersey colony, what are they left with?"

"The *Gettysburg*," Hudson answered. "The Russians still have a chance at pirating a treasure trove of scientific data."

"By snatching the shuttle out of the air?" Simmons stated sarcastically. "News to me they have Buck Rogers on their side."

"They don't need him," Hudson retorted. "It's technically possible to program a deviation into the flight guidance systems. The computers can be fooled into sending the wrong signal to the drive elevons, the thrusters, and other equipment to control the *Gettysburg*. There are a thousand different way to nudge the shuttle off its course a few degrees. Depending on the distance from touchdown, it could be thrown off as far as a thousand miles from the Kennedy spaceport at Cape Canaveral."

"But the pilots can override the automated system and land on manual control," protested Post.

"Not if they're conned into thinking Houston Control is monitoring their return flight path."

"Is this possible?" asked the President incredulously.

Alan Mercier nodded. "Providing the Soviets have local transmitters with the capacity to overpower the shuttle's internal electronics and jam all signals from Houston Control."

The President exchanged grim looks with Brogan.

"Cayo Santa María," Brogan muttered miserably.

"An island north of Cuba containing a powerful transmission and listening facility with the necessary muscle to do the job," the President explained to the others.

"Maybe they haven't caught on that our colonists have left the moon," Fawcett said hopefully.

"They know," replied Hudson. "Once their eavesdropping satellites were aimed toward Jersey Colony, they've monitored every one of our transmissions."

"We'll have to come up with a plan to neutralize the island's equipment," suggested Post.

Brogan smiled. "Just so happens there is an operation in the works."

Post smiled back. "If you're scheming what I'm thinking, all I'd like to know is *when*."

"There is talk—purely a rumor, mind you—that Cuban military forces are going to launch an attack-and-destroy mission sometime after midnight tonight."

"And the departure time of the shuttle for home?" asked Alan Mercier.

"0500 tomorrow," Post answered.

"That settles it," said the President. "Inform the commander of *Columbus* to hold *Gettysburg* on the docking platform until we can guarantee its safe return."

Everyone around the table seemed satisfied for the moment, except Hudson. He had the look of a boy who had just lost his puppy to the county dogcatcher.

"I just wish," he muttered to no one in particular, "it was all that easy."

52

VELIKOV AND MAISKY stood on a balcony three levels above the electronic listening center and looked down on a small army of men and women who manned the sophisticated electronic receiving equipment. Twenty-four hours a day, giant antennas on Cuba intercepted United States civilian telephone calls and military radio signals, relaying them to Cayo Santa María, where they were fed into the computers for decoding and analysis.

"A truly superb job, General," said Maisky. "The reports on your installation have been far too modest."

"A day doesn't go by when we don't continue the expansion," Velikov said proudly. "Besides the business end of the complex there is a well-supplied dining room and a physical conditioning center with exercise equipment and a sauna. We even have an entertainment room and a barber shop."

Maisky's gaze rose to two screens, each ten by fifteen feet, on different walls. The left screen contained computer-generated displays while the right showed various data and intricate graphs.

"Have your people discovered the status of the moon colonists yet?"

The general nodded and picked up a telephone. He spoke a few words into the receiver while looking down on the busy equipment floor. A staff member at a console looked up and waved a hand. Then the two screens went dark for a brief instant and returned to life with a new data display.

"A complete rundown," said Velikov, pointing to the right screen. "We can monitor almost everything that is transmitted between their astronauts and Houston Control. As you can see, the moon colonists' lunar transporter docked three hours ago at the space station."

Maisky was fascinated as his eyes traveled over the display information. He could not bring himself to accept the fact that American intelligence undoubtedly knew as much if not more about Soviet space efforts.

"Do they transmit in code?" he asked.

"Occasionally, if it is a military mission, but NASA usually talks to their astronauts quite openly."

"As you can see on the data display, the Houston Ground Control Center has ordered the *Gettysburg* to postpone its scheduled departure for tomorrow morning."

"I don't like the look of that."

"I see nothing suspicious. The President probably wants time to mount a massive propaganda campaign to announce another American space triumph."

"Or they may be wise to our intentions." Maisky then became quiet, lost in thought. His eyes had a worried look, and he clasped and unclasped his hands nervously.

Velikov looked at him with amusement. "If this in any way upsets your plans, I could break in on Houston Control's frequency and issue a false command."

"You can do that?"

"I can."

"Simulate an order for the shuttle to depart the space station for reentry?"

"Yes."

"And deceive the commanders of the station and the shuttle into believing they're hearing a familiar voice?"

"They'll never detect the difference. Our computerized synthesizers have more than enough taped transmissions to perfectly imitate voice, accent, and verbal mannerisms of at least twenty different officials of NASA."

"What's to stop Houston Control from countermanding the order?"

"I can scramble their transmissions until it's too late for them to stop the shuttle. Then, if the instructions you gave us from our space scientists are correct, we'll override the craft's flight systems and bring her down at Santa Clara."

Maisky looked at Velikov long and steadily. Then he said, "Do it."

The President was dead asleep when the phone beside his bed softly chimed. He rolled over and read the luminous dial on his wristwatch. Ten minutes after one in the morning. Then he answered. "Go ahead."

The voice that replied was Dan Fawcett's. "Sorry to wake you, Mr. President, but something has come up that I thought you'd want to know about."

"I'm listening. What is it?"

"I've just received a call from Irwin Mitchell at NASA. He said the *Gettysburg* has cast off from *Columbus* and is orbiting in preparation for reentry."

The President sat bolt upright, waking his wife beside him. "Who gave the order?" he demanded.

"Mitchell can't say. All communication between Houston and the space station is down because of some strange interference."

"Then how has he confirmed the shuttle's departure?"

"General Fisher has been tracking and monitoring *Columbus* at the Space Operations Center in Colorado Springs since Steinmetz left Jersey Colony. The sensitive cameras at the center caught the movement when *Gettysburg* left the station's dock. He called me as soon as he was informed."

The President pounded the mattress in dismay. "Damn!"

"I took the liberty of alerting Jess Simmons. He's already scrambled two Air Force tactical squadrons into the air to fly escort and protect the shuttle as soon as she drops through the atmosphere."

"How much time do we have before the *Gettysburg* lands?"

"From initial descent preparation to touchdown, about two hours."

"The Russians are behind this."

"The general consensus," acknowledged Fawcett. "We can't be sure yet, but all indications point to Cuba as the source of Houston's radio interference problem."

"When does Brogan's special team hit Cayo Santa María?"

"0200 hours."

"Who's leading them in?"

"One moment while I look up the name in yesterday's CIA report." Fawcett left the line for no more than thirty seconds before he returned. "The mission is being directed by Marine Colonel Ramon Kleist."

"I know the name. Kleist was a Congressional Medal of Honor winner."

"Here's something else."

"What?"

"Kleist's men are being guided by Dirk Pitt."

The President sighed almost sadly. "He's already given too much. Is his presence absolutely required?"

"It was Pitt or nobody," said Fawcett.

"Can they destroy the jamming center in time?"

"In all honesty, I'd have to say it's a toss-up."

"Tell Jess Simmons to stand by in the War Room," said the President solemnly. "If anything goes wrong, I fear the only alternative left for us to keep the *Gettysburg* and her valuable cargo out of Soviet hands is to shoot her down. Do you read me, Dan?"

"Yes, sir," Fawcett said, his face suddenly white. "I'll give him your message."

53

"ALL STOP," ORDERED KLEIST. He rechecked the readings on the Navstar satellite instrument and tapped a pair of dividers on a flattened chart. "We're seven miles due east of Cayo Santa María. This is close as we dare move the SPUT."

Major Quintana, wearing mottled gray and black battle dress, stared at the yellow mark on the chart. "Should take us about forty minutes to swing around to the south and land from the Cuban side."

"The wind is calm and the sea is only running at two feet. Another blessing is no moon. It's pitch black topside."

"Good as well as bad news," said Quintana heavily. "Makes us tough to spot, but we won't be able to see any wandering guards either. Our main problem, as I see it, is not having an exact fix on the compound. We could land miles from it."

Kleist turned and stared at a tall, commanding figure leaning against a bulkhead. He was dressed in the same night battle fatigues as Quintana. The piercing green eyes met Kleist's stare.

"You still can't pinpoint the location?"

Pitt straightened, smiled his congenial indifferent smile, and said simply, "No."

"You're not very encouraging," Quintana said nastily.

"Maybe, but at least I'm honest."

Kleist spoke with forbearance. "We regret, Mr. Pitt, that visual conditions were not ideal during your escape. But we'd be grateful if you were a bit more specific."

Pitt's smile faded. "Look, I landed in the middle of a hurricane and left in the middle of the night. Both events took place on the opposite side of the island from where we're supposed to land. I didn't measure distances, nor did I sprinkle breadcrumbs along my trail. The land was flat, no hills or streams for landmarks. Just palm trees, brush, and sand. The antenna was a half mile west of the village. The compound, a good mile beyond. Once we strike the road the compound will be to the left. That's the best I can offer."

Quintana gave a resigned nod. "Under the circumstances we can't ask for more than that."

A crewman dressed sloppily in cutaway jeans and T-shirt stepped through the hatchway into the control room. He silently handed a decoded communication to Kleist and left.

"Better not be a last-minute cancellation," Pitt said sharply.

"Far from it," Kleist muttered. "More like a new twist."

He studied the message a second time, a frown crossing his normally impassive face. He handed it to Quintana, who stared at the wording and then tightened his lips in annoyance before passing the paper to Pitt. It read:

SPACE SHUTTLE GETTYSBURG HAS DEPARTED STATION AND OR-
BITING IN PREPARATION FOR REENTRY. ALL CONTACT LOST. YOUR
TARGET'S ELECTRONICS HAVE PENETRATED GUIDANCE COM-
PUTERS AND TAKEN COMMAND. EXPECT COURSE DEVIATION
TO SET CRAFT DOWN IN CUBA AT 0340. SPEED CRITICAL. DIRE
CRISIS IF COMPOUND NOT DESTROYED IN TIME. LUCK.

"Nice of them to warn us at the last minute," said Pitt grimly. "0340 is less than two hours away."

Quintana looked at Kleist severely. "Can the Soviets actually do this thing and get away with it?"

Kleist wasn't listening. His gaze returned to the chart and he made a little pencil line that marked a course to the southern shore of Cayo Santa María. "Where approximately do you put the antenna?"

Pitt took the pencil and made a tiny dot on the sperm-shaped island at the base of the tail. "A wild guess at best."

"All right. We'll equip you with a small waterproof radio sender and receiver. I'll convert the position on the chart and program it into the Navstar computer, then maintain a fix on your signal and guide you in."

"You won't be the only one who can put a fix on us."

"A small gamble, but one that will save valuable time. You should be able to blow the antenna and cut off their radio command of the *Gettysburg* much faster than fighting your way inside the compound and destroying its brain center."

"Makes sense."

"Since you agree," said Kleist quietly, "I suggest you gentlemen shove off."

The special-purpose underwater transporter looked nothing like any submarine Pitt had ever seen. The craft was slightly over three hundred feet long and shaped like a chisel turned sideways. The horizontal wedgelike bow tapered quickly to an almost square hull that ended abruptly at a boxed-off stern. Her upper deck was completely smooth without any projections.

No man stood at her helm. She was totally automated with nuclear power that turned twin propellers or, when required, soundless pumps that took in water from the forward momentum and thrust it silently through vents along the sides.

The SPUT was specifically designed for the CIA to support covert arms smuggling, undercover agent infiltration, and hit-and-run raids. She could travel as deep as eight hundred feet at fifty knots, but also had the capability of running onto a beach, spreading her bows, and disgorging a two-hundred-man landing force with several vehicles.

The ship broke the surface, her flat deck only two feet above the black water. Quintana's team of Cuban exiles scrambled from the hatches and quickly began lifting the water Dashers that were passed up from below.

Pitt had ridden a Dasher at a resort in Mexico. A water-propulsion vehicle, it was manufactured in France for seaside recreation. Called the sports car of the sea, the sleek little machine had the look of two torpedoes attached side by side. The operator lay back with each leg stretched out in one of the twin hulls and controlled the movement with an automobile-type steering wheel. Power came from a high-performance battery that could propel the craft by means of water jets over smooth seas at twenty knots for three hours before recharging.

After Pitt proposed using them to cruise under the Cuban radar network, Kleist hurriedly negotiated a special purchase from the factory and arranged to have them flown by Air Force transport to San Salvador within fifteen hours.

The early morning air was warm and a light rain squall passed over. As each man slipped into his Dasher, he was shoved across the wet deck, over the low freeboard, and into the sea. Shaded blue lights had been mounted in the sterns so each man could follow the one in front.

Pitt took a few moments and stared into the darkness toward Cayo Santa María, desperately hoping he wasn't too late to save his friends. An early gull wheeled crying over his head, invisible in the murky sky.

Quintana gripped him by the arm. "You're next." He paused and stared through the gloom. "What in hell is that?"

Pitt held up a wooden shaft in one hand. "A baseball bat."

"What do you need that for? You were issued an AK-74."

"It's a gift for a friend."

Quintana shook his head in bewilderment. "Let's get going. You'll lead off. I'll bring up the rear and catch stragglers."

Pitt nodded and eased into his Dasher and adjusted a tiny receiver in one ear. Just before the SPUT crew pushed him over the side Colonel Kleist bent down and shook Pitt's hand. "Get them to the target," he said tensely.

Pitt gave him a sober grin. "I aim to."

Then his Dasher was in the water. He adjusted the power lever to half speed and eased clear of the ship. There was no use in turning to check if the others were following. He couldn't have seen them anyway. The only light came from the stars, and they were too dim to sparkle the water.

He increased speed and studied the luminescent dial of the compass strapped to one wrist. He maintained a heading of due east until Kleist's voice came through his earpiece: "Bear 270 degrees."

Pitt made the correction and kept on the course for ten miles, keeping a few knots below the Dasher's full speed to allow the men behind to close up if they strayed out of line. He was certain the sensitive underwater sensors would pick up the raiding party's approach, but he counted on the Russians to dismiss the readings on their recording instruments as a school of fish.

A long way off to the south toward Cuba, a good four miles perhaps, a searchlight from a patrol boat blazed on and swept the water like a scythe, cutting the night, searching for intruding vessels. The far-off glow dimly lit them up, but they were two small and low in the water to be seen at that distance.

Pitt received a new bearing from Kleist, and altered course to the north. The night was as dark as a crypt, and he could only hope the other thirty men were hugging his stern. The Dasher's twin bows dipped into a series of rising waves, tossing spray into his face, and he tasted the strong saltiness of the sea.

The slight turbulence from the Dasher's passage through the water

caused flecks of sparkling phosphorus that briefly flashed like an armada of fireflies before dying in his wake. Pitt was finally beginning to relax a bit when Kleist's voice came through his ear again: "I put you about two hundred yards from shore."

Pitt slowed his little boat and eased ahead cautiously. Then he stopped, drifting with the current. He waited, eyes strained against the dark, tense and listening. Five minutes went by, and Cayo Santa María's outline vaguely loomed ahead, black and ominous. The surf was nearly nonexistent on the inside waters of the island, and its soft lapping on the beach was the only sound he could hear.

He gently pressed the power pedal and went forward dead slow, ready to turn hard and speed out to sea if they were detected. Seconds later, the Dasher bumped noiselessly into the sand. Immediately Pitt stepped out and dragged the light craft across the beach and into the underbrush beneath a line of palm trees. Then he waited until Quintana and his men rose up like wraiths and silently grouped around him in a tight knot, indistinct blurs in the gloom, thankful to a man their feet were on solid land again.

As insurance against Murphy's law, Quintana took precious time to account for every man and briefly check his equipment. Finally satisfied, he turned to Pitt. "After you, amigo."

Pitt took a reading from the compass, and then led the way inland on a slight angle to his left. He held the baseball bat out in front of him like a blind man with a cane. Less than two hundred feet from the staging area, the end of the bat met with the electrified fence. He stopped abruptly and the man in his rear bumped into him.

"Easy!" Pitt hissed. "Pass it on, we're at the fence."

Two men with shovels came forward and attacked the soft sand. In no time they had excavated a hole that was large enough to push a small burro through.

Pitt crawled under first. For a moment he was uncertain which way he should go. He hesitated, sniffing at the wind. Then, suddenly, he knew exactly where he was.

"We screwed up," he murmured to Quintana. "The compound is only a few hundred yards to our left. The antenna is a good mile in the opposite direction."

"How can you tell?"

"Use your nose. You can smell exhaust fumes from the diesel engines that run the generators."

Quintana inhaled deeply. "You're right. A breeze is carrying it from the northwest."

"So much for a quick solution. It'll take your men a good half hour to reach the antenna and set the charges."

"Then we'll go for the compound."

"Safer to play both ends against the middle. Send your strongest runners to blow the antenna and the rest of us will try for the electronics center."

Quintana took less than a second to make up his mind. He went through the ranks and quickly selected five men. He returned with a small, indistinct figure whose head hardly reached Pitt's shoulders.

"This is Sergeant López. He'll need directions to the antenna."

Pitt stripped the compass off his wrist and handed it to the sergeant. López didn't speak English and Quintana had to translate. The little sergeant was a quick study. He repeated Pitt's instructions flawlessly in Spanish. Then López flashed a smile, gave a curt order to his men, and vanished into the night.

Pitt and the rest of Quintana's force took off at a run. The weather began to deteriorate. Clouds blanketed the stars, and the raindrops that splattered against the palm fronds made a strange drumming sound. They wound through trees gracefully curved from the fury of hurricane winds. Every few yards someone stumbled and fell but was helped up by others. Soon their breathing came more heavily and the sweat flowed down their bodies and soaked their battle fatigues. Pitt set a fast pace, driven on by desperate anticipation of finding Jessie, Giordino, and Gunn still alive. His mind remained remote from the discomfort and growing exhaustion by envisioning the agonies Foss Gly must have inflicted on them. His ugly thoughts were interrupted when he stepped out of the underbrush onto the road.

He turned left toward the compound, making no attempt at stealth or concealment, using the flat surface to make time. The feel of the land felt more familiar to Pitt now. He slowed to a walk and whispered for Quintana. When he felt a hand on one shoulder, he gestured at a dim light barely visible through the trees. "The guardhouse at the gate."

Quintana slapped Pitt's back in acknowledgment and gave instructions in Spanish to the next man in line, who slipped away toward the light.

Pitt didn't have to ask. He knew the security guards manning the gate had only another two minutes to live.

He skirted the wall and crept into the culvert, vastly relieved to find the bars still bent as he had left them. They scrambled through

and wormed their way to the air vent above the compound's motor pool. This was as far as Pitt was supposed to go. Kleist's firm instructions were for him to guide Quintana's force to the air vent and go no further. He was to step out of the way, return alone to the landing beach, and wait for the others to withdraw.

Kleist should have guessed that when Pitt offered no argument the orders were not about to be carried out, but the colonel had too many problems on his mind to become suspicious. And good old Pitt, quite naturally, had been the very model of cooperation when he laid out a diagram of the entry into the compound.

Before Quintana could reach out and stop him, Pitt dropped through the vent onto the support girder over the parked vehicles and disappeared like a shadow down the exit shaft to the cells far below.

54

DAVE JURGENS, flight commander of the *Gettysburg*, was mildly disturbed. He shared the elation with everyone in the space station at the unexpected arrival of Steinmetz and his men from the moon. And he found nothing amiss in the sudden orders to carry the colonists to earth as soon as their scientific cargo could be loaded into the shuttle's payload bay.

What disturbed him was the abrupt demand by Houston Control to make a night landing at Cape Canaveral. His request to wait a few hours until the sun rose was met with a cold refusal. He was given no reason why NASA officials had suddenly reversed their strict policy of daylight touchdowns for the first time in nearly thirty years.

He looked over at his copilot, Carl Burkhart, a twenty-year veteran of the space program. "We won't have much of a view of the Florida swamps on this approach."

"You see one alligator, you've seen them all," the laconic Burkhart replied.

"Our passengers all tucked in?"

"Like corn in a bin."

"Computers programmed for reentry?"

"Set and ticking."

Jurgens briefly scanned the three TV screens in the center of the main panel. One gave the status on all the mechanical systems, while the other two gave data on trajectory and guidance control. He and Burkhart began to run through the de-orbit and entry procedure checklist.

"Ready when you are, Houston."

"Okay, Don," replied ground control. "You are go for de-orbit burn."

"Out of sight, out of mind," said Jurgens. "Is that it?"

"We don't read, come again."

"When I left earth, my name was Dave."

"Sorry about that, Dave."

"Who's on the line?" asked Jurgens, his curiosity aroused.

"Merv Foley. You don't recognize my resonant vowel sounds?"

"After all our scintillating conversations, you've forgotten my name. For shame."

"A slip of the tongue," said the familiar voice of Foley. "Shall we cut the small talk and get back to procedures."

"Whatever you say, Houston." Jurgens briefly pressed his intercom switch. "Ready to head home, Mr. Steinmetz?"

"We're all looking forward to the trip," Steinmetz answered.

In the Spartan living quarters below the flight deck and cockpit the shuttle specialists and Jersey colonists were packed together in every foot of available space. Behind them the sixty-foot-long payload bay was loaded two-thirds full with data records, geological specimens, cases containing the results of more than a thousand medical and chemical experiments—the bonanza accumulated by the colonists that would take scientists two decades to fully analyze. The bay also carried the body of Dr. Kurt Perry.

The *Gettysburg* was traveling through space backward and upside down at over 15,000 knots per hour. The small reaction-control jets were fired and joggled the craft over from orbit as thrusters pitched it to a nose-high attitude so the insulated belly could absorb the reentry friction of the atmosphere. Over Australia, two secondary engines burned briefly to slow the shuttle's orbit speed from twenty-five times the speed of sound. Thirty minutes later, they hit the atmosphere shortly before Hawaii.

As the atmosphere grew denser, the heat turned the *Gettysburg*'s belly a vivid orange. The thrusters lost their effectiveness and the elevons and the rudder began to clutch the heavier air. The computers controlled the entire flight. Jurgens and Burkhart had little to do except monitor the TV data and systems indicators.

Suddenly a warning tone sounded in their headsets and a master alarm light came on. Jurgens quickly reacted by punching a computer keyboard to call up details of the problem while Burkhart notified ground control.

"Houston, we have a warning light."

"We read nothing here, *Gettysburg*. All systems look great."

"Something is going on, Houston," persisted Burkhart.

"Can only be computer error."

"Negative. All three navigation and guidance computers agree."

"I have it," said Jurgens. "We're showing a course error."

The cool voice at the Johnson Space Center returned. "Disregard, Dave. You're right on the beam. Do you copy?"

"I copy, Foley, but bear with me while I go to the backup computer."

"If it will make you happy. But all systems are go."

Jurgens quickly punched a request for navigation data from the backup computer. Less than thirty seconds later he hailed Houston.

"Merv, something's fishy. Even the backup shows us coming down four hundred miles south and fifty east of Canaveral."

"Trust me, Dave," Foley said in a bored tone. "All tracking stations show you on course."

Jurgens looked out his side window and saw only blackness below. He switched off his radio and turned to Burkhart. "I don't give a damn what Houston says. We're off our approach course. There's nothing but water under us when we should be seeing lights over the Baja California peninsula."

"Beats me," said Burkhart, shifting restlessly in his seat. "What's the plan?"

"We'll stand by to take over manual control. If I didn't know better, I'd swear Houston was setting us down in Cuba."

"She's coming in like a kite on a string," said Maisky, his expression wolfish.

Velikov nodded. "Three more minutes and the *Gettysburg* will be past the point of no return."

"No return?" Maisky repeated.

"To bank and still glide to the runway at the Kennedy Space Center."

Maisky rubbed the palms of his hands together in nervous anticipation. "An American space shuttle in Soviet hands. This has to be the intelligence coup of the century."

"Washington will scream like a village of raped virgins, demanding we return it."

"They'll get their billion-dollar super-machine back. But not before our space engineers have explored and photographed every square inch of her."

"And then there's the wealth of information from their moon colonists," Velikov reminded him.

"An incredible feat, General. The Order of Lenin will be in this for you."

"We're not out of the woods yet, Comrade Maisky. We cannot predict the President's reaction."

Maisky shrugged. "His hands are tied if we offer to negotiate. Our only problem as I see it is the Cubans."

"Not to worry. Colonel General Kolchak has placed a screen of fifteen hundred Soviet troops around the runway at Santa Clara. And, since our advisers are in command of Cuba's aircraft defenses, the shuttle has a clear path to land."

"Then she's as good as in our hands."

Velikov nodded. "I think you can safely say that."

The President sat in a bathrobe behind his desk in the Oval Office, chin lowered, elbows on the arms of his chair. His face was tired and drawn.

He looked up abruptly and said, "Is it certain, Houston can't make contact with the *Gettysburg?*"

Martin Brogan nodded. "That's the word from Irwin Mitchell at NASA. Their signals are being drowned out by outside interference."

"Is Jess Simmons standing by at the Pentagon?"

"We have him on a direct line," answered Dan Fawcett.

The President hesitated, and when he spoke it was in a whisper. "Then you'd better tell him to order the pilots in those fighters to stand by."

Fawcett nodded gravely and picked up the phone. "Any word from your people, Martin?"

"The latest is they've landed on the beach," Brogan said helplessly. "Beyond that, nothing."

The President felt weighted with despair. "My God, we're trapped in limbo."

One of four phones rang and Fawcett snatched it up. "Yes, yes, he's here. Yes, I'll tell him." He replaced the receiver in its cradle, his expression grim. "That was Irwin Mitchell. The *Gettysburg* has deviated too far south to reach Cape Canaveral."

"She might still make a water landing," said Brogan without enthusiasm.

"Providing she can be warned in time," added Fawcett.

The President shook his head. "No good. Her landing speed is over two hundred miles an hour. She'd tear herself to pieces."

The others stood silent, searching for the right words. The President swiveled in his chair and faced the window, sick at heart.

After a few moments he turned to the men standing expectantly around his desk. "God help me for signing a death warrant on all those brave men."

55

PITT DROPPED OUT of the exit shaft and hit the corridor at a dead run. He twisted the handle and threw open the door to the cell that housed Giordino and Gunn with such a force that he nearly tore it from the hinges.

The tiny room was empty.

The noise betrayed him. A guard rushed around the corner from a side passage and stared at Pitt in astonishment. That split-second hesitation cost him. Even as he was lifting the barrel of his weapon, the baseball bat caught him on the side of the head. Pitt had grabbed the unfortunate guard around the waist and was dragging him into a convenient cell before he hit the floor. Pitt threw him on a bed and looked down into the face of the young Russian who had escorted him to Velikov's study. The boy was breathing normally, and Pitt figured the damage was no more than a concussion.

"You're lucky, kid. I never shoot anyone under the age of twenty-one."

Quintana was just coming out of the exit shaft as Pitt locked the guard in the cell and took off running again. He did not bother to be careful of concealing his presence. He would have welcomed the chance to bash the head of another guard. He reached the door to Jessie's cell and kicked it open.

She was missing too.

Dread swept through him like a wave. He plunged on through the corridors until he came to room six. There was nothing inside but the stench of torture.

Dread was replaced by cold, ungovernable rage. Pitt became someone else, a man without conscience or moral code, no longer in control of his emotions, a man for whom danger was merely a force to be ignored. Fear of dying had totally ceased to exist.

Quintana hurried up to Pitt and clutched his arm. "Damn you, get back to the beach! You know the orders—"

He got no further. Pitt shoved the stubby barrel of the AK-74 into Quintana's gut and slowly pushed him back and against a wall. Quintana had stood face to face with death many times before this moment, but staring at the ice-cold expression on the craggy face, seeing the pure look of murderous indifference in the green eyes, he knew he had one foot in a coffin.

Pitt did not speak. He pulled back the gun, raised the baseball bat to his shoulder, and pushed his way through Quintana's men. Suddenly he halted in his tracks and turned back. "The elevator is this way," he said quietly.

Quintana motioned his men to follow. Pitt took a fast head count. There were twenty-five, including himself. He hurried toward the elevator that rose to the upper levels. No more guards appeared in their way. The passages were deserted. With the prisoners dead, Pitt reasoned, Velikov probably saw no purpose in stationing more than one guard in the lower storage area.

They reached the elevator and he was about to push the Up button when the motors began to hum. He motioned everyone against the wall. They waited, listening to the elevator stop at a level above, hearing a murmur of voices and soft laughter. They stood frozen and watched the interior light shine through the crack between the doors as it descended.

It was all over in ten seconds. The doors opened and two technicians in white coats stepped outside and died without the slightest whisper of a sound from knives thrust into their hearts. Pitt was amazed at the efficiency of the act. None of the Cubans wore the slightest expression of remorse in their eyes.

"Decision time," said Pitt. "The elevator can hold only ten men."

"Only fourteen minutes until the space shuttle lands," Quintana said urgently. "We've got to find and cut off the compound's power source."

"There are four levels above us. Velikov's study is on the top. So are the living quarters. Take your pick of the other three."

"Like drawing to an inside straight."

"What else," Pitt said quickly. "We're also bunched-up fish in a barrel. My advice is to split up into three groups and take each level. You'll cover more territory faster."

"Sounds good," Quintana hastily agreed. "We've come this far without a greeting. They won't be expecting visitors to pop up on the inside at the same time in different areas."

"I'll go with the first eight men to level two and send the elevator down for the next team, who will hit level three, and so on."

"Fair enough." Quintana wasted no time arguing. He hurriedly selected eight men and ordered them into the elevator with Pitt. Just before the doors closed he snapped, "You stay alive, damn you!"

The ride up seemed endless. None of the men looked into the eyes of the others. A few dabbed at the sweat trickling down their faces. Some scratched at imagined itches. All had a finger poised on a trigger.

At last the elevator settled to a stop and the door parted. The Cubans poured out into an operations room staffed by nearly twenty Soviet GRU officers and four women who were also in uniform. Most died behind their desks in a hail of gunfire, dying in dazed disbelief. In a few seconds the office resembled a charnel house with blood and tissue sprayed everywhere.

Pitt took no time to see more. He punched the Level 1 button on the panel and rose alone in the elevator to Velikov's study. Pressing his back against the front wall, weapon in the raised position, he stole one quick glance around the opening doors. The sight inside the study struck him with a mixed force of elation and savage anger.

Seven GRU officers were siting in a semicircle, watching in rapt fascination as Foss Gly performed his sadistic act. They seemed oblivious to the muted thump of gunfire from the level below, their senses deadened, Pitt concluded, by the emptied contents of several wine bottles.

Rudi Gunn lay off to one side, his face nearly battered into pulp, trying desperately out of some burning pride to hold up his head in contempt. One officer held a small automatic pistol on a bleeding Al Giordino who was tied in a metal chair. The brawny little Italian sagged forward with his head almost on his knees, shaking it slowly from side to side as if to clear his vision and rid himself of the pain. One of the men lifted his leg and kicked Giordino in the side, knocking him and the chair sideways to the floor. Raymond LeBaron sat beside and slightly behind Gly. The once dynamic financier had the look of a man who was worn to a shadow, his spirit torn from his body. The eyes were sightless, the face expressionless. Gly had pressured and twisted him into a decaying vegetable.

Jessie LeBaron knelt in the center of the room, staring at Gly in defiance. Her hair had ben crudely lopped short. She clutched a blanket around her shoulders. Ugly red welts and dark bruises covered her exposed legs and arms. She looked to be beyond suffering, her mind deadened to any further pain. Despite her pitiful appearance she was incredibly beautiful, with a serenity and poise that were remarkable.

Foss and the other men turned at the arrival of the elevator, but seeing that it was apparently empty, they turned back to their sport.

Just as the doors began to close Pitt stepped into the room with an almost inhuman icy calm, his AK-74 held at eye level, the muzzle erupting fire.

His first carefully aimed shots took the man who had kicked Giordino onto the floor. The second blast struck the chest of the bemedaled officer seated next to Gunn, pitching him backward into a bookcase. The third and fourth bursts swept away three men sitting in a tight group. He was swinging the gun barrel in an arc, lining up on Foss Gly, but the massively built turncoat reacted more quickly than the others.

Gly yanked Jessie to her feet and held her in front of him as a shield. Pitt delayed just long enough for the seventh Russian, who was sitting almost at his elbows, to unholster an automatic pistol and snap off a wild shot.

The bullet struck the breech of Pitt's gun, shattered it, and then ricocheted into the ceiling. Pitt raised the useless weapon and sprang at the same moment he saw the muzzle flash from the second shot. Everything seemed to slow down. Even the frightened expression on the Russian's face as he squeezed the trigger for the third time, but the blast never came. The frame of the AK-74 sliced the air and caved the side of his head in.

At first Pitt thought the second bullet had missed, but then he felt the blood dripping down his neck from the nick taken out of his left ear. He stood there rooted, his fury still burning as Gly rudely shoved Jessie sprawling on the carpet.

A satanic grin spread across Gly's evil face along with an expression of unholy expectation. "You came back."

"Very perceptive—for a cretin, that is."

"I promised you would die slowly when we met again," said Gly menacingly. "Have you forgotten?"

"No, I didn't forget," said Pitt. "I even remembered to bring a big club."

Pitt had no doubts that Gly meant to crush the life out of him with

his massive hands. And he knew that his only real advantage, besides
the bat, was a total lack of fear. Gly was used to seeing his victims
helpless and naked, intimidated by his brute strength. Pitt's lips
matched the satanic grin, and he began to stalk Gly, observing with
cold satisfaction the look of confusion in his opponent's eyes.

Pitt went into a baseball crouch and swung the bat, aiming for a
low pitch, and struck Gly in the knee. The blow smashed Gly's
kneecap and he grunted in pain but didn't go down. He recovered
in the blink of an eye and lurched at Pitt, receiving a blow in the
ribs that knocked the breath from his body with an agonized gasp.
For a moment he stood still warily watching Pitt, feeling the broken
ribs, sucking painful intakes of air.

Pitt stepped back and lowered the bat. "Does the name Brian Shaw
do anything for you?" he asked calmly.

The twisted look of hate slowly changed to puzzlement. "The British agent? You knew him?"

"Six months ago, I saved his life on a tugboat in the Saint Lawrence
River. Remember? You were crushing him to death when I came up
from behind and brained you with a wrench."

Pitt relished the savage glare in Gly's eyes.

"That was you?"

"A final thought to take with you," Pitt said, smiling fiendishly.

"The confession of a dead man." There was no contempt, no in-
solence in Gly's voice, just simple belief.

Without another word the two men began circling each other like
a pair of wolves, Pitt with the bat raised, Gly dragging his injured
leg. An eerie quiet settled over the room. Gunn struggled through a
sea of pain to reach the fallen automatic pistol, but Gly caught the
movement out of the corner of one eye and kicked the gun aside.
Still tied to the chair, Giordino struggled weakly against his bonds
in helpless frustration, while Jessie lay rigid, staring in morbid fascination.

Pitt took a step forward and was in the act of swinging when one
foot slipped in the blood of a slain Russian. The bat should have
caught Gly on the side of his head, but the arc was thrown off by six
inches. On reflex Gly threw up his arm and absorbed the impact
with king-size biceps.

The wooden shaft quivered in Pitt's hands as if he had struck it
against a car bumper. Gly lashed out with his free hand, grabbed the
end of the bat, and heaved like a weightlifter. Pitt gripped the handle
for dear life as he was lifted into the air like a small child and slung

halfway across the room against a wall of bookshelves, where he crashed to the floor amid an avalanche of leather-bound volumes.

Sadly, despairingly, Jessie and the others knew Pitt could never shake off the jarring collision with the wall. Even Gly relaxed and took his time about approaching the body on the floor, triumph fairly glowing on his gargoyle face, lips spread in sharkish anticipation of the extermination to come.

Then Gly stopped and stared incredulous as Pitt rose up from under a mountain of books like a quarterback who had been sacked, dazed, and slightly disoriented but ready for the next play. What Pitt knew, and no one else realized, was that the books had cushioned his impact. He hurt like hell but suffered no crippling damage to flesh and bone. Lifting the bat he moved to meet the advancing iron man, and rammed the blunt end with all his strength into the sneering face.

But he misjudged the giant's unholy strength. Gly side-stepped and met the bat with his fist, knocking it aside and taking advantage of Pitt's forward momentum to clench iron arms around his back. Pitt twisted violently and brought his knee up into Gly's groin, a savage blow that would have doubled over any other man. But not Gly. He gave a slight gasp, blinked, and then increased the pressure in a vicious bear hug that would crush the life out of Pitt.

Gly stared unblinking into Pitt's eyes from a distance of four inches. There wasn't the slightest display of physical exertion on his face. The only expression was the sneer that was locked in place. He lifted Pitt from his feet and kept squeezing, anticipating the contorted terror that would spread across his victim's face just before the end.

The air was choked off from Pitt's lungs and he gasped for breath. The room began to blur as the pain inside his chest ruptured into flaming agony. He could hear Jessie screaming, Giordino shouting something, but he couldn't distinguish the words. Through the pain his mind remained curiously sharp and clear. He refused to accept death and coldly devised a simple way to cheat it.

One arm was free, while the other, the one still clutching the baseball bat, was caught in Gly's relentless grip. The black curtain was beginning to drop over his eyes for the last time, and he realized death was only seconds away when he performed his last desperate act.

He brought up his hand until it was even with Gly's face and thrust the full length of the thumb into one eye, driving inward through the skull and twisting deeply into the brain.

Shock wiped the sneer off Gly's face, the shock of atrocious pain and unbelief. The dark features contorted in an anguished mask, and he instinctively released his arms from around Pitt and threw his hands up to his eye, filling the air with a horrible scream.

In spite of the terrible injury, Gly remained on his feet, thrashing around the room like a crazed animal. Pitt could not believe the monster was still alive, he almost believed Gly was indestructible—until a deafening roar drowned the agonized cries.

Once, twice, three times, calmly and quite coldly, Jessie pulled the trigger on the fallen automatic pistol and shot Foss Gly in the groin. The shells thudded into him, and he staggered backward a few steps, then stood grotesquely for a few moments as if held by puppet strings. Finally he collapsed and crashed to the floor like a falling tree. The one eye was still open, black and as evil in death as it had been in life.

56

MAJOR GUS HOLLYMAN was flying scared. A career Air Force pilot with almost three hundred hours of flight time, he was suffering acute pangs of doubt, and doubt was one of a pilot's worst enemies. Lack of confidence in himself, his aircraft, or the men on the ground could prove deadly.

He couldn't bring himself to believe his mission to shoot down the space shuttle *Gettysburg* was anything more than a crazy exercise dreamed up by some egghead general with a fetish for far-out war games. A simulation, he told himself for the tenth time, it had to be a simulation that would terminate at the last minute.

Hollyman stared up at the stars through the canopy of the F-15E night attack fighter and wondered if he could actually obey an order to destroy the space shuttle and all those on board.

His eyes dropped to the instruments that glowed on the panel in front of him. His altitude was just over 50,000 feet. He would have less than three minutes to close on the rapidly descending space shuttle and lock in before firing a radar-guided Modoc missile. He automatically went through the procedure in his mind, hoping it would get no further than a mental event.

"Anything yet?" he asked his radar observer, a gum-chewing lieutenant named Regis Murphy.

"Still out of range," replied Murphy. "The last update from the space center in Colorado puts her altitude at twenty-six miles, speed approximately six thousand and slowing. She should reach our sector in five minutes, forty seconds, at a speed of twelve hundred."

Hollyman turned and scanned the black sky behind, spotting the faint exhaust glow of the two aircraft following his tail. "Do you copy, Fox Two?"

"Roger, Fox Leader."

"Fox Three?"

"We copy."

A cloud of oppression seemed to fill Hollyman's cockpit. None of this was right. He hadn't dedicated his life to defending his country, hadn't spent years in intensive training, simply to blast an unarmed aircraft carrying innocent scientists out of the air. Something was horribly wrong.

"Colorado Control, this is Fox Leader."

"Go ahead, Fox Leader."

"I request permission to terminate exercise, over."

There was a long pause. Then: "Major Hollyman, this is General Allan Post. Do you read me?"

So this was the egghead general, Hollyman mused. "Yes, General, I read you."

"This is not an exercise. I repeat, this is not an exercise."

Hollyman did not mince words. "Do you realize what you're asking me to do, sir?"

"I'm not asking, Major. I'm giving you a direct order to bring down the *Gettysburg* before she lands in Cuba."

There had been no time for a full briefing when Hollyman was ordered to scramble his flight into the air. He was stunned and bewildered at Post's sudden revelation. "Forgive me for asking, General, but are you acting by higher command? Over."

"Is a directive straight from your Commander in Chief in the White House good enough for you?"

"Yes, sir," he said slowly. "I guess it is."

God, Hollyman thought despairingly, there was no getting around it.

"Altitude twenty-two miles, nine minutes to touchdown." Burkhart was reading off the instruments for Jurgens. "We've got lights off to our right."

"What's going down, Houston?" asked Jurgens, his face set in a frown. "Where in hell are you putting us?"

"Stay cool," replied the impassive voice of Flight Director Foley. "You're lined up just fine. Just sit tight and we'll bring you in."

"Radar and navigation indicators say we're touching down in the middle of Cuba. Please cross-check."

"No need, *Gettysburg*, you're on final approach."

"Houston, I'm not getting through to you. I repeat, where are you setting us down?"

There was no reply.

"Listen to me," said Jurgens in near desperation. "I'm going to full manual."

"Negative, Dave. Remain in auto. All systems are committed to the landing site."

Jurgens clenched his fists in futility. "Why?" he demanded. "Why are you doing this?"

There was no reply.

Jurgens looked over at Burkhart. "Move the speed brakes back to zero percent. We're going on TAEM.* I want to keep this ship in the air as long as I can until we get some straight answers."

"You're only prolonging the inevitable by a couple of minutes," said Burkhart.

"We can't just sit here and accept this."

"It's out of our hands," Burkhart replied miserably. "We've no place else to go."

The real Merv Foley sat at a console in the Houston control center in helpless rage. His face, the color of chalk, showed an expression of incredulity. He pounded a fist against the edge of the console.

"We're losing them," he muttered hopelessly.

Irwin Mitchell of the "inner core" stood directly behind him. "Our communications people are doing the best they can to get through."

"Too damned late!" Foley burst out. "They're on final approach." He turned and grabbed Mitchell by the arm. "For Christ's sake, Irv, beg the President to let them land. Give the shuttle to the Russians, let them take whatever they can get out of it. But in the name of God don't let those men die."

Mitchell stared up dully at the data display screens. "Better this way," he said, his voice vague.

"The moon colonists—those are your people. After all they've achieved, the years of struggling just to stay alive in a murderous environment, you can't simply write them off this close to home."

"You don't know those men. They'd never allow the results of their efforts to be given away to a hostile government. If I was up there

*Terminal-area energy management, a process for conserving speed and altitude.

and Eli Steinmetz was down here, he wouldn't hesitate to blow the *Gettysburg* to ashes."

Foley looked at Mitchell for a long moment. Then he turned away and buried his head in his hands, stricken with grief.

57

JESSIE LIFTED HER HEAD and gazed at Pitt, the coffee-brown eyes misted, teardrops rolling past the bruises on her cheeks. She was shuddering now, shuddering from the death around her and immense relief. Pitt unashamedly embraced her, saying nothing, and gently removed the gun from her hand. Then he released her, quickly cut Giordino's bonds, gave Gunn a reassuring squeeze on the shoulder, and stepped up to the huge wall map.

He rapped his knuckles against it, gauging the thickness. Then he moved back and lashed out with his foot at the center of the Indian Ocean. The hidden panel gave way, swung on its hinges, and smashed against the wall.

"I'll be back," he said, and disappeared into a passageway.

The interior was well lit and carpeted. He rushed incautiously, the gun held out in front of him. The passage was air-conditioned and cool, but the sweat was flowing through his pores more heavily than ever before. He rubbed a sleeve over his forehead, blocking his view for a brief moment, and almost died.

At that exact moment he reached a cross passage, and like a scene from an old Mack Sennett silent movie he collided with two guards who were walking around the corner.

Pitt crashed through them, knocking them to the sides, then whirled and dropped to the floor. The advantage of surprise was on his side. The guards hadn't expected to meet a foe so close to General Velikov's study. Pitt did. The automatic in his hand spat four times before the startled guards had a chance to trigger their rifles. He leaped to his feet while they were still falling.

For two seconds, perhaps three—it seemed an hour—he stared at the inert figures, curiously unaffected by their death but stunned that it all happened so fast. Mentally and emotionally he was exhausted, physically he felt reasonably fit. He sucked in deep lungfuls of air until his mind struggled through the haze, and he turned it to figuring which passage ran toward the electronic center of the compound.

The side passages had concrete floors, so he stuck with the one with the carpet and forged ahead. He had run only fifty feet when his brain cells finally came back on line and he cursed his sluggishness for not thinking to snatch one of the guard's rifles. He pulled out the clip of the automatic. It was empty, only one shell remained in the chamber. He wrote off the mistake and kept going.

It was then he saw a backwash of light ahead and heard voices. He slowed and ghosted up to a portal and peered out with the wariness of a mouse peeking from a knothole for a cat.

Six feet away was a railing on a balcony overlooking a vast room crammed with banks of computers and consoles stretched in neat rows beneath two large data display screens. At least ten technicians and engineers sat and calmly monitored the array of electronics while another five or six stood in agitated conversation.

The few uniformed guards who were present were crouched at one end of the room, their rifles aimed at a heavy steel door. A barrage of gunfire was coming from the other side, and Pitt knew Quintana and his men were about to break through. Now he was really sorry he hadn't taken the guns from the dead guards. He was about to turn and run back for them when a thunderous roar engulfed the room, followed by a great shower of dust and debris as the shattered door twisted crazily and burst into jagged fragments.

Before the cloud settled, the Cubans charged through the opening, guns blazing. The first three inside the room went down from the fire of the guards. Then the Russians seemed to melt away before the murderous onslaught. The din inside the concrete-walled room was deafening, but even so, above it all Pitt could hear the screams of the wounded. Most of the technicians hid under their consoles. Those who resisted were unmercifully shot down.

Pitt moved out along the balcony, keeping his back flattened against the wall. He saw two men standing about thirty feet away, staring in rapt horror at the carnage below. He recognized one of them as General Velikov and began edging closer, stalking his prey. He had only moved a short distance when Velikov pulled back from the balcony railing and turned. He looked at Pitt blankly for an instant, and his eyes widened in recognition, and then incredibly he smiled. The man seemed to have no nerves at all.

Pitt raised the automatic and took deliberate aim.

Velikov moved with the swiftness of a cat, jerking the other man in front of him, a fraction of a second before the hammer fell on the cartridge.

The bullet caught Lyev Maisky in the chest. The deputy chief of the KGB stiffened in shock and stood there staring in petrified astonishment before staggering backward and tumbling over the railing to the floor below.

Pitt unconsciously pulled the trigger again, but the gun was empty. In a futile gesture he threw it at Velikov, who easily deflected it with an arm.

Velikov nodded, his face revealing more curiosity than fear. "You're an amazing man, Mr. Pitt."

Before Pitt could reply or take a step, the general lurched sideways through an open door and slammed it shut. Pitt threw himself against the door, but he was too late. The lock was on the inside and Velikov had snapped the latch. There would be no kicking this one in. The heavy bolt was firmly embedded in a metal frame. He raised his fist to punch the door, thought better of it, swung around and ran down a stairway to the floor below.

He crossed the room through the confusion, stepping over the bodies until he reached Quintana, who was emptying the magazine of his AK-74 into a bank of computers.

"Forget that!" Pitt shouted in Quintana's ear. He gestured to the radio console. "If your men haven't destroyed the antenna, let me try to make contact with the shuttle."

Quintana lowered his rifle and looked at him. "The controls are in Russian. Can you operate it?"

"Never know till I try," said Pitt. He sat at the radio console and quickly studied the confusing sea of lights and switches labeled in the Cyrillic alphabet.

Quintana leaned over Pitt's shoulder. "You'll never find the right frequency in time."

"You Catholic?"

"Yes. Why?"

"Then call up the saint who guides lost souls and pray this thing is already set on the shuttle's frequency."

Pitt placed the tiny headset over one ear and kept pressing switches until he received a tone. Then he adjusted the microphone and pressed what he guessed and fervently hoped was the Transmit switch.

"Hello, *Gettysburg*, do you read me? Over." Then he pushed what he was sure was the Receive switch.

Nothing.

He tried a second, and a third. "*Gettysburg,* do you read? Over."

He pushed a fourth switch. "*Gettysburg. Gettysburg,* please respond," Pitt implored. "Do you read me? Over."

Silence, and then: "This is *Gettysburg.* Who the hell are you? Over."

The sudden reply, so clear and distinct, surprised Pitt, and he took nearly three seconds to answer.

"Not that it matters, the name is Dirk Pitt. For the love of God, *Gettysburg,* sheer off. I repeat, sheer off. You are on a glide path for Cuba."

"So what else is new?" said Jurgens. "I can only keep this bird in the air a few more minutes and must make a touchdown attempt at the nearest landing strip. We've run out of options."

Pitt did not reply immediately. He closed his eyes and tried to think. Suddenly something clicked in his mind.

"*Gettysburg,* can you possibly make Miami?"

"Negative. Over."

"Try for the Key West Naval Air Station. It lies at the tip of the Keys."

"We copy. Our computers show it one hundred ten miles north and slightly east of us. Very doubtful. Over."

"Better to pile it up in the water than hand it to the Russians."

"That's easy for you to say. We've got over a dozen people on board. Over."

Pitt wrestled with his conscience for a moment, struggling whether or not to play God. Then he said urgently, "*Gettysburg,* go for it! Go for the Keys."

He couldn't have known it but Jurgens was about to make the same decision. "Why not? What have we got to lose but a billion-dollar airplane and our lives. Keep your fingers crossed."

"When I go off the air you should be able to reestablish communications with Houston," said Pitt. "Good luck, *Gettysburg.* Come home safe. Out."

Pitt sat there, drained. There was a strange silence in the devastated room, a silence only intensified by the low moans of the wounded. He looked up at Quintana and smiled thinly. His part in the act was over, he thought vaguely, all that was left was to gather up his friends and return home.

But then his mind recalled the La Dorada.

58

THE GETTYSBURG MADE A FAT target as she glided quietly through the night. There was no glow from the exhaust pods of her dead engines, but she was lit from bow to tail by flashing navigation lights. She was only a quarter of a mile ahead and slightly below Hollyman's attack fighter. He knew now that nothing could save the shuttle and the men inside. Her fiery end was only seconds away.

Hollyman went through the mechanical motions of planning his attack. The visual displays on his forward panel and windshield showed the necessary speed and navigation data along with the status and firing cues of his missile delivery systems. A digital computer automatically tracked the space shuttle, and he had little to do except press a button.

"Colorado Control, I am locked on target."

"Roger, Fox Leader. Four minutes to touchdown. Begin your attack."

Hollyman was torn by indecision. He felt such a wave of revulsion that he was temporarily incapable of movement, his mind sick with the realization of the terrible act he was about to commit. He had nurtured a forlorn hope the whole thing was some horrible mistake and the Gettysburg, like a condemned convict about to be executed in an old movie, would be saved by a last-minute reprieve from the President.

Hollyman's distinguished career in the Air Force was finished. Despite the fact he was carrying out orders, he would forever be branded as the man who blasted the Gettysburg and her crew out of the sky. He experienced a fear and an anger he had never known before.

He could not accept his lot as hard luck, or that fate chose him to play executioner. He softly cursed the politicians who made the military decisions, and who had brought him to this moment.

"Repeat, Fox Leader. Your transmission was garbled."

"Nothing, Control. It was nothing."

"What is your delay?" asked General Post. "Begin your attack immediately."

Hollyman's fingers hovered over the fire button. "God forgive me," he whispered.

Suddenly the digits on his tracking display began to change. He studied them briefly, drawn by curiosity. Then he stared at the space shuttle. It appeared to be rolling.

"Colorado Control!" he shouted into his microphone. "This is Fox Leader. *Gettysburg* has broken off her approach heading. Do you copy? *Gettysburg* is banking left and turning north."

"We copy, Fox Leader," replied Post, relief evident in his voice. "We have the course change on our tracking display. Take up position and stay with shuttle. Those guys are going to need all the moral support they can get."

"With pleasure," said Hollyman gleefully. "With pleasure."

A pall of silence hung over the Johnson Space Center control room. Unaware of the near-fatal drama played out by the Air Force, the ground team of four controllers and a growing crowd of NASA scientists and administrators hung in a purgatory of gloom. Their tracking network displayed the sudden turn to the north by the shuttle, but it could have merely indicated a roll or an S-turn in preparation for landing.

Then with startling abruptness, Jurgens' voice cracked the silence. "Houston, this is *Gettysburg*. Do you read? Over."

The control room erupted in a pandemonium of cheering and applause. Merv Foley reacted swiftly and replied. "Roger, *Gettysburg*. Welcome back to the fold."

"Am I talking to the real Merv Foley?"

"If there are two of us, I hope they catch the other guy quick before he signs our names to a lot of checks."

"You're Foley, all right."

"What is your status, Dave? Over."

"Are you tracking?"

"All systems have been go except communications and guidance control since you departed the space station."

"Then you know our altitude is 44,000 feet, speed 1,100. We're going to try for a touchdown at Key West Naval Air Station, over."

Foley looked up at Irwin Mitchell, his face strained.

Mitchell nodded and lightly tapped Foley's shoulder. "Let's pull out all the stops and bring those guys home."

"She's a good four hundred miles outside the cross-range," said Foley dejectedly. "We've got a hundred-ton aircraft with a descent rate of 10,000 feet a minute on a glide slope seven times steeper than a commercial airliner's. We'll never do it."

"Never say never," Mitchell replied. "Now tell them we're getting on it. And try to sound cheerful."

"Cheerful?" Foley took a few seconds to brace himself, and then he pressed the Transmit switch. "Okay, Dave, we're going to work on the problem and get you to Key West. Are you on TAEM? Over."

"Affirmative. We're pulling every trick in the book to conserve altitude. Our normal pattern approach will have to be deleted to extend our reach, over."

"Understood. All air and sea rescue units in the area are being alerted."

"Might not be a bad idea to let the Navy know we're dropping in for breakfast."

"Will do," Foley said. "Stand by."

He punched in tracking data on the display screen of his console. The *Gettysburg* was dropping past 39,500 feet, and she still had eighty miles to go.

Mitchell walked over, his eyes staring at the trajectory display on the giant wall screen. He adjusted his headset and called Jurgens.

"Dave, this is Irwin Mitchell. Go back to auto. Do you copy? Over."

"I copy, Irv, but I don't like it."

"Better the computers handle this stage of the approach. You can go back to manual ten miles from touchdown."

"Roger, out."

Foley looked up at Mitchell expectantly. "How close?" was all he asked.

Mitchell took a deep breath. "Paper thin."

"They can do it?"

"If the wind doesn't get temperamental, they stand a hairline chance. But if it veers into a five-knot crosswind, they buy the farm."

There was no fear in the cockpit of the *Gettysburg*. There was no time for it. Jurgens followed the descent trajectory on the computer display screens very closely. He flexed his fingers like a piano player before a concert, anxiously awaiting the moment he took over manual control for the final landing maneuvers.

"We've got an escort," said Burkhart.

For the first time, Jurgens turned his eyes from the instruments and gazed out the windows. He could just make out an F-15 fighter flying alongside about two hundred yards away. As he watched, the pilot switched on his navigation lights and waggled his wings. Two other aircraft in formation followed suit. Jurgens reset his radio to a military frequency.

"Where did you guys come from?"

"Just cruising the neighborhood for girls and spotted your flying machine," answered Hollyman. "Anything we can do to assist? Over."

"Got a towrope? Over."

"Fresh out."

"Thanks for hanging around, out."

Jurgens felt a small measure of comfort. If they fell short of Key West and had to ditch, at least the fighters could stand by and guide rescuers to their position. He turned his attention back to the flight indicators and idly wondered why Houston hadn't put him in communication with the Key West Naval Air Station.

"What in hell do you mean Key West is shut down?" Mitchell shouted at a white-faced engineer standing at his side, who was holding a phone. Without waiting for an answer, Mitchell grabbed the receiver. "Who am I talking to?" he demanded.

"This is Lieutenant Commander Redfern."

"Are you fully aware of the seriousness of this situation?"

"It has been explained, sir, but there is nothing we can do. A fuel tanker crashed into our power lines earlier this evening and blacked out the field."

"What about your emergency generators?"

"The diesel-engine power source ran fine for about six hours and then failed from a mechanical problem. They're working on it now and should have it back in service in an hour."

"That's too damned late," Mitchell snapped. "The *Gettysburg* is two minutes away. How can you guide them in on the final approach?"

"We can't," answered the commander. "All our equipment is shut down."

"Then line the runway with car and truck headlights, anything that will illuminate the surface."

"We'll do our best, sir, but with only four men on flight line duty this time of the morning it won't be much. I'm sorry."

"You're not the only one who's sorry," Mitchell grunted, and slammed down the phone.

"We should have the runway on visual by now," said Burkhart uneasily. "I see the city lights of Key West but no sign of the air station."

For the first time, a faint gleam of sweat appeared on Jurgens' brow. "Damned odd we haven't heard from their control tower."

At that moment, Mitchell's strained voice broke in. "*Gettysburg,* Key West station has a power outage. They are making an effort to light the runway with vehicles. We are directing your approach from the east to land on a westerly heading. Your runway is seven thousand feet. If you overshoot you wind up in a recreation park. Do you copy? Over."

"Roger, Control. We copy."

"We show you at 11,300 feet, Dave. Speed 410. One minute, ten seconds and six miles to touchdown. You are go for full manual, over."

"Roger, going to manual."

"Do you have the runway on visual?"

"Nothing yet."

"Excuse the interruption, *Gettysburg.*" It was Hollyman cutting in on the NASA frequency. "But I think my boys and I can play Rudolph to your sleigh. We'll go ahead and light the way, over."

"Much obliged, little buddy," said Jurgens gratefully.

He watched as the F-15s accelerated past, dropped their noses, and pointed them toward Key West. They fell into line as if playing follow the leader and switched on their landing lights. At first the brilliant rays only reflected on water, and then they lit up a salt flat before sweeping up the naval air station runway.

The effort of concentration showed on Jurgens' face. The shuttle went right where he aimed it, but it was never meant to soar through the air like a paper glider. Burkhart read out the airspeed and altitude so Jurgens could center his attention on flying.

"*Gettysburg,* you are three hundred feet under minimum," said Foley.

"If I pull up another inch, she'll stall."

The runway seemed to take forever to grow larger. The shuttle was only four miles out, but it looked like a hundred. Jurgens believed he could make it. He had to make it. Every brain cell in his skull willed the *Gettysburg* to hang in the air.

"Speed 320, altitude 1,600, three miles to runway," reported Burkhart. His voice had a trace of hoarseness.

Jurgens could see the flashing lights from the fire and rescue equipment now. The fighters were hovering above him, shining their landing lights on the concrete ribbon 1.5 miles long by 200 feet wide.

The shuttle was eating up her glide slope. Jurgens flared her out as much as he dared. The landing lights glinted on the shoreline no more than ninety feet below. He held on to the last possible second before he pushed the switch and deployed the landing gear. Normal landing procedure required the wheels to touch 2,760 feet down the runway, but Jurgens held his breath, hoping against hope that they would even reach the concrete.

The salt flat flashed past under the blinding beams and was lost in the darkness behind. Burkhart gripped his seat rests and droned off the diminishing numbers.

"Speed 205. Main gear at ten feet...five feet...three feet...two feet...one, contact."

The four huge tires of the main landing gear thumped on the hard surface and protested at the sudden friction with a puff of smoke. A later measurement would show that Jurgens touched the shuttle down only forty-seven feet from the end of the runway. Jurgens gently pitched the bow down until the nose wheel made contact and then pushed both brake pedals. He rolled the spacecraft to a stop with a thousand feet to spare.

"They made it!" Hollyman whooped over his radio.

"*Gettysburg* to Houston Control," said Jurgens with an audible sigh. "The wheels have stopped."

"Magnificent! Magnificent!" shouted Foley.

"Congratulations, Dave," added Mitchell. "Nobody could have done it better."

Burkhart looked over at Jurgens and said nothing, simply gave a thumbs-up sign.

Jurgens sat there, his adrenaline still flowing, basking in his triumph over the odds. His weary mind began to wander and he found himself wondering who Dirk Pitt was. Then he pressed the intercom switch.

"Mr. Steinmetz."

"Yes, Commander?"

"Welcome back to earth. We're home."

59

PITT TOOK ONE QUICK comprehensive look as he stepped back into Velikov's study. Everyone was kneeling, clustered around Raymond LeBaron, who was stretched out on the floor. Jessie was holding his hand and murmuring to him. Gunn looked up at Pitt's approach and shook his head.

"What happened?" Pitt asked blankly.

"He jumped to his feet to help you and caught the bullet that cut your ear," Giordino replied.

Before kneeling, Pitt stared down a moment at the mortally wounded millionaire. The clothing that covered the upper abdomen bloomed in a spreading stain of crimson. The eyes still had life and were focused on Jessie's face. His breath came in rapid and shallow pants. He tried to raise his head and say something to her, but the effort was too great and he fell back.

Slowly Pitt sank on one knee beside Jessie. She turned and looked at him with tears trickling down her discolored cheeks. He stared back at her briefly without speaking. He could think of nothing to say to her, his mind was played out.

"Raymond tried to save you," she said huskily. "I knew they could never completely turn him inside out. In the end he came back."

LeBaron coughed, a strange rasping kind of cough. He gazed up at Jessie, his eyes dulled, face white and drained of blood. "Take care of Hilda," he whispered. "I leave everything in your hands."

Before he could say more, the room trembled as the rumble of explosives came from deep below; Quintana's team had begun destroying the electronic equipment inside the compound. They would have to leave soon, and there would be no taking Raymond LeBaron with them.

Pitt thought of all the newspaper stories and magazine articles glorifying the dying man on the carpet as a steel-blooded power merchant who could make or break executive officers of giant corporations or high-level politicians in government, a wizard at manipulating the financial markets of the world, a vindictive and cold man whose trail was littered with the bones of competing businesses he had crushed and their thousands of employees who were cast out on the streets. Pitt had read all that, but all he saw was a dying old man, a paradox of human frailty, who had stolen his best friend's wife and then killed him for a fortune in treasure. Pitt could feel no pity for such a man, no flicker of emotion.

Now the slender thread holding LeBaron on to life was about to break. He leaned over and placed his lips close to the old power broker's ear.

"La Dorada," Pitt whispered. "What did you do with her?"

LeBaron looked up, and his eyes glistened for an instant as his clouding mind took a final look at the past. His voice was faint as he summoned up the strength to answer. The words came almost as he died.

"What did he say?" asked Giordino.

"I'm not sure," replied Pitt, his expression bewildered. "It sounded like 'Look on the main sight.'"

To the Cubans across the bay on the main island the detonations sounded like distant thunder and they paid no attention. No spouting volcano of red and orange lit the horizon, no fiery column of flame reaching hundreds of feet through the black sky attracted their curiosity. The sounds came strangely muffled as the compound was destroyed from within. Even the belated destruction of the great antenna went without notice.

Pitt helped Jessie to the staging area on the beach, followed by Giordino and Gunn, who was carried on a stretcher by the Cubans. Quintana joined them and dropped all caution as he shined a pencil-thin flashlight in Pitt's face.

"You'd better get a patch on that ear."

"I'll survive until we reach the SPUT."

"I had to leave two men behind, buried where they'll never be found. But there are still more going out than came in. Some of you will have to double up on the water Dashers. Dirk, you carry Mrs. LeBaron. Mr. Gunn can ride with me. Sergeant López can—"

"The sergeant can ride alone," Pitt interrupted.

"Alone?"

"We left a man behind too," said Pitt.

Quintana quickly swept the narrow beam at the others. "Raymond LaBaron?"

"He won't be coming."

Quintana gave a slight shrug, bowed his head at Jessie, and said simply, "I'm sorry." Then he turned away and began assembling his men for the trip back to the mother ship.

Pitt held Jessie close to him and spoke gently. "He asked you to take care of his first wife, Hilda, who still lives."

He couldn't see the surprise on her face, but he could feel her body tense.

"How did you know?" she asked incredulously.

"I met and talked with her a few days ago."

She seemed to accept that and did not ask him how he came to be at the rest home. "Raymond and I went through the ceremony and played out our roles as man and wife, but he could never completely give up or divorce Hilda."

"A man who loved two women."

"In different, special ways. A tiger in business, a lamb on the home front, Raymond was lost when Hilda's mind and body began to deteriorate. He desperately needed a woman to lean on. He used his influence to fake her death and place her in a rest home under a former married name."

"Your cue to walk on the scene." He did not like being cold, but he was not sorry.

"I was already part of his life," she said without hurt. "I was one of the senior editors of the *Prosperteer*. Raymond and I had carried on an affair for years. We felt comfortable together. His proposal bordered on a business proposition, a staged marriage of convenience, but it soon grew into more, much more. Do you believe that?"

"I've no talent for rendering verdicts," Pitt replied quietly.

Quintana detached himself from the shadows and touched Pitt's arm. "We're moving out. I'll take the radio receiver and lead off." He moved close to Jessie and his voice softened. "Another hour and you'll be safe. Do you think you can hold on a little longer?"

"I'll be fine. Thank you for your concern."

The Dashers were dragged across the beach and set in the water. At Quintana's command everyone mounted and set off across the black water. This time Pitt brought up the rear as Quintana, headset in place, homed in on the SPUT from headings transmitted by Colonel Kleist.

They left an island of dead in their wake. The huge compound was reduced to great broken slabs of concrete that crumbled inward. The vast array of electronic equipment and the ornate furnishings smoldered like the dying core of a volcano deep beneath the sun-bleached coral sand. The giant antenna lay in a thousand twisted pieces, shattered beyond any possible repair. Within hours hundreds of Russian soldiers, led by agents of the GRU, would be crawling over the ruins, searching and sifting the sands for incriminating evidence of the forces responsible for the destruction. But the only bits and pieces their probing investigation would turn up pointed directly to the cunning mind of Fidel Castro and not the CIA.

Pitt kept his eyes locked on the shaded blue light of the Dasher straight in front of him. They were going against the tide now and the tiny craft nosed into the wave troughs and bounced over the crests like a roller coaster. Jessie's added weight slowed their speed, and he kept the accelerator pressed against its stop to keep from falling behind.

They had only traveled about a mile when Pitt felt one of Jessie's hands loosen from his waist.

"Are you all right?" he asked.

His answer was the feel of a cold gun muzzle against his chest just beneath the armpit. He dipped his head very slowly and looked down under his arm. There was indeed the black outline of an automatic pistol pressed into his rib cage, a 9-millimeter Makarov, and the hand that held it was rock steady.

"If I'm not being too forward," he said in genuine surprise, "may I ask what's on your mind?"

"A change in plan," she replied, her voice low and tense. "Our job is only half done."

Kleist paced the deck of the SPUT as Quintana's team of raiders were lifted on board and the Dashers quickly stowed through a large hatch and down a ramp to the cavernous cargo bay. Quintana circled the ship, riding herd until there was no one left in the water; only then did he climb onto the low deck.

"How did it go?" Kleist asked anxiously.

"As they say on Broadway, a smash hit. The destruction was complete. You can tell Langley the GRU is off the air."

"Nice work," said Kleist. "You'll receive a fat bonus and long vacation. Courtesy of Martin Brogan."

"Pitt deserves a major share of the credit. He led us straight into the parlor before the Russians woke up. He also went on the radio and warned off the space shuttle."

"Unfortunately, there are no brass bands for part-time help," said Kleist vaguely. Then he asked, "And what of General Velikov?"

"Presumed dead and buried in the rubble."

"Any casualties?"

"I lost two men." He paused. "We also lost Raymond LeBaron."

"The President won't be happy when he hears that news."

"More of an accident really. He made a very brave but foolhardy attempt to save Pitt's life and was shot for his effort."

"So the old bastard went out a hero." Kleist stepped to the edge of the deck and peered into the darkness. "And what of Pitt?"

"A slight wound, nothing serious."

"And Mrs. LeBaron?"

"A few days' rest and some cosmetics to cover the bruises, and she'll look as good as new."

Kleist turned briskly. "When did you see them last?"

"When we left the beach. Pitt was carrying her on his Dasher. I kept the speed low so they could keep up."

Quintana couldn't see it, but Kleist's eyes turned fearful, fearful with the sudden realization that something was terribly amiss. "Pitt and Mrs. LeBaron have not come on board."

"They must have," Quintana said uneasily. "I'm the last one in."

"Neither has been accounted for," said Kleist. "They're still out there somewhere. And since Pitt didn't carry the radio receiver on the return trip, we can't guide them home."

Quintana put a hand to his forehead. "My fault. I was responsible."

"Maybe, maybe not. If something went wrong, if his Dasher broke down, Pitt would have called out, and you would have surely heard him."

"We might pick them up on radar," Quintana offered hopefully.

Kleist doubled his fists and rapped them together. "We'd better hurry. It's suicide to drift around here much longer."

He and Quintana hurried down the ramp to the control room. The radar operator was sitting in front of a blank scope. He looked up as the two officers flanked his sides, their faces strained.

"Raise the antenna," ordered Kleist.

"We'll be targeted by every radar unit on the Cuban coast," the operator protested.

"Raise it!" Kleist demanded sharply.

Topside, a section of the deck parted and a directional antenna unfolded and rose on the top of a mast that telescoped nearly fifty feet into the sky. Below, six pairs of eyes watched as the screen glowed into life.

"What are we looking for?" asked the operator.

"Two of our people are missing," answered Quintana.

"They're too small to show on the screen."

"What about computer enhancement?"

"We can try."

"Go for it."

After half a minute, the operator shook his head. "Nothing within two miles."

"Increase the range to five."

"Still nothing."

"Go to ten."

The operator ignored the radar screen and stared intently at the enhanced computer display. "Okay, I have a tiny object that's a possible. Nine miles southwest, bearing two-two-two degrees."

"They must be lost," muttered Kleist.

The radar operator shook his head. "Not unless they're blind or plain stupid. The skies are clear as crystal. Any tenderfoot Boy Scout knows where the North Star lies."

Quintana and Kleist straightened and stared at each other in mute astonishment, unable to fully comprehend what they knew to be true. Kleist was the first to ask the inescapable question.

"Why?" he asked dumbly. "Why would they deliberately go to Cuba?"

PART V

The Amy Bigalow

Gulf

Morro Castle

Tunnel

Castillo de la Punta

MALECON

MARTI (PRADO)

CESPEDES

City Hall

Presidential Palace

Castilla de Fuerza Real and Templete

Refinery

Santa Clara Convent

Ozero Baykai

Capitol

PUERTO

Havana Bay

SIMON BOLIVAR

CARLOS III

Parque de Colón

Maine

Ozero Zaysan

Amy Bigalow

MONTE

DESEMPARADOS

Atarés Inlet

INFANTA

Atarés Castle

Guasabacoa Inlet

IODE OCTUBRE

Luyano River

TO AIRPORT

VIA BLANCA

LUYANO

CENTRAL

60

PITT AND JESSIE EVADED a prowling Cuban patrol boat and were within a thousand yards of the Cuban shoreline when the battery on the Dasher died. He pulled the drain plugs, and they swam away as the little sport craft slipped under the sea and sank to the bottom. His combat boots were a tight fit and allowed little water to seep inside, so he left them on, well aware they would be essential once he stepped on shore.

The water felt comfortably warm and the waves remained low. An early morning quarter-moon slipped over the horizon two hours ahead of the sun. With the added light Pitt could easily keep Jessie in view. She coughed as if she had taken in some water but appeared to be treading without effort.

"How's your backstroke?" he asked.

"Good." She sputtered and spit for a moment and said, "I took third in an all-state high school meet."

"What state?"

"Wyoming."

"I didn't know Wyoming had a swimming pool."

"Funny man."

"The tide is running in our favor, so let's get moving before it turns."

"It'll be light soon," she said.

"All the more reason to make shore and find cover."

"What about sharks?"

"They never breakfast before six o'clock," he said impatiently. "Now come on, no more talk."

They set off with the elementary backstroke, arms thrown back, legs thrusting in a whip kick. The incoming tide pushed them along at close to a knot, and they made good time. Jessie was a strong swimmer. She matched Pitt stroke for stroke, staying right alongside him. He marveled at her endurance after all she had been through the past six days and felt pity for the aches and exhaustion he knew she was suffering. But he could not allow her to slack off now, not until they reached shore and found a small measure of safety.

She had not offered a reason for forcing him to turn for Cuba, and Pitt had not asked. He didn't have to be clairvoyant to know she had a definite purpose in mind that went beyond mere insanity. This lady had very definite ideas and the stubbornness to back them up. He could have disarmed her by capsizing the Dasher during a fast turn on the down slope of a wave, and he was also reasonably certain she wouldn't have pulled the trigger if he had refused.

But it was business as usual for Pitt. "In for a penny, in for a pound / It's love that makes the world go round." Only he wasn't in love—attracted, yes, but not swept away. Curiosity overrode any passionate urge. He could never resist sticking his foot through a door to the unknown. And then there was the lure of the La Dorada treasure. LeBaron's clue was meager, but the statue had to be somewhere in Cuba. The only snag was that he could easily get killed.

Pitt stopped and dove straight down, touching bottom at what he reckoned was ten feet. He reached out and accidentally brushed one of Jessie's legs as he surfaced. She shrieked, thinking she was being attacked by something big with a triangular fin, unseeing eyes, and a mouth that only a dentist could appreciate.

"Quiet!" he rasped. "You'll alert every guard patrol for miles."

"Oh, God, it was you!" she groaned in dazed fright.

"Keep it low," he murmured close to her ear. "Sound carries over water. We'll rest awhile and watch for signs of activity."

There was no answer from her, simply a light touch of her hand on his shoulder in agreement. They treaded water for several minutes, peering into the darkness. The dim moonlight softly illuminated the coastline of Cuba, the narrow strip of white sand and the dark shadows of the growth behind. About two miles to their right they could see lights from cars passing on a road that cut close to the shore. Five miles beyond an incandescent glow revealed a small port city.

Pitt could not detect any indication of movement. He gestured forward and began swimming again, using a breaststroke this time so he could keep his eyes trained ahead. Heights and shapes, angles and contours became nebulous silhouettes as they moved closer. After fifty yards he extended his feet downward and touched sand. He stood and the water came up to his chest.

"You can stand," he said softly.

There was a momentary pause, then she whispered tiredly, "Thank heavens, my arms feel like lead."

"As soon as we reach the shallows you lie still and take it easy. I'm going to scout around."

"Please be careful."

"Not to worry," he said, breaking into a wide grin. "I'm getting the hang of it. This is the second enemy beach I've landed on tonight."

"Are you ever serious?"

"When the occasion demands. Like now, for instance. Give me the gun."

She hesitated. "I think I lost it."

"You think?"

"When we went in the water..."

"You dropped it."

"I dropped it," she repeated in innocent regret.

"You don't know what a joy it's been working with you," Pitt said in abject exasperation.

They swam the remaining distance in silence until the low surf diminished and it was only a few inches deep. He motioned for Jessie to stay put. For the next minute Pitt lay rigid and unmoving, then abruptly, without a word, he leaped to his feet, ran across the sand, and vanished into the shadows.

Jessie fought to keep from nodding off. Her whole body was going numb from exhaustion, and she gratefully became aware that the pain from the bruises caused by Foss Gly's hands were fading away. The soothing lap of the water against her lightly clad body relaxed her like a sedative.

And then she froze, fingers digging into the wet sand, her heart catching in her throat.

One of the bushes had moved. Ten, maybe twelve yards away, a dark mass detached itself from the surrounding shadows and advanced along the beach just above the tideline.

It was not Pitt.

The pale light from the moon revealed a figure in a uniform carrying a rifle. She lay paralyzed, acutely aware of her naked help-lessness. She pressed her body into the sand and slid backward slowly into deeper water, an inch at a time.

Jessie shrank in a vain attempt to make herself smaller as the beam from a flashlight suddenly speared the dark and played on the beach above the waterline. The Cuban sentry swept the light back and forth as he walked toward her, intently examining the ground. With a fearful certainty Jessie realized that he was following footprints. She felt a sudden anger at Pitt for leaving her alone, and for leaving a trail that led straight to her.

The Cuban approached within ten yards and would have seen the upper outline of her shape if he had only turned a fraction in her direction. The beam stopped its sweep and held steady, probing at the impressions left by Pitt on his dash across the beach. The guard swung to his right and crouched, aiming the flashlight into the bor-dering undergrowth. Then, inexplicably, he spun around to his left and the beam caught Jessie full in its glare. The light blinded her.

For a second the Cuban stood startled, then his free hand lifted the barrel of the automatic rifle that was was slung over his shoulder and he pointed the muzzle directly at Jessie. Too terrified to speak, she clamped her eyes closed as if the mere act would shut out the horror and impact of the bullets.

She heard a faint thud, followed by a convulsive grunt. The bullets never came. There was only a strange silence, and then she sensed the light had gone out. She opened her eyes and stared vaguely at a pair of legs that stood ankle deep in the water, straddling her head, and through them she saw the inert body of the Cuban sentry stretched out on the sand.

Pitt leaned down and gently hoisted Jessie to her feet. He smoothed back her dripping hair and said, "It seems I can't turn my back for a minute without you getting into trouble."

"I thought I was dead," she said, as her heartbeat gradually slowed.

"You must have thought the same thing at least a dozen times since we left Key West."

"Fear of death takes a while to get used to."

Pitt picked up the Cuban's flashlight, hooded it in his hand, and began stripping off the uniform. "Fortunately he's a short little rascal, about your size. Your feet will probably swim in his boots, but better too large than too small."

"Is he dead?"

"Just a small dent in the skull from a rock. He'll come around in a few hours."

She wrinkled her nose as she caught the thrown fatigue uniform. "I don't think he ever bathed."

"Launder it in the sea and put it on wet," he said briskly. "And be quick about it. This is no time to play fashionable rich bitch. The sentry at the next post will wonder why he hasn't shown up. His relief and sergeant of the guard are bound to come along pretty soon."

Five minutes later Jessie stood dripping in the uniform of a Cuban armed forces patrol guard. Pitt was right, the boots were two sizes too big. She lifted her damp hair and neatly tucked it under the cap. She turned and stared at Pitt as he emerged from the trees and bushes carrying the Cuban's rifle and a palm frond.

"What did you do with him?" she asked.

"Stashed him a ways inland under a bush." Pitt's voice betrayed a sense of urgency. He pointed at a tiny beam of light about a quarter of mile down the beach. "They're coming. No time for a volleyball game. Get a move on."

He roughly pushed her toward the trees and followed, walking backward brushing away their footprints with the palm frond. After nearly seventy yards, he dropped the frond and they hurried through the jungle growth, putting as much distance between them and the beach as possible before daylight.

They had covered five miles when the eastern sky began to brighten from black to orange. A sugarcane field rose up out of the fading darkness, and they skirted its border until it ended beside a paved two-lane highway. No headlights played on the asphalt in either direction. They walked along the shoulder, ducking into the brush whenever a car or truck approached. Pitt noticed that Jessie's steps were beginning to falter and her breathing was coming in rapid gasps. He halted, placed his handkerchief over the lens of the flashlight, and shone it in her face. He didn't require the credentials of a sports physician to see that she was done in. He put his arm around her waist and pushed on until they reached the steep sides of a small ravine.

"Catch your breath, I'll be right back."

Pitt dropped down the slope into a dry creek bed that threaded a jagged course around a low hill littered with large boulders and scrub pine. It passed under the highway through a concrete pipe three feet in diameter and spread into a fenced pasture on the other side. He scrambled back up to the road, silently took Jessie's hand, and led her stumbling and sliding to the gravelly bottom of the ravine. He flicked the beam of the flashlight inside the drainpipe.

"The only vacant room in town," he said in a voice as cheerful as he could make it under the circumstances.

It was no penthouse suite, but the curved bottom of the pipe held a good two inches of soft sand, and it was a safer haven than Pitt could have hoped for. Any pursuing guards who eventually came on their trail and followed it to the highway would assume the landing party met a prearranged ride.

Somehow they managed to find a comfortable position in the cramped darkness. Pitt set the gun and flashlight within easy reach and finally relaxed.

"Okay, lady," he said, his words echoing through the drainpipe. "I think the time has come for you to tell me what in hell we're doing here."

But Jessie didn't answer.

Oblivious to her clammy, ill-fitting uniform, oblivious even to aching feet and sore joints, she was curled in a fetal position sound asleep.

61

"DEAD? ALL DEAD?" Kremlin boss Antonov repeated angrily. "The entire facility destroyed and no survivors, none at all?"

Polevoi nodded heavily. "The captain of the submarine that detected the explosions and the colonel in command of the security forces sent ashore to investigate reported that they found no one alive. They retrieved the body of my chief deputy, Lyev Maisky, but General Velikov has yet to be found."

"Were secret codes and documents missing?"

Polevoi was not about to put his head on the block and take responsibility for an intelligence disaster. As it was, he stood within a hair of losing his lofty position and quickly becoming a forgotten bureaucrat in charge of a labor camp

"All classified data were destroyed by General Velikov's staff before they died fighting."

Antonov accepted the lie. "The CIA," he said, brooding. "They're behind this foul provocation."

"I don't think we can make the CIA the scapegoat on this one. The preliminary evidence points to a Cuban operation."

"Impossible," Antonov snapped. "Our friends in Castro's military would have warned us well in advance of any ambitious plan to attack the island. Besides, a daring and imaginative operation of this magnitude goes far beyond any Latin brain."

"Perhaps, but our best intelligence minds do not believe the CIA was remotely aware of our communications center on Cayo Santa María. We haven't uncovered the slightest indication of surveillance. The CIA is good, but its people are not gods. They could not have possibly planned, rehearsed, and carried out the raid in the few short hours from the time the shuttle left the space station until it suddenly veered off our programmed flight path to Cuba."

"We lost the shuttle too?"

"Our monitoring of the Johnson Space Center revealed that it landed safely in Key West."

"With the American moon colonists," he added flatly.

"They were on board, yes."

For seconds, too furious to react, Antonov sat there, his lips taut, unblinking eyes staring into nothingness. "How did they do it?" he growled at last. "How did they save their precious space shuttle at the last minute?"

"Fool's luck," said Polevoi, again relying on the Communist dogma of casting blame elsewhere. "Their asses were saved by the devious interference of the Castros."

Antonov's eyes suddenly focused on Polevoi. "As you've so often reminded me, Comrade Director, the Castro brothers can't go to the toilet without the KGB knowing how many squares of paper they use. You tell me how they suddenly crawled in bed with the President of the United States without your agents becoming aware of it."

Polevoi had unwittingly dug himself into a hole and now he shrewdly climbed out of it by switching the course of the briefing. "Operation Rum and Cola is still in progress. We may have been cheated out of the space shuttle and a rich source of scientific data, but it is an acceptable loss compared to gaining total mastery of Cuba."

Antonov considered Polevoi's words, and swallowed the bait. "I have my doubts. Without Velikov to direct the operation its chances for success are cut in half."

"The general is no longer crucial to Rum and Cola. The plan is ninety percent complete. The ships will enter Havana Harbor to-morrow evening, and Castro's speech is set for the following morning. General Velikov performed admirably in laying the groundwork. Ru-mors of a new CIA plot to assassinate Castro have already been spread throughout the Western world, and we have prepared evidence show-ing American involvement. All that's left to do is push a button."

"Our people in Havana and Santiago are alerted?"

"They're prepared to move in and form a new government as soon as the assassination is confirmed."

"And the next leader?"

"Alicia Cordero."

Antonov's mouth hung half open. "A woman, you're telling me? We're naming a woman to rule Cuba after Fidel Castro's death?"

"The perfect choice," said Polevoi firmly. "She is secretary of the Central Committee and secretary of the Council of State. Most important, she is a close confidante of Fidel and is idolized by the people for the success of her family economic programs and fiery oratory. She has a charm and charisma that matches Fidel's. Her loyalty to the Soviet Union is unquestionable, and she will have the total backing of the Cuban military."

"Who work for us."

"Who belong to us," Polevoi corrected.

"So we are committed."

"Yes, Comrade President."

"And then?" Antonov prompted.

"Nicaragua, Peru, Chile, and yes, Argentina," said Polevoi, warming to his subject. "No more messy revolutions, no more bloody guerrilla movements. We infiltrate their governments and subtly erode from within, careful to arouse no hostility from the United States. When they finally wake up it will be too late. South and Central America will be solid extensions of the Soviet Union."

"And not the party?" Antonov asked reproachfully. "Are you forgetting the glory of our Communist heritage, Polevoi?"

"The party is the base to build upon. But we cannot continue to be chained to an archaic Marxist philosophy that has taken a hundred years to prove unworkable. The twenty-first century is only a decade away. The day of cold realism is now. I quote you, Comrade President, when you said, 'I envision a new era of socialism that will wipe the hated scourge of capitalism from the earth.' Cuba is the first step in fulfilling your dream of a world society dominated by the Kremlin."

"And Fidel Castro is the barrier in our path."

"Yes," said Polevoi with a sinister smile. "But only for another forty-eight hours."

Air Force One lifted off from Andrews Air Force Base and turned south over the historic hills of Virginia. The early morning sky was clear and blue with only a few scattered thunderclouds. The Air Force colonel, who had piloted the Boeing jet under three Presidents, leveled off at 34,000 feet and gave the arrival time at Cape Canaveral over the cabin intercom.

"Breakfast, gentlemen?" asked the President, motioning toward a small dining compartment recently modified into the plane. His wife had hung a Tiffany lampshade over an art deco table, lending an informal, relaxed atmosphere. "Our galley can provide champagne if anyone wishes to celebrate."

"I wouldn't mind a hot cup of black coffee," said Martin Brogan. He sat down and removed a file from his briefcase before sliding it under the table.

Dan Fawcett pulled up a chair beside him, while Douglas Oates sat opposite, next to the President. A white-coated Air Force sergeant served guava juice, the President's favorite, and coffee. Each man gave his order and relaxed, waiting for the President to launch the conversation.

"Well," he said, smiling, "we've got a lot to get through before we land at the Cape and congratulate everyone. So let's get started. Dan, fill us in on the status of the *Gettysburg* and the moon colonists."

"I've been on the phone all morning with NASA officials," said Fawcett, excitement evident in his tone. "As we all know, Dave Jurgens put the spacecraft down in Key West by the skin of his teeth. A remarkable job of flying. The naval air station has been closed to all air and car traffic. The gates and fences are under heavy Marine guard. The President has ordered a temporary news blackout on the situation until he can announce the existence of our new moon base."

"The reporters must be screaming like wounded vultures," said Oates, "demanding to know why the shuttle made an unscheduled arrival so far off course."

"That goes without saying."

"When do you plan to make the announcement?" asked Brogan.

"In two days," replied the President. "We need time to sort out the immense implications and debrief Steinmetz and his people before we throw them to the news media."

"If we delay any longer," added Fawcett, "someone in the White House press corps is bound to hit on a leak."

"Where are the moon colonists now?"

"Undergoing tests at the Kennedy Space Center medical facility," answered Fawcett. "They were flown out of Key West along with Jurgens' crew shortly after the *Gettysburg* touched down."

Brogan looked at Oates. "Any word from the Kremlin?"

"Only silence so far."

"Be interesting to see how they react to having their nationals shot down for a change."

"Antonov is a wily old bear," said the President. "He'll reject a propaganda blitz accusing us of murdering his cosmonauts in favor

of secret talks where he'll demand restitution in the form of shared scientific data."

"Will you give it to him?"

"The President is morally bound to comply," said Oates.

Brogan looked appalled, and so did Fawcett.

"This is not a political matter," Brogan said in a low voice. "There is nothing in the book that says we have to throw away secrets vital to our national defense."

"We're cast as the villains this time around, not the Russians," protested Oates. "We're within inches of a SALT IV agreement to halt all future nuclear missile placement. If the President ignored Antonov's claims, the Soviet negotiators would take one of their famous walks only hours before signing the treaty."

"You may be right," said Fawcett. "But everyone connected with the Jersey Colony didn't struggle for two decades just to give it all away to the Kremlin."

The President had followed this exchange without interrupting. Now he held up a hand. "Gentlemen, I am not about to sell out the store. But there is an enormous wealth of information we can share with the Russians and the rest of the world in the interests of humanity. Medical findings, geological and astronomical data must be freely passed around. However, you may rest easy. I'm not about to compromise our space and defense programs. That area will remain firmly in our hands. Do I make myself clear?"

Silence descended on the dining compartment as the steward delivered three steaming plates of eggs, ham, and hotcakes. He refilled the coffee cups. As soon as he returned to the galley, the President sighed deeply and looked at the table in front of Brogan.

"You're not eating, Martin?"

"I usually skip breakfast. Lunch is my big meal."

"You don't know what you're missing. These hotcakes are light as a feather."

"No, thanks. I'll just stick with coffee."

"While the rest of us dig in, why don't you brief us on the Cayo Santa María operation."

Brogan took a sip from his cup, opened the file, and condensed the contents in a few concise statements. "A special combat team under the command of Colonel Ramon Kleist and led by Major Angelo Quintana landed on the island at 0200 hours this morning. By 0430 the Soviet radio jamming and listening facility, including its antenna, was destroyed and all personnel terminated. The timing

was most fortunate, as the final radio transmission warned off the *Gettysburg* only minutes before it would have landed on Cuban soil."

"Who gave the warning?" interrupted Fawcett.

Brogan stared across the table and smiled. "He gave his name as Dirk Pitt."

"My God, the man is everywhere," the President exclaimed.

"Jessie LeBaron and two of Admiral Sandecker's NUMA people were rescued," Brogan continued. "Raymond LeBaron was killed."

"Is that confirmed?" asked the President, his expression turned solemn.

"Yes, sir, it was confirmed."

"A great pity. He deserved recognition for his contribution to the Jersey Colony."

"Still, the mission was a great success," Brogan said quietly. "Major Quintana recovered a wealth of intelligence material, including the Soviets' latest codes. It arrived only an hour ago. Analysts at Langley are sifting through it now."

"Congratulations are in order," said the President. "Your people performed an incredible feat."

"You may not be so hasty with praise, Mr. President, after you hear the full story."

"Okay, Martin, let's have it."

"Dirk Pitt and Jessie LeBaron..." Brogan paused and gave a dejected shrug of his shoulders. "They didn't return to the mother ship with Major Quintana and his men."

"Were they killed on the island along with Raymond LeBaron?"

"No, sir. They departed with the others, but veered away and headed for Cuba."

"Cuba," the President repeated in a soft voice. He looked across the table at Oates and Fawcett, who stared back incredulously. "Good lord, Jessie is still trying to deliver our reply to the proposed U.S.–Cuban pact."

"Is it possible she can somehow make contact with Castro?" asked Fawcett.

Brogan shook his head doubtfully. "The island is teeming with security forces, police and militia units who check every mile of road. They'd be arrested inside an hour, assuming they get past patrols on the beach."

"Maybe Pitt will get lucky," Fawcett muttered hopefully.

"No," said the President gravely, his features shrouded with concern. "The man has used up whatever luck he had."

In a small office at the CIA headquarters at Langley, Bob Thornburg, chief documents analyst, sat with his feet crossed on his desk and read through a pile of material that had been flown in from San Salvador. He puffed a veil of blue pipe smoke and translated the Russian typing.

He quickly scanned three folders and picked up a fourth. The title intrigued him. The phrasing was peculiarly American. It was a covert action named after a mixed drink. He quickly glanced through to the end and sat there a moment, stunned. Then he set the pipe in an ashtray, removed his feet from the desktop, and read the contents of the folder more carefully, picking it apart sentence by sentence and making notes on a yellow legal pad.

Nearly two hours later, Thornburg picked up his phone and dialed an internal number. A woman answered, and he asked for the deputy director.

"Eileen, this is Bob Thornburg. Is Henry available?"

"He's on another line."

"Have him ring me first chance, this is urgent."

"I'll tell him."

Thornburg assembled his notes and was restudying the folder for the fifth time when the chime of his phone interrupted him. He sighed and picked up the receiver.

"Bob, this is Henry. What have you got?"

"Can we meet right away? I've just been going over part of the intelligence data from the Cayo Santa María operation."

"Something of value?"

"Let's say it's a blockbuster."

"Can you give me a hint?"

"Concerns Fidel Castro."

"What no good is he up to now?"

"He's going to die the day after tomorrow."

62

As soon as Pitt woke up he looked at his watch. The time was 12:18. He felt refreshed, in good spirits, even optimistic.

When he reflected on it, Pitt found his cheerful outlook grimly amusing. His future was not exactly bright. He had no Cuban currency or identification papers. He was in a Communist country without even one friendly contact or an excuse for being there. And he was wearing the wrong uniform. He would be lucky if he made it through the day without getting shot as a spy.

He reached over and gently shook Jessie by the shoulder. Then he crawled from the drainage pipe, warily surveyed the area, and began doing stretching exercises to relieve his stiff muscles.

Jessie opened her eyes and woke up slowly, languidly, from a deep luxurious sleep, gradually fitting her world into perspective. Uncurling and extending her arms and legs like a cat, she moaned softly at the pain, but was thankful it spurred her mind into motion.

She thought of silly things at first—who to invite to her next party, planning a menu with her chef, reminding the gardener to trim the hedges bordering the walks—and then memories of her husband began passing in front of her inner eye. She wondered how a woman could work and live with a man for twenty years and still not come to grips with his inner moods. Yet she more than anyone saw Raymond LeBaron simply as a human being no worse or no better than other men, and with a mind that could radiate compassion, pettiness, brilliance, or ruthlessness almost on cue to suit the moment.

She closed her eyes tightly to shut out his death. Think of someone or something else, she told herself. Think of how to survive the next few days. Think of...Dirk Pitt.

Who was he, she wondered. What kind of man? She looked at him through the drainpipe as he bent and flexed his body and for the first time since meeting him felt a sexual attraction toward him. It was ridiculous, she reasoned, she was older by at least fifteen years. And besides, he had not shown any interest in her as a desirable woman, never once cast a suggestive insinuation or made a flirtatious overture. She decided Pitt was an enigma, the type of man who intrigued women, incited them to wanton behavior, but could never be owned or beguiled by their feminine ploys.

Jessie was snapped back to reality as Pitt leaned into the pipe and smiled. "How are you feeling?"

She looked away nervously. "Battered but ready to meet the day."

"Sorry about not having breakfast ready," he said, his voice hollow through the pipe. "The room service leaves much to be desired hereabouts."

"I'd sell my soul for a cup of coffee."

"According to a road sign I spotted a few hundred yards up the road, we're ten kilometers from the next town."

"What time is it?"

"Twenty minutes to one."

"The day is half gone," she said, rolling to her hands and knees, and beginning to crawl toward the light. "We have to get moving."

"Stay where you are."

"Why?"

He didn't answer, but returned and sat down beside her. He gently took her face in his hands and kissed her mouth.

Jessie's eyes widened, and then she returned his kiss hungrily. After a long moment, he pulled back. She waited expectantly, but he made no further move, just sat there and stared into her eyes.

"I want you," she said.

"Yes."

"Now."

He drew her to him, pressing against her body, and kissed her again. Then he broke away from her. "First things first."

She gave him a hurt, curious look. "Like what things?"

"Like why did you hijack me to Cuba?"

"You have a strange sense of timing."

"I don't usually conduct foreplay in a drainpipe either."

"What do you want to know?"

"Everything."

"And if I don't tell you?"

He laughed. "We shake hands and part company."

For a few seconds she lay against the side of the pipe, considering how far she would get without him. Probably no farther than the next town, the first suspicious policeman or security guard. Pitt seemed an incredibly resourceful man. He had proven that several times over. There was no avoiding the hard fact that she needed him more than he needed her.

She tried to find the right words to explain, an introduction that made some kind of sense. Finally she gave up and blurted it out. "The President sent me to meet with Fidel Castro."

His deep green eyes examined her with honest curiosity. "That's a good start. I'd like to hear the rest."

Jessie took a deep breath and continued.

She revealed Fidel Castro's genuine offer of a pact and his bizarre manner of sending it past the watchful eyes of Soviet intelligence.

She told of her secret meeting with the President after the unexpected return of the *Prosperteer* and his request for her to convey his reply by retracing her husband's flight in the blimp, a guise Castro would have recognized.

She admitted the deception in recruiting Pitt, Giordino, and Gunn, and she asked Pitt's forgiveness for a plan gone wrong by the surprise attack from the Cuban helicopter.

And last, she described General Velikov's narrowing suspicion of the true purpose behind the botched attempt to reach Castro and his demand for answers through Foss Gly's torture methods.

Pitt listened to the whole story without comment.

His response was the part she dreaded. She feared what he would say or do now that he had discovered how he had been used, lied to, and misled, battered bloody and nearly killed on several occasions for a mission he knew nothing about. She felt he had every right to strangle her.

She could think of nothing further to say except "I'm sorry."

Pitt did not strangle her. He held out his hand. She grasped it, and he pulled her toward him. "So you conned me all up and down the line," he said.

God, those green eyes, she thought. She wanted to dive into them. "I can't blame you for being angry."

He embraced her for several moments silently.

"Well?"

"Well what?"

"Aren't you going to say something?" she asked timidly. "Aren't you even mad?"

He unbuttoned the shirt of the uniform and lightly touched her breasts. "Lucky for you I'm not one to harbor a grudge."

Then they made love as the traffic rumbled over the highway above.

Jessie felt incredibly calm. The warm feeling had stayed with her for the last hour as they walked openly along the road's shoulder. It spread like an anesthetic, deadening her fear and sharpening her confidence. Pitt had accepted her story and agreed to help her reach Castro. And now she walked along beside him as he led her through the backcountry of Cuba as though he owned it, feeling secure and warm in the afterglow of their intimacy.

Pitt scrounged some mangoes, a pineapple, and two half-ripened tomatoes. They ate as they walked. Several vehicles, mostly trucks loaded with sugarcane and cirtrus fruits, passed them. Once in a while a military transport carrying militia swept by. Jessie would tense and look down at her tightly laced boots nervously while Pitt lifted his rifle in the air and shouted *"Saludos amigos!"*

"A good thing they can't hear you clearly," she said.

"Why is that?" he asked in mock indignation.

"Your Spanish is awful."

"It always got me by at the dog races in Tijuana."

"It won't do here. You'd better let me do the talking."

"You think your Spanish is better than mine?"

"I can speak it like a native. I can also converse fluently in Russian, French, and German."

"I'm continually amazed at your talents," Pitt said sincerely. "Did Velikov know you spoke Russian?"

"We'd have all been dead if he had."

Pitt started to say something and suddenly gestured ahead. They were rounding a curve, and he pointed at a car parked by the highway. The hood was up and someone was leaning over the fender, his head and shoulders lost in the engine compartment.

Jessie hesitated, but Pitt took her by the hand and tugged her along. "You handle this," he said softly. "Don't be frightened. We're both in military uniform, and mine belongs to an elite assault force."

"What should I say?"

"Play along. This may be a chance to get a ride."

Before she could protest, the driver heard their feet on the gravel and turned at their approach. He was a short man in his fifties with thick black hair and dark skin. He was shirtless and wore only shorts and sandals. Military uniforms were so common in Cuba he scarcely gave them any notice. He flashed a broad smile. *"Hola."*

"Having motor trouble?" Jessie asked in Spanish.

"Third time this month." He gave a helpless shrug. "She just stopped."

"Do you know the problem?"

He held up a short length of wire that had rotted apart in three different places and was barely hanging together by its insulation. "Runs from the coil to the distributor."

"You should have replaced it with a new one."

He looked at her suspiciously. "Parts for old cars like this one are impossible to find. You must know that."

Jessie caught her mistake and, smiling sweetly, quickly played on Latin *machismo*. "I'm only a woman. What would I know about mechanics?"

"Ah," he said, smiling graciously, "but a very pretty woman."

Pitt paid little attention to the conversation. He was walking around the car, examining its lines. He leaned over the front end and studied the engine for a moment. Then he straightened and stepped back.

"A fifty-seven Chevy," he said admiringly in English. "One damned fine automobile. Ask him if he has a knife and some tape."

Jessie's mouth dropped open in shock.

The driver looked at him uncertainly, unsure of what to do. Then he asked in broken English, "You no speak Spanish?"

"Faith and what's the matter?" Pitt boomed. "Haven't you ever laid eyes on an Irishman before?"

"Why an Irelander wearing a Cuban uniform?"

"Major Paddy O'Hara, Irish Republican Army, on assignment as an adviser to your militia."

The Cuban's face lit up like a camera flash, and Pitt was pleased to see that the man was duly impressed.

"Herberto Figueroa," he said, offering his hand. "I learn English many years ago when the Americans were here."

Pitt took it and nodded at Jessie. "Corporal María López, my aide and guide. She also interprets my fractured Spanish."

Figueroa dipped his head and noticed Jessie's wedding ring. "Señora López." He tilted his head to Pitt. "She understand English?" pronouncing it "chee unnarstan Englaise?"

"A little," Pitt answered. "Now then, if you can give me a knife and some tape, I think I can get you going again."

"Sure, sure," said Figueroa. He pulled a pocketknife from the glove compartment and found a small roll of friction tape in a toolbox in the trunk.

Pitt reached down into the engine, cut a few excess lengths of wire from the spark plug leads, and spliced the ends back together. Then he did the same with the extra pieces until he had a wire that stretched from the coil to the distributor.

"Okay, give her a try."

Figueroa turned the ignition key and the big 283-cubic-inch V-8 coughed once, twice, and settled into a throaty roar.

"*Magnífico!*" shouted Figueroa happily. "Can I give you a ride?"

"How far you going?"

"Havana. I live there. My sister's husband died in Nuevitas. I went to help her with the funeral. Now I'm on my way home."

Pitt nodded to Jessie. This was their lucky day. He tried to picture the shape of Cuba, and he rightly calculated that Havana was very nearly two hundred miles to the northeast as the crow flies, more like three hundred by road.

He held the front seat forward as Jessie climbed in the rear. "We're grateful to you, Herberto. My staff car developed an oil leak and the engine froze up about two miles back. We were traveling to a training camp east of Havana. If you can drop us off at the Ministry of Defense, I'll see that you get paid for your trouble."

Jessie's jaw dropped and she stared at Pitt with a classic expression of distaste. He knew that in her mind she was calling him a cocky bastard.

"Your bad luck is my good luck," said Figueroa, happy at the prospect of picking up a few extra pesos.

Figueroa spun gravel on the shoulder as he quickly moved onto the asphalt, shifting through the gears until the Chevy was spinning along at a respectable seventy miles an hour. The engine sounded smooth, but the body rattled in a dozen places and the exhaust fumes leaked through the rusted floorboards.

Pitt stared at Jessie's face in the rearview mirror. She seemed uncomfortable and out of her element. A limousine was more to her liking. Pitt positively enjoyed himself. For the moment, his love of old cars overcame any thoughts of danger.

"How many miles do you have on her?" he asked.

"Over six hundred and eighty thousand kilometers," Figueroa answered.

"She's still got good power."

"If the Yankees ever dropped their trade embargo, I might be able to buy new parts and keep her going. But she can't last forever."

"Do you have any trouble at the checkpoints?"

"I'm always waved on through."

"You must have influence. What do you do in Havana?"

Figueroa laughed. "I'm a cabdriver."

Pitt did not try to suppress a smile. This was even better than he had hoped. He sat back and relaxed, enjoying the scenery like a tourist. He tried to apply his mind to LeBaron's cryptic direction to the treasure of La Dorada, but his thinking was clouded with remorse.

He knew that at some time, somewhere along the road he might have to take what little money Figueroa carried and steal his cab. Pitt hoped he would not have to kill the friendly little man in the bargain.

63

THE PRESIDENT RETURNED to the White House from the Kennedy Space Center late in the evening and went directly to the Oval Office. After secretly meeting with Steinmetz and the moon colonists and hearing the enthusiastic reports of their explorations, he felt exhilarated. Sleep was forgotten as he walked into his office alone, inspired to plan a new range of space goals.

He sat down behind the big desk and opened a lower drawer. He lifted out a walnut humidor and removed a large cigar. He peeled off the cellophane, stared a moment at the dark brown, tightly wrapped leafy cover, and inhaled the heady aroma. It was a Montecristo, the finest cigar Cuba made, and banned from American import by the trade embargo on Cuban goods.

The President relied on an old trusted school pal to smuggle him a box every two months from Canada. Even his wife and closest aides were unaware of his cache. He clipped one end and exactingly lit the other, wondering as he always did what kind of uproar the public would raise if they discovered his clandestine and slightly illegal indulgence.

Tonight he did not give a damn. He was riding high. The economy was holding, and Congress had finally got around to passing tough budget cuts and a flat-tax law. The international scene had entered a cooling-off period, however temporary, and his popularity polls showed him up five percentage points. And now he was about to make a political profit on his predecessors' foresight, just as Nixon did after the success of the Apollo program. The stunning success of the moon colony would be the high-water mark of his administration.

His next goal was to enhance his image on Latin American affairs. Castro had cracked open the door with his offer of a treaty. Now, if the President could slip his foot over the threshold before it slammed shut again, he might have a fighting chance to neutralize Marxist influence in the Americas.

The prospects appeared gloomy at the moment. It was most likely that Pitt and Jessie LeBaron had been either shot or arrested. If they had not, then it was only a matter of hours before the inevitable happened. The only course of action was to slip someone else into Cuba to make contact with Castro.

His intercom buzzed. "Yes?"

"Sorry to interrupt you, Mr. President," said a White House operator, "but Mr. Brogan is calling and he says it is urgent he speak with you."

"It's quite all right. Please put him on."

There was a slight click and Martin Brogan said, "Did I catch you in bed?"

"No, I'm still up. What's on your mind that couldn't wait until tomorrow's briefing?"

"I'm still at Andrews Field. My deputy was waiting for me with a translated document that was taken from Cayo Santa María. It contains some pretty hot material."

"Can you fill me in?"

"The Russians are going to knock off Castro the day after tomorrow. The operation is code-named 'Rum and Cola.' It details the complete takeover of the Cuban government by Soviet agents."

The President watched the blue smoke from the Havana cigar curl toward the ceiling. "They're making their move sooner than we figured," he said thoughtfully. "How do they intend to eliminate Castro?"

"The wild part of the plan," said Brogan. "The GRU arm of the KGB intends to blitz the city along with him."

"Havana?"

"A damned good chunk of it."

"Jesus Christ, you're talking a nuclear bomb."

"I've got to be honest and say the document does not state the exact means, but it's quite clear that some kind of explosive device is being smuggled into the harbor by ship that can level four square miles."

Depression settled around the President and dampened his high spirits. "Does the document give the name of the ship?"

"It mentions three ships but none by name."

"And when is the blast supposed to be set off?"

"During an Education Day celebration. The Russians are counting on Castro making an unscheduled appearance and giving his usual two-hour harangue."

"I can't believe Antonov is a party to such horror. Why not send in a local team of hit men and gun Castro down? What's to be gained by taking a hundred thousand innocent victims with him?"

"Castro is a cult figure to the Cubans," explained Brogan. "A cartoon Communist to us maybe, but a revered god to them. A simple assassination will ignite an overwhelming ground swell of resentment against the Soviet-backed parties who replace him. But a major disaster—that would give the new leaders a rallying cry and a cause to incite the people to close ranks behind a new government, particularly if it was proven the United States was the culprit, specifically the CIA."

"I still can't conceive of such a monstrous scheme."

"I assure you, Mr. President, everything is spelled out in black and white." Brogan paused to scan a page of the document. "Odd thing, it's vague about the details of the explosion, but very specific in listing the step-by-step propaganda campaign to blame us. It even lists the names of the Soviet cohorts and the positions they are to move into after they seize control. You may be interested to learn that Alicia Cordero is to be the new President."

"God help us. She's twice the fanatic Fidel is."

"In any case, the Soviets win and we lose."

The President laid the cigar in an ashtray and closed his eyes. The problems never end, he mused. One begets another. The triumphs of office do not last very long. The pressure and the frustrations never let up.

"Can our Navy stop those ships?" he asked.

"According to the schedule, two of them have already docked in Havana," answered Brogan. "The third should be entering the harbor any hour. I had the same idea but we're an inch early and a mile late."

"We must have the names of those ships."

"I've already got my people checking on all shipping arrivals in Havana Harbor. They should have identification within the hour."

"Of all the times for Castro to hide out," the President said in exasperation.

"We found him."

"Where?"

"At his country retreat. He's cut off all contact with the outside world. Even his closest advisers and the Soviet bigwigs can't reach him."

"Who do we have on our team who can meet him face to face?"

Brogan grunted. "No one."

"There must be somebody we can send in."

"If Castro was in a communicative mood, I can think of at least ten people on our payroll who could get through the front gate. But not as things stand now."

The President toyed with the cigar, fumbling for inspiration. "How many Cubans can you trust in Havana who work the docks and have maritime experience?"

"I'd have to check."

"Guess."

"Off the top of my head, maybe fifteen or twenty."

"All right," the President said. "Round them up. Have them get on board those ships somehow and find which one is carrying the bomb."

"Someone who knows what he's doing will have to defuse it."

"We'll cross that bridge when we learn where it's hidden."

"A day and a half isn't much time," Brogan said glumly. "Better we concentrate on sorting out the mess afterward."

"You'd better get the show moving. Keep me informed every two hours. Turn everyone you've got in the Cuban department loose on this thing."

"What about warning Castro?"

"My job. I'll handle it."

"Good luck, Mr. President."

"Same to you, Martin."

The President hung up. His cigar had gone out. He relit it, then picked up the phone again and placed a call to Ira Hagen.

64

THE GUARD WAS YOUNG, no more than sixteen, eager and dedicated to Fidel Castro and committed to revolutionary vigilance. He glowed with self-importance and official arrogance as he swaggered to the car window, rifle slung tightly over one shoulder, and demanded to see identification papers.

"It had to happen," Pitt muttered under his breath.

The guards at the first three checkpoints had lazily waved Figueroa through when he flashed his taxi driver's permit. They were *campesinos* who chose the routine of a military career over a dead-end life of working in the fields or factories. And like soldiers in every army of the world, they found sentry duty tedious, eventually losing all suspicions except when their superiors arrived for an inspection.

Figueroa handed the youngster his permit.

"This only covers the Havana city borders. What are you doing in the country?"

"My brother-in-law died," Figueroa said patiently. "I went to his funeral."

The guard bent down and looked through the driver's open window. "Who are these others?"

"Are you blind?" Figueroa snapped. "They're military like you."

"We have orders to be on the watch for a man wearing a stolen militia uniform. He is suspected of being an imperialist spy who landed on a beach one hundred miles east of here."

"Because *she* is wearing a militia uniform," said Figueroa, pointing to Jessie in the backseat, "you think the Yankee imperialists are sending women to invade us?"

"I want to see their identification papers," the guard persisted.

Jessie rolled down the rear window and leaned out. "This is Major O'Hara of the Irish Republican Army, on assignment as an adviser.

I'm Corporal López, his aide. Enough of this nonsense. Pass us through."

The guard kept his eyes on Pitt. "If he's a major, why isn't he showing his rank?"

For the first time it occurred to Figueroa that there was no insignia on Pitt's uniform. He stared at Pitt, a doubtful frown spreading across his face.

Pitt sat there without taking part in the exchange. Then he slowly turned and gazed into the guard's eyes and gave him a friendly smile. When he spoke his voice was soft, but it carried total authority.

"Get this man's name and rank. I wish to have him commended for his attention to duty. General Raúl Castro has often said Cuba needs men of this caliber."

Jessie translated and watched with relief as the guard stood erect and smiled.

Then Pitt's tone turned glacial, and so did his eyes. "Now tell him to stand clear or I'll arrange to have him sent as a volunteer to Afghanistan."

The young guard seemed to shrink perceptibly as Jessie repeated Pitt's words in Spanish. He stood lost, undecided what to do as a long black car pulled up and stopped behind the old cab. Pitt recognized it as a Zil, a seven-seater luxury limousine built in Russia for high-ranking government and military officials.

The Zil's driver honked his horn impatiently, and the guard seemed frozen with indecision. He turned and stared pleadingly at another guard, but his partner was occupied with traffic traveling in the other direction. The limousine's driver honked again and shouted out his side window.

"Move that car aside and let us pass!"

Then Figueroa got into the act and began yelling at the Russians. "Stupid Russo, shut up and take a bath! I can smell you from here!"

The Soviet driver pushed open his door, leaped from behind the wheel, and shoved the guard aside. He was built like a bowling pin, huge, beefy body and small head. His rank indicated that he was a sergeant. He stared at Figueroa through eyes burning with malice.

"Idiot," he snarled. "Move this wreck."

Figueroa shook his fist in the Russian's face. "I'll go when my countryman tells me to."

"Please, *please*," Jessie pleaded, shaking Figueroa's shoulder "We don't want any trouble."

"Discretion isn't a Cuban virtue," Pitt murmured. He cradled the assault rifle in his arms with the muzzle pointed at the Russian and eased the door open.

Jessie turned and peered cautiously through the rear window at the limousine, just in time to see a Soviet officer, followed by two armed bodyguards, climb from the backseat and gaze with an amused smile at the shouting match taking place beside the taxicab. Jessie's mouth dropped open and she gasped.

General Velikov, looking tired and haggard, and wearing a badly fitted borrowed uniform, approached from the rear of the Chevrolet as Pitt slid out of his seat and stepped around the front end before Jessie could warn him.

Velikov's attention was focused on his driver and Figueroa, and he paid scant notice to what appeared to be another Cuban soldier emerging from the other side of the car. The argument was heating up as he came alongside.

"What is the problem?" he asked in fluent Spanish.

His answer did not come from his driver, but from a totally unexpected source.

"Nothing we can't settle like gentlemen," Pitt said acidly in English.

Velikov stared at Pitt for a long moment, the amused smile dying on his lips, his face as expressionless as ever. The only sign of astonished recognition was a sudden hardness of the flat cold eyes.

"We are survivors, are we not, Mr. Pitt?" he replied.

"Lucky. I'd say we were lucky," Pitt answered in a steady voice.

"I congratulate you on your escape from the island. How did you manage it?"

"A makeshift boat. And you?"

"A helicopter concealed near the installation. Fortunately, your friends failed to discover it."

"An oversight."

Velikov glanced out of the corner of his eye, noting with irritation the relaxed stance of his bodyguards. "Why have you come to Cuba?"

Pitt's hand tightened around the rifle's grip, muzzle pointing in the sky just above Velikov's head, finger poised on the trigger. "Why bother to ask when you've established the fact I'm a habitual liar?"

"I also know you only lie if there is a purpose. You didn't come to Cuba to drink rum and lie in the sun."

"What now, General?"

"Look around you, Mr. Pitt. You're hardly in a position of strength. The Cubans do not take kindly to spies. You would be wise to lay down your gun and place yourself under my protection."

"No, thank you. I've been under your protection. His name was Foss Gly. You remember him. He got high by pounding his fists on flesh. I'm happy to report he's no longer in the pain business. One of his victims shot him where it hurts most."

"My men can kill you where you stand."

"It's obvious they don't understand English and haven't got any idea of what's being said between us. Don't try to alert them. This is what's known as a Mexican standoff. You so much as pick your nose and I'll put a bullet up the opposite nostril."

Pitt glanced around him. Both the Cuban checkpoint guard and the Soviet driver were listening dumbly to the English conversation. Jessie was crouched down in the backseat of the Chevy, only the top of the fatigue cap showing above the side window. Velikov's guards stood lax, their eyes and minds turning to the landscape, automatic pistols snapped securely in their holsters.

"Get in the car, General. You'll be riding with us."

Velikov stared coldlly at Pitt. "And if I refuse?"

Pitt stared back with grim conviction. "You die first. Then your bodyguards. After them, the Cuban sentries. I'm prepared to kill. They're not. Now, if you please..."

The Soviet bodyguards stood rooted and looked on in rapt amazement as Velikov silently followed Pitt's gesture and entered the front passenger's seat. He turned briefly and gazed curiously at Jessie.

"Mrs. LeBaron?"

"Yes, General."

"You're with this madman?"

"I am."

"But why?"

Figueroa opened his mouth to interrupt, but Pitt roughly shouldered the Soviet driver aside, firmly gripped the friendly Cuban's arm, and pulled him from the car.

"This is as far as you go, *amigo*. Tell the authorities we abducted you and hijacked your taxi." Then he passed his rifle to Jessie through the open window and angled his long frame behind the wheel. "If the general so much as twitches, shoot him through the head."

Jessie nodded and placed the gun barrel against the base of Velikov's skull.

Pitt shifted the Chevy into first gear and accelerated smoothly as if he was on a Sunday drive, watching the figures at the checkpoint through the rearview mirror. He was gratified to see that they milled around in confusion, not sure of what to do. Then Velikov's driver and bodyguards finally woke up to what was happening, ran to the black limousine, and took up the chase.

Pitt skidded to a stop and took the gun from Jessie. He fired several shots at a pair of telephone wires where they ran through insulators at the top of a pole. The car was burning rubber on the asphalt before the parted ends of the wire dropped to the ground.

"That should buy us half an hour," he said.

"The limousine is only a hundred yards behind and gaining." Jessie's voice was high-pitched and apprehensive.

"You'll never shake them" said Velikov calmly. "My driver is an expert at high speeds, and the car is powered by a seven-liter 425-horsepower engine."

For all of Pitt's offhandedness and casual speech there was an icy competence and an unmistakable air about him of someone who knew exactly what he was doing.

He offered Velikov a reckless smile and said, "The Russians haven't built a car that can take a 'fifty-seven Chevy."

As if to hammer home the point he mashed the gas pedal to the floor and the tired old car seemed to reach into the depths of her worn parts for a burst of power she hadn't known in thirty years. The big roaring lump of iron could still go. She gathered speed and ate up the highway, the steady roar of her squat V-8 meant business.

Pitt's entire mind was concentrated on his driving and on studying the road two, even three turns ahead. The Zil clung tenaciously to the smokescreen that poured from the Chevy's tailpipe. He threw the car around a series of hairpin turns as they climbed through forested hills. He was skirting the fine edge of disaster. The brakes were awful and did little but smell and smoke when Pitt stood on them. Their lining was gone and metal ground against metal inside the drums.

At ninety miles an hour a front-wheel wobble set in with eyeball-rattling proportions. The steering wheel shuddered in Pitt's hands. The shock absorbers were long gone and the Chevy sponged around the bends, leaning precariously, tires screeching like wild turkeys.

Velikov sat stiff as wood, his eyes trained straight ahead, one hand gripping the door handle with white knuckles as if ready to eject before the inevitable crash.

Jessie was frankly terrified, closing her eyes as the car drifted and swayed wildly along the road. She braced her knees on the back of the front seat to keep from being thrown from side to side and steadied the rifle aimed at Velikov's lower hairline.

If Pitt was aware of the considerable anguish he was causing his passengers, he gave no sign of it. A half-hour head start was the most he could hope for before the Cuban sentries made contact with their superiors and reported the kidnapping of the Soviet general. A helicopter would be the first sign the Cuban military was closing in and preparing a trap. When and how far ahead they would set up a roadblock was a matter of pure conjecture. A tank or a small fleet of armored cars suddenly appearing around a hidden curve and the ride would be over. Only Velikov's presence forestalled a massacre.

The driver of the Zil was no lightweight. He gained on Pitt in the turns, but dropped back in the straights as the burning acceleration of the old Chevy took hold. Out of the corner of one eye Pitt caught a small sign indicating they were approaching the port city of Cárdenas. Houses and small roadside businesses began to hug the highway and the traffic increased.

He glanced at the speedometer. The wavering needle hovered around 85. He backed off until it dropped to 70, keeping the Zil at bay as he weaved in and out of the traffic, one hand heavy on the horn. A policeman made a futile attempt to wave him to the curb as he careened around the Plaza Colón and a high bronze statue of Columbus. Luckily the streets were broad and he had little trouble staying clear of pedestrians and other vehicles.

The city lay just inland of a shallow, circular bay, and as long as he kept the sea on his right he figured he was still heading toward Havana. Somehow he managed to stay on the main road, and less than ten minutes later the car was flying from the major portion of the city and entering the countryside again.

During the high-speed run through the streets the Zil had closed to within fifty yards. One of the bodyguards leaned out the window and fired his pistol.

"They're shooting at us," Jessie announced in the tone of someone who was emotionally washed out.

"He's not aiming at us," Pitt replied. "They're trying for our tires."

"You're as good as caught," said Velikov. Those were the first words he had uttered in fifty miles. "Give it up. You can't get away."

"I'll quit when I'm dead." Pitt's cool composure was staggering.

It was not the answer Velikov was expecting. If all Americans were like Pitt, he thought, the Soviet Union was in for a rough time. Velikov prided himself on his skills in manipulating men, but this was clearly one man he would never dent.

They soared over a dip in the road and landed heavily on the other side. The muffler was torn away and the sudden thunder of exhaust was startling, almost shattering in its unexpected fury of sound. Their eyes began to water from the fumes, and the interior of the car became a steam bath under the combined onslaught of the heat from the engine and humid climate outside. The floorboards were almost hot enough to melt the soles of Pitt's boots. Between the noise and the heat, he felt as though he were working overtime in a boiler room.

The Chevy was becoming a mechanical bedlam. The teeth on the transmission were ground down to their nubs, and they howled in protest at the high revolutions. Strange knocking sounds began to emanate from the engine's bowels. But she was still vicious, and with that old deep-throated Chevy sound, she barreled along almost as if she knew this would be her last ride.

Pitt had carefully slowed ever so slightly and allowed the Russian driver to pull up within three car lengths. Pitt swung the Chevy back and forth across the road to throw off the bodyguard's aim. He eased his foot off the accelerator a hair until the Zil had come within twenty feet of the Chevy's rear bumper.

Then Pitt stood on the brakes.

The sergeant driving the Zil was good, but he wasn't that good. He snapped the steering wheel to the left and almost swung clear. But there was no time and even less distance. The Zil crashed into the rear of the Chevy with a scream of steel and an eruption of glass, crushing the radiator against the engine as the tail end whipped around in a corkscrew motion.

The Zil, madly out of control, and now nothing but three tons of metal bent on its own destruction, sideswiped a tree and caromed across the road to smash into an empty, broken-down bus at a speed of eighty miles an hour. Orange flame burst from the car as it flipped crazily end over end for over a hundred yards before coming to rest on its roof, all four tires still spinning. The Russians were trapped inside and had no hope of escape as the orange flames transformed into a thick cloud of black smoke.

The faithful, battered Chevy was still running on little but mechanical guts. Steam and oil were streaming from under the hood, second gear was gone along with the brakes, and the twisted rear bumper was dragging on the road, throwing out a spray of sparks.

The plume of smoke would draw the searchers. The net was closing. The next mile, the next curve in the highway, might reveal a roadblock. Pitt was sure a helicopter would appear any minute over the treetops bordering the road. Now was the time to ditch the car. It was senseless to play on his luck any longer. Like a bandit running from a posse, the time had come to trade horses.

He slowed down to fifty as he approached the outskirts of the city of Matanzas. He spotted a fertilizer plant and turned into the parking lot. Stopping the dying Chevy under a large tree, he looked around, and not seeing anyone, killed the engine. The crackling of burning metal and hissing steam replaced the ear-blasting drone of the exhaust.

"What's your next scheme?" asked Jessie. She was coming back on balance now. "You *do* have another scheme up your sleeve, I hope."

"The Artful Dodger has nothing on me," said Pitt with a reassuring grin. "Sit tight. If our friend the general hiccups, kill him."

He walked through the parking lot. It was a weekday and it was filled with the workers' cars. The stench from the plant had a sickening smell about it that filled the air for miles. He stood near the main gate as a stream of trucks loaded with ammonium sulphate, potassium chloride, and animal manure rumbled into the plant and trucks carrying the processed fertilizer in paper bags drove out. He had an idea and strolled casually down the dirt road that led to the highway. He waited for about fifteen minutes until a Russian-built truck filled with raw manure turned in and headed for the plant. He stood in the middle of the road and waved it to a stop.

The driver was alone. He looked down from the cab questioningly. Pitt motioned him out and pointed vigorously under the truck. Curious, the driver stepped to the ground and crouched down next to Pitt, who was staring intently at the drive shaft. Seeing nothing wrong, the driver turned just as Pitt chopped him on the back of the neck.

The driver went limp and Pitt caught him over a shoulder. He heaved the unconscious Cuban into the truck's cab and quickly climbed in. The engine was running and he shifted it into gear and drove toward the tree that shielded the Chevy from the air.

"Everyone climb aboard," he said, jumping down from the cab.

Jessie shrank back in disgust. "God, what's in there?"

"The polite word is manure."

"You expect me to wallow in filth?" demanded Velikov.

"Not only wallow," Pitt replied, "you're going to bury yourselves in it." He took the assault rifle from Jessie and prodded the general none too gently in the kidneys. "Up you go, General. You've probably rubbed many a KGB victim in slime. Now it's your turn."

Velikov shot Pitt a malignant look, and then climbed into the back of the truck. Jessie reluctantly followed as Pitt began stripping off the driver's clothes. They were several sizes too small and he had to leave the shirt unbuttoned and the pants fly unzipped to get into them. He quickly slipped his combat fatigues on the Cuban and dragged him up into the back with the others. He handed the rifle back to Jessie. She needed no instructions and placed the muzzle against Velikov's head. He found a shovel in a rack beside the cab and began to cover them.

Jessie gagged and fought to keep from retching. "I don't think I can take this."

"Be thankful it came from horses and cattle and not the city sewer."

"That's easy for you to say, you're driving."

When they were all invisible but could still breathe, Pitt returned to the cab and drove the truck back to the highway. He paused before turning as a flight of three military helicopters whirled overhead and a transport convoy of armed troops sped in the direction of the wrecked Zil.

Pitt waited and then turned left onto the highway. He was about to enter the city limits of Matanzas when he came to a roadblock manned by an armored car and nearly fifty soldiers, all looking very grim and purposeful.

He stopped and held out the papers he had taken off the driver. His scheme worked even better than he had imagined. The guards never came near the obnoxious-smelling truck. They waved him through, glad to see him on his way and happy to breathe fresh air again.

An hour and a half later the sun had fallen in the west and the lights of Havana twinkled to life. Pitt arrived in the city and drove up the Via Blanca. Except for the truck's aroma, he felt safely anonymous in the noisy, bustling, rush-hour traffic. He also felt more secure entering the city during the evening.

With no passport and no money his only option was to make contact with the American mission at the Swiss Embassy. They could take Jessie off his hands and keep him hidden until his passport and entry papers were sent by diplomatic courier from Washington. Once he became an official tourist, he could search for the riddle of the La Dorada treasure.

Velikov presented no problem. Alive, the general was a dangerous menace. He would go on murdering and torturing. Dead, he was only a memory. Pitt decided to kill him with one quick shot in a deserted alley. Anyone curious enough to investigate would simply chalk the blast up to a backfire from the truck.

He turned into a narrow road between a row of deserted warehouses near the dock area and stopped the truck. He left the engine running and stepped to the rear of the truck. As he climbed over the tailgate, he saw Jessie's head and arms protruding from the load of manure. Blood was seeping from a small gash in her temple and her right eye was swelling and turning purple. The only signs of Velikov and the Cuban driver were hollowed-out indentations where Pitt had buried them.

They were gone.

He eased her out of the muck and brushed it away from her cheeks. Her eyes fluttered open and focused on him, and after a moment she slowly shook her head from side to side. "I'm sorry, I messed things up."

"What happened?" he asked.

"The driver came to and attacked me. I didn't yell to you for help because I was afraid we might arouse suspicion and be stopped by police. We wrestled for the gun and it was lost over the side of the truck. Then the general grabbed my arms and the driver beat me until I passed out." Something suddenly occurred to her and she looked around wildly. "Where are they?"

"Must have jumped from the truck," he answered. "Can you remember where or how long ago it took place?"

The effort of concentration showed on her face. "I think it was about the time we were coming into the city. I recall hearing the sound of heavy traffic."

"Less than twenty minutes ago."

He helped her to the side of the truck bed and gently lowered her to the ground. "Best if we leave the truck here and catch a cab."

"I can't go anywhere smelling like this," she said in surprise. "And look at you. You look ridiculous. Your whole front end is open."

Pitt shrugged. "Oh, well, I won't be arrested for indecent exposure. I still have my shorts on."

"We can't catch a cab," she said in exasperation. "We don't have any Cuban pesos."

"The American mission at the Swiss Embassy will take care of it. Do you know where they're located?"

"It's called the Special Interests Section. Cuba has the same setup in Washington. The building faces the water on a boulevard called the Malecón."

"We'll hide out until it gets dark. Maybe we can find a water faucet and clean you up. Velikov will launch a full-scale search of the city for us. They'll probably watch the embassy, so we'll have to figure a way to sneak in. You feel strong enough to start walking?"

"You know something," she said with a pained smile, "I'm getting awfully tired of you asking that question."

65

IRA HAGEN STEPPED OFF the aircraft and entered the terminal of José Martí Airport. He had prepared himself for a hassle with the immigration officials, but they simply glanced at his diplomatic passport and passed him through with a minimum of formality. As he walked to the baggage claim, a man in a seersucker suit hailed him.

"Mr. Hagen?"

"I'm Hagen."

"Tom Clark, chief of the Special Interests Section. I was alerted to your arrival by Douglas Oates himself."

Hagen measured Clark. The diplomat was an athletic thirty-five or so, with a tan face, Errol Flynn moustache, thinning red hair neatly combed forward to hide the spreading bare front, blue eyes, and a nose that had been broken more than once. He pumped Hagen's hand heartily a good seven times.

"I don't suppose you greet many Americans down here," said Hagen.

"Very few since President Reagan placed the island off limits to tourists and businessmen."

"I assume you've been apprised of the reason for my visit."

"Better we wait and discuss it in the car," said Clark, nodding toward an unobtrusive fat woman sitting nearby with a small suitcase on her lap.

Hagen didn't need a blueprint to recognize a stakeout with a disguised receiver that recorded their every word.

After close to an hour, Hagen's suitcase was finally cleared and they made for Clark's car, a Lincoln sedan with a driver. A light rain was falling, but Clark was prepared with an umbrella. The driver placed the suitcase in the trunk and they set off toward the Swiss Embassy, where the U.S. Special Interests Section was housed.

Hagen had honeymooned in Cuba several years before the revo-

lution and he found that Havana looked much the same as he remembered it. The pastel colors of the stucco buildings gracing the
palm-lined avenues seemed faded but little changed. It was a nos-
talgic trip. The streets were teeming with 1950s automobiles, makes
that stirred old memories—Kaisers, Studebakers, Packards, Hudsons,
and even one or two Edsels. They mingled with the newer Fiats
from Italy and Ladas from Russia.

The city thrived, but not with the passions of the Batista years.
The beggars, prostitutes, and slums were gone, replaced with an
austere shabbiness that was the hallmark of Communist countries.
Marxism was a wart on the rectum of mankind, Hagen decided.

He turned to Clark. "How long have you been in the diplomatic
service?"

"Never," Clark answered. "I'm with the company."

"CIA."

Clark nodded. "If you prefer."

"That line about Douglas Oates?"

"For the benefit of the airport eavesdropper. I was informed of
your mission by Martin Brogan."

"Where do you stand on finding and disarming the device?"

Clark smiled darkly. "You can call it a bomb. No doubt a low-yield
bomb, but having enough punch to level half of Havana and start a
firestorm that will incinerate every flimsy house and hut in the sub-
urbs. And no, we haven't found it. We've got an undercover team of
twenty men probing the dock areas and the three ships in question.
Nothing has turned up. They might as well be looking for a shoe in
a swamp. The celebration ceremonies and parade are less than eighteen hours away. It would take an army of two thousand searchers
to find the bomb in time. And to make matters worse, our tiny force
is handicapped by having to work around Cuban and Russian security
measures. As things look, I'd have to say the detonation is inevitable."

"If I can get through to Castro and give him the President's warning—"

"Castro won't talk to anybody," said Clark. "Our most trusted officials in the Cuban government—we own five who hold top-level
positions—can't make contact. I hate to say it, but your job is more
hopeless than mine."

"Are you going to evacuate your people?"

There was a look of deep sadness in Clark's eyes. "No. We're all
going to stay on this thing to the end."

Hagen was silent as the driver turned off the Malecón and through the entrance of what had once been the United States Embassy but was now officially occupied by the Swiss. Two guards in Swiss Army uniforms swung open the high iron gate.

Suddenly, with no warning, a taxicab whipped directly behind the limousine and followed it through the gate before the startled guards could react and push it closed. The cab was still rolling when a woman in a militia uniform and a man clad in rags jumped out. The guards quickly recovered and came running over as the stranger confronted them, crouching in a part-boxing, part-judo stance. They stopped, fumbling for their holstered automatic pistols. The delay was enough for the woman to yank open a rear door to the Lincoln and climb in.

"Are you American or Swiss?" she demanded.

"American," replied Clark, as stunned by the disgusting aroma that hung on her as by her abrupt appearance. "What do you want?"

Her answer was entirely unexpected. She began to laugh hysterically. "American or Swiss. My God, I sound like I'm asking for cheese."

The chauffeur finally woke up to the intrusion, leaped from the car, and grabbed her around the waist.

"Wait!" ordered Hagen, seeing that the woman's face was badly bruised. "What's going on?"

"I'm an American," she blurted after gaining a measure of control. "My name is Jessie LeBaron. Please help me."

"Good lord," Hagen muttered. "You're not Raymond LeBaron's wife?"

"Yes. Yes, I am." She motioned wildly at the struggle that was erupting in the driveway of the embassy. "Stop them. He's Dirk Pitt, special projects director for NUMA."

"I'll handle it," said Clark. By the time he was able to intercede, Pitt had flattened one guard and was wrestling with the other. The Cuban cab driver danced about wildly waving his arms and shouting for his fare. Several plainclothes policemen also added to the confusion by appearing from nowhere on the street side of the closed gate and demanding that Pitt and Jessie be turned over to them. Clark ignored the police, stopped the fight, and paid off the driver. Then he led Pitt over to the Lincoln.

"Where in hell did you come from?" Hagen asked. "The President thought you were either dead or arrested—"

"Not now!" Clark interrupted. "We'd better get out of sight before the police forget the sanctity of the embassy and turn ugly."

He quickly hustled everyone inside and through a corridor to the American section of the building. Pitt was shown to a spare room where he could take a shower and shave. One of the staff who was about his size lent him some casual clothes. Jessie's uniform was burned in the trash, and she thankfully bathed off the stench of the manure. A Swiss Embassy doctor gave her a thorough examination and treated her cuts and bruises. He arranged for a hearty meal and ordered her to rest for a few hours before being interviewed by Special Interests Section officials.

Pitt was escorted to a small conference room. As he entered, Hagen and Clark rose and formally introduced themselves. They offered him a chair and everyone got comfortable around a heavy-legged table hand-carved from pine.

"We haven't time for lengthy explanations," said Clark without preamble. "Two days ago, my superiors at Langley briefed me about your planned covert raid on Cayo Santa María. They confided in me so I would be prepared if it failed and there was fallout here in Havana. I was not told of its success until Mr. Hagen—"

"Ira," Hagen cut in.

"Until Ira just now showed me a top-secret document taken from the island installation. He also has a directive from Martin Brogan and the President asking me to be on the lookout for you and Mrs. LeBaron. I was ordered to notify them immediately in the event you were caught and arrested."

"Or executed," Pitt added.

"That too," acknowledged Clark.

"Then you also know why Jessie and I cut out and came to Cuba."

"Yes. She carries an urgent message from the President to Castro."

Pitt relaxed and slouched in his chair. "Fine. My part in the affair is finished. I'd appreciate it if you could arrange to fly me back to Washington after I've had a few days to take care of some personal business."

Clark and Hagen exchanged stares, but neither could look Pitt square in the eyes.

"Sorry to screw up your plans," said Clark. "But we have a crisis on our hands, and your experience with ships might prove helpful."

"I'd be no good to you. I'm washed out."

"Can we take a few minutes and tell you what we're dealing with here?"

"I'm willing to listen."

Clark nodded, satisfied. "Okay, Ira has come direct from the President. He's better qualified to explain the situation than I am." He turned to Hagen. "You've got the floor."

Hagen took off his coat, removed a handkerchief from his hip pocket, and wiped his perspiring forehead. "The situation is this, Dirk. Do you mind if I call you Dirk?"

"It's my name."

Hagen was an expert judge of men, and he liked what he saw. This guy didn't seem the type who could be conned. There was also a look about him that suggested trust. Hagen laid the cards on the table and spelled out the Russian plot to murder the Castros and assume control of Cuba. He waded through the details in concise terms, explaining how the nuclear explosive was smuggled into the harbor and the projected time of its detonation.

When Hagen finished, Clark outlined the operation to find the bomb. There was no time to bring in a highly trained nuclear-device search team, nor would the Cubans allow them to step foot in the city. He had only twenty men with the most primitive radiation-detection equipment. He had the horrifying responsibility of leading the search, and it didn't require much imagination for him to get across the futility of his substandard efforts. Finally he paused.

"Do you follow me, Dirk?"

"Yes..." Pitt said slowly. "I follow. Thank you."

"Any questions?"

"Several, but one is uppermost in my mind. What happens to all of us if this thing isn't found and disarmed?"

"I think you know the answer," said Clark.

"Okay, but I want to hear it from you."

Clark's face took on the look of a mourner at a funeral. "We all die," he said simply.

"Will you help us?" asked Hagen.

Pitt looked at Clark. "How much time is left?"

"Roughly sixteen hours."

Pitt rose from his chair and began pacing the floor, his instincts beginning to sift through the maze of information. After a minute of silence as Hagen and Clark watched him expectantly, he suddenly leaned across the table and said, "I need a map of the dock area."

One of Clark's staff quickly produced one.

Pitt smoothed it out on the table and peered at it. "You say you can't alert the Cubans?" he asked as he studied the docking facilities of the bay.

"No," Hagen replied. "Their government is riddled with Soviet agents. If we were to warn them, they'd ignore it and squelch our search operation."

"What about Castro?"

"Penetrating his security and warning him is my job," said Hagen.

"And the United States receives the blame."

"Soviet disinformation will see to that."

"May I have a pencil, please?"

Clark obliged and sat back quietly while Pitt made a circle on the map.

"My guess is the ship with the bomb is docked in the Antares Inlet."

Clark's eyebrows raised. "How could you know that?"

"The obvious place for an explosion to cause the most damage. The inlet cuts almost into the heart of the city."

"Good thinking," said Clark. "Two of the suspected ships are docked there. The other is across the bay."

"Give me a rundown on the vessels?"

Clark examined the page of the document pertaining to the ship arrivals. "Two belong to the Soviet Union merchant fleet. The third sails under Panamanian registry and is owned by a corporation run by Cuban anti-Castro exiles."

"The last is a phony front set up by the KGB," said Hagen. "They'll claim the Cuban exiles are an arm of the CIA, making us the villains of the destruction. There won't be a nation in the world who will believe our noninvolvement."

"A sound plan," said Clark. "They'd hardly use one of their own vessels to carry the bomb."

"Yes, but why destroy two ships and their cargoes for no purpose?" asked Pitt.

"I admit it doesn't add up."

"Ships' names and cargoes?"

Clark extracted another page from the document and quoted from it. "The *Ozero Zaysan*, Soviet cargo ship carrying military supplies and equipment. The *Ozero Baykai*, a 200,000-ton oil tanker. The bogus Cuban-operated ship is the *Amy Bigalow*, bulk carrier with a cargo of 25,000 tons of ammonium nitrate."

Pitt stared at the ceiling as if mesmerized. "The oil tanker, is she the one moored across the bay?"

"Yes, at the oil refinery."

"Have any of the cargoes been unloaded?"

Clark shook his head. "There has been no activity around the two cargo carriers, and the tanker still sits low in the water."

Pitt sat down again and gave the other two men in the room a cold, hard stare. "Gentlemen, you've been had."

Clark looked at Pitt in dark speculation. "What are you talking about?"

"You overestimated the Russians' grandstand tactics and underestimated their cunning," said Pitt. "There is no nuclear bomb on any of those ships. For what they plan to do, they don't need one."

66

COLONEL GENERAL VIKTOR KOLCHAK, chief of the fifteen thousand Soviet military forces and advisers based on Cuban soil, came from behind his desk and embraced Velikov warmly.

"General, you don't know how glad I am to see you alive."

"The feeling is mutual, Colonel General," said Velikov, returning Kolchak's bear hug.

"Sit down, sit down, we have much to discuss. Whoever was behind the destruction of our island surveillance facility will pay. A communication from President Antonov assures me he will not take this outrage sitting down."

"No one agrees more than me," said Velikov. "But we have another urgent matter to discuss."

"Care for a glass of vodka?"

"I can do without," Velikov replied brusquely. "Rum and Cola takes place tomorrow morning at ten-thirty. Are your preparations complete?"

Kolchak poured a small shot of vodka for himself. "Soviet officials and our Cuban friends are discreetly slipping out of the city in small groups. Most of my military forces have already left to begin sham maneuvers forty miles away. By dawn, all personnel, equipment, and important documents will have been quietly evacuated."

"Leave some behind," Velikov said casually.

Kolchak peered over his rimless glasses like a grandmother hearing a four-letter word from a child. "Leave what behind, General?"

Velikov brushed off the derisive look. "Fifty Soviet civilian personnel, wives and families, and two hundred of your military forces."

"Do you know what you're asking?"

"Precisely. We cannot lay blame on the CIA for a hundred thousand deaths without suffering casualties ourselves. Russians dying beside

Cubans. We'll reap propaganda rewards that will go far in smoothing the path for our new government."

"I can't bring myself to throw away the lives of two hundred and fifty countrymen."

"Conscience never bothered your father when he cleared German mine fields by marching his men over them."

"That was war."

"Only the enemy has changed," Velikov said coldly. "We have been at war with the United States since 1945. The cost in lives is small compared to increasing our hold in the Western Hemisphere. There is no room for argument, General. You will be expected to do your duty."

"I don't need the KGB lecturing me on my duty to the motherland," Kolchak said without rancor.

Velikov shrugged indifferently. "We all do our part. Getting back to Rum and Cola; after the explosion your troops will return to the city and assist in medical and relief operations. My people will oversee the orderly transition of government. I'll also arrange for international press coverage showing benevolent Soviet soldiers caring for the injured survivors."

"As a soldier I have to say I find this entire operation abhorrent. I can't believe Comrade Antonov is a party to it."

"His reasons are valid, and I for one do not question them."

Kolchak leaned against the edge of his desk, his shoulders sagging. "I'll have a list made up of those who will stay."

"Thank you, Colonel General."

"I assume all preparations are complete?"

Velikov nodded. "You and I will accompany the Castro brothers to the parade reviewing stand. I will be carrying a pocket transmitter that will detonate the explosives in the primary ship. When Castro begins his usual marathon speech, we will make an unobtrusive exit to a waiting staff car. Once we are safely out of range—allowing about thirty minutes to drive fifteen miles—I'll activate the signal and the blast will follow."

"How do we explain our miraculous escape?" Kolchak asked sarcastically.

"First reports will have us dead and missing. Later, we'll be discovered among the injured."

"How badly injured?"

"Just enough to look convincing. Torn uniforms, a little blood, and some artificial wounds covered by bandages."

"Like two hooligans who vandalized the dressing rooms of a theater."

"Hardly the metaphor that comes to mind."

Kolchak turned and sadly looked out the window of his headquarters over the busy city of Havana.

"Impossible to believe that tomorrow at this time," he said in a morbid tone, "all this will be a smoldering, twisted sea of misery and death."

The President worked at his desk late. Nothing was cut-and-dried, black or white. The job of Chief Executive was one compromise after another. His wins over Congress were diluted by tacked-on amendments, his foreign policies picked apart by world leaders until little remained of the original proposals. Now he was trying to save the life of a man who had viewed the United States as his number one enemy for thirty years. He wondered what difference any of it would make two hundred years from now.

Dan Fawcett walked in with a pot of coffee and sandwiches. "The Oval Office never sleeps," he said with forced cheerfulness. "Your favorite, tuna with bacon." He offered the President a plate and then poured the coffee. "Can I help you with anything?"

"No thanks, Dan. Just editing my speech for tomorrow's news conference."

"I can't wait to see the faces of the press corps when you lay the existence of the moon colony on them, and then introduce Steinmetz and his people. I previewed some of the videotapes they brought back of their lunar experiments. They're incredible."

The President set the sandwich aside and thoughtfully sipped the coffee. "The world is upside down."

Fawcett paused in midbite. "Pardon?"

"Think of the terrible incongruity. I'll be informing the world of man's greatest modern achievement at the same time that Havana is being blown off the map."

"Any late word from Brogan since Pitt and Jessie LeBaron popped up at our Special Interests Section?"

"Not in the past hour. He's keeping a vigil at his office too."

"How in the world did they ever manage it?"

"Two hundred miles through a hostile nation. Beats me."

The direct phone line to Langley rang. "Yes."

"Martin Brogan, Mr. President. Havana reports that searchers have not yet detected a positive radioactive reading in any of the ships."

"Did they get on board?"

"Negative. Security is too heavy. They can only drive by the two ships tied to the docks. The other one, an oil tanker, is moored in the bay. They circled it in a small boat."

"What are you telling me, Martin? The bomb was unloaded and hidden in the city?"

"The ships have been under tight surveillance since arriving in the harbor. No cargo has come off."

"Maybe the radiation can't leak through the steel hulls of the ships."

"The experts at Los Alamos assure me it can. The problem is our people in Havana are not professional radiation experts. They're also hamstrung having to use commercial Geiger counters that aren't sensitive enough to measure a light reading."

"Why didn't we get qualified experts with the right equipment in there?" the President demanded.

"It's one thing to send in one man on a diplomatic mission with a small suitcase like your friend Hagen. It's something else to smuggle a team with five hundred pounds of electronic equipment. If we had more time, something might have been arranged. Covert boat landings and parachute drops stand little chance through Cuba's defense screen. Smuggling by ship is the best method, but we're talking at least a month's preparation."

"You make it sound like we're a guy with an unknown disease and no known cure."

"That about sums it up, Mr. President," said Brogan. "About all we can do is sit and wait...and watch it happen."

"No, I won't have that. In the name of humanity we have to do something. We can't let all those people die." He paused, feeling a knot growing in his stomach. "God, I can't believe the Russians will actually set off a nuclear bomb in a city. Doesn't Antonov realize he's plunging us deeper into a morass there can be no backing out of?"

"Believe me, Mr. President, our analysts have run every conceivable contingency through computers. There is no easy answer. Asking the Cubans to evacuate the city through our radio networks will accomplish nothing. They'll simply ignore any warnings coming from us."

"There is still hope Ira Hagen can get to Castro in time."

"Do you really think Fidel will take Hagen at face value? Not very likely. He'll think it's only a plot to discredit him. I'm sorry, Mr. President, we have to steel ourselves against the disaster, because there isn't a damned thing we can do about it.''

The President wasn't listening anymore. His face reflected grim despair. We put a colony on the moon, he thought, and yet the world's inhabitants still insist on murdering each other for asinine reasons.

"I'm calling a cabinet meeting tomorrow early, before the moon colony announcement," he said in a defeated voice. "We'll have to create a plan to counter Soviet and Cuban accusations of guilt and pick up the pieces as best we can."

67

LEAVING THE SWISS EMBASSY was ridiculously easy. A tunnel had been dug twenty years before that dropped over a hundred feet below the streets and sewer pipes, far beneath any shafts Cuban security people might have sunk around the block. The walls were sealed to keep out water, but silent pumps were kept busy draining away the seepage.

Clark led Pitt down a long ladder to the bottom, and then through a passage that ran for nearly two city blocks before ending at a shaft. They climbed up and emerged in a fitting room of a women's dress shop.

The shop had closed six hours earlier and the window displays effectively blocked any view of the interior. Sitting in the storeroom were three exhausted, haggard-looking men who gave barely a sign of recognition to Clark as he entered with Pitt.

"No need to know real names," said Clark. "May I present Manny, Moe, and Jack."

Manny, a huge black with a deeply trenched face, wearing an old faded green shirt and khaki trousers, lit a cigarette and merely glanced at Pitt with world-weary detachment. He looked like a man who had experienced the worst of life and had no illusions left.

Moe was peering through spectacles at a Russian phrase book. He wore the image of an academic—lost expression, unruly hair, neatly sculptured beard. He silently nodded and gave an offhand smile.

Jack was the stereotype Latin out of a 1930s movie—flashing eyes, compact build, fireworks teeth, triangular moustache. All he was missing was a bongo drum. He gave the only words of recognition. "*Hola*, Thomas. Come to pep-talk the troops?"

"Gentlemen, this is...ah...Sam. He's come up with an angle that throws new light on the search."

"It better be damned well worth it to drag us off the docks," grunted Manny. "We've got little time to waste on asshole theories."

"You're no closer now to finding the bomb than you were twenty-four hours ago," Clark said patiently. "I suggest you listen to what he has to say."

"Screw you," Manny said. "Just when we found a way to slip on board one of the freighters, you call us back."

"You could have searched every inch of those ships and never found a ton-and-a-half nuclear device," said Pitt.

Manny turned his attention to Pitt, eyes traveling from feet to hair, like a linebacker sizing up an opposing halfback. "Okay, smartass, where's our bomb?"

"Three bombs," Pitt corrected, "and none of them nuclear."

There was silence in the room. Everyone but Clark appeared skeptical.

Pitt pulled the map from under his shirt and unfolded it. He borrowed some pins from a mannikin and stuck it on one wall. He was not put off by the indifferent attitude of the group of CIA agents. His eyes showed him these men were alert, precise, and competent. He knew they possessed a remarkable variety of skills and the absolute determination of men who did not take failure lightly.

"The *Amy Bigalow* is the first link in the holocaust chain. Her cargo of twenty-five thousand tons of ammonium nitrate—"

"That's nothing but *fertilizer*," said Manny.

"—is also a highly volatile chemical," Pitt continued. "If that amount of ammonium nitrate were to explode, its force would be far greater than the bombs dropped on Hiroshima and Nagasaki. They were air drops and much of their destructive power was lost in the atmosphere. When the *Amy Bigalow* blows at ground level, most of her power will sweep through Havana like a hurricane of molten lava. The *Ozero Zaysan*, whose manifest claims she's carrying military supplies, is probably crammed to the top of her holds with munitions. She'll unleash her destructive horror in a sympathetic explosion with the *Amy Bigalow*. Next, the *Ozero Baykai* and her oil will ignite, adding to the devastation. Fuel storage tanks, refineries, chemical plants, any factory with volatile materials, will go up. The conflagration can conceivably last for days."

Outwardly, Manny, Moe, and Jack appeared uncomprehending, the expressions on their faces inscrutable. Inwardly, they were stunned by the unthinkable horror of Pitt's vision of hell.

Moe looked at Clark. "He's on dead center, you know."

"I agree. Langley misread the Soviets' intent. The same results can be achieved without resorting to nuclear terror."

Manny rose and clasped Pitt's shoulders between two great clamshell hands. "Man, I gotta hand it to you. You really know where the crap flows."

Jack spoke up for the first time. "Impossible to unload those ships before the celebration tomorrow."

"But they can be moved," said Pitt.

Manny considered that for a moment. "The freighters might clear the harbor, but I wouldn't bet on getting the tanker under way in time. We'd need a tug just to shove her bows toward the channel."

"Every mile we put between those ships and the harbor means a hundred thousand lives spared," said Pitt.

"Might give us extra time to look for the detonators," said Moe.

"If they can be found before we reach open sea, so much the better."

"And if not," Manny muttered grimly, "we'll all be committin' suicide."

"Save your wife the cost of a funeral," said Jack with a death's-head smile. "There won't be anything left to bury."

Moe looked doubtful. "We're way short of hands."

"How many ship's engineers can you scrape up?" asked Pitt.

Moe nodded across the room. "Manny there used to be a chief engineer. Who else can you name, Manny?"

"Enrico knows his way around an engine room. So does Hector when he's sober."

"That's three," said Pitt. "What about deckhands?"

"Fifteen, seventeen including Moe and Jack," answered Clark.

"That's twenty, and I make twenty-one," said Pitt. "What about harbor pilots?"

"Every one of them bastards is in Castro's pocket," snorted Manny. "We'll have to steer the ships clear ourselves."

"Wait just a damned minute," interjected Moe. "Even if we overpowered the security force guarding the docks, we'd still have the ships' crews to fight."

Pitt turned to Clark. "If your people take care of the guards, I'll eliminate the crews."

"I'll personally lead a combat team," replied Clark. "But I'm curious as to how you intend to accomplish your end of the bargain."

"Already done," Pitt said with a wide grin. "The ships are abandoned. I'll guarantee that the crews have been quietly evacuated to a safe place outside the destruction zone."

"The Soviets might spare the lives of their own people," said Moe. "But they'd hardly give a damn about the foreign crew on the *Amy Bigalow*."

"Sure, but on the other hand, they couldn't risk a nosy crewman hanging around while the detonating device was placed in position."

Jack thought a moment, then said, "Two and two make four. This guy is sharp."

Manny gazed at Pitt with a newfound respect in his eyes. "You with the company?"

"No, NUMA."

"Second-guessed by an amateur," Manny sighed. "Time to take my pension."

"How many men do you estimate are patrolling the ships?" Clark asked him.

Manny took out a soiled handkerchief and blew his nose like a honking goose before answering. "About a dozen guarding the *Bigalow*. Same number around the *Zaysan*. A small patrol boat is moored next to the oil tanker. Probably no more than six or seven in her crew."

Clark began to pace back and forth as he spoke. "So that's it. Gather up your crews. My team will take out the guards and protect the operation. Manny, you and your men will get the *Amy Bigalow* under way. Moe, take the *Ozero Zaysan*. The tugboat is your department, Jack. Just make sure there isn't an alarm when you pirate it. We've got six hours of daylight left. Let's make good use of every minute." He stopped and looked around. "Any questions?"

Moe raised a hand. "After we make open water, what happens to us?"

"Take your ship's motor launch and beat it as fast and as far as you can before the explosions."

No one made a comment. They all knew their chances bordered on hopeless.

"I'd like to volunteer to go with Manny," said Pitt. "I'm pretty fair with a helm."

Manny came to his feet and slapped a hand on Pitt's back that knocked the wind from him. "By God, Sam, I think I might learn to like you."

Pitt gave him a heavy stare. "Let's hope we live long enough to find out."

68

THE AMY BIGALOW lay moored alongside a long modern wharf that had been built by Soviet engineers. Beyond her, a few hundred yards across the dock channel, the cream-colored hull of the *Ozero Zaysan* sat dark and deserted. The lights of the city sparkled across the black waters of the harbor. A few clouds drifted down from the mountains, crossing the city and heading out to sea.

The Russian-built command car turned off the Boulevard Desemparados, followed by two heavy military trucks. The convoy moved slowly through the dock area and stopped at the boarding ramp of the *Amy Bigalow*. A sentry stepped from inside a guard shack and cautiously approached the car.

"Do you have permission to be in this area?" he asked.

Clark, wearing the uniform of a Cuban colonel, gave the sentry an arrogant stare. "Send for the officer of the guard," he ordered sharply. "And say *sir* when you address an officer."

Recognizing Clark's rank under the yellowish, sodium vapor lights that illuminated the waterfront, the sentry stiffened to attention and saluted. "Right away, sir. I'll call him."

The sentry ran back to the guard shack and picked up a portable transmitter. Clark shifted in his seat uneasily. Deception was vital, strong-arm tactics fatal. If they had stormed the ships with guns blazing, alarms would have sounded throughout the city's military garrisons. Once alerted, and with their backs to the wall, the Russians would have been forced to set off the explosions ahead of schedule.

A captain came through a door of a nearby warehouse, paused a moment to study the parked column, and then walked up to the passenger side of the command car and addressed Clark.

"Captain Roberto Herras," he said, saluting. "How can I help you, sir?"

"Colonel Ernesto Pérez," replied Clark. "I've been ordered to relieve you and your men."

Herras looked confused. "My orders were to guard the ships until noon tomorrow."

"They've been changed," Clark said curtly. "Have your men assemble for departure back to their barracks."

"If you don't mind, Colonel, I wish to confirm this with my commanding officer."

"And he'll have to call General Melena, and the general is asleep in bed." Clark stared at him with narrowed, cold eyes. "A letter attesting to your insubordination won't look good when your promotion to major comes due."

"Please, sir, I'm not refusing to obey a superior."

"Then I suggest you accept my authority."

"Yes, Colonel. I—I'm not doubting you..." He caved in. "I'll assemble my men."

"You do that."

Ten minutes later Captain Herras had his twenty-four-man security force lined up and ready to move out. The Cubans took the change of guard willingly. They were all happy to be relieved and returned to their barracks for a night's sleep. Herras did not seem to notice that the colonel's men remained hidden inside the darkness of the lead truck.

"This your entire unit?" asked Clark.

"Yes, sir. They're all accounted for."

"Even the men guarding the next ship?"

"Sorry, Colonel. I left sentries at the boarding ramp to make sure no one boarded until your men were dispersed. We can drive by and pick them up as we leave."

"Very well, Captain. The rear truck is empty. Order them to board. You can take my car. I'll have my aide pick it up later at your headquarters."

"That's good of you, sir. Thank you."

Clark had his hand on a tiny .25-caliber silenced automatic that was sitting loose in his pants pocket, but he left it in place. The Cubans were already climbing over the tailgate of the truck under the direction of a sergeant. Clark offered his seat to Herras and casually strolled toward the silent truck containing Pitt and the Cuban seamen.

The vehicles had turned around and were leaving the dock area when a staff car carrying a Russian officer drove up and stopped. He leaned out the window of the rear seat and stared, a suspicious frown on his face.

"What's going on here?"

Clark slowly approached the car and passed around the front end, assuring himself that the only occupants were the Russian and his driver.

"Changing of the guard."

"I know of no such orders."

"They came from General Velikov," said Clark, halting no more than two feet from the rear door. He could now see the Russian was also a colonel.

"I've just come from the general's headquarters to inspect security. Nothing was said about changing the guard." The colonel opened the door as if to get out of the car. "There must be a mistake."

"No mistake," said Clark. He pressed the door shut with his knees and shot the colonel between the eyes. Then he coldly put two bullets in the back of the driver's head.

Minutes later the car was set in gear and rolled into the dark waters between the wharves.

Manny led the way, followed by Pitt and four Cuban merchant seamen. They rushed up the boarding ramp to the main deck of the *Amy Bigalow* and split up. Pitt climbed the ladder topside while the rest dropped down a companionway to the engine room. The wheelhouse was dark, and Pitt left it that way. He spent the next half hour checking the ship's electronic controls and speaker system with a flashlight until he had every lever and switch firmly planted in his mind.

He picked up the ship's phone and rang the engine room. A full minute went by before Manny answered.

"What in the hell do you want?"

"Just checking in," said Pitt. "Ready when you are."

"You got a long wait, mister."

Before Pitt could reply, Clark stepped into the wheelhouse. "You talking to Manny?" he asked.

"Yes."

"Get him up here, now."

Pitt passed on Clark's brusque command, and received a barrage of four-letter words before ringing off.

Less than a minute later, Manny burst through the door reeking of sweat and oil. "Make it quick," he snapped to Clark. "I got a problem."

"Moe has it even worse."

"I already know. The engines have been shut down."

"Are yours in running shape?"

"Why wouldn't they be?"

"The Soviet crew took sledgehammers to every valve on the *Ozero Zaysan*," said Clark heavily. "Moe says it would take two weeks to make repairs."

"Jack will have to tow him out to sea with the tug," Pitt said flatly.

Manny spat through the wheelhouse door. "He'll never make it back in time to move the oil tanker. The Russians ain't blind. They'll catch on to the game soon as the sun comes up."

Clark nodded his head in slow understanding. "I fear he's right."

"Where do you stand?" Pitt asked Manny.

"If this tub had diesels, I could start her up in two hours. But she's got steam turbines."

"How much time do you need?"

Manny looked down at the deck, his mind running over the lengthy and complicated procedures. "We're starting with a dead plant. First thing we did was get the emergency diesel generator going and light off the burners in the furnace to heat the fuel oil. The lines have to be drained of condensation, the boilers fired up, and the auxiliaries put on line. Then wait for the steam pressure to rise enough to operate the turbines. We're looking at four hours—providin' everything goes right."

"Four hours?" Clark felt dazed.

"Then the *Amy Bigalow* can't clear the harbor before daylight," said Pitt.

"That wraps it." There was a tired certainty in Clark's voice.

"No, that doesn't wrap it," said Pitt firmly. "If we get even one ship past the harbor entrance we cut the death toll by a third."

"And we all die," added Clark. "There'll be no escape. Two hours ago I'd have given us a fifty-fifty chance of surviving. Not now, not when your old friend Velikov spots his monstrous plan steaming over the horizon. And lest we forget the Soviet colonel sitting on the bottom of the bay, he'll be missed before long and a regiment will come looking for him."

"And there's that captain of the security guards," said Manny. "He'll wise up damned quick when he catches hell for leaving his duty area without proper orders."

The thump of heavy diesel engines slowly amplified outside and a ship's bell gave off three muted rings.

Pitt peered through the bridge windows. "Jack's coming alongside with the tug."

He turned and faced the lights of the city. They reminded him of a vast jewelry box. He began to think of the multitude of children who went to bed looking forward to the holiday celebrations. He wondered how many of them would never wake up.

"There's still hope," he said at last. Quickly he outlined what he thought would be the best solution for reducing the devastation and saving most of Havana. When he finished, he looked from Manny to Clark. "Well, is it workable?"

"Workable?" Clark was numb. "Myself and three others holding off half the Cuban Army for three hours? It's downright homicidal."

"Manny?"

Manny stared at Pitt, trying to make something of the craggy face that was barely visible from the lights on the wharf. Why would an American throw away his life for people who would shoot him on sight? He knew he'd never find the answer in the darkened wheelhouse of the *Amy Bigalow,* and he shrugged in slow finality.

"We're wastin' time," he said as he turned and headed back to the ship's engine room.

69

THE LONG BLACK LIMOUSINE eased to a quiet stop at the main gate of Castro's hunting lodge in the hills southeast of the city. One of the two flags mounted on the front bumper symbolized the Soviet Union and the other marked the passenger as a high-ranking military officer.

The visitors' house outside the fenced estate was the headquarters for Castro's elite bodyguard force. A man in a tailored uniform but showing no insignia walked slowly up to the car. He looked at the shadowed form of a big Soviet officer sitting in the darkness of the backseat and at the identification that was held out the window.

"Colonel General Kolchak. You do not have to prove yourself to me." He threw a wavelike salute. "Juan Fernández, chief of Fidel's security."

"Don't you ever sleep?"

"I'm a night owl," said Fernández. "What brings you here at this ungodly hour?"

"A sudden emergency."

Fernández waited for further elaboration, but none came. He began to feel uneasy. He knew that only a critical situation could bring the Soviets' highest-ranking military representative out at three-thirty in the morning. He wasn't sure how to deal with it.

"I'm very sorry, sir, but Fidel left strict orders not to be disturbed by anyone."

"I respect President Castro's wishes. However, it's Raúl I must speak with. Please tell him I'm here on a matter of extreme urgency that must be dealt with face to face."

Fernández mulled over the request for a moment and then nodded. "I'll phone up to the lodge and tell his aide you're on your way."

"Thank you."

Fernández waved to an unseen man in the visitors' house and the electronically operated gate swung open. The limousine drove up a curving road that hugged the hills for about two miles. Finally, it pulled up in front of a large Spanish-style villa that overlooked a panorama of dark hills dotted by distant lights.

The driver's boot crunched on the gravel drive as he stepped around to the passenger's door. He did not open it but stood there for nearly five minutes, casually observing the guards that patrolled the grounds. At last, Raúl Castro's chief of staff came yawning through the front door.

"Colonel General, what an unexpected pleasure," he said without enthusiasm. "Please come in. Raúl is on his way down."

Without replying, the Soviet officer heaved his bulk from the car and followed the aide over a wide patio and into the foyer of the lodge. He held a handkerchief over his face and snorted into it. His driver came also, keeping a few steps behind. Castro's aide stood aside and gestured toward the trophy room. "Please make yourselves comfortable. I'll order some coffee."

Left alone, the two stood silently with their backs to the open doorway and stared at an army of boar heads mounted on the walls and the dozens of stuffed birds perched around the room.

Raúl Castro soon entered in pajamas and silk paisley robe. He halted in midstride as his guests turned and faced him. His brows knitted together in surprise and curiosity.

"Who the devil are you?"

"My name is Ira Hagen, and I bear a most important message from the President of the United States." Hagen paused and nodded at his driver, who doffed her cap, allowing a mass of hair to fall to her shoulders. "May I present Mrs. Jessie LeBaron. She's endured great hardship to deliver a personal reply from the President to your brother regarding his proposed U.S.–Cuban friendship pact."

For a moment the silence in the room was so total that Hagen became conscious of the ticking of an elaborate grandfather clock standing against the far wall. Raúl's dark eyes darted from Hagen to Jessie and held.

"Jessie LeBaron is dead," he said in quiet astonishment.

"I survived the crash of the blimp and torture by General Peter Velikov." Her voice was calm and commanding. "We carry documented evidence that he intends to assassinate you and Fidel tomorrow morning during the Education Day celebration."

The directness of the statement, the tone of authority behind it, made an impression on Raúl.

He hesitated thoughtfully. Then he nodded. "I'll wake Fidel and ask him to listen to what you have to say."

Velikov watched as a file cabinet from his office was jostled onto a handcart and taken by elevator down to the fireproof basement of the Soviet Embassy. His second-ranking KGB officer entered the disarranged room, brushed some papers from a chair, and sat down.

"Seems a shame to burn all of this," he said tiredly.

"A new and finer building will rise from the ashes," said Velikov with a cunning smile. "Gift of a grateful Cuban government."

The phone buzzed and Velikov quickly answered. "What is it?"

The voice of his secretary replied. "Major Borchev wishes to talk to you."

"Put him on."

"General?"

"Yes, Borchev, what's your problem?"

"The captain in command of waterfront security has left his post along with his men and returned to their base outside the city."

"They left the ships unguarded?"

"Well . . . not exactly."

"Did they or did they not desert their post?"

"He claims he was relieved by a guard force under the command of a Colonel Ernesto Pérez."

"I issued no such order."

"I'm aware of that, General. Because if you had, it would have most certainly come to my attention."

"Who is this Pérez and what military unit is he assigned to?"

"My staff has checked Cuban military files. They find no record of him."

"I personally sent Colonel Mikoyan to inspect security measures around the ships. Make contact and ask him what in hell is happening down there."

"I've tried to raise him for the past half hour," said Borchev. "He doesn't respond."

Another line buzzed, and Velikov placed Borchev on hold.

"What is it?" he snapped.

"Juan Fernández. General, I thought you should know that Colonel General Kolchak just arrived for a meeting with Raúl Castro."

"Not possible."

"I checked him through the gate myself."

This new development added fuel to Velikov's confusion. A stunned look gripped his face and he expelled his breath in an audible hiss. He had only four hours' sleep in the last thirty-six and his mind was becoming woolly.

"You there, General?" asked Fernández anxiously at the silence.

"Yes, yes. Listen to me, Fernández. Go to the lodge and find out what Castro and Kolchak are doing. Listen in to their conversation and report back to me in two hours."

He didn't wait for an acknowledgment, but punched into Borchev's line. "Major Borchev, form a detachment and go to the dock area. Lead it yourself. Check out this Pérez and his relief force and report back to me as soon as you find out anything."

Then Velikov buzzed his secretary. "Get me Colonel General Kolchak's headquarters."

His deputy straightened in the chair and stared at him curiously. He had never seen Velikov in a state of nervousness before.

"Something wrong?"

"I don't know yet," Velikov muttered.

The familiar voice of Colonel General Kolchak suddenly burst from the other end of the phone line. "Velikov, how are things progressing with the GRU and KGB?"

Velikov stood stunned for several moments before recovering. "Where are you?"

"Where am I?" Kolchak repeated. "Trying to clear classified documents and equipment from my headquarters, the same as you. Where did you think I was?"

"I just received a report you were meeting with Raúl Castro at the hunting lodge."

"Sorry, I haven't mastered being in two places at the same time," said Kolchak imperturbably. "Sounds to me your intelligence agents are starting to see ghosts."

"Most strange. The report came from a usually reliable source."

"Is Rum and Cola in any danger?"

"No, it is continuing as planned."

"Good. Then I take it the operation is running smoothly."

"Yes," Velikov lied with a fear tainted by uncertainty, "everything is under control."

70

THE TUGBOAT WAS CALLED the *Pisto* after a Spanish dish of stewed red peppers, zucchini, and tomatoes. The name was appropriate, as her sides were streaked red with rust and her brass coated with verdigris. Yet, despite the neglect to her outer structure, the big 3,000-horsepower diesel engine that throbbed in her bowels was as bright and glossy as a polished bronze sculpture.

Hands gripping the big teakwood wheel, Jack stared through the moisture-streaked windows at the gigantic mass looming up in the blackness. She was as cold and dark as the other two carriers of death tied to the docks. No navigation lights indicated her presence in the bay, only the patrol boat that circled her 1,100-foot length and 160-foot beam served as a warning for other craft to stay clear.

Jack eased the *Pisto* abreast of the *Ozero Baykai* and cautiously edged toward the aft anchor chain. The patrol boat quickly spotted them and came alongside. Three men rushed from the bridge and manned a rapid-fire gun on the bow. Jack rang the engine room for All Stop, an act that was strictly for show as the tug's bow wave was already dying away to a ripple.

A young lieutenant with a beard leaned out of the wheelhouse of the patrol boat and raised a bullhorn.

"This is a restricted area. You don't belong here. Move clear."

Jack cupped his hands to his mouth and shouted, "I've lost all power to my generators and my diesel just died on me. Can you give me a tow?"

The lieutenant shook his head in exasperation. "This is a military boat. We do not give tows."

"Can I come aboard and use your radio to call my boss? He'll send another tug to tow us clear."

"What's wrong with your emergency battery power?"

"Worn out." Jack made a gesture of helplessness. "No parts for repair. I'm on the waiting list. You know how it is."

The boats were so close now they were almost touching. The lieutenant laid aside the bullhorn and replied in a rasping voice, "I cannot allow that."

"Then I'll have to anchor right here until morning," Jack replied nastily.

The lieutenant angrily threw up his hands in defeat. "Come aboard and make your call."

Jack dropped down a ladder to the deck and jumped across the four-foot gap between the boats. He looked around him with a slow, salty indifference, carefully noting the relaxed attitude of the three-man gun crew, the mate standing by the helm casually lighting a cigar, the tired look on the lieutenant's face. The only man who was missing, he knew, was the engineer below.

The lieutenant came up to him. "Make it quick. You're interfering with a military operation."

"Forgive me," said Jack slavishly, "but it's not my doing."

He reached forward as if wanting to shake hands and pumped two bullets from a silenced automatic into the lieutenant's heart. Then he calmly shot the helmsman.

The trio around the bow gun crumpled and died under a flight of three precisely aimed arrows, fired by Jack's crew with crossbows. The engineer never felt the bullet that struck him in the temple. He fell over the boat's diesel engine, lifeless hands gripping a rag and a wrench.

Jack and his crewmen carried the bodies below and then swiftly opened all drain plugs and sea cocks. They returned to the tug and paid no more attention to the sinking patrol boat as it drifted away on the tide into the darkness.

There was no gangway down, so a pair of grappling hooks were thrown over the tanker's deck railing. Jack and two others clambered up the sides and then hauled up portable acetylene tanks and a cutting torch.

Forty-five minutes later the anchor chains were cut away and the little *Pisto,* like an ant trying to move an elephant, buried her heavy rope bow fender against the huge stern of the *Ozero Baykai.* Inch by inch, almost imperceptibly at first, and then yard by yard the tug began nudging the tanker away from the refinery and toward the middle of the bay.

• • • •

Pitt observed the slothful movement of the *Ozero Baykai* through a pair of night glasses. Fortunately the ebb tide was working in their favor, pulling the behemoth farther from the core of the city.

He had found a self-contained breathing unit and searched the holds for any sign of a detonating device, but could find nothing. He came to the conclusion it must have been buried somewhere under the ammonium nitrate in one of the middle cargo holds. After nearly two hours, he climbed to the main deck and thankfully breathed in the cool breeze off the sea.

Pitt's watch read 4:30 when the *Pisto* came about and returned to the docks. She made straight for the munitions ship. Jack backed her in until Moe's men hauled in the tow wire that was unreeled from the great winch on the stern of the tug and made fast to the *Ozero Zaysan*'s aft bollards. The lines were cast off, but just as the *Pisto* prepared to pull, a military convoy of four trucks came roaring onto the wharf.

Pitt dropped down the gangway and hit the dock at a dead run. He dodged around a loading crane and stopped at the stern line. He heaved the fat, oily rope off the bollard and let it fall in the water. There was no time to cast off the bow line. Heavily armed men were dropping from the trucks and forming into combat teams. He climbed the gangway and engaged the electric winch that lifted it level with the deck to prevent any assault from the wharf.

He snatched up the bridge phone and rang the engine room. "Manny, they're here" was all he said.

"I've got vacuum and enough steam in one boiler to move her."

"Nice work, my friend. You shaved off an hour and a half."

"Then let's haul ass."

Pitt walked over to the ship's telegraph and moved the pointers to Stand By. He threw the helm over so the stern would swing away from the pier first. Then he rang for Dead Slow Astern.

Manny rang back from the engine room and Pitt could feel the engines begin to vibrate beneath his feet.

Clark realized with sudden dismay that his small group of men were greatly outnumbered and any escape route cut off. He also discovered that they were not up against ordinary Cuban soldiers but an elite force of Soviet marines. At best he might gain a few minutes' grace—enough time for the ships to move clear of the docks.

He reached into a canvas bag hanging from his belt and took out a grenade. He stepped from the shadows and lobbed the grenade into the rear truck. The explosion came like a dull thump, followed by a brilliant flash of flame as the fuel tank burst. The truck seemed to blossom outward, and men were thrown across the dock like fiery bowling pins.

He ran through the dazed and disorganized Russians, leaping over the screaming injured who were rolling around the dock desperately trying to douse their flaming clothing. The next detonations came in rapid succession, echoing across the bay, as he heaved three more grenades under the remaining trucks.

Fresh flame and clouds of smoke billowed above the roofs of the warehouses. The marines frantically abandoned their vehicles and scrambled for their lives out of the holocaust. A few were galvanized into action and began firing into the darkness at anything that vaguely resembled a human form. The ragged fusillade mingled with the sound of shattering glass as the windows of the warehouses were blown away.

Clark's small team of six fighters held their fire. The few shots that came in their direction went over their heads. They waited as Clark mingled in the disorganized melee, unsuspected in his Cuban officer's uniform, cursing in fluent Russian and ordering the marines to regroup and charge up the wharf.

"Form up! Form up!" he shouted excitedly. "They're running away. Move, damn you, before the traitors escape!"

He broke off suddenly as he came face to face with Borchev. The Soviet major's mouth fell open in total incredulity and before he could close it Clark grabbed him by the arm and hurled him over the dock into the water. Fortunately, no one took notice amid the confusion.

"Follow me!" Clark yelled, and began running up the dock where it passed between two warehouses. Individually, and in groups of four or five, the Soviet marines raced after him, crouching and zigzagging in highly trained movements across the wharf, laying down a sheet of fire as they advanced.

They seemed to have overcome the paralyzing shock of surprise and were determined to retaliate against their unseen enemy, never knowing they were escaping from one nightmare and entering another. No one questioned Clark's orders. Without their commander to tell them otherwise, the noncoms exhorted their men to follow the officer in the Cuban uniform who was leading the attack.

When the marines had dodged their way between the warehouses, Clark threw himself flat as though hit. It was the signal for his men to open up. The Soviets were hit from all sides. Many were cut off their feet. They made perfect targets, silhouetted by the blazing pyre of the trucks. Those who survived the scything sweep of death returned the fire. The staccato crash of sound was deafening as shells thudded into wooden walls and human flesh or missed and richocheted, whining into the night.

Clark rolled violently toward the cover of a packing crate, but was struck in the thigh and again by a bullet that passed through both wrists.

Badly battered, but still fighting, the Soviet marines began to pull back. They made a futile attempt to break out of the dock area and reach the safety of a concrete wall running along the main boulevard, but two of Clark's men laid down a hail of fire that stopped them in their tracks.

Clark lay there behind the crate, blood streaming from shattered veins, his life draining away, and he was helpless to stop it. His hands hung like broken tree limbs, and there was no feeling in his fingers. Blackness was already closing in when he dragged himself to the edge of the pier and stared out over the harbor.

The last sight his eyes were to ever see was the outline of the two cargo ships against the lights on the opposite shore. They were swinging clear of the docks and turning toward the harbor entrance.

71

WHILE THE BATTLE WAS RAGING on the wharf, the little *Pisto* took the tow and began pulling the *Ozero Zaysan* into the harbor stern first. Struggling mightily, she buried her huge single propeller in the oily water and boiled it into a cauldron of foam.

The 20,000-ton vessel began to move, her formless bulk animated by orange flames as she slipped into open water. Once free of the docks Jack made a wide 180-degree sweep, pivoting the munitions ship until her bow faced the harbor entrance. Then the tow wire was released and winched in.

In the wheelhouse of the *Amy Bigalow* Pitt gripped the helm and hoped something would give. He tensed, scarcely daring to breathe. The still-fastened bowline came taut and creaked from the tremendous stress placed on it by the backing vessel and stoutly refused to snap. Like a dog straining at a leash, the *Amy Bigalow* tucked her bow slightly, increasing the tension. The rope held, but the bollard was torn from its dock mountings with a loud crunch of splintered wood.

A tremor ran through the ship and she gradually began to back away into the harbor. Pitt put the wheel over and slowly the bows came around until she had turned broadside to the receding dock. The vibration from the engine smoothed out and soon they were quietly gliding astern with a light wisp of smoke rising from the funnel.

The whole waterfront seemed to be ablaze, the flames from the burning trucks casting an eerie, flickering light inside the wheelhouse. All hands except Manny came up from the engine room and stood by on the bow. Now that he had room to maneuver, Pitt spun the wheel hard to starboard and rang Slow Ahead on the telegraph.

Manny answered and the *Amy Bigalow* lost sternway and began to creep slowly forward.

The stars in the east were beginning to lose their sparkle as the shadowy hull of the *Ozero Zaysan* drew abeam. Pitt ordered All Stop as the tugboat came about under the bows. The *Pisto*'s crew flung up a light heaving rope that was tied to a graduated series of heavier lines. Pitt watched from the bridge as they were hauled on board. Then the thick tow cable was taken up by a forward winch and made fast.

The same act was repeated on the stern, only this time with the port anchor chain from the dead and drifting *Ozero Zaysan*. After the chain was winched across, its links were tied to the after bits. The two-way connection was made. The three vessels were now tethered together, with the *Amy Bigalow* in the middle.

Jack gave a blast on the *Pisto*'s air horn, and the tug began to ease ahead, taking up the slack. Pitt stood on the bridge wing and stared aft. When one of Manny's men signaled that the tow chain on the stern was taut, Pitt gave a slight pull on the steam whistle and swung the telegraph to Full Ahead.

The final step in Pitt's plan had been completed. The oil tanker was left behind, floating nearer the oil storage tanks on the opposite shore of the harbor, but a good mile farther from the more populated center of the city. The other two ships and their deadly cargoes were gathering way in their dash for the open sea, the tugboat adding her power to that of the *Amy Bigalow* to raise the speed of the marine caravan.

Behind them the great column of smoke and flame spiraled up into the early blue of morning. Clark had bought them enough time for a fighting chance, but he had paid with his life.

Pitt did not look back. His eyes were drawn like a magnet on the beacon from the lighthouse above the gray walls of Morro Castle, that grim fortress guarding the entrance to Havana Harbor. It lay three miles away, but it seemed thirty.

The die was cast. Manny raised power to the other engine and the twin screws thrashed the water. The *Amy Bigalow* began to pick up speed. Two knots became three. Three became four. She beat toward the channel below the lighthouse like a Clydesdale in a pulling contest.

They were forty minutes away from reaching home free. But the warning was out and the unthinkable was yet to come.

• • •

Major Borchev dodged the burning embers that fell and hissed in the water. Floating there under the pilings, he could hear the roar of automatic weapons fire and see the flames leap into the sky. The dirty water between the docks felt tepid and reeked of dead fish and diesel oil. He gagged and vomited up the foul backwash he had swallowed when the strange Cuban colonel shoved him over the side.

He swam for what seemed a mile before he found a ladder and climbed to the top of an abandoned pier. He spat out the disgusting taste and jogged toward the burning convoy.

Blackened and smoldering bodies littered the dock. The gunfire had stopped after Clark's few surviving men escaped in a small outboard boat. Borchev walked cautiously through the carnage. Except for two wounded men who had taken refuge behind a forklift, the rest were dead. His entire detachment had been wiped out.

Half crazed with anger, Borchev staggered among the victims, searching, until he came upon the body of Clark. He rolled the CIA agent over on his back and looked down into sightless eyes.

"Who are you?" he demanded senselessly. "Who do you work for?"

The answers had died with Clark.

Borchev took the limp body by the belt and dragged it to the edge of the pier. Then he kicked it into the water.

"See how you like it!" he shouted insanely.

Borchev wandered aimlessly amid the massacre for another ten minutes before he regained his balance. He finally realized he had to report to Velikov. The only transmitter had melted inside the lead truck, and he began to run around the waterfront, feverishly hunting for a telephone.

He found a sign on a building identifying a dockworkers' recreation room. He lunged at the door and smashed it open with his shoulder. He fumbled along the wall, found the light switch, and turned it on. The room was furnished with old stained sofas. There were checkerboards and dominoes and a small refrigerator. Posters of Castro, Che Guevara haughtily smoking a cigar, and a somber Lenin stared down from one wall.

Borchev entered the office of a supervisor and snatched up the telephone on a desk. He dialed several times without getting through. Finally he raised the operator, cursing the retarded efficiency of the Cuban phone system.

The clouds above the eastern hills were beginning to glow orange and the sirens of the city's fire squads were converging on the waterfront when he was finally connected to the Soviet Embassy.

Captain Manuel Pinon stood on the bridge wing of the Russian-built Riga-class patrol frigate and steadied his binoculars. He had been awakened by his first officer soon after the fighting and conflagration had broken out in the commercial dock area. He could see little through the binoculars because his vessel was moored to the naval dock around a point just below the channel and his vision was blocked by buildings.

"Shouldn't we investigate?" asked his first officer.

"The police and fire crews can handle it," answered Pinon.

"Sounds like gunshots."

"Probably a warehouse blaze that's ignited military supplies. Better we stay clear of the fireboats." He handed the glasses to the first officer. "Keep a watch on it. I'm going back to bed."

Pinon was just about to enter his stateroom when his first officer came running up the passageway.

"Sir, you'd better return to the bridge. Two ships are attempting to leave the harbor."

"Without clearance?"

"Yes, sir."

"Could be they're moving to a new mooring."

The first officer shook his head. "Their heading is taking them into the main channel."

Pinon groaned. "The gods are against me getting any sleep."

The first officer grinned sardonically. "A good Communist does not believe in gods."

"Tell that to my white-haired mother."

On the bridge wing once again, Pinon yawned and peered through the early-morning haze. Two ships under tow were about to enter the Entrada Channel for open seas.

"What in hell—" Pinon refocused the glasses. "Not a flag, not a navigation light showing, no lookouts on the bridge—"

"Nor do they respond to our radio signals requesting their intent. Almost looks like they're trying to sneak out."

"Counterrevolutionary scum trying to reach the United States," Pinon growled. "Yes, that must be it. Can't be anything else."

"Shall I give the order to cast off and get under way?"

"Yes, immediately. We'll come around across their bows and block their way."

Even as he spoke, the first officer's hand was reaching for the siren switch that whooped the crew to action stations.

Ten minutes later the thirty-year-old ship, retired by the Russian Navy after it had been replaced by a newer, modified class of frigate, drifted broadside across the channel. Her four-inch guns turned and aimed almost point-blank at the rapidly approaching phantom vessels.

Pitt gazed at the blinking signal lamp on the frigate. He was tempted to turn on the radio, but it was agreed upon from the beginning that the convoy would remain silent in case an alert port authority official or security post receiver happened to tune in on the same frequency. Pitt's international Morse code was rusty, but he deciphered the message as "Stop immediately and identify."

He kept a sharp eye on the *Pisto*. He was aware that any sudden evasive move would have to originate with Jack. Pitt called down to the engine room and alerted Manny to the frigate blocking their course, but the brass telegraph pointers remained locked on Full Ahead.

They were so close now he could see the Cuban naval ensign standing stiffly in the offshore breeze. The vanes on the signal lamp flipped up and down again. "Stop immediately or we will open fire."

Two men appeared on the stern of the *Pisto* and frantically began reeling out more cable. At the same time the tug lost way, made a sharp turn to starboard, and heaved to. Then Jack stepped out of the wheelhouse and hailed the frigate through a bullhorn.

"Give way, you sea cow's ass. Can't you see I have a tow?"

Pinon ignored the insult. He expected no less from a tug captain. "Your movement is unauthorized. I am sending over a boarding party."

"I'll be damned if I let any candy-ass Navy boy step foot on my ship."

"You'll be dead if you don't," Pinon replied in good humor. He was uncertain now whether this was a mass escape attempt by dissidents, but the strange actions of the tug and unlit ships required an investigation.

He leaned over the bridge railing and ordered the ship's motor cutter and boarding crew to lower away. When he turned back to face the unidentified convoy, he froze in horror.

Too late. In the dusky light he had failed to see that the ship behind the tug was not a dead tow. It was under way and boring down on the frigate at a good eight knots. He stared dazedly for several seconds before his reeling mind took hold.

"Full ahead!" he shrieked. "Guns fire!"

His command was followed by a deafening blast as shells streaked across the narrowing gap, tore into the bow and superstructure of the *Amy Bigalow*, and exploded in a burst of flame and shattered steel. The port side of the wheelhouse seemed to melt away as if ripped open by a junkyard mangling machine. Glass and debris felt like pellets out of a shotgun. Pitt ducked and kept his grip on the wheel with a determination tied to blind stubbornness. He was lucky to emerge with only a few cuts and a bruised thigh.

The second salvo blew away the chart room and sliced the forward mast in two. The top half fell over the side and was dragged for a hundred feet before the cables parted and it floated clear. The funnel was shattered and turned to scrap, and a shell burst inside the starboard anchor locker, scattering a cloud of salt-rusted links like shrapnel.

There would be no third salvo.

Pinon stood absolutely still, hands tightly clenched on the bridge rail. He stared up at the menacing black bows of the *Amy Bigalow* as they rose ponderously over the frigate, his face white and his eyes sick with a certainty that his ship was about to die.

The frigate's screws beat the water in a frenzy, but they could not push her out of the way soon enough. There was no question of the *Amy Bigalow* missing and no doubt as to Pitt's intentions. He was compensating and cutting the angle toward the frigate's midsection. Those of the crew who were topside and could see the approaching disaster gazed numb with horror before finally reacting and throwing themselves over the sides.

The *Amy Bigalow*'s sixty-foot-high stem slashed through the frigate just forward of her rear turret, shredding the plates and penetrating the hull for nearly twenty feet. Pinon's ship might have survived the collision and made shore before settling in the water, but with a terrible screech of grinding steel the bow of the *Amy Bigalow* rose up from the gaping wound until her barnacled keel was exposed. She hung there for an instant, and then dropped, crushing the frigate in two and pile-driving the stern section out of sight beneath the surface.

Instantly, the sea poured into the amputated stern, sweeping through

941

the twisted bulkheads and flooding the open compartments. As the cataract surged into the doomed frigate's hull she quickly began to settle astern. Her dying agony did not last long. By the time the *Ozero Zaysan* was towed over the collision site, she was gone, leaving a pitiful few of her crew struggling in the water.

72

"YOU WALKED INTO A TRAP?" Velikov's voice came flat and hard over the phone.

Borchev felt uncomfortable. He couldn't very well admit that he was one of the only three survivors out of forty and lacked even a scratch. "An unknown force of at least two hundred Cubans opened fire with heavy equipment before we could evacuate the trucks."

"You certain they were Cubans?"

"Who else could have planned and carried it out? Their commanding officer was wearing a Cuban Army uniform."

"Pérez?"

"Can't say. We'll need time to make an identification."

"Might have been a blunder by green troops who opened fire out of stupidity or panic."

"They were far from stupid. I can recognize highly trained combat troops when I see them. They knew we were coming and laid a well-prepared ambush."

Velikov's face went completely blank and then quickly reddened. The assault on Cayo Santa María passed before his eyes. He could scarcely contain his rage. "What was their objective?"

"A delaying action to take possession of the ships."

Borchev's answer staggered Velikov. He felt as if his body had turned to ice. The questions came spilling out of his mouth. "The Rum and Cola operation ships were seized? Are they still moored to their docks?"

"No, a tugboat towed off the *Ozero Zaysan*. The *Amy Bigalow* steamed clear under her own power. I lost sight of them after they rounded the point. A little later I heard what sounded like naval gunfire near the entrance channel."

Velikov had heard the rumble of heavy guns too. He stared at a blank wall with unbelieving eyes, trying to envision the circle of men dogging his intricately planned operations. He refused to believe that intelligence units loyal to Castro had the knowledge and expertise. Only the long arm of the Americans and their Central Intelligence Agency could have destroyed Cayo Santa María and wrecked his scheme to terminate the Castro regime. Only one individual could have been responsible for the leak of information.

Dirk Pitt.

A deep look of concentration tensed Velikov's face. The mud was clearing from the water. He knew what he had to do in the little time left.

"Are the ships still in the harbor?" he demanded of Borchev.

"If they were trying to escape to the sea, I'd put them somewhere in the Entrada Channel."

"Find Admiral Chekoldin and tell him I want those ships stopped and headed back to the inner harbor."

"I thought all Soviet naval ships have stood out to sea."

"The admiral and his flagship aren't due to depart until eight o'clock. Don't use the telephone. Convey my request in person and stress the urgency."

Before Borchev could reply, Velikov threw down the receiver and rushed to the main entrance of the embassy, ignoring the busy staff preparing for evacuation. He ran outside to the embassy limousine and shoved aside the chauffeur, who was standing by to drive the Soviet ambassador to safety.

He turned the ignition key and threw the transmission into drive the instant the engine fired. The rear wheels spun and shrieked furiously as the car leaped out of the embassy courtyard into the streets.

Two blocks later Velikov was stopped dead.

A military roadblock barred his way. Two armored cars and a company of Cuban soldiers stretched across the broad boulevard. An officer stepped up to the car and shone a flashlight in the window.

"May I see your identification papers, please?"

"I am General Peter Velikov, attached to the Soviet Military Mission. I'm in a great hurry to reach Colonel General Kolchak's headquarters. Stand aside and let me pass."

The officer studied Velikov's face for a moment as if satisfying himself. He switched off the flashlight and motioned for two of his men to enter the backseat. Then he came around and climbed into the front passenger's seat.

"We've been waiting for you, General," he said in a cold but courteous tone. "Please follow my directions and turn left at the next cross street."

Pitt stood, feet slightly apart, both hands on the helm, his craggy face thrust forward, as he watched the lighthouse at the harbor entrance slip past with terrible slowness. His whole mind and body, every nerve was concentrated on moving the ship as far away from the populated city as possible before the ammonium nitrate was detonated.

The water turned from gray-green to emerald and the ship started to roll slightly as it plowed into the swells marching in from the sea. The *Amy Bigalow* was taking in water through her ripped bow plates, but she still answered her helm and chased after the tailing wake of the tugboat.

His whole body ached from exhaustion. He drove himself on with sheer willpower. The blood from the cuts he received from the blast of the frigate's guns had hardened into dark red streaks down his face. He was oblivious to the sweat and the clothes sticking to his body.

He closed his eyes for a moment and wished he was back in his hangar apartment with a Bombay gin martini, sitting in a steaming shower. God, he was tired.

A sudden gust of wind blew in through the shattered bridge windows and he opened his eyes again. He studied the shorelines both port and starboard. The hidden gun emplacements around the harbor remained silent and there were still no signs of aircraft or patrol vessels. Despite the battle with the naval frigate no alarm had been given. The confusion and lack of intelligence among the Cuban military security forces were working in their favor.

The still sleeping city lingered behind as if tied to the trailing ship's stern. The sun was up now and the convoy in naked view up and down the coast.

A few more minutes, a few more minutes, he said in his mind over and over.

Velikov was ordered to stop on a quiet corner near Cathedral Square in old Havana. He was led into a shabby building with dusty and cracked windows, past glass cases displaying faded posters of 1940s movie stars staring at the camera while seated at the bar inside.

A one-time watering hole patronized by wealthy American celebrities, Sloppy Joe's was now only a dingy hole in the wall, long forgotten except by an elderly few. Four people were seated off to one side of the tarnished and neglected bar.

The interior was dark and smelled of disinfectant and decay. Velikov didn't recognize his hosts until he was halfway across the unswept floor. Then he stopped short and stared unbelieving, a sudden nausea growing within him.

Jessie LeBaron was sitting between a strange fat man and Raúl Castro. The fourth party stared back ominously.

"Good morning, General," said Fidel Castro. "I'm happy you could join us."

73

PITT'S EARS PICKED UP the drone of an aircraft. He released his hold on the wheel and stepped to the door of the bridge wing.

A pair of helicopter gunships were beating along the shore from the north. His gaze swung back to the harbor entrance. A gray warship was charging through the channel at full speed, throwing up a big bow wave. A Soviet destroyer this time, pencil-thin, forward guns trained on the creeping, defenseless death ships. The chase that nobody could win was on.

Jack stepped out onto the deck of the tugboat and looked up at the broken, twisted wreck of the *Amy Bigalow*'s bridge. He marveled that anyone was still alive and manning the helm. He made a gesture to his ear and waited until a hand waved back in understanding. He watched as a crewman hurried to the freighter's stern and gave the same signal to Moe on board the *Ozero Zaysan*. Then he returned inside and called out on the radio.

"This is *Pisto*. Do you read? Over."

"Loud and clear," replied Pitt.

"I've got you," Moe added.

"This is as good a time as any to tie your helms and abandon ship," said Jack.

"Good riddance," Moe snorted. "Let these hell buckets go up by themselves."

"We'll leave our engines running at full ahead," said Pitt. "What about the *Pisto*?"

"I'll man her a few more minutes to make sure the ships don't circle back to shore," replied Jack.

"Better not be late. Castro's boys are coming through the slot."

"I see them," said Jack. "Good luck. Out."

Pitt locked the helm in the Dead Ahead position and called up

Manny. The tough chief engineer needed no urging. He and his men were swinging the ship's motor launch out in its davits three minutes later. They scrambled aboard and were beginning to lower it when Pitt jumped over the railing and dropped in.

"Almost left you behind," shouted Manny.

"I radioed the destroyer and told her to stand clear or we'd blow up the munitions ship."

Before Manny could reply, there was an echoing thunderlike rumble. A few seconds later a shell plunged into the sea fifty yards in front of the *Pisto*.

"They didn't buy your bill of goods," Manny grunted. He started the boat's engine and engaged the gearbox to equal the ship's headway when they hit the water. The falls were cast off and they were thrown broadside into the wash, almost swamping the launch. The *Amy Bigalow* swept past on her final voyage, deserted and destined for obliteration.

Manny turned and saw that Moe and his crew were lowering the *Ozero Zaysan*'s launch. It smashed into a swell and was thrown against the steel sides with such force that the seams on the starboard side were sprung and the bottom half awash, drowning the engine.

"We've got to help them," said Pitt.

"Right you are," Manny agreed.

Before they could come about, Jack had appraised the situation and yelled through his bullhorn, "Leave them be. I'll pick them up after I cut loose. Look to yourselves and head for shore."

Pitt took the pilot's chair from a crewman who had smashed his fingers in the davit ropes. He sheered the launch toward the tall buildings lining the Malecón waterfront and crammed the throttle against its stop.

Manny was looking back at the tug and the drifting launch that carried Moe's crew. His face went gray as the destroyer fired again and twin columns of water straddled the *Pisto*. The spray crashed down on her upper works, but she shook off the deluge and plowed on.

Moe turned away with a feeling of dread that he did not show. He knew he would never see his friends alive again.

Pitt was gauging the distance between the retreating ships and the shore. They were still close enough for the explosives to devastate a major share of Havana, he judged grimly, way too close.

• • •

"Did President Antonov agree to your plan for my assassination?" Fidel Castro asked.

Velikov stood with arms crossed. He was not offered a chair. He glared back at Castro with cold contempt. "I am a ranking military office of the Soviet Union. I demand to be treated accordingly."

The black, angry eyes of Raúl Castro flashed. "This is Cuba. You don't demand anything here. You're nothing but KGB scum."

"Enough, Raúl, enough," cautioned Fidel. He looked at Velikov. "Don't toy with us, General. I've studied your documents. Rum and Cola is no longer a secret."

Velikov played out his hand. "I'm fully aware of the operation. Another vicious CIA attempt to undermine the friendship between Cuba and the Soviet Union."

"If that is so, why didn't you warn me?"

"There was no time."

"You found time enough to clear out Russian nationals," Raúl snapped. "Why were you running away at this time in the morning?"

A look of arrogance crossed Velikov's face. "I won't bother to answer your questions. Need I remind you I have diplomatic immunity. You have no right to interrogate me."

"How do you intend to set off the explosives?" asked Castro calmly.

Velikov stood silent. The corners of his lips turned up slightly in a smile at the sound of the distant rumble of heavy gunfire. Fidel and Raúl exchanged glances, but nothing was said between them.

Jessie shuddered as the tension mounted in the small barroom. For a moment she wished she was a man so she could beat the truth out of the general. She suddenly felt sick and wanted to scream because of the costly time that was drifting away.

"Please tell them what they want to know," she begged. "You can't stand there and allow thousands of children to die for a senseless political cause."

Velikov did not argue. He remained unmoved.

"I'll be happy to take him out back," said Hagen.

"You needn't soil your hands, Mr. Hagen," said Fidel. "I have experts in painful interrogation waiting outside."

"You wouldn't dare," Velikov snapped.

"It is my duty to warn you that if you do not halt the detonation you'll be tortured. Not with simple injections like political prisoners at your mental hospitals in Russia, but unspeakable tortures that will continue day and night. Our finest medical specialists will keep you alive. No nightmare can do justice to your suffering, General. You will scream until you can scream no more. Then, when you are little more than a vegetable without sight, speech, or hearing, you will be transported and dumped in a slum somewhere in North Africa where you will survive or die, and where no one will rescue or pity a crippled beggar living in filth. You will become what you Russians call a nonperson."

Velikov's shell cracked, but very thinly. "You waste your breath. You are dead. I am dead. We are all dead."

"You're mistaken. The ships carrying the munitions and ammonium nitrate have been removed from the harbor by the very people you blame. At this minute agents of the CIA are sailing them out to sea where the explosive force will only kill the fish."

Velikov quickly pressed his slim advantage. "No, *Señor Presidente*, it is you who are mistaken. The sound of guns you heard a few moments ago came from a Soviet vessel stopping the ships and turning them back inside the harbor. They may explode too early for your celebration speech, but they will still accomplish the end results."

"You're lying," Fidel said uneasily.

"Your reign as the great father of the revolution is over," said Velikov, his voice sly and baiting. "I'll gladly die for the Russian motherland. Will you sacrifice your life for Cuba? Maybe when you were young and had nothing to lose, but you're soft now and too used to having others do your dirty work for you. You've got the good life and you're not about to let it slip away. But it's finished. Tomorrow you'll only be another photograph on a wall and a new president will sit in your place. One whose loyalties extend to the Kremlin."

Velikov stepped back a few paces and took out a small case from his pocket.

Hagen recognized it immediately. "An electronic transmitter. He can send a signal to detonate the explosives from here."

"Oh, God!" Jessie cried despairingly. "Oh, my God, he's going to do it, he's really going to do it."

"Don't bother to call your bodyguards," said Velikov. "They'll never react in time."

Fidel stared at him with cold bleak eyes. "Remember what I said."

Velikov stared back contemptuously. "Can you really picture me screaming in agony in one of your dirty prisons?"

"Give me the transmitter and you will be free to leave Cuba unharmed."

"And return to Moscow a cowardly figure? I think not."

"It's on your head," said Fidel, his expression a curious blend of anger and fear. "You know your fate if you detonate the explosives and live."

"Little chance of that," Velikov sneered. "This building sits less than five hundred yards from the harbor channel. There will be nothing left of us." He paused, his face as hard as a chiseled gargoyle. Then he said, "Goodbye, *Señor Presidente*."

"You bastard—" Hagen leaped over the table in an incredible display of agility for his huge bulk and was only inches away from Velikov when the Russian pressed the transmitter's Activate switch.

74

THE *AMY BIGALOW* VAPORIZED.

The *Ozero Zaysan* waited only a fraction of a second longer before blowing herself out of existence. The combined force of the volatile cargoes inside the two ships threw up a mountainous column of fiery debris and smoke that thrust five thousand feet into the tropical sky. A vast vortex opened in the sea as a gigantic geyser of maddened water and steam shot up into the smoke and then burst outward.

The brilliant red-white glare flashed across the water with the blinding intensity of ten suns, followed by a thunderous clap that lashed and flattened the wave tops.

The sight of the gallant little *Pisto* as the blast flung her two hundred feet into the air like a disintegrating skyrocket was locked forever in Pitt's mind. He watched stunned as her shredded remains along with Jack and his crew splattered into the maelstrom like burning hail.

Moe and his crew in the drifting launch simply vanished off the face of the sea.

The explosive fury blew the two helicopter gunships out of the air. Seagulls within two miles were crushed by the concussion. The propeller from the *Ozero Zaysan* whirled across the sea and smashed into the control castle of the Soviet destroyer, killing every man on the bridge. Twisted steel plates, rivets, chain links, and deck gear pelted the city, tearing through walls and roofs like cannon shells. Telephone poles and streetlights were lashed and broken off at the base.

Hundreds of people perished in their beds while still asleep. Many were terribly gashed by flying glass or crushed by pancaked ceilings. Early-morning workers and pedestrians were picked up off their feet and crushed against buildings.

The shock wave struck the city with twice the force of any recorded hurricane, flattening wooden structures near the shore as though they were paper toys, collapsing storefronts, shattering a hundred thousand windows, and hurling parked automobiles into buildings.

Inside the harbor the monstrous *Ozero Baykai* went up.

At first, flames shot from her hull like blowtorches. Then the whole oil tanker burst open in a giant fireball. A surge of flaming oil swamped the surrounding waterfront structures and launched a chain reaction of explosions from combustible cargoes sitting on the docks. Fiery metal plunged into oil and gas storage tanks on the east side of the harbor. One after another they blew up like a time-sequence fireworks display, spewing gigantic black smoke clouds over the city.

An oil refinery exploded, then a chemical company blew, followed by blasts at a paint company and fertilizer plant. Two nearby freighters, under way and heading for sea, collided, caught fire, and began to blaze. A fiery hunk of steel from the destroyed tanker plummeted into one of ten railroad tank cars containing propane and sent them up like a string of firecrackers.

Another blast...then another...and another.

Four miles of waterfront were turned into a holocaust. Ashes and soot covered the city like a black snowfall. Few stevedores working the docks survived. Fortunately, the refineries and the chemical plant were nearly abandoned. Loss of life would have been many times higher if it had not been a national holiday.

The worst of the disaster inside the harbor was past, but the nightmare still facing the rest of the city had yet to arrive.

An immense fifty-foot tidal wave rose up out of the vortex and hurtled toward shore. Pitt and the others stared in awe as the green and white mountain roared after them. They sat there waiting, no panic, just staring and waiting for the frail little launch to become a shattered piece of wreckage and the water their tomb.

The seawall along the Malecón was only thirty yards away when the horizontal avalanche engulfed the launch. The crest curled and burst right over them. It tore Manny and three men from their seats, and Pitt watched them sail through the crashing spray like roof shingles in a tornado. The seawall rushed closer but the momentum of the wave lifted the launch over the top and slung it across the wide boulevard.

Pitt clutched the helm with such strength that it was torn away from its mounting and he was swept clear. He thought this was the end, but with a conscious effort of will he took a deep breath and held it as he was pulled under. As if in a dream he could look down through the strangely clear and demoniac water, seeing cars tumbling in crazy gyrations as if thrown by a giant hand.

Buried deep in the boiling turmoil, he felt strangely detached. It struck him as ludicrous that he was about to drown on a city street. His desire for life still clung tenaciously, but he did not struggle senselessly and waste precious oxygen. He went lax and vainly tried to peer through the froth, his mind somehow working with uncanny clarity. He knew that if the wave swept him against a concrete building the rushing tons of water would mash him into the same consistency as a watermelon dropped from an airplane.

His fear would have been heightened if he had seen the launch smash into the second story of an apartment building that housed Soviet technicians. The impact collapsed the hull as if the planking were no stronger than an eggshell. The four-cylinder diesel engine was tossed through a broken window by the cascade and ended up in a stairwell.

Mercifully, Pitt was swept into a narrow side street like a log through a chute. The flood carried everything before it in a great tumbling mass of wreckage. But even as it curled around the buildings strong enough to withstand the onslaught, the wave was already beginning to die. Within seconds the leading edge would reach its high mark and then recede, the retreating torrent sucking human bodies and loose debris back to the sea.

Pitt began to see stars as his brain starved for oxygen. His senses began to shut down one by one. He felt a jarring blow as his shoulder struck a fixed object. He whipped an arm around it, trying to hang on, but he was thrust forward by the force of the wave. He ran into another flat surface, and this time he reached out and clutched it in a death grip, not recognizing it as a sign over a jeweler's shop.

The thinking, feeling equipment of his body slowed and shut down as if its electrical current had switched off. His head was pounding and blackness was covering the stars bursting behind his eyes. He existed only on instinct, and soon even that would desert him.

The wave had reached its outer limit and began to fall in on itself, rushing back to the sea. It was too late for Pitt, he was slipping away from consciousness. His brain somehow managed to send out one last message. An arm clumsily jammed its way between the sign and its support shaft that protruded from the building, and wedged there.

Then his bursting lungs could take no more, and he began to drown.

The great rumble from the explosions echoed away into the hills and sea. There was no sunlight over the city, no real sunlight. It was hidden by a smoke-blackened pall of incredible density. The whole harbor seemed afire; the docks, ships, storage tanks, and three square miles of oil-coated water were bristling with orange and blue flame that streaked up into the dark canopy.

The dreadfully wounded city began to shake off the shock and stagger to its feet. Sirens began to match the noisy intensity of the crackling fires. The tidal wave had flowed back into the Gulf of Mexico, dragging a great mass of splintered debris and bodies in its wake.

Survivors began to stumble dazed and injured into the streets, like bewildered sheep, shocked at the enormous devastation around them, wondering what had happened. Some wandered in shock, unfeeling of their wounds. Others stared dumbly at the huge piece of the *Amy Bigalow*'s rudder that had crashed through the bus station and mashed four of the vehicles and several people who were waiting to board.

A piece of the *Ozero Zaysan*'s forward mast was found embedded in the center of Havana Stadium's soccer field. A one-ton winch landed in a wing of University Hospital and squashed the only three beds not occupied in a forty-bed ward. It was to be widely talked about as only one of a hundred miracles that happened that day. A great boon to the Catholic Church and a small setback to Marxism.

Rescue parties began to form as firefighters and police converged on the waterfront. Army units were called out along with the militia. There was panic amid the chaos at first. The military forces turned their backs on rescue work and manned island defenses under the mistaken belief the United States was invading. The injured seemed to be everywhere, some screaming in pain, most hobbling or walking away from the flaming harbor.

The earthshaking quake died with the shock waves. The ceiling of Sloppy Joe's had fallen in, but the walls still stood. The barroom was a shambles. Wooden beams, fallen plaster, overturned furniture, and broken bottles lay scattered under a thick cloud of dust. The swinging door had been ripped from its hinges and hung at a crazy angle over Castro's bodyguards, who lay groaning under a small hill of bricks.

Ira Hagen hoisted himself painfully to his feet and shook his head to clear it from the ringing of the concussion. He wiped his eyes to penetrate the dust cloud and clutched a wall for support. He looked up through the now open ceiling and saw pictures still hanging on the walls of the floor above.

His first thought was of Jessie. She was lying partially under the table that still stood in the center of the room. Her body was crumpled in a curled position. Hagen knelt and gently turned her over.

She lay motionless, appearing lifeless under the coating of white plaster dust, but there was no blood or serious wounds. Her eyes were half open and she groaned. Hagen smiled with relief and removed his coat. He folded and placed it under her head.

She reached up and grasped his wrist more tightly than he believed possible and stared up at him.

"Dirk is dead," she whispered.

"He might have survived," said Hagen softly, but there was no optimism in his tone.

"Dirk is dead," she repeated.

"Don't move," he said. "Just lie easy while I check out the Castros."

Then he rose unsteadily and began searching through the fallen debris. The sound of coughing came from his left and he climbed over the rubble until he bumped into the bar.

Raúl Castro was hanging on to the raised edge of the bar with both hands, dazed and in shock, hacking the dust from his throat. Blood was trickling from his nose and a nasty cut on his chin.

Hagen marveled at how close everyone had been sitting before the explosions and how scattered they were now. He uprighted a fallen chair and helped Raúl to sit down.

"Are you all right, sir?" Hagen asked, genuinely concerned.

Raúl nodded weakly. "I'm all right. Fidel? Where is Fidel?"

"Sit tight. I'll find him."

Hagen moved off through the rubble until he found Fidel Castro. The Cuban leader was on his stomach and twisted sideways, shoulders propped up by one arm. Hagen stared in fascination at the scene on the floor.

Castro's eyes were trained on an upturned face only a foot away. General Velikov was spread-eagled on his back, a large beam crushing his legs. The expression on his face was a mixture of defiance and apprehension. He stared up at Castro through eyes bitter with the taste of defeat.

There was not a flicker of emotion in Castro's expression. The plaster dust made him look as though he were sculpted in marble. The rigidity of the face, masklike, the total concentration, was almost inhuman.

"We live, General," he murmured triumphantly. "We both live."

"Not right," Velikov uttered through clenched teeth. "We should all be dead."

"Dirk Pitt and the others somehow got the ships through your naval units and out to sea," explained Hagen. "The destructive force of the explosion was only one-tenth of what it might have been if they remained in the harbor."

"You have failed," said Castro. "Cuba remains Cuba."

"So near and yet—" Velikov shook his head resignedly. "And now for the revenge you vowed to take on me."

"You will die for every one of my countrymen you murdered," Castro promised, in a voice as cold as an open grave. "If it takes a thousand deaths or a hundred thousand. You will suffer them all."

Velikov grinned crookedly. He seemed to have no nerves at all. "Another man, another time, and you will surely be killed, Fidel. I know. I helped create five alternative plans in case this one failed."

PART VI

Eureka! the La Dorada

75

MARTIN BROGAN WALKED into the early-morning cabinet meeting late. The President and the men seated around the large kidney-shaped table looked up expectantly.

"The ships were detonated four hours ahead of schedule," he informed them while still standing.

His announcement was greeted with solemn silence. Every man at the table had been told of the unbelievable plan by the Soviets to remove Castro, and the news struck them more as an inevitable tragedy than a shocking catastrophe.

"What are the latest reports on loss of life?" asked Douglas Oates.

"Too early to tell," replied Brogan. "The whole harbor area is in flames. The deaths could conceivably total in the thousands. The devastation, however, is not nearly as severe as we first projected. It appears our agents in Havana seized two of the ships and sailed them out of the harbor before they exploded."

As they listened in contemplative quiet, Brogan read from the initial reports sent from the Special Interests Section in Havana. He recounted the details of the plan to move the ships and the sketchy details of the actual operation. Before he had finished, one of his aides entered and slipped him an updated report. He scanned it silently and then read the first line.

"Fidel and Raúl Castro are alive." He paused to gaze at the President. "Your man, Ira Hagen, says he is in direct contact with the Castros and they have requested any assistance we can offer in the way of disaster relief, including medical personnel and supplies, firefighting equipment, food and clothing, and also morgue and embalming experts."

The President looked at General Clayton Metcalf, chairman of the Joint Chiefs of Staff. "General?"

"After your call last night, I alerted Air Transport Command. We can begin the airlift as soon as the people and supplies arrive at the airfields and are loaded on board."

"Any approach by American military aircraft had better be coordinated or the Cubans will cut loose with their surface-to-air missiles," pointed out Secretary of Defense Simmons.

"I'll see to it a line of communication is opened with their Foreign Ministry," said Secretary of State Oates.

"Better make it clear to Castro that any relief we send is organized under the umbrella of the Red Cross," added Dan Fawcett. "We don't want to scare him into slamming the door."

"An angle we can't overlook," said the President.

"Almost a crime to take advantage of a terrible disaster," mused Oates. "Still, we can't deny it's a heaven-sent opportunity to cement relations with Cuba and defuse revolutionary fever throughout the Americas."

"I wonder if Castro has ever studied Símon Bolívar?" the President asked no one in particular.

"The Great Liberator of South America is one of Castro's idols," replied Brogan. "Why do you ask?"

"Then perhaps he's finally heeded one of Bolívar's quotations."

"Which quotation is that, Mr. President?"

The President looked from face to face around the table before answering. "'He who serves a revolution plows the sea.'"

76

THE CHAOS SLOWLY SUBSIDED and the rescue work began as the population of Havana recovered from the shock. Hurricane emergency procedures were put into operation. Army and militia units along with paramedics sifted through the rubble, lifting the bodies of the living into ambulances and the dead into trucks.

The Santa Clara convent, dating from 1643, was taken over as a temporary hospital and quickly filled. The wards and corridors of University Hospital soon overflowed. The elegant old Presidential Palace, now the museum of the revolution, was turned into a morgue.

Injured people walked the streets bleeding, staring vacantly or searching desperately for loved ones. A clock on top of a building in Cathedral Square of old Havana sat frozen at 6:21. Some residents who had fled their homes during the havoc began to drift back. Others who had no homes to return to walked through the streets, picking their way around the bodies, carrying small bundles containing salvaged possessions.

Every fire unit for a hundred miles streamed into the city and vainly fought the fires spreading throughout the waterfront. A tank of chlorine gas exploded, adding its poison to the ravages of the blaze. Twice the hundreds of firefighters had to run for cover when a change of wind whipped the blistering heat in their faces.

Even while the rescue operations were being organized, Fidel Castro launched a purge of disloyal government officials and military officers. Raúl personally directed the roundup. Most had abandoned the city, having been forewarned of Rum and Cola by Velikov and the KGB. One by one they were arrested, each one stunned by the news the Castro brothers were still alive. By the hundreds they were transported under heavy guard to a secret prison compound deep in the mountains, never to be seen again.

At two o'clock in the afternoon the first U.S. Air Force heavy cargo plane landed at Havana's international airport. Soon a constant stream of aircraft were arriving. Fidel Castro was on hand to greet the volunteer doctors and nurses. He personally saw to it that Cuban relief committees stood by to receive the supplies and cooperate with the incoming Americans.

By early evening, Coast Guard and firefighting vessels from the port of Miami began to stream over the smoke-filled horizon. Bulldozers, heavy equipment, and oil-fire experts from Texas moved into the fiery wreckage along the harbor and wasted no time in attacking the flames.

Despite past political differences the imagination of the United States and Cuba seemed to leap to the occasion and everyone worked together closely on the specific emergencies to be met.

Admiral Sandecker and Al Giordino stepped off a NUMA jet late in the afternoon. They hitched a ride on a truck, loaded with bed linen and military cots, as far as a distribution depot, where Giordino hot-wired and *borrowed* an abandoned Fiat.

The false sunset from the flames tinted their faces red through the windshield as they gazed incredulously at the gigantic smoke cloud and great sea of fire.

After nearly an hour of winding their way through the city and being directed by police through complicated detours to avoid streets choked with debris and rescue vehicles, they finally reached the Swiss Embassy.

"We have our job cut out," said Sandecker, staring at the ruined buildings and the wreckage littering the wide boulevard of the Malecón.

Giordino nodded sadly. "He may never be found."

"Still, we owe it to him to try."

"Yes," Giordino said heavily. "We owe Dirk that."

They turned and walked through the battered entrance of the embassy and were directed to the communications room of the Special Interests Section.

The room was jammed with news correspondents, waiting their turn to transmit reports of the disaster. Sandecker shouldered his way through the throng and found a heavyset man dictating to a radio operator. When the man finished, Sandecker tapped him on the arm.

"You Ira Hagen?"

"Yes, I'm Hagen." The hoarse voice matched the tired lines in the face.

"Thought so," said Sandecker. "The President described you in some detail."

Hagen patted his rotund stomach and forced a smile. "I'm not hard to pick out in a crowd." Then he paused and looked at Sandecker strangely. "You say the President—"

"I met with him four hours ago in the White House. My name is James Sandecker and this is Al Giordino. We're with NUMA."

"Yes, Admiral, I know the name. What can I do for you?"

"We're friends of Dirk Pitt and Jessie LeBaron."

Hagen closed his eyes for a second and then gazed at Sandecker steadily. "Mrs. LeBaron is one hell of a woman. Except for a few small cuts and bruises, she came out of the explosion in good shape. She's helping out at an emergency hospital for children in the old cathedral. But if you're looking for Pitt, I'm afraid you're wasting your time. He was at the helm of the *Amy Bigalow* when she blew up."

Giordino suddenly felt sick at heart. "There's no chance he might have escaped?"

"Of the men who fought off the Russians on the docks while the ships slipped out to sea, only two survived. Every one of the crew on board the ships and tugboat is missing. There's little hope any of them made it clear in time. And if the explosions didn't kill them, they surely must have drowned in the tidal wave."

Giordino clenched his fists in frustration. He turned and faced away so the others couldn't see the tears rimming his eyes.

Sandecker shook his head in sorrow. "We'd like to make a search of the hospitals."

"I hate to sound heartless, Admiral, but you'd do better to look in the morgues."

"We'll do both."

"I'll ask the Swiss to arrange a diplomatic pass so you can move freely about the city."

"Thank you."

Hagen looked at both men, his eyes filled with compassion. "If it's any consolation, your friend Pitt was responsible for saving a hundred thousand lives."

Sandecker stared back, a sudden proud look on his face. "And if you knew Dirk Pitt, Mr. Hagen, you'd have expected no less."

77

WITH NOT MUCH OPTIMISM, Sandecker and Giordino began looking for Pitt in the hospitals. They stepped over countless wounded who lay in rows on the floors as nurses administered what aid they could and teams of exhausted doctors labored in the operating rooms. Numerous times they stopped and helped move stretcher cases before continuing the hunt.

They could not find Pitt among the living.

Next they searched through the makeshift morgues, some with trucks waiting in front containing bodies stacked four and five deep. A small army of embalmers worked feverishly to prevent the spread of disease. The dead lay everywhere like cordwood, their faces bare, staring vacantly at the ceilings. Many were too burned and mutilated to identify and were later buried in a mass ceremony in the Colón cemetery.

One harried morgue attendant showed them the remains of a man reported to have been washed in from the sea. It was not Pitt, and they failed to identify Manny because they did not know him.

The early-morning sun rose over the ravaged city. More injured were found and carried to the hospitals, more dead to the morgues. Troops with fixed bayonets walked the streets to prevent looting. Flames still raged in the dock area, but the firefighters were making headway. The vast cloud still bloomed black in the sky, and airline pilots reported that easterly winds had carried it as far as Mexico City.

Sickened by the sights they witnessed that night, Sandecker and Giordino were glad to see daylight again. They drove to within three blocks of Cathedral Plaza and were stopped by wreckage blocking the streets. They walked the rest of the way to the temporary children's hospital to find Jessie.

She was soothing a small girl who was whimpering as a doctor encased a slim brown leg in a cast. Jessie looked up at the admiral and Giordino as they approached. Unconsciously her eyes wandered over their faces, but her weary mind did not recognize them.

"Jessie," said Sandecker softly. "It's Jim Sandecker and Al Giordino."

She looked at them for a few seconds and then it began to register. "Admiral. Al. Oh, thank God you've come." She whispered something in the girl's ear, and then stood and embraced them both, crying uncontrollably.

The doctor nodded at Sandecker. "She's been working like a demon for twenty hours straight. Why don't you see to it she takes a breather."

Each man took an arm and eased her outside. They gently lowered her to a sitting position on the cathedral steps.

Giordino sat down in front of Jessie and looked at her. She was still dressed in combat fatigues. The camouflage pattern was now blotched with bloodstains. Her hair was damp with perspiration and tangled, her eyes red from the pervasive smoke.

"I'm so glad you found me," she said finally. "Did you just arrive?"

"Last night," replied Giordino. "We've been looking for Dirk."

She gazed blankly at the great smoke cloud. "He's gone," she said as if in a trance.

"The bad penny always turns up," Giordino muttered absently.

"They're all gone—my husband, Dirk, so many others." Her voice died.

"Is there coffee anywhere?" said Sandecker, changing the tack of the conversation. "I think we could all use a cup."

Jessie nodded weakly toward the entrance to the cathedral. "A poor woman whose children are badly injured has been making some for the volunteers."

"I'll get it," said Giordino. He rose and disappeared inside.

Jessie and the admiral sat there for several moments, listening to the sirens and watching the flames leap in the distance.

"When we return to Washington," Sandecker said at last, "if I can help in any way..."

"You're most kind, Admiral, but I can manage." She hesitated. "There is one thing. Do you think that Raymond's body might be found and shipped home for burial?"

"I'm sure after all you've done, Castro will cut through any red tape."

"Strange how we became drawn into all this because of the treasure."

"The La Dorada?"

Jessie's eyes stared at a group of figures walking toward them in the distance, but she gave no sign of seeing them. "Men have been beguiled by her for nearly five hundred years, and most have died because of their lust to own her. Stupid...stupid to waste lives over a statue."

"She is still considered the greatest treasure of them all."

Jessie closed her eyes tiredly. "Thank heavens it's hidden. Who knows how many men would kill for it."

"Dirk would never climb over someone's bones for money," Sandecker said. "I know him too well. He was in it for the adventure and the challenge of solving a mystery, not for profit."

Jessie did not reply. She opened her eyes and finally took notice of the approaching party. She could not see them clearly. One of them seemed seven feet tall through the yellow haze from the smoke. The others were quite small. They were singing, but she couldn't make out the tune.

Giordino returned with a small board holding three cups. He stopped and stared for a long moment at the group threading their way through the rubble in the plaza.

The figure in the middle wasn't seven feet tall, but a man with a small boy perched on his shoulders. The boy looked frightened and tightly laced his hands around the man's forehead, obscuring the upper part of his face. A young girl was cradled in one muscled arm, while the opposite hand was clutched by a girl no more than five. A string of ten or eleven other children followed close behind. They sounded as if they were singing in halting English. Three dogs trotted alongside and yapped in accompaniment.

Sandecker looked at Giordino curiously. The barrel-chested Italian blinked away the eye-watering smoke and gazed with an intense wondering expression at the strange and pathetic sight.

The man looked like an apparition, exhausted, desperately so. His clothes were in tatters and he walked with a limp. The eyes were sunken and the gaunt face was streaked with dried blood. Yet his jaw was determined, and he led the children in song with a booming voice.

"I must go back to work," said Jessie, struggling to her feet. "Those children will need care."

They were close enough now so that Giordino could make out the song they were singing.

I'm a Yankee Doodle Dandy. A Yankee Doodle do or die...

Giordino's jaw dropped and his eyes widened in disbelief. He pointed in uncomprehending awe. Then he threw the coffee cups over his shoulder and bounded down the steps of the cathedral like a madman.

"It's him!" he shouted.

A real live nephew of my Uncle Sam. Born on the fourth of July.

"What was that?" Sandecker shouted after him. "What did you say?"

Jessie jumped to her feet, suddenly oblivious to the wrenching fatigue, and ran after Giordino. "He's come back!" she cried.

Then Sandecker took off.

The children stopped in midchorus and huddled around the man, frightened at the sudden appearance of three people shouting and running toward them. They clung to him as life itself. The dogs closed ranks around his legs and began barking louder than ever.

Giordino halted and stood there only two feet away, not sure of what to say that was meaningful. He smiled and smiled in immense delight and relief. At last he found his tongue.

"Welcome back, Lazarus."

Pitt grinned impishly. "Hello, pal. You wouldn't happen to have a dry martini in your pocket?"

78

Six hours later Pitt was sleeping like a stone in an empty alcove of the cathedral. He had refused to go down until the children were cared for and the dogs fed. Then he insisted that Jessie get some rest too.

They lay a few feet apart on double blankets that served as pads against the hard tile floor. Faithful Giordino sat in a wicker chair at the entrance of the alcove, guarding against invasion of their sleep, shushing an occasional band of children who played too close and too loud.

He stiffened at the sight of Sandecker approaching with a group of uniformed Cubans at his heels. Ira Hagen was among them, looking older and far more tired than when Giordino had last seen him, hardly twenty hours previously. The man next to Hagen and directly behind the admiral, Giordino recognized immediately. He rose to his feet as Sandecker nodded toward the sleeping figures.

"Wake them up," he said quietly.

Jessie struggled up from the depths and moaned. Giordino had to shake her by the shoulder several times to keep her from slipping back again. Still bone-tired and drugged from sleep, she sat up and shook her head to clear the blurriness.

Pitt came awake almost instantly, his mind triggered like an alarm clock. He twisted around and elbowed himself to a sitting position, eyes alert and sweeping the men standing around him in a half circle.

"Dirk," said Sandecker. "This is President Fidel Castro. He was making an inspection tour of the hospitals and was told you and Jessie were here. He'd like to talk to you."

Before Pitt could make a remark, Castro stepped forward, took his hand, and pulled him to his feet with surprising strength. The magnetic brown eyes met with piercing opaline green. Castro wore neat, starched olive fatigues with a commander in chief's shoulder insignia, in contrast to Pitt, who still had on the same ragged and dirty clothes as when he arrived at the cathedral.

"So this is the man who made idiots out of my security police and saved the city," said Castro in Spanish.

Jessie translated, and Pitt made a negative gesture. "I was only one of the luckier men who survived. At least two dozen others died trying to prevent the tragedy."

"If the ships had exploded while still tied to the docks, most of Havana would now be a leveled wasteland. A tomb for myself as well as half a million people. Cuba is grateful and wishes to make you a Hero of the Revolution."

"There goes my standing in the neighborhood," muttered Pitt.

Jessie threw him a distasteful look and didn't translate.

"What did he say?" asked Castro.

Jessie cleared her throat. "Ah...he said he is honored to accept."

Castro then asked Pitt to describe the seizing of the ships. "Tell me what you saw," he said politely. "Everything you know that happened. From the beginning."

"Starting with the time we left the Swiss Embassy?" Pitt asked, his eyes narrowed in furtive but shrewd reflection.

"If you wish," answered Castro, comprehending the look.

As Pitt narrated the desperate fight on the docks and the struggle to move the *Amy Bigalow* and the *Ozero Zuysun* from the harbor, Castro interrupted with a barrage of questions. The Cuban leader's curiosity was insatiable. The report took almost as long as the actual event.

Pitt related the facts as straight and unemotionally as he could, knowing he could never do justice to the incredible courage of men who selflessly gave their lives for people of another country. He told of Clark's magnificent holding action against overwhelming odds; how Manny and Moe and their crews struggled in the dark bowels of the ships to get them under way, knowing they could be blown into atoms at any moment. He told how Jack and his crew stayed with the tugboat, towing the death ships out to sea until it was too late to escape. He wished they could all be there to tell their own stories, and he wondered what they might have said. He smiled to himself, knowing how Manny would have turned the air blue with pungent language.

At last Pitt told of being swept into the city by the tidal wave and blacking out, and how he regained consciousness hanging upside down from an overhead jewelry-shop sign. He related how staggering through the debris he heard a little girl crying, and pulled her and a brother from under the wreckage of a collapsed apartment building. After that he seemed to attract lost children like a magnet. Rescue workers added to his collection during the night. When no more could be found alive, a policeman directed Pitt to the children's hospital and relief center, where he was discovered by his friends.

Suddenly Pitt's voice trailed off and he dropped his hands limply to his sides. "That's all there is to tell."

Castro looked at Pitt steadily, his face filled with emotion. He stepped forward and embraced him. "Thank you," he murmured in a broken voice. Then he kissed Jessie on both cheeks and shook Hagen's hand. "Cuba thanks you all. We will not forget."

Pitt looked at Castro slyly. "I wonder if I might ask a favor?"

"You have but to name it," Castro quickly answered.

Pitt hesitated, then he said, "There is this taxi driver named Herberto Figueroa. If I were to find him a restored 'fifty-seven Chevrolet in the States and have it shipped, do you suppose you could arrange for him to take delivery. Herberto and I would both be very grateful."

"But of course. I'll personally see to it he receives your gift."

"There is one more favor," said Pitt.

"Don't push your luck," whispered Sandecker.

"What is it?" Castro asked courteously.

"I wonder if I could borrow a boat with a crane?"

79

THE BODIES OF MANNY and three of his crew were identified. Clark
was fished out of the channel by a fishing boat. Their remains were
flown back to Washington for burial. Nothing of Jack, Moe, and the
rest ever turned up.

The fire was finally under control four days after the death ships
were blown out of existence. The final, stubborn blaze would not be
extinguished until a week later. Another six weeks would pass before
the last of the dead were found. Many were never found at all.

The Cubans were meticulous in their accounting. They eventually
compiled a complete list of casualities. The known dead came to
732. The injured totaled 3,769. The missing were calculated at 197.

At the President's urging, Congress passed an emergency aid bill
of $45 million to help the Cubans rebuild Havana. The President
also, as a gesture of goodwill, lifted the thirty-five-year-old trade
embargo. At last Americans could legally smoke good Havana cigars
again.

After the Russians were expelled, their only representation in Cuba
was a Special Interests Section in the Polish Embassy. The Cuban
people shed no tears at their departure.

Castro still remained a Marxist revolutionary at heart, but he was
mellowing. After agreeing in principle to the U.S.–Cuban friendship
pact, he unhesitantly accepted an invitation to visit with the President at the White House and make an address before Congress,
although he did grumble when asked to keep his speech to twenty
minutes.

At dawn on the third day after the explosions an old peeling,
weather-worn vessel dropped anchor almost in the exact center of

the harbor. Fireboats and salvage craft swept past her as though she were a disabled car in the center of a highway. She was a squat workboat, broad and beamy, about sixty feet in length with a small derrick on the stern whose boom extended over the water. Her crew seemed oblivious to the frenzy of activity going on around them.

Most of the flames in the dock area had been extinguished, but firemen were still pouring thousands of gallons of water on the smoldering debris inside the heat-twisted framework of the warehouses. Several blackened oil storage tanks across the harbor sputtered with stubborn flame, and the acrid pall of smoke reeked of burned oil and rubber.

Pitt stood on the bleached deck of the workboat and squinted through the smoky yellow haze at the wreck of the oil tanker. All that remained of the *Ozero Baykai* was the scorched superstructure on the stern that rose grotesque and distorted above the oily water. He turned his attention to a small compass he held in one hand.

"Is this the spot?" asked Admiral Sandecker.

"Cross bearings on the landmarks check out," Pitt answered.

Giordino stuck his head out the wheelhouse window. "The magnetometer is going crazy. We're right over a heavy mass of iron."

Jessie was sitting on a hatch. She wore gray shorts and a pale blue blouse and looked like her old luscious self.

She flashed a curious look at Pitt. "You still haven't told me why you think Raymond hid the La Dorada on the bottom of the harbor and how you know exactly where to look."

"I was stupid not catch on immediately," explained Pitt. "The words sound the same, and I misinterpreted them. I thought his last words were 'Look on the m-a-i-n s-i-g-h-t.' What he was really trying to say was 'Look on the M-a-i-n-e s-i-t-e.'"

Jessie looked confused. "Maine site?"

"Remember Pearl Harbor, the Alamo, and the *Maine*. On or about this spot in 1898 the battleship *Maine* blew up and launched the Spanish-American War."

An edge of excitement began to form inside her. "Raymond threw the statue on top of an old shipwreck?"

"Shipwreck site," Pitt corrected her. "The hulk of the *Maine* was raised and towed out to sea, where she was sunk with flag flying in 1912."

"But why would Raymond deliberately throw the treasure away?"

"It all goes back to when he and his marine salvage partner, Hans Kronberg, discovered the *Cyclops* and salvaged the La Dorada. It should have been a triumph for two friends who fought the odds together and stole the most sought-after treasure in history from a possessive sea. And it should have had a happy ending. But the tale turned sour. Raymond LeBaron was in love with Kronberg's wife."

Jessie's face tensed in understanding. "Hilda."

"Yes. Hilda. He had two motives for wanting to get rid of Hans. The treasure and a woman. Somehow he must have talked Hans into making another dive after the La Dorada was raised. Then he cut the lifeline, leaving his friend to die a horrible death. Can you imagine what it must have been like, strangling in agony deep inside a steel crypt like the *Cyclops?*"

Jessie averted her eyes. "I can't bring myself to believe you."

"You saw Kronberg's body with your own eyes. Hilda was the real key. She outlined most of the sordid story. I only had to fill in a few details."

"Raymond could never commit murder."

"He could and he did. With Hans out of the picture he went one step further. He dodged the Internal Revenue Service—who can blame him when you remember the federal government collected over eighty percent of income above $150,000 in the late fifties— and sidestepped a time-consuming lawsuit from Brazil, which would have rightly claimed the statue as a stolen national treasure. He kept quiet and set a course for Cuba. A shifty man, your lover.

"The problem he now faced was how to dispose of it. Who could afford to pay even a fraction of twenty to fifty million dollars for an art object? He was also afraid that once the word was out the current Cuban dictator, Fulgencio Batista, a racketeer of the first magnitude, would have it seized. And if Batista didn't grab it for himself, the army of Mafia hoods he invited into Cuba after the Second World War would. So Raymond decided to carve up the La Dorada and sell it bit by bit.

"Unfortunately for him, his timing was bad. He sailed his salvage boat into Havana on the same day that Castro and his rebels swarmed into town after toppling Batista's corrupt government. The revolutionary forces immediately closed down the harbors and airports to stop Batista's cronies from fleeing the country with uncountable wealth."

"LeBaron got nothing?" asked Sandecker. "He lost it all?"

"Not entirely. He realized he was trapped and it was only a question of time before the revolutionaries searched his salvage boat and found the La Dorada. His only option was to hack out whatever he could carry and catch the next plane back to the States. Under cover of night he must have slipped his salvage boat into the harbor, hoisted the statue overboard, and dumped it on top of the site where the battleship *Maine* had blown up seventy years before. Naturally he planned to come back and retrieve it after the chaos died down, but Castro didn't play according to LeBaron's rules. Cuba's honeymoon with the United States soon fell apart and he could never return and raise three tons of priceless treasure under the eyes of Castro's security."

"What piece of the statue did he remove?" Jessie asked.

"According to Hilda, he pried out the ruby heart. Then, after he smuggled it home, he discreetly had it cut, faceted, and sold through brokers. Now he had enough leverage to reach the pinnacle of high finance with Hilda at his side. Raymond LeBaron had arrived in fat city."

For a long moment they were quiet, each with his own thoughts, envisioning a desperate LeBaron throwing the golden woman over the side of his boat thirty years ago.

"The La Dorada," said Sandecker, breaking the silence. "Her weight would have pushed her deep beneath the soft silt of the harbor bottom."

"The admiral has a point," said Giordino. "LeBaron failed to consider that finding her again would be a major operation."

"I admit that bothered me too," said Pitt. "He must have known that after the Army Corps of Engineers stripped and removed the main hull section of the *Maine* hundreds of tons of wreckage were left embedded in the mud, making her almost impossible to find. The most sophisticated metal detector that money can buy won't pick out one particular object in a junkyard."

"So the statue will lie down there forever," said Sandecker. "Unless someday, someone comes along and dredges up half the harbor until he strikes it."

"Maybe not," Pitt said thoughtfully, his mind seeing something only he could see. "Raymond LeBaron was a canny character. He was also a professional salvage man. I believe he knew exactly what he was doing."

"What are you aiming at?" asked Sandecker.

"He put the statue over the side, all right. But I'm betting he very slowly lowered her feet first so she came down on the bottom standing up."

Giordino stared down at the deck. "Might be," he said slowly. "Might be. How tall is she?"

"About eight feet, including the base."

"Thirty years for three tons to settle in the mud..." mused Sandecker. "It's possible a couple of feet of her may still be protruding from the harbor floor."

Pitt smiled distantly. "We'll know as soon as Al and I dive down and run a search pattern."

As if on cue they all became quiet and gazed over the side into the water, oil-slicked and ash-coated, dark and secretive. Somewhere in the sinister green depths La Dorada beckoned.

80

PITT STOOD IN FULL DIVE GEAR and watched the bubbles rising from the deep and bursting on the surface. He glanced at his watch, marking the time. Giordino had been down nearly fifty minutes at a depth of forty feet. He went on watching the bubbles and saw them gradually travel in a circle. He knew that Giordino had enough air left for one more 360-degree sweep around the descent line tied to a buoy about thirty yards from the boat.

The small crew of Cubans Sandecker had recruited were very quiet. Pitt looked along the deck and saw them lined up at the rail beside the admiral, staring as though hypnotized at the glitter from the bubbles.

Pitt turned to Jessie, who was standing beside him. She hadn't said a word or moved in the last five minutes, her face tense with deep concentration, her eyes shining with excitement. She was swept up in the anticipation of seeing a legend. Then suddenly she called out. "Look!"

A dark form rose from the depths amid a cloud of bubbles, and Giordino's head broke the water near the buoy. He rolled over on his back and paddled easily with his fins until he reached the ladder. He handed up his weight belt and twin air cylinder before climbing to the deck. He pulled off his face mask and spit over the side.

"How did it go?" asked Pitt.

"Okay," Giordino answered. "Here's the situation. I made eight sweeps around the base point where the buoy's descent line is anchored. Visibility is less than three feet. We may have a little luck. The bottom is a mixture of sand and mud, so it's not real soft. The statue may not have sunk over her head."

"Current?"

"About a knot. You can live with it."

"Any obstructions?"

"A few bits and pieces of rusted wreckage protrude from the bottom, so be careful not to snag your distance line."

Sandecker came up behind Pitt and made a final check of his gear. Pitt stepped through an opening in the rail and set the air regulator's mouthpiece between his teeth.

Jessie gave his arm a gentle squeeze through the protective dry suit. "Luck," she said.

He winked at her through the face mask and then took a long step forward. The bright sunlight was diffused by a sudden burst of bubbles as he was engulfed by the green void. He swam out to the buoy and started down the descent line. The yellow nylon braid faded and vanished a few feet below in the opaque murk.

Pitt followed the line cautiously, taking his time. He paused once to clear his ears. Less than a minute later the bottom abruptly seemed to lift up toward him and meet his outstretched hand. He again paused to adjust his buoyancy compensator vest and check his watch for the time, compass for direction, and air pressure gauge. Then he took the distance line Giordino had attached to the descent line by a clip and moved out along the radius.

After swimming about twenty-four feet his hand came in contact with a knot in the line Giordino had tied to measure the outer perimeter of his last sweep. After a short distance, Pitt spied an orange stake standing in the muck that marked the starting point for his circular search pattern. Then he moved out another six-foot increment, held the line taut, and began his sweep, his eyes taking in the three-foot visibility on both sides.

The water was desolate and lifeless and smelled of chemicals. He passed over colonies of dead sea life, crushed by the concussion from the bursting oil tanker, their bodies rolling across the bottom with the tide like leaves under a gentle breeze. He had sweated inside his dry suit under the sun on the boat, and he was sweating inside it now forty feet below the surface. He could hear the sounds of the rescue boats racing back and forth across the harbor, the roar of their exhaust and cavitation of their propellers magnified by the density of the water.

Yard by yard he scanned the barren harbor until he completed a full circle. He moved the marker out and started another sweep in the opposite direction.

Divers often experience great loneliness when swimming over an underwater desert with nothing to see beyond a hand's reach. The real world with people, less than fifty feet away on the surface, ceases to exist. They experience a careless abandon and an indifference toward the unknown. Their perception becomes distorted and they began to fantasize.

Pitt felt none of those things, except maybe a touch of a fantasy. He was drunk with the hunt and so absorbed in seeing the treasured statue in his mind, gleaming gold and brilliant green, that he almost missed a vague form looming up through the mist on his right.

Rapidly kicking his fins, he swam toward it. The object was round and indistinct and partly buried. The two feet that protruded from the silt were coated with slime and strands of sea growth that waved with the current.

A hundred times Pitt had wondered how he'd feel, how he would react when he confronted the golden woman. What he really felt was fear, fear that it was only a false alarm and the search might never end.

Slowly, apprehensively, he wiped away the slimy growth with his gloved hands. Tiny particles of vegetation and silt billowed in a brown swirl, obscuring the thing. He waited under an eerie silence until the cloud melted into the watery gloom.

He moved closer, floating just above the bottom, until his face was only a few inches away from the mysterious object. He stared through his face mask, his mouth suddenly going dry, his heart pounding like a calypso drum.

With a look of timeless melancholy, a pair of emerald-green eyes stared back at him.

Pitt had found La Dorada.

81

January 4, 1990
Washington, D.C.

THE PRESIDENT'S ANNOUNCEMENT of the Jersey Colony and the exploits of Eli Steinmetz and his moon team electrified the nation and caused a worldwide sensation.

Every evening for a week television viewers were treated to spectacular scenes of the lunar landscape never viewed during the brief Apollo landings. The struggle of the men to survive while constructing a livable habitat was also shown in dramatic detail.

Steinmetz and the others became the heroes of the hour. They were feted across the country, interviewed on countless television talk shows, and given the traditional ticker tape parade in New York.

The cheers for the moon colonists' triumph had the ring of old-fashioned patriotism, but the impact went deeper, broader. Now there was something tangible beyond the short, showy flights above the earth's atmosphere, a permanence in space, solid proof that man could live a life far from his home planet.

The President looked buoyant at a private dinner party he hosted in honor of the "inner core" and the colonists. His mood was far different from the first time he had confronted the men who conceived and launched the moon base. He held out a glass of champagne to Hudson, who was staring absently through the roomful of people as though it were silent and empty.

"Your mind lost in space, Leo?"

Hudson's eyes fixed on the President for a moment, and then he nodded. "My apologies. A nasty habit of mine, tuning out at parties."

"I'll bet you're hatching plans for a new settlement on the moon."

Hudson smiled wryly. "Actually, I was thinking of Mars."

"So the Jersey Colony is not the end."

"There will never be an end, only the beginning of another beginning."

"Congress will ride with the mood of the country and vote funding to expand the colony. But an outpost on Mars—you're talking heavy money."

"If we don't do it now, the next generation will."

"Got a name for the project?"

Hudson shook his head. "Haven't given it much thought."

"I've often wondered," the President said, "where you came up with 'Jersey Colony.'"

"You didn't guess?"

"There's the state of New Jersey, the isle of Jersey off the French coast, Jersey sweaters..."

"It's also a breed of cow."

"A what?"

"The nursery rhyme, 'Hey diddle diddle,/The cat and the fiddle,/The cow jumped over the moon.'"

The President looked blank for a moment, and then he broke out laughing. When he recovered he said, "My God, there's irony for you. Man's greatest achievement was named after a Mother Goose cow."

"She's truly exquisite," said Jessie.

"Yes, gorgeous," agreed Pitt. "You never tire of looking at her."

They gazed in rapt fascination at the La Dorada, which now stood in the East Building central court of Washington's National Gallery. The burnished golden body and the polished emerald head gleamed under the sun's rays that shone through the great skylight. The dramatic effect was awesome. Her unknown Indian sculptor had portrayed her with compelling beauty and grace. She stood in a relaxed posture, one leg in front of the other, arms slightly bent at the elbows with hands extended outward from the sides.

Her rose quartz pedestal sat atop a five-foot-high solid block of Brazilian rosewood. The missing heart had been replaced by one crafted out of crimson glass that almost matched the splendor of the original ruby.

Throngs of people stared in wonder at the dazzling sight. A line stretched outside the gallery by the mall for nearly a quarter of a mile. La Dorada even surpassed the attendance record for the King Tut artifacts.

Every dignitary in the capital appeared to pay homage. The President and his wife escorted Hilda Kronberg-LeBaron to the preopening viewing. She sat in her wheelchair, a content old lady with sparkling eyes who smiled and smiled as the President honored the two men in her past with a short dedication speech. When he lifted her out of her chair so she could touch the statue, there wasn't a dry eye in the house.

"Strange," Jessie murmured, "when you think about how it all began with the shipwreck of the *Cyclops* and ended on the shipwreck of the *Maine*."

"Only for us," Pitt said distantly. "For her it began four hundred years ago in a Brazilian jungle."

"Hard to imagine such a thing of beauty has caused so many deaths."

He wasn't listening and didn't reply.

She flashed a curious look at him. He was staring intently at the statue, his mind lost in another time, another place.

"Rich the treasure, sweet the pleasure," she quoted.

He slowly turned and looked at her, his eyes refocusing on the present. The spell was broken. "I'm sorry," he said.

Jessie couldn't help smiling. "When are you going to give it a try?"

"Try?"

"Rush off to search for La Dorada's lost city?"

"No need to rush," Pitt replied, suddenly laughing. "It's not going anywhere."

Other authors with bestselling omnibus collections
from Random House Value Publishing:

SUE GRAFTON

MARY HIGGINS CLARK

COLLEEN McCULLOUGH

DEAN KOONTZ

MICHAEL CRICHTON

NELSON DeMILLE

ROSAMUND PILCHER